THE AMAZING JOY BUZZARDS

THE AMAZING JOY BUZZARDS
ISBN: 978-1-58240-918-4
FIRST PRINTING

PUBLISHED BY IMAGE COMICS, INC. OFFICE OF PUBLICATION: 1942 UNIVERSITY AVENUE, SUITE 305, BERKELEY, CALIFORNIA 94704. COPYRIGHT © 2008 MARK ANDREW SMITH & DAN HIPP. INCORPORATES PORTIONS OF AMAZING JOY BUZZARDS, VOL. 1 #1-4 AND AMAZING JOY BUZZARDS VOL. 2 #1-4. ALL RIGHTS RESERVED. THE AMAZING JOY BUZZARDS™ (INCLUDING ALL PROMINENT CHARACTERS FEATURED HEREIN), ITS LOGO AND ALL CHARACTER LIKENESSES ARE TRADEMARKS OF MARK ANDREW SMITH & DAN HIPP, UNLESS OTHERWISE NOTED. IMAGE COMICS® IS A TRADEMARK OF IMAGE COMICS, INC. ALL RIGHTS RESERVED. NO PART OF THIS PUBLICATION MAY BE REPRODUCED OR TRANSMITTED, IN ANY FORM OR BY ANY MEANS (EXCEPT FOR SHORT EXCERPTS FOR REVIEW PURPOSES) WITHOUT THE EXPRESS WRITTEN PERMISSION OF IMAGE COMICS, INC. ALL NAMES, CHARACTERS, EVENTS AND LOCALES IN THIS PUBLICATION ARE ENTIRELY FICTIONAL. ANY RESEMBLANCE TO ACTUAL PERSONS (LIVING OR DEAD), EVENTS OR PLACES, WITHOUT SATIRIC INTENT, IS COINCIDENTAL. PRINTED IN CANADA

IMAGE COMICS, INC.

Erik Larsen - *Publisher*
Todd McFarlane - *President*
Marc Silvestri - *CEO*
Jim Valentino - *Vice-President*

Eric Stephenson - *Executive Director*
Joe Keatinge - *PR & Marketing Coordinator*
Branwyn Bigglestone - *Accounts Manager*
Paige Richardson - *Administrative Assistant*
Traci Hui - *Traffic Manager*
Allen Hui - *Production Manager*
Drew Gill - *Production Artist*
Jonathan Chan - *Production Artist*
Monica Garcia - *Production Artist*

www.imagecomics.com

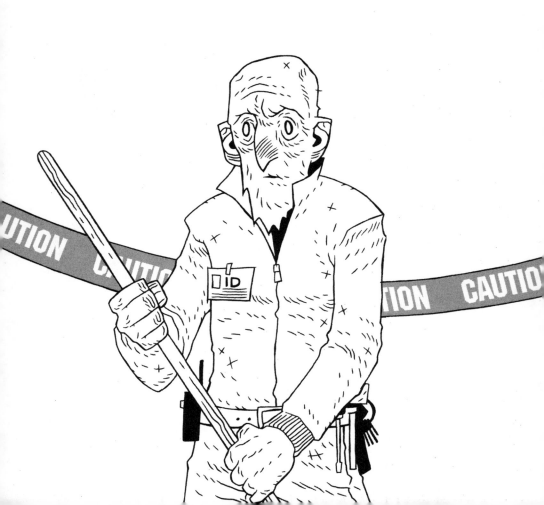

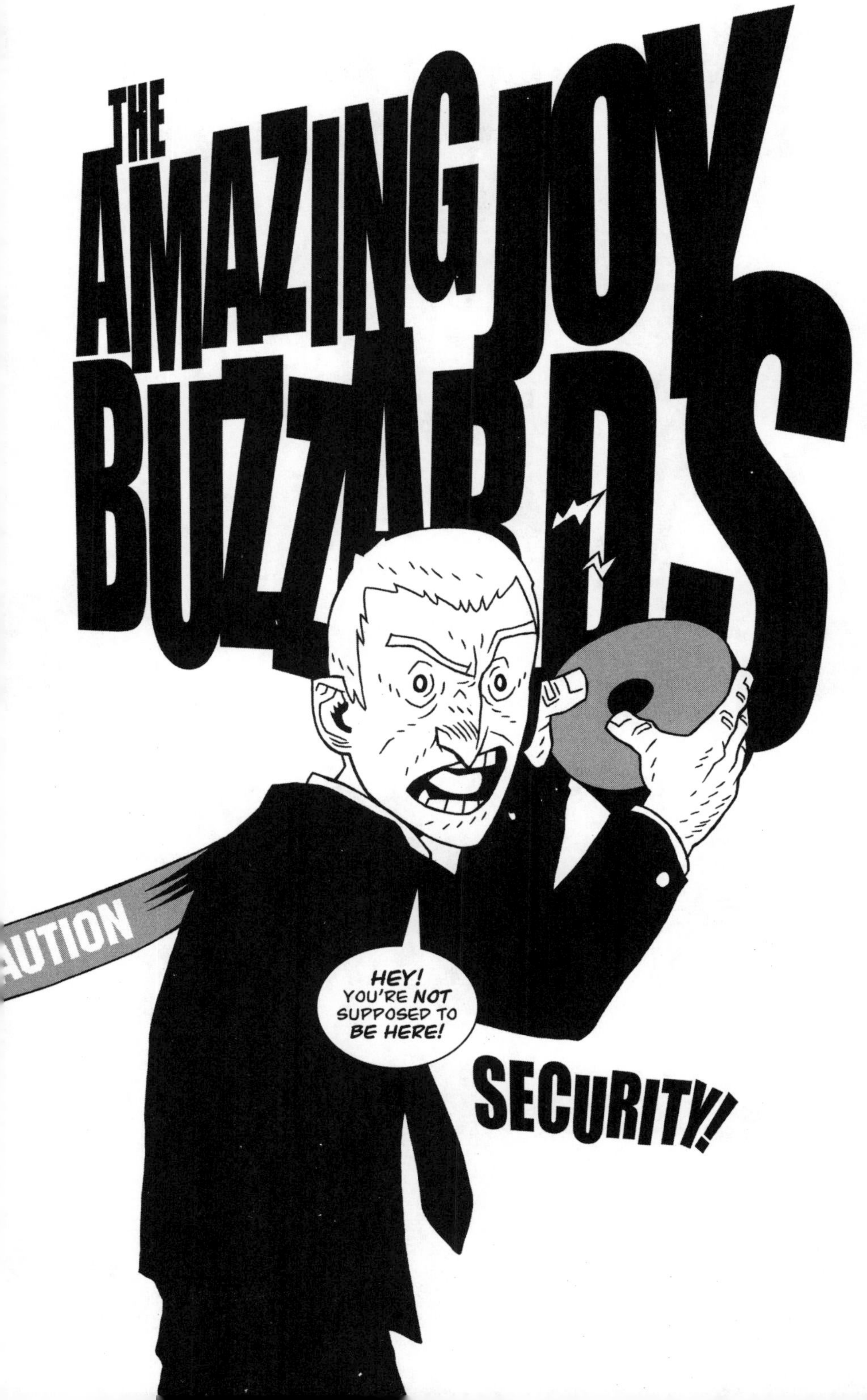
THE AMAZING JOY BUZZARDS
AUTION
HEY! YOU'RE NOT SUPPOSED TO BE HERE!
SECURITY!

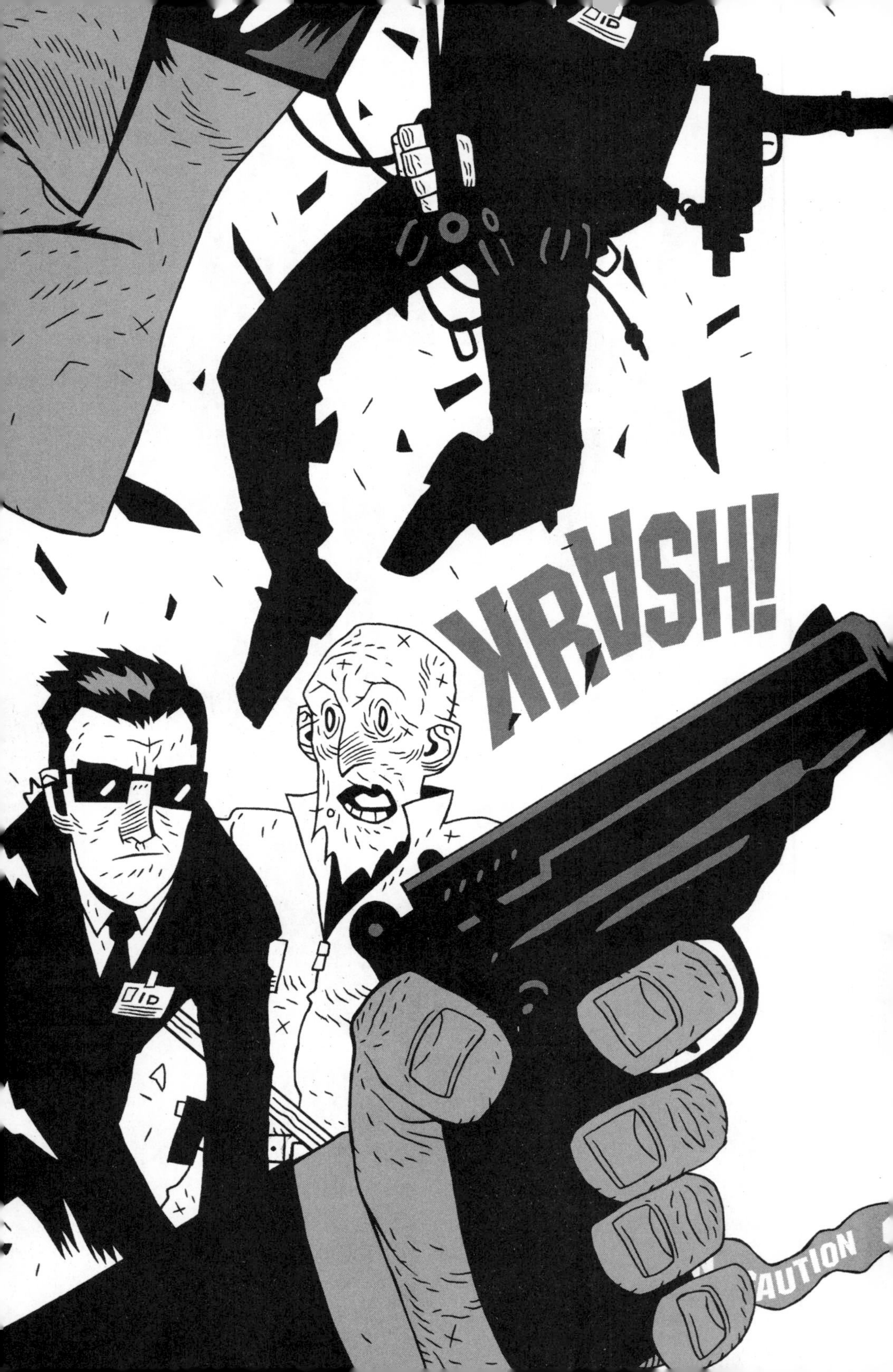
ID
KRASH!
ID
CAUTION

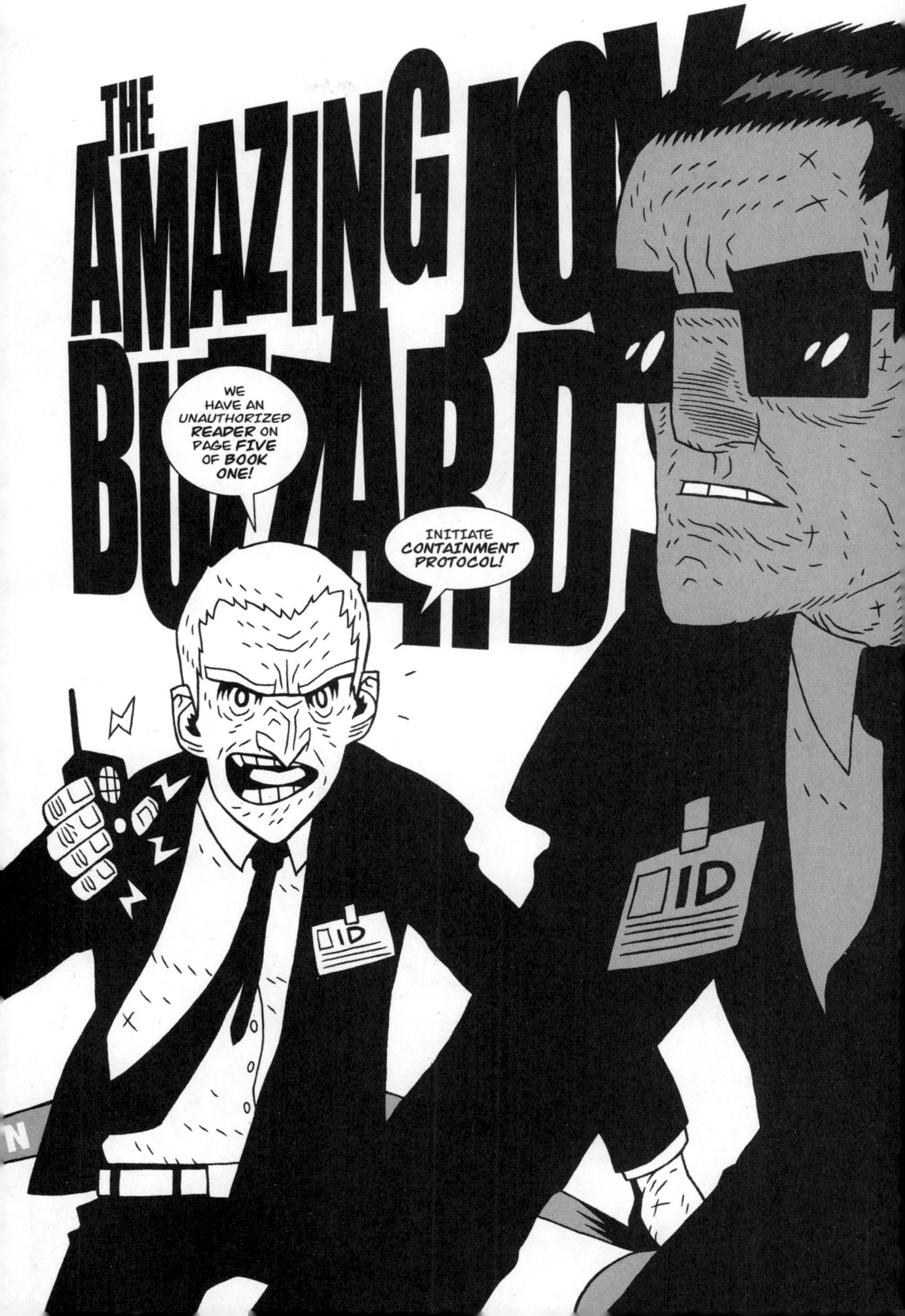
THE
AMAZING
WE HAVE AN UNAUTHORIZED READER ON PAGE FIVE OF BOOK ONE!
INITIATE CONTAINMENT PROTOCOL!
ID
ID

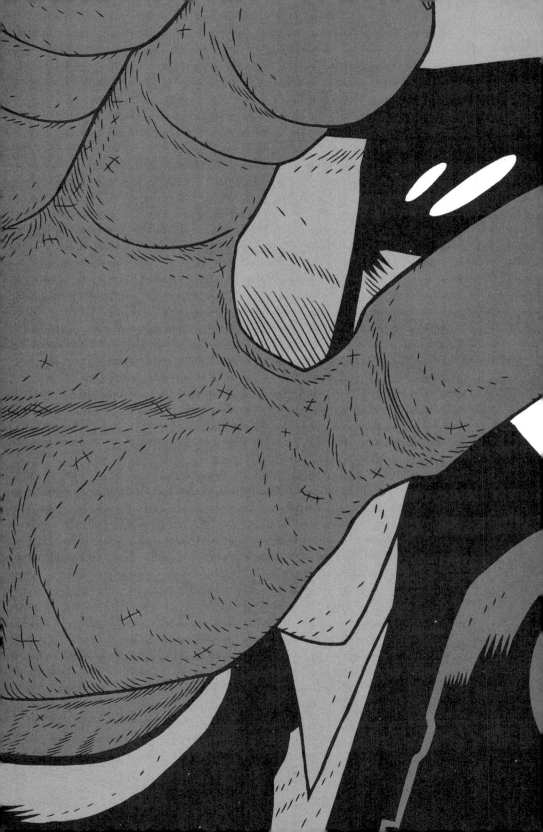

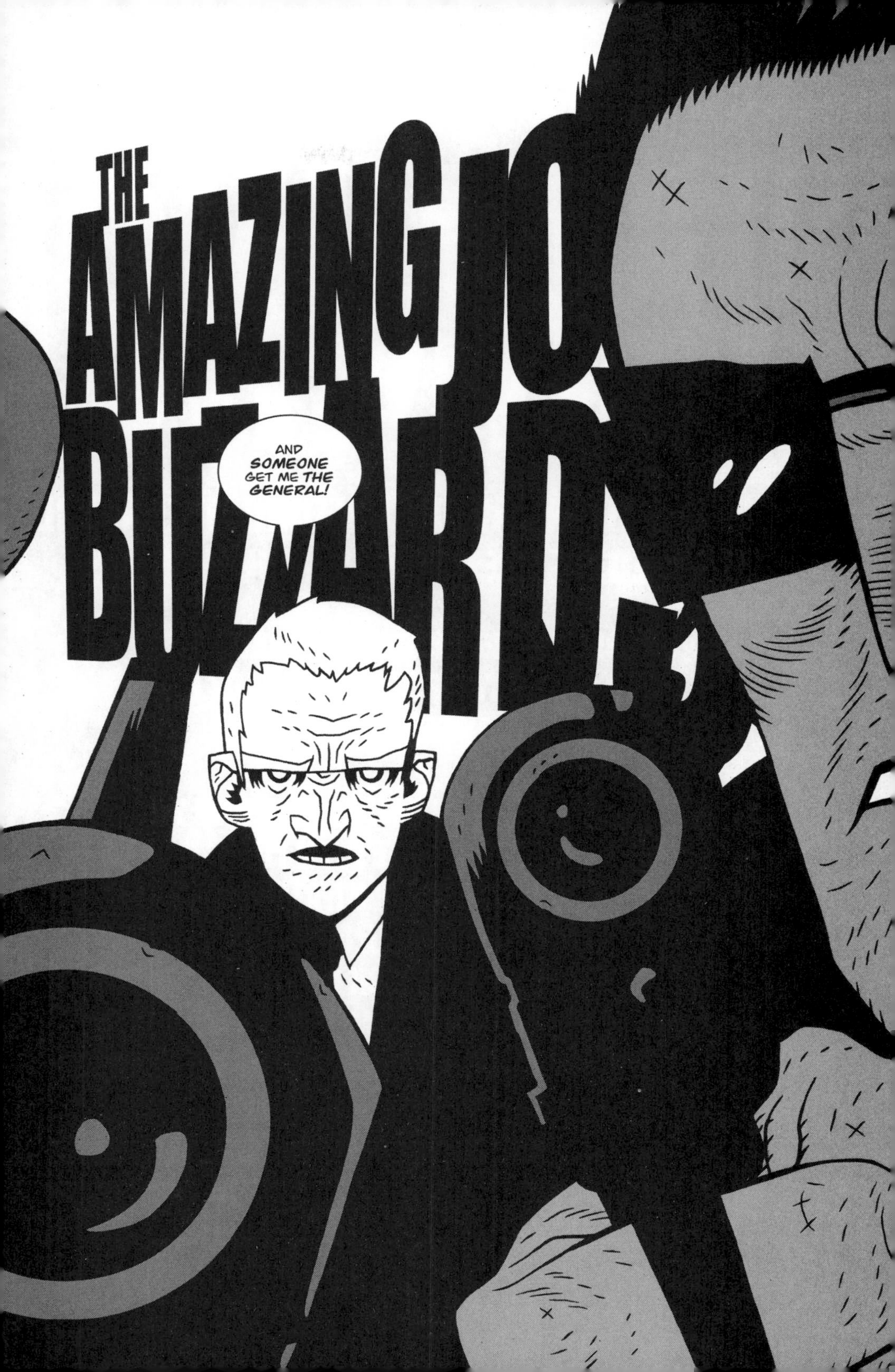
THE AMAZING JOE BIZZARRO
AND SOMEONE GET ME THE GENERAL!

FEDERAL ALERT #MD001

WARNING!

YOU HAVE BEEN CAUGHT READING LITERATURE
BANNED BY THE FEDERAL GOVERNMENT.

AN OFFENSE PUNISHABLE BY JAILTIME
AND OR DEATH, IF DEEMED AN ACT OF
TREASON BY SECRET TRIBUNAL.

AUTHORITIES HAVE BEEN ALERTED AND YOUR
PERSONAL RECORDS HAVE BEEN TURNED OVER
TO THE FEDERAL GOVERNMENT, ALONG WITH ANY
AND ALL INTERNET AND CELLULAR PHONE HISTORIES.
THE ISBN CODE ON THE BACK OF THIS BOOK HAS
BEEN ACTIVATED AND YOUR MOVEMENT AND
ACTIVITIES ARE BEING MONITERED BY SATELLITE.

FURTHER READING OF SAID LITERATURE, BEYOND
THIS FEDERAL ALERT, WILL RESULT IN YOUR
DETAINMENT AND AFOREMENTIONED PENALTIES.

END FEDERAL ALERT #MD001

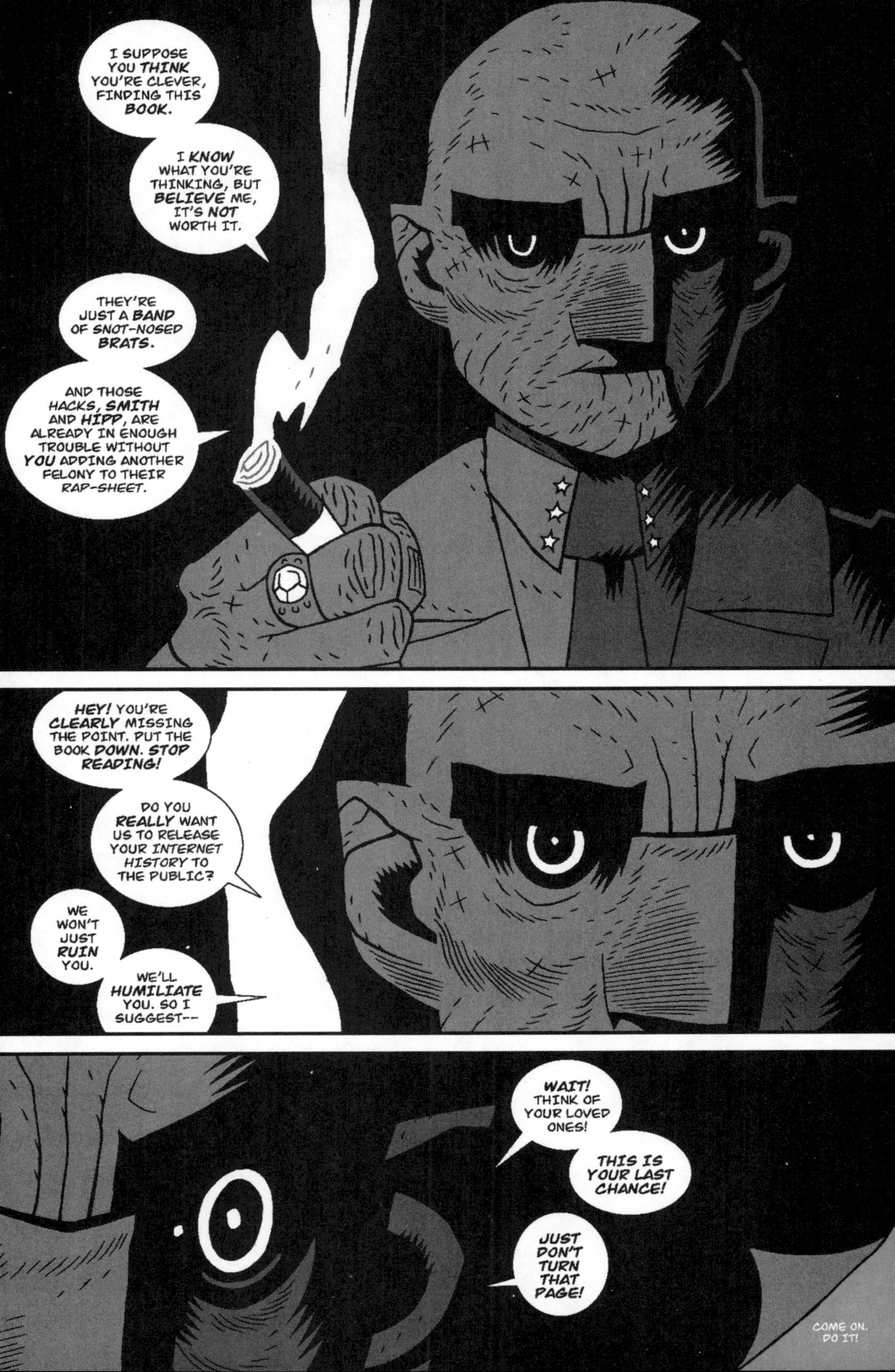
I SUPPOSE YOU THINK YOU'RE CLEVER, FINDING THIS BOOK.
I KNOW WHAT YOU'RE THINKING, BUT BELIEVE ME, IT'S NOT WORTH IT.
THEY'RE JUST A BAND OF SNOT-NOSED BRATS.
AND THOSE HACKS, SMITH AND HIPP, ARE ALREADY IN ENOUGH TROUBLE WITHOUT YOU ADDING ANOTHER FELONY TO THEIR RAP-SHEET.
HEY! YOU'RE CLEARLY MISSING THE POINT. PUT THE BOOK DOWN. STOP READING!
DO YOU REALLY WANT US TO RELEASE YOUR INTERNET HISTORY TO THE PUBLIC?
WE WON'T JUST RUIN YOU.
WE'LL HUMILIATE YOU. SO I SUGGEST--
WAIT! THINK OF YOUR LOVED ONES!
THIS IS YOUR LAST CHANCE!
JUST DON'T TURN THAT PAGE!
COME ON. DO IT!

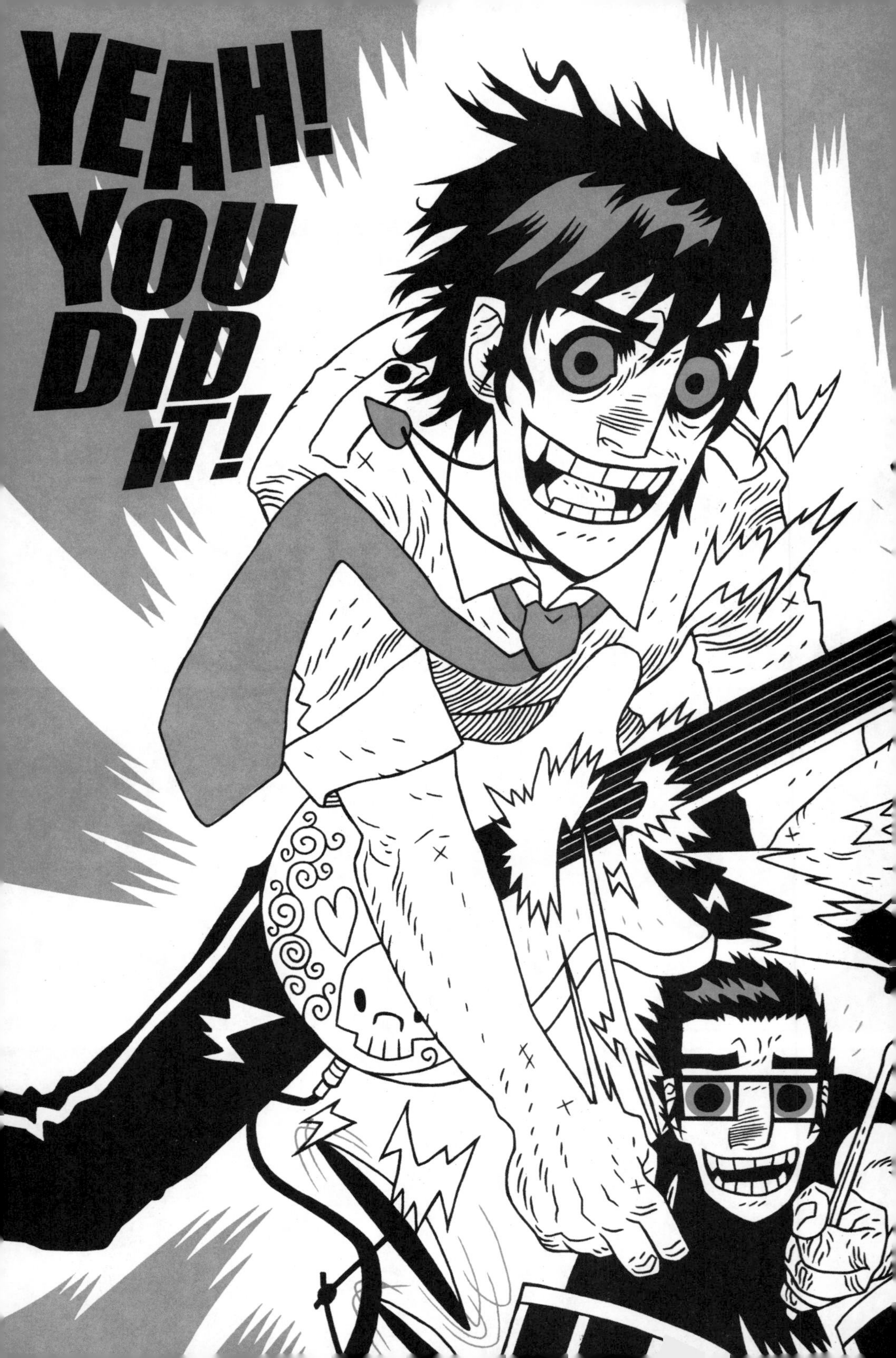
YEAH! YOU DID IT!

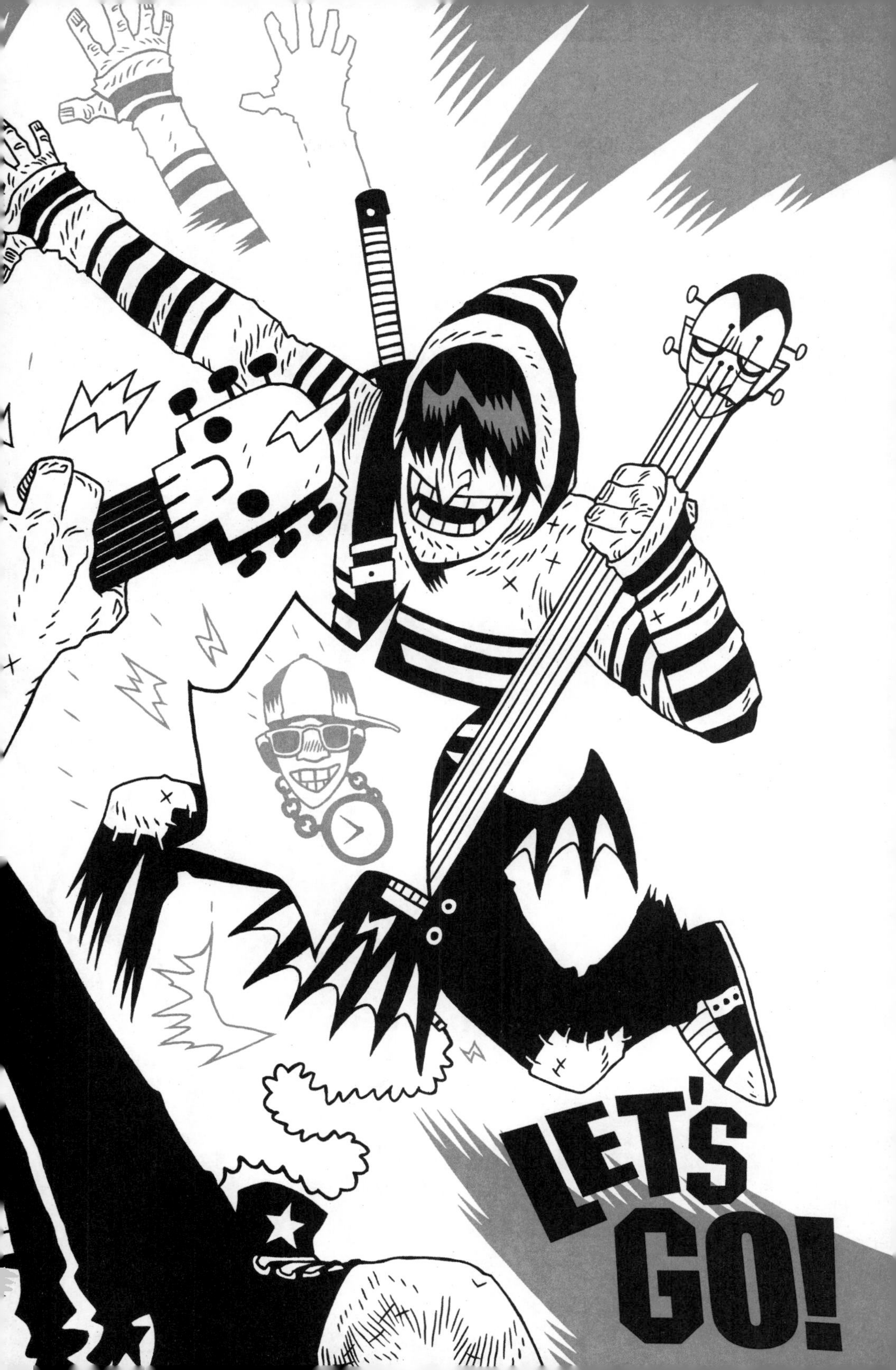
LET'S GO!

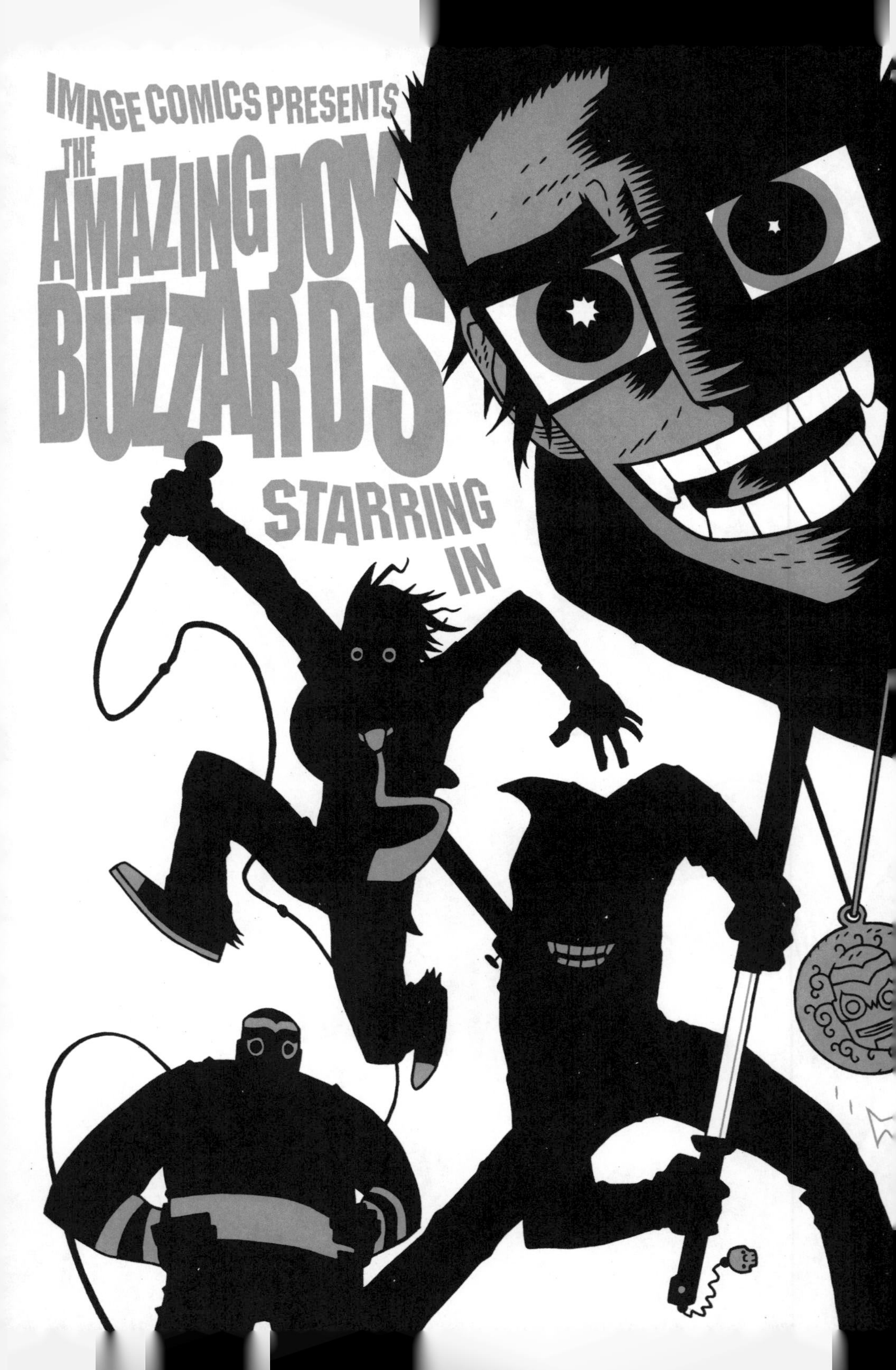
IMAGE COMICS PRESENTS
THE AMAZING JOY BUZZARDS
STARRING
IN

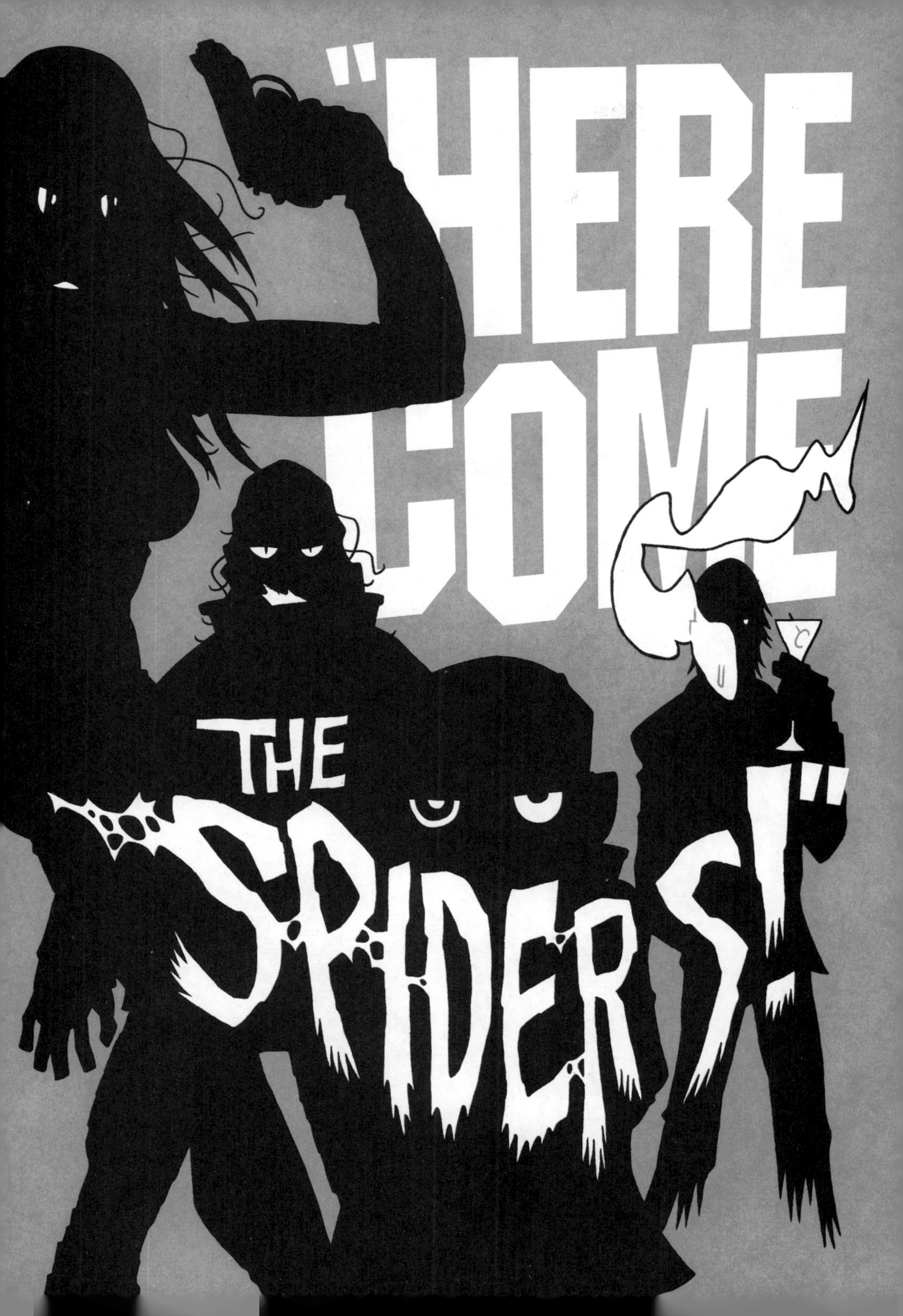
"HERE COME
THE SPIDERS!"

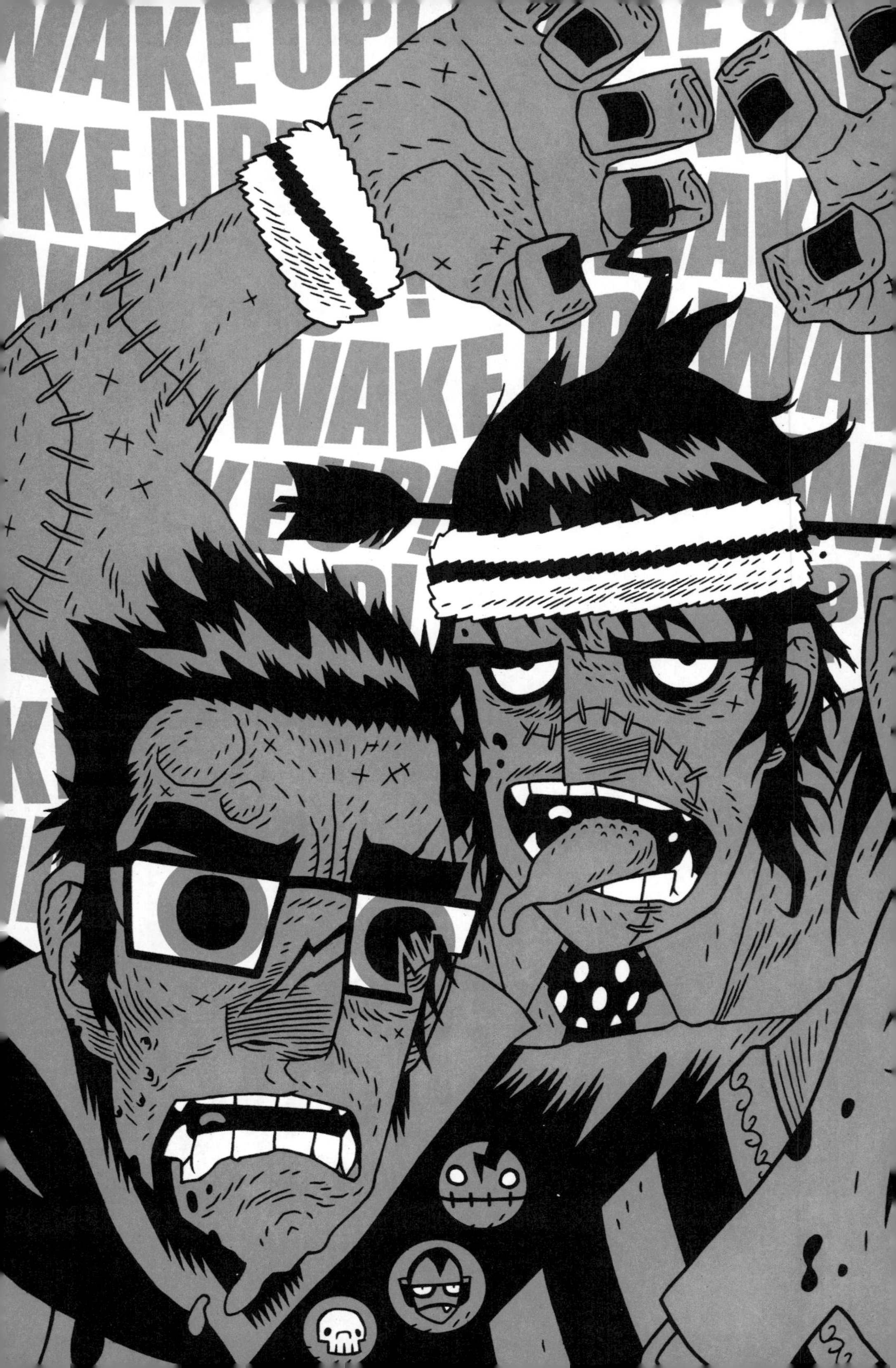
WAKE UP!

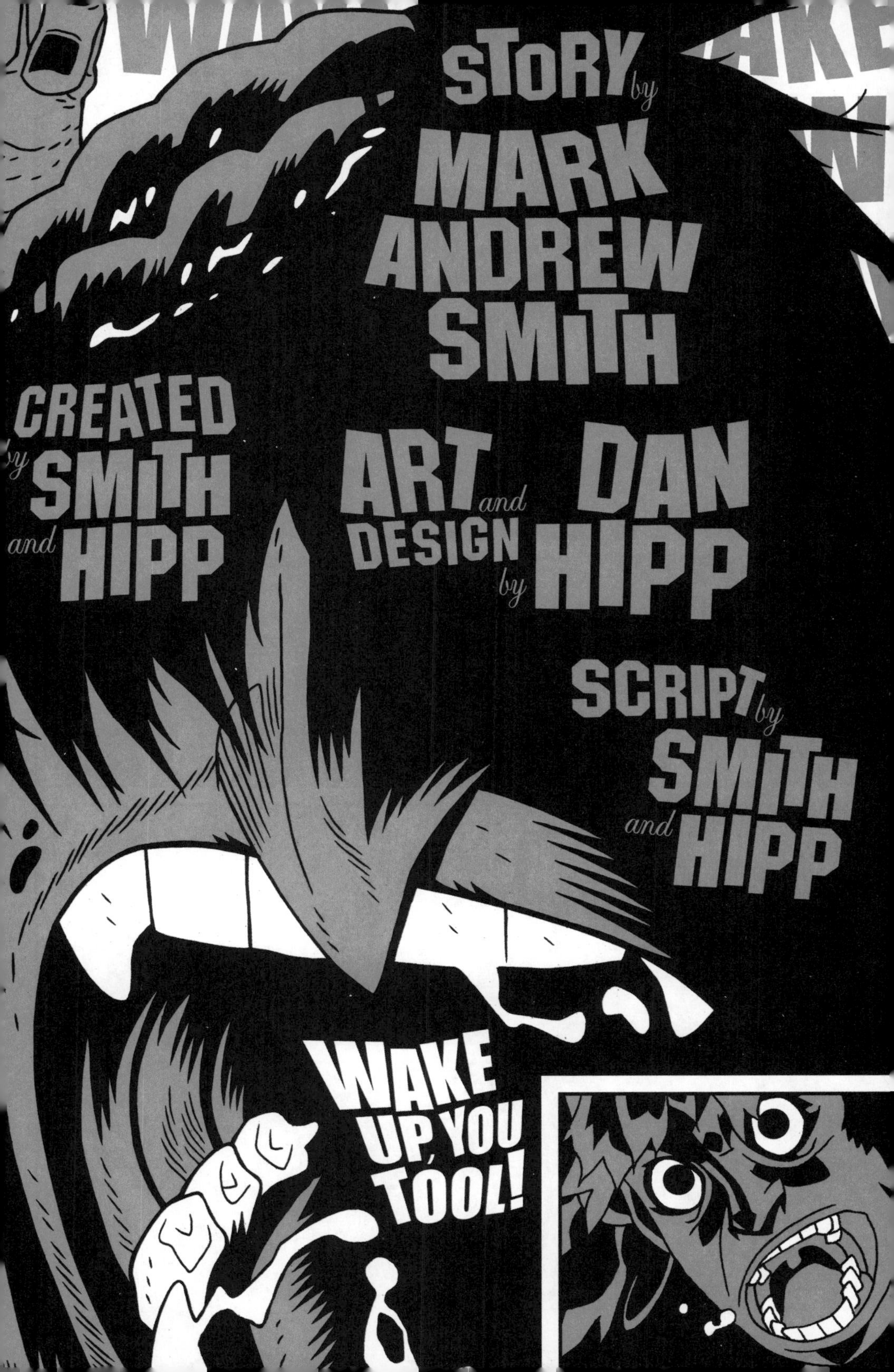

STORY by MARK ANDREW SMITH
CREATED by SMITH and HIPP
ART and DESIGN by DAN HIPP
SCRIPT by SMITH and HIPP
WAKE UP, YOU TOOL!

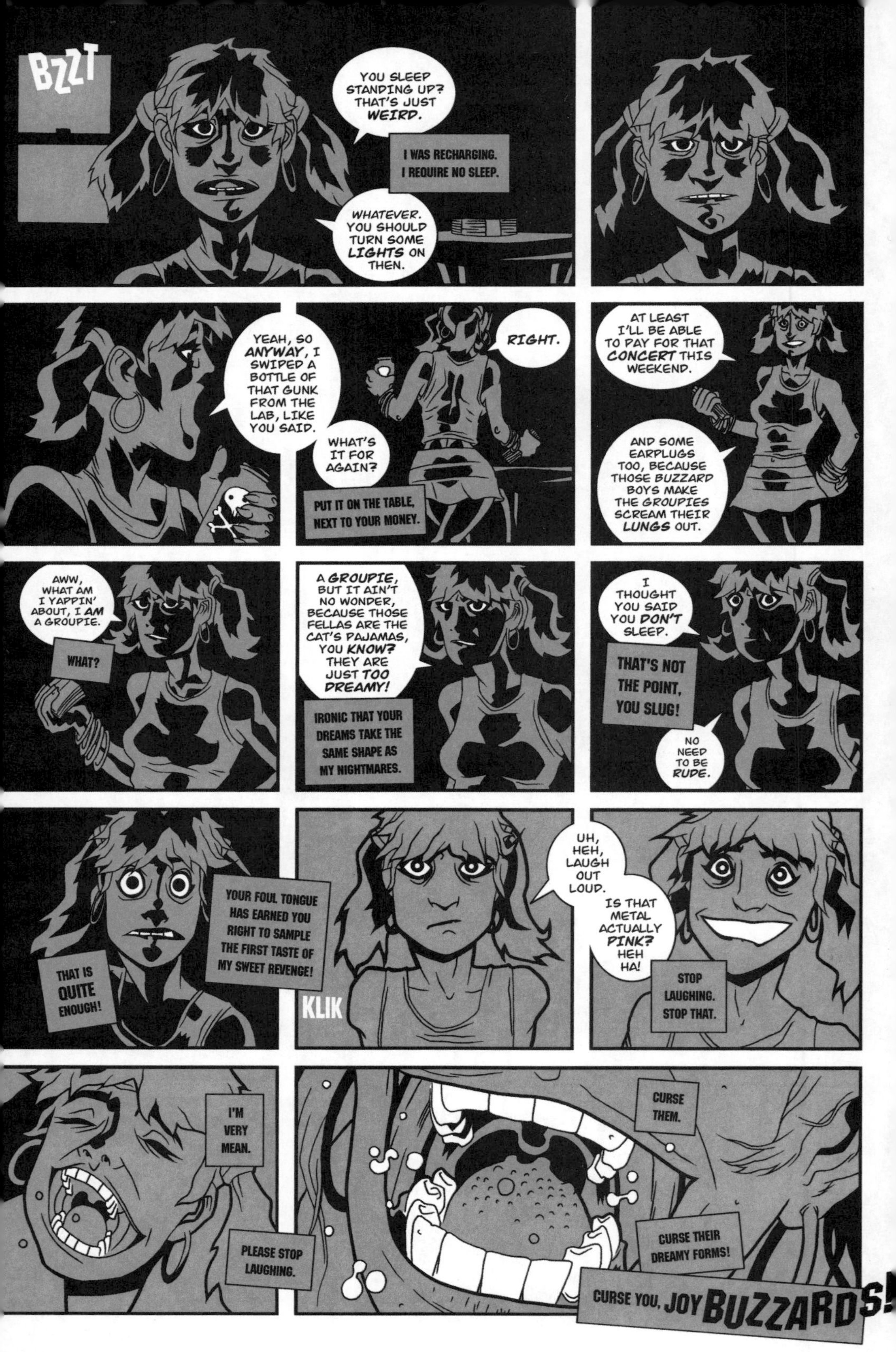
BZZT
YOU SLEEP STANDING UP? THAT'S JUST WEIRD.
I WAS RECHARGING. I REQUIRE NO SLEEP.
WHATEVER. YOU SHOULD TURN SOME LIGHTS ON THEN.
YEAH, SO ANYWAY, I SWIPED A BOTTLE OF THAT GUNK FROM THE LAB, LIKE YOU SAID.
RIGHT.
WHAT'S IT FOR AGAIN?
PUT IT ON THE TABLE, NEXT TO YOUR MONEY.
AT LEAST I'LL BE ABLE TO PAY FOR THAT CONCERT THIS WEEKEND.
AND SOME EARPLUGS TOO, BECAUSE THOSE BUZZARD BOYS MAKE THE GROUPIES SCREAM THEIR LUNGS OUT.
AWW, WHAT AM I YAPPIN' ABOUT, I AM A GROUPIE.
WHAT?
A GROUPIE, BUT IT AIN'T NO WONDER, BECAUSE THOSE FELLAS ARE THE CAT'S PAJAMAS, YOU KNOW? THEY ARE JUST TOO DREAMY!
IRONIC THAT YOUR DREAMS TAKE THE SAME SHAPE AS MY NIGHTMARES.
I THOUGHT YOU SAID YOU DON'T SLEEP.
THAT'S NOT THE POINT, YOU SLUG!
NO NEED TO BE RUDE.
YOUR FOUL TONGUE HAS EARNED YOU RIGHT TO SAMPLE THE FIRST TASTE OF MY SWEET REVENGE!
THAT IS QUITE ENOUGH!
KLIK
UH, HEH, LAUGH OUT LOUD.
IS THAT METAL ACTUALLY PINK? HEH HA!
STOP LAUGHING. STOP THAT.
I'M VERY MEAN.
PLEASE STOP LAUGHING.
CURSE THEM.
CURSE THEIR DREAMY FORMS!
CURSE YOU, JOY BUZZARDS!

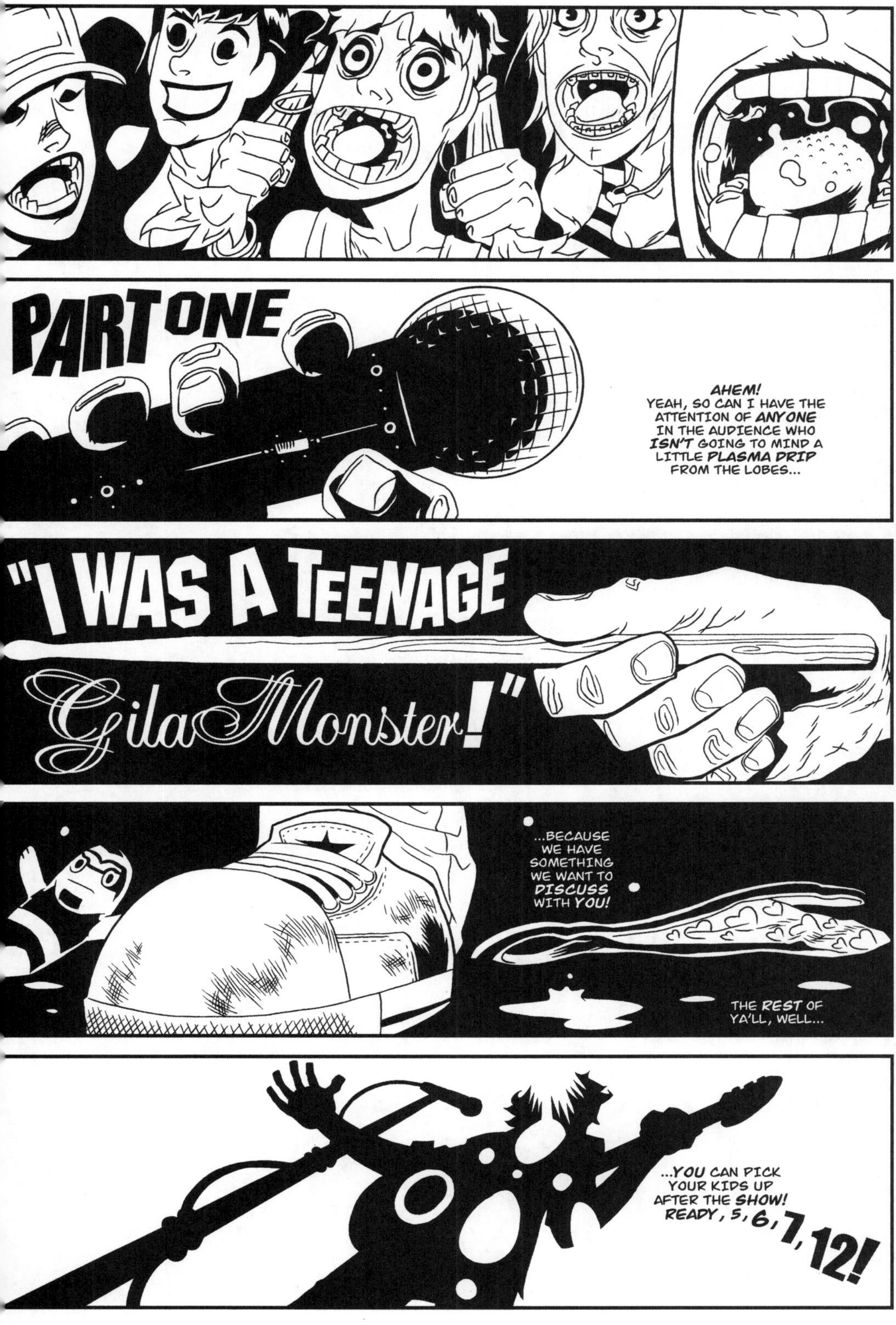
PART ONE
AHEM!
YEAH, SO CAN I HAVE THE ATTENTION OF ANYONE IN THE AUDIENCE WHO ISN'T GOING TO MIND A LITTLE PLASMA DRIP FROM THE LOBES...
"I WAS A TEENAGE Gila Monster!"
...BECAUSE WE HAVE SOMETHING WE WANT TO DISCUSS WITH YOU!
THE REST OF YA'LL, WELL...
...YOU CAN PICK YOUR KIDS UP AFTER THE SHOW!
READY, 5, 6, 7, 12!

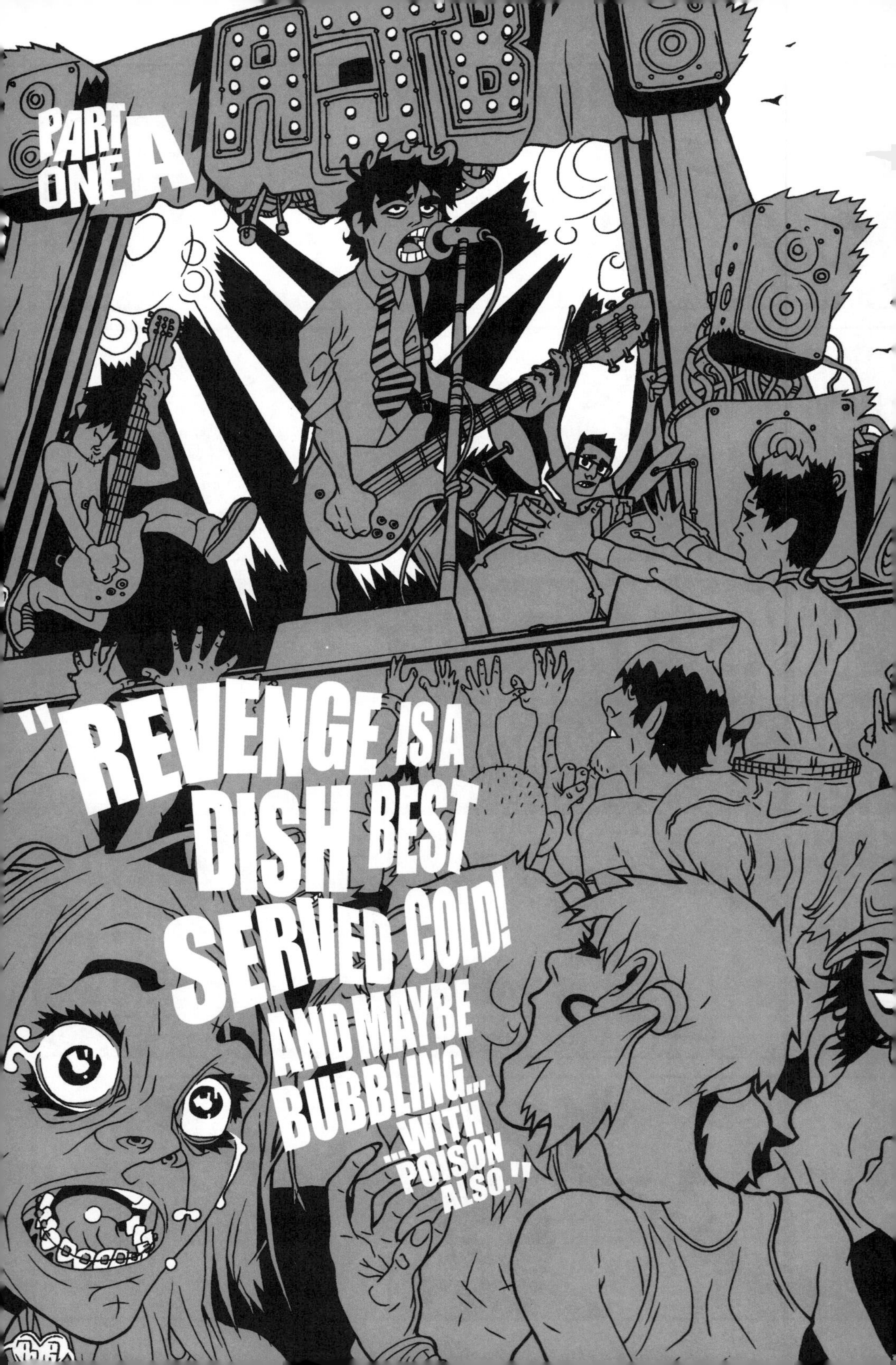
PART ONE A
"REVENGE IS A DISH BEST SERVED COLD!
AND MAYBE BUBBLING...
...WITH POISON ALSO."

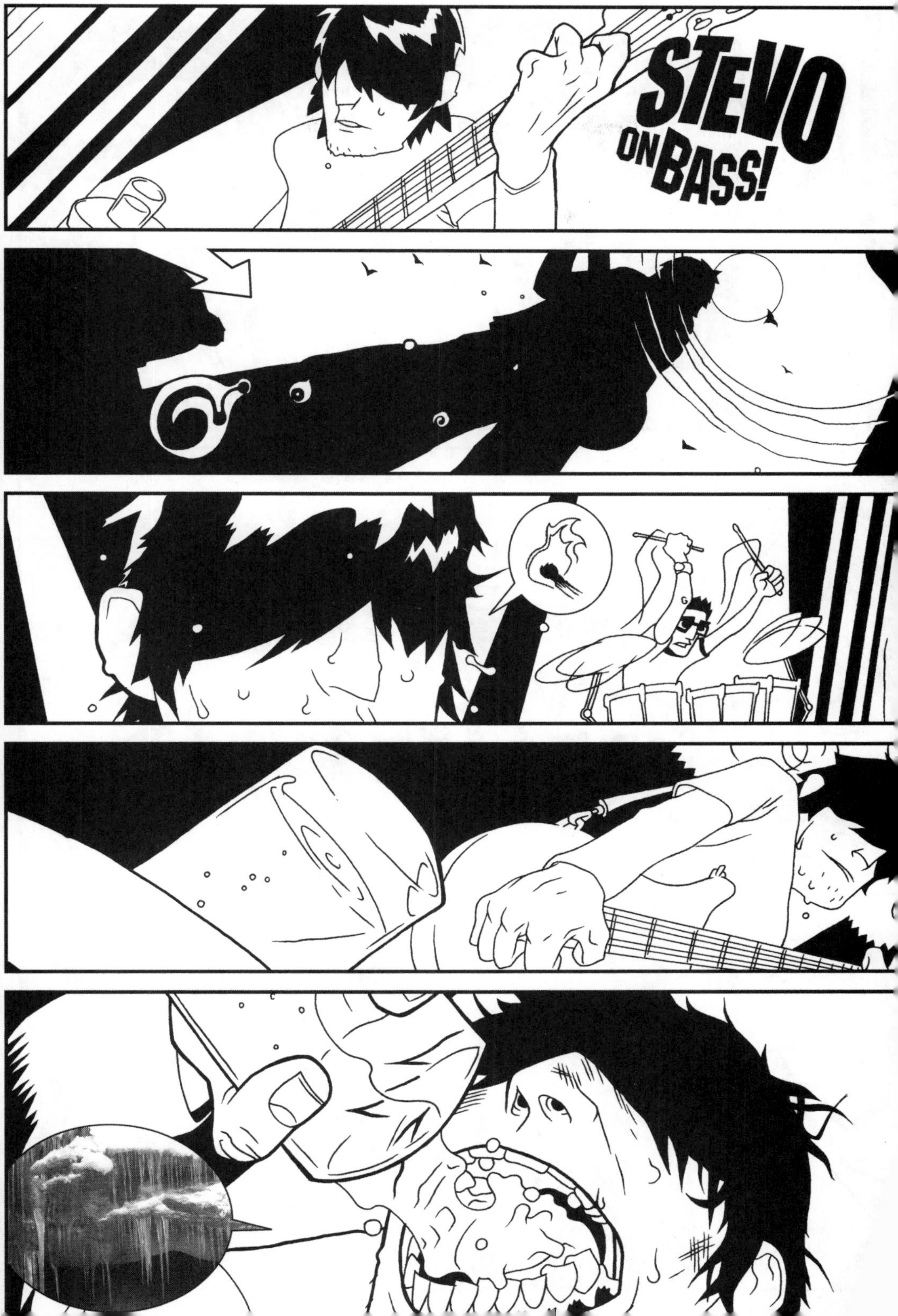
STEVO ON BASS!

BIFF ON VOCALS AND GUITAR!

WITH GABE ON DRUMS!

'RE SO DREAMY! HAVE MY BABY, STEVO! DID YOU HEAR ABOUT... ...THEY RESCUED FROM BURNING DOW ULD JUST DIE NOW, THEY'RE SO PERFECT! ROCK ON, JOY BUZZ... ...LOVE THOSE SEX...S! I HEARD T HT BE ROBOTS, THEY'RE JUST TOO GOOD! DO YOU THINK THEY... GO... ...RS I'LL BET T... E GOT SUPER E MY BOYFRIEND GET A PAIR OF GLASSES SO HE'D LOOK LIKE GABE, ...NP! OH GOD CO... THEY BE ANY C ST ...M LOVE THEM I TELL YOU! MOM, CALM DOWN! BI... IS MY... ...SHUT UP, HE S... INE... NO HE'S M ...M TO... ...HE'S M...! ...NE, B... STEVO ...NO STEVO ...ND SO IS BIFF A... GA... JUST ...M TO... ...OT...ATTE... W! DO YOU ...INK THAT B... ...ER ...AN ...TA...CIDE! THEY... LOO...

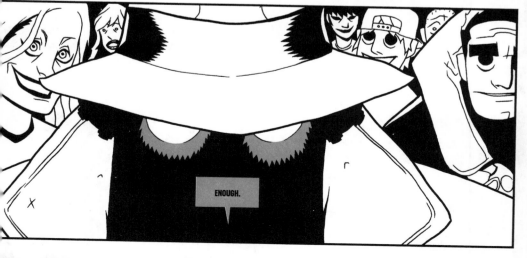

ENOUGH.

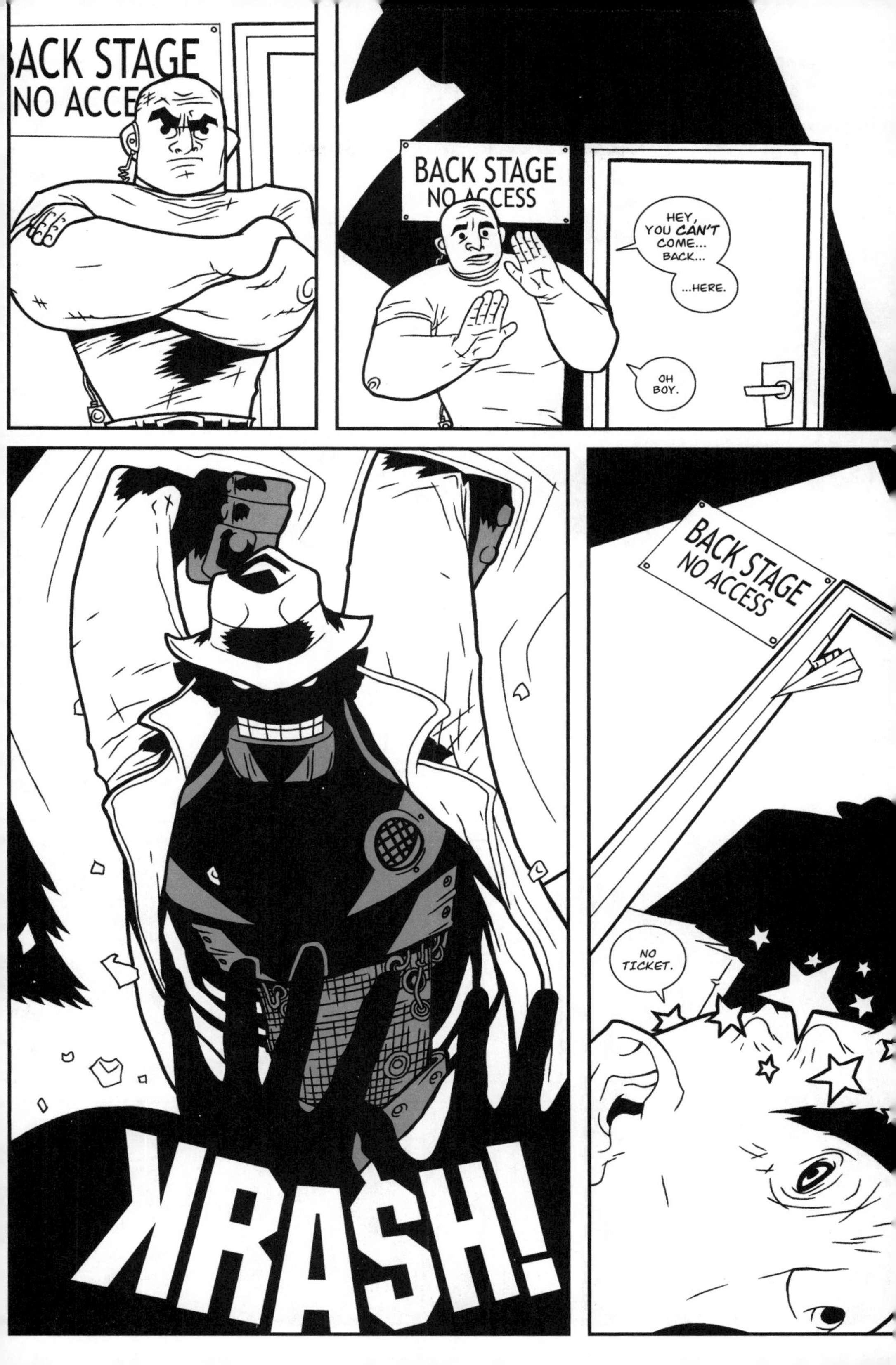
BACK STAGE
NO ACCESS
BACK STAGE
NO ACCESS
HEY, YOU CAN'T COME... BACK...
...HERE.
OH BOY.
KRASH!
BACK STAGE
NO ACCESS
NO TICKET.

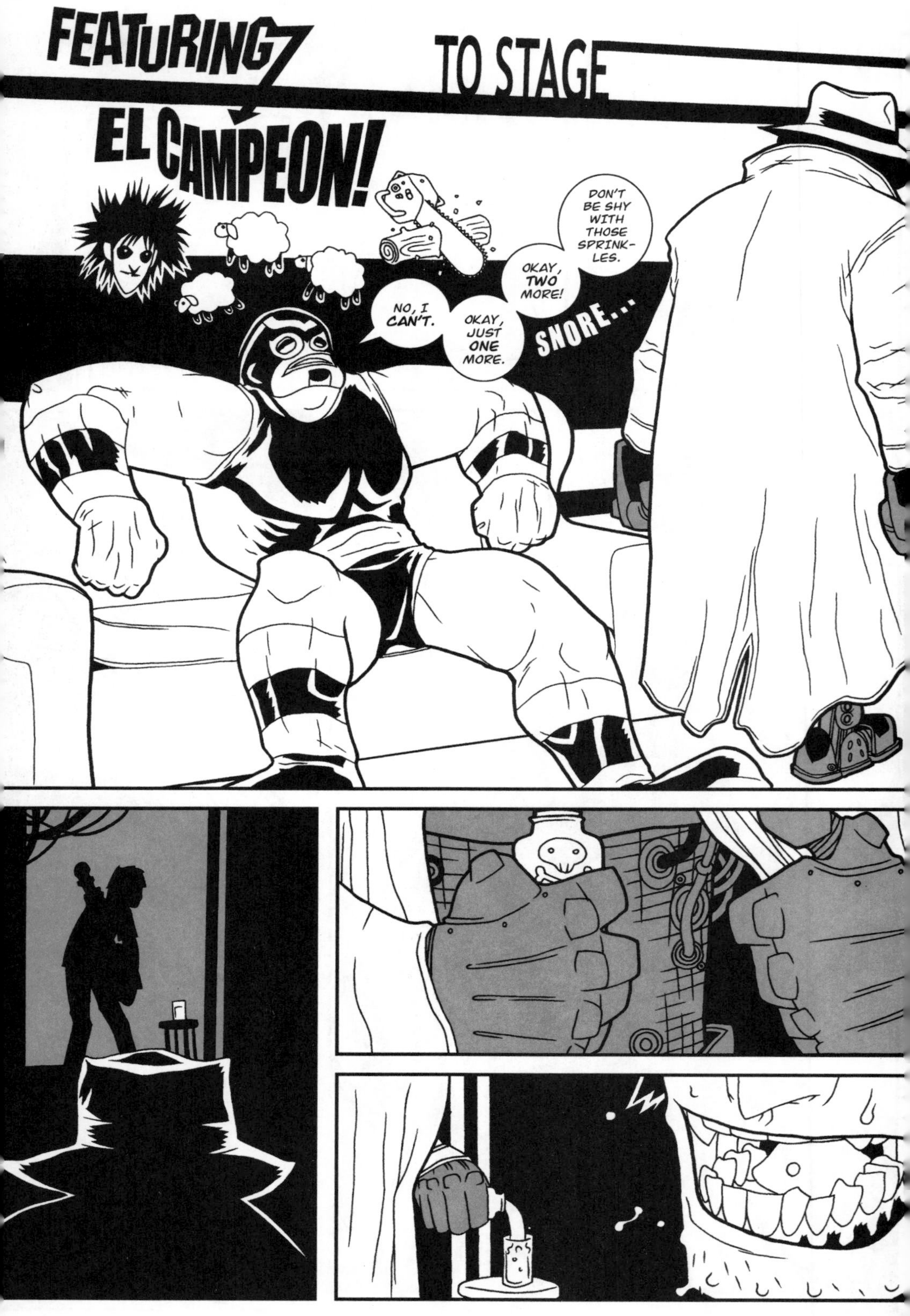
FEATURING
EL CAMPEON!
TO STAGE
DON'T BE SHY WITH THOSE SPRINK-LES.
OKAY, TWO MORE!
NO, I CAN'T.
OKAY, JUST ONE MORE.
SNORE...

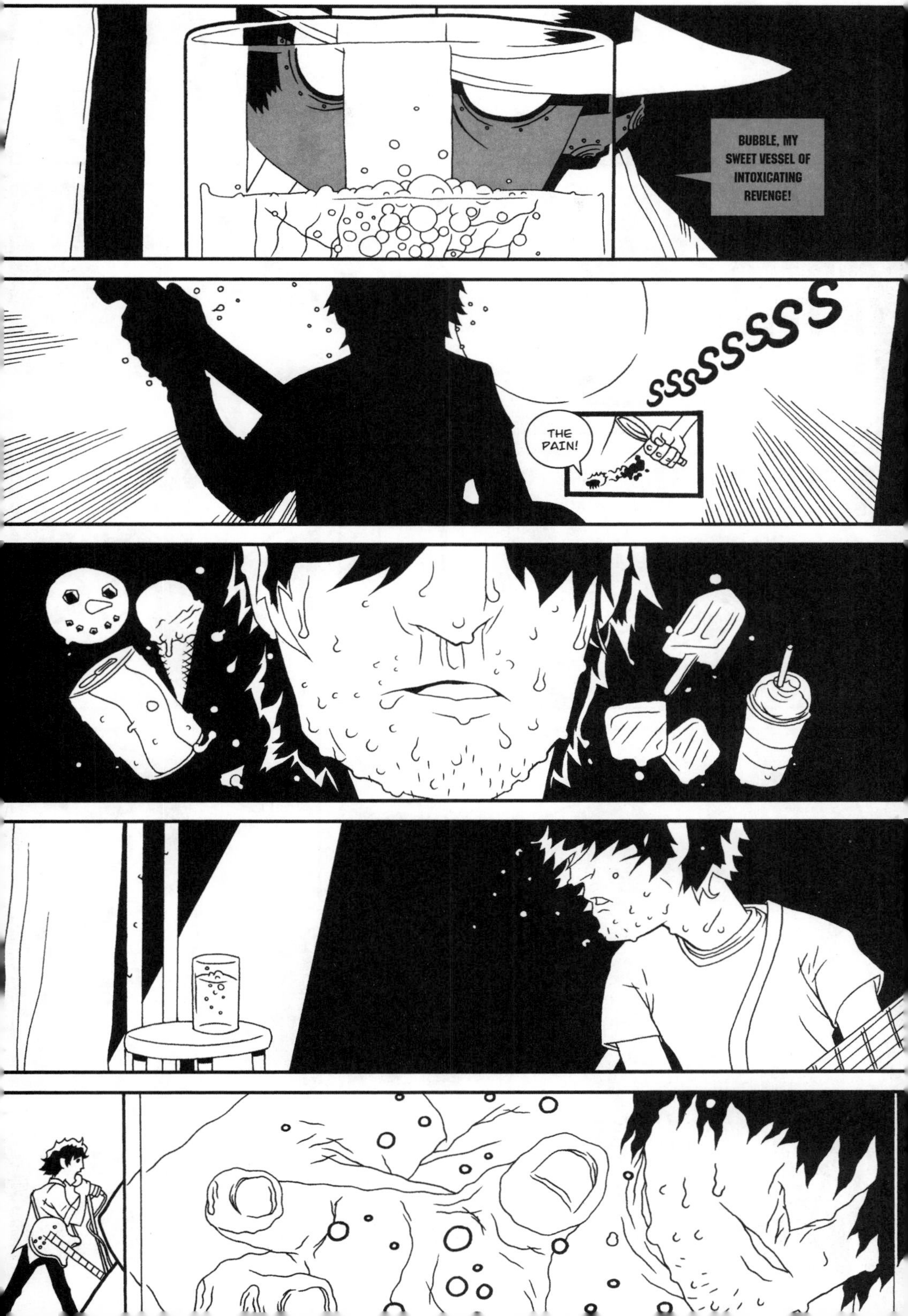
BUBBLE, MY SWEET VESSEL OF INTOXICATING REVENGE!
SSSSSSSS
THE PAIN!

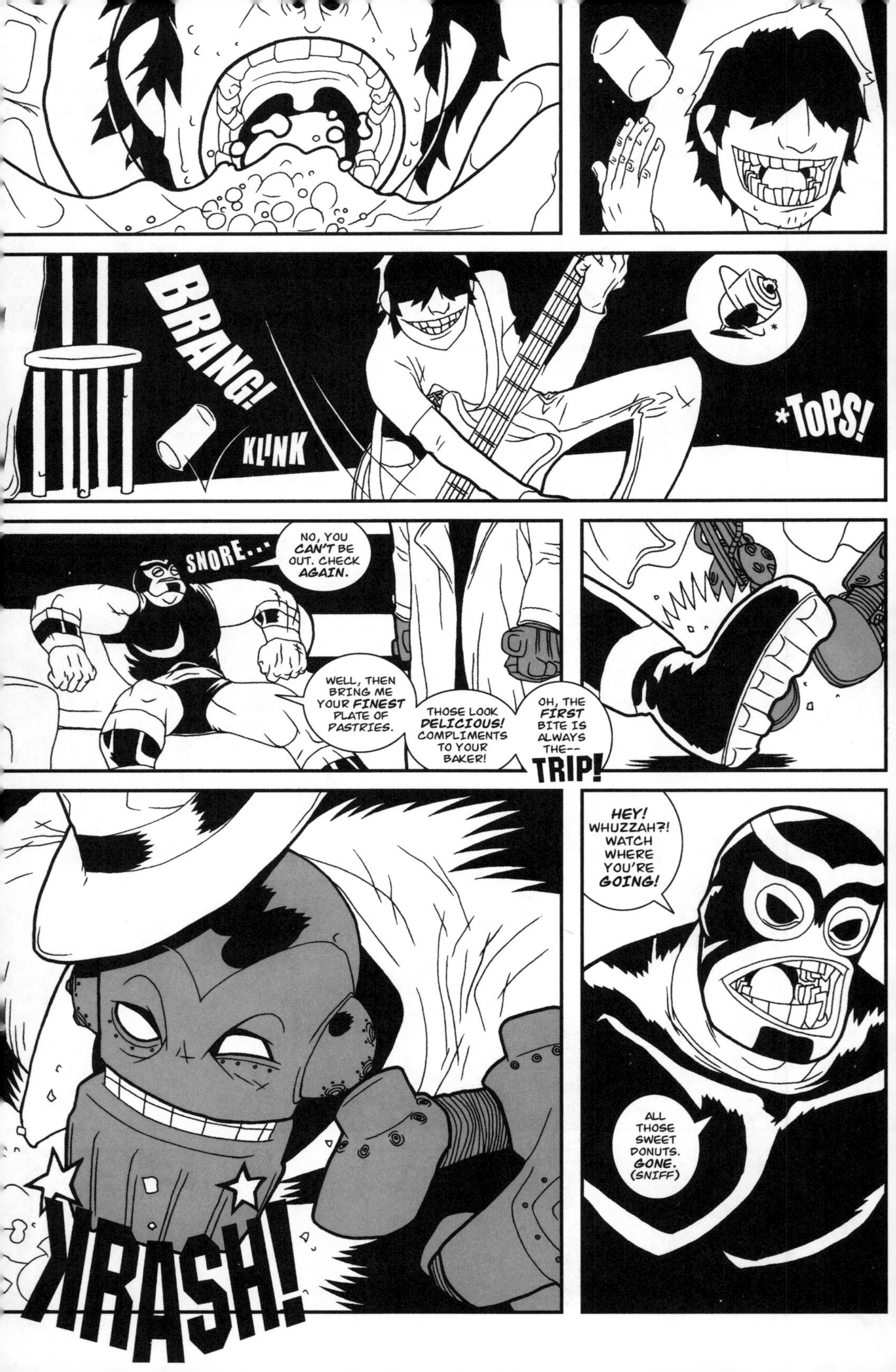
BRANG!
KLINK
*TOPS!
SNORE...
NO, YOU CAN'T BE OUT. CHECK AGAIN.
WELL, THEN BRING ME YOUR FINEST PLATE OF PASTRIES.
THOSE LOOK DELICIOUS! COMPLIMENTS TO YOUR BAKER!
OH, THE FIRST BITE IS ALWAYS THE--
TRIP!
KRASH!
HEY! WHUZZAH?! WATCH WHERE YOU'RE GOING!
ALL THOSE SWEET DONUTS. GONE. (SNIFF)

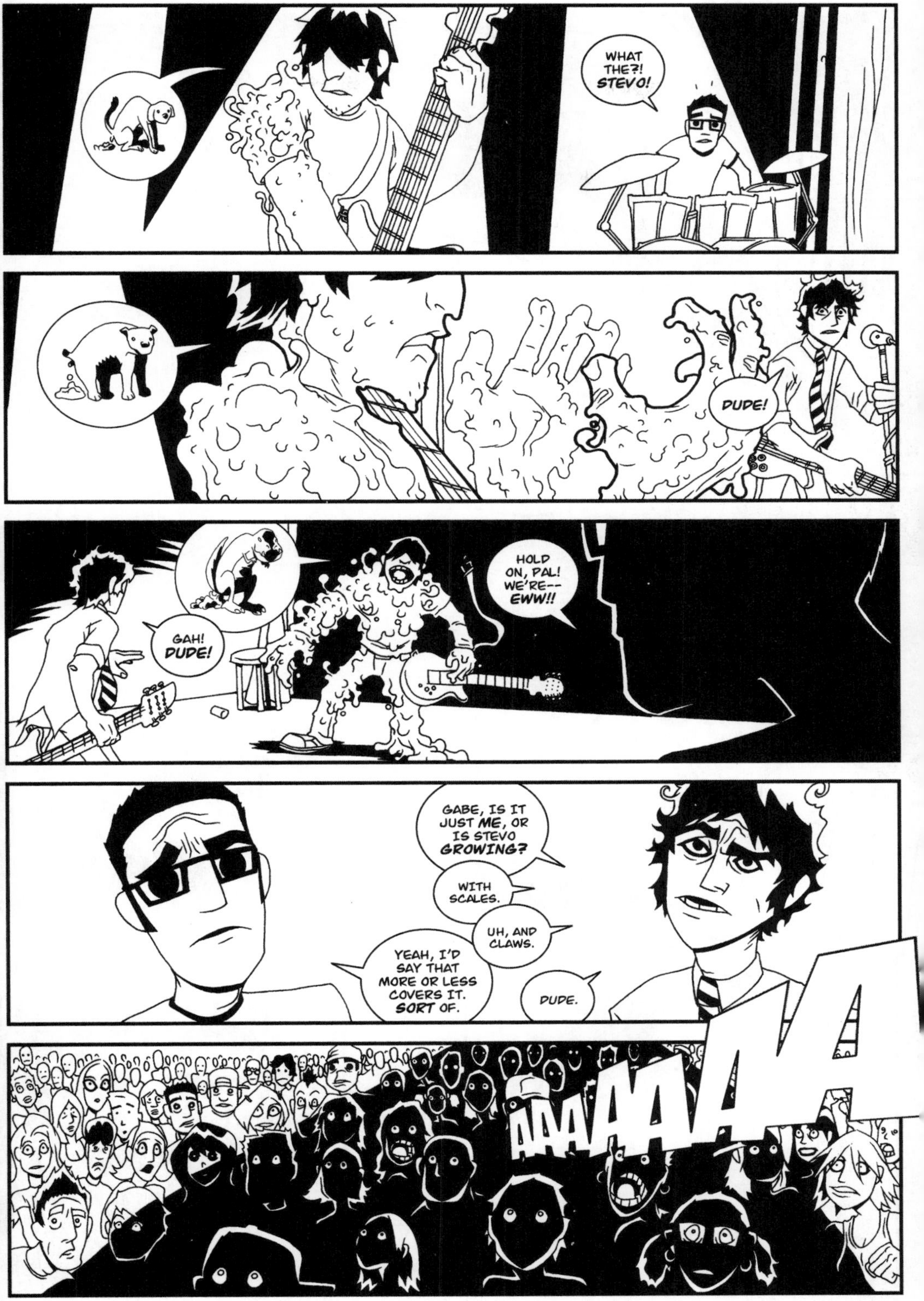
WHAT THE?! STEVO!
DUDE!
GAH! DUDE!
HOLD ON, PAL! WE'RE-- EWW!!
GABE, IS IT JUST ME, OR IS STEVO GROWING?
WITH SCALES.
UH, AND CLAWS.
YEAH, I'D SAY THAT MORE OR LESS COVERS IT. SORT OF.
DUDE.
AAAAAAA

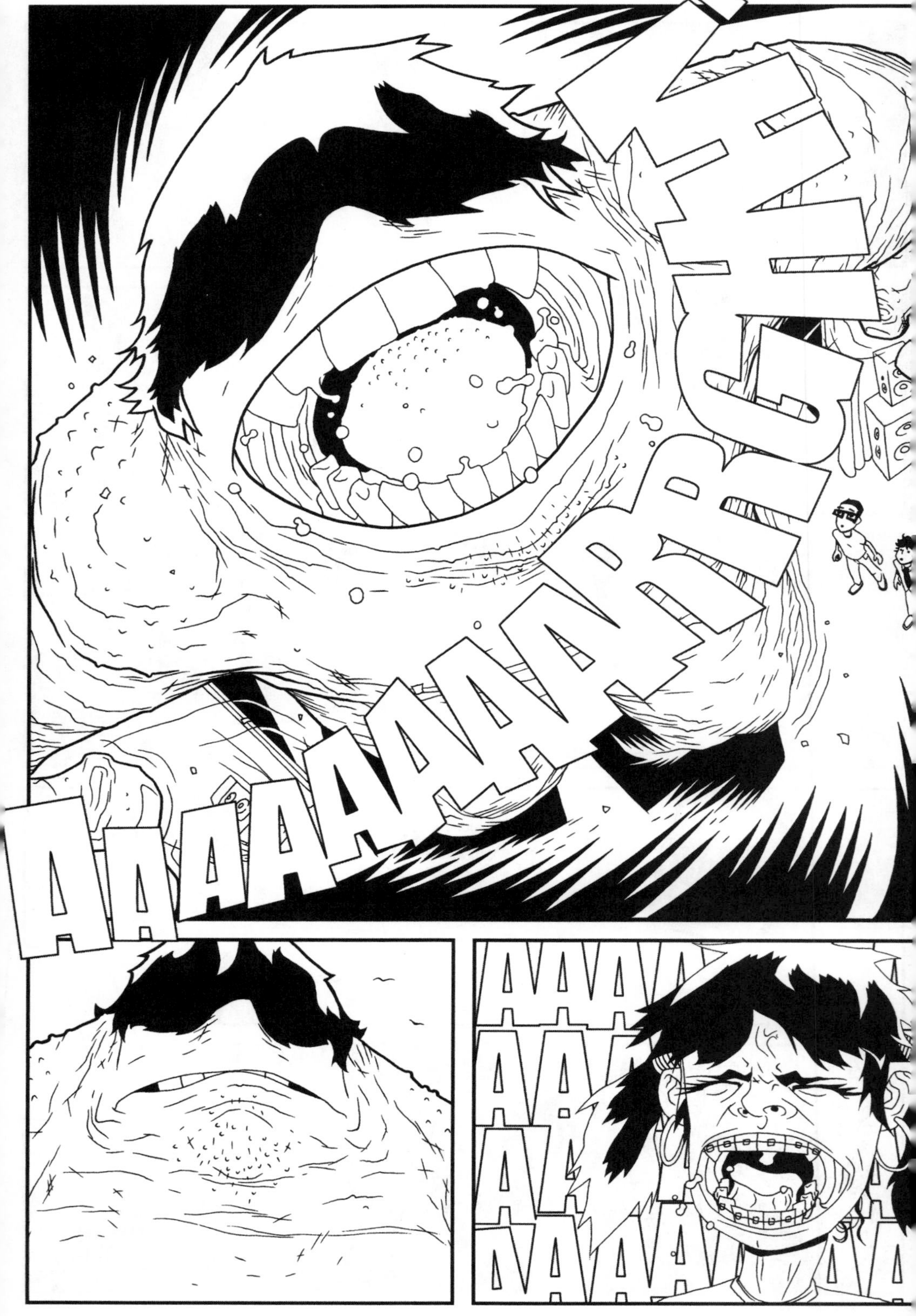
AAAAAAAARRGH!
AAAAAAAAAAAAAAAAAAAA

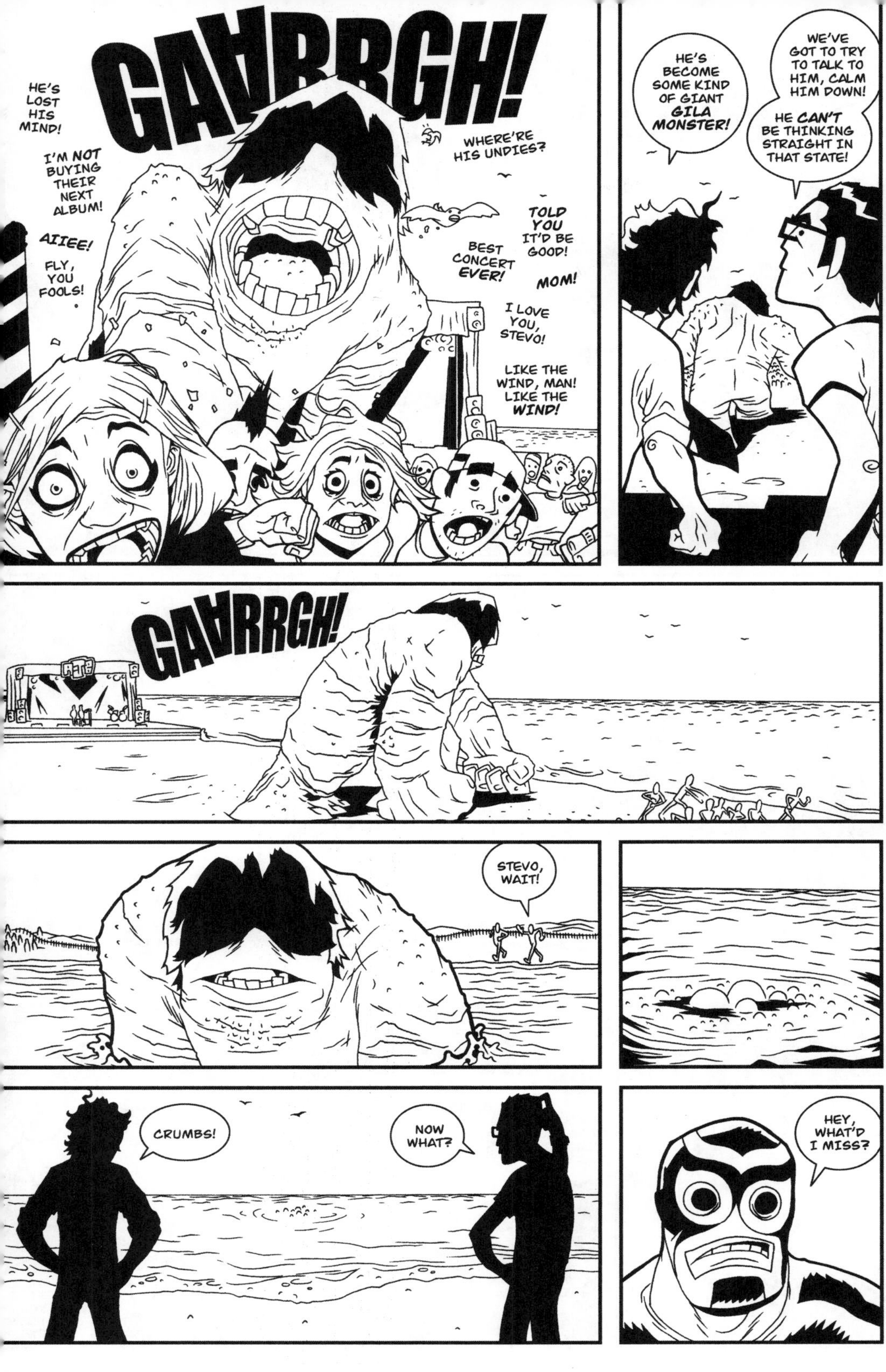
GAAARRGH!
HE'S LOST HIS MIND!
I'M NOT BUYING THEIR NEXT ALBUM!
AIIEE!
FLY, YOU FOOLS!
WHERE'RE HIS UNDIES?
TOLD YOU IT'D BE GOOD!
BEST CONCERT EVER!
MOM!
I LOVE YOU, STEVO!
LIKE THE WIND, MAN! LIKE THE WIND!
HE'S BECOME SOME KIND OF GIANT GILA MONSTER!
WE'VE GOT TO TRY TO TALK TO HIM, CALM HIM DOWN!
HE CAN'T BE THINKING STRAIGHT IN THAT STATE!
GAARRGH!
STEVO, WAIT!
CRUMBS!
NOW WHAT?
HEY, WHAT'D I MISS?

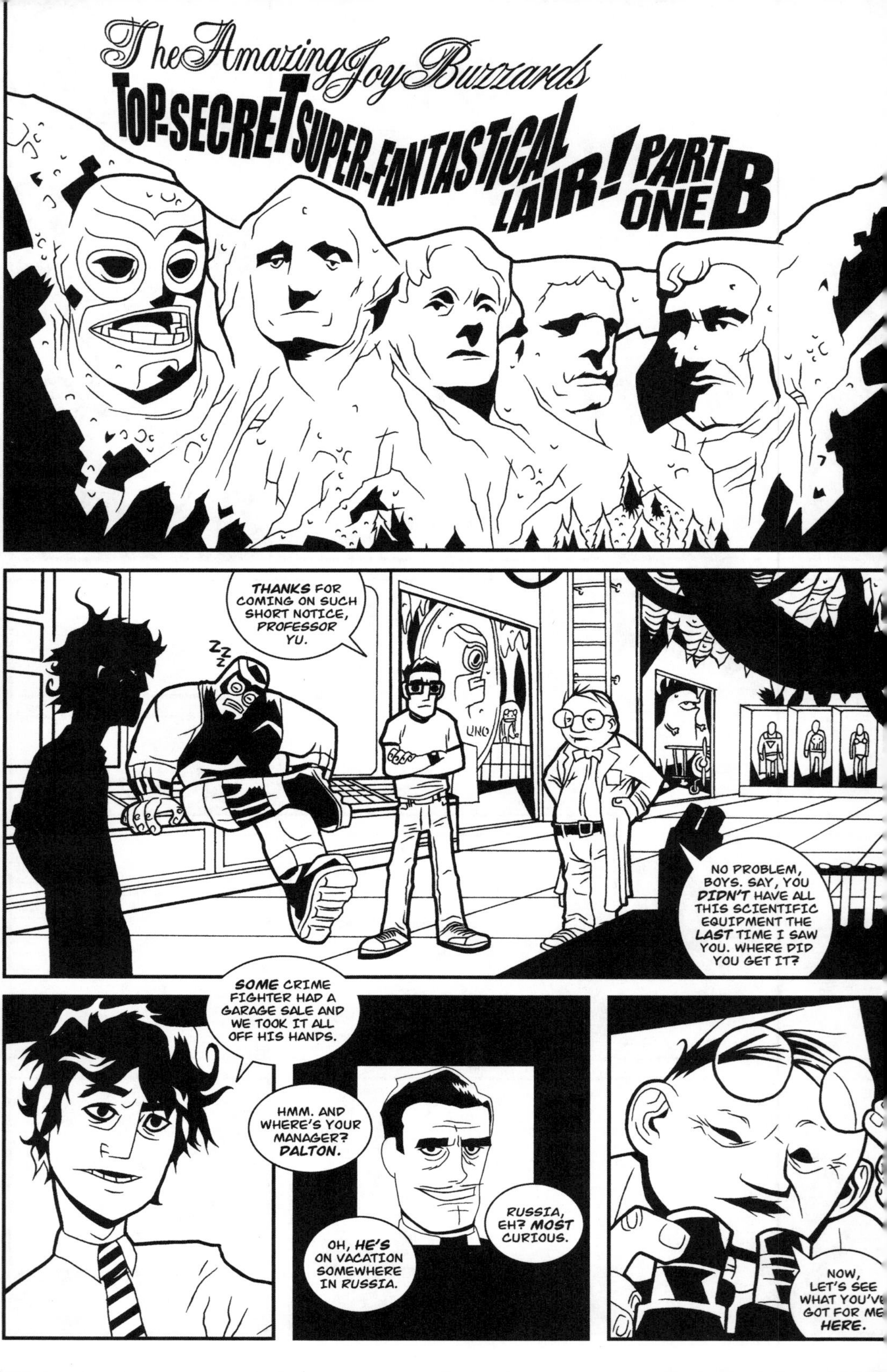

The Amazing Joy Buzzards
TOP-SECRET SUPER-FANTASTICAL LAIR! PART ONE B
ZZZ
THANKS FOR COMING ON SUCH SHORT NOTICE, PROFESSOR YU.
UNO
NO PROBLEM, BOYS. SAY, YOU DIDN'T HAVE ALL THIS SCIENTIFIC EQUIPMENT THE LAST TIME I SAW YOU. WHERE DID YOU GET IT?
SOME CRIME FIGHTER HAD A GARAGE SALE AND WE TOOK IT ALL OFF HIS HANDS.
HMM. AND WHERE'S YOUR MANAGER? DALTON.
OH, HE'S ON VACATION SOMEWHERE IN RUSSIA.
RUSSIA, EH? MOST CURIOUS.
NOW, LET'S SEE WHAT YOU'VE GOT FOR ME HERE.

NOW, YOU SAY THIS WAS A PIECE OF THE RESIDUE LEFT ON STAGE BY THE GILA-STEVO?

BASED ON THIS SAMPLE, I *SHOULD* BE ABLE TO CREATE AN ANTIDOTE, TRANSFORMING HIM *BACK* TO NORMAL.

BUT *WHAT* DO YOU SUPPOSE CAUSED THE TRANSFORMATION IN THE *FIRST* PLACE?

YOU MEAN *WHO* COULD HAVE CAUSED IT, BIFF. WE'VE MADE A *LOT* OF ENEMIES LATELY.

NOW *THINK!* DID ANYONE SEE *ANYTHING* STRANGE AT ALL DURING THE SHOW?

HEY! *WAIT* A MINUTE! I SAW A *ROBOT!*

IN A *TRENCH COAT!*

AND GET THIS...

...IT LOOKED *PINK!*

HA HA *PINK!*

WHO'S EVER HEARD OF *THAT?*

A PINK ROBOT! I'M *KILLIN'* ME HERE.

HOLD UP! EL CAMPEON, YOU SAW A *ROBOT* BACKSTAGE AND YOU DIDN'T *STOP* IT?!

HEY, I WAS TAKING MY *NAP.*

AND I WAS DREAMING.

IT WAS A *DONUT* DREAM.

MMM.

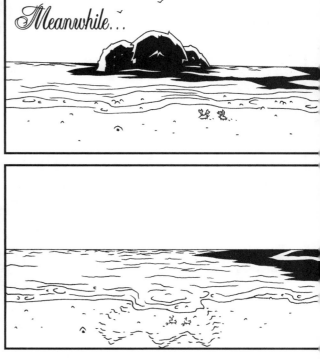

Meanwhile...

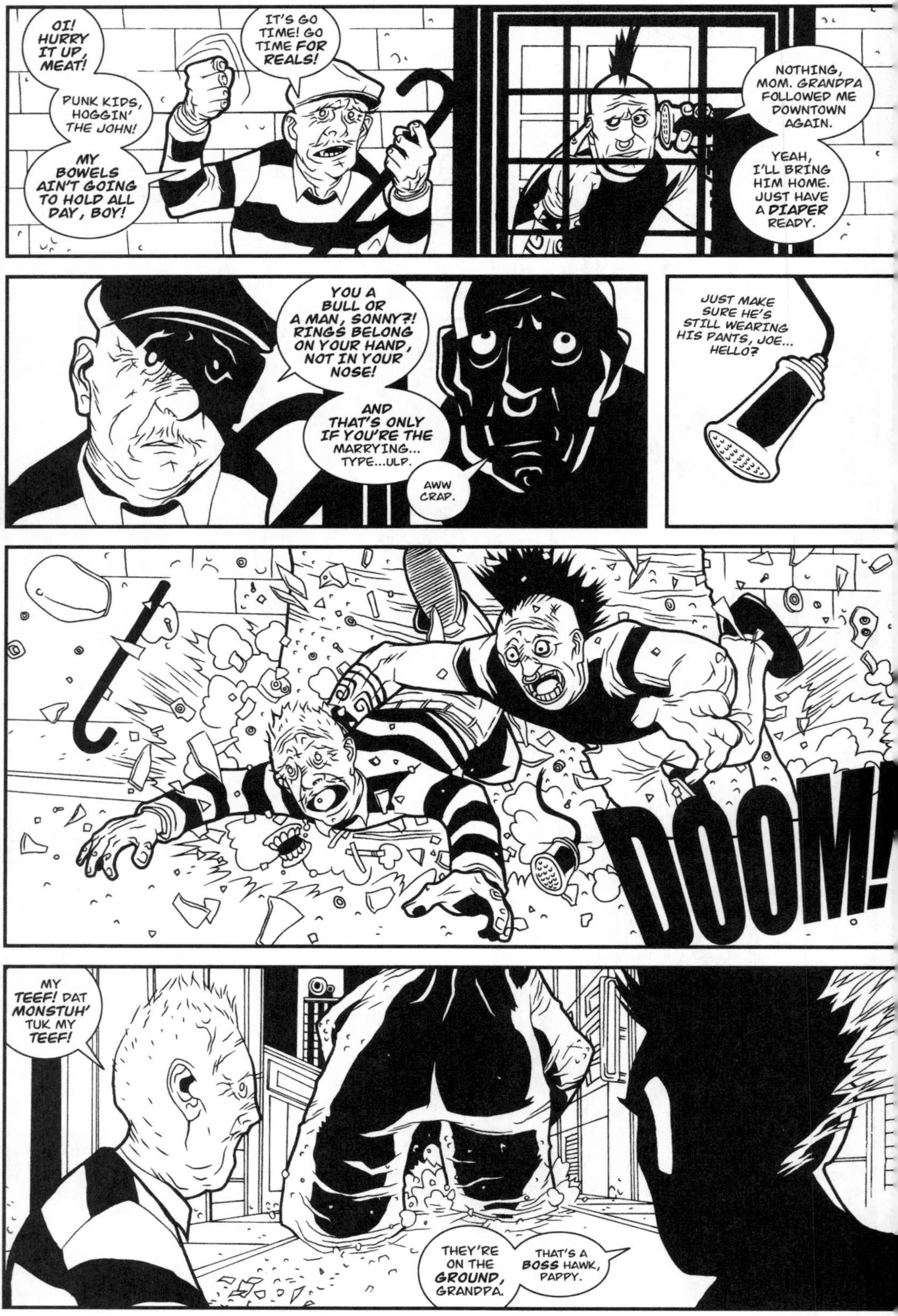
OI! HURRY IT UP, MEAT!
PUNK KIDS, HOGGIN' THE JOHN!
MY BOWELS AIN'T GOING TO HOLD ALL DAY, BOY!
IT'S GO TIME! GO TIME FOR REALS!
NOTHING, MOM. GRANDPA FOLLOWED ME DOWNTOWN AGAIN.
YEAH, I'LL BRING HIM HOME. JUST HAVE A DIAPER READY.
YOU A BULL OR A MAN, SONNY?! RINGS BELONG ON YOUR HAND, NOT IN YOUR NOSE!
AND THAT'S ONLY IF YOU'RE THE MARRYING... TYPE...ULP.
AWW CRAP.
JUST MAKE SURE HE'S STILL WEARING HIS PANTS, JOE... HELLO?
DOOM!
MY TEEF! DAT MONSTUH' TUK MY TEEF!
THEY'RE ON THE GROUND, GRANDPA.
THAT'S A BOSS HAWK, PAPPY.

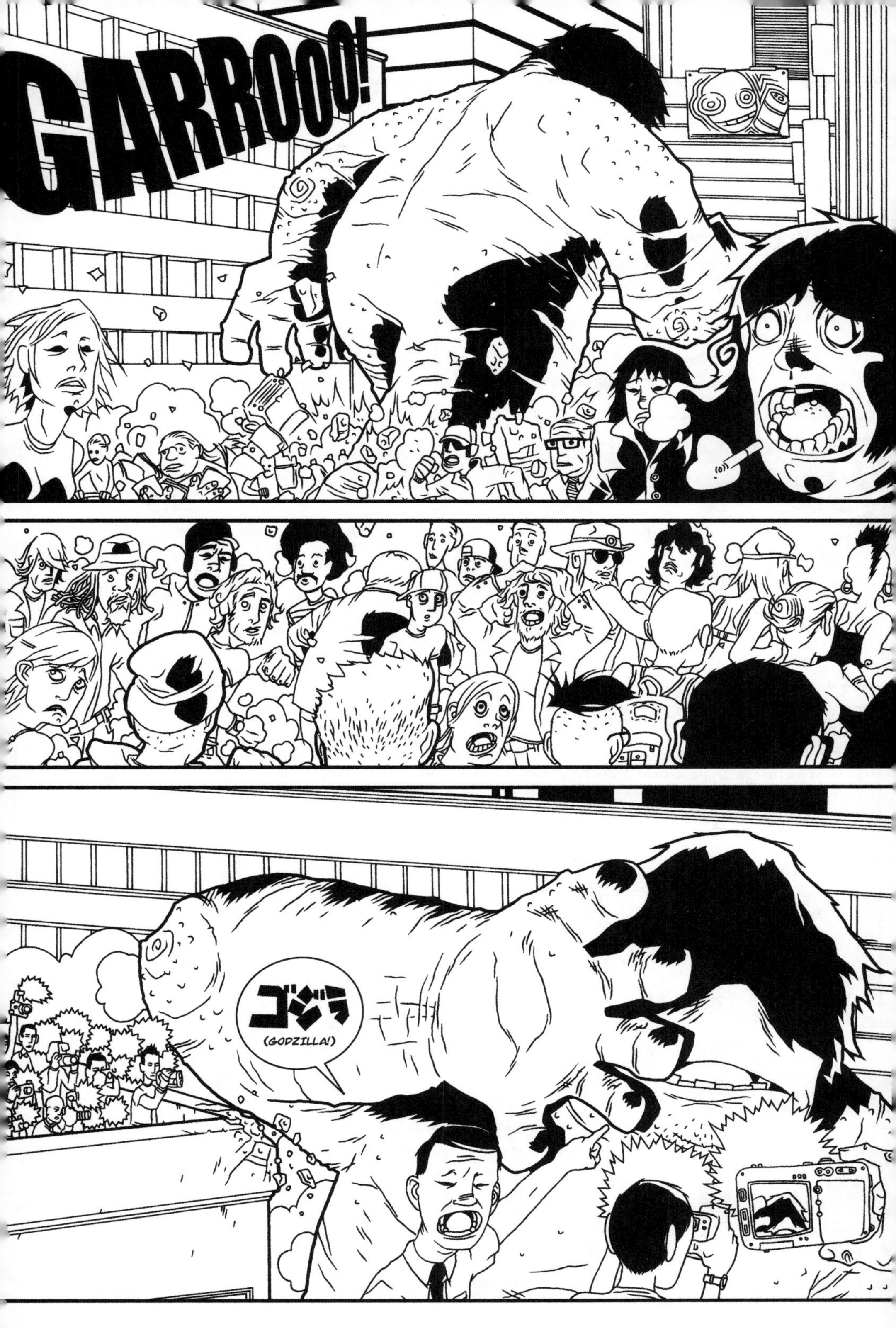
GARROOO!
ゴジラ
(GODZILLA!)

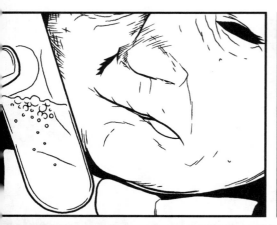

EXCELLENT! I'VE DONE IT!

EH?

WE'LL TAKE IT FROM HERE, PROFESSOR. WE HAVE THE SERUM, NOW WE NEED TO FIND STEVO.

AND I KNOW HOW. LET'S GO!

GOOD LUCK, LADS! HAVE FUN SAVING STEVO! AND THE CITY FOR THAT MATTER. NOT TO MENTION ALL THE ORGANIC LIFE FORMS, AND THE BLAH BLAH BLAH...

READY!...

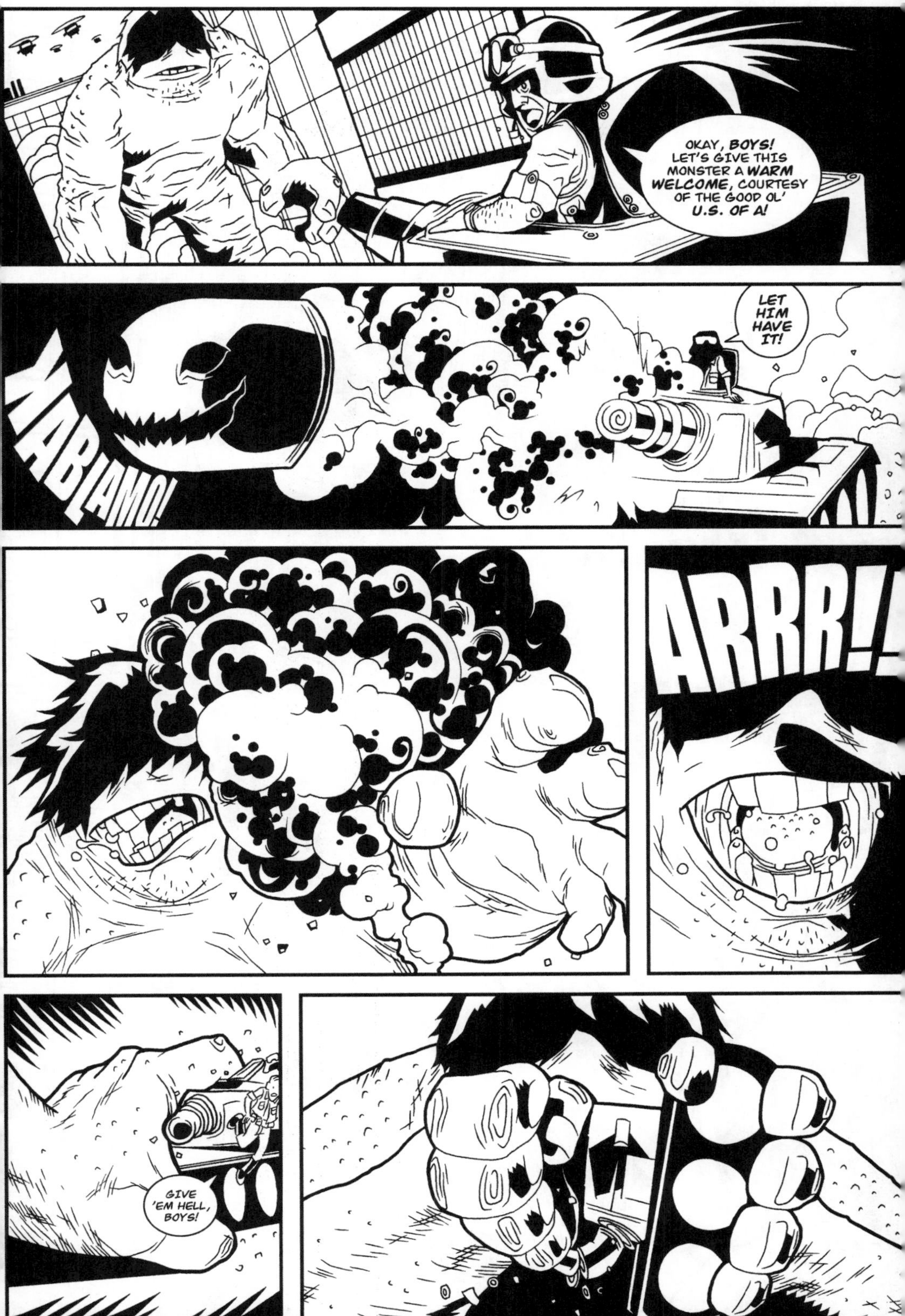
OKAY, BOYS! LET'S GIVE THIS MONSTER A WARM WELCOME, COURTESY OF THE GOOD OL' U.S. OF A!
LET HIM HAVE IT!
KABLAMO!
ARRR!!
GIVE 'EM HELL, BOYS!

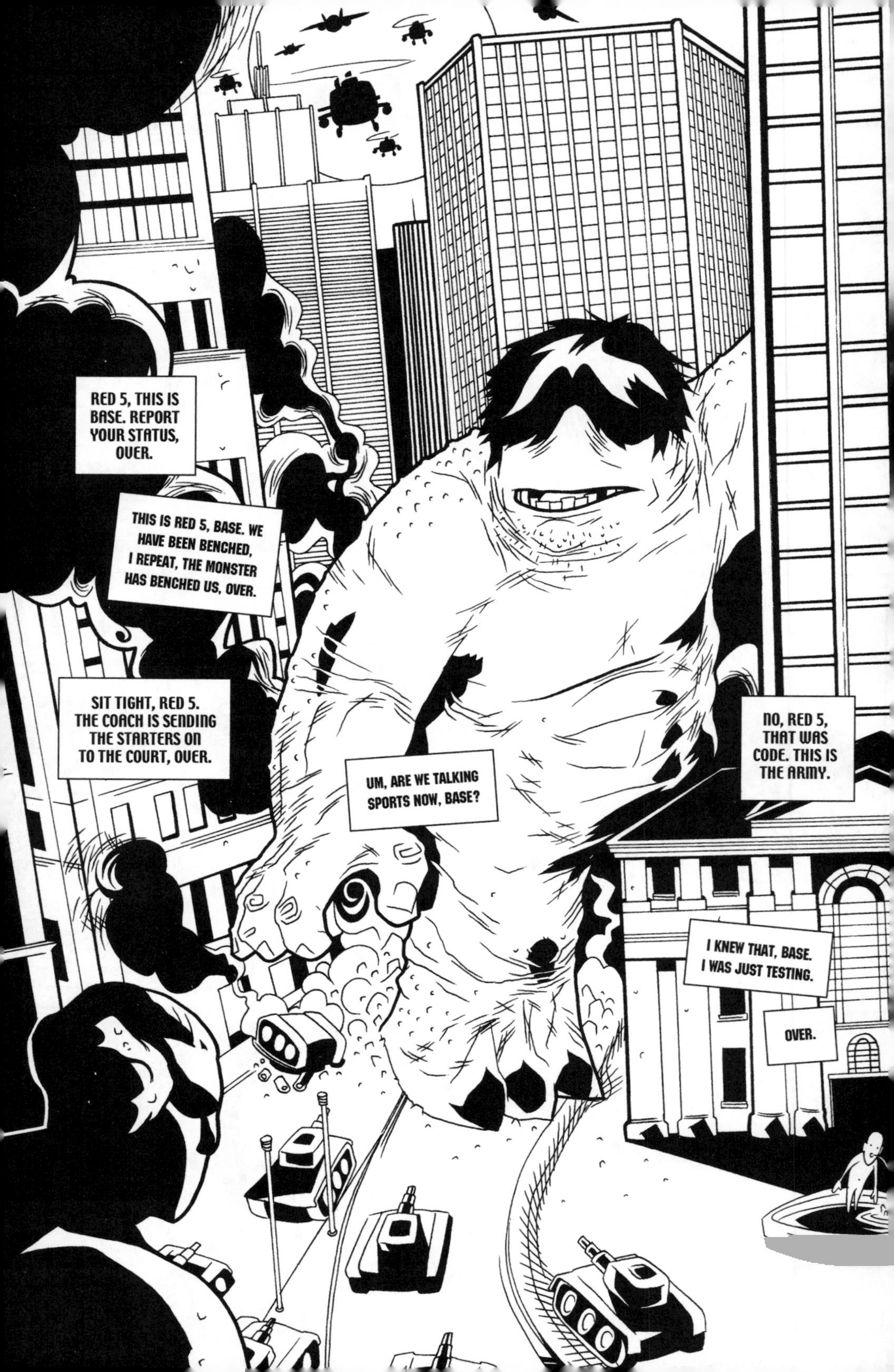
RED 5, THIS IS BASE. REPORT YOUR STATUS, OVER.
THIS IS RED 5, BASE. WE HAVE BEEN BENCHED, I REPEAT, THE MONSTER HAS BENCHED US, OVER.
SIT TIGHT, RED 5. THE COACH IS SENDING THE STARTERS ON TO THE COURT, OVER.
UM, ARE WE TALKING SPORTS NOW, BASE?
NO, RED 5, THAT WAS CODE. THIS IS THE ARMY.
I KNEW THAT, BASE. I WAS JUST TESTING.
OVER.

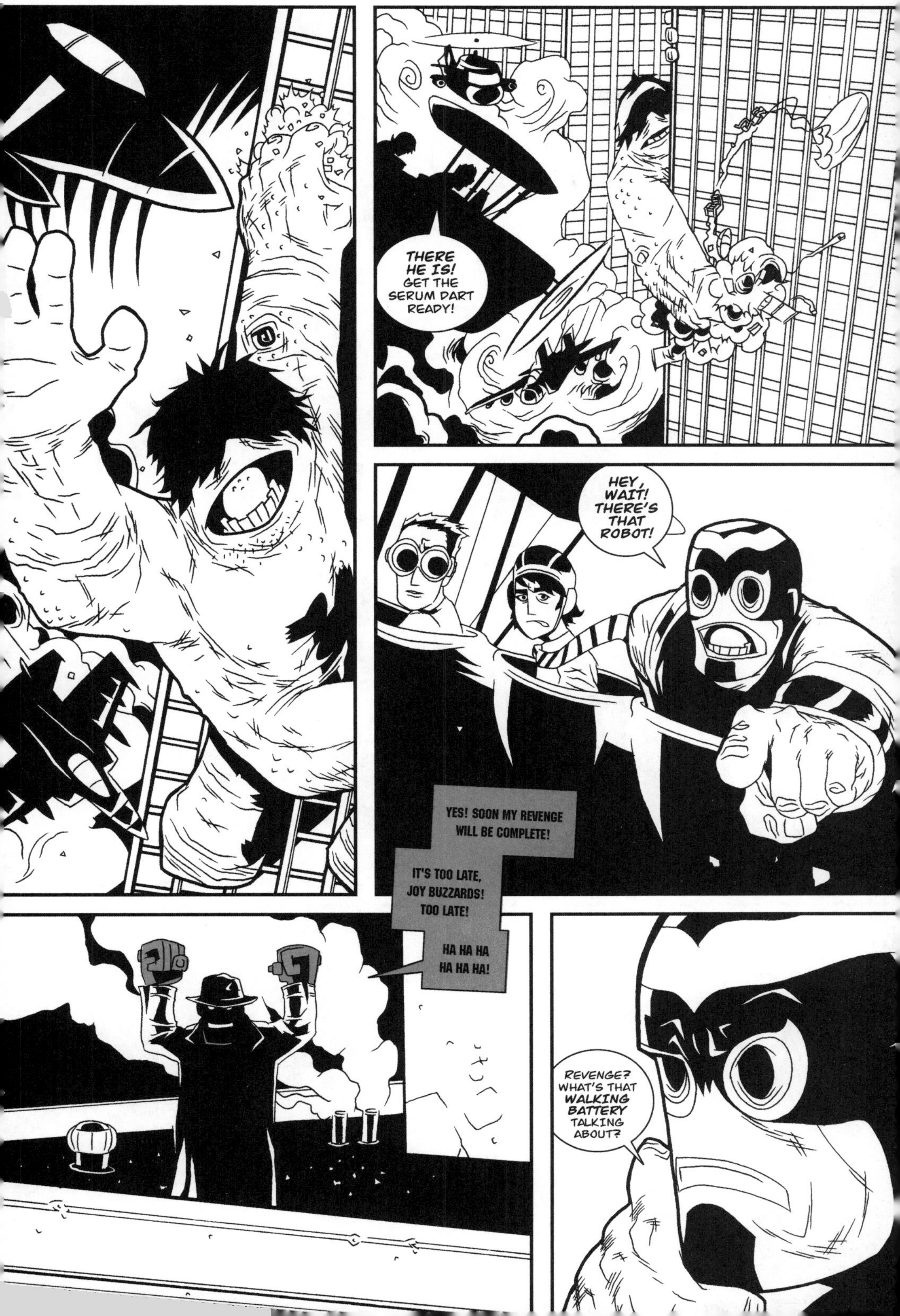
THERE HE IS! GET THE SERUM DART READY!
HEY, WAIT! THERE'S THAT ROBOT!
YES! SOON MY REVENGE WILL BE COMPLETE!
IT'S TOO LATE, JOY BUZZARDS! TOO LATE!
HA HA HA HA HA HA!
REVENGE? WHAT'S THAT WALKING BATTERY TALKING ABOUT?

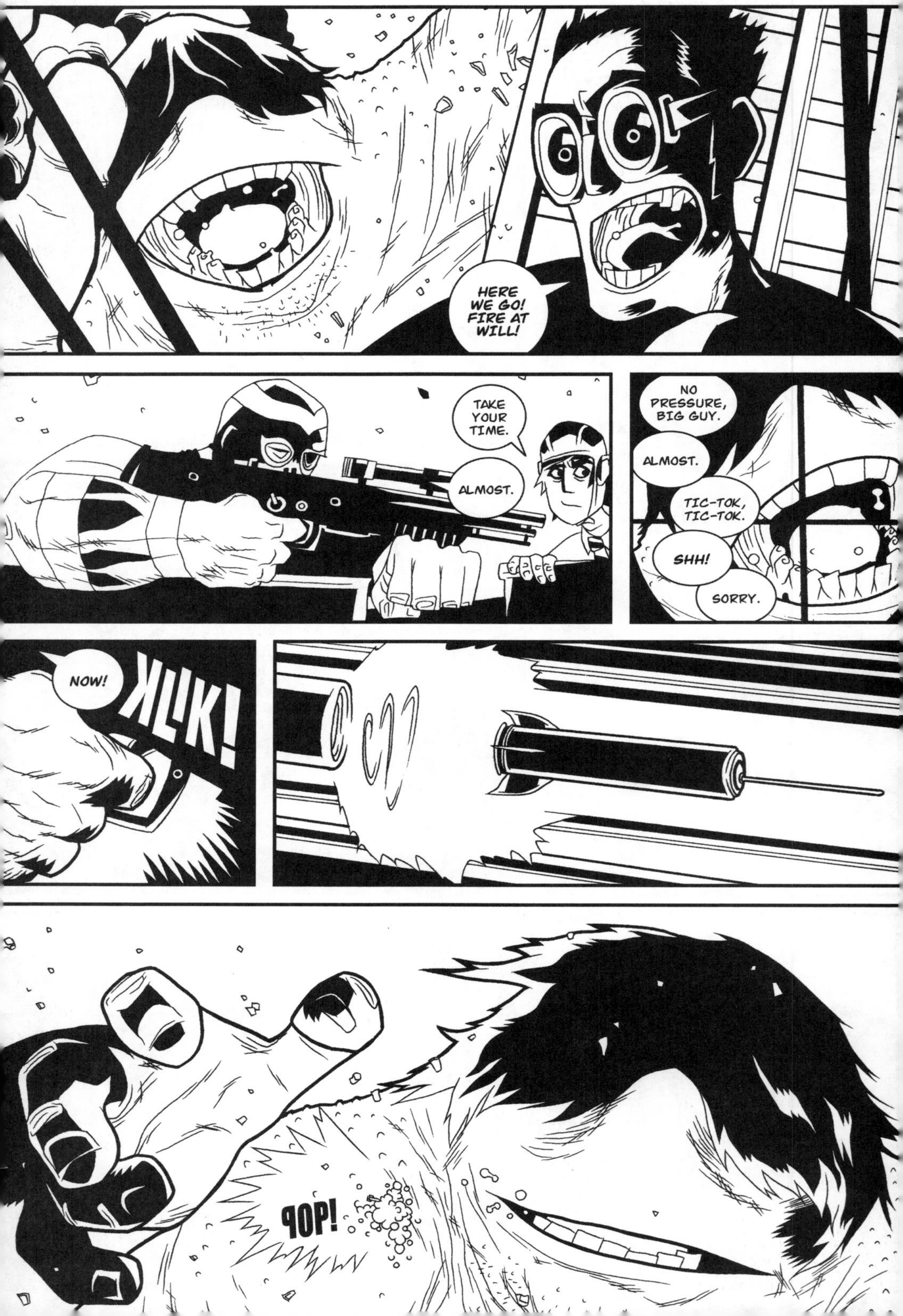
HERE WE GO! FIRE AT WILL!
TAKE YOUR TIME.
ALMOST.
NO PRESSURE, BIG GUY.
ALMOST.
TIC-TOK, TIC-TOK.
SHH!
SORRY.
NOW!
KLIK!
POP!

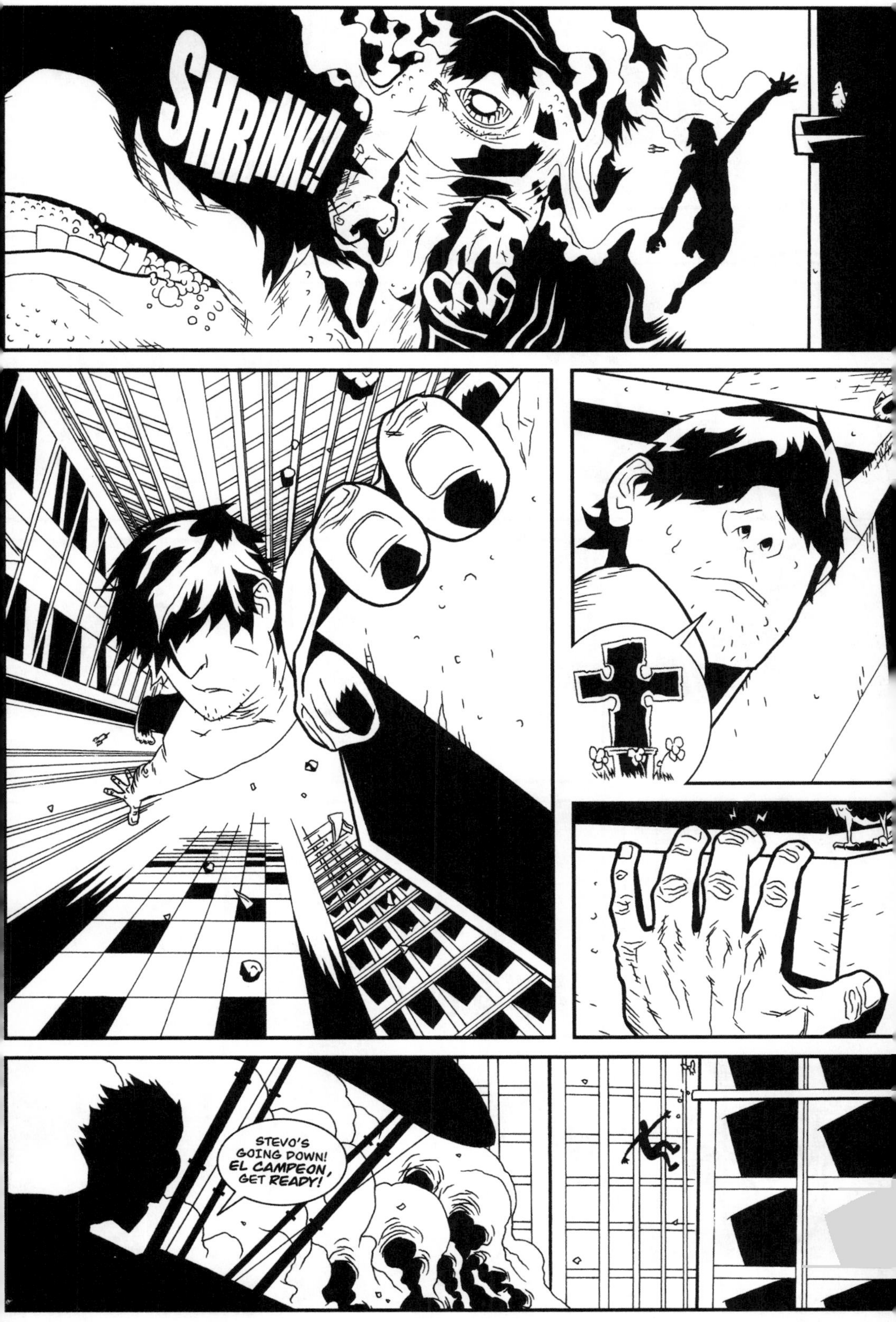
SHRINK!!
STEVO'S GOING DOWN! EL CAMPEON, GET READY!

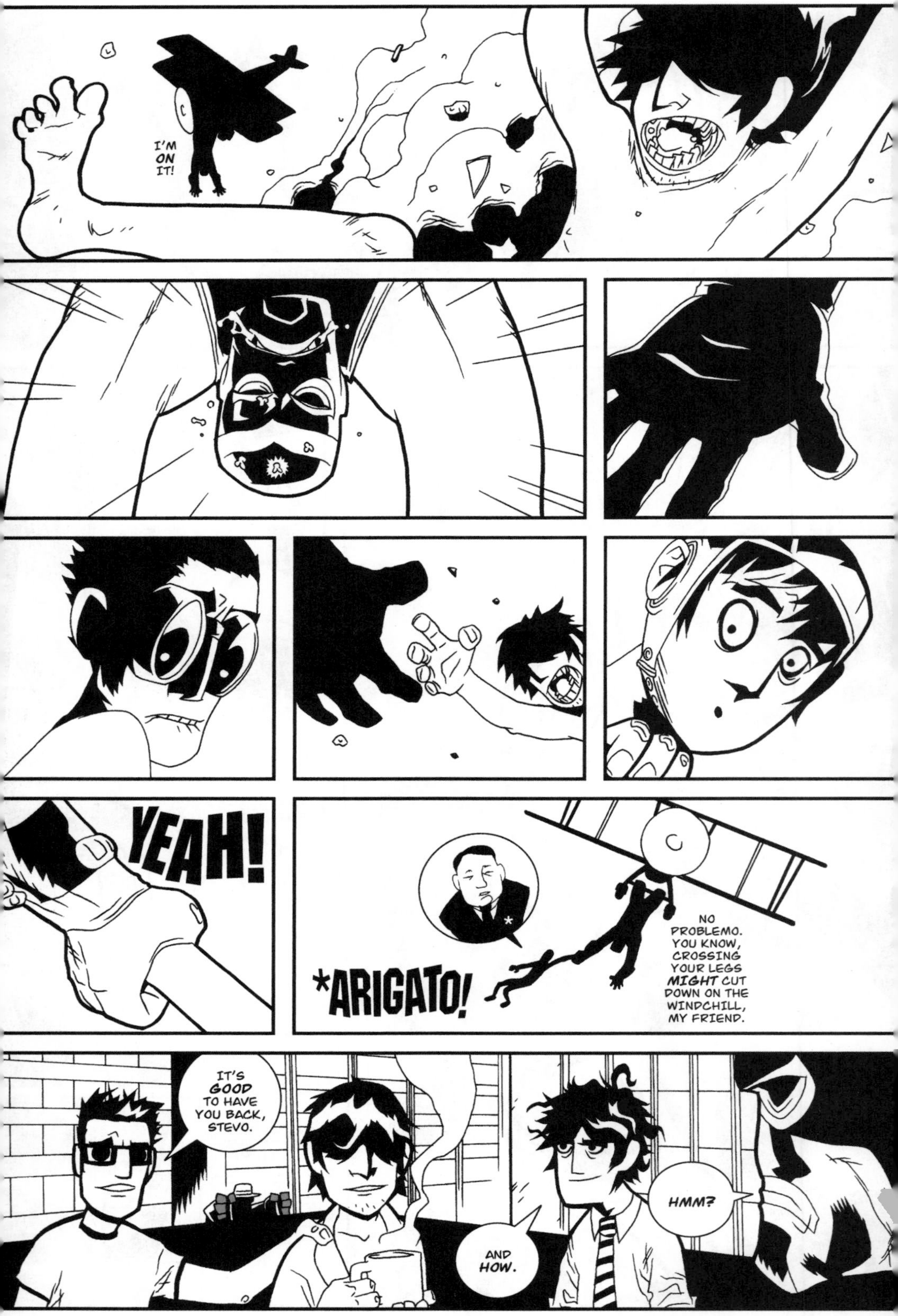

I'M ON IT!
YEAH!
*ARIGATO!
NO PROBLEMO. YOU KNOW, CROSSING YOUR LEGS MIGHT CUT DOWN ON THE WINDCHILL, MY FRIEND.
IT'S GOOD TO HAVE YOU BACK, STEVO.
AND HOW.
HMM?

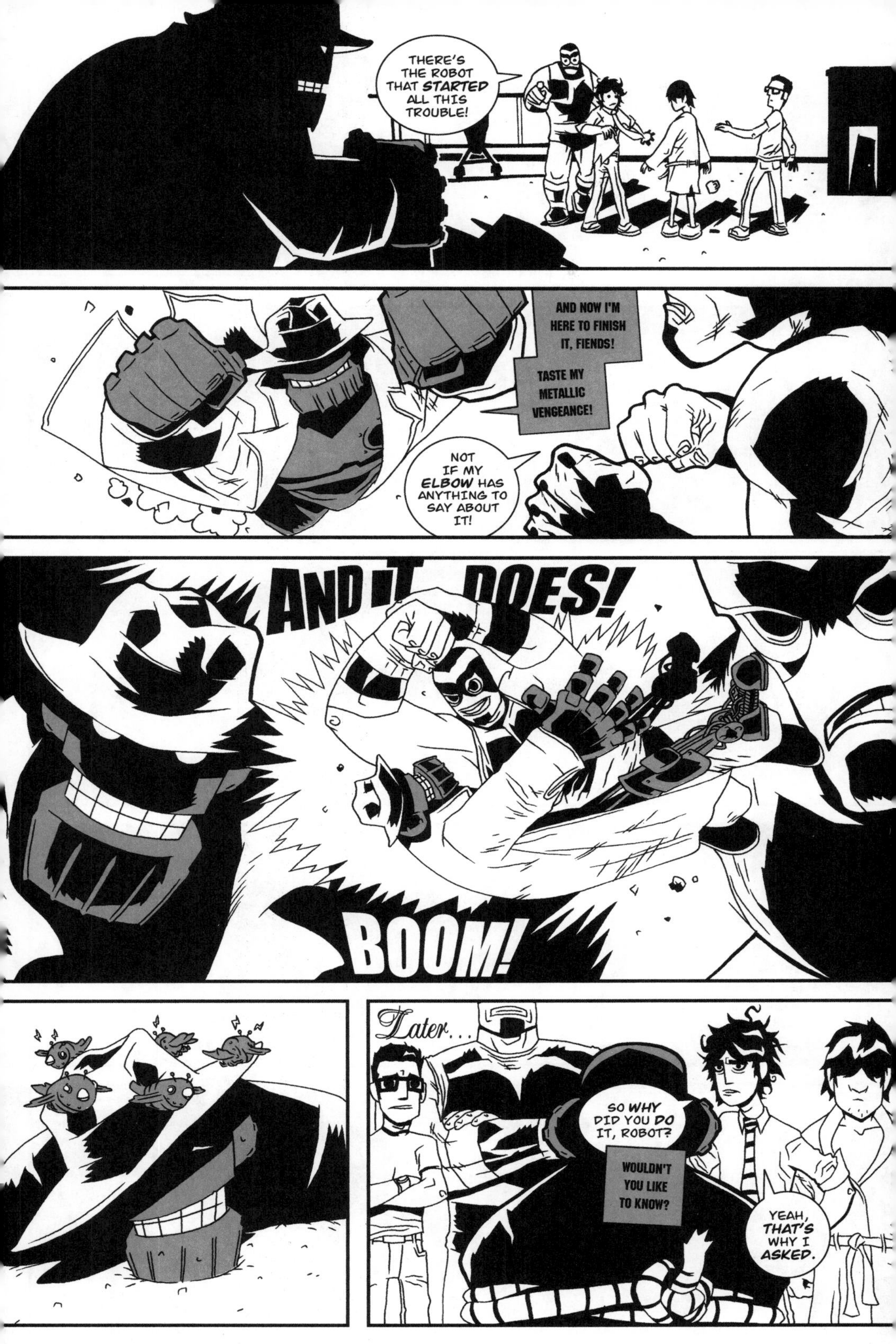

THERE'S THE ROBOT THAT STARTED ALL THIS TROUBLE!
AND NOW I'M HERE TO FINISH IT, FIENDS!
TASTE MY METALLIC VENGEANCE!
NOT IF MY ELBOW HAS ANYTHING TO SAY ABOUT IT!
AND IT DOES!
BOOM!
Later...
SO WHY DID YOU DO IT, ROBOT?
WOULDN'T YOU LIKE TO KNOW?
YEAH, THAT'S WHY I ASKED.

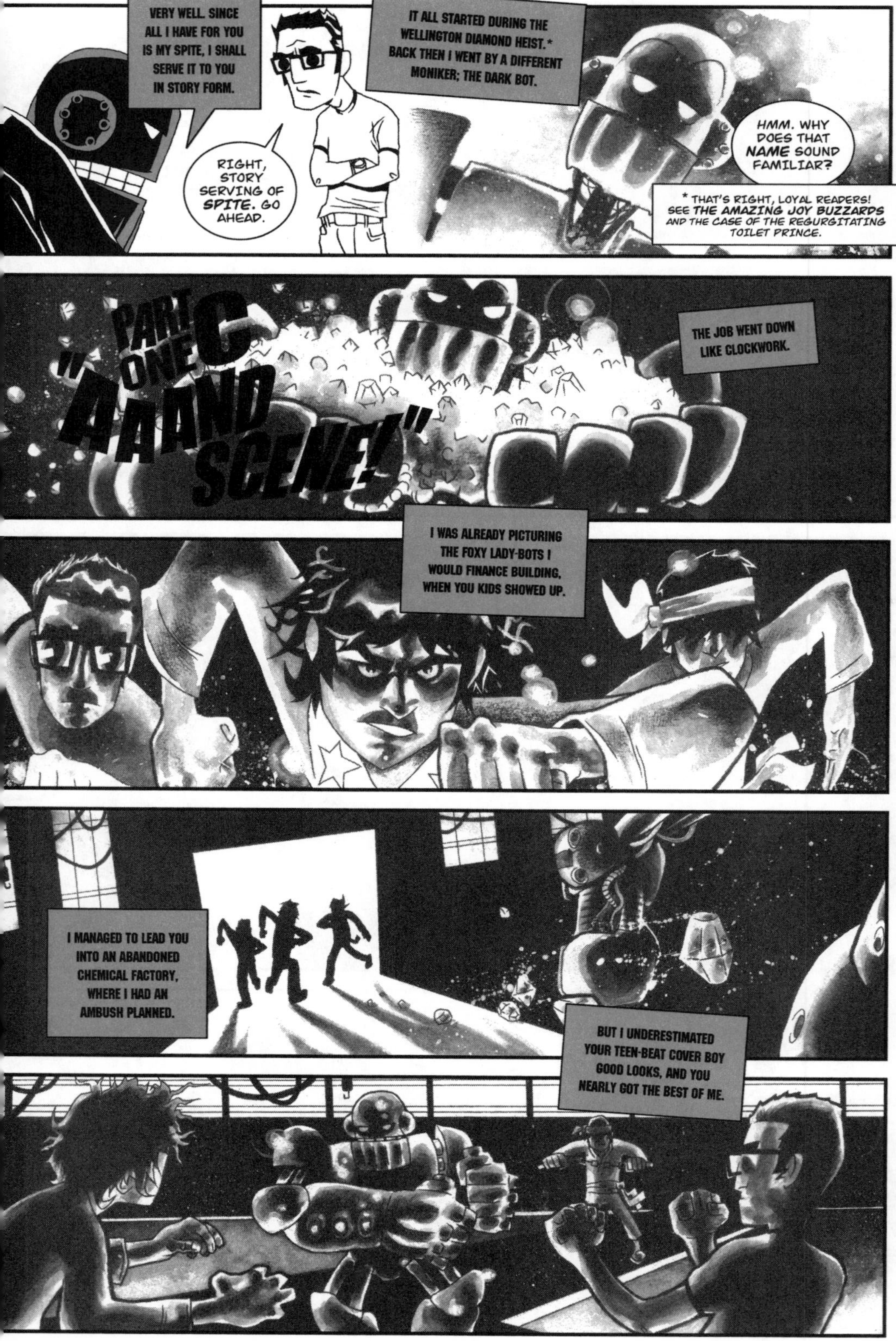
VERY WELL. SINCE ALL I HAVE FOR YOU IS MY SPITE, I SHALL SERVE IT TO YOU IN STORY FORM.
RIGHT, STORY SERVING OF SPITE. GO AHEAD.
IT ALL STARTED DURING THE WELLINGTON DIAMOND HEIST.* BACK THEN I WENT BY A DIFFERENT MONIKER; THE DARK BOT.
HMM. WHY DOES THAT NAME SOUND FAMILIAR?
* THAT'S RIGHT, LOYAL READERS! SEE THE AMAZING JOY BUZZARDS AND THE CASE OF THE REGURGITATING TOILET PRINCE.
PART ONE C
"AAAND SCENE!"
THE JOB WENT DOWN LIKE CLOCKWORK.
I WAS ALREADY PICTURING THE FOXY LADY-BOTS I WOULD FINANCE BUILDING, WHEN YOU KIDS SHOWED UP.
I MANAGED TO LEAD YOU INTO AN ABANDONED CHEMICAL FACTORY, WHERE I HAD AN AMBUSH PLANNED.
BUT I UNDERESTIMATED YOUR TEEN-BEAT COVER BOY GOOD LOOKS, AND YOU NEARLY GOT THE BEST OF ME.

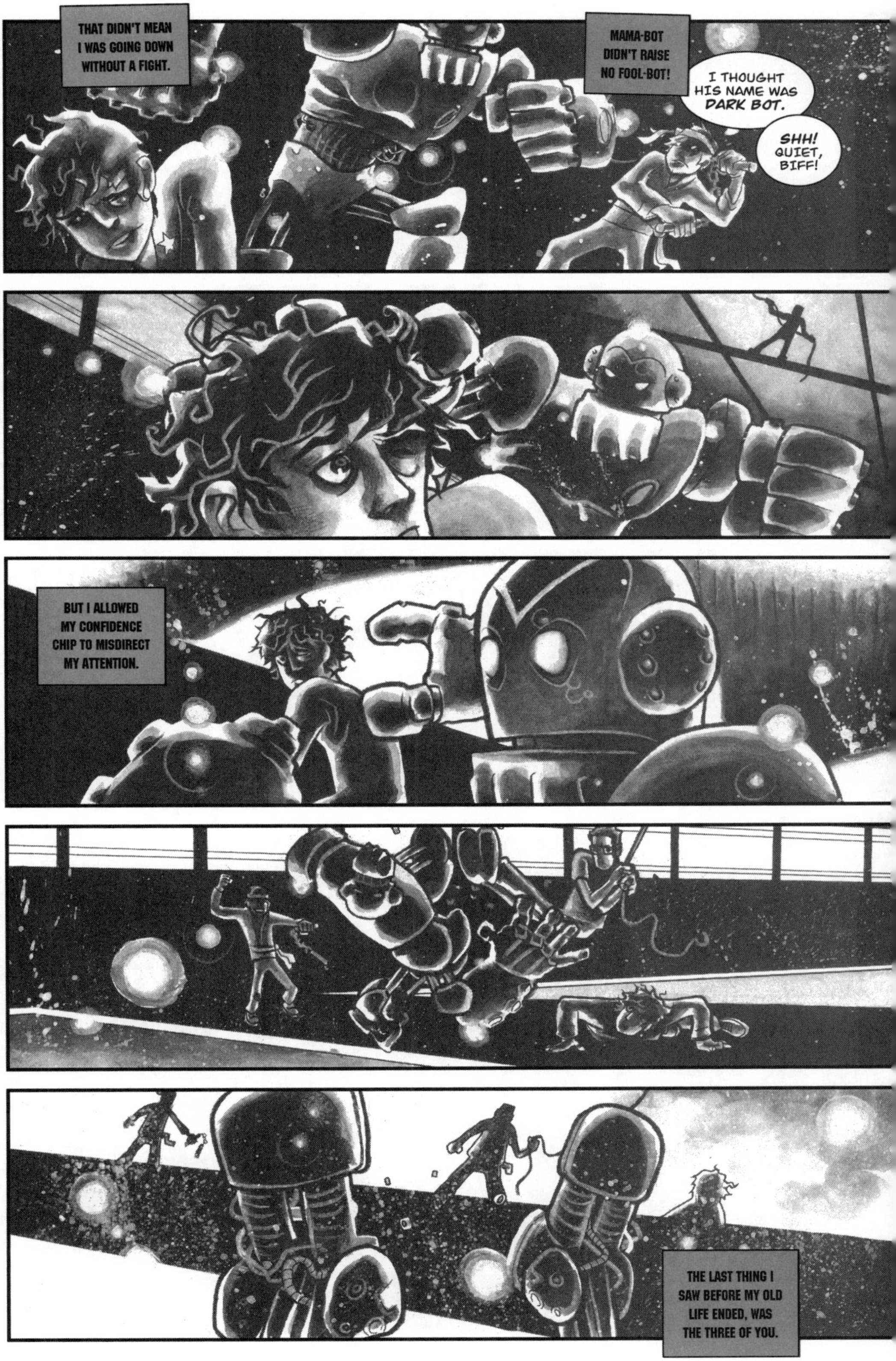
THAT DIDN'T MEAN I WAS GOING DOWN WITHOUT A FIGHT.
MAMA-BOT DIDN'T RAISE NO FOOL-BOT!
I THOUGHT HIS NAME WAS DARK BOT.
SHH! QUIET, BIFF!
BUT I ALLOWED MY CONFIDENCE CHIP TO MISDIRECT MY ATTENTION.
THE LAST THING I SAW BEFORE MY OLD LIFE ENDED, WAS THE THREE OF YOU.

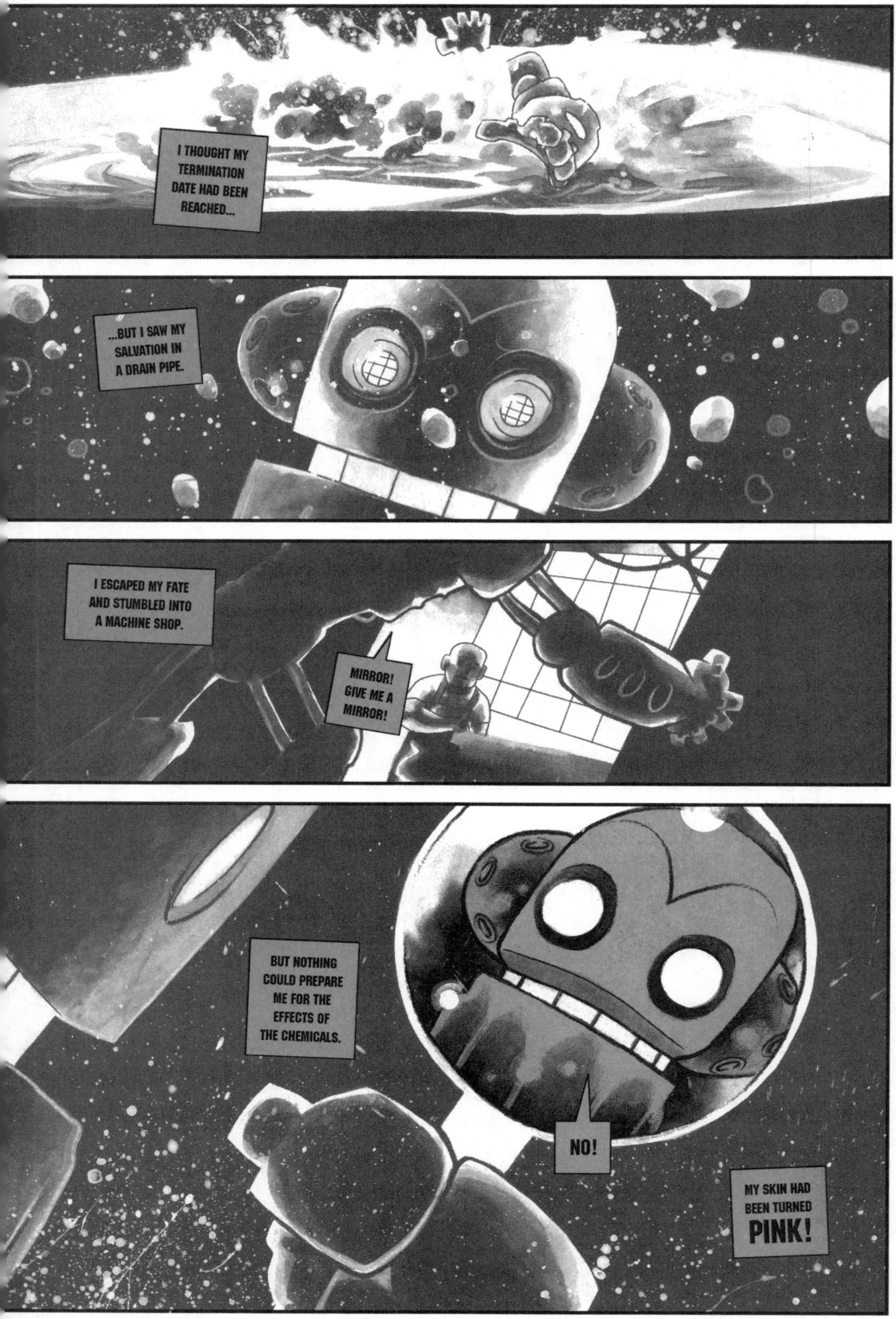
I THOUGHT MY TERMINATION DATE HAD BEEN REACHED...
...BUT I SAW MY SALVATION IN A DRAIN PIPE.
I ESCAPED MY FATE AND STUMBLED INTO A MACHINE SHOP.
MIRROR! GIVE ME A MIRROR!
BUT NOTHING COULD PREPARE ME FOR THE EFFECTS OF THE CHEMICALS.
NO!
MY SKIN HAD BEEN TURNED PINK!

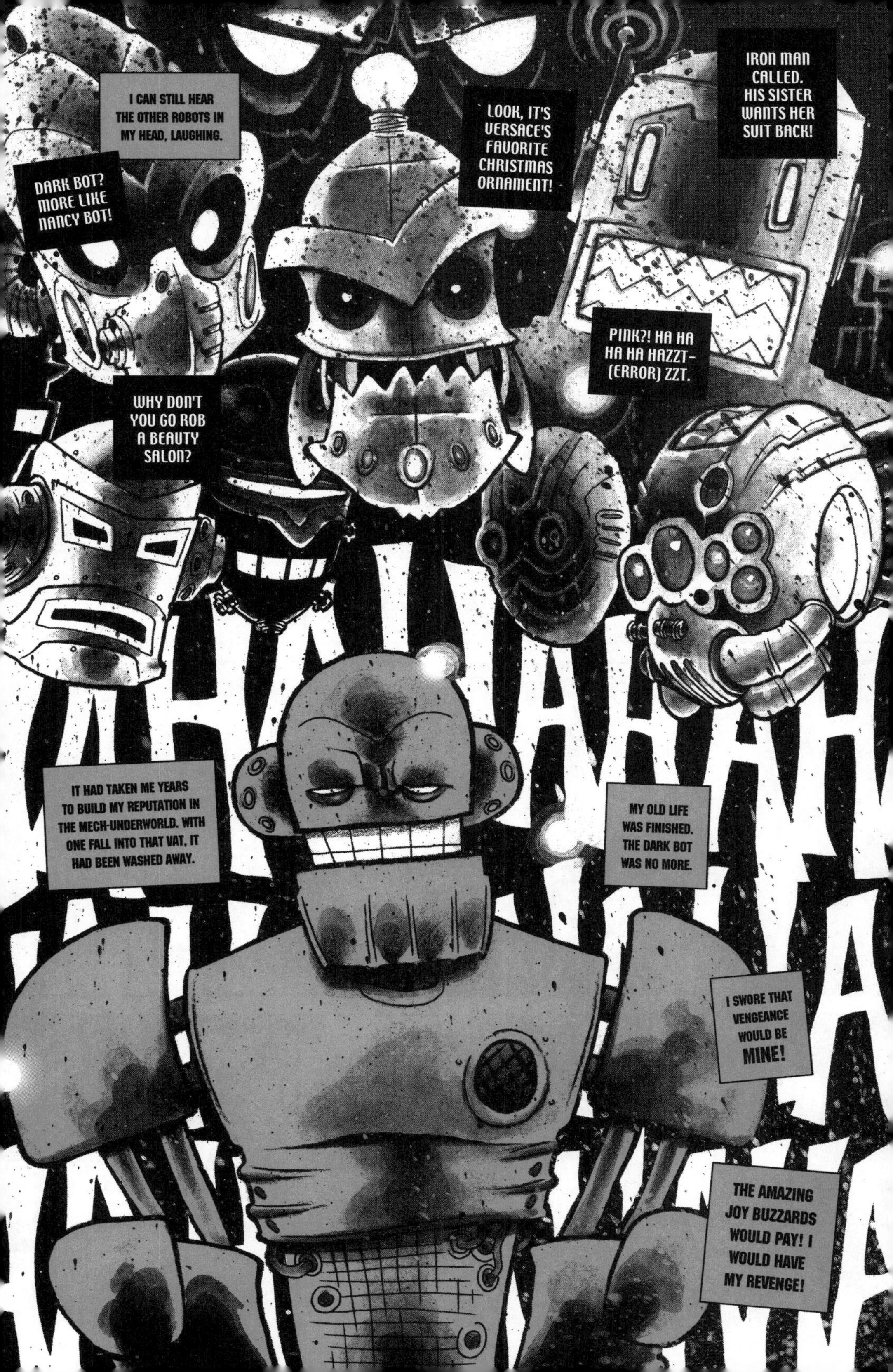
I CAN STILL HEAR THE OTHER ROBOTS IN MY HEAD, LAUGHING.
DARK BOT? MORE LIKE NANCY BOT!
LOOK, IT'S VERSACE'S FAVORITE CHRISTMAS ORNAMENT!
IRON MAN CALLED. HIS SISTER WANTS HER SUIT BACK!
PINK?! HA HA HA HA HAZZT-(ERROR) ZZT.
WHY DON'T YOU GO ROB A BEAUTY SALON?
IT HAD TAKEN ME YEARS TO BUILD MY REPUTATION IN THE MECH-UNDERWORLD. WITH ONE FALL INTO THAT VAT, IT HAD BEEN WASHED AWAY.
MY OLD LIFE WAS FINISHED. THE DARK BOT WAS NO MORE.
I SWORE THAT VENGEANCE WOULD BE MINE!
THE AMAZING JOY BUZZARDS WOULD PAY! I WOULD HAVE MY REVENGE!

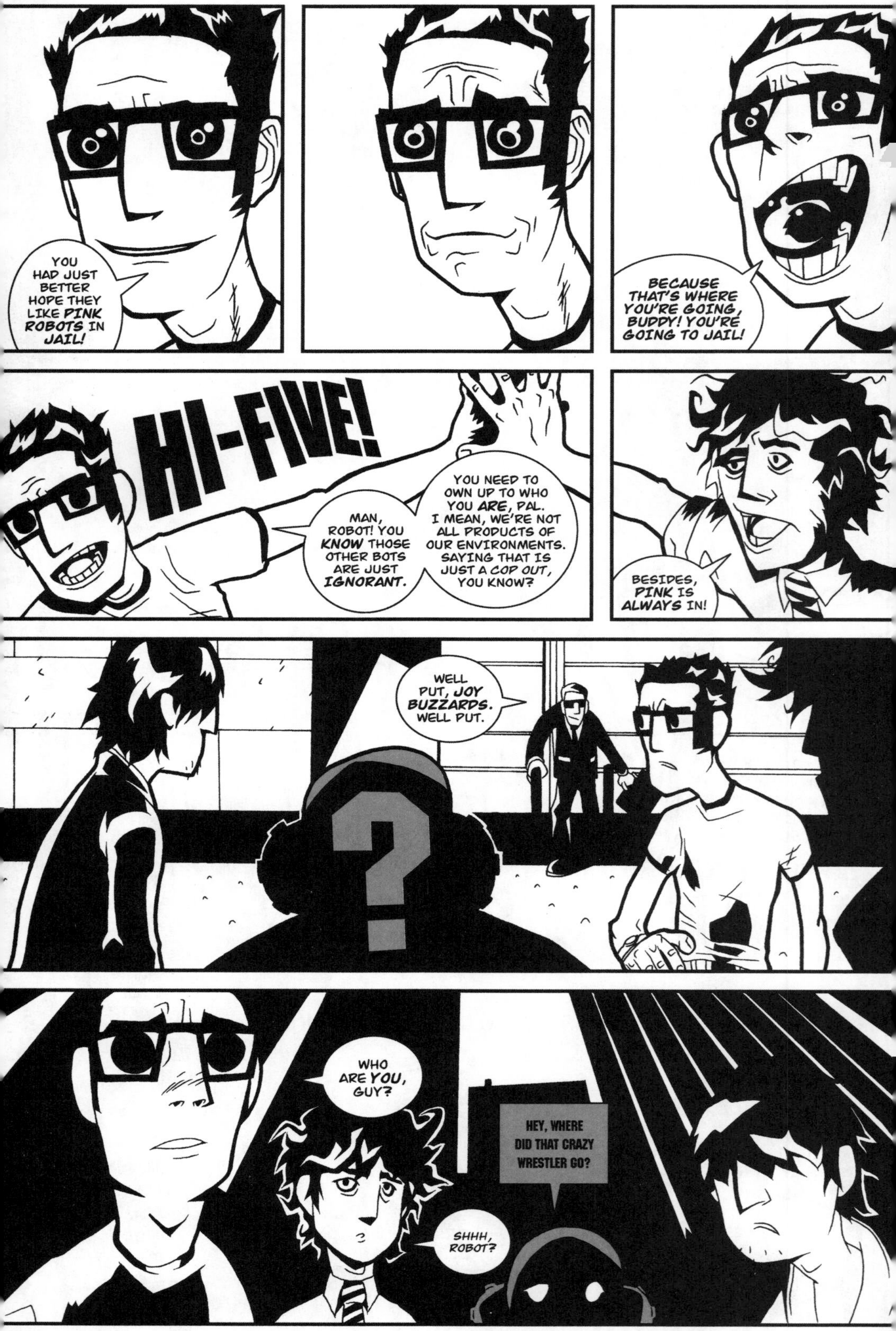
YOU HAD JUST BETTER HOPE THEY LIKE PINK ROBOTS IN JAIL!
BECAUSE THAT'S WHERE YOU'RE GOING, BUDDY! YOU'RE GOING TO JAIL!
HI-FIVE!
MAN, ROBOT! YOU KNOW THOSE OTHER BOTS ARE JUST IGNORANT.
YOU NEED TO OWN UP TO WHO YOU ARE, PAL. I MEAN, WE'RE NOT ALL PRODUCTS OF OUR ENVIRONMENTS. SAYING THAT IS JUST A COP OUT, YOU KNOW?
BESIDES, PINK IS ALWAYS IN!
WELL PUT, JOY BUZZARDS. WELL PUT.
?
WHO ARE YOU, GUY?
HEY, WHERE DID THAT CRAZY WRESTLER GO?
SHHH, ROBOT?

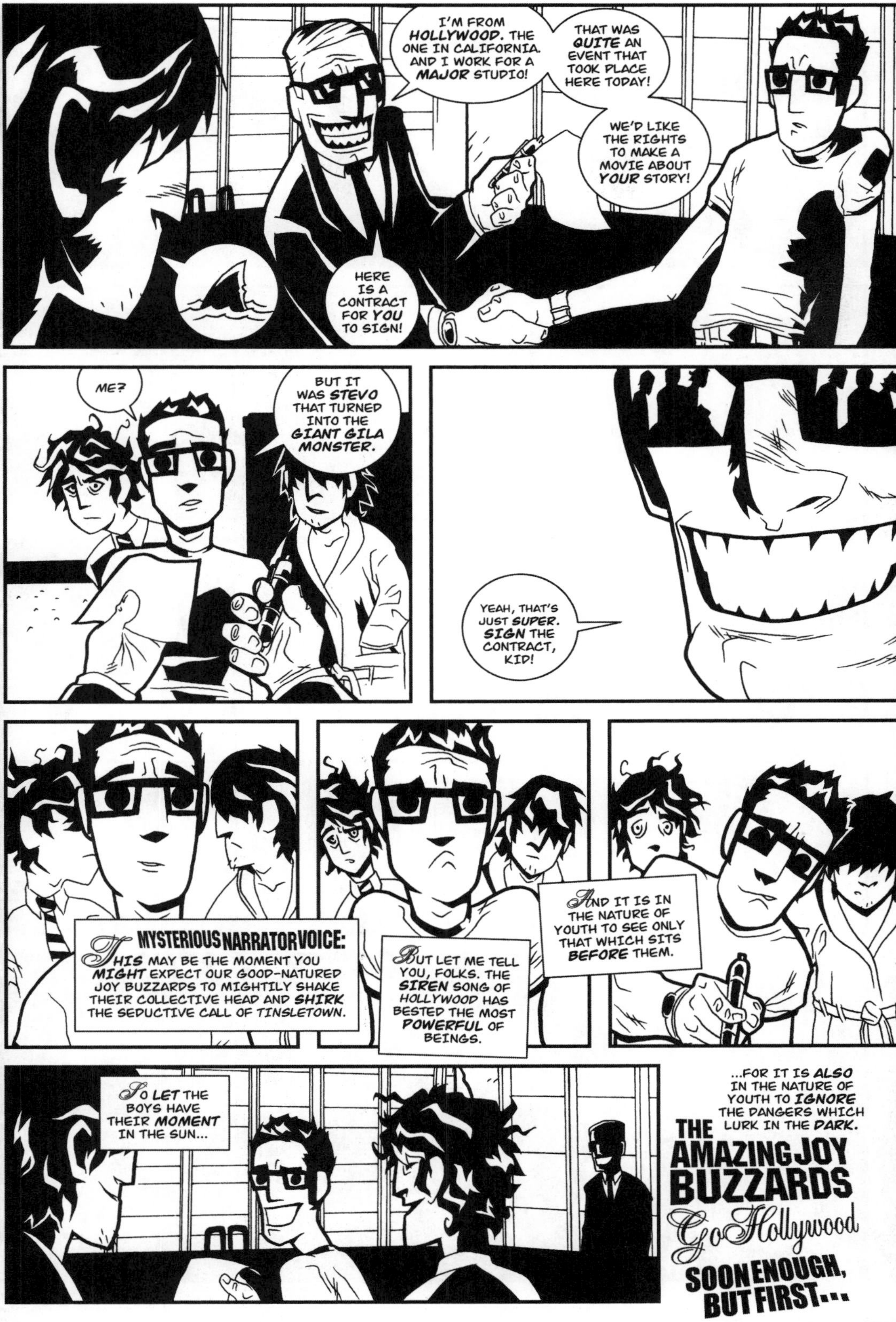
I'M FROM HOLLYWOOD. THE ONE IN CALIFORNIA. AND I WORK FOR A MAJOR STUDIO!
THAT WAS QUITE AN EVENT THAT TOOK PLACE HERE TODAY!
WE'D LIKE THE RIGHTS TO MAKE A MOVIE ABOUT YOUR STORY!
HERE IS A CONTRACT FOR YOU TO SIGN!
ME?
BUT IT WAS STEVO THAT TURNED INTO THE GIANT GILA MONSTER.
YEAH, THAT'S JUST SUPER. SIGN THE CONTRACT, KID!
MYSTERIOUS NARRATOR VOICE: THIS MAY BE THE MOMENT YOU MIGHT EXPECT OUR GOOD-NATURED JOY BUZZARDS TO MIGHTILY SHAKE THEIR COLLECTIVE HEAD AND SHIRK THE SEDUCTIVE CALL OF TINSLETOWN.
BUT LET ME TELL YOU, FOLKS. THE SIREN SONG OF HOLLYWOOD HAS BESTED THE MOST POWERFUL OF BEINGS.
AND IT IS IN THE NATURE OF YOUTH TO SEE ONLY THAT WHICH SITS BEFORE THEM.
SO LET THE BOYS HAVE THEIR MOMENT IN THE SUN...
...FOR IT IS ALSO IN THE NATURE OF YOUTH TO IGNORE THE DANGERS WHICH LURK IN THE DARK.
THE AMAZING JOY BUZZARDS
Go Hollywood
SOON ENOUGH, BUT FIRST...

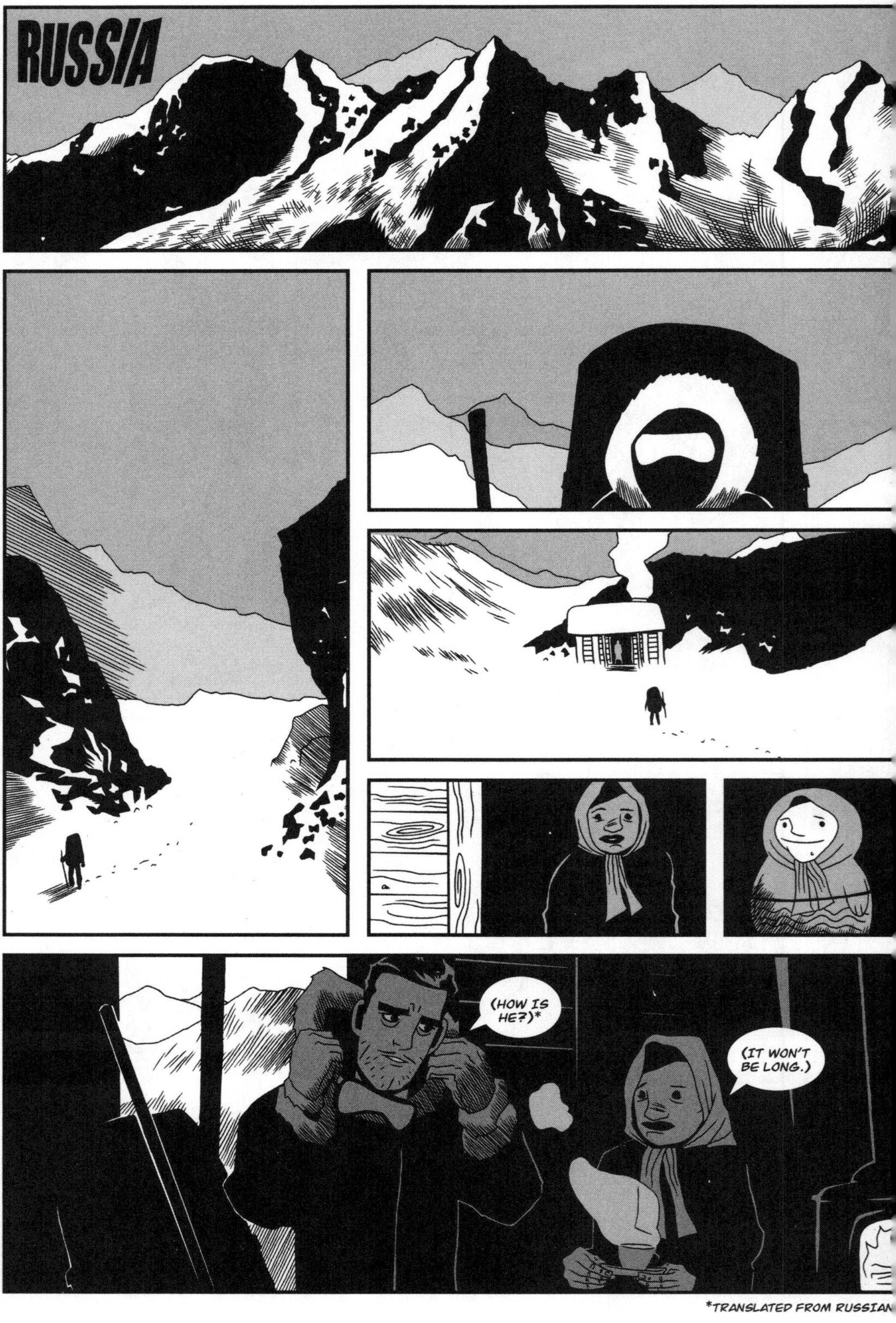
RUSSIA
(HOW IS HE?)*
(IT WON'T BE LONG.)

*TRANSLATED FROM RUSSIAN

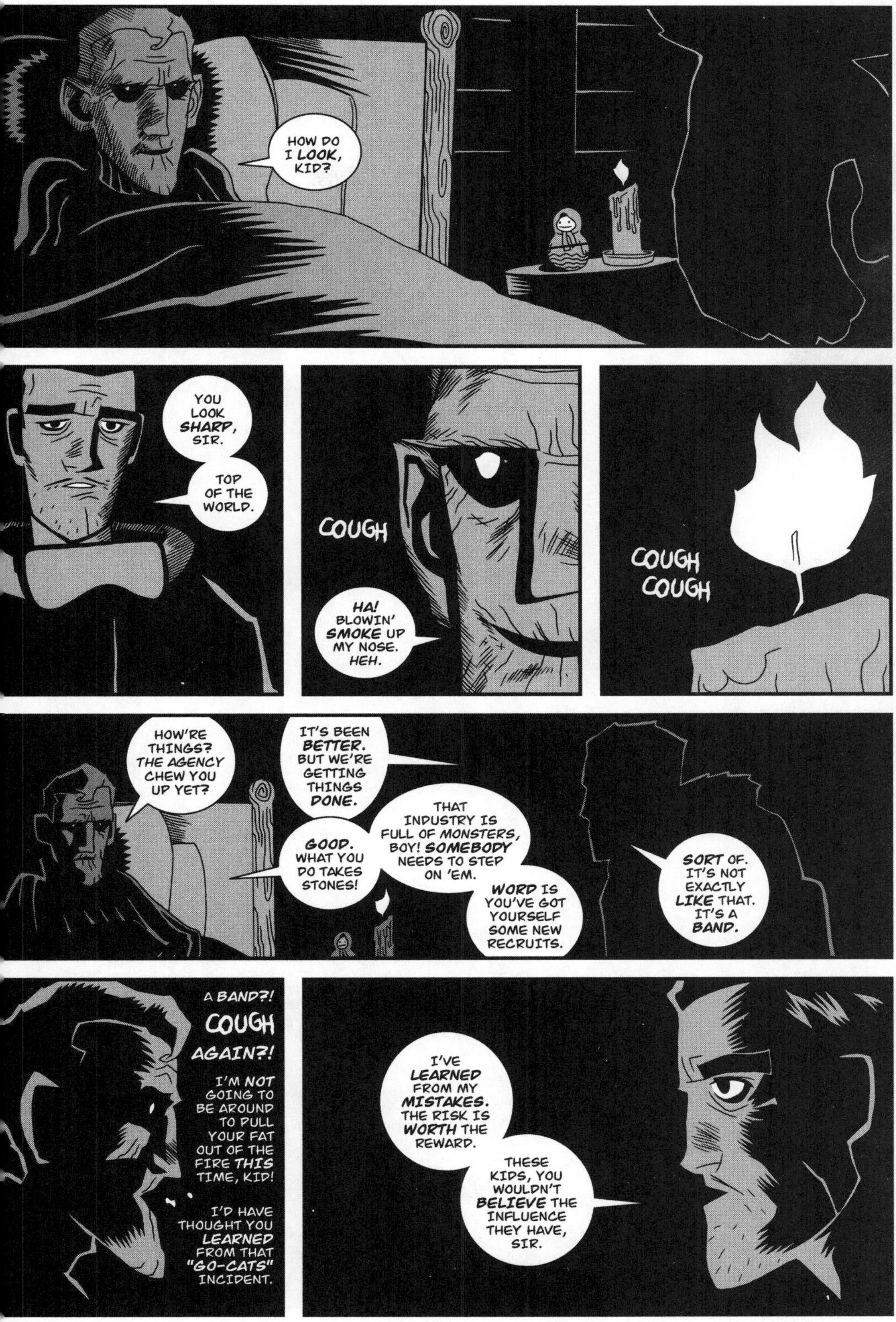

HOW DO I LOOK, KID?
YOU LOOK SHARP, SIR.
TOP OF THE WORLD.
COUGH
HA! BLOWIN' SMOKE UP MY NOSE. HEH.
COUGH COUGH
HOW'RE THINGS? THE AGENCY CHEW YOU UP YET?
IT'S BEEN BETTER. BUT WE'RE GETTING THINGS DONE.
GOOD. WHAT YOU DO TAKES STONES!
THAT INDUSTRY IS FULL OF MONSTERS, BOY! SOMEBODY NEEDS TO STEP ON 'EM.
WORD IS YOU'VE GOT YOURSELF SOME NEW RECRUITS.
SORT OF. IT'S NOT EXACTLY LIKE THAT. IT'S A BAND.
A BAND?!
COUGH
AGAIN?!
I'M NOT GOING TO BE AROUND TO PULL YOUR FAT OUT OF THE FIRE THIS TIME, KID!
I'D HAVE THOUGHT YOU LEARNED FROM THAT "GO-CATS" INCIDENT.
I'VE LEARNED FROM MY MISTAKES. THE RISK IS WORTH THE REWARD.
THESE KIDS, YOU WOULDN'T BELIEVE THE INFLUENCE THEY HAVE, SIR.

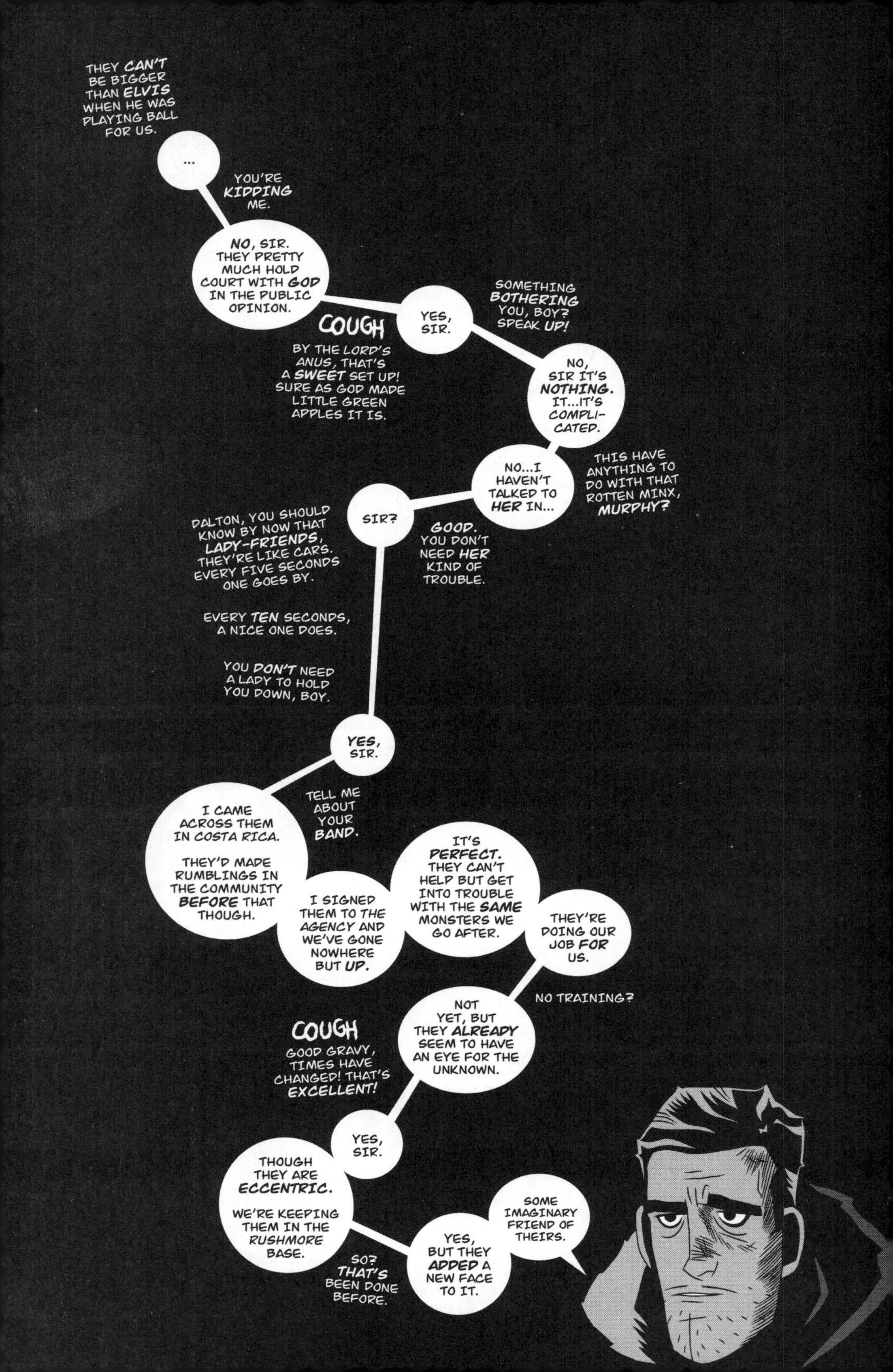

THEY CAN'T BE BIGGER THAN ELVIS WHEN HE WAS PLAYING BALL FOR US.
...
YOU'RE KIDDING ME.
NO, SIR. THEY PRETTY MUCH HOLD COURT WITH GOD IN THE PUBLIC OPINION.
COUGH
BY THE LORD'S ANUS, THAT'S A SWEET SET UP! SURE AS GOD MADE LITTLE GREEN APPLES IT IS.
YES, SIR.
SOMETHING BOTHERING YOU, BOY? SPEAK UP!
NO, SIR IT'S NOTHING. IT...IT'S COMPLI-CATED.
THIS HAVE ANYTHING TO DO WITH THAT ROTTEN MINX, MURPHY?
NO...I HAVEN'T TALKED TO HER IN...
GOOD. YOU DON'T NEED HER KIND OF TROUBLE.
SIR?
DALTON, YOU SHOULD KNOW BY NOW THAT LADY-FRIENDS, THEY'RE LIKE CARS. EVERY FIVE SECONDS ONE GOES BY.
EVERY TEN SECONDS, A NICE ONE DOES.
YOU DON'T NEED A LADY TO HOLD YOU DOWN, BOY.
YES, SIR.
TELL ME ABOUT YOUR BAND.
I CAME ACROSS THEM IN COSTA RICA.
THEY'D MADE RUMBLINGS IN THE COMMUNITY BEFORE THAT THOUGH.
I SIGNED THEM TO THE AGENCY AND WE'VE GONE NOWHERE BUT UP.
IT'S PERFECT. THEY CAN'T HELP BUT GET INTO TROUBLE WITH THE SAME MONSTERS WE GO AFTER.
THEY'RE DOING OUR JOB FOR US.
NO TRAINING?
NOT YET, BUT THEY ALREADY SEEM TO HAVE AN EYE FOR THE UNKNOWN.
COUGH
GOOD GRAVY, TIMES HAVE CHANGED! THAT'S EXCELLENT!
YES, SIR.
THOUGH THEY ARE ECCENTRIC.
WE'RE KEEPING THEM IN THE RUSHMORE BASE.
SO? THAT'S BEEN DONE BEFORE.
YES, BUT THEY ADDED A NEW FACE TO IT.
SOME IMAGINARY FRIEND OF THEIRS.

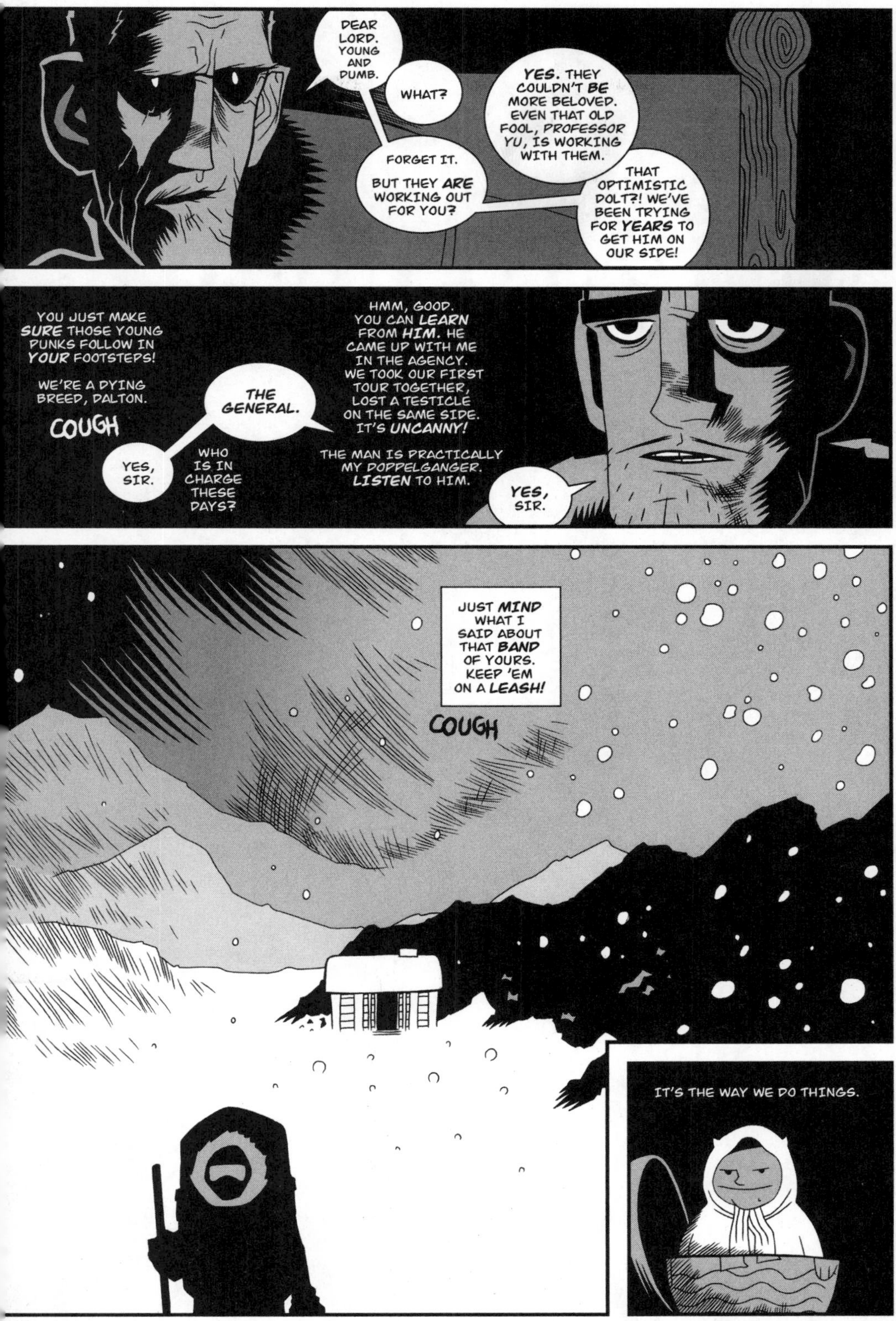
DEAR LORD. YOUNG AND DUMB.
WHAT?
FORGET IT.
BUT THEY ARE WORKING OUT FOR YOU?
YES. THEY COULDN'T BE MORE BELOVED. EVEN THAT OLD FOOL, PROFESSOR YU, IS WORKING WITH THEM.
THAT OPTIMISTIC DOLT?! WE'VE BEEN TRYING FOR YEARS TO GET HIM ON OUR SIDE!
YOU JUST MAKE SURE THOSE YOUNG PUNKS FOLLOW IN YOUR FOOTSTEPS!
WE'RE A DYING BREED, DALTON.
COUGH
YES, SIR.
WHO IS IN CHARGE THESE DAYS?
THE GENERAL.
HMM, GOOD. YOU CAN LEARN FROM HIM. HE CAME UP WITH ME IN THE AGENCY. WE TOOK OUR FIRST TOUR TOGETHER, LOST A TESTICLE ON THE SAME SIDE. IT'S UNCANNY!
THE MAN IS PRACTICALLY MY DOPPELGANGER. LISTEN TO HIM.
YES, SIR.
JUST MIND WHAT I SAID ABOUT THAT BAND OF YOURS. KEEP 'EM ON A LEASH!
COUGH
IT'S THE WAY WE DO THINGS.

CUE CURTAIN!

PART TWO

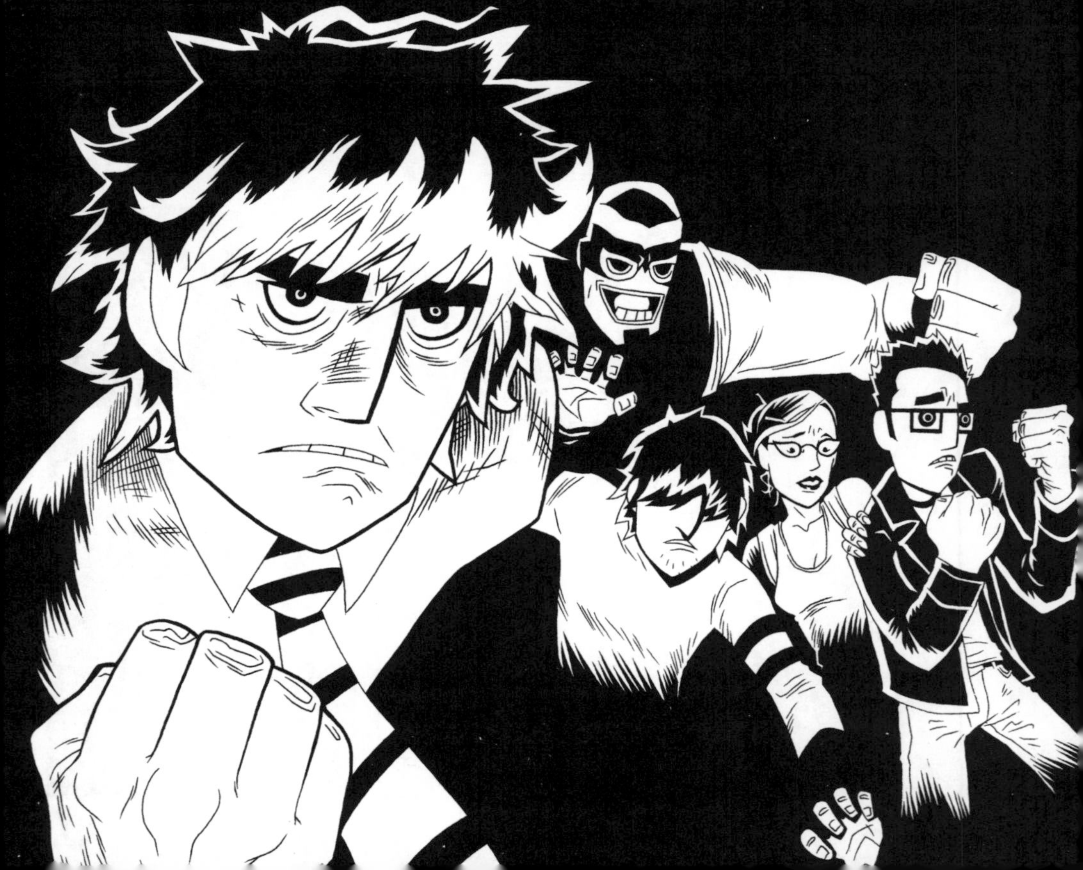

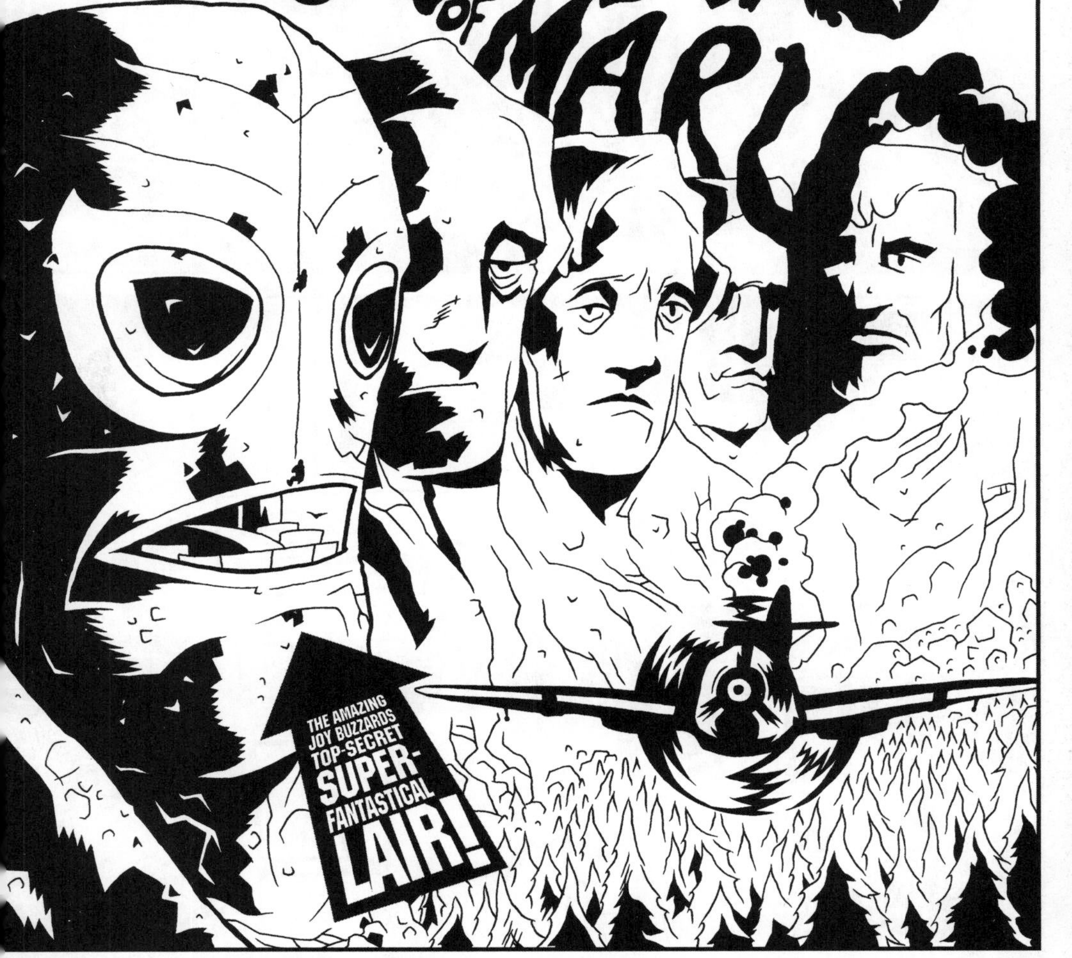
THE AMAZING JOY BUZZARDS IN THE .. ISLAND OF MARLO
THE AMAZING JOY BUZZARDS TOP-SECRET SUPER-FANTASTICAL LAIR!

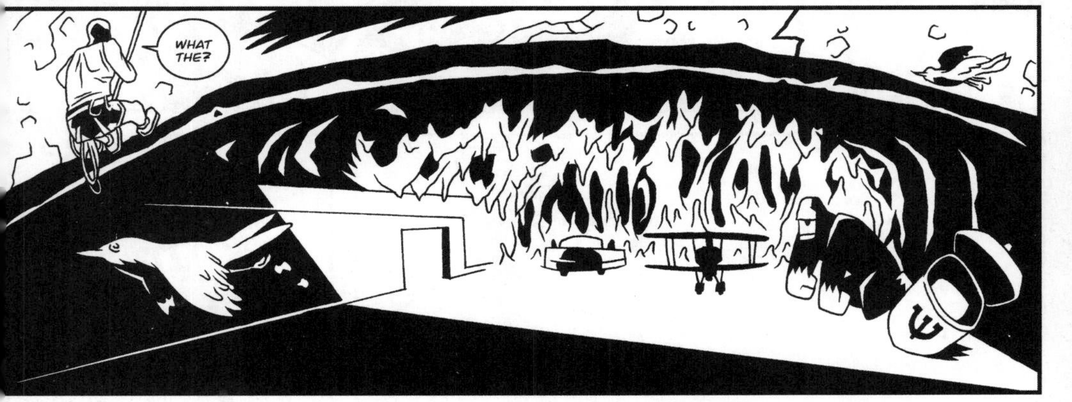
WHAT THE?

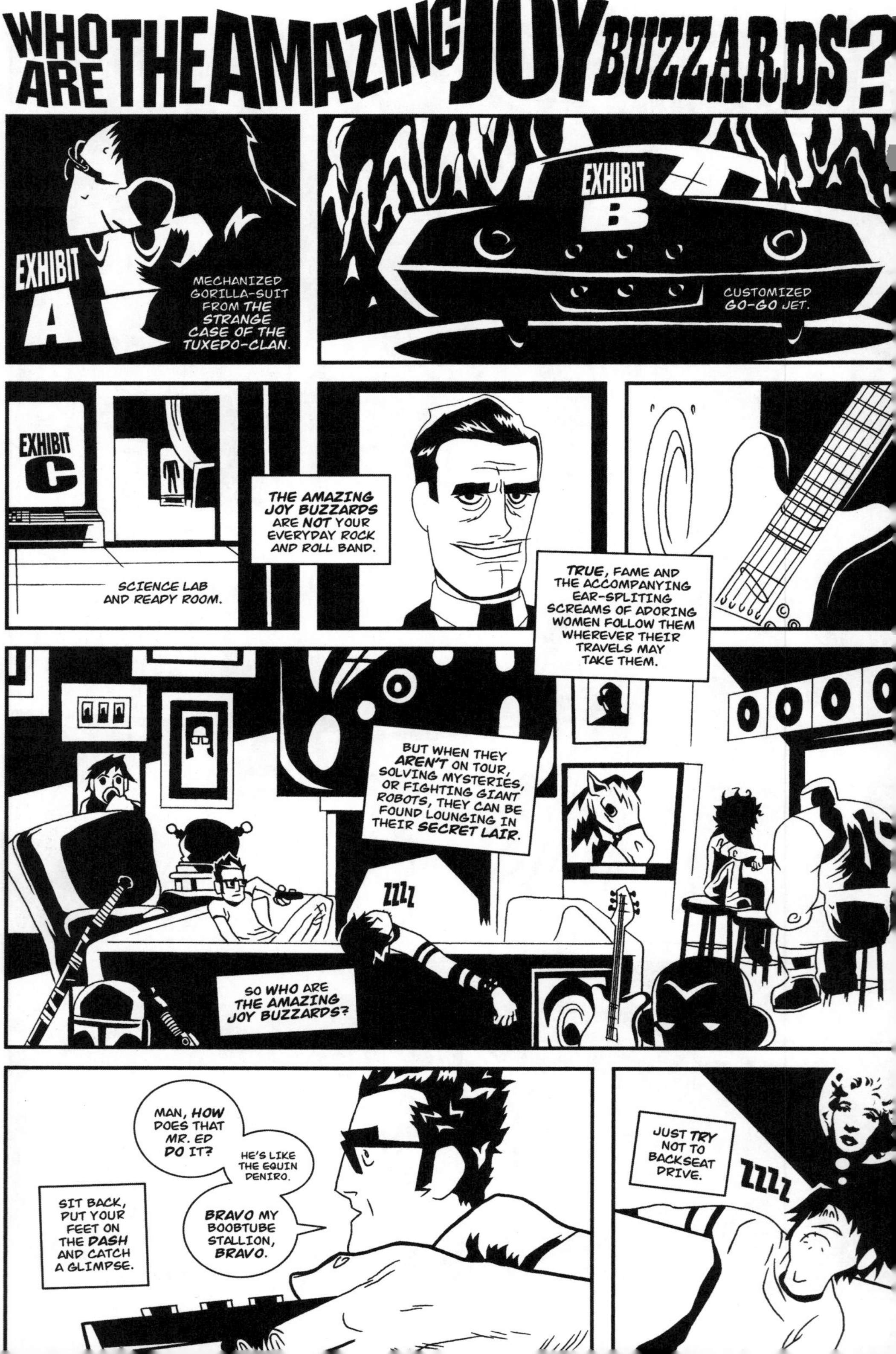
WHO ARE THE AMAZING JOY BUZZARDS?
EXHIBIT A
MECHANIZED GORILLA-SUIT FROM THE STRANGE CASE OF THE TUXEDO-CLAN.
EXHIBIT B
CUSTOMIZED GO-GO JET.
EXHIBIT C
SCIENCE LAB AND READY ROOM.
THE AMAZING JOY BUZZARDS ARE NOT YOUR EVERYDAY ROCK AND ROLL BAND.
TRUE, FAME AND THE ACCOMPANYING EAR-SPLITING SCREAMS OF ADORING WOMEN FOLLOW THEM WHEREVER THEIR TRAVELS MAY TAKE THEM.
BUT WHEN THEY AREN'T ON TOUR, SOLVING MYSTERIES, OR FIGHTING GIANT ROBOTS, THEY CAN BE FOUND LOUNGING IN THEIR SECRET LAIR.
ZZZZ
SO WHO ARE THE AMAZING JOY BUZZARDS?
SIT BACK, PUT YOUR FEET ON THE DASH AND CATCH A GLIMPSE.
MAN, HOW DOES THAT MR. ED DO IT?
HE'S LIKE THE EQUIN DENIRO.
BRAVO MY BOOBTUBE STALLION, BRAVO.
JUST TRY NOT TO BACKSEAT DRIVE.
ZZZZ

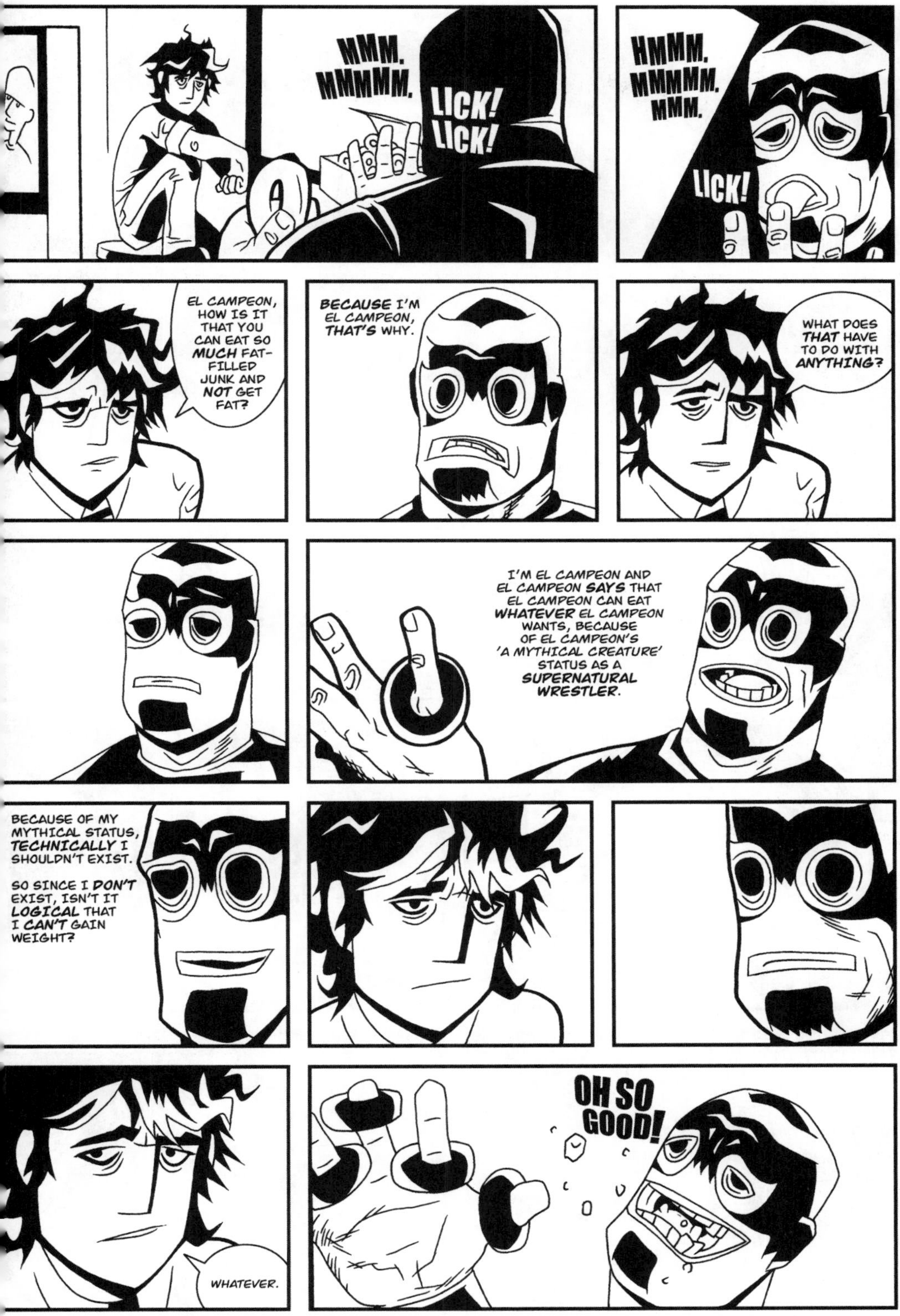

MMM.
MMMMM.
LICK!
LICK!
HMMM.
MMMMM.
MMM.
LICK!
EL CAMPEON, HOW IS IT THAT YOU CAN EAT SO MUCH FAT-FILLED JUNK AND NOT GET FAT?
BECAUSE I'M EL CAMPEON, THAT'S WHY.
WHAT DOES THAT HAVE TO DO WITH ANYTHING?
I'M EL CAMPEON AND EL CAMPEON SAYS THAT EL CAMPEON CAN EAT WHATEVER EL CAMPEON WANTS, BECAUSE OF EL CAMPEON'S 'A MYTHICAL CREATURE' STATUS AS A SUPERNATURAL WRESTLER.
BECAUSE OF MY MYTHICAL STATUS, TECHNICALLY I SHOULDN'T EXIST.
SO SINCE I DON'T EXIST, ISN'T IT LOGICAL THAT I CAN'T GAIN WEIGHT?
WHATEVER.
OH SO GOOD!

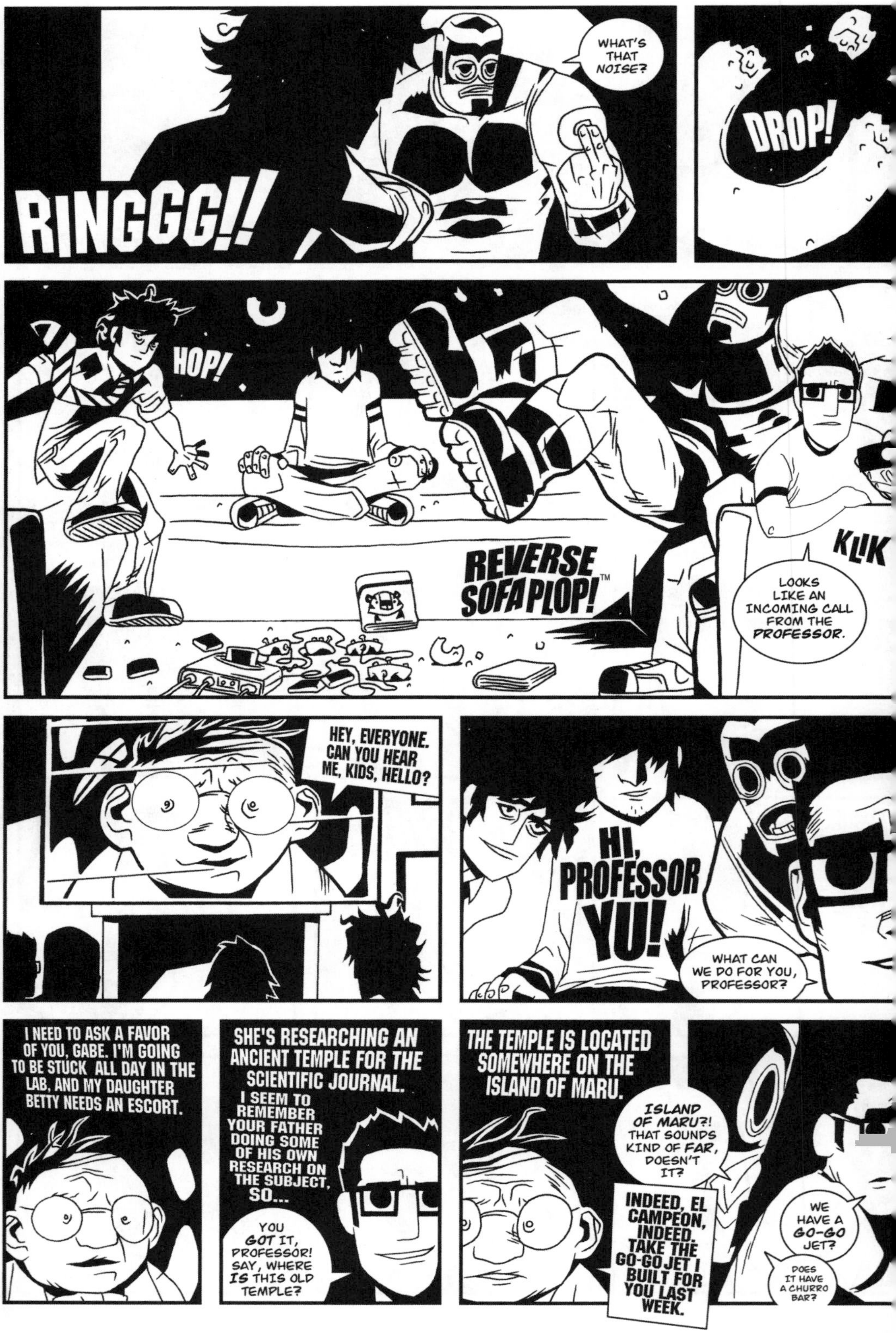

WHAT'S THAT NOISE?
RINGGG!!
DROP!
HOP!
REVERSE SOFA PLOP!™
KLIK
LOOKS LIKE AN INCOMING CALL FROM THE PROFESSOR.
HEY, EVERYONE. CAN YOU HEAR ME, KIDS, HELLO?
HI, PROFESSOR YU!
WHAT CAN WE DO FOR YOU, PROFESSOR?
I NEED TO ASK A FAVOR OF YOU, GABE. I'M GOING TO BE STUCK ALL DAY IN THE LAB, AND MY DAUGHTER BETTY NEEDS AN ESCORT.
SHE'S RESEARCHING AN ANCIENT TEMPLE FOR THE SCIENTIFIC JOURNAL.
I SEEM TO REMEMBER YOUR FATHER DOING SOME OF HIS OWN RESEARCH ON THE SUBJECT, SO...
YOU GOT IT, PROFESSOR! SAY, WHERE IS THIS OLD TEMPLE?
THE TEMPLE IS LOCATED SOMEWHERE ON THE ISLAND OF MARU.
ISLAND OF MARU?! THAT SOUNDS KIND OF FAR, DOESN'T IT?
INDEED, EL CAMPEON, INDEED. TAKE THE GO-GO JET I BUILT FOR YOU LAST WEEK.
WE HAVE A GO-GO JET?
DOES IT HAVE A CHURRO BAR?

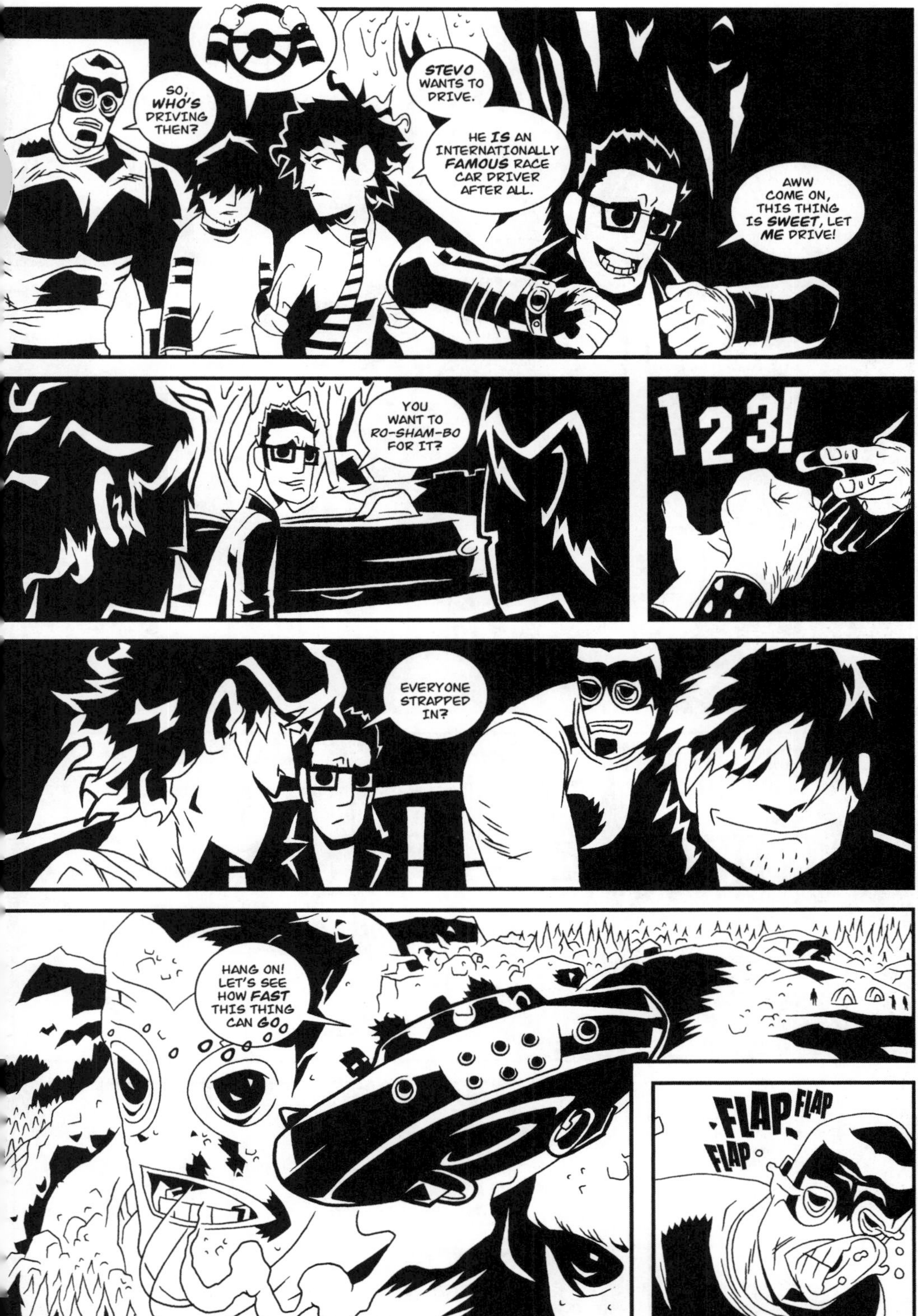
SO, WHO'S DRIVING THEN?
STEVO WANTS TO DRIVE.
HE IS AN INTERNATIONALLY FAMOUS RACE CAR DRIVER AFTER ALL.
AWW COME ON, THIS THING IS SWEET, LET ME DRIVE!
YOU WANT TO RO-SHAM-BO FOR IT?
1 2 3!
EVERYONE STRAPPED IN?
HANG ON! LET'S SEE HOW FAST THIS THING CAN GO
FLAP FLAP
FLAP

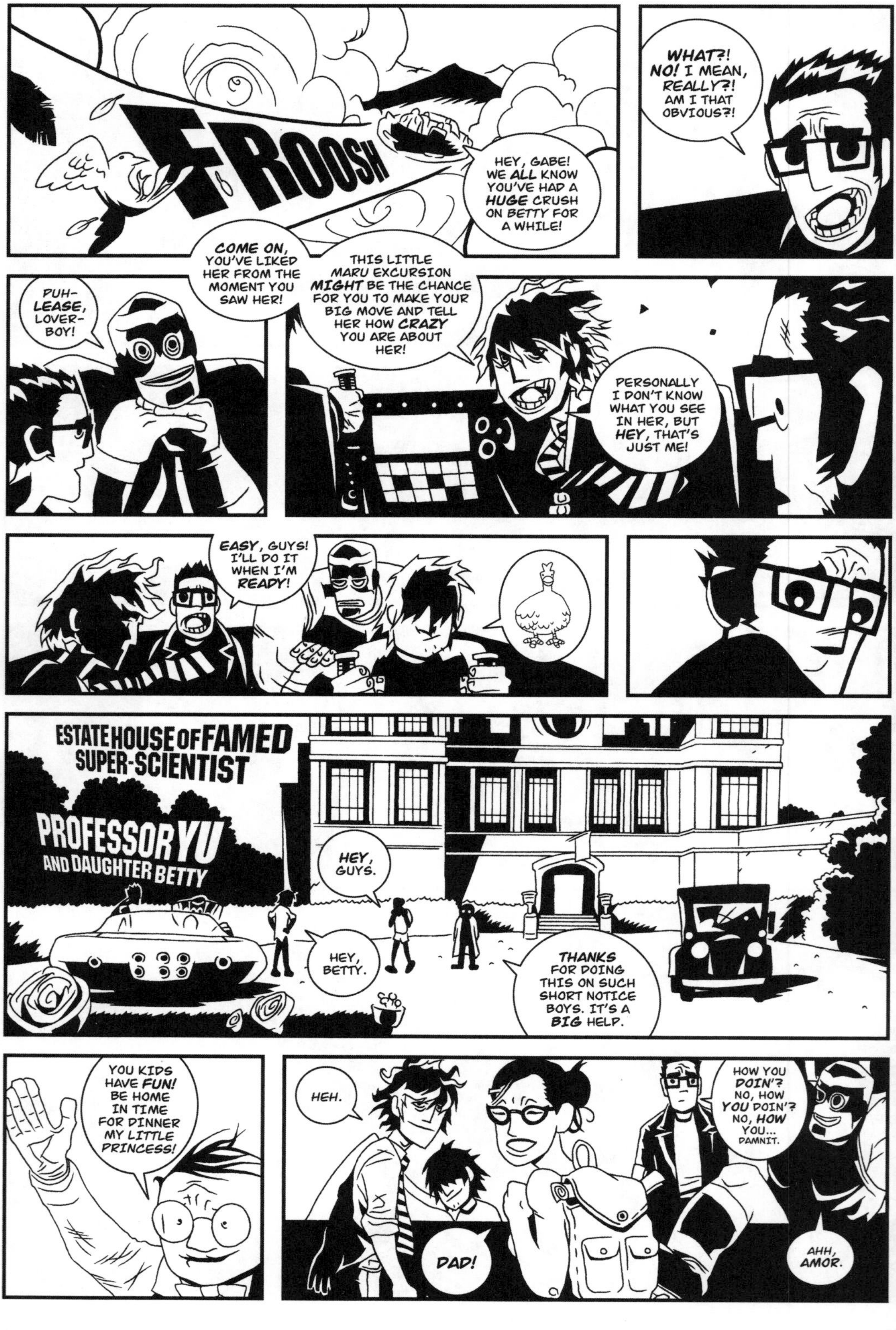
FROOSH
HEY, GABE! WE ALL KNOW YOU'VE HAD A HUGE CRUSH ON BETTY FOR A WHILE!
WHAT?! NO! I MEAN, REALLY?! AM I THAT OBVIOUS?!
PUH-LEASE, LOVER-BOY!
COME ON, YOU'VE LIKED HER FROM THE MOMENT YOU SAW HER!
THIS LITTLE MARU EXCURSION MIGHT BE THE CHANCE FOR YOU TO MAKE YOUR BIG MOVE AND TELL HER HOW CRAZY YOU ARE ABOUT HER!
PERSONALLY I DON'T KNOW WHAT YOU SEE IN HER, BUT HEY, THAT'S JUST ME!
EASY, GUYS! I'LL DO IT WHEN I'M READY!
ESTATE HOUSE OF FAMED SUPER-SCIENTIST
PROFESSOR YU
AND DAUGHTER BETTY
HEY, GUYS.
HEY, BETTY.
THANKS FOR DOING THIS ON SUCH SHORT NOTICE BOYS. IT'S A BIG HELP.
YOU KIDS HAVE FUN! BE HOME IN TIME FOR DINNER MY LITTLE PRINCESS!
HEH.
HOW YOU DOIN'? NO, HOW YOU DOIN'? NO, HOW YOU... DAMNIT.
DAD!
AHH, AMOR.

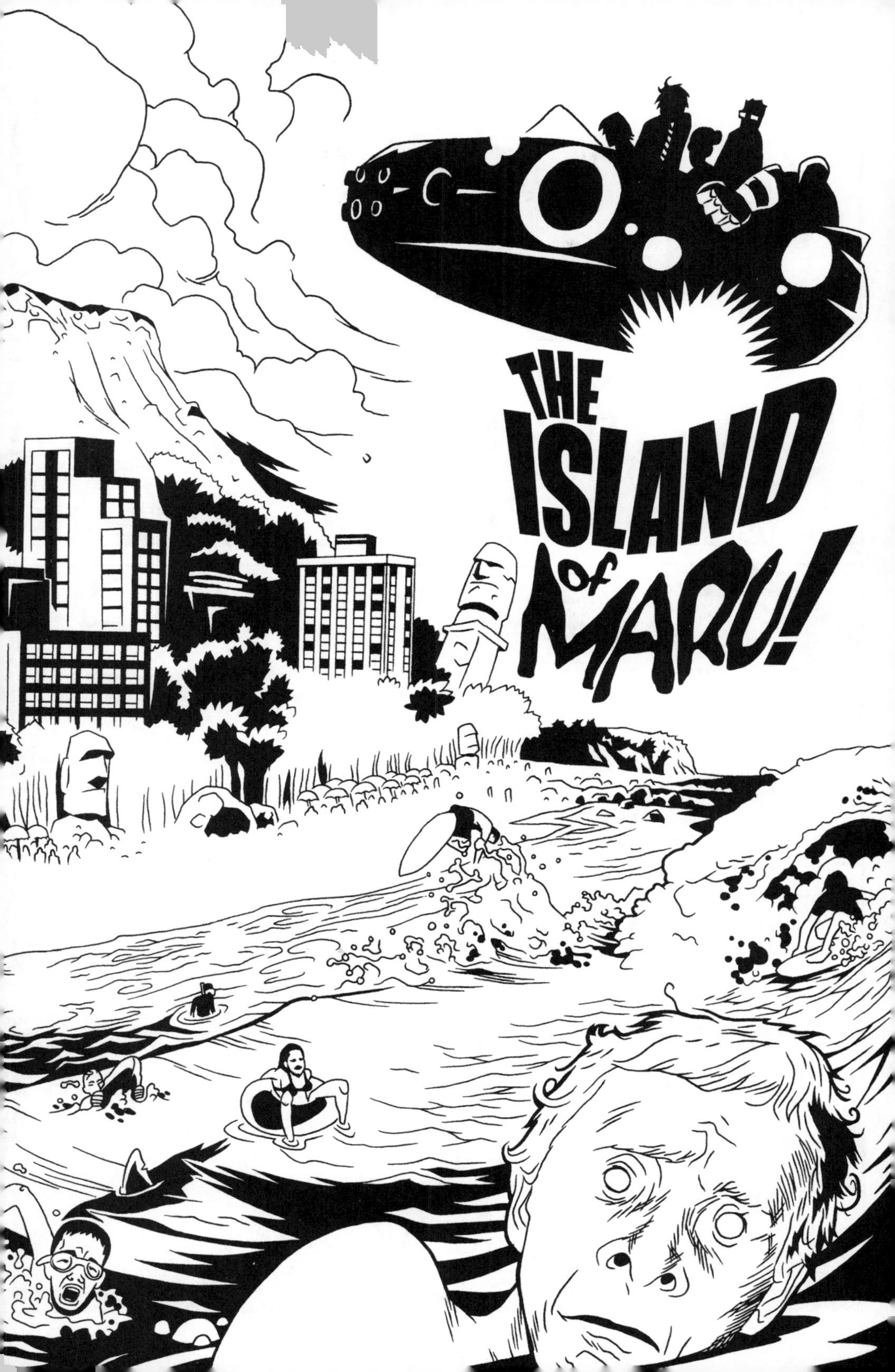
THE
ISLAND
of
MARU!

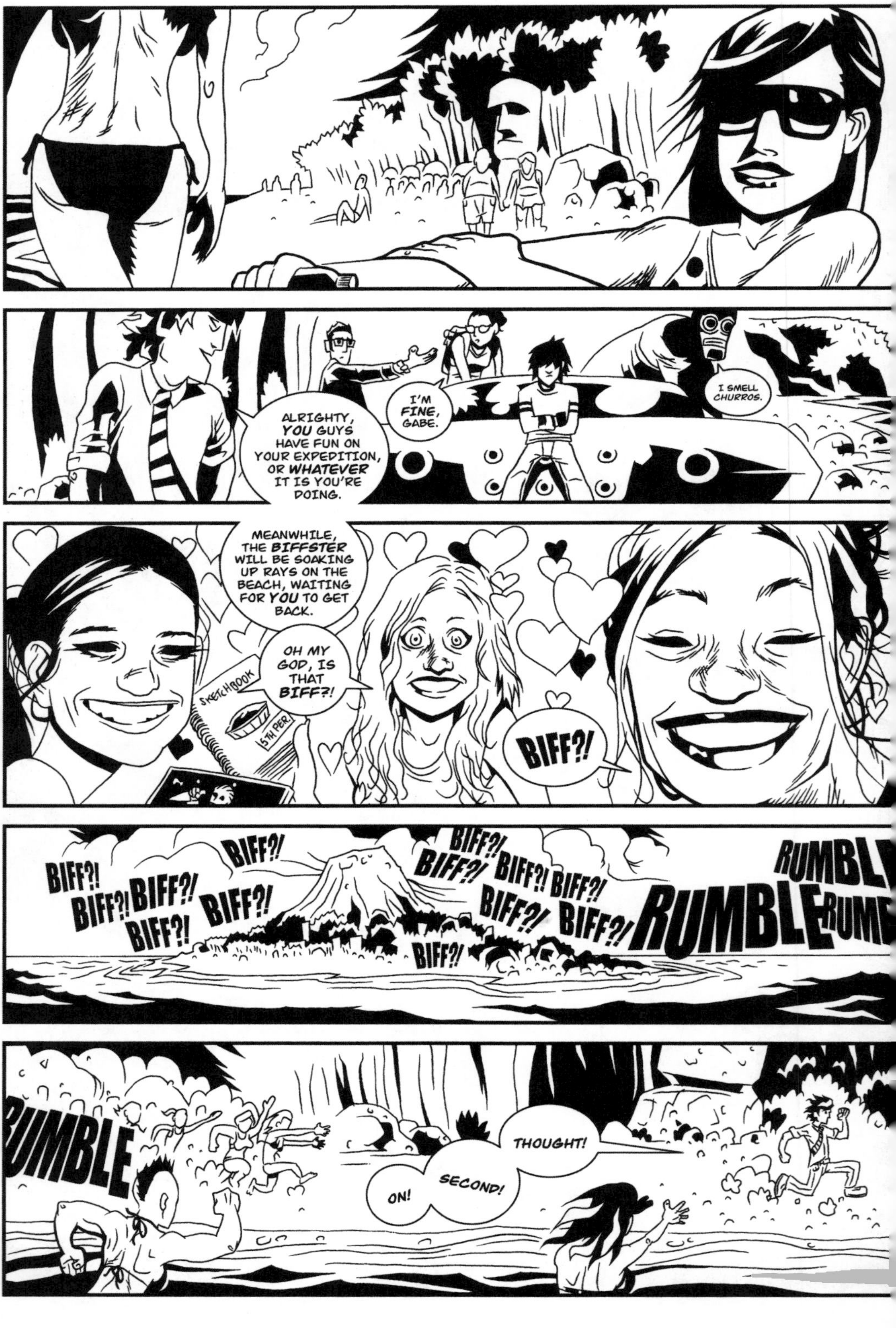

ALRIGHTY, YOU GUYS HAVE FUN ON YOUR EXPEDITION, OR WHATEVER IT IS YOU'RE DOING.
I'M FINE, GABE.
I SMELL CHURROS.
MEANWHILE, THE BIFFSTER WILL BE SOAKING UP RAYS ON THE BEACH, WAITING FOR YOU TO GET BACK.
SKETCHBOOK
5TH PER
OH MY GOD, IS THAT BIFF?!
BIFF?!
BIFF?! BIFF?! BIFF?! BIFF?! BIFF?! BIFF?! BIFF?! BIFF?! BIFF?! BIFF?! BIFF?! BIFF?! BIFF?!
RUMBLE RUMBLE
RUMBLE
THOUGHT!
SECOND!
ON!

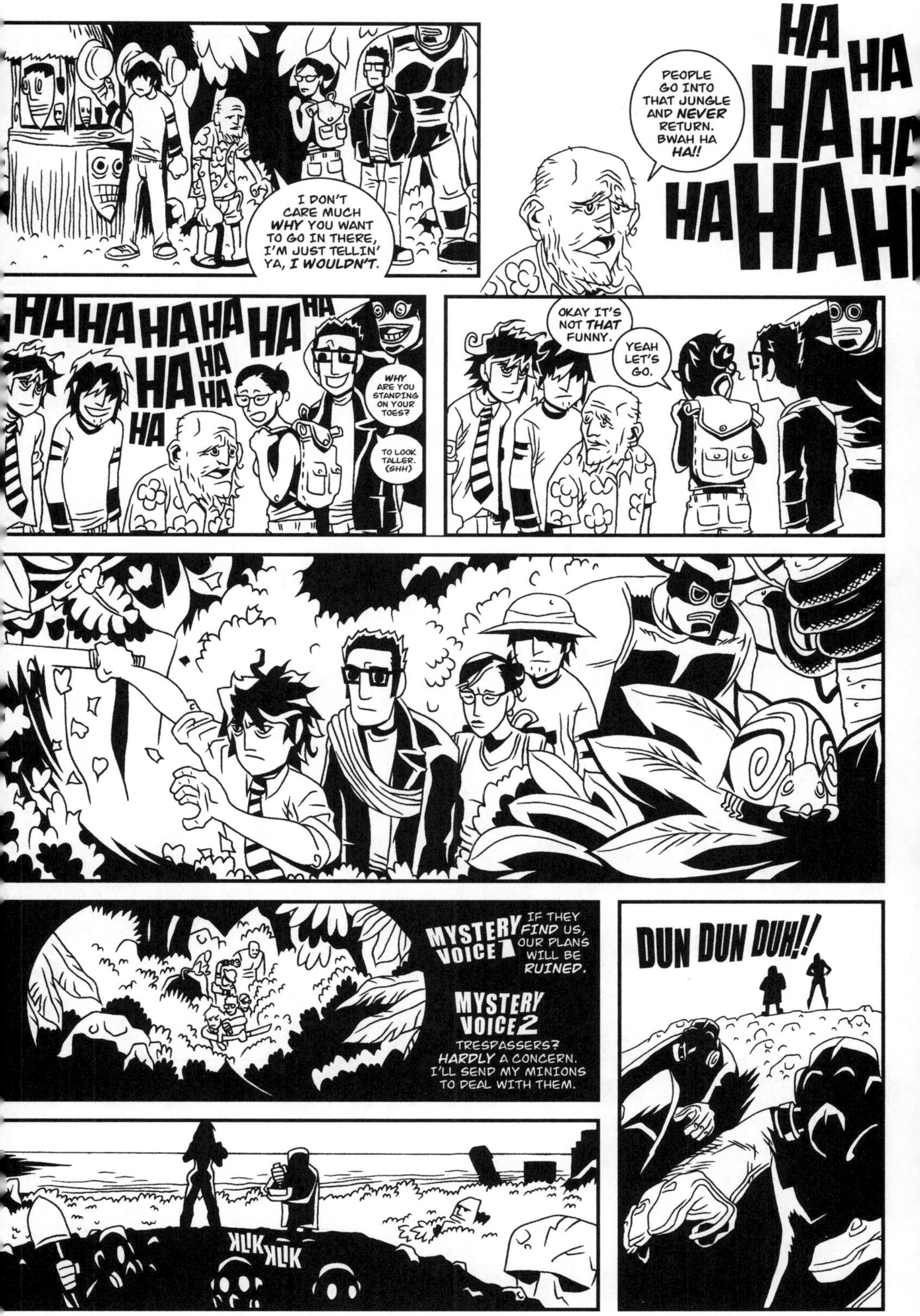
I DON'T CARE MUCH WHY YOU WANT TO GO IN THERE, I'M JUST TELLIN' YA, I WOULDN'T.
PEOPLE GO INTO THAT JUNGLE AND NEVER RETURN. BWAH HA HA!!
HA HA HA HA HA HA HA HA
HA HA HA HA HA HA HA HA HA HA HA HA HA HA
WHY ARE YOU STANDING ON YOUR TOES?
TO LOOK TALLER. (SHH)
OKAY IT'S NOT THAT FUNNY.
YEAH LET'S GO.
MYSTERY VOICE 1
IF THEY FIND US, OUR PLANS WILL BE RUINED.
MYSTERY VOICE 2
TRESPASSERS? HARDLY A CONCERN. I'LL SEND MY MINIONS TO DEAL WITH THEM.
KLIK KLIK
DUN DUN DUH!!

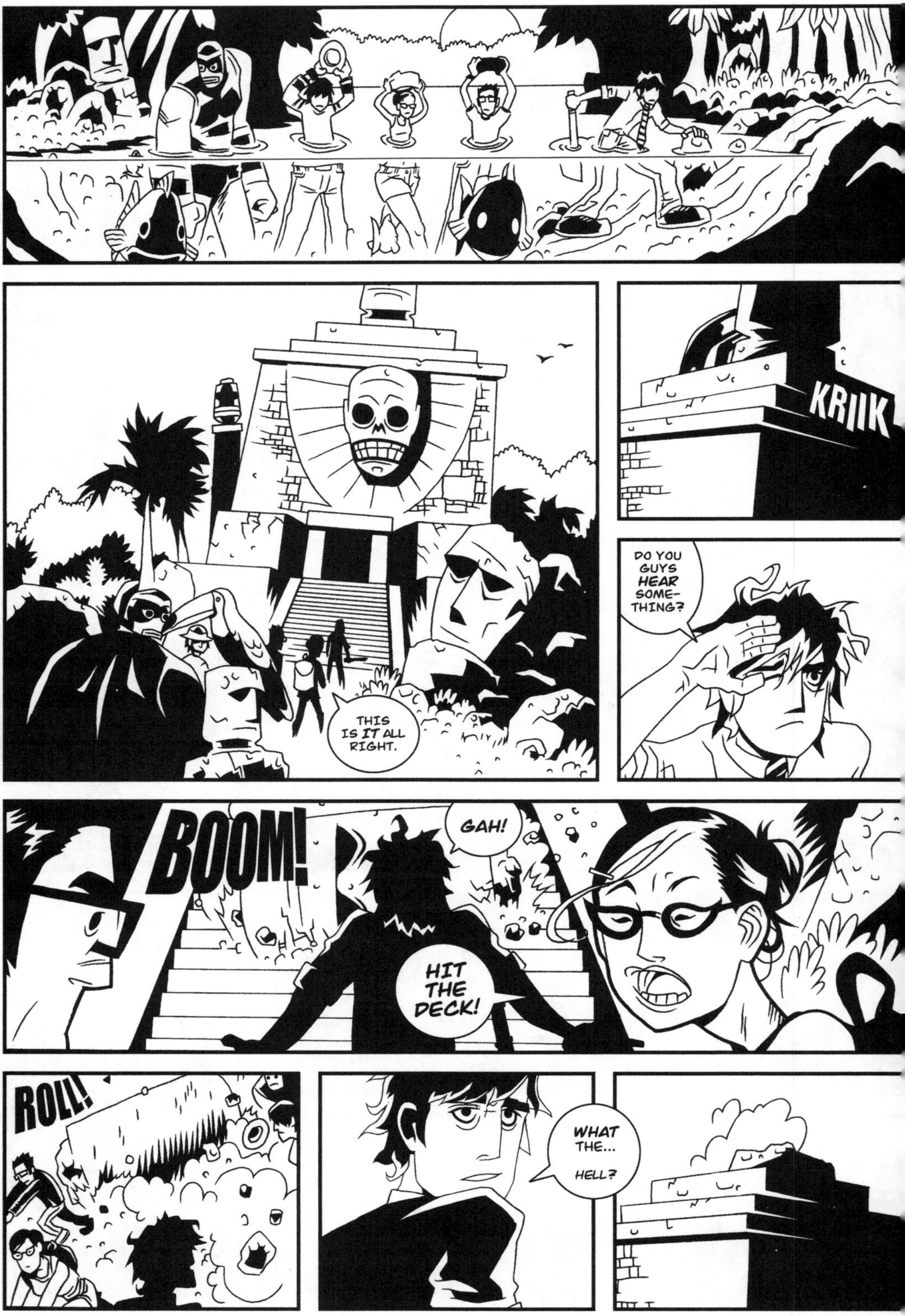
KRIIK
THIS IS IT ALL RIGHT.
DO YOU GUYS HEAR SOME-THING?
BOOM!
GAH!
HIT THE DECK!
ROLL!
WHAT THE...
HELL?

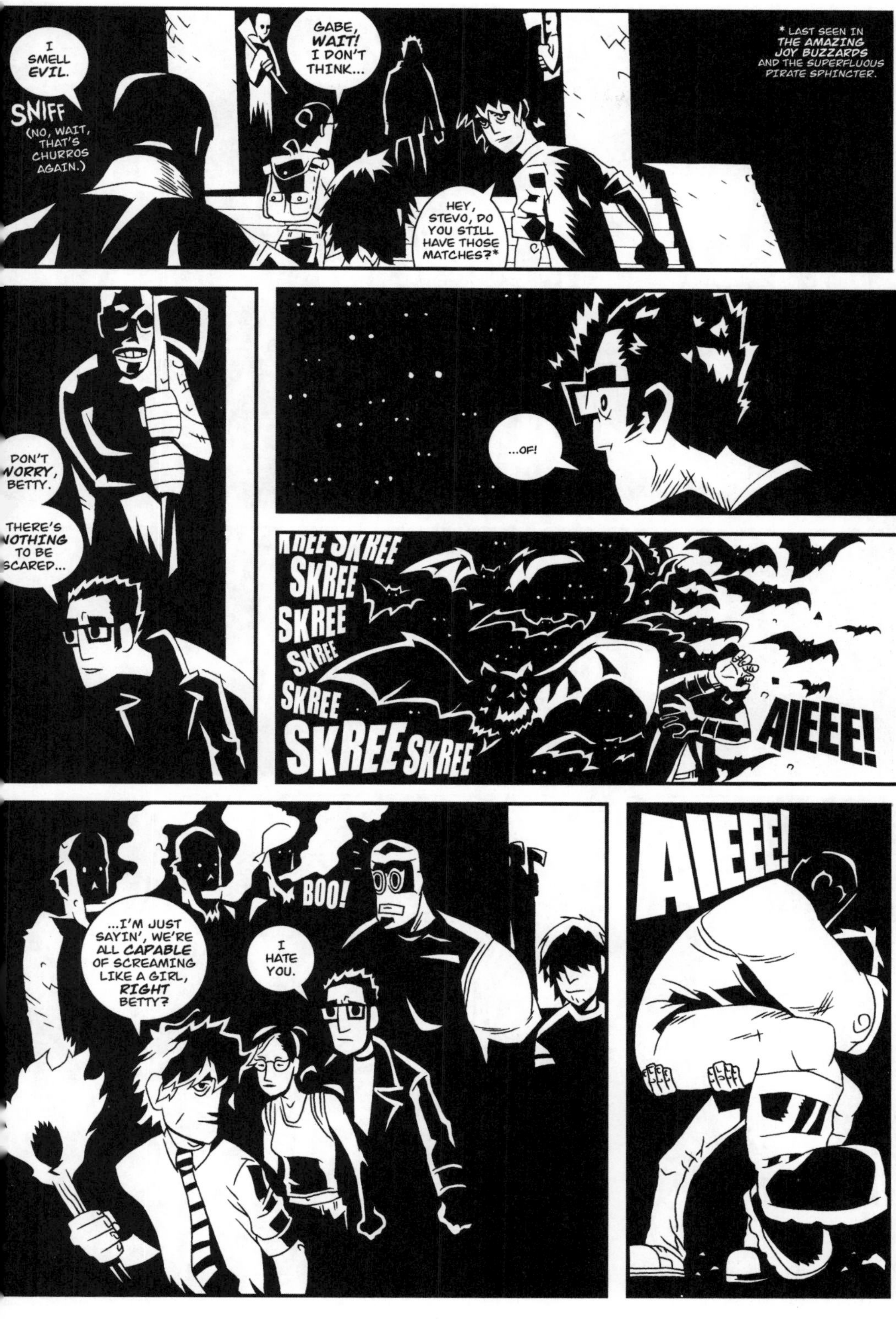
I SMELL EVIL.
SNIFF
(NO, WAIT, THAT'S CHURROS AGAIN.)
GABE, WAIT! I DON'T THINK...
HEY, STEVO, DO YOU STILL HAVE THOSE MATCHES?*
* LAST SEEN IN THE AMAZING JOY BUZZARDS AND THE SUPERFLUOUS PIRATE SPHINCTER.
DON'T WORRY, BETTY.
THERE'S NOTHING TO BE SCARED...
...OF!
SKREE SKREE
SKREE
SKREE
SKREE
SKREE
SKREE SKREE
AIEEE!
...I'M JUST SAYIN', WE'RE ALL CAPABLE OF SCREAMING LIKE A GIRL, RIGHT BETTY?
I HATE YOU.
BOO!
AIEEE!

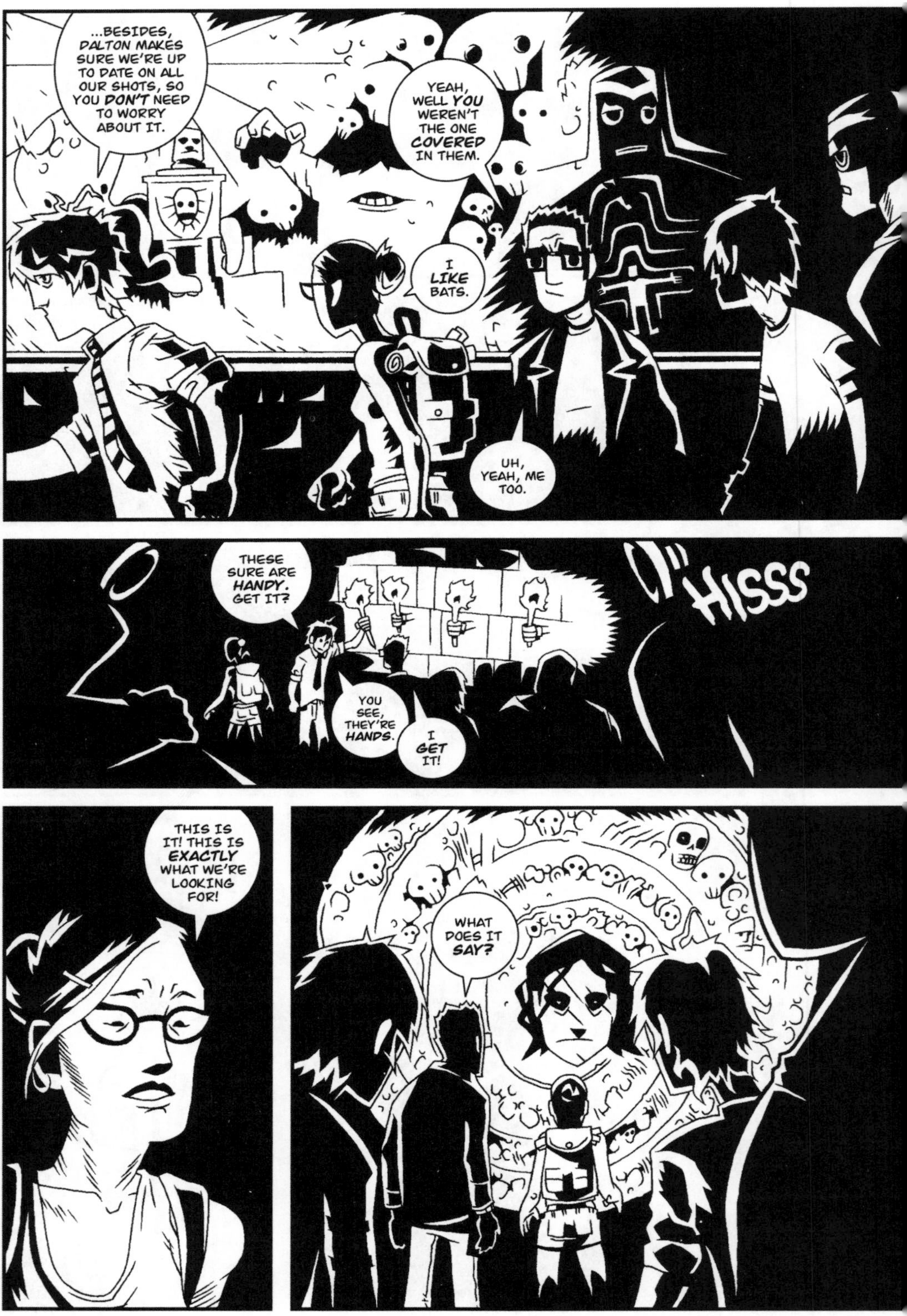
...BESIDES, DALTON MAKES SURE WE'RE UP TO DATE ON ALL OUR SHOTS, SO YOU DON'T NEED TO WORRY ABOUT IT.
YEAH, WELL YOU WEREN'T THE ONE COVERED IN THEM.
I LIKE BATS.
UH, YEAH, ME TOO.
THESE SURE ARE HANDY. GET IT?
YOU SEE, THEY'RE HANDS.
I GET IT!
HISSS
THIS IS IT! THIS IS EXACTLY WHAT WE'RE LOOKING FOR!
WHAT DOES IT SAY?

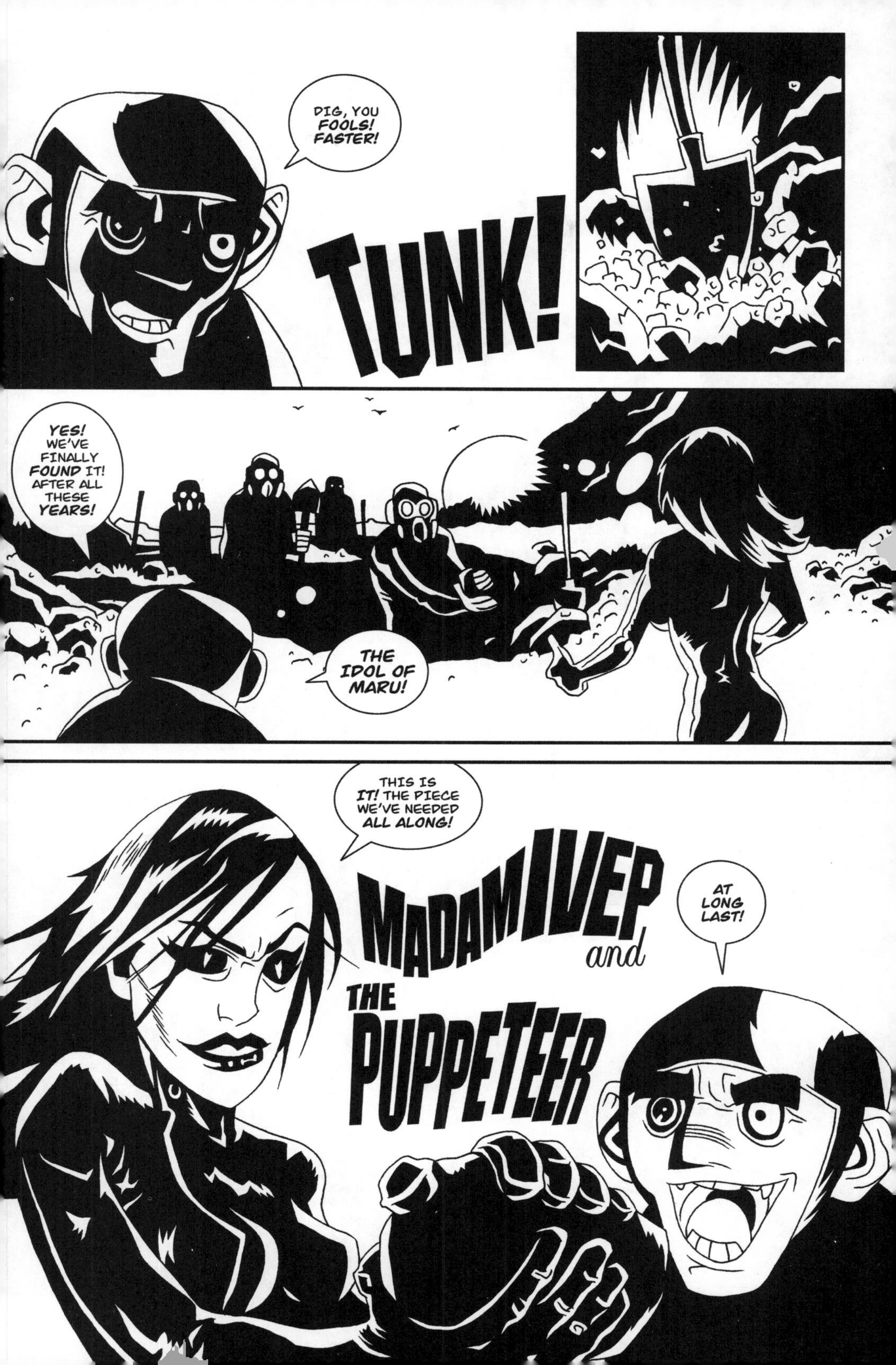
DIG, YOU FOOLS! FASTER!
TUNK!
YES! WE'VE FINALLY FOUND IT! AFTER ALL THESE YEARS!
THE IDOL OF MARU!
THIS IS IT! THE PIECE WE'VE NEEDED ALL ALONG!
AT LONG LAST!
MADAM IVEP and THE PUPPETEER

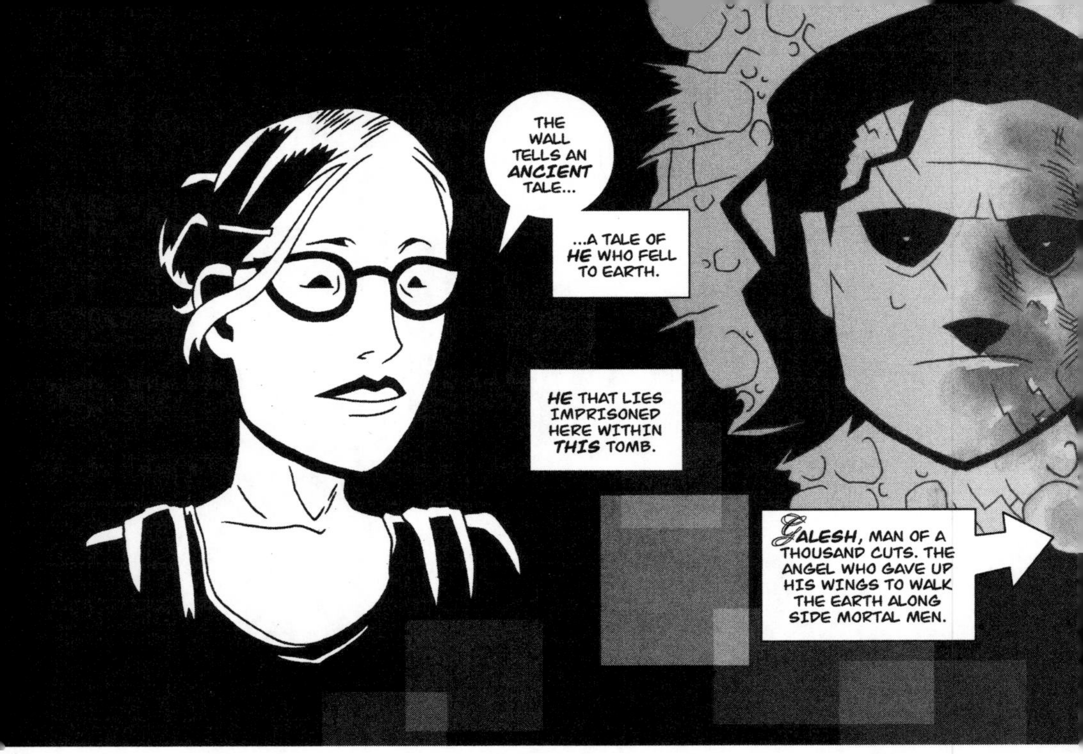
THE WALL TELLS AN ANCIENT TALE...
...A TALE OF HE WHO FELL TO EARTH.
HE THAT LIES IMPRISONED HERE WITHIN THIS TOMB.
GALESH, MAN OF A THOUSAND CUTS. THE ANGEL WHO GAVE UP HIS WINGS TO WALK THE EARTH ALONG SIDE MORTAL MEN.

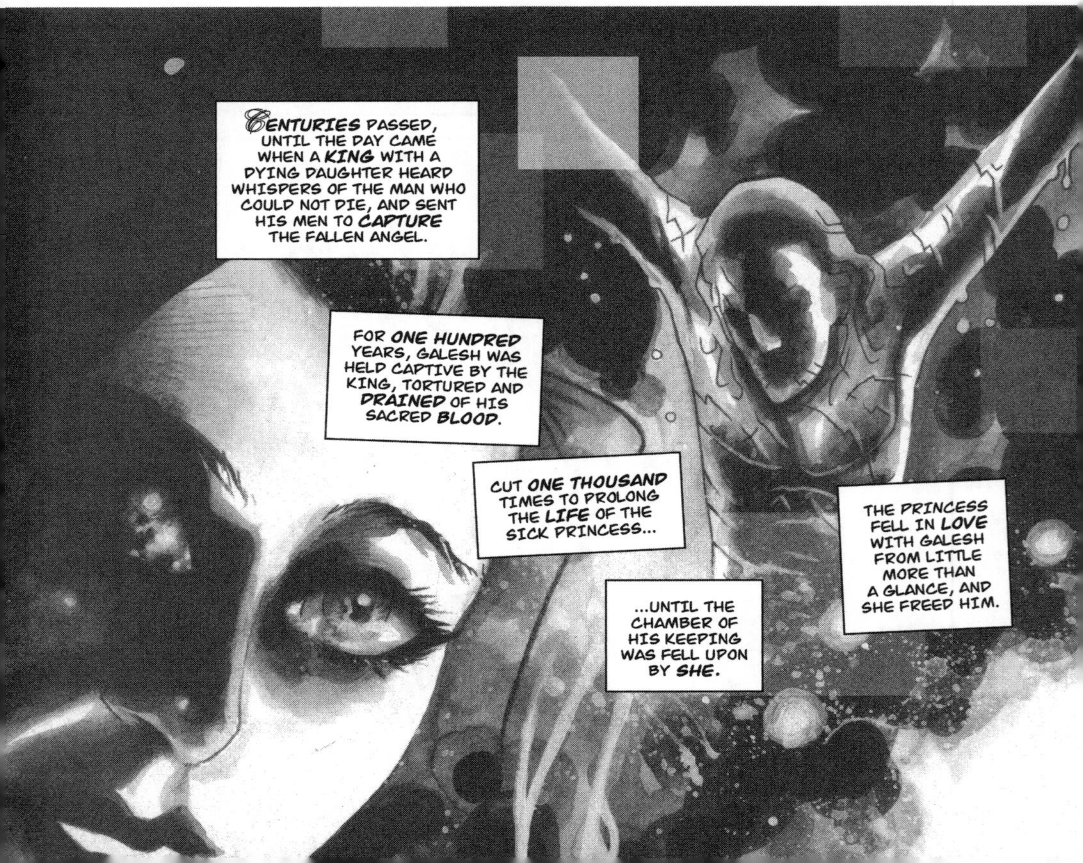
CENTURIES PASSED, UNTIL THE DAY CAME WHEN A KING WITH A DYING DAUGHTER HEARD WHISPERS OF THE MAN WHO COULD NOT DIE, AND SENT HIS MEN TO CAPTURE THE FALLEN ANGEL.
FOR ONE HUNDRED YEARS, GALESH WAS HELD CAPTIVE BY THE KING, TORTURED AND DRAINED OF HIS SACRED BLOOD.
CUT ONE THOUSAND TIMES TO PROLONG THE LIFE OF THE SICK PRINCESS...
...UNTIL THE CHAMBER OF HIS KEEPING WAS FELL UPON BY SHE.
THE PRINCESS FELL IN LOVE WITH GALESH FROM LITTLE MORE THAN A GLANCE, AND SHE FREED HIM.

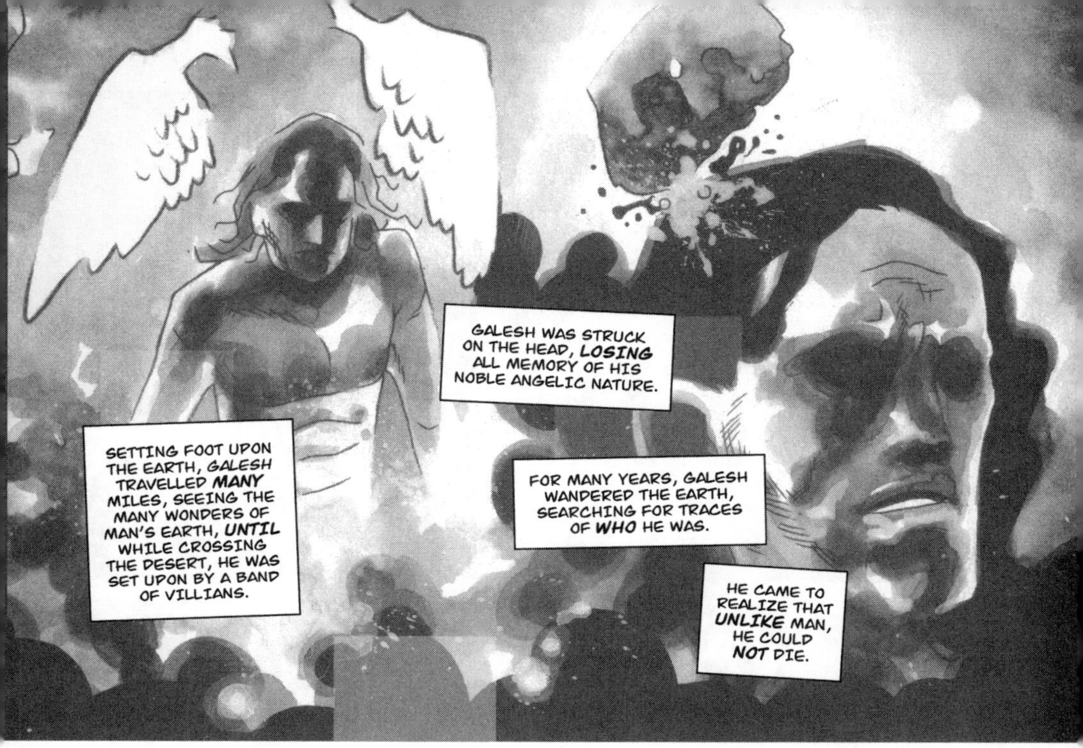
SETTING FOOT UPON THE EARTH, GALESH TRAVELLED MANY MILES, SEEING THE MANY WONDERS OF MAN'S EARTH, UNTIL WHILE CROSSING THE DESERT, HE WAS SET UPON BY A BAND OF VILLIANS.
GALESH WAS STRUCK ON THE HEAD, LOSING ALL MEMORY OF HIS NOBLE ANGELIC NATURE.
FOR MANY YEARS, GALESH WANDERED THE EARTH, SEARCHING FOR TRACES OF WHO HE WAS.
HE CAME TO REALIZE THAT UNLIKE MAN, HE COULD NOT DIE.

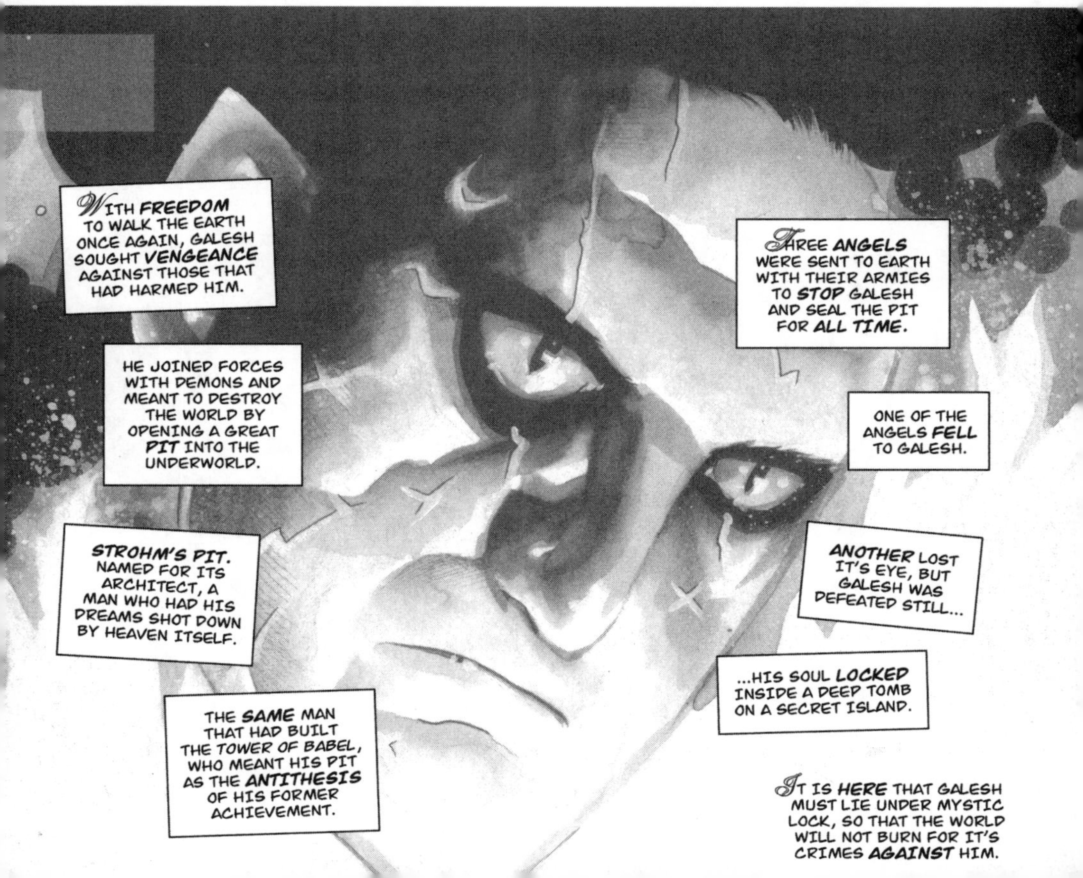
WITH FREEDOM TO WALK THE EARTH ONCE AGAIN, GALESH SOUGHT VENGEANCE AGAINST THOSE THAT HAD HARMED HIM.
HE JOINED FORCES WITH DEMONS AND MEANT TO DESTROY THE WORLD BY OPENING A GREAT PIT INTO THE UNDERWORLD.
STROHM'S PIT. NAMED FOR ITS ARCHITECT, A MAN WHO HAD HIS DREAMS SHOT DOWN BY HEAVEN ITSELF.
THE SAME MAN THAT HAD BUILT THE TOWER OF BABEL, WHO MEANT HIS PIT AS THE ANTITHESIS OF HIS FORMER ACHIEVEMENT.
THREE ANGELS WERE SENT TO EARTH WITH THEIR ARMIES TO STOP GALESH AND SEAL THE PIT FOR ALL TIME.
ONE OF THE ANGELS FELL TO GALESH.
ANOTHER LOST IT'S EYE, BUT GALESH WAS DEFEATED STILL...
...HIS SOUL LOCKED INSIDE A DEEP TOMB ON A SECRET ISLAND.
IT IS HERE THAT GALESH MUST LIE UNDER MYSTIC LOCK, SO THAT THE WORLD WILL NOT BURN FOR IT'S CRIMES AGAINST HIM.

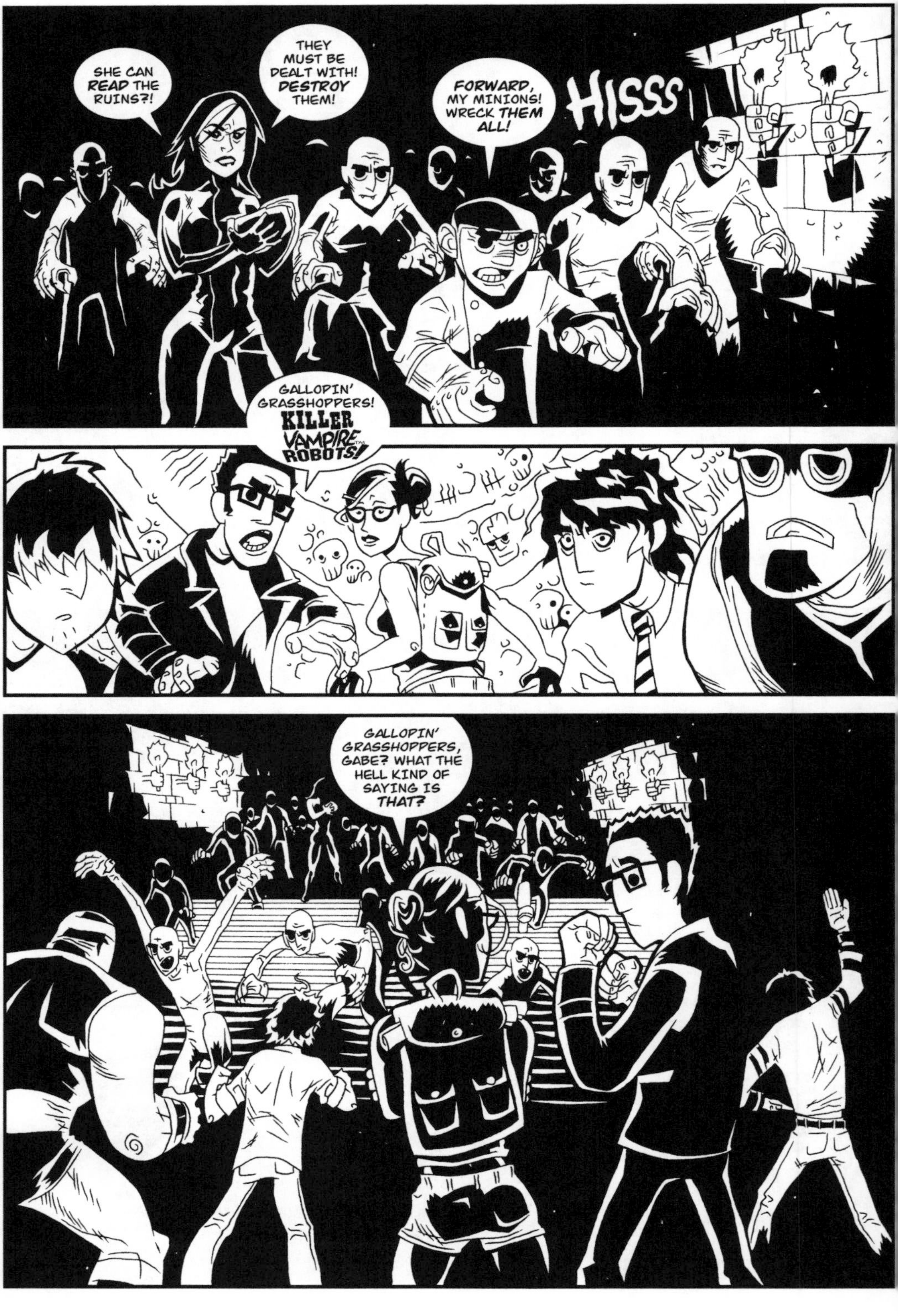
SHE CAN READ THE RUINS?!
THEY MUST BE DEALT WITH! DESTROY THEM!
FORWARD, MY MINIONS! WRECK THEM ALL!
HISSS
GALLOPIN' GRASSHOPPERS! KILLER VAMPIRE ROBOTS!
GALLOPIN' GRASSHOPPERS, GABE? WHAT THE HELL KIND OF SAYING IS THAT?

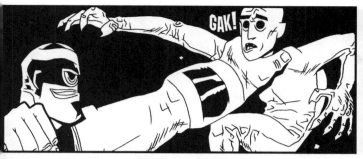

GAK!

LET'S RUMBLE!

BETTY, WATCH OUT!

JUST STAY HERE, BEHIND--

--ME?

KRAK!

YEAH!

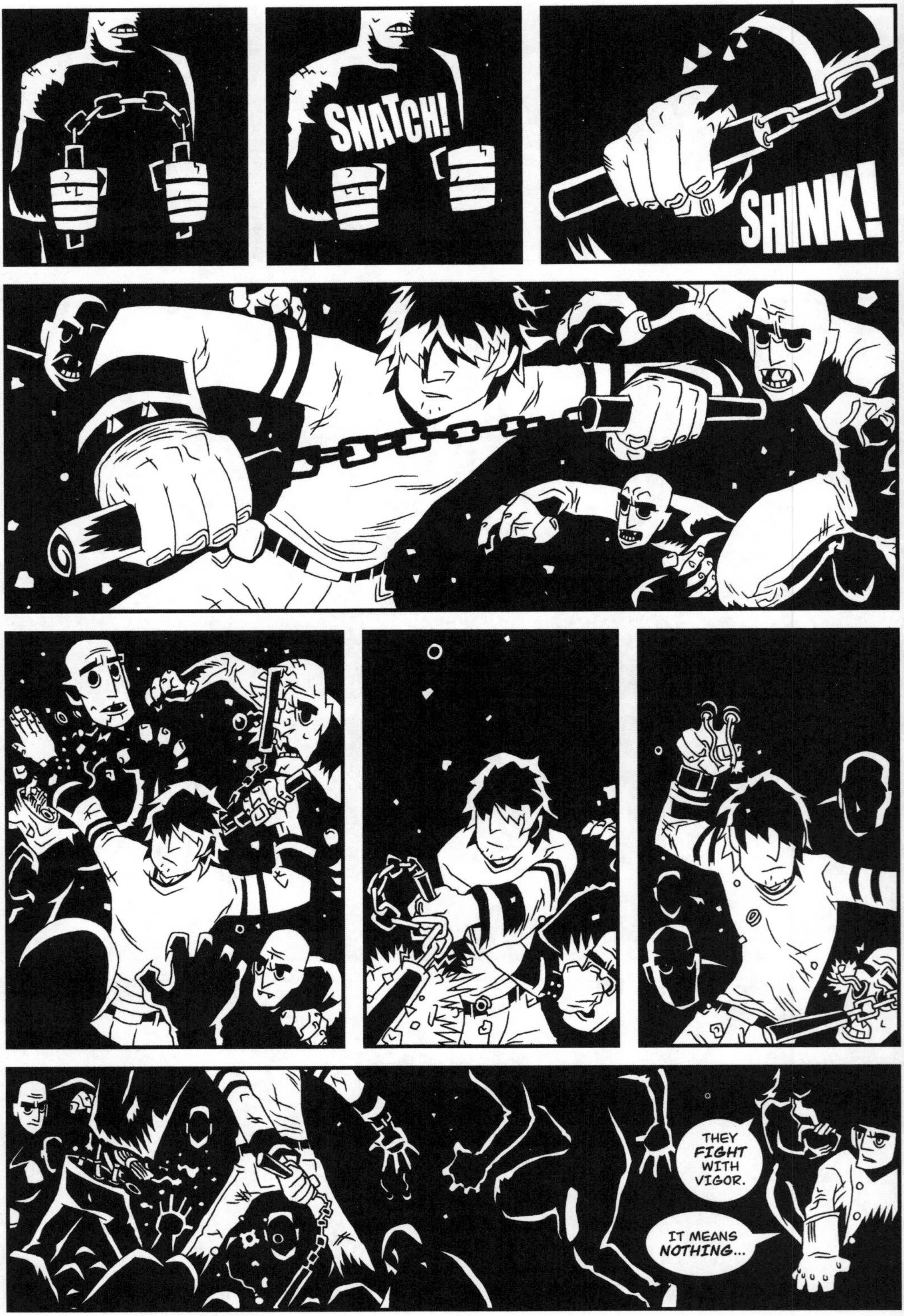
SNATCH!
SHINK!
THEY FIGHT WITH VIGOR.
IT MEANS NOTHING...

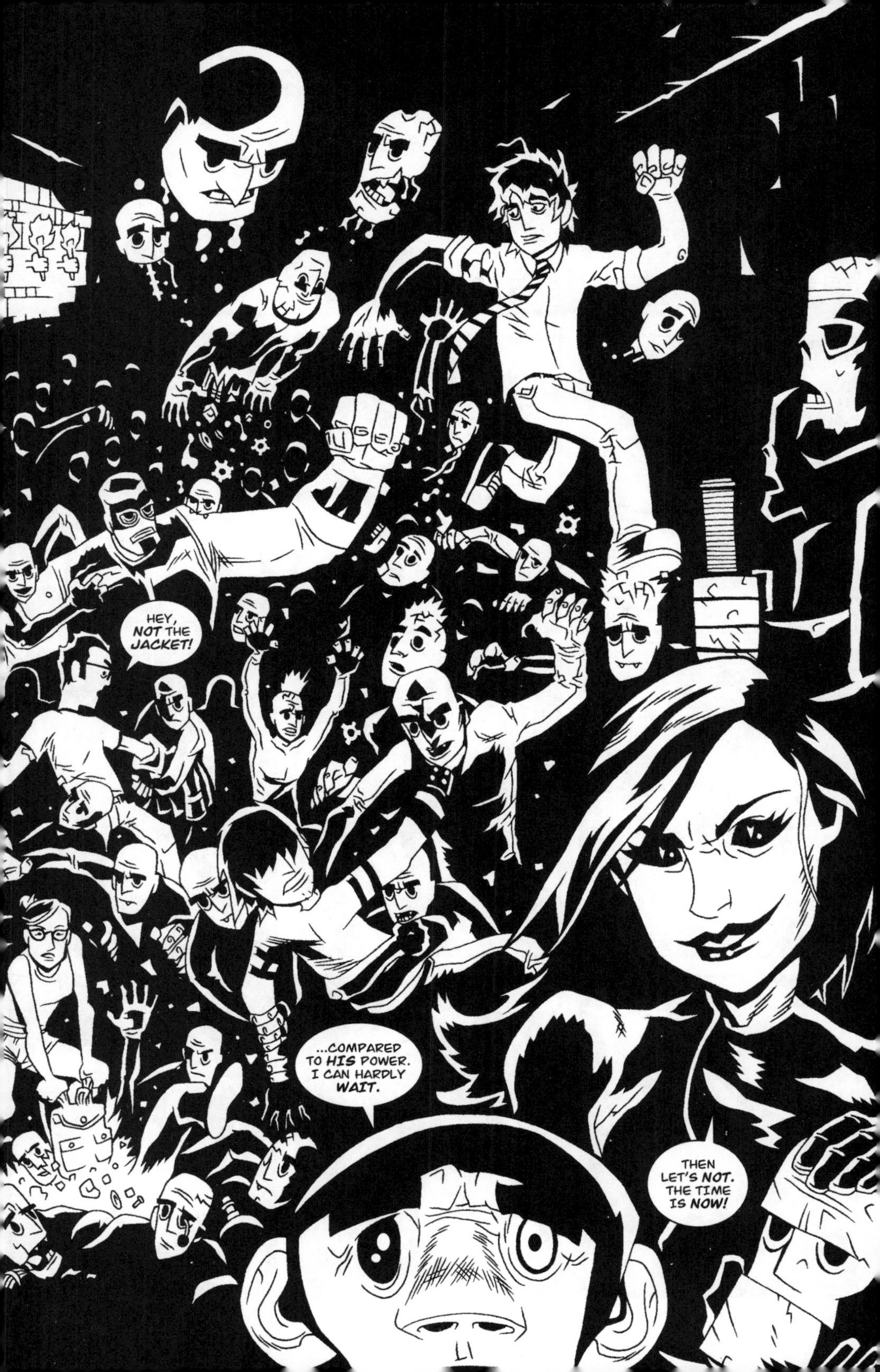
HEY, NOT THE JACKET!
...COMPARED TO HIS POWER. I CAN HARDLY WAIT.
THEN LET'S NOT. THE TIME IS NOW!

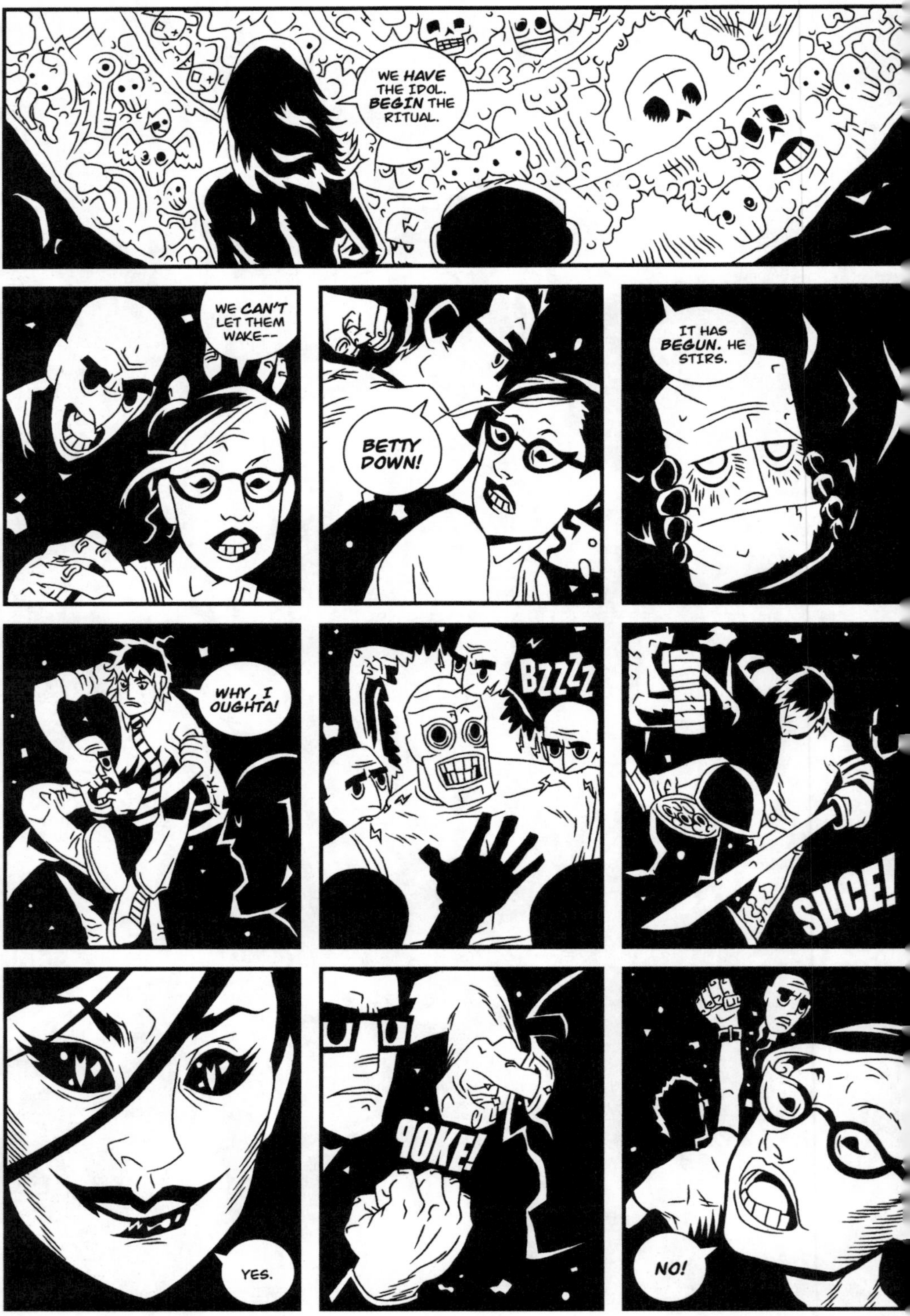
WE HAVE THE IDOL. BEGIN THE RITUAL.
WE CAN'T LET THEM WAKE--
BETTY DOWN!
IT HAS BEGUN. HE STIRS.
WHY, I OUGHTA!
BZZZZ
SLICE!
YES.
POKE!
NO!

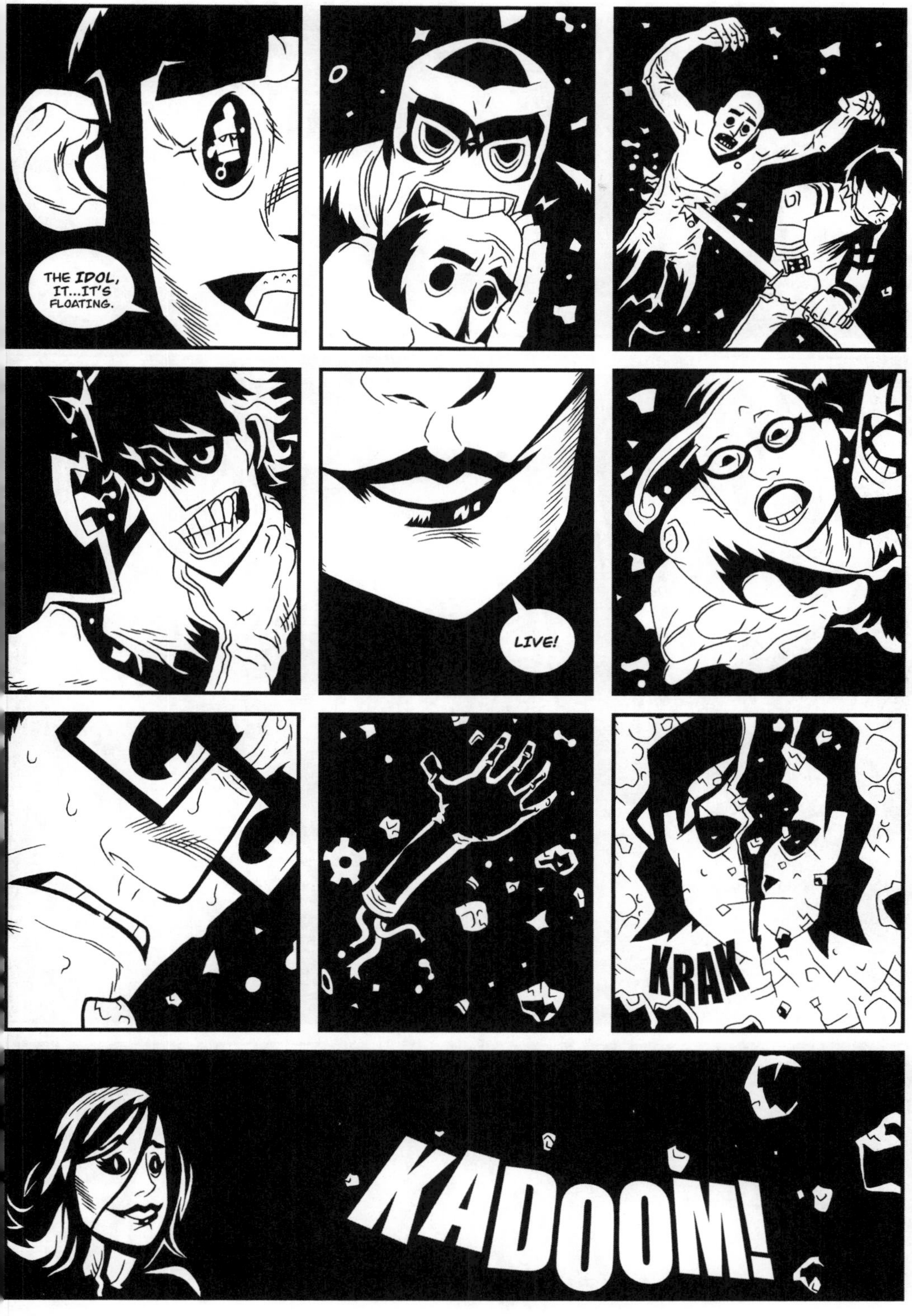
THE IDOL, IT...IT'S FLOATING.
LIVE!
KRAK
KADOOM!

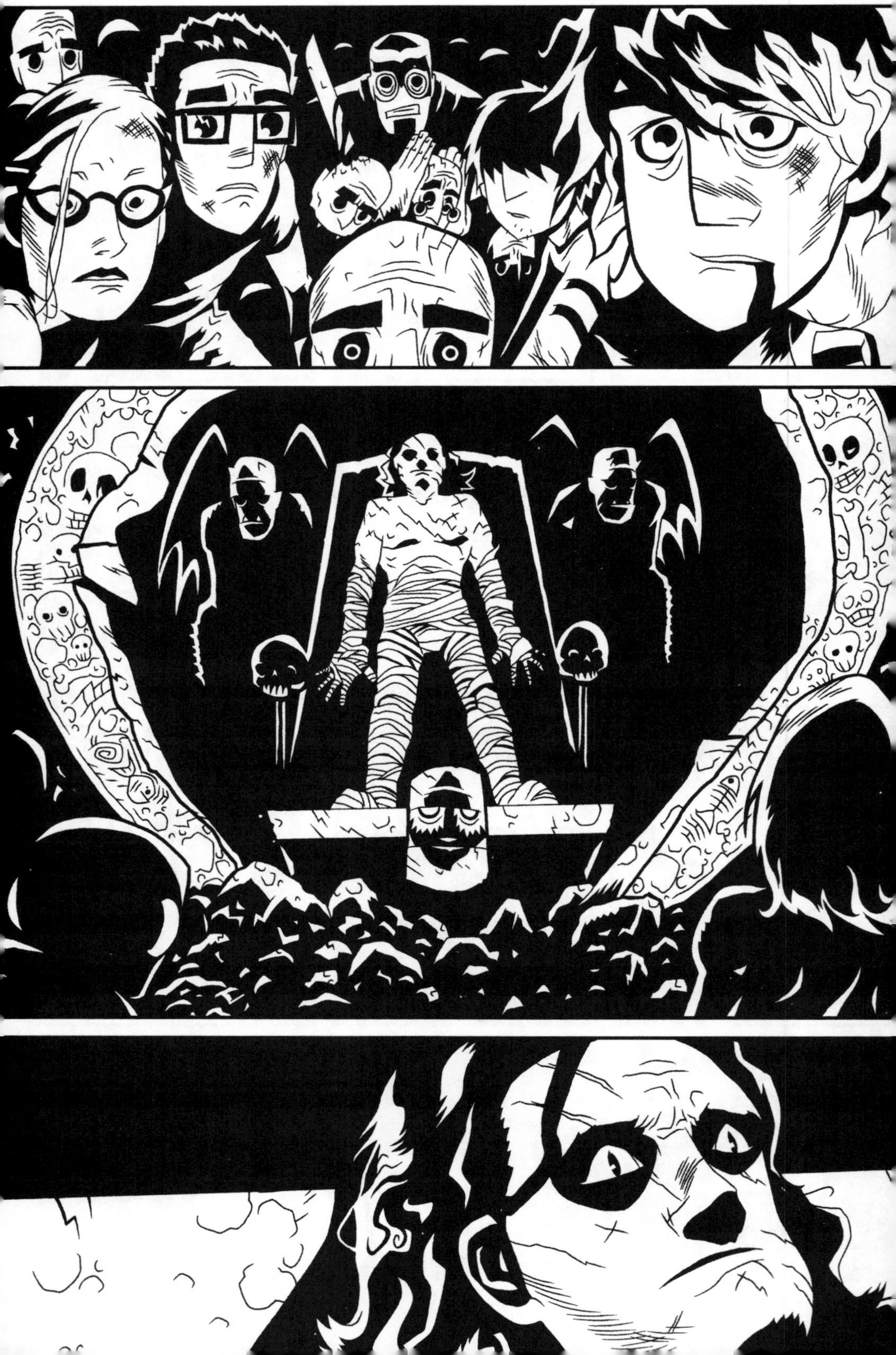

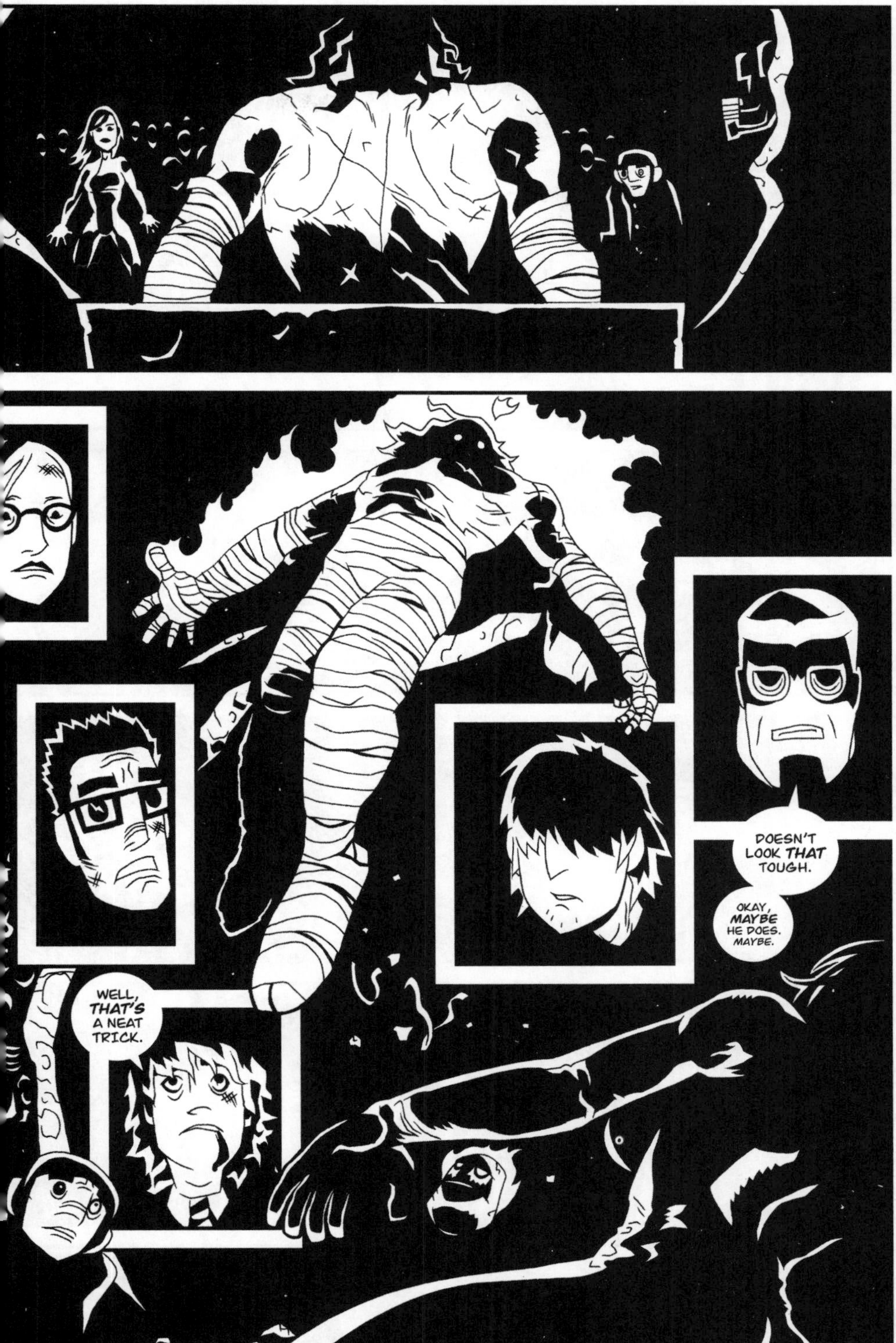
DOESN'T LOOK THAT TOUGH.
OKAY, MAYBE HE DOES. MAYBE.
WELL, THAT'S A NEAT TRICK.

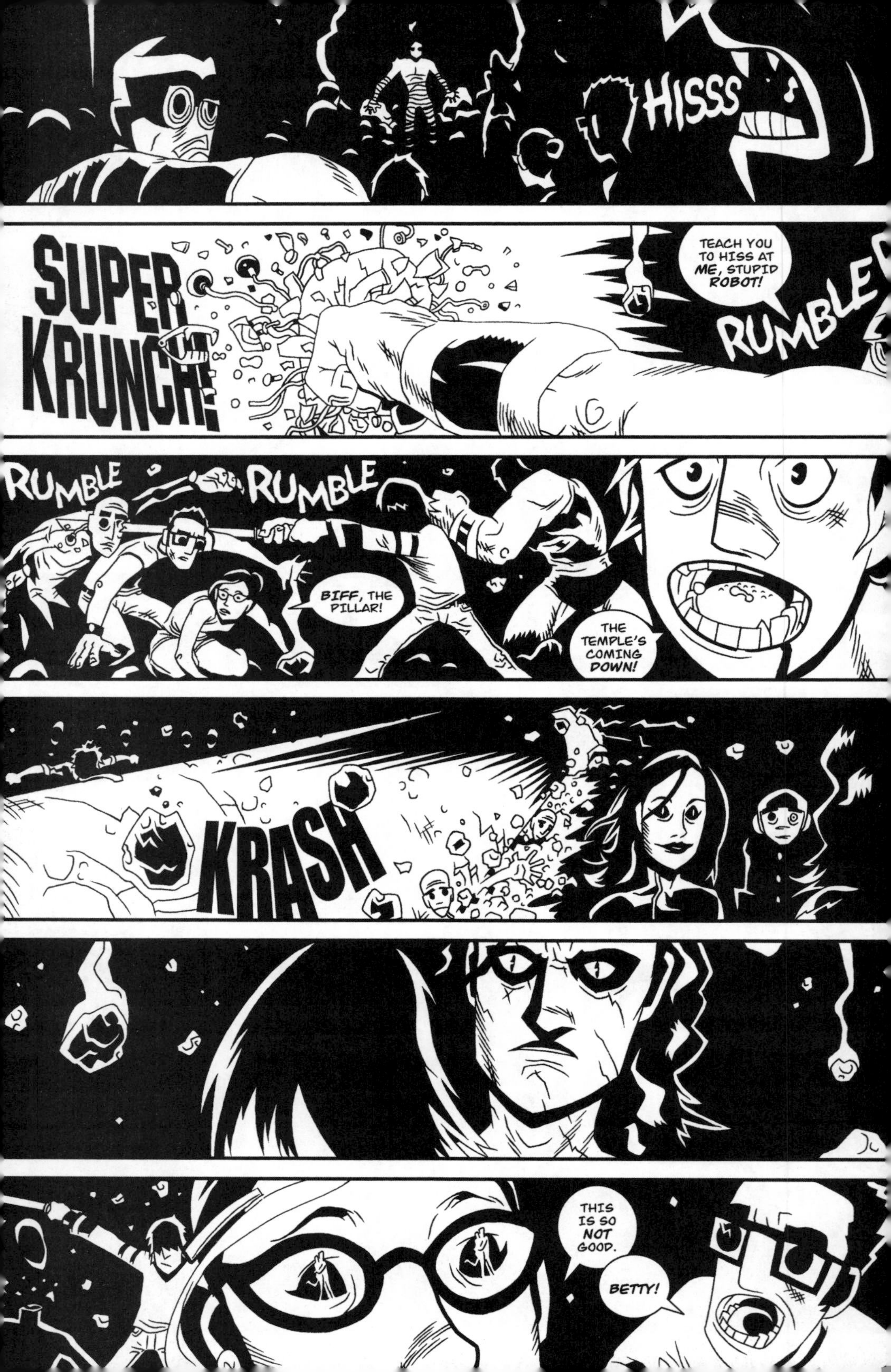
HISSS
SUPER KRUNCH!
TEACH YOU TO HISS AT ME, STUPID ROBOT!
RUMBLE
RUMBLE
RUMBLE RUMBLE
BIFF, THE PILLAR!
THE TEMPLE'S COMING DOWN!
KRASH
THIS IS SO NOT GOOD.
BETTY!

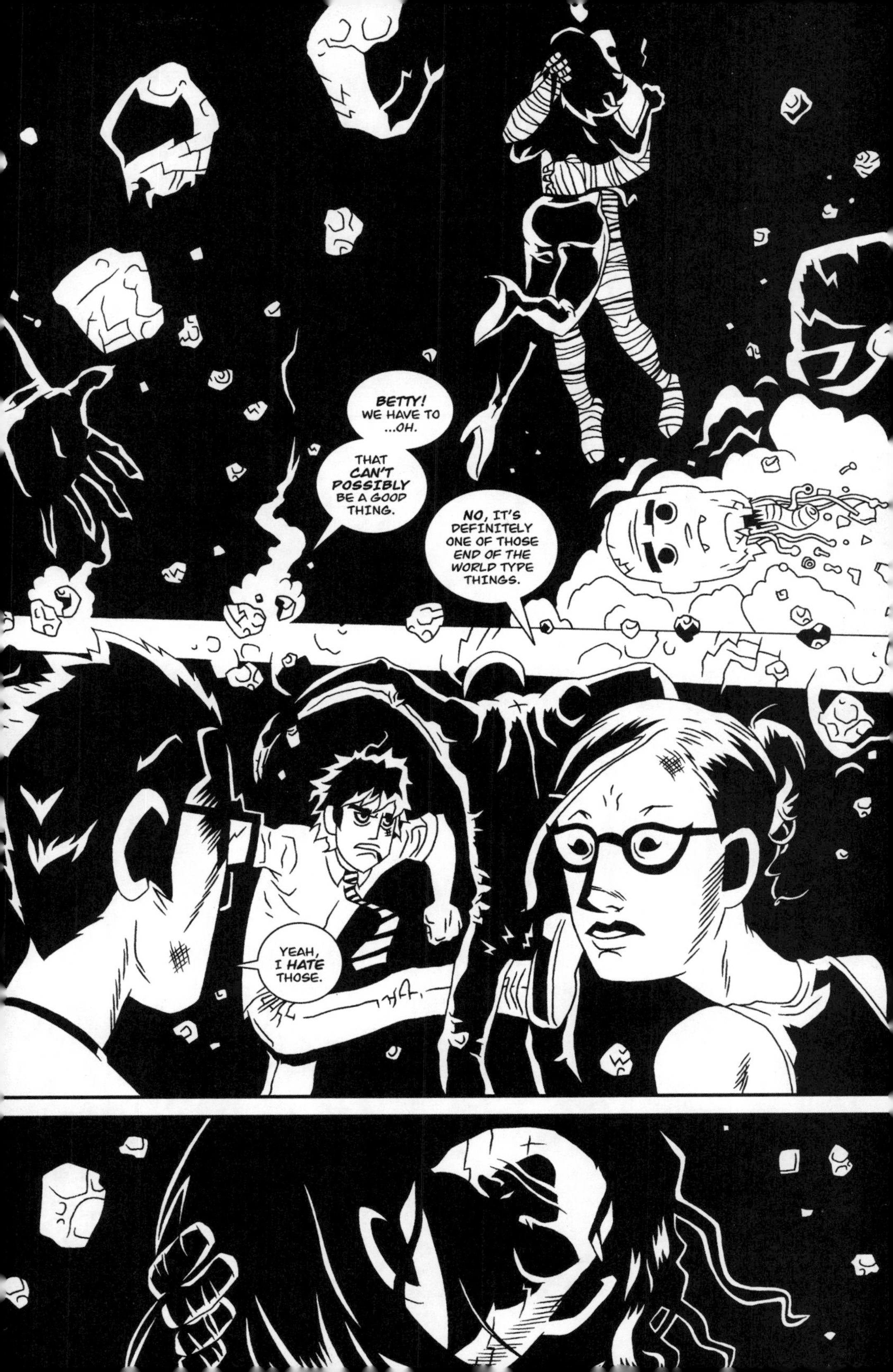
BETTY! WE HAVE TO ...OH.
THAT CAN'T POSSIBLY BE A GOOD THING.
NO, IT'S DEFINITELY ONE OF THOSE END OF THE WORLD TYPE THINGS.
YEAH, I HATE THOSE.

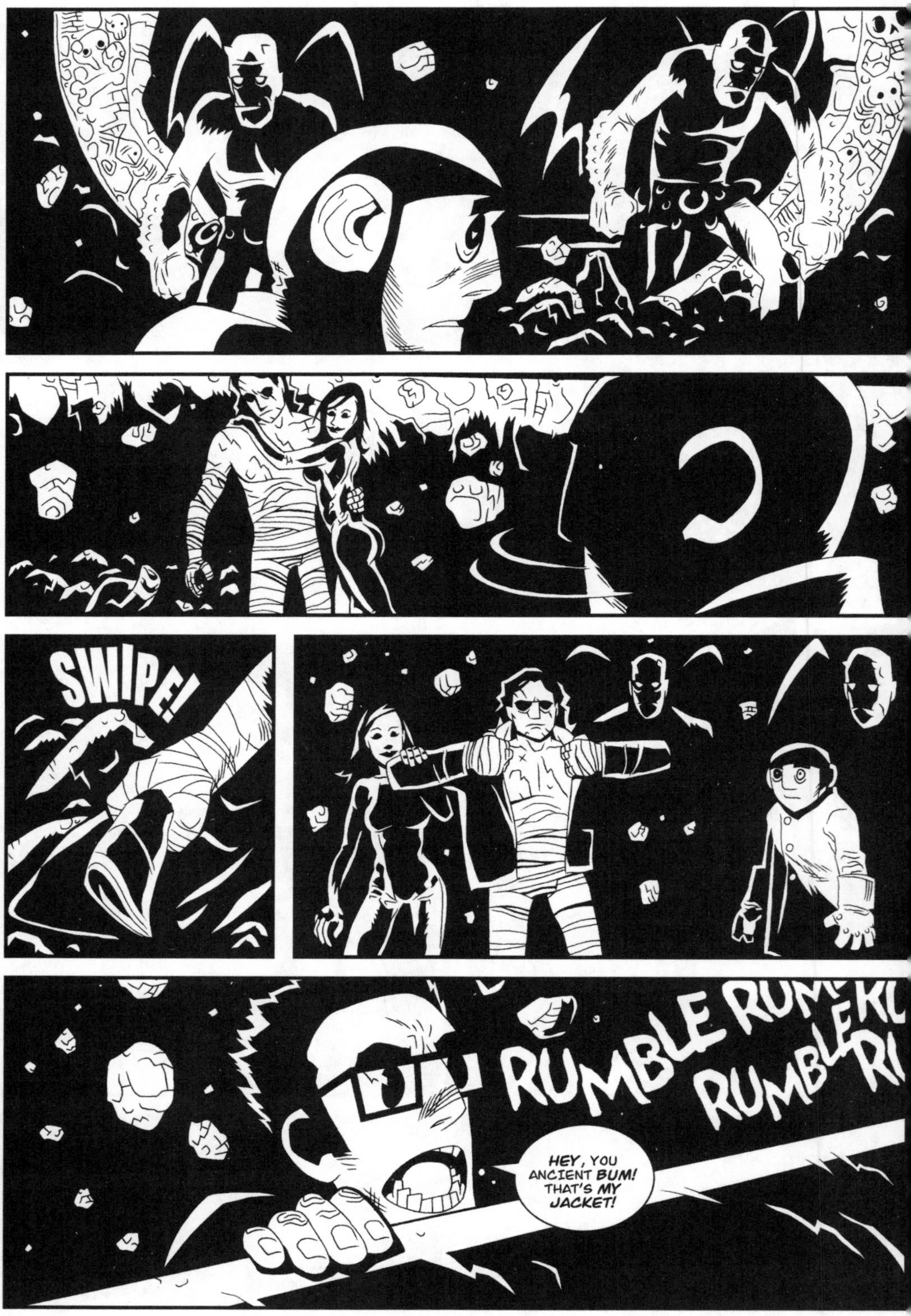
SWIPE!
RUMBLE RUMBLE
RUMBLE
HEY, YOU ANCIENT BUM! THAT'S MY JACKET!

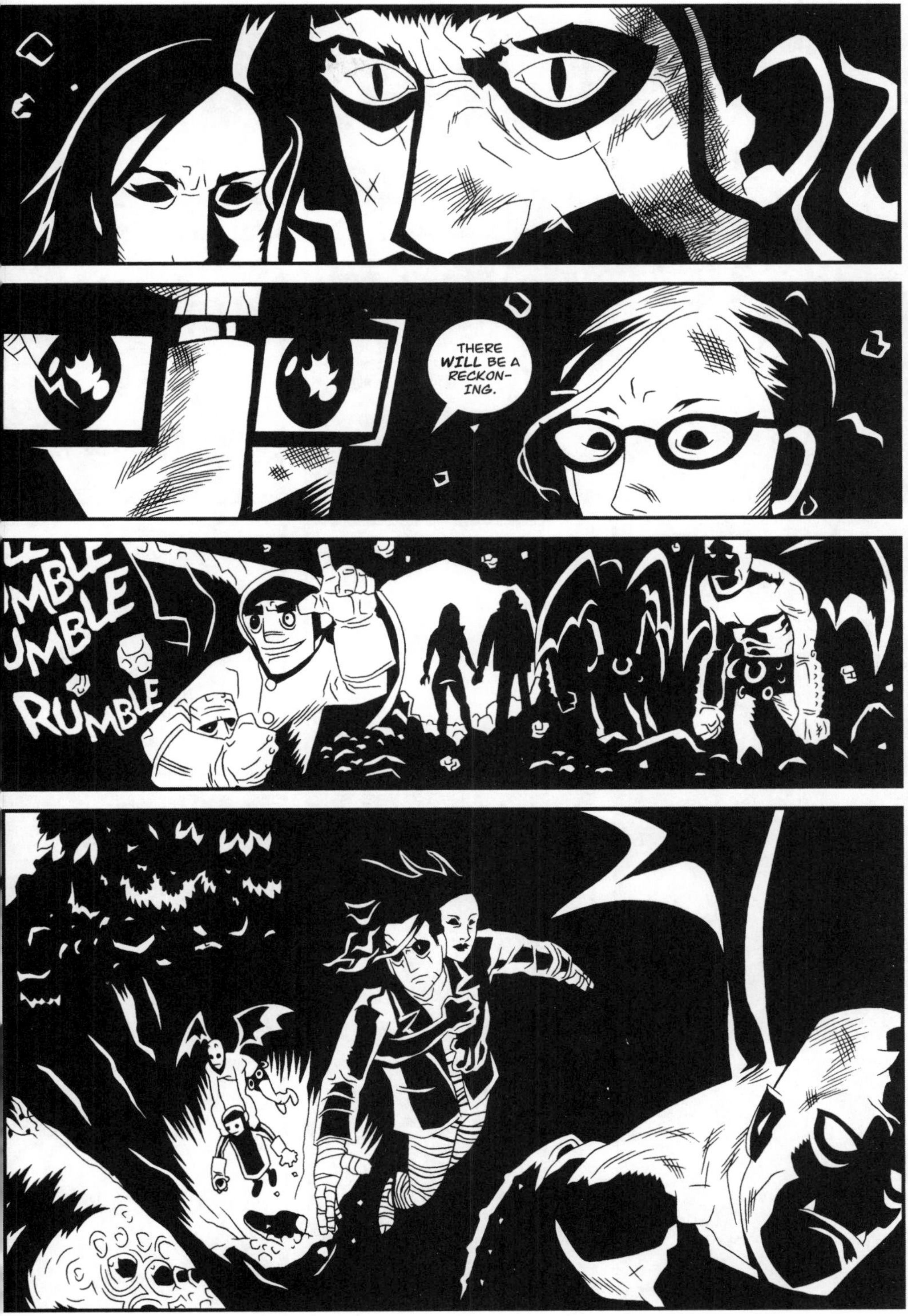
THERE WILL BE A RECKONING.
UMBLE
UMBLE
UMBLE
RUMBLE

WHAT THE HELL JUST HAPPENED?
GABE, LOOK OUT!
OH NO.
KRAK!
AHGG! MY NODE!
GUYD! I CAN'D DEE!
GUYD?
STEVO, WATCH YOUR BACK!
EL CAMPEON, THAT PILLAR IS BLOCKING THE ONLY WAY OUT!
ON IT!
QUICKLY, MY FRIENDS! I CAN'T HOLD IT FOR LONG.
STUPID ROBOT!
OW! BIFF, THAT'S ME!
WAID, DOND LEAVE!
EVERYONE HEAD FOR THE OPENING!
WAID!
CLASP!

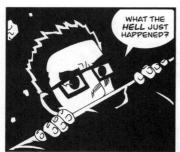

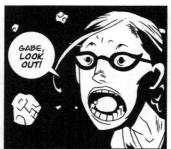

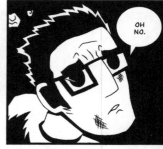

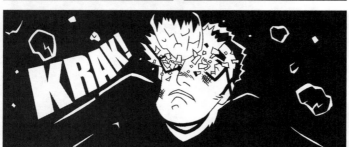

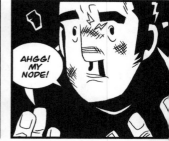

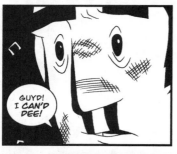

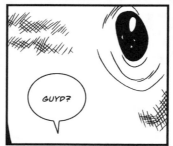

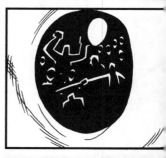

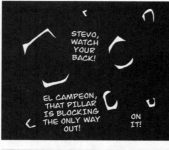

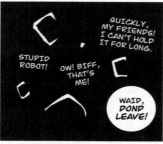

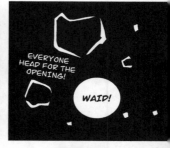

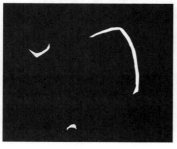

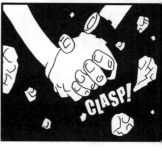

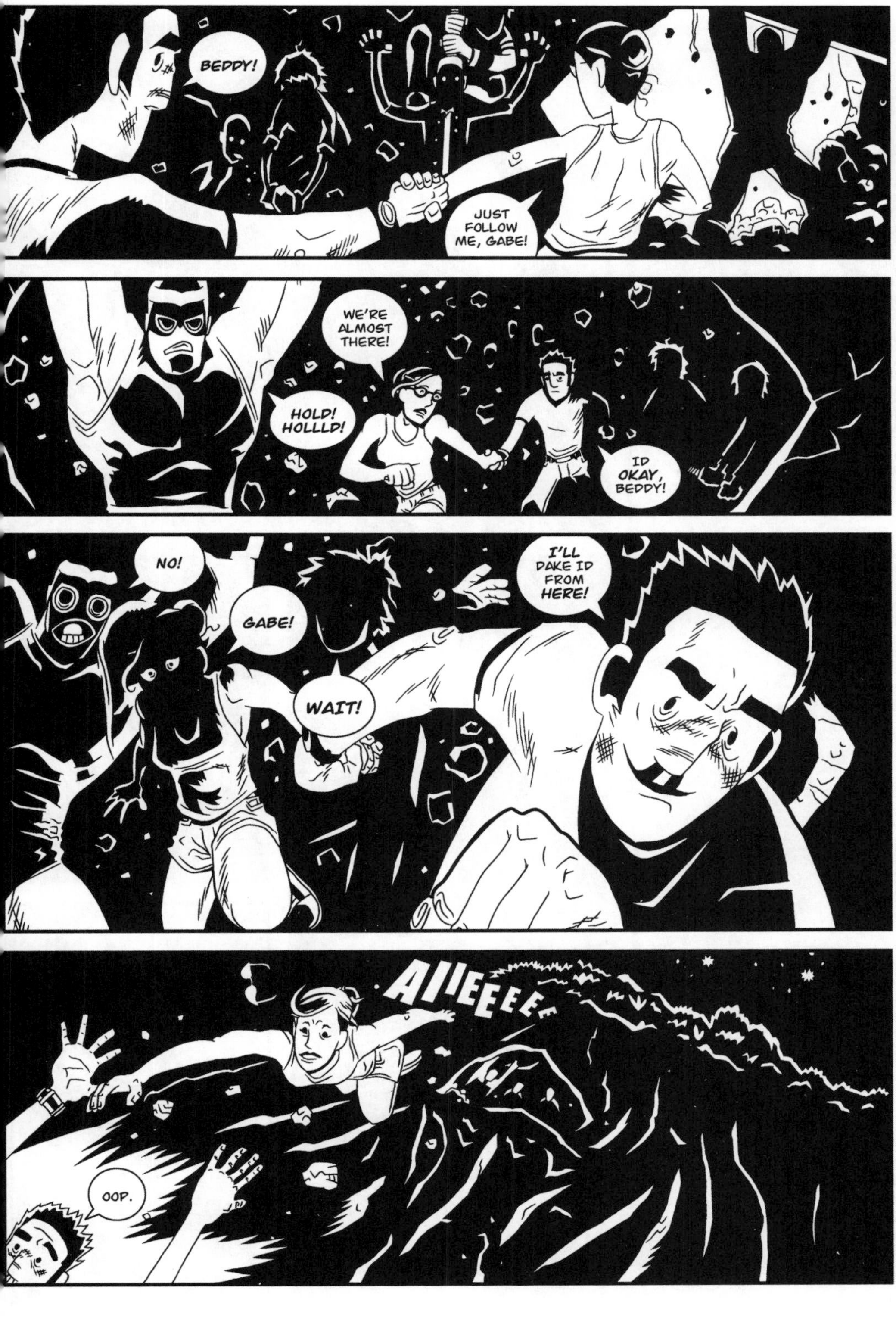

BEDDY!
JUST FOLLOW ME, GABE!
WE'RE ALMOST THERE!
HOLD! HOLLLD!
ID OKAY, BEDDY!
NO!
GABE!
WAIT!
I'LL DAKE ID FROM HERE!
AIIEEEEE
OOP.

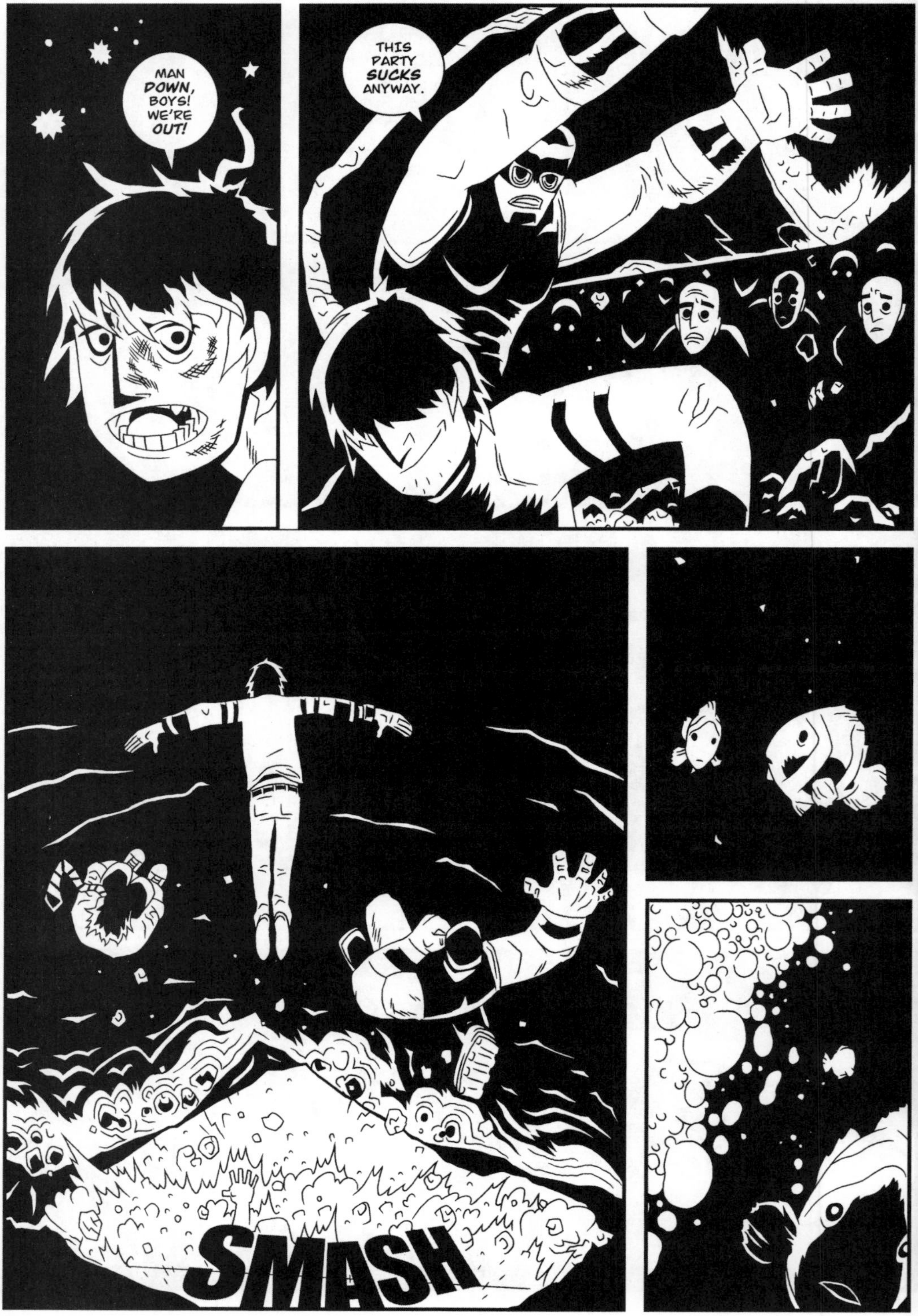
MAN DOWN, BOYS! WE'RE OUT!
THIS PARTY SUCKS ANYWAY.
SMASH

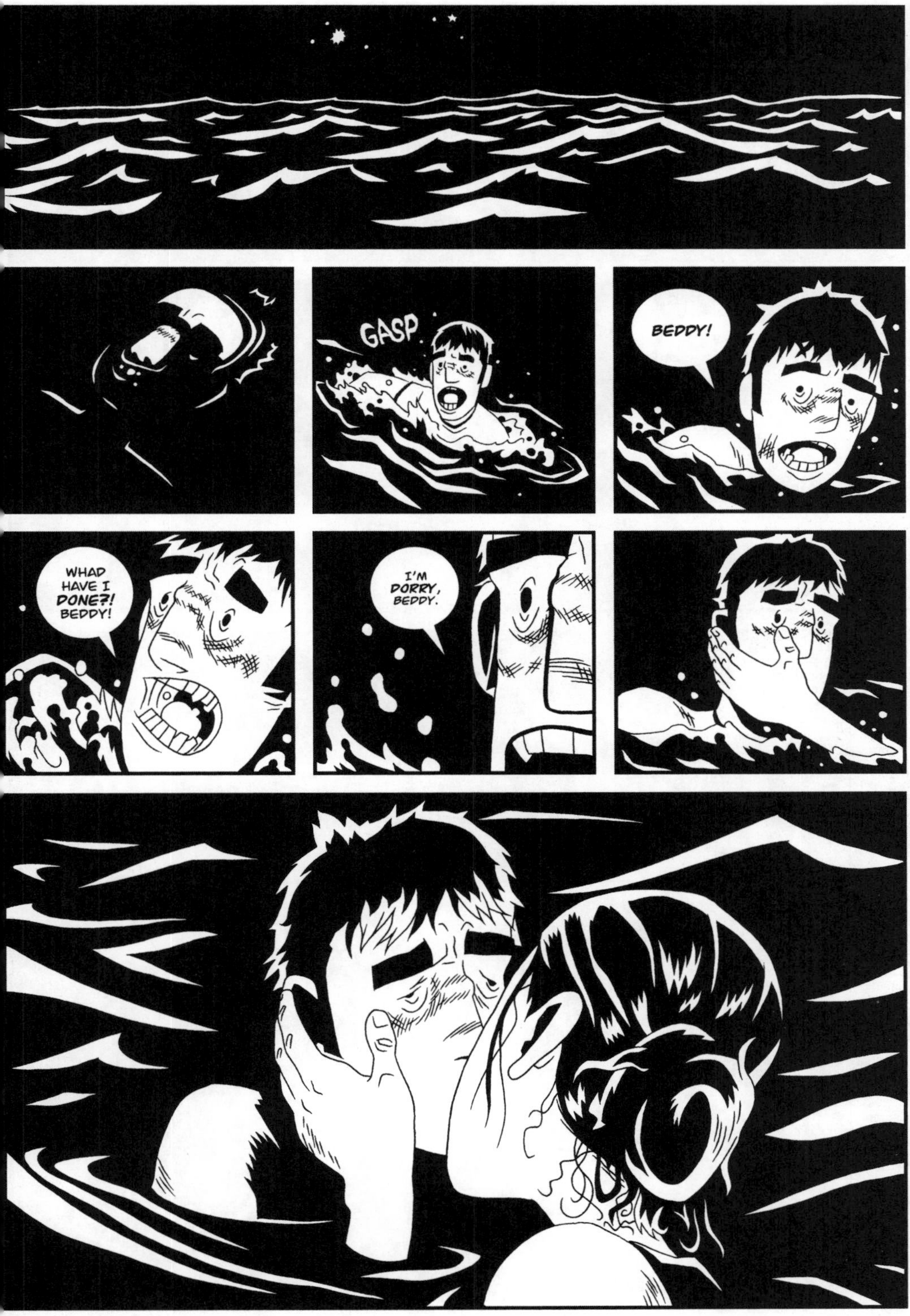
GASP
BEDDY!
WHAD HAVE I DONE?! BEDDY!
I'M DORRY, BEDDY.

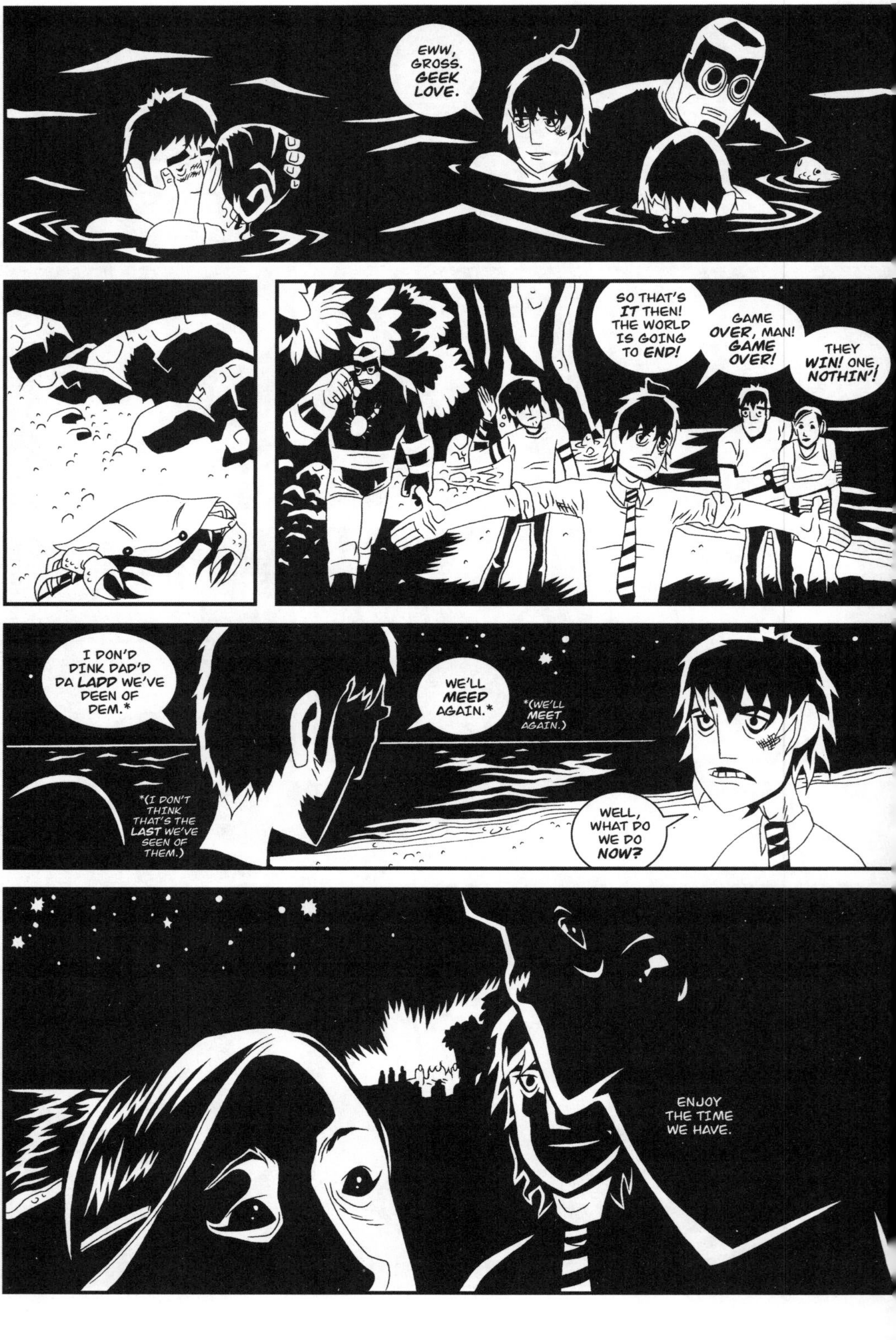
EWW, GROSS. GEEK LOVE.
SO THAT'S IT THEN! THE WORLD IS GOING TO END!
GAME OVER, MAN! GAME OVER!
THEY WIN! ONE, NOTHIN'!
I DON'D DINK DAD'D DA LADD WE'VE DEEN OF DEM.*
*(I DON'T THINK THAT'S THE LAST WE'VE SEEN OF THEM.)
WE'LL MEED AGAIN.*
*(WE'LL MEET AGAIN.)
WELL, WHAT DO WE DO NOW?
ENJOY THE TIME WE HAVE.

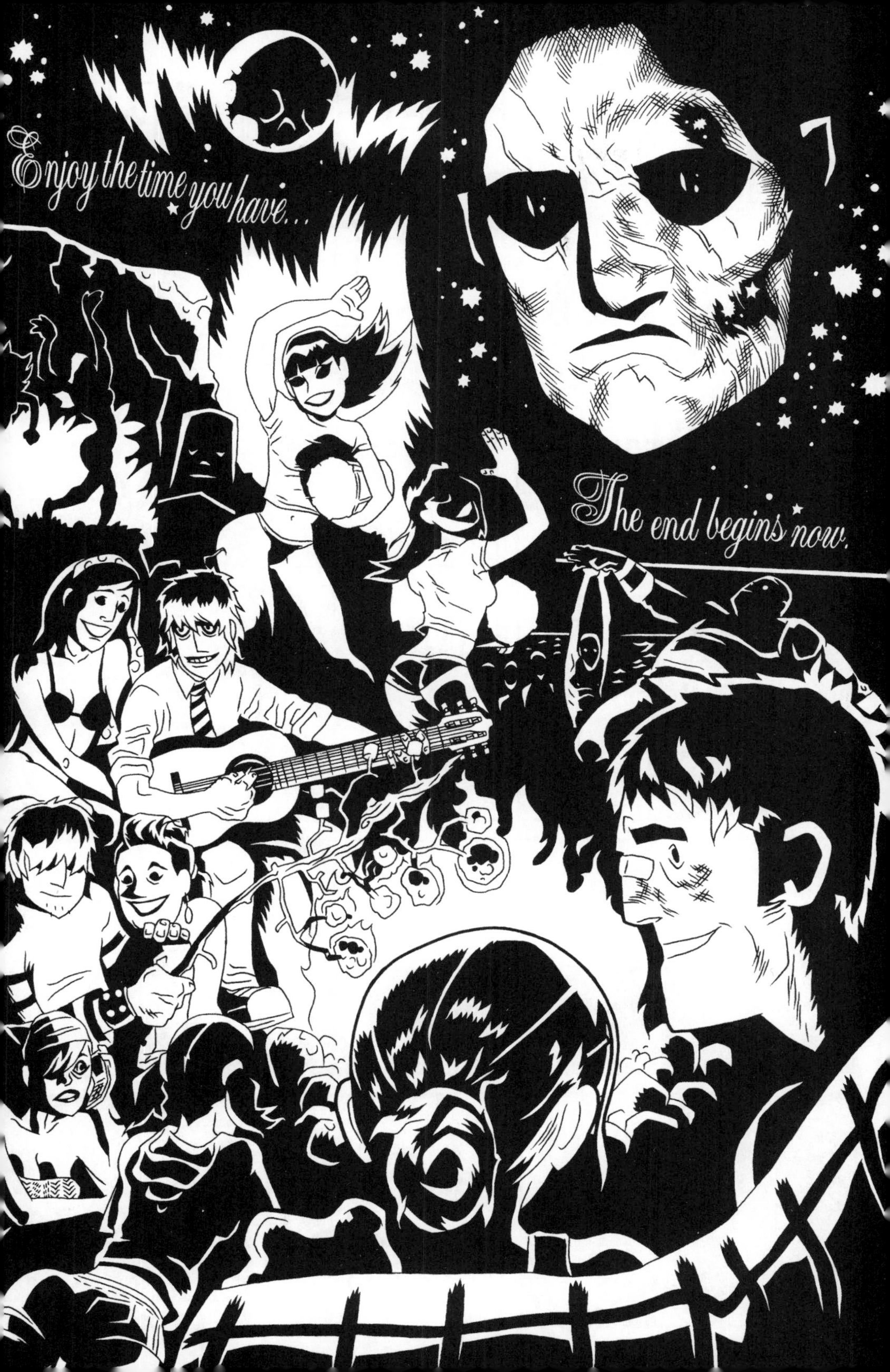
Enjoy the time you have...
The end begins now.

Somewhere else entirely...

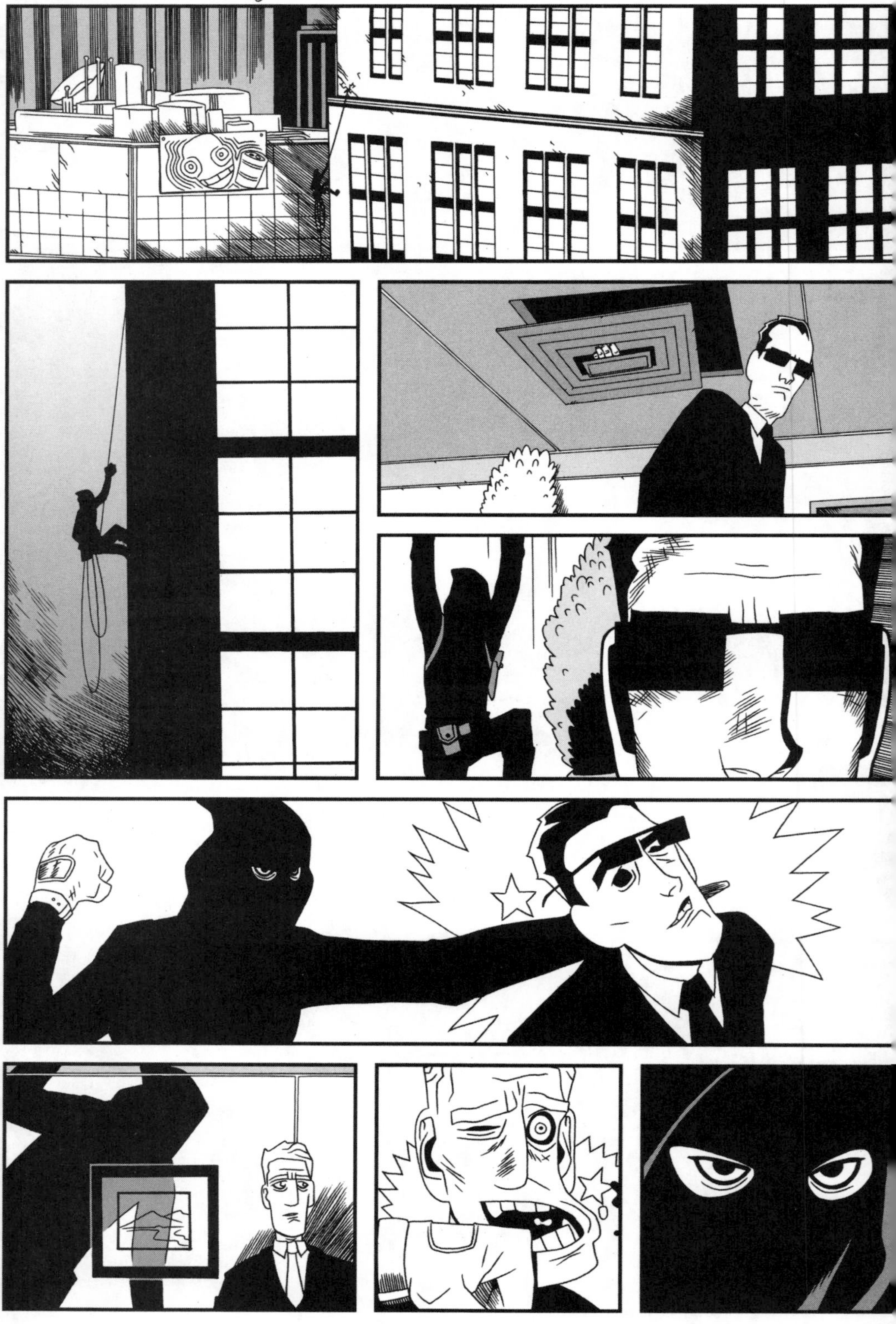

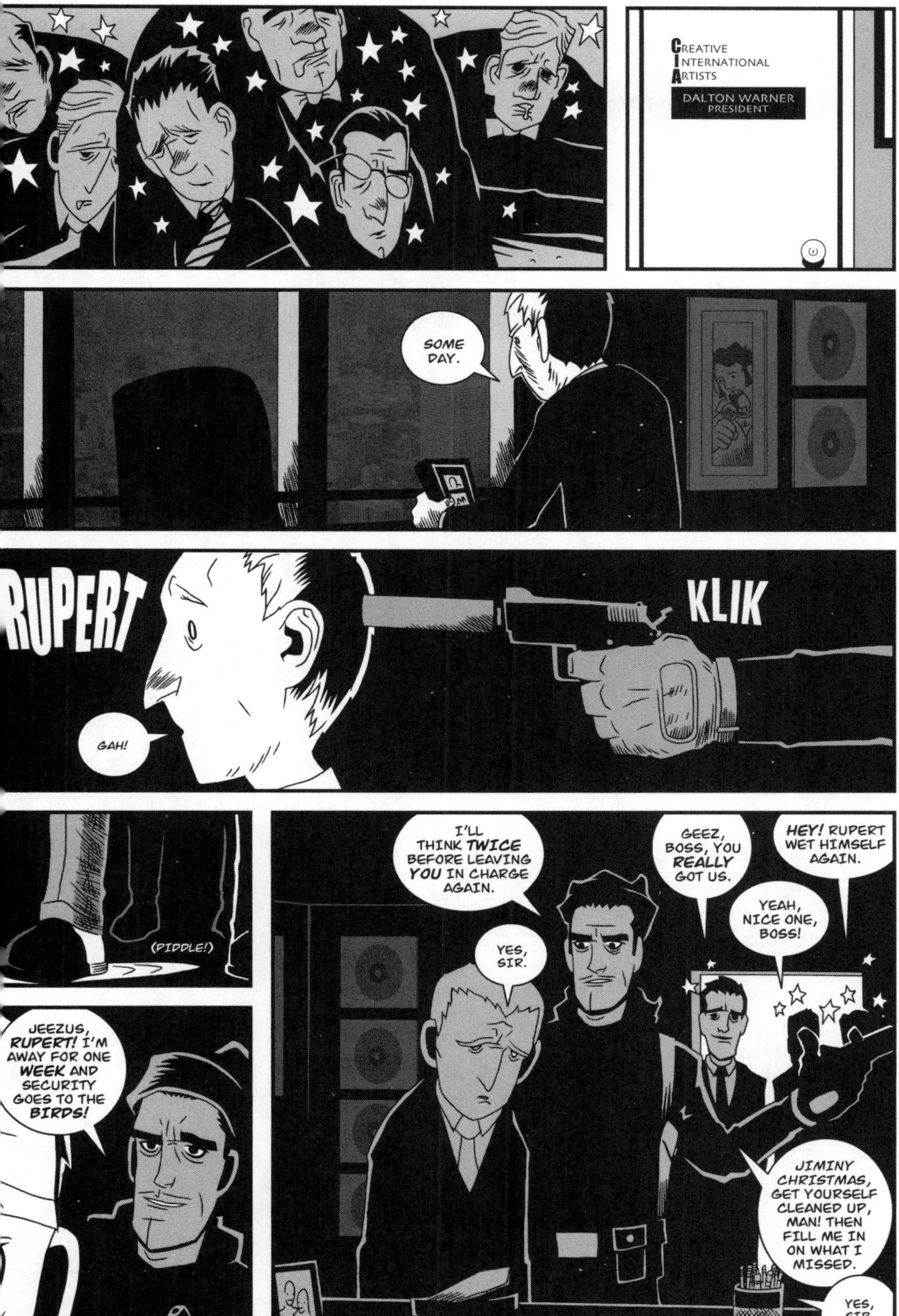
CREATIVE INTERNATIONAL ARTISTS
DALTON WARNER PRESIDENT
SOME DAY.
RUPERT
KLIK
GAH!
(PIDDLE!)
JEEZUS, RUPERT! I'M AWAY FOR ONE WEEK AND SECURITY GOES TO THE BIRDS!
I'LL THINK TWICE BEFORE LEAVING YOU IN CHARGE AGAIN.
YES, SIR.
GEEZ, BOSS, YOU REALLY GOT US.
HEY! RUPERT WET HIMSELF AGAIN.
YEAH, NICE ONE, BOSS!
JIMINY CHRISTMAS, GET YOURSELF CLEANED UP, MAN! THEN FILL ME IN ON WHAT I MISSED.
YES, SIR.
(KEEP YOUR HEAD UP, RUPERT. NOW BACK TO THE SHOW!)

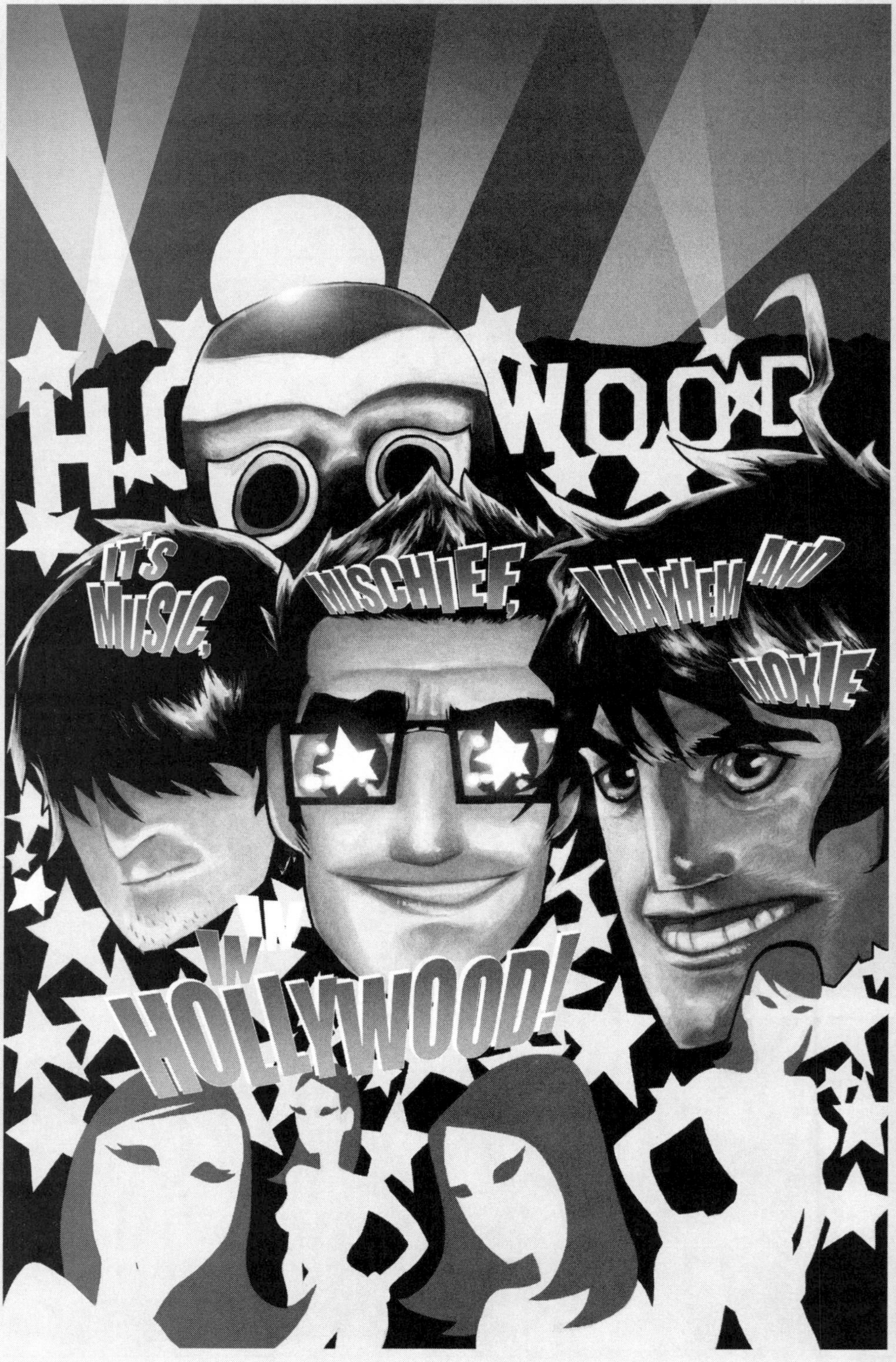
H WOOD
IT'S MUSIC,
MISCHIEF,
MAYHEM AND
MOXIE
IN
HOLLYWOOD!

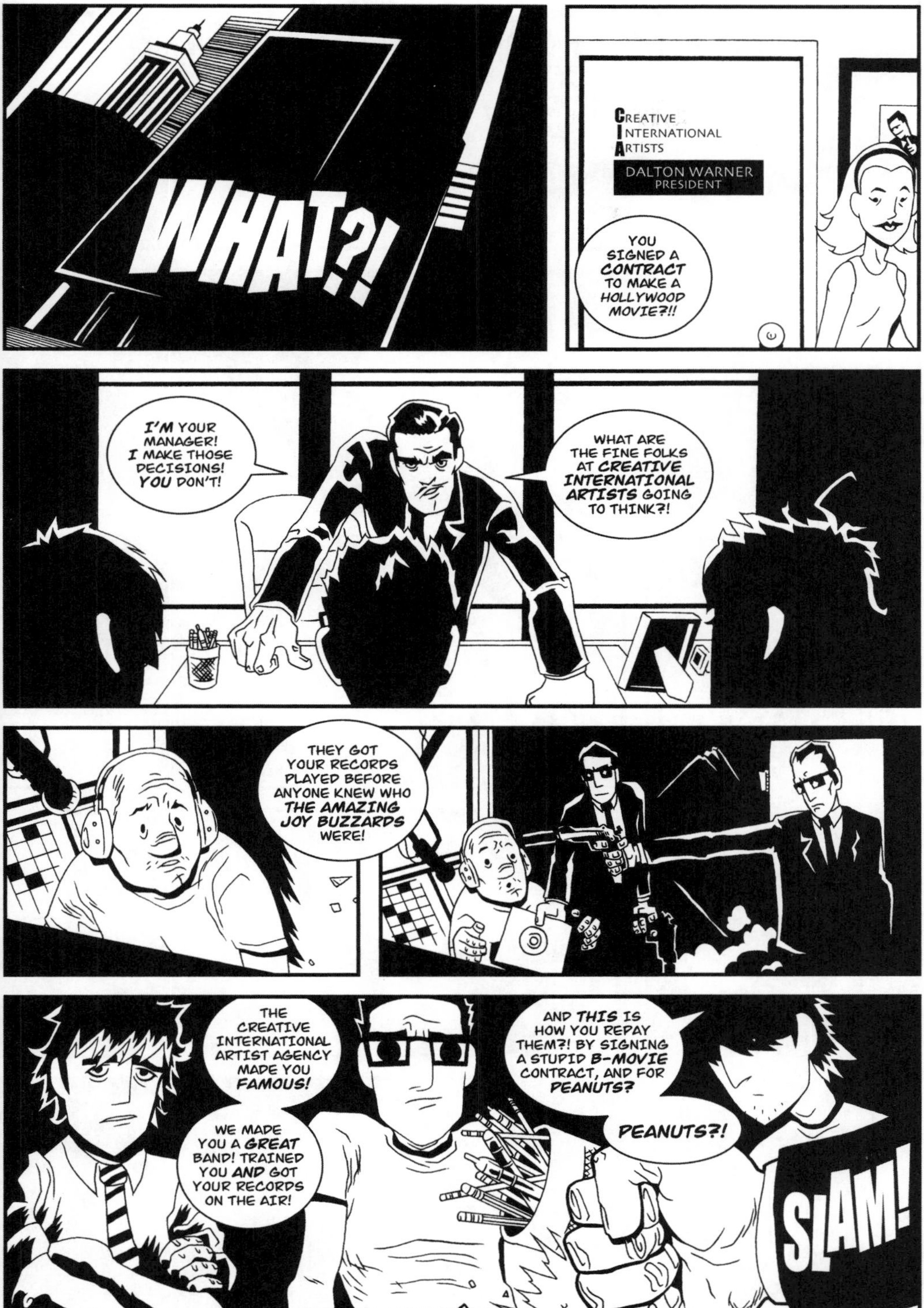
WHAT?!
CREATIVE INTERNATIONAL ARTISTS
DALTON WARNER PRESIDENT
YOU SIGNED A CONTRACT TO MAKE A HOLLYWOOD MOVIE?!!
I'M YOUR MANAGER! I MAKE THOSE DECISIONS! YOU DON'T!
WHAT ARE THE FINE FOLKS AT CREATIVE INTERNATIONAL ARTISTS GOING TO THINK?!
THEY GOT YOUR RECORDS PLAYED BEFORE ANYONE KNEW WHO THE AMAZING JOY BUZZARDS WERE!
THE CREATIVE INTERNATIONAL ARTIST AGENCY MADE YOU FAMOUS!
WE MADE YOU A GREAT BAND! TRAINED YOU AND GOT YOUR RECORDS ON THE AIR!
AND THIS IS HOW YOU REPAY THEM?! BY SIGNING A STUPID B-MOVIE CONTRACT, AND FOR PEANUTS?
PEANUTS?!
SLAM!

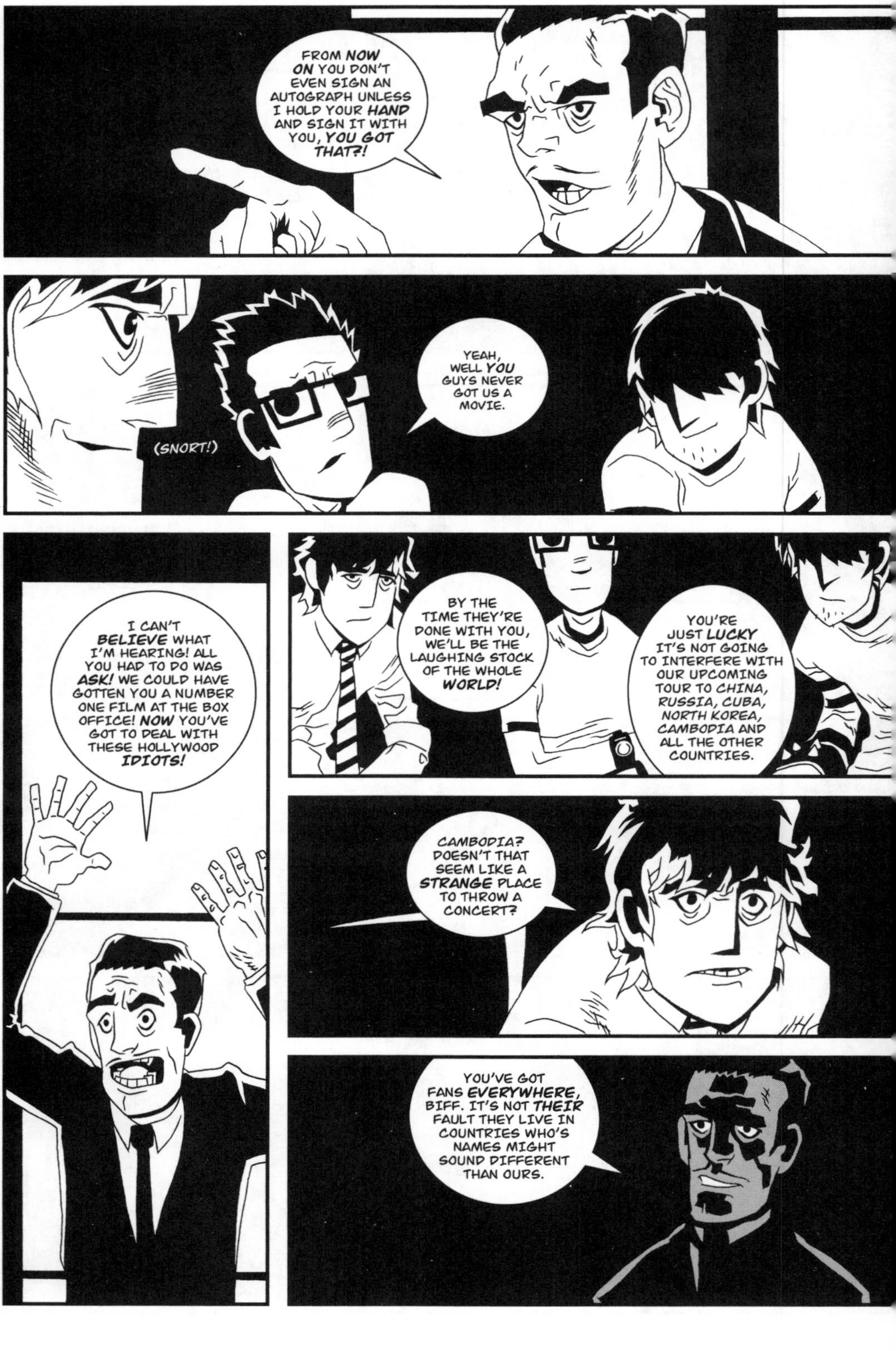
FROM NOW ON YOU DON'T EVEN SIGN AN AUTOGRAPH UNLESS I HOLD YOUR HAND AND SIGN IT WITH YOU, YOU GOT THAT?!
(SNORT!)
YEAH, WELL YOU GUYS NEVER GOT US A MOVIE.
I CAN'T BELIEVE WHAT I'M HEARING! ALL YOU HAD TO DO WAS ASK! WE COULD HAVE GOTTEN YOU A NUMBER ONE FILM AT THE BOX OFFICE! NOW YOU'VE GOT TO DEAL WITH THESE HOLLYWOOD IDIOTS!
BY THE TIME THEY'RE DONE WITH YOU, WE'LL BE THE LAUGHING STOCK OF THE WHOLE WORLD!
YOU'RE JUST LUCKY IT'S NOT GOING TO INTERFERE WITH OUR UPCOMING TOUR TO CHINA, RUSSIA, CUBA, NORTH KOREA, CAMBODIA AND ALL THE OTHER COUNTRIES.
CAMBODIA? DOESN'T THAT SEEM LIKE A STRANGE PLACE TO THROW A CONCERT?
YOU'VE GOT FANS EVERYWHERE, BIFF. IT'S NOT THEIR FAULT THEY LIVE IN COUNTRIES WHO'S NAMES MIGHT SOUND DIFFERENT THAN OURS.

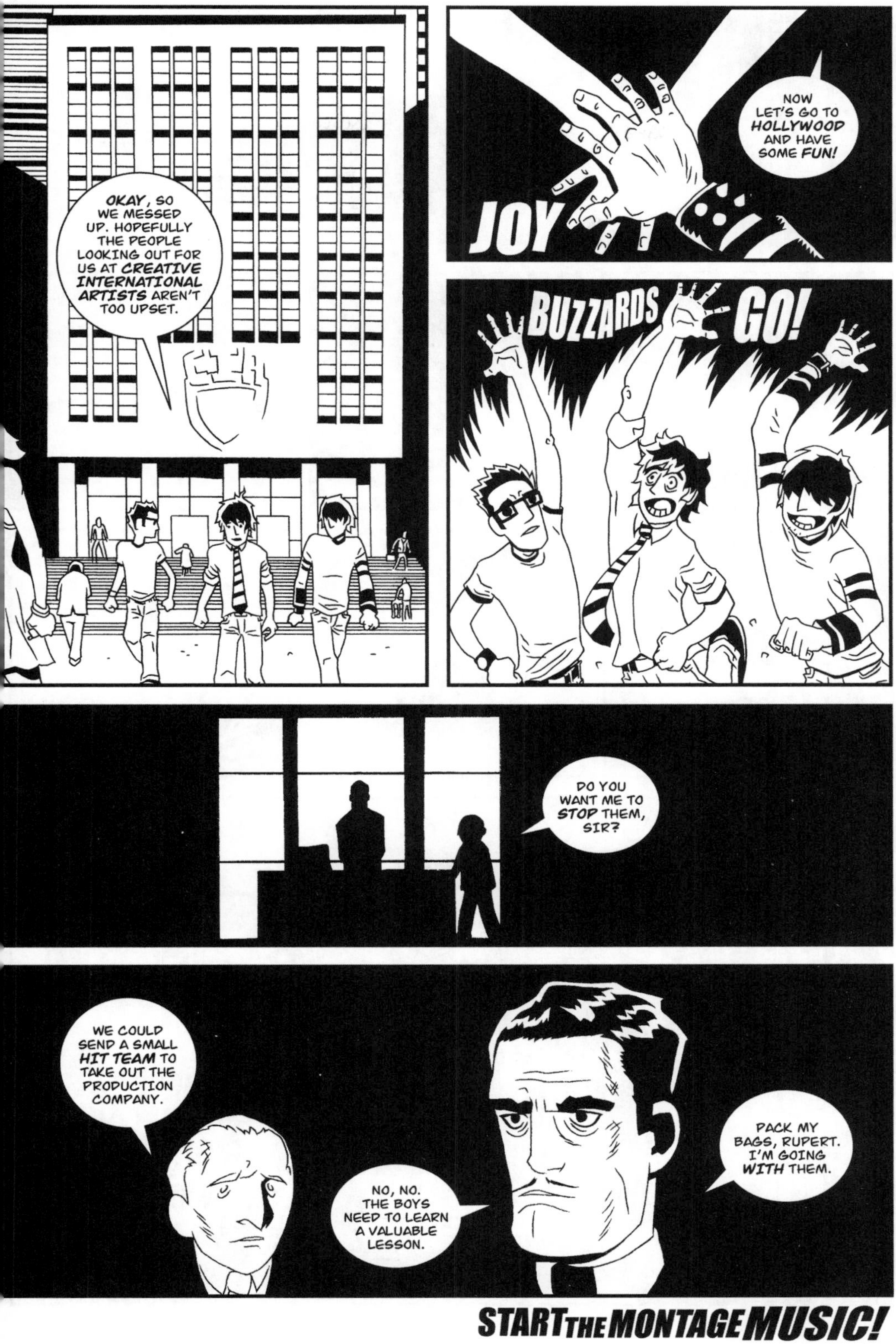
OKAY, SO WE MESSED UP. HOPEFULLY THE PEOPLE LOOKING OUT FOR US AT CREATIVE INTERNATIONAL ARTISTS AREN'T TOO UPSET.
NOW LET'S GO TO HOLLYWOOD AND HAVE SOME FUN!
JOY
BUZZARDS
GO!
DO YOU WANT ME TO STOP THEM, SIR?
WE COULD SEND A SMALL HIT TEAM TO TAKE OUT THE PRODUCTION COMPANY.
NO, NO. THE BOYS NEED TO LEARN A VALUABLE LESSON.
PACK MY BAGS, RUPERT. I'M GOING WITH THEM.
START THE MONTAGE MUSIC!

PART THREE

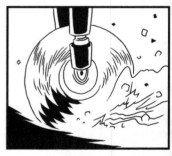

NEVER FEAR, HOLLYWOOD!

THE AMAZING JOY BUZZARDS ARE HERE!

ACTUALLY, THIS IS JUST LOS ANGELES, BIFF.

SAME THING.

OF A SMITH AND HIPP PRODUCTION

BIFF!

BIFF!

BIFF!

BIFF!

BIFF!

BIFF!

BIFF!

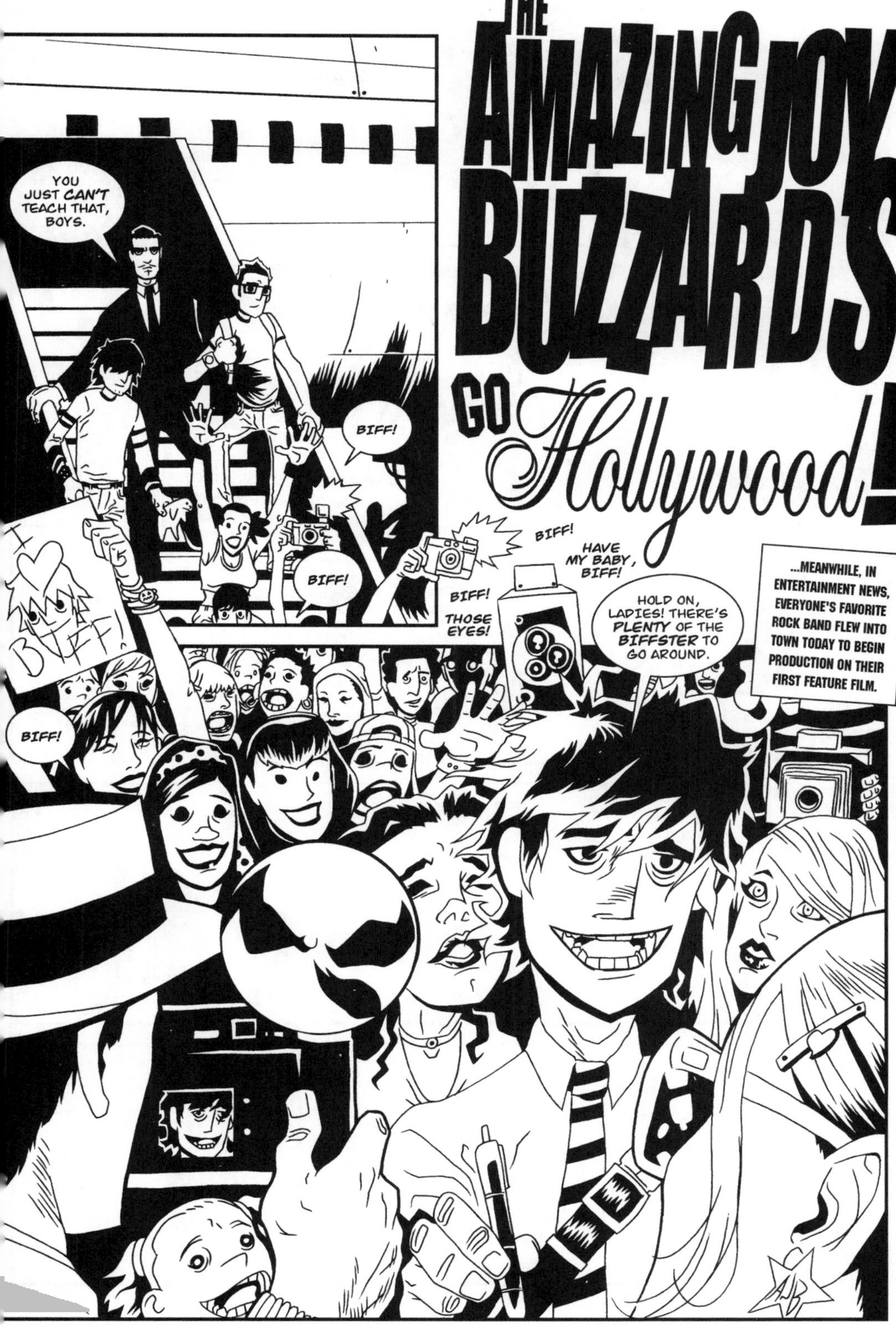
THE AMAZING JOY BUZZARDS GO Hollywood!
YOU JUST CAN'T TEACH THAT, BOYS.
BIFF!
BIFF!
BIFF!
HAVE MY BABY, BIFF!
BIFF!
THOSE EYES!
HOLD ON, LADIES! THERE'S PLENTY OF THE BIFFSTER TO GO AROUND.
...MEANWHILE, IN ENTERTAINMENT NEWS, EVERYONE'S FAVORITE ROCK BAND FLEW INTO TOWN TODAY TO BEGIN PRODUCTION ON THEIR FIRST FEATURE FILM.
I ♥ BIFF!
BIFF!

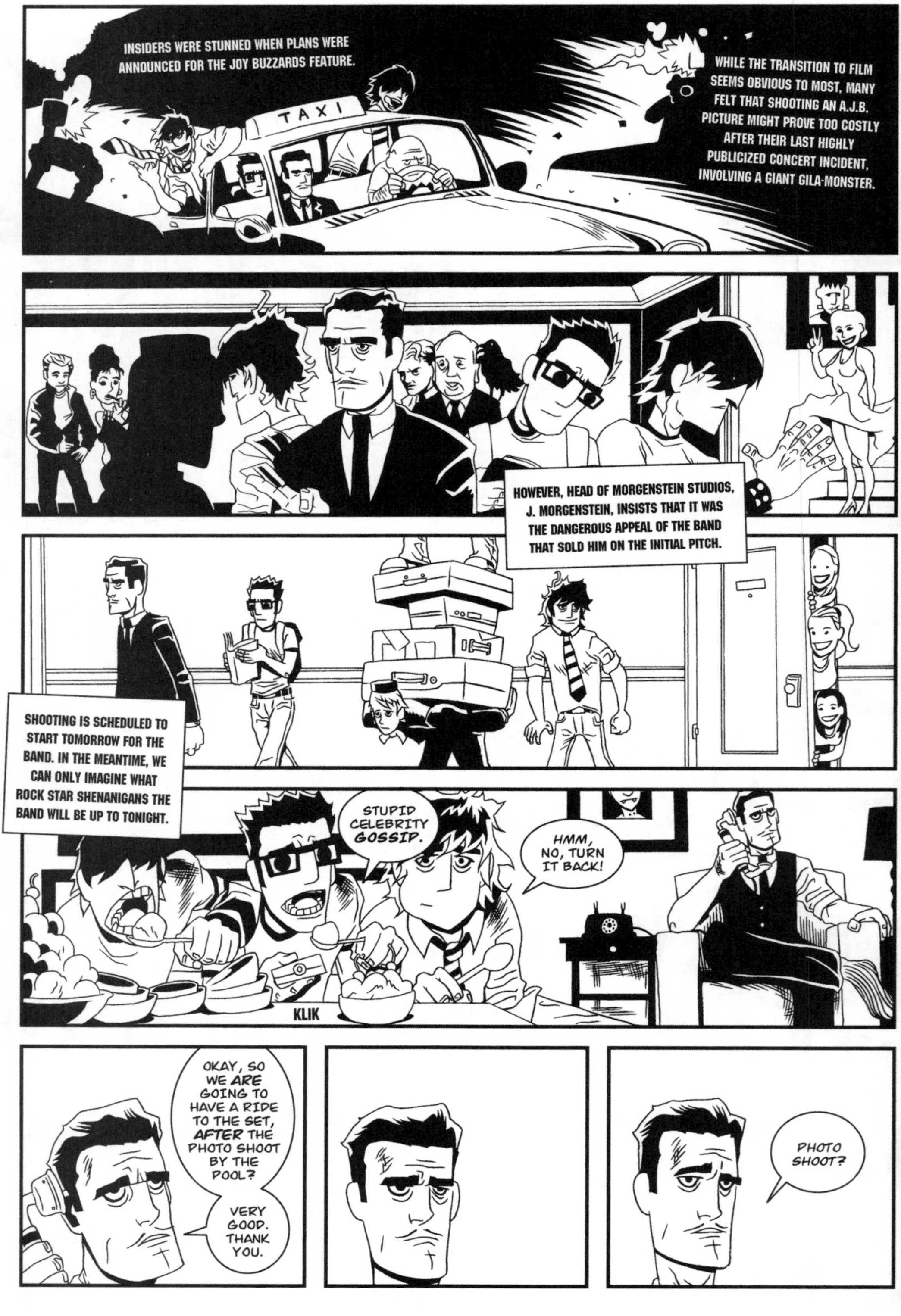
INSIDERS WERE STUNNED WHEN PLANS WERE ANNOUNCED FOR THE JOY BUZZARDS FEATURE.
TAXI
WHILE THE TRANSITION TO FILM SEEMS OBVIOUS TO MOST, MANY FELT THAT SHOOTING AN A.J.B. PICTURE MIGHT PROVE TOO COSTLY AFTER THEIR LAST HIGHLY PUBLICIZED CONCERT INCIDENT, INVOLVING A GIANT GILA-MONSTER.
HOWEVER, HEAD OF MORGENSTEIN STUDIOS, J. MORGENSTEIN, INSISTS THAT IT WAS THE DANGEROUS APPEAL OF THE BAND THAT SOLD HIM ON THE INITIAL PITCH.
SHOOTING IS SCHEDULED TO START TOMORROW FOR THE BAND. IN THE MEANTIME, WE CAN ONLY IMAGINE WHAT ROCK STAR SHENANIGANS THE BAND WILL BE UP TO TONIGHT.
STUPID CELEBRITY GOSSIP.
HMM, NO, TURN IT BACK!
KLIK
OKAY, SO WE ARE GOING TO HAVE A RIDE TO THE SET, AFTER THE PHOTO SHOOT BY THE POOL?
VERY GOOD. THANK YOU.
PHOTO SHOOT?

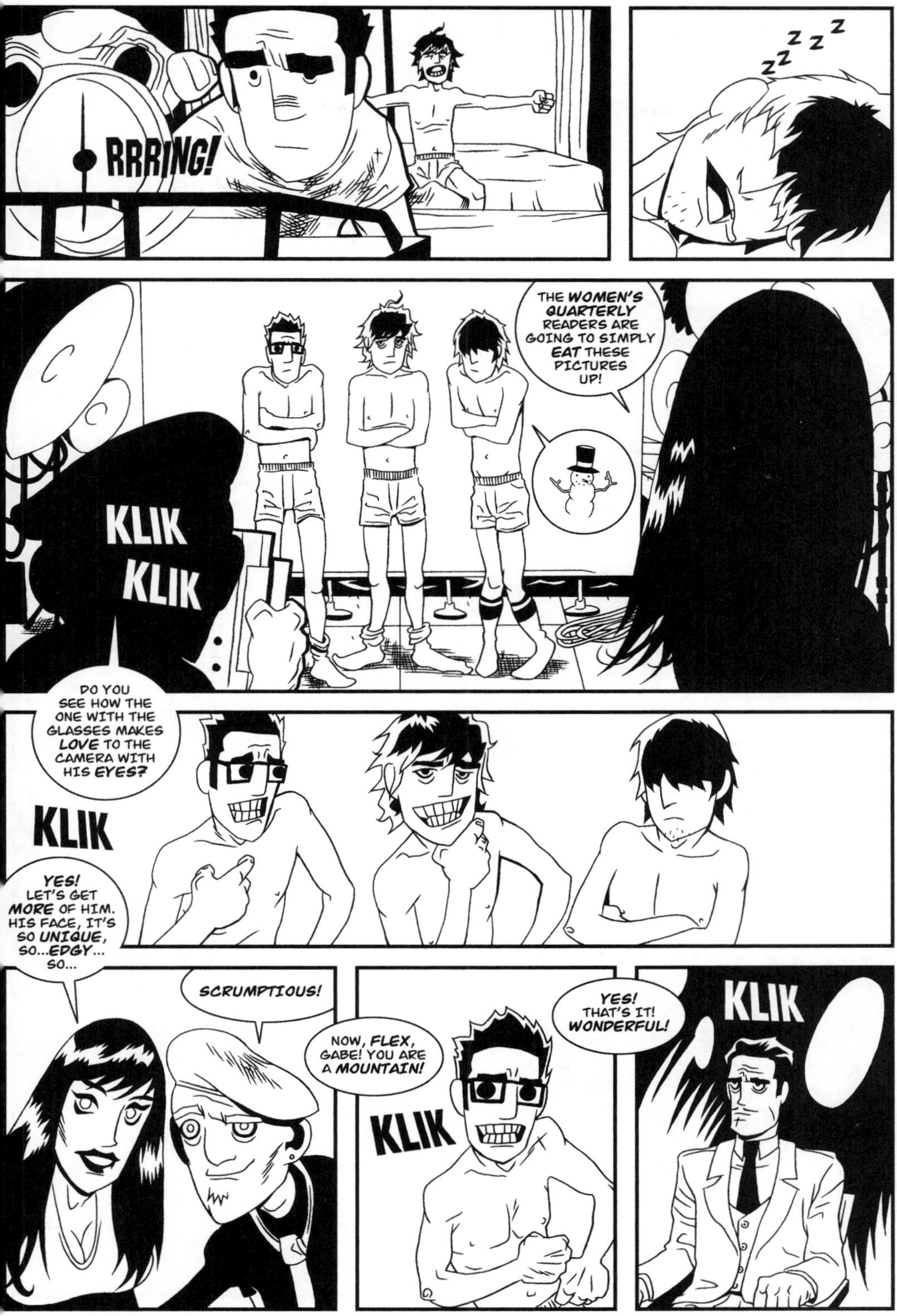
RRRING!
Z Z Z Z
THE WOMEN'S QUARTERLY READERS ARE GOING TO SIMPLY EAT THESE PICTURES UP!
KLIK
KLIK
DO YOU SEE HOW THE ONE WITH THE GLASSES MAKES LOVE TO THE CAMERA WITH HIS EYES?
KLIK
YES! LET'S GET MORE OF HIM. HIS FACE, IT'S SO UNIQUE, SO...EDGY... SO...
SCRUMPTIOUS!
NOW, FLEX, GABE! YOU ARE A MOUNTAIN!
KLIK
YES! THAT'S IT! WONDERFUL!
KLIK

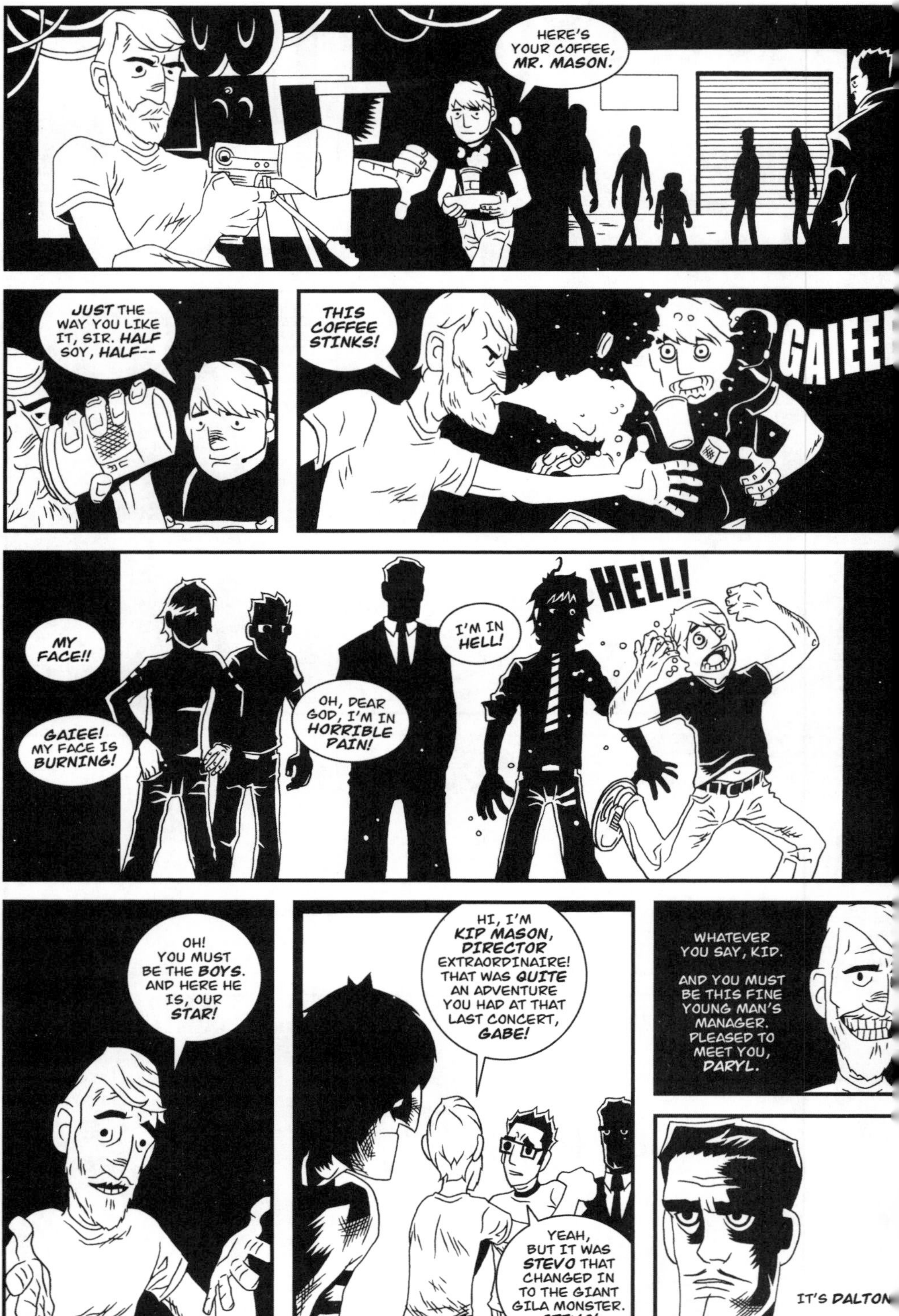
HERE'S YOUR COFFEE, MR. MASON.
JUST THE WAY YOU LIKE IT, SIR. HALF SOY, HALF--
THIS COFFEE STINKS!
GAIEEE
MY FACE!!
GAIEE! MY FACE IS BURNING!
OH, DEAR GOD, I'M IN HORRIBLE PAIN!
I'M IN HELL!
HELL!
OH! YOU MUST BE THE BOYS. AND HERE HE IS, OUR STAR!
HI, I'M KIP MASON, DIRECTOR EXTRAORDINAIRE! THAT WAS QUITE AN ADVENTURE YOU HAD AT THAT LAST CONCERT, GABE!
YEAH, BUT IT WAS STEVO THAT CHANGED IN TO THE GIANT GILA MONSTER. STEVO!
WHATEVER YOU SAY, KID.
AND YOU MUST BE THIS FINE YOUNG MAN'S MANAGER. PLEASED TO MEET YOU, DARYL.
IT'S DALTON

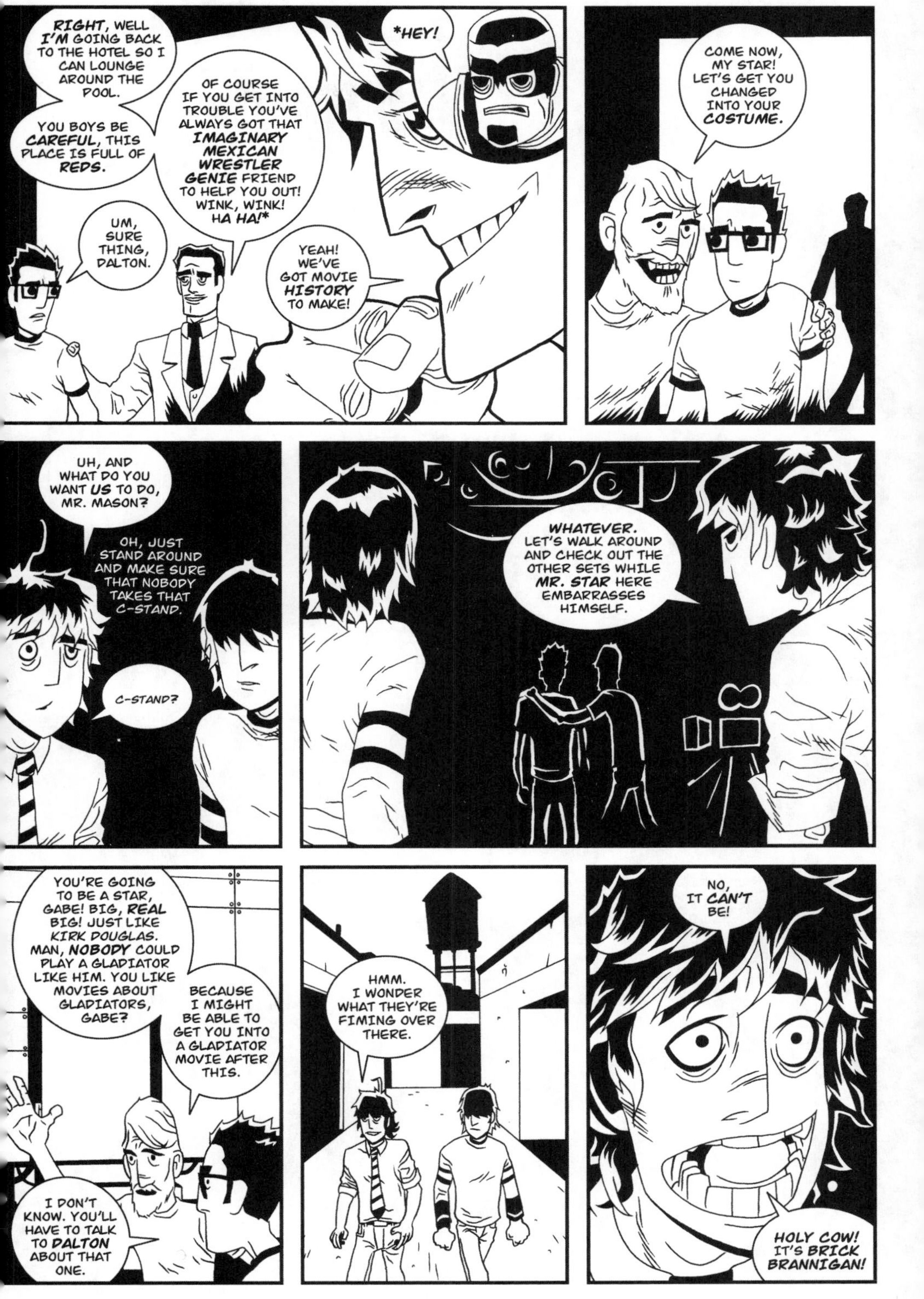
RIGHT, WELL I'M GOING BACK TO THE HOTEL SO I CAN LOUNGE AROUND THE POOL.
YOU BOYS BE CAREFUL, THIS PLACE IS FULL OF REDS.
OF COURSE IF YOU GET INTO TROUBLE YOU'VE ALWAYS GOT THAT IMAGINARY MEXICAN WRESTLER GENIE FRIEND TO HELP YOU OUT! WINK, WINK! HA HA!*
*HEY!
UM, SURE THING, DALTON.
YEAH! WE'VE GOT MOVIE HISTORY TO MAKE!
COME NOW, MY STAR! LET'S GET YOU CHANGED INTO YOUR COSTUME.
UH, AND WHAT DO YOU WANT US TO DO, MR. MASON?
OH, JUST STAND AROUND AND MAKE SURE THAT NOBODY TAKES THAT C-STAND.
C-STAND?
WHATEVER. LET'S WALK AROUND AND CHECK OUT THE OTHER SETS WHILE MR. STAR HERE EMBARRASSES HIMSELF.
YOU'RE GOING TO BE A STAR, GABE! BIG, REAL BIG! JUST LIKE KIRK DOUGLAS. MAN, NOBODY COULD PLAY A GLADIATOR LIKE HIM. YOU LIKE MOVIES ABOUT GLADIATORS, GABE?
BECAUSE I MIGHT BE ABLE TO GET YOU INTO A GLADIATOR MOVIE AFTER THIS.
I DON'T KNOW. YOU'LL HAVE TO TALK TO DALTON ABOUT THAT ONE.
HMM. I WONDER WHAT THEY'RE FIMING OVER THERE.
NO, IT CAN'T BE!
HOLY COW! IT'S BRICK BRANNIGAN!

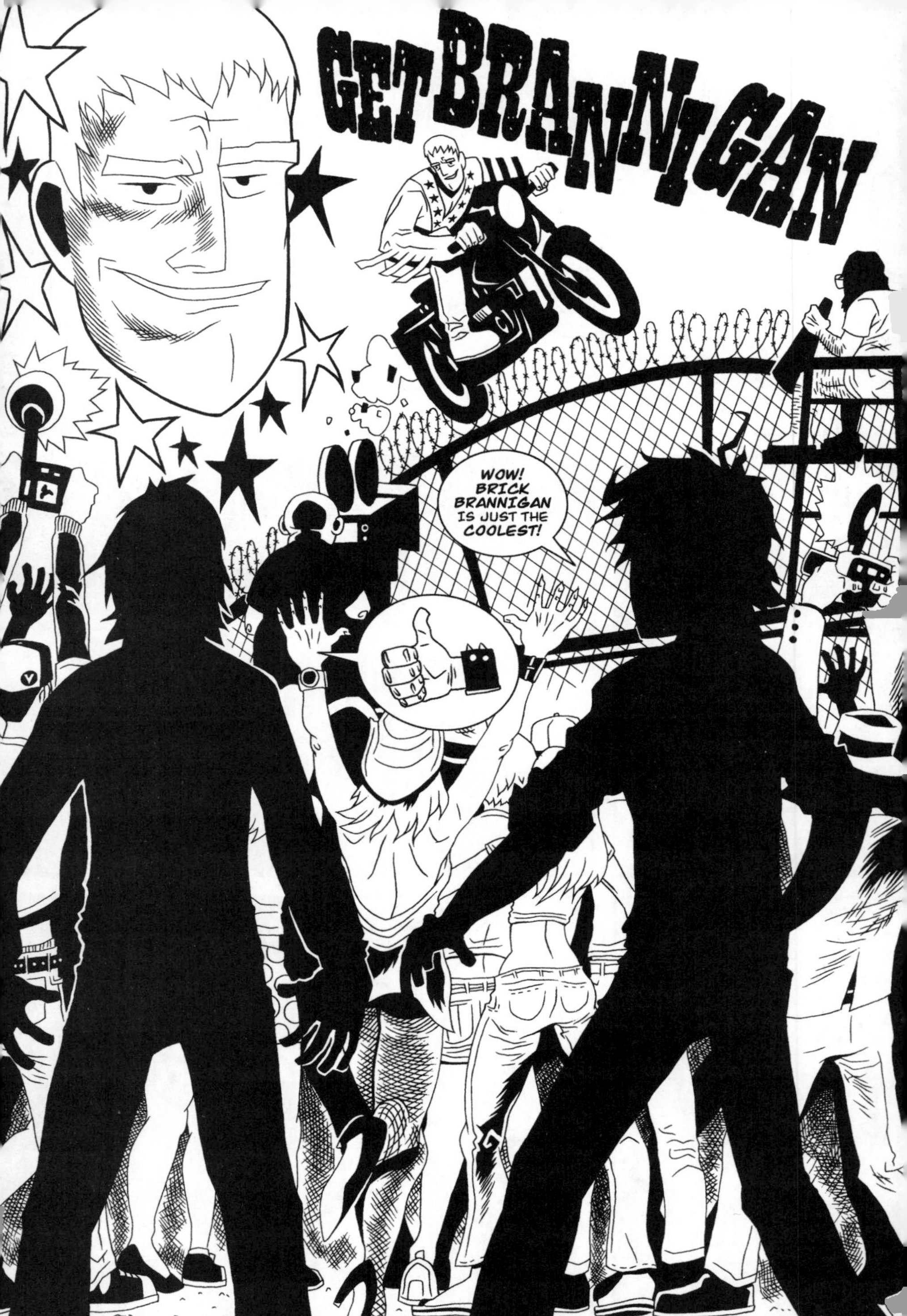
GET BRANNIGAN
WOW! BRICK BRANNIGAN IS JUST THE COOLEST!

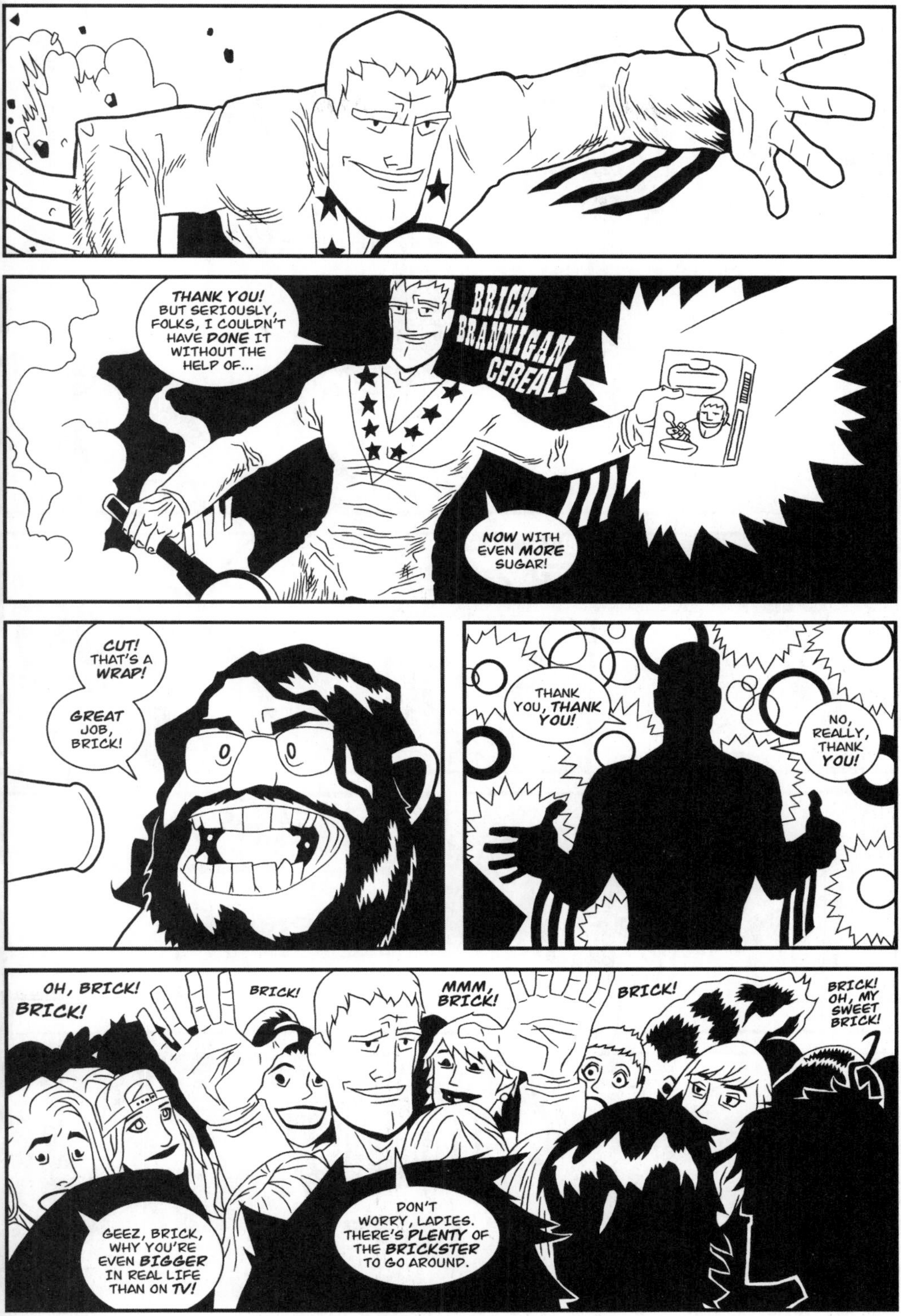
THANK YOU! BUT SERIOUSLY, FOLKS, I COULDN'T HAVE DONE IT WITHOUT THE HELP OF...
BRICK BRANNIGAN CEREAL!
NOW WITH EVEN MORE SUGAR!
CUT! THAT'S A WRAP!
GREAT JOB, BRICK!
THANK YOU, THANK YOU!
NO, REALLY, THANK YOU!
OH, BRICK!
BRICK!
BRICK!
MMM, BRICK!
BRICK!
BRICK! OH, MY SWEET BRICK!
GEEZ, BRICK, WHY YOU'RE EVEN BIGGER IN REAL LIFE THAN ON TV!
DON'T WORRY, LADIES. THERE'S PLENTY OF THE BRICKSTER TO GO AROUND.

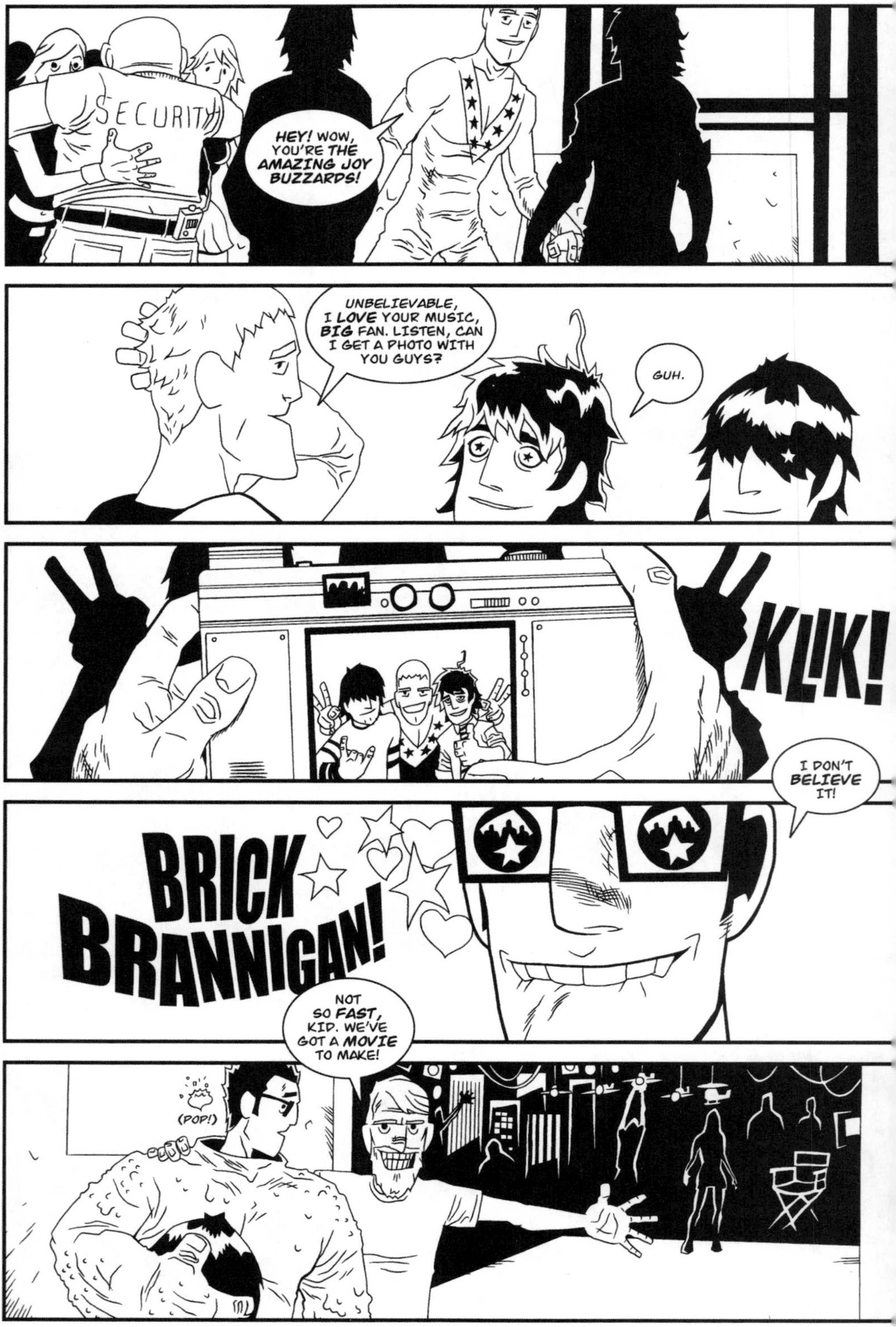
SECURITY
HEY! WOW, YOU'RE THE AMAZING JOY BUZZARDS!
UNBELIEVABLE, I LOVE YOUR MUSIC, BIG FAN. LISTEN, CAN I GET A PHOTO WITH YOU GUYS?
GUH.
KLIK!
I DON'T BELIEVE IT!
BRICK BRANNIGAN!
NOT SO FAST, KID. WE'VE GOT A MOVIE TO MAKE!
(POP!)

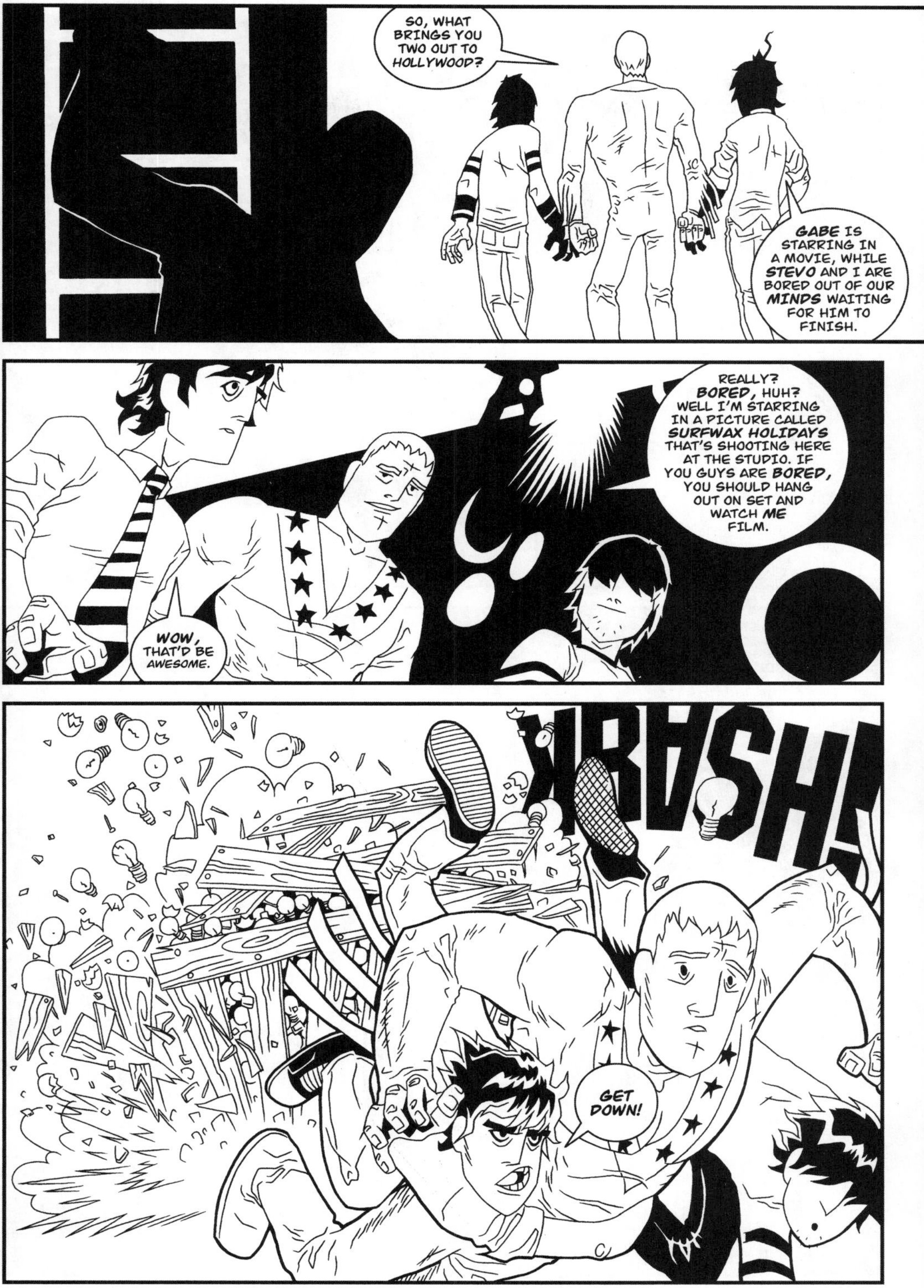
SO, WHAT BRINGS YOU TWO OUT TO HOLLYWOOD?
GABE IS STARRING IN A MOVIE, WHILE STEVO AND I ARE BORED OUT OF OUR MINDS WAITING FOR HIM TO FINISH.
REALLY? BORED, HUH? WELL I'M STARRING IN A PICTURE CALLED SURFWAX HOLIDAYS THAT'S SHOOTING HERE AT THE STUDIO. IF YOU GUYS ARE BORED, YOU SHOULD HANG OUT ON SET AND WATCH ME FILM.
WOW, THAT'D BE AWESOME.
GET DOWN!

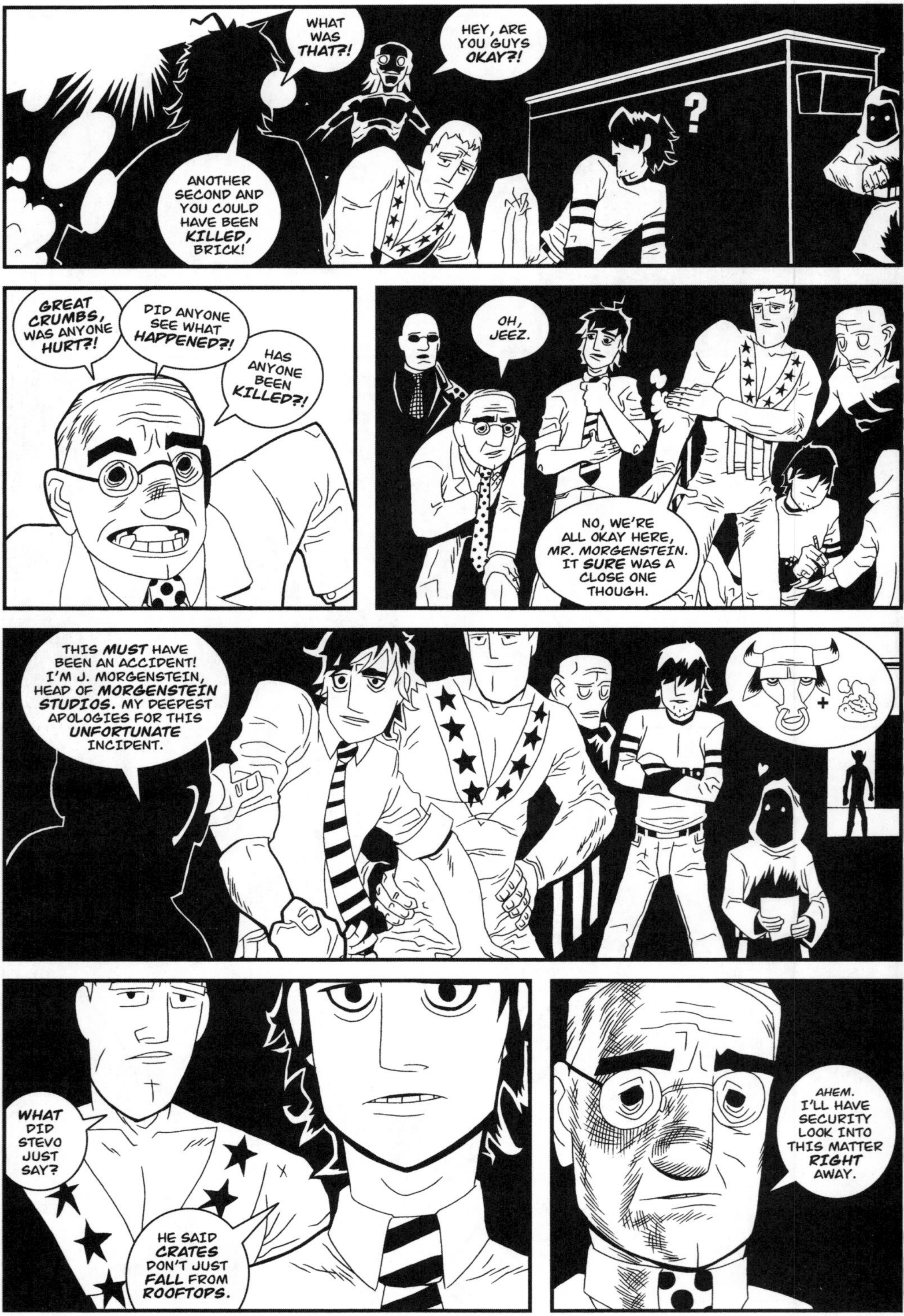
WHAT WAS THAT?!
HEY, ARE YOU GUYS OKAY?!
?
ANOTHER SECOND AND YOU COULD HAVE BEEN KILLED, BRICK!
GREAT CRUMBS, WAS ANYONE HURT?!
DID ANYONE SEE WHAT HAPPENED?!
HAS ANYONE BEEN KILLED?!
OH, JEEZ.
NO, WE'RE ALL OKAY HERE, MR. MORGENSTEIN. IT SURE WAS A CLOSE ONE THOUGH.
THIS MUST HAVE BEEN AN ACCIDENT! I'M J. MORGENSTEIN, HEAD OF MORGENSTEIN STUDIOS. MY DEEPEST APOLOGIES FOR THIS UNFORTUNATE INCIDENT.
+
WHAT DID STEVO JUST SAY?
HE SAID CRATES DON'T JUST FALL FROM ROOFTOPS.
AHEM. I'LL HAVE SECURITY LOOK INTO THIS MATTER RIGHT AWAY.

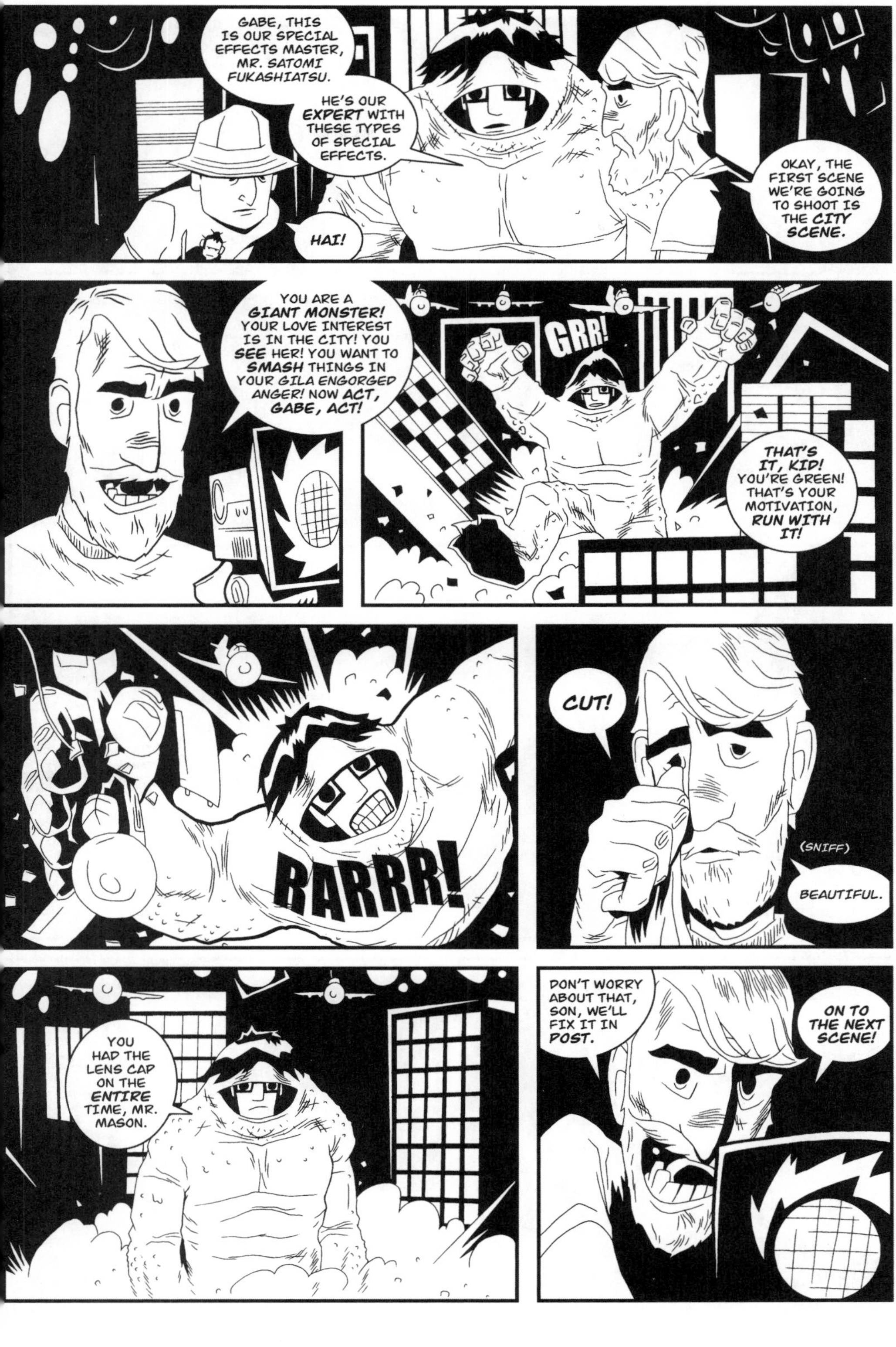
GABE, THIS IS OUR SPECIAL EFFECTS MASTER, MR. SATOMI FUKASHIATSU.
HE'S OUR EXPERT WITH THESE TYPES OF SPECIAL EFFECTS.
HAI!
OKAY, THE FIRST SCENE WE'RE GOING TO SHOOT IS THE CITY SCENE.
YOU ARE A GIANT MONSTER! YOUR LOVE INTEREST IS IN THE CITY! YOU SEE HER! YOU WANT TO SMASH THINGS IN YOUR GILA ENGORGED ANGER! NOW ACT, GABE, ACT!
GRR!
THAT'S IT, KID! YOU'RE GREEN! THAT'S YOUR MOTIVATION, RUN WITH IT!
RARRR!
CUT!
(SNIFF)
BEAUTIFUL.
YOU HAD THE LENS CAP ON THE ENTIRE TIME, MR. MASON.
DON'T WORRY ABOUT THAT, SON, WE'LL FIX IT IN POST.
ON TO THE NEXT SCENE!

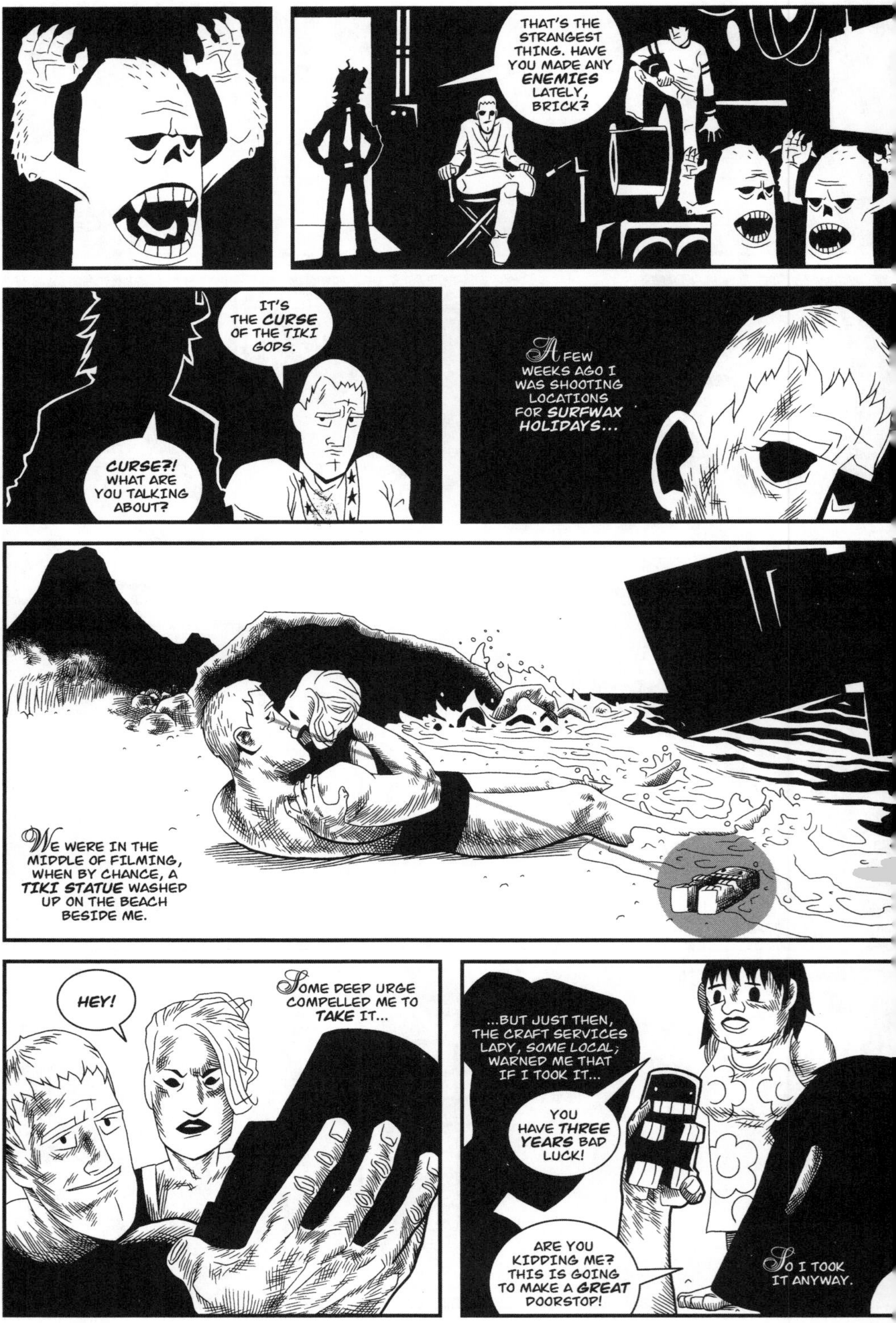

THAT'S THE STRANGEST THING. HAVE YOU MADE ANY ENEMIES LATELY, BRICK?
IT'S THE CURSE OF THE TIKI GODS.
CURSE?! WHAT ARE YOU TALKING ABOUT?
A FEW WEEKS AGO I WAS SHOOTING LOCATIONS FOR SURFWAX HOLIDAYS...
WE WERE IN THE MIDDLE OF FILMING, WHEN BY CHANCE, A TIKI STATUE WASHED UP ON THE BEACH BESIDE ME.
HEY!
SOME DEEP URGE COMPELLED ME TO TAKE IT...
...BUT JUST THEN, THE CRAFT SERVICES LADY, SOME LOCAL, WARNED ME THAT IF I TOOK IT...
YOU HAVE THREE YEARS BAD LUCK!
ARE YOU KIDDING ME? THIS IS GOING TO MAKE A GREAT DOORSTOP!
SO I TOOK IT ANYWAY.

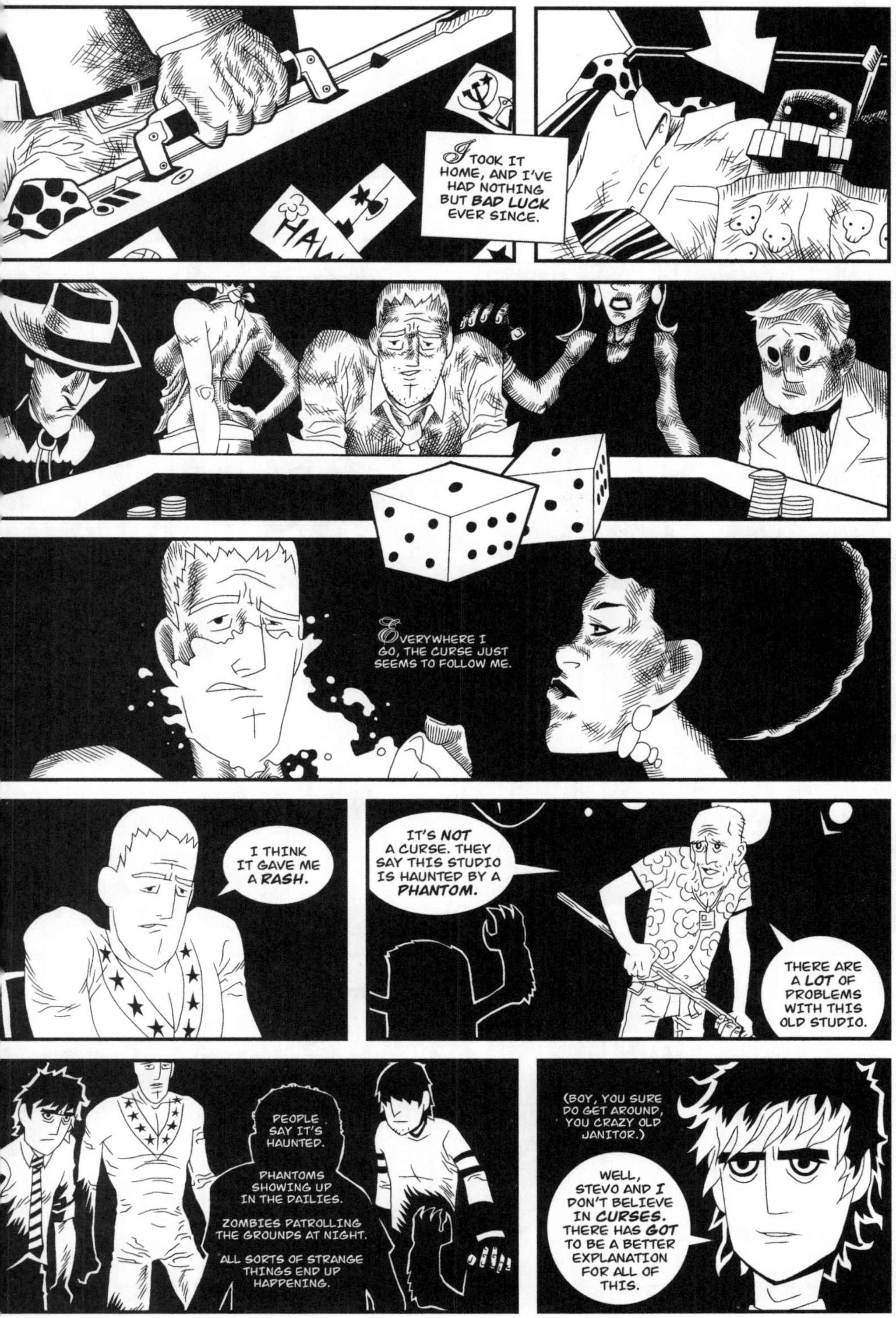
HAW
I TOOK IT HOME, AND I'VE HAD NOTHING BUT BAD LUCK EVER SINCE.
EVERYWHERE I GO, THE CURSE JUST SEEMS TO FOLLOW ME.
I THINK IT GAVE ME A RASH.
IT'S NOT A CURSE. THEY SAY THIS STUDIO IS HAUNTED BY A PHANTOM.
THERE ARE A LOT OF PROBLEMS WITH THIS OLD STUDIO.
PEOPLE SAY IT'S HAUNTED.
PHANTOMS SHOWING UP IN THE DAILIES.
ZOMBIES PATROLLING THE GROUNDS AT NIGHT.
ALL SORTS OF STRANGE THINGS END UP HAPPENING.
(BOY, YOU SURE DO GET AROUND, YOU CRAZY OLD JANITOR.)
WELL, STEVO AND I DON'T BELIEVE IN CURSES. THERE HAS GOT TO BE A BETTER EXPLANATION FOR ALL OF THIS.

Interlude...

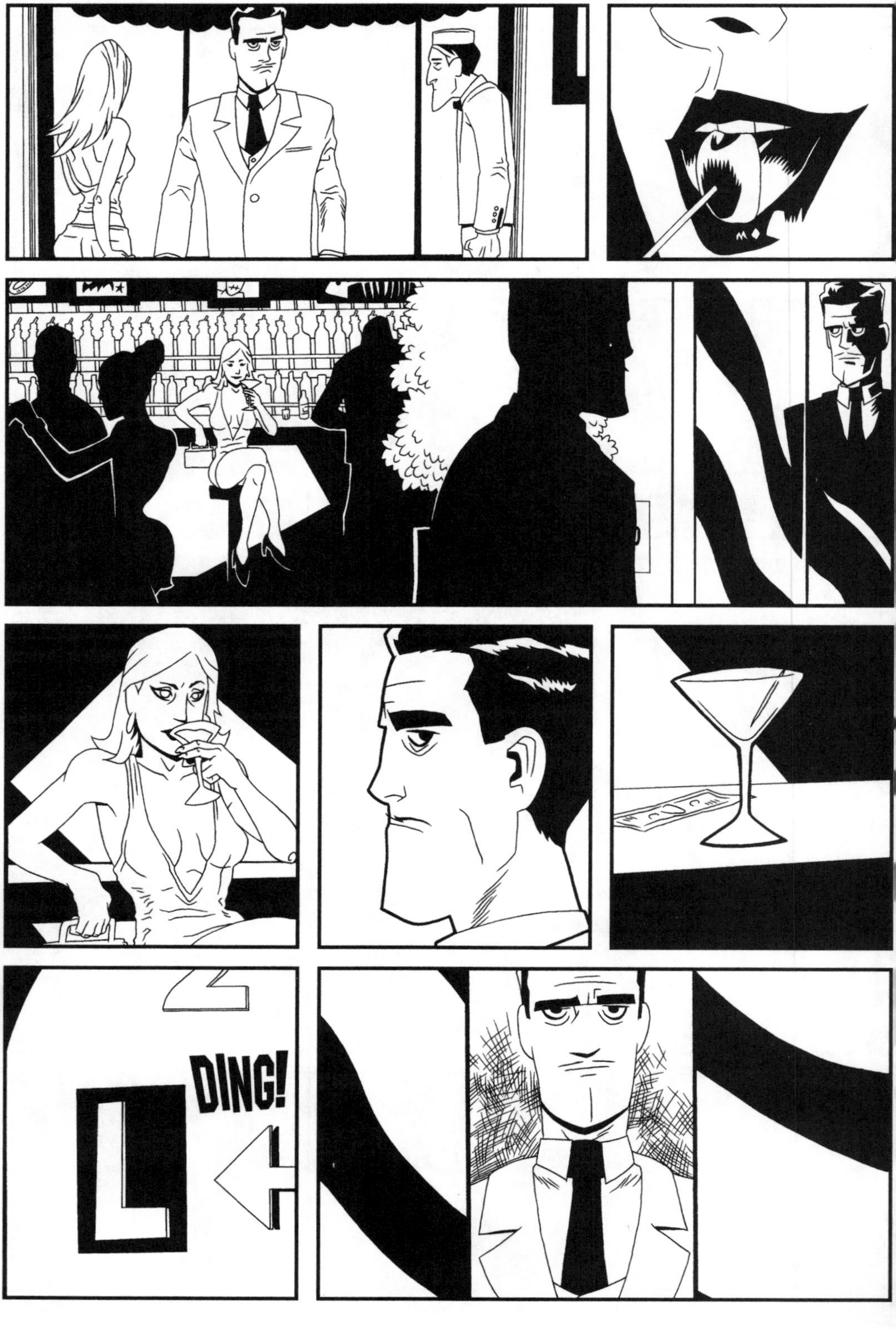
DING!
L

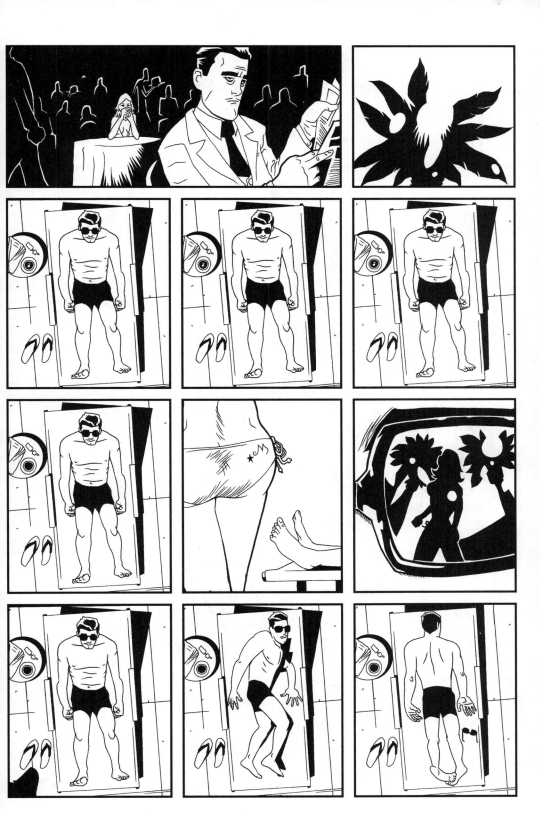

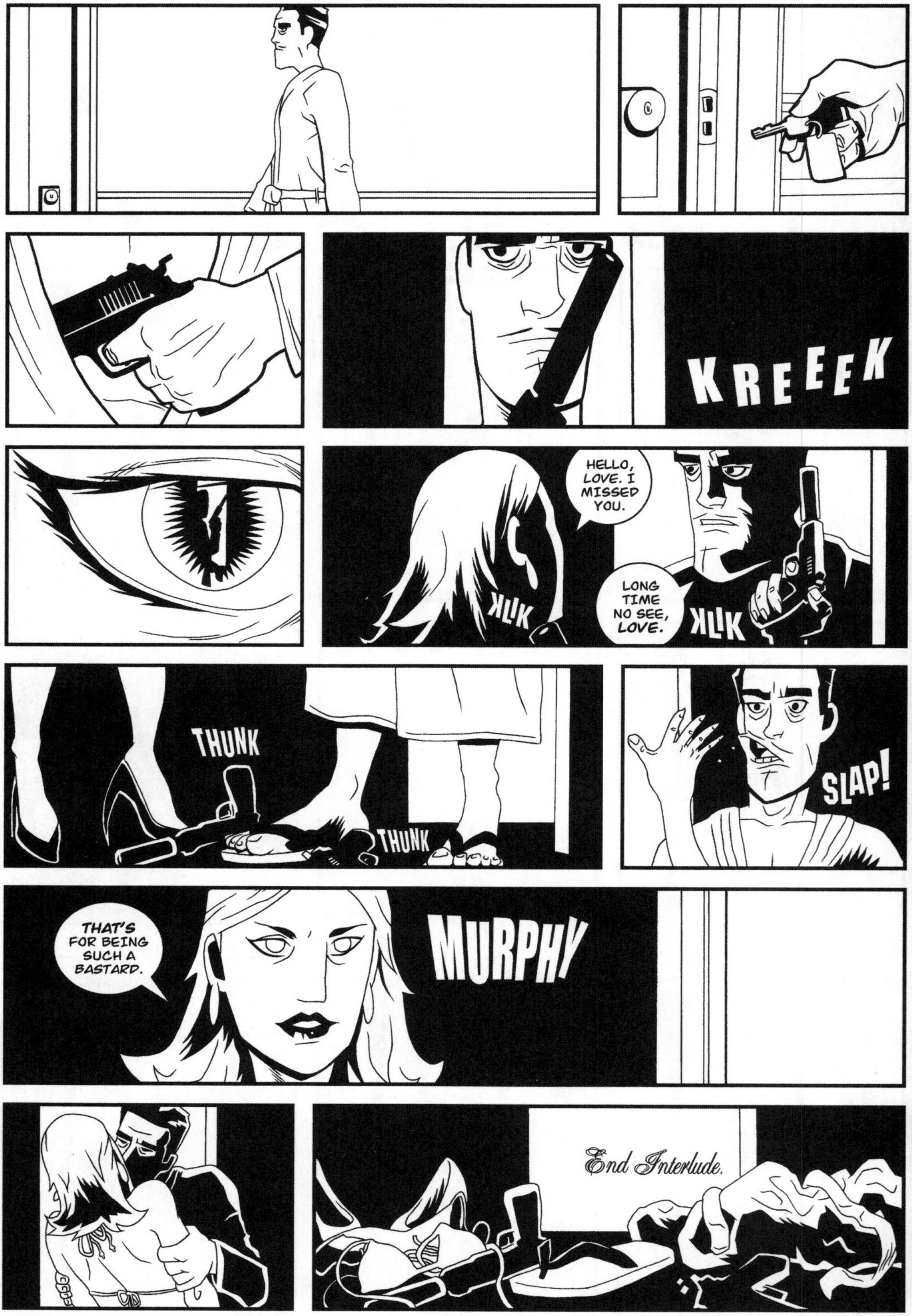
KREEEK
HELLO, LOVE. I MISSED YOU.
LONG TIME NO SEE, LOVE.
KLIK
KLIK
THUNK
THUNK
SLAP!
THAT'S FOR BEING SUCH A BASTARD.
MURPHY
End Interlude.

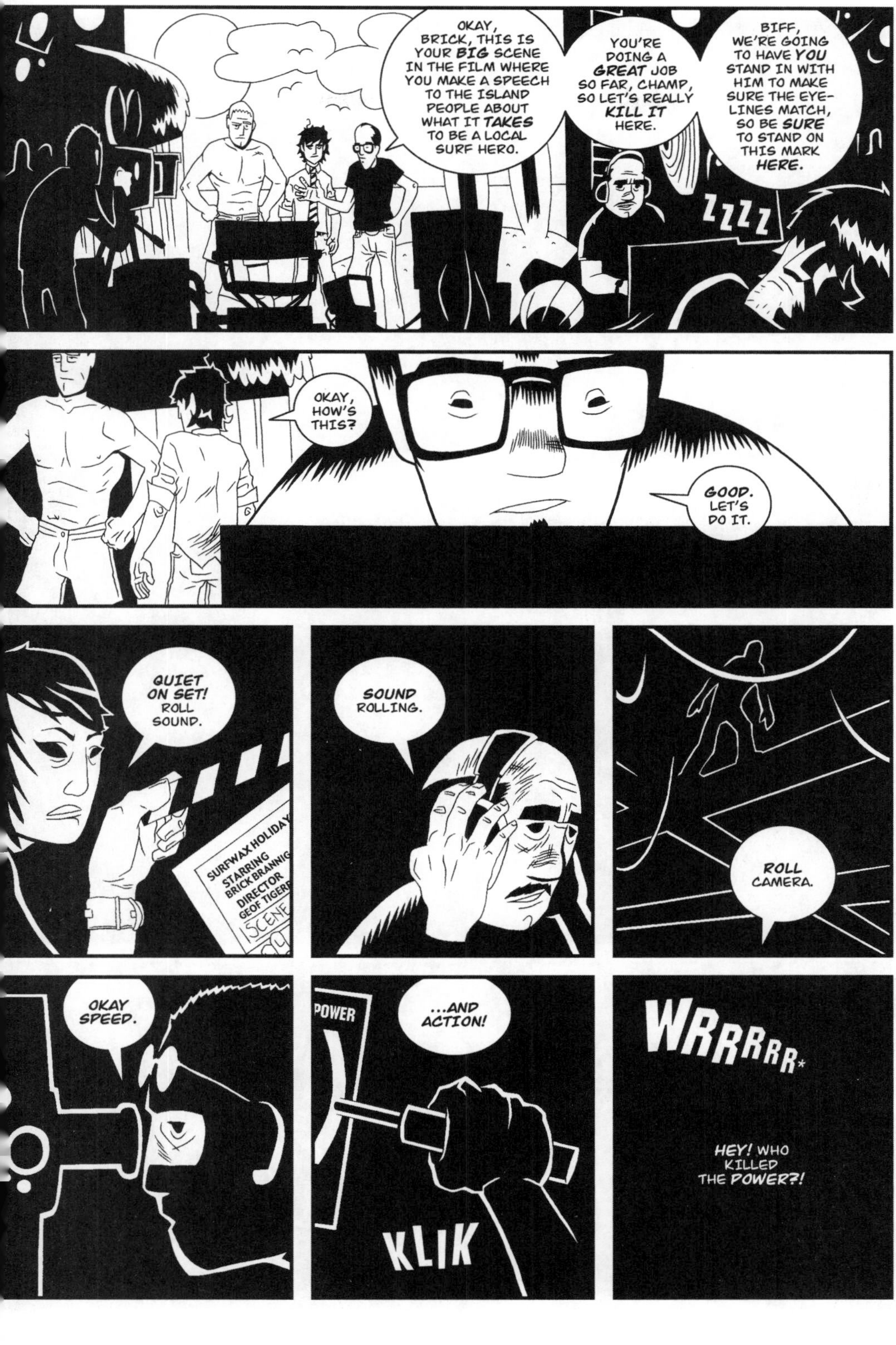
OKAY, BRICK, THIS IS YOUR BIG SCENE IN THE FILM WHERE YOU MAKE A SPEECH TO THE ISLAND PEOPLE ABOUT WHAT IT TAKES TO BE A LOCAL SURF HERO.
YOU'RE DOING A GREAT JOB SO FAR, CHAMP, SO LET'S REALLY KILL IT HERE.
BIFF, WE'RE GOING TO HAVE YOU STAND IN WITH HIM TO MAKE SURE THE EYE-LINES MATCH, SO BE SURE TO STAND ON THIS MARK HERE.
ZZZZ
OKAY, HOW'S THIS?
GOOD. LET'S DO IT.
QUIET ON SET! ROLL SOUND.
SURFWAX HOLIDAY
STARRING BRICK BRANNIG
DIRECTOR GEOF TIGER
SCENE
SOUND ROLLING.
ROLL CAMERA.
OKAY SPEED.
POWER
...AND ACTION!
KLIK
WRRRRR*
HEY! WHO KILLED THE POWER?!

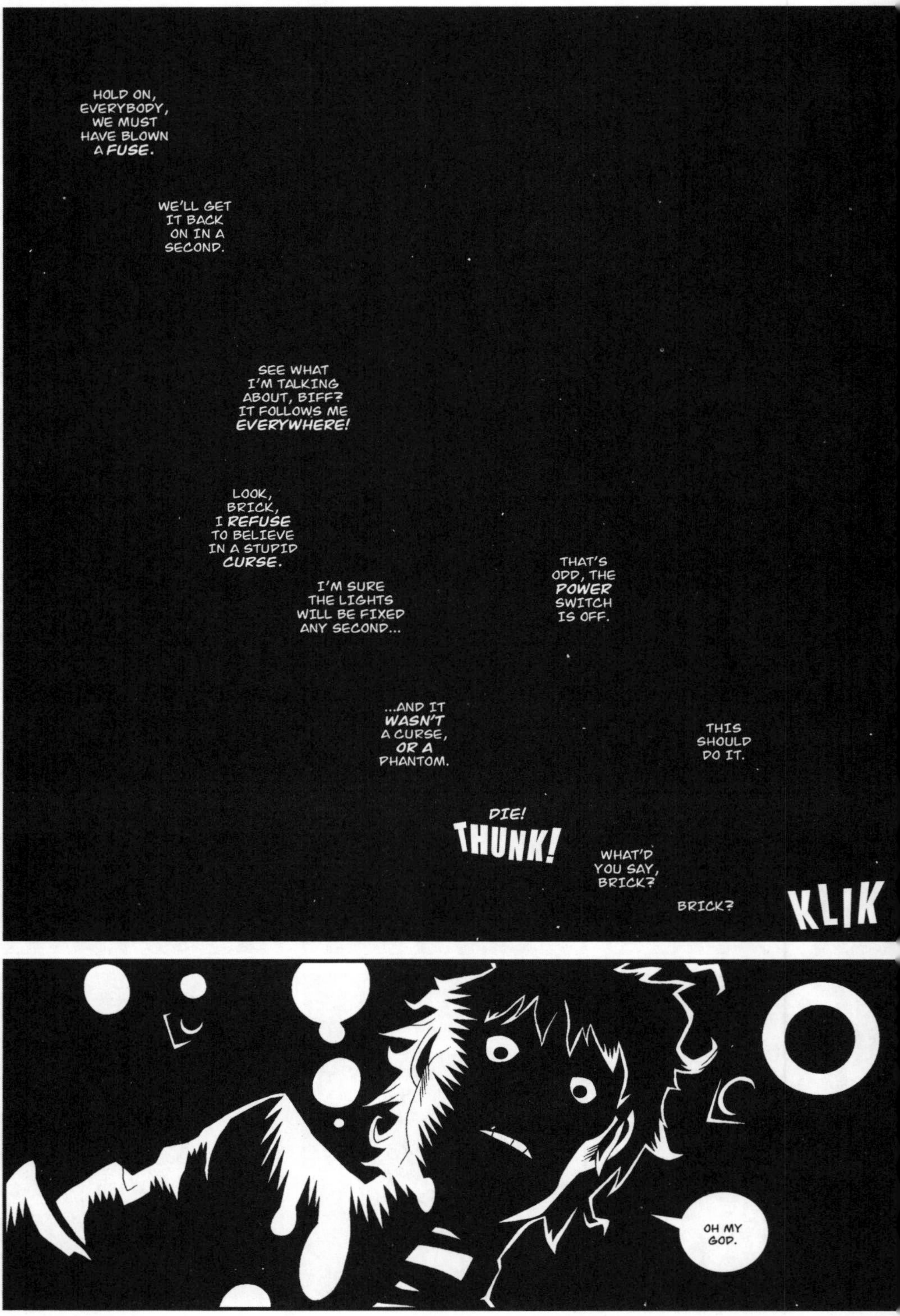

HOLD ON, EVERYBODY, WE MUST HAVE BLOWN A FUSE.
WE'LL GET IT BACK ON IN A SECOND.
SEE WHAT I'M TALKING ABOUT, BIFF? IT FOLLOWS ME EVERYWHERE!
LOOK, BRICK, I REFUSE TO BELIEVE IN A STUPID CURSE.
I'M SURE THE LIGHTS WILL BE FIXED ANY SECOND...
THAT'S ODD, THE POWER SWITCH IS OFF.
...AND IT WASN'T A CURSE, OR A PHANTOM.
THIS SHOULD DO IT.
DIE!
THUNK!
WHAT'D YOU SAY, BRICK?
BRICK?
KLIK
OH MY GOD.

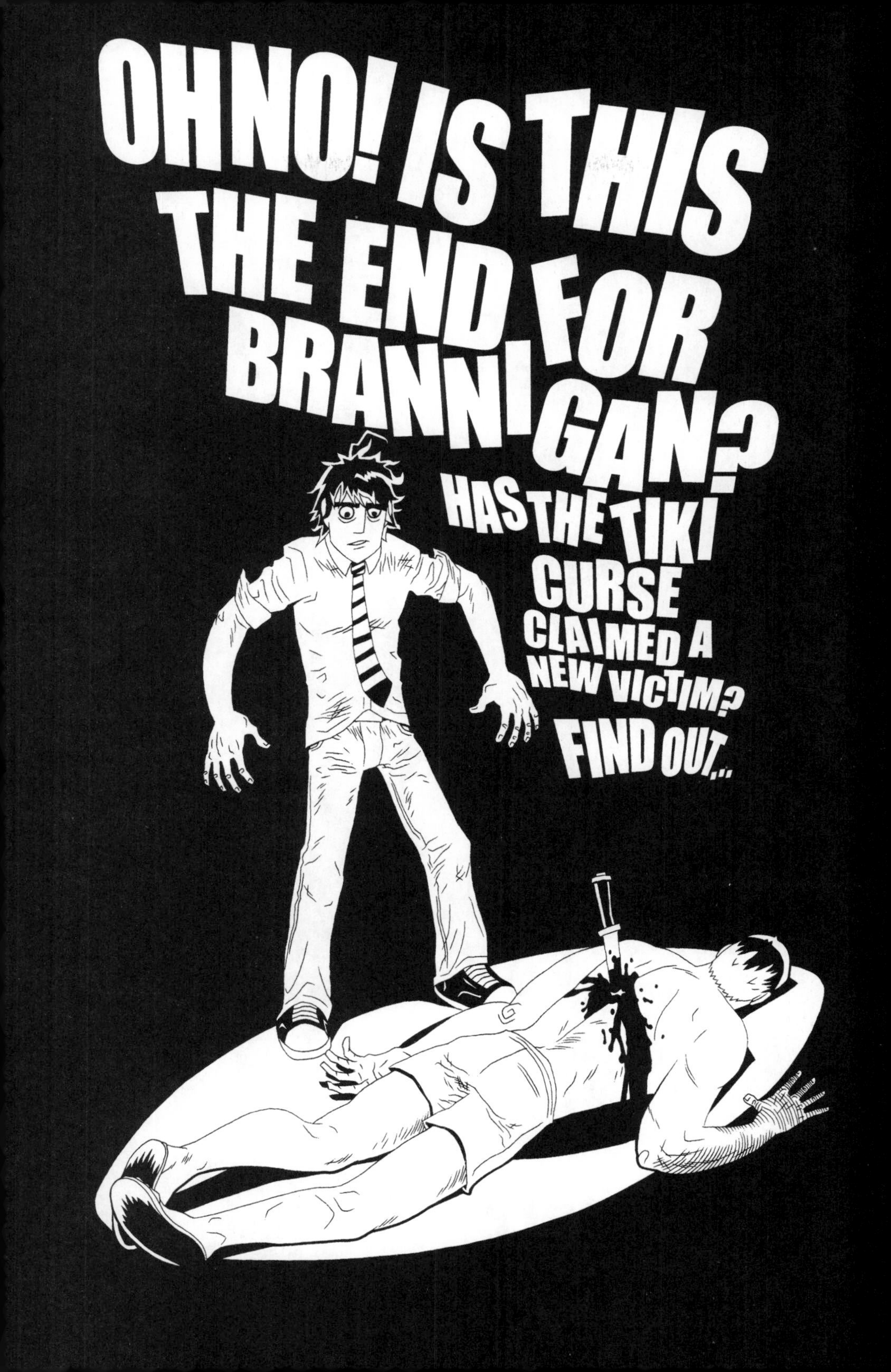
OHNO! IS THIS THE END FOR BRANNIGAN?
HAS THE TIKI CURSE CLAIMED A NEW VICTIM?
FIND OUT...

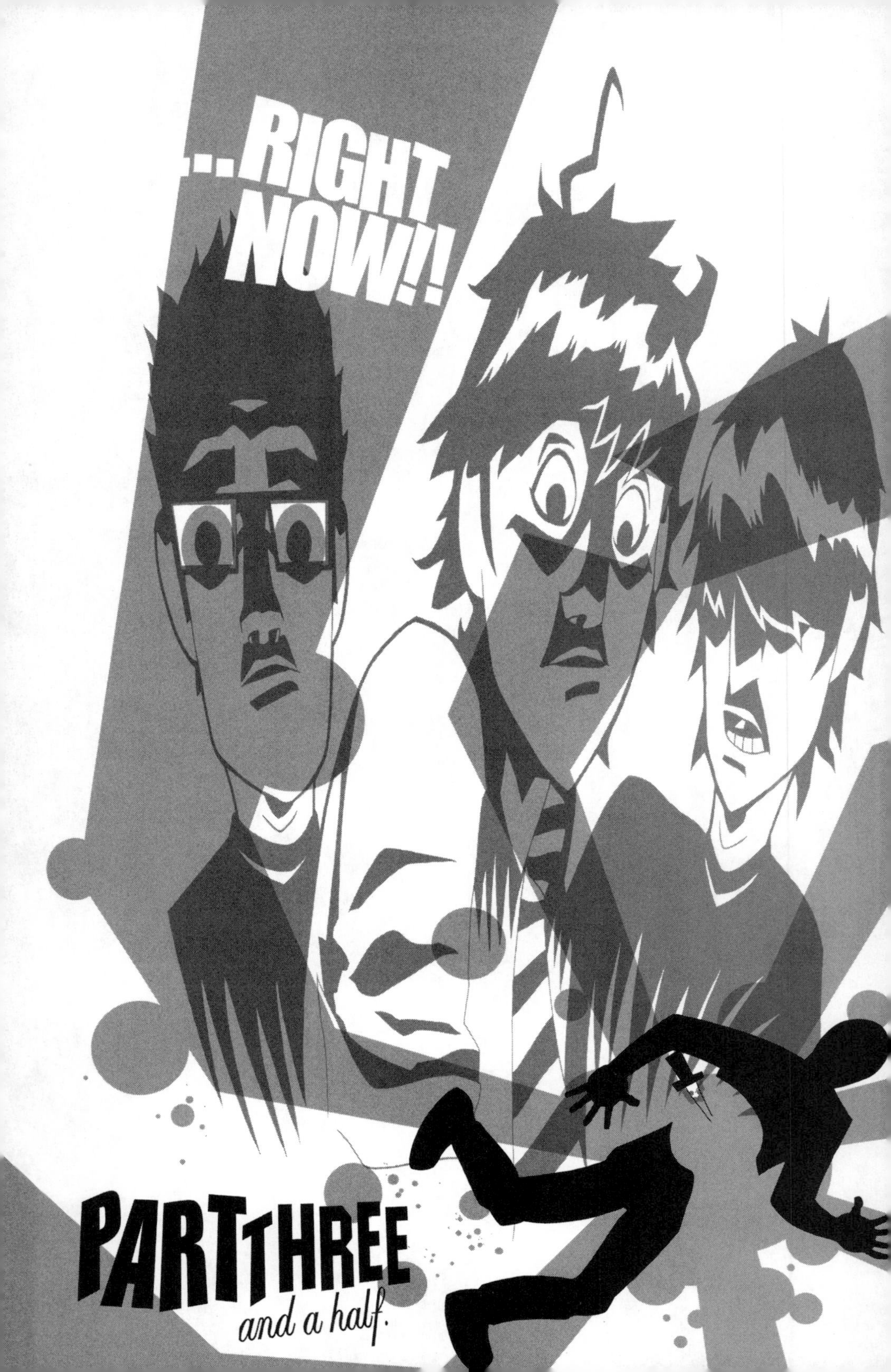
...RIGHT NOW!!!
PART THREE
and a half.

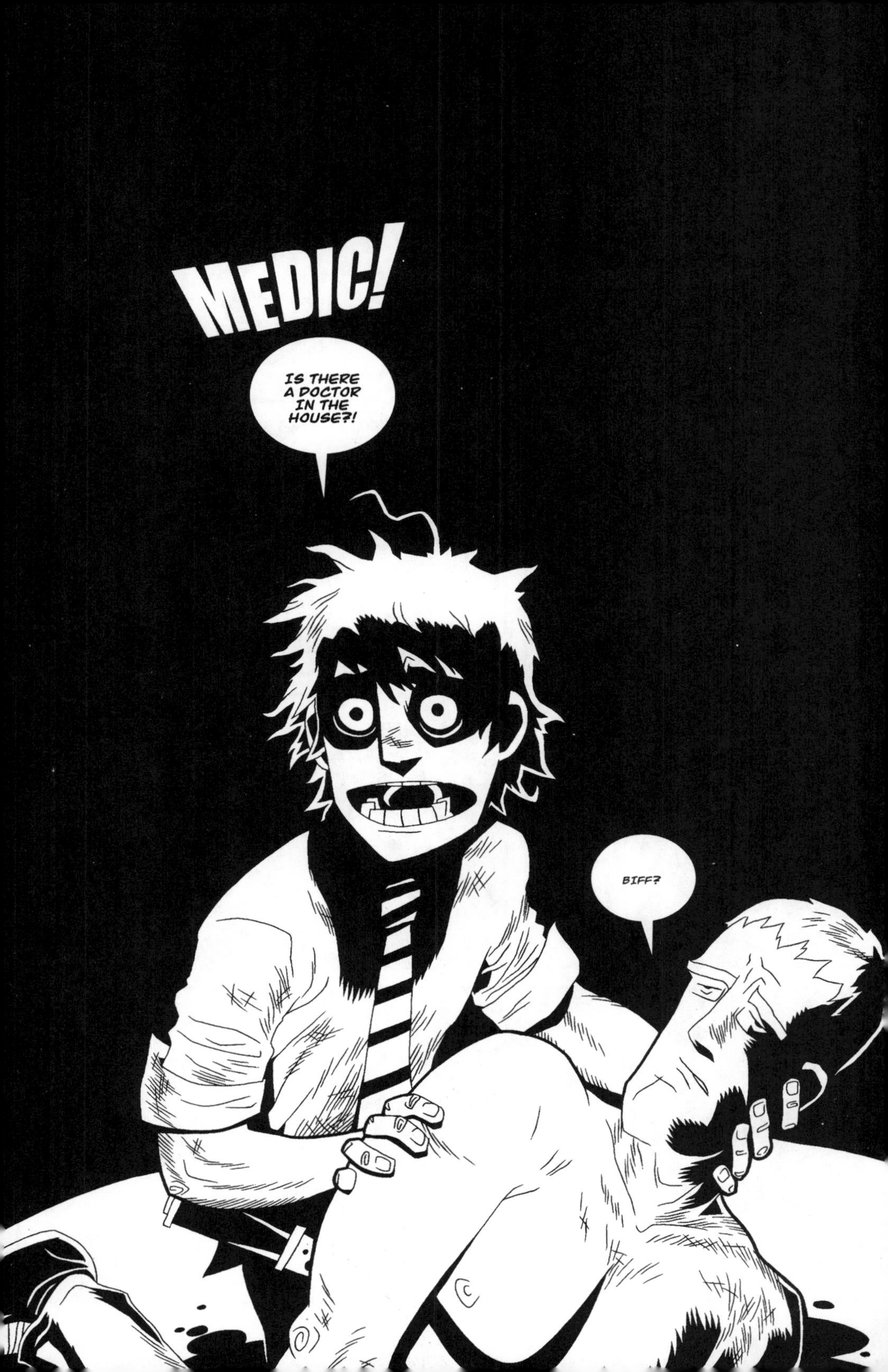
MEDIC!
IS THERE A DOCTOR IN THE HOUSE?!
BIFF?

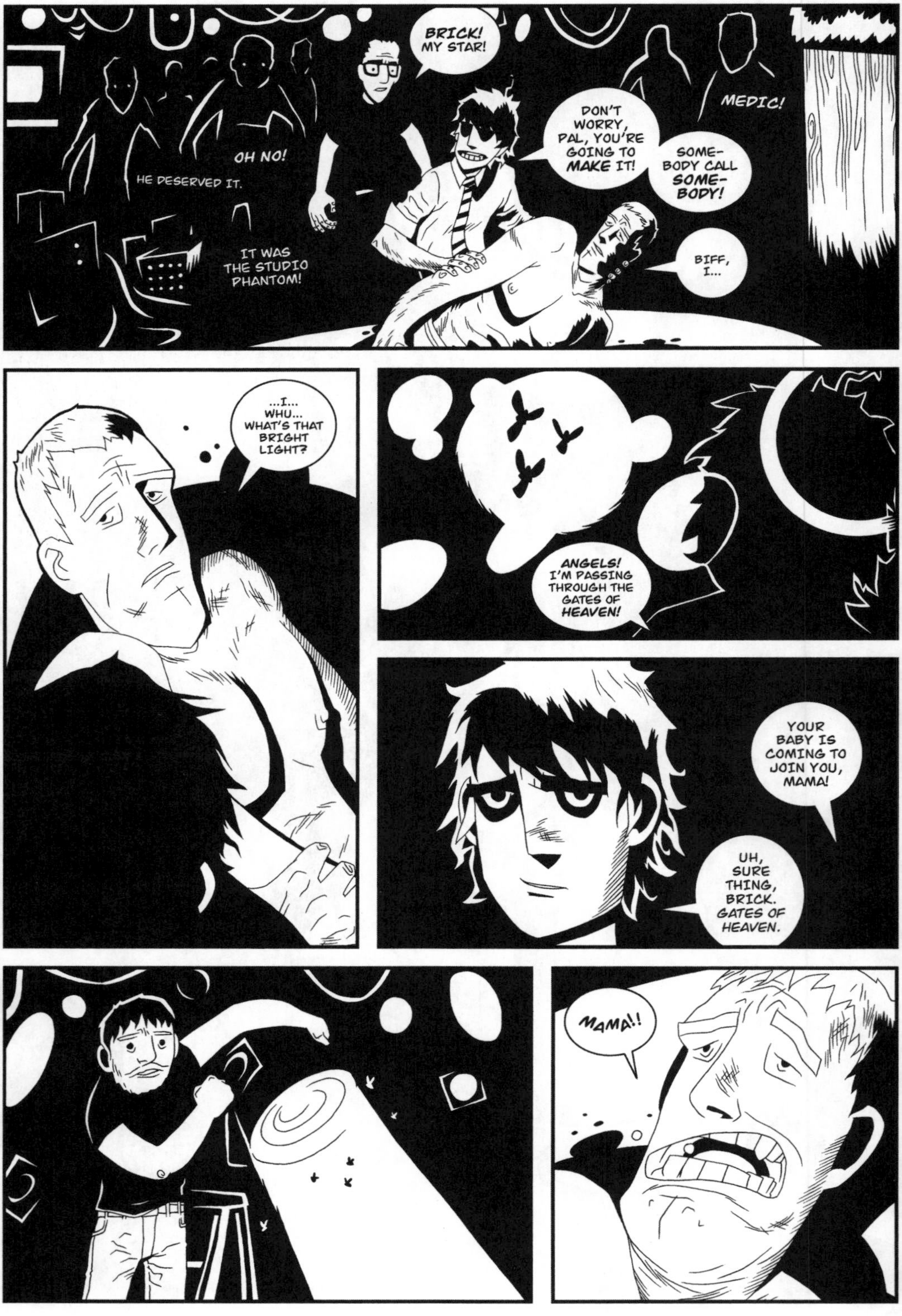
BRICK! MY STAR!
OH NO!
HE DESERVED IT.
IT WAS THE STUDIO PHANTOM!
DON'T WORRY, PAL, YOU'RE GOING TO MAKE IT!
MEDIC!
SOME-BODY CALL SOME-BODY!
BIFF, I...
...I... WHU... WHAT'S THAT BRIGHT LIGHT?
ANGELS! I'M PASSING THROUGH THE GATES OF HEAVEN!
YOUR BABY IS COMING TO JOIN YOU, MAMA!
UH, SURE THING, BRICK. GATES OF HEAVEN.
MAMA!!

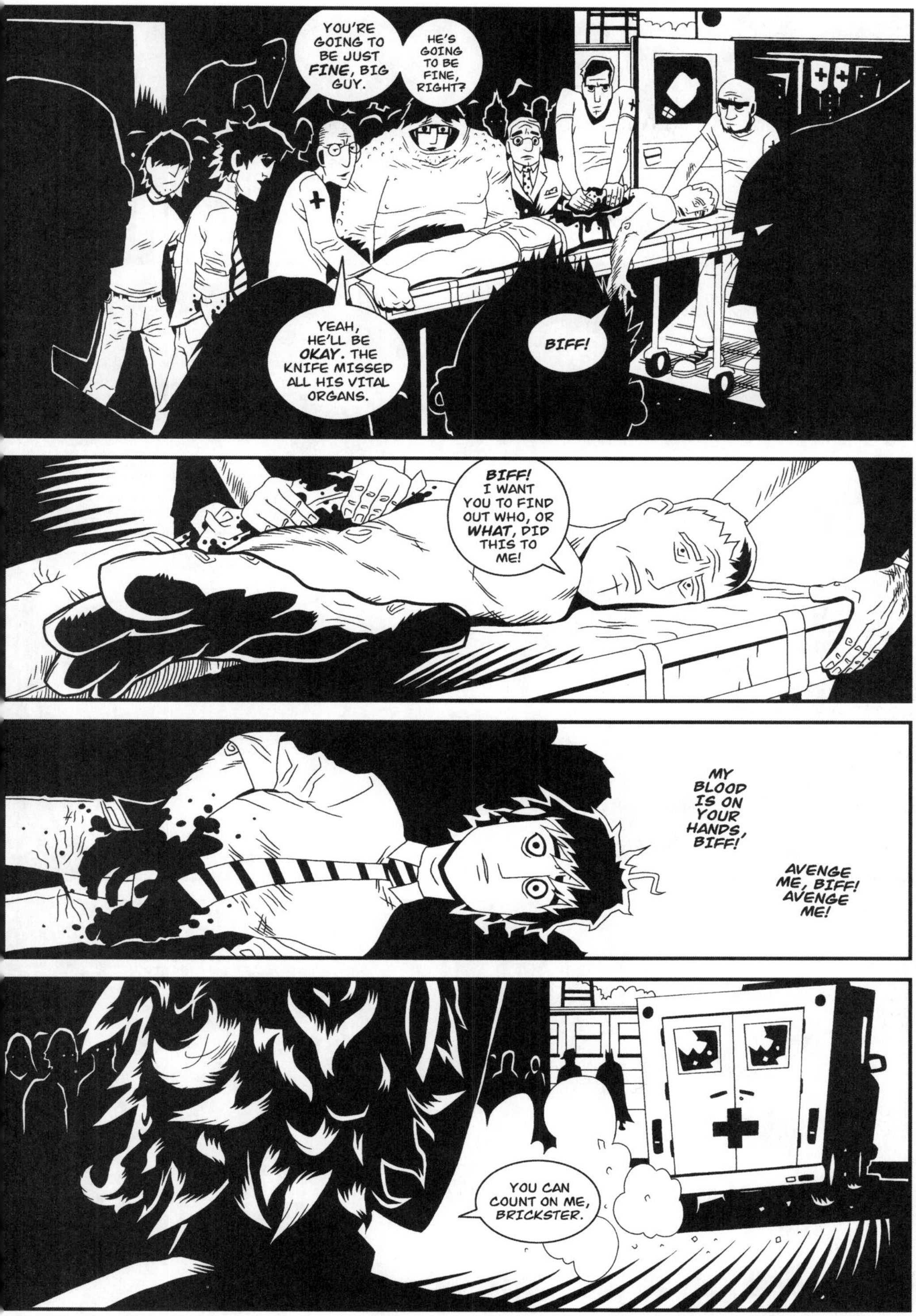
YOU'RE GOING TO BE JUST FINE, BIG GUY.
HE'S GOING TO BE FINE, RIGHT?
YEAH, HE'LL BE OKAY. THE KNIFE MISSED ALL HIS VITAL ORGANS.
BIFF!
BIFF! I WANT YOU TO FIND OUT WHO, OR WHAT, DID THIS TO ME!
MY BLOOD IS ON YOUR HANDS, BIFF!
AVENGE ME, BIFF! AVENGE ME!
YOU CAN COUNT ON ME, BRICKSTER.

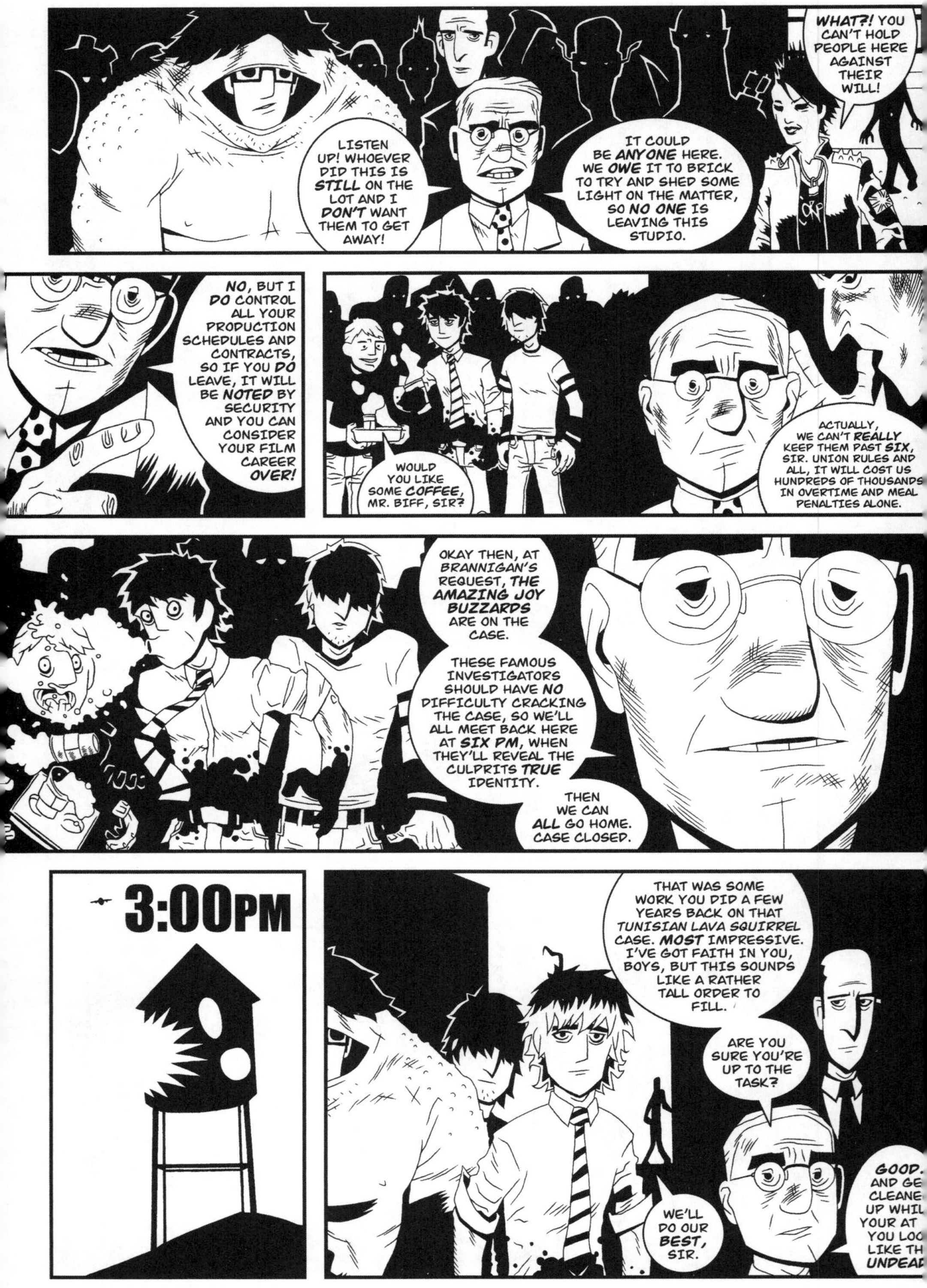

LISTEN UP! WHOEVER DID THIS IS STILL ON THE LOT AND I DON'T WANT THEM TO GET AWAY!
IT COULD BE ANYONE HERE. WE OWE IT TO BRICK TO TRY AND SHED SOME LIGHT ON THE MATTER, SO NO ONE IS LEAVING THIS STUDIO.
WHAT?! YOU CAN'T HOLD PEOPLE HERE AGAINST THEIR WILL!
NO, BUT I DO CONTROL ALL YOUR PRODUCTION SCHEDULES AND CONTRACTS, SO IF YOU DO LEAVE, IT WILL BE NOTED BY SECURITY AND YOU CAN CONSIDER YOUR FILM CAREER OVER!
WOULD YOU LIKE SOME COFFEE, MR. BIFF, SIR?
ACTUALLY, WE CAN'T REALLY KEEP THEM PAST SIX, SIR. UNION RULES AND ALL, IT WILL COST US HUNDREDS OF THOUSANDS IN OVERTIME AND MEAL PENALTIES ALONE.
OKAY THEN, AT BRANNIGAN'S REQUEST, THE AMAZING JOY BUZZARDS ARE ON THE CASE.
THESE FAMOUS INVESTIGATORS SHOULD HAVE NO DIFFICULTY CRACKING THE CASE, SO WE'LL ALL MEET BACK HERE AT SIX PM, WHEN THEY'LL REVEAL THE CULPRITS TRUE IDENTITY.
THEN WE CAN ALL GO HOME. CASE CLOSED.
3:00PM
THAT WAS SOME WORK YOU DID A FEW YEARS BACK ON THAT TUNISIAN LAVA SQUIRREL CASE. MOST IMPRESSIVE. I'VE GOT FAITH IN YOU, BOYS, BUT THIS SOUNDS LIKE A RATHER TALL ORDER TO FILL.
ARE YOU SURE YOU'RE UP TO THE TASK?
WE'LL DO OUR BEST, SIR.

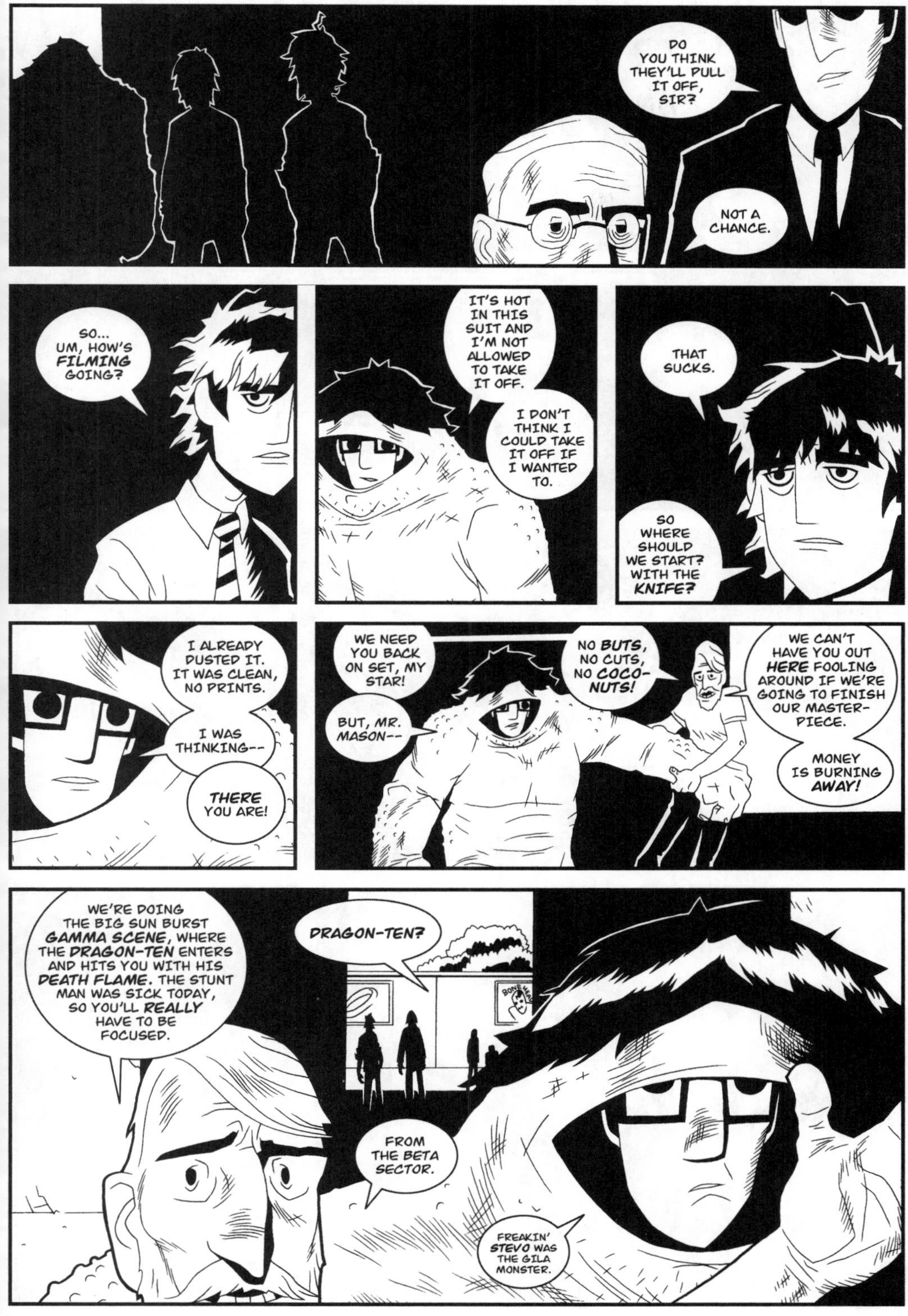
DO YOU THINK THEY'LL PULL IT OFF, SIR?
NOT A CHANCE.
SO... UM, HOW'S FILMING GOING?
IT'S HOT IN THIS SUIT AND I'M NOT ALLOWED TO TAKE IT OFF.
I DON'T THINK I COULD TAKE IT OFF IF I WANTED TO.
THAT SUCKS.
SO WHERE SHOULD WE START? WITH THE KNIFE?
I ALREADY DUSTED IT. IT WAS CLEAN, NO PRINTS.
I WAS THINKING--
THERE YOU ARE!
WE NEED YOU BACK ON SET, MY STAR!
BUT, MR. MASON--
NO BUTS, NO CUTS, NO COCONUTS!
WE CAN'T HAVE YOU OUT HERE FOOLING AROUND IF WE'RE GOING TO FINISH OUR MASTERPIECE.
MONEY IS BURNING AWAY!
WE'RE DOING THE BIG SUN BURST GAMMA SCENE, WHERE THE DRAGON-TEN ENTERS AND HITS YOU WITH HIS DEATH FLAME. THE STUNT MAN WAS SICK TODAY, SO YOU'LL REALLY HAVE TO BE FOCUSED.
DRAGON-TEN?
FROM THE BETA SECTOR.
FREAKIN' STEVO WAS THE GILA MONSTER.

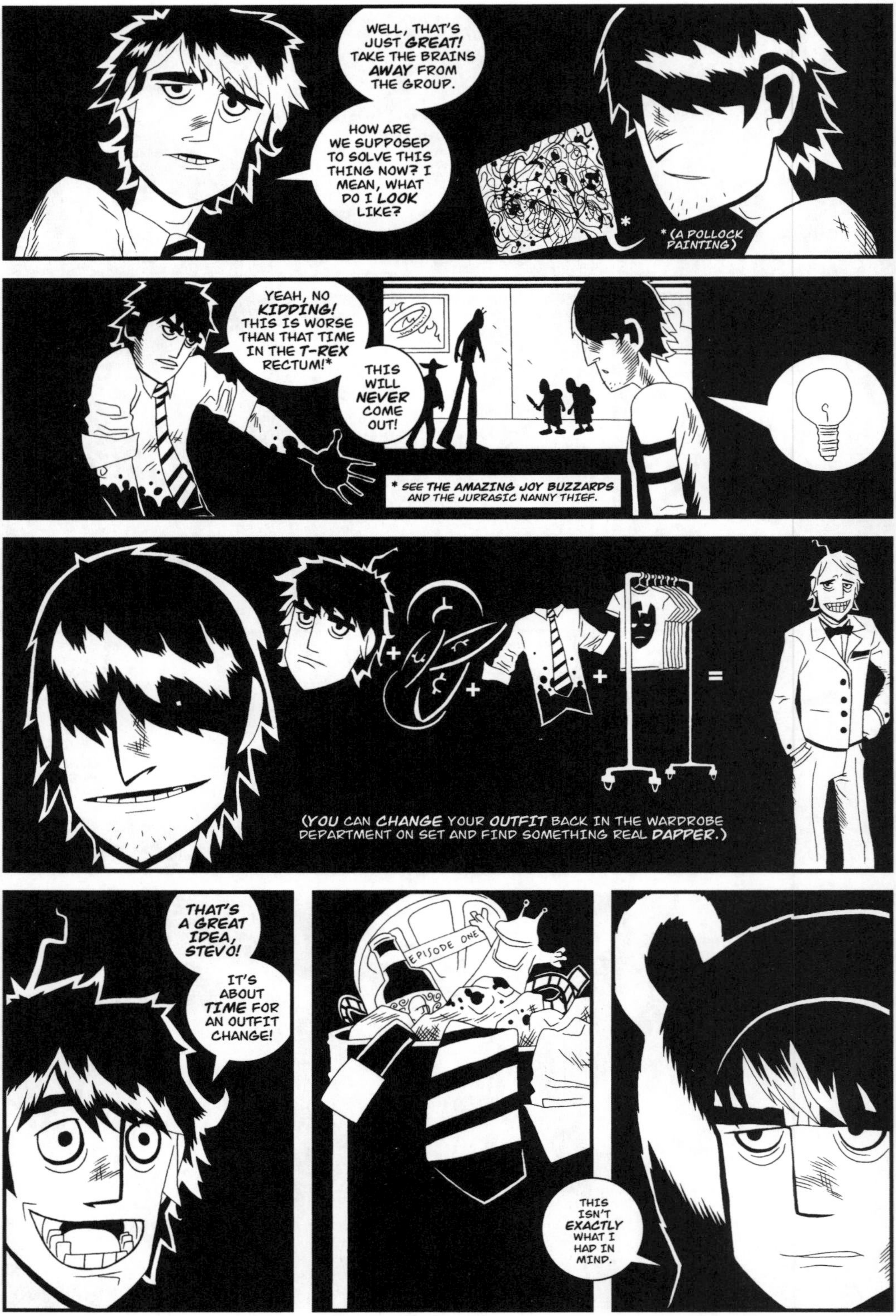
WELL, THAT'S JUST GREAT! TAKE THE BRAINS AWAY FROM THE GROUP.
HOW ARE WE SUPPOSED TO SOLVE THIS THING NOW? I MEAN, WHAT DO I LOOK LIKE?
*
*(A POLLOCK PAINTING)
YEAH, NO KIDDING! THIS IS WORSE THAN THAT TIME IN THE T-REX RECTUM!*
THIS WILL NEVER COME OUT!
* SEE THE AMAZING JOY BUZZARDS AND THE JURRASIC NANNY THIEF.
+
+
+
=
(YOU CAN CHANGE YOUR OUTFIT BACK IN THE WARDROBE DEPARTMENT ON SET AND FIND SOMETHING REAL DAPPER.)
THAT'S A GREAT IDEA, STEVO!
IT'S ABOUT TIME FOR AN OUTFIT CHANGE!
EPISODE ONE
THIS ISN'T EXACTLY WHAT I HAD IN MIND.

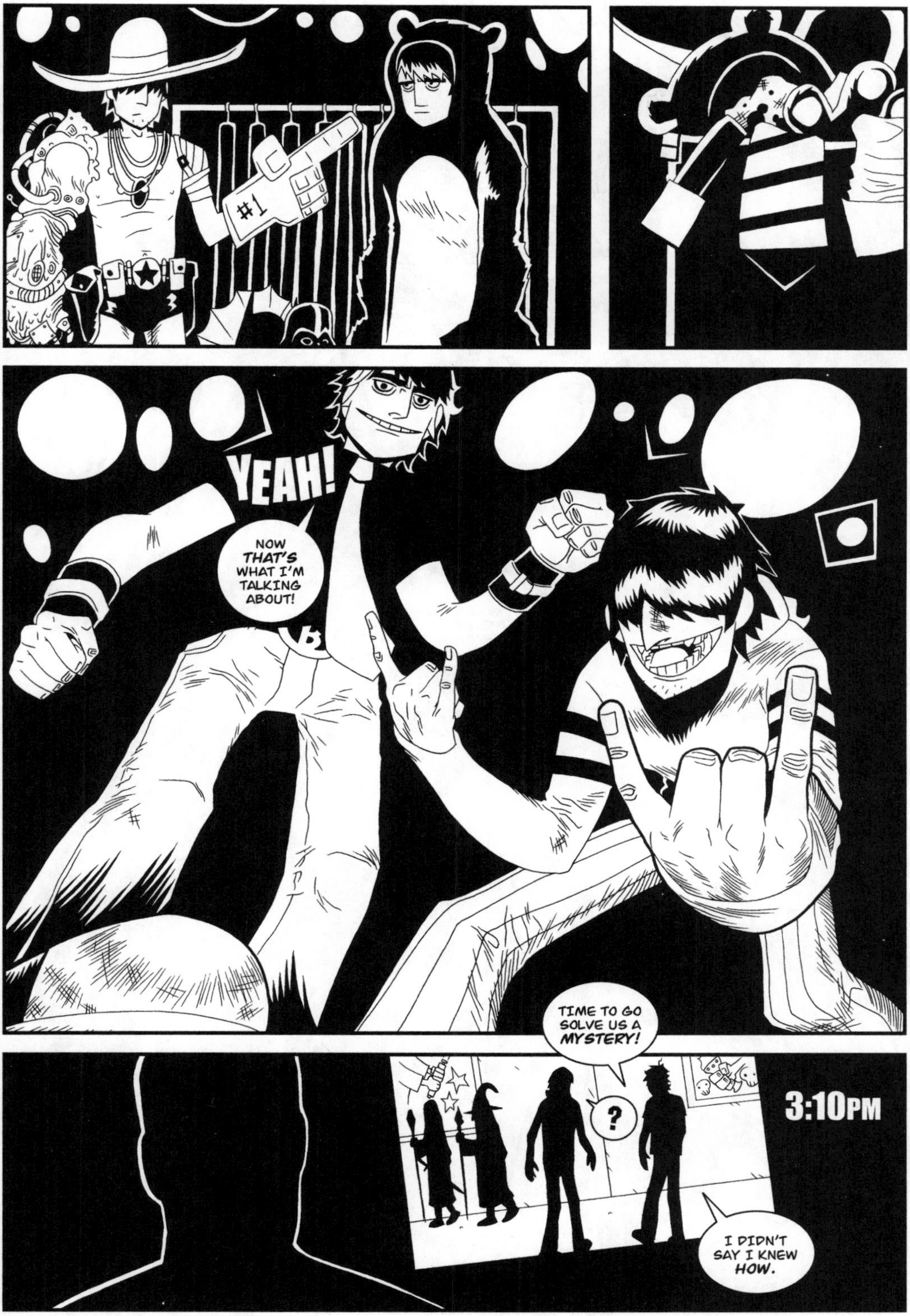
YEAH!
NOW THAT'S WHAT I'M TALKING ABOUT!
TIME TO GO SOLVE US A MYSTERY!
?
I DIDN'T SAY I KNEW HOW.
3:10PM

Sounds like it might be time for another...

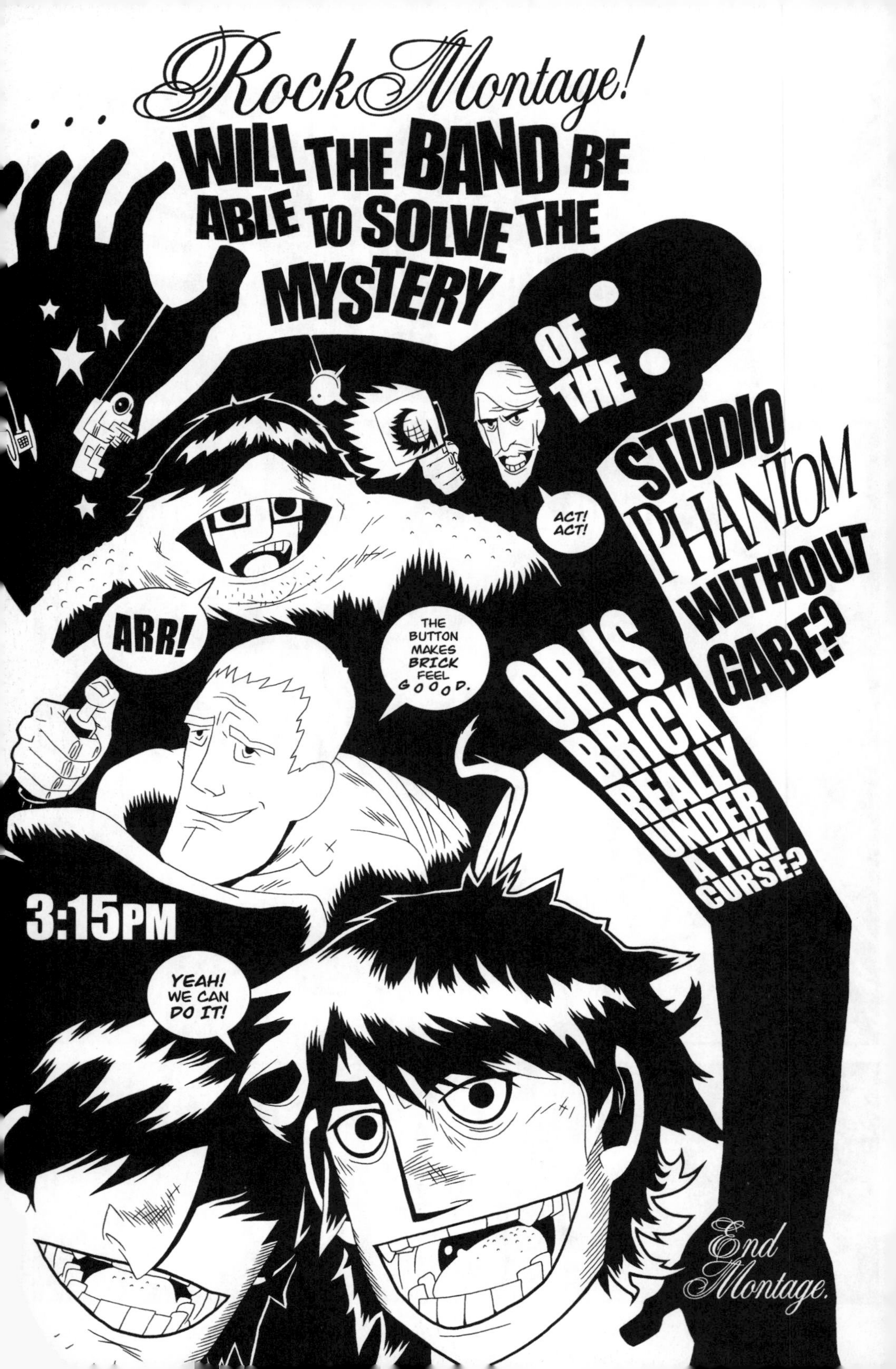

Rock Montage!
. . . WILL THE BAND BE ABLE TO SOLVE THE MYSTERY OF THE STUDIO PHANTOM WITHOUT GABE?
ACT! ACT!
ARR!
THE BUTTON MAKES BRICK FEEL GOOOOD.
OR IS BRICK REALLY UNDER A TIKI CURSE?
3:15PM
YEAH! WE CAN DO IT!
End Montage.

PART FOUR
"GET BRANNIGAN!"

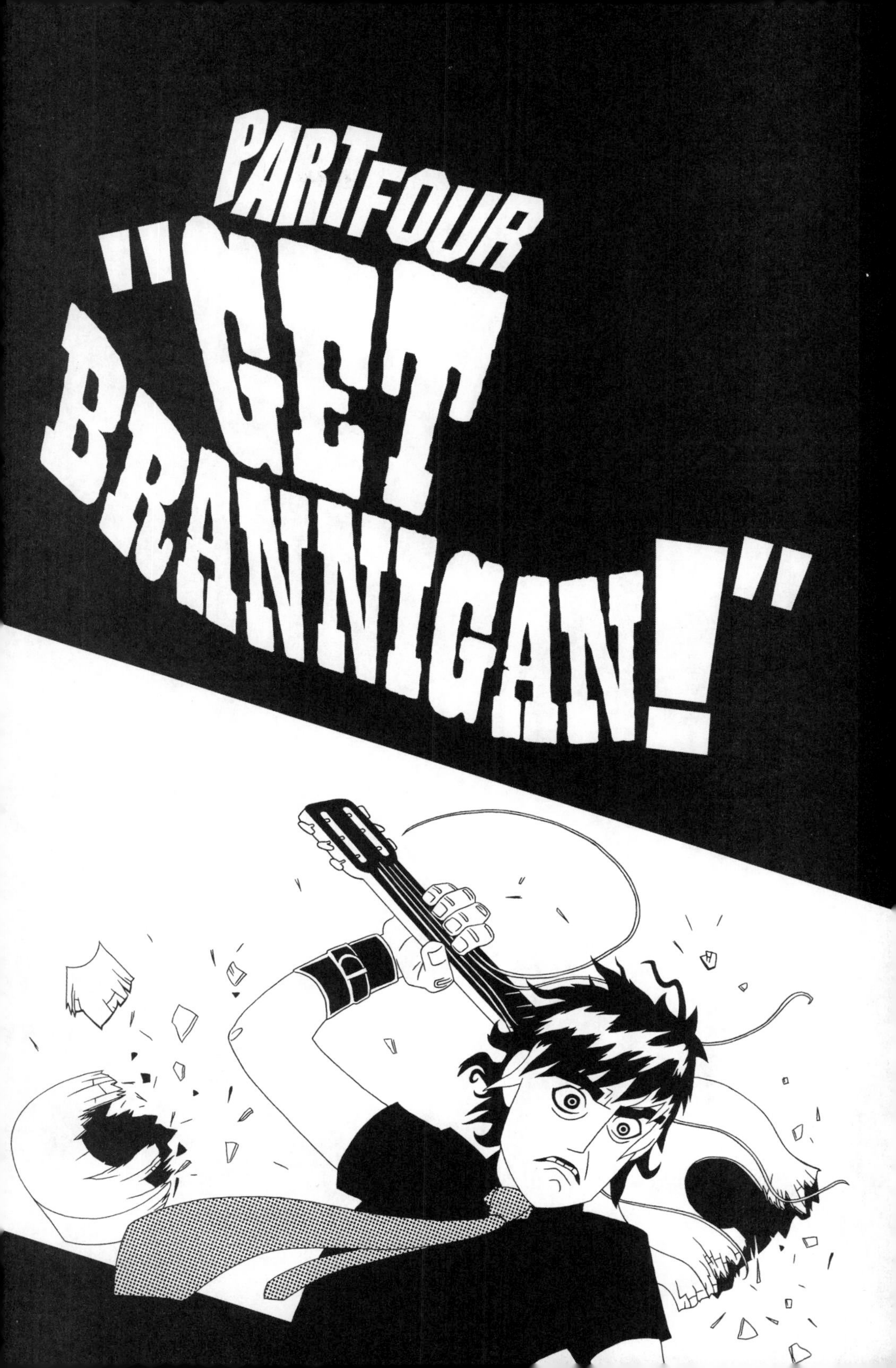

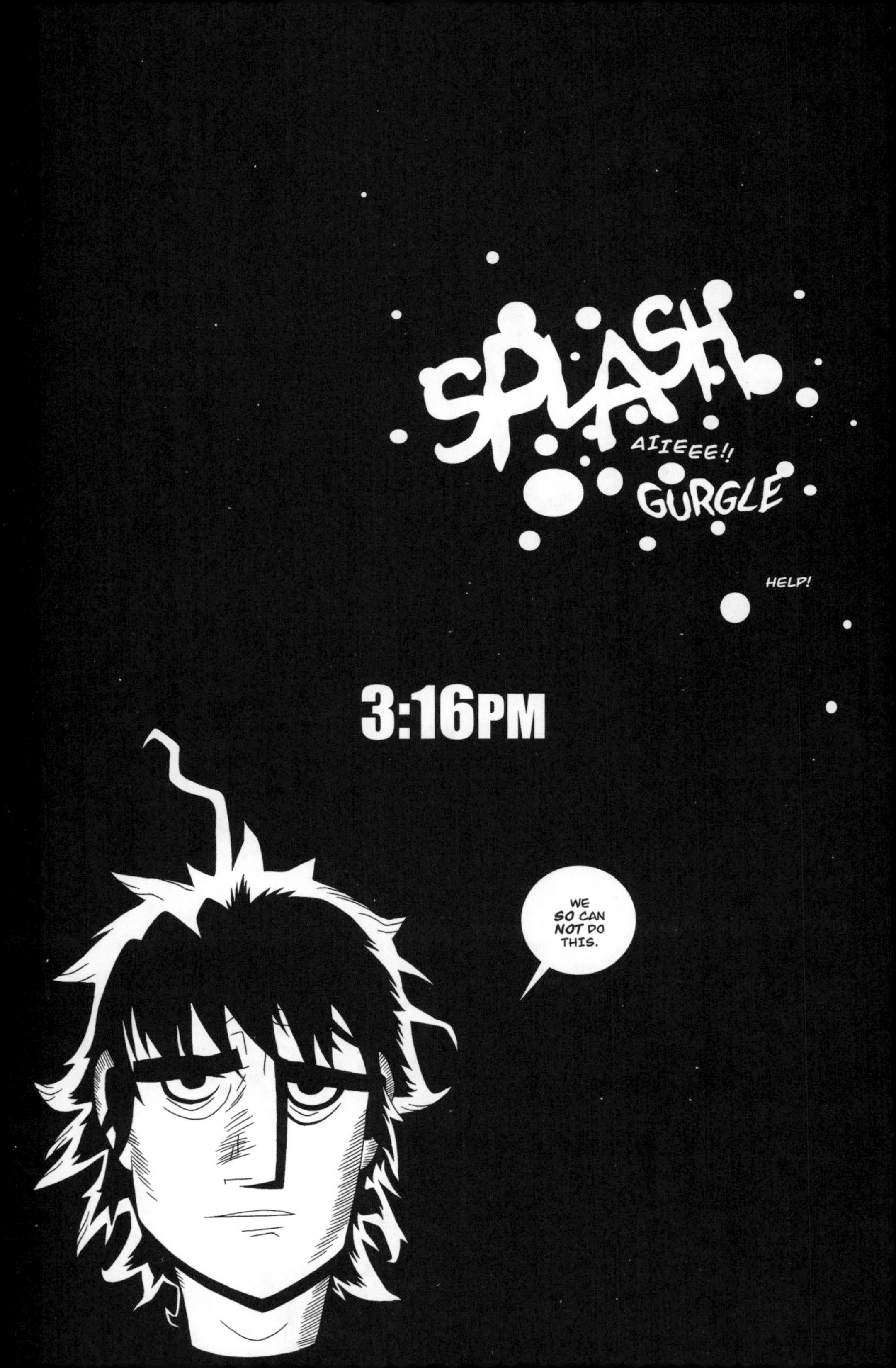
SPLASH
AIIEEE!!
GURGLE
HELP!
3:16PM
WE SO CAN NOT DO THIS.

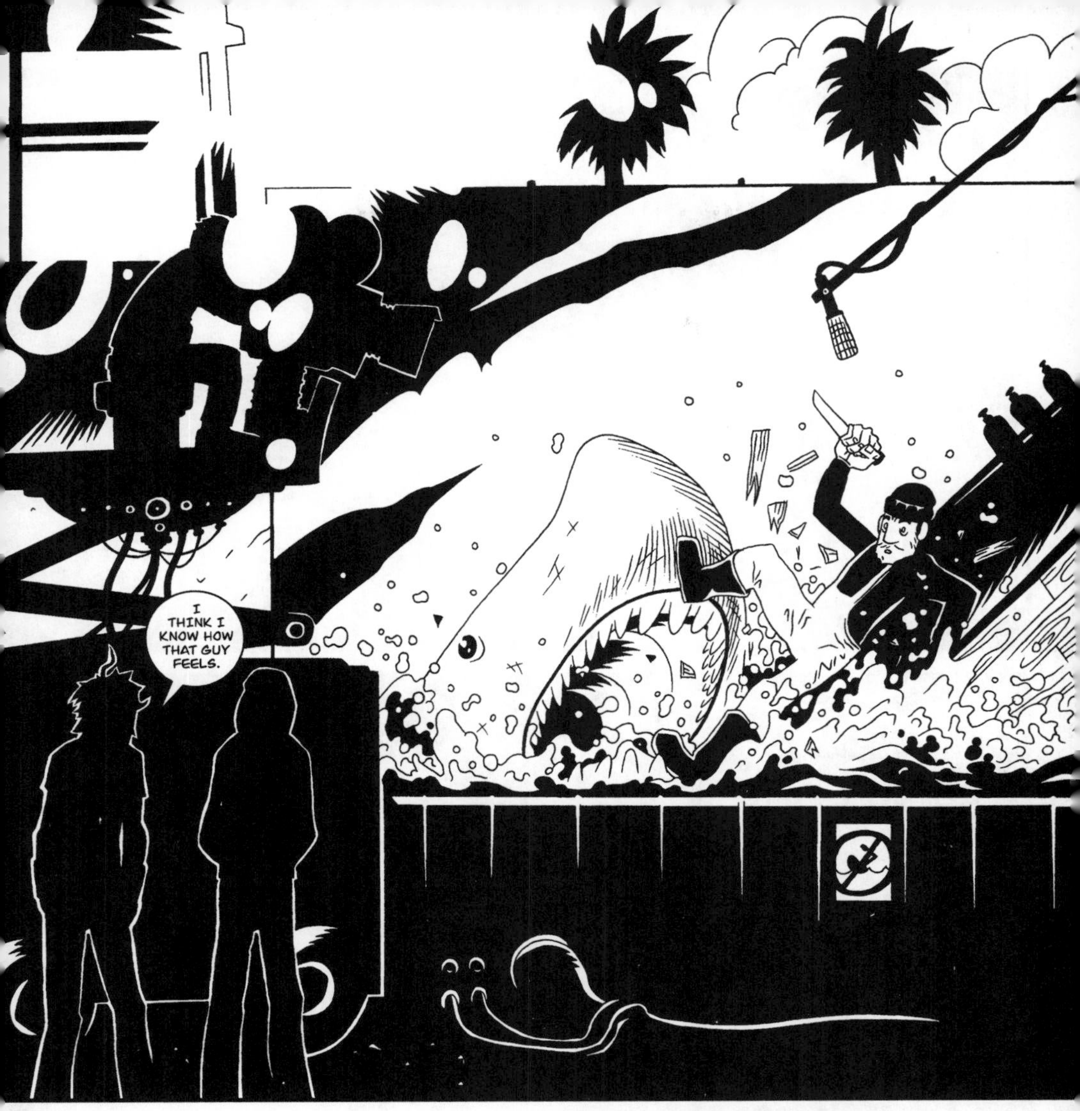
I THINK I KNOW HOW THAT GUY FEELS.

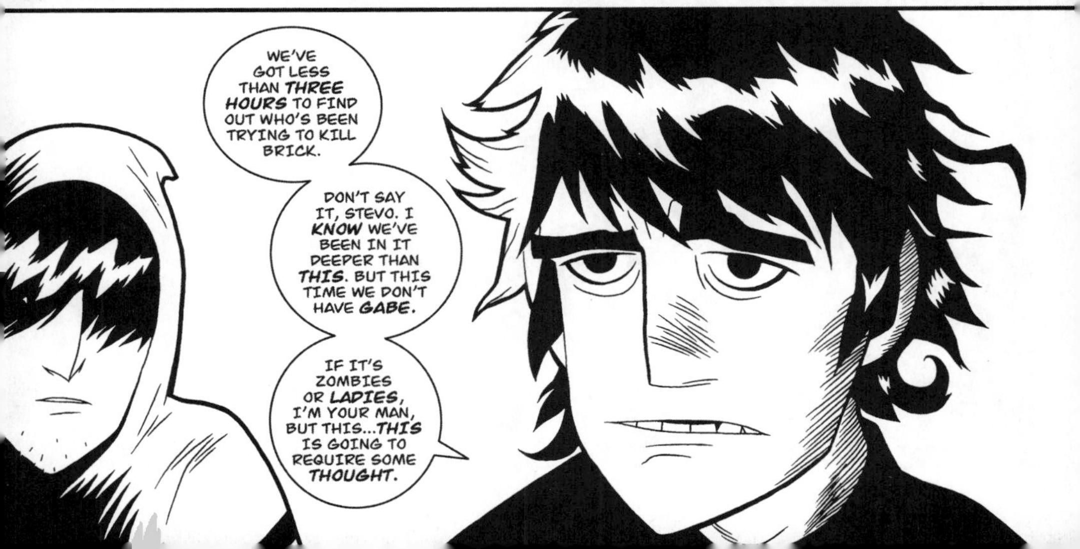
WE'VE GOT LESS THAN THREE HOURS TO FIND OUT WHO'S BEEN TRYING TO KILL BRICK.
DON'T SAY IT, STEVO. I KNOW WE'VE BEEN IN IT DEEPER THAN THIS. BUT THIS TIME WE DON'T HAVE GABE.
IF IT'S ZOMBIES OR LADIES, I'M YOUR MAN, BUT THIS...THIS IS GOING TO REQUIRE SOME THOUGHT.

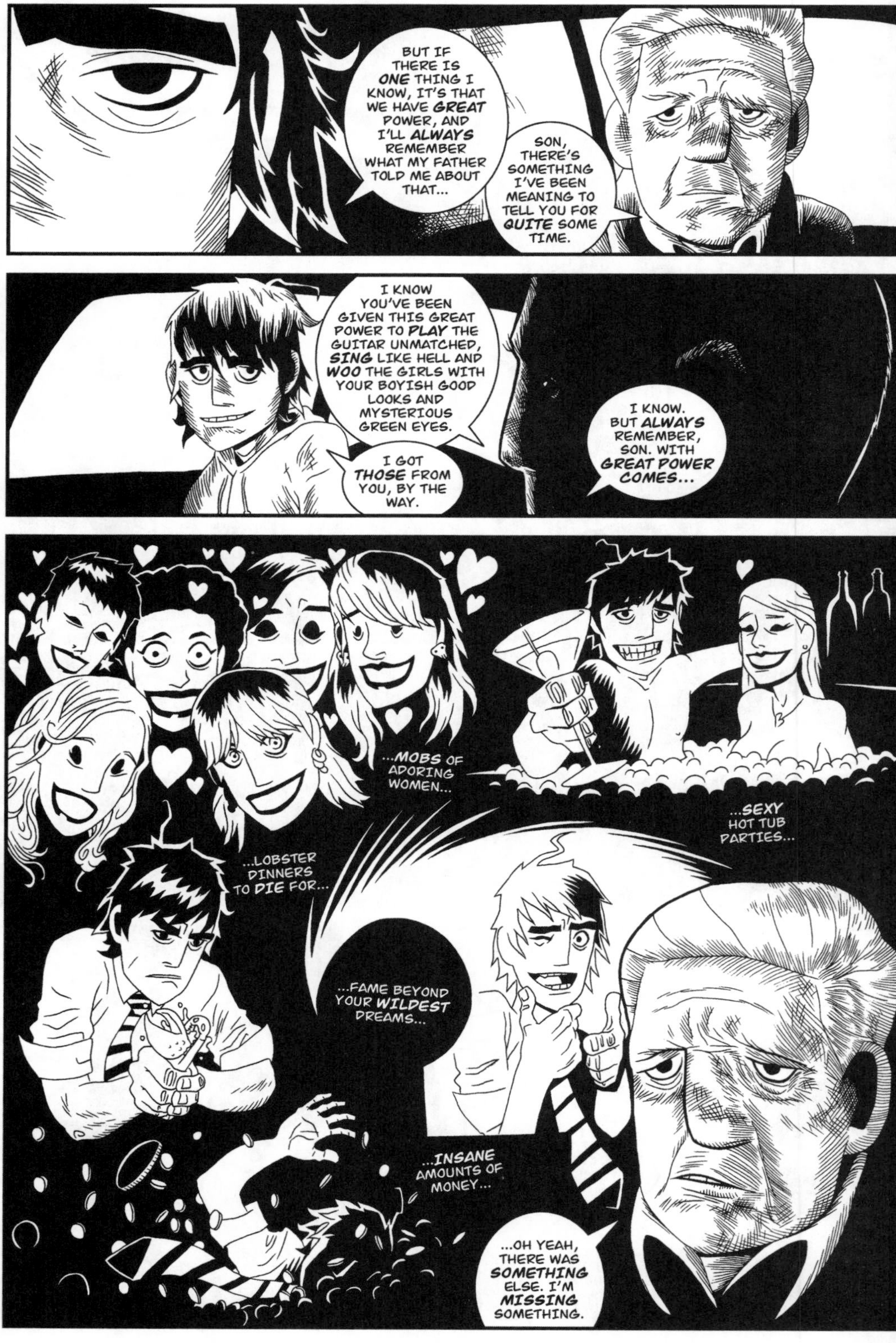
BUT IF THERE IS ONE THING I KNOW, IT'S THAT WE HAVE GREAT POWER, AND I'LL ALWAYS REMEMBER WHAT MY FATHER TOLD ME ABOUT THAT...
SON, THERE'S SOMETHING I'VE BEEN MEANING TO TELL YOU FOR QUITE SOME TIME.
I KNOW YOU'VE BEEN GIVEN THIS GREAT POWER TO PLAY THE GUITAR UNMATCHED, SING LIKE HELL AND WOO THE GIRLS WITH YOUR BOYISH GOOD LOOKS AND MYSTERIOUS GREEN EYES.
I GOT THOSE FROM YOU, BY THE WAY.
I KNOW. BUT ALWAYS REMEMBER, SON. WITH GREAT POWER COMES...
...MOBS OF ADORING WOMEN...
...SEXY HOT TUB PARTIES...
...LOBSTER DINNERS TO DIE FOR...
...FAME BEYOND YOUR WILDEST DREAMS...
...INSANE AMOUNTS OF MONEY...
...OH YEAH, THERE WAS SOMETHING ELSE. I'M MISSING SOMETHING.

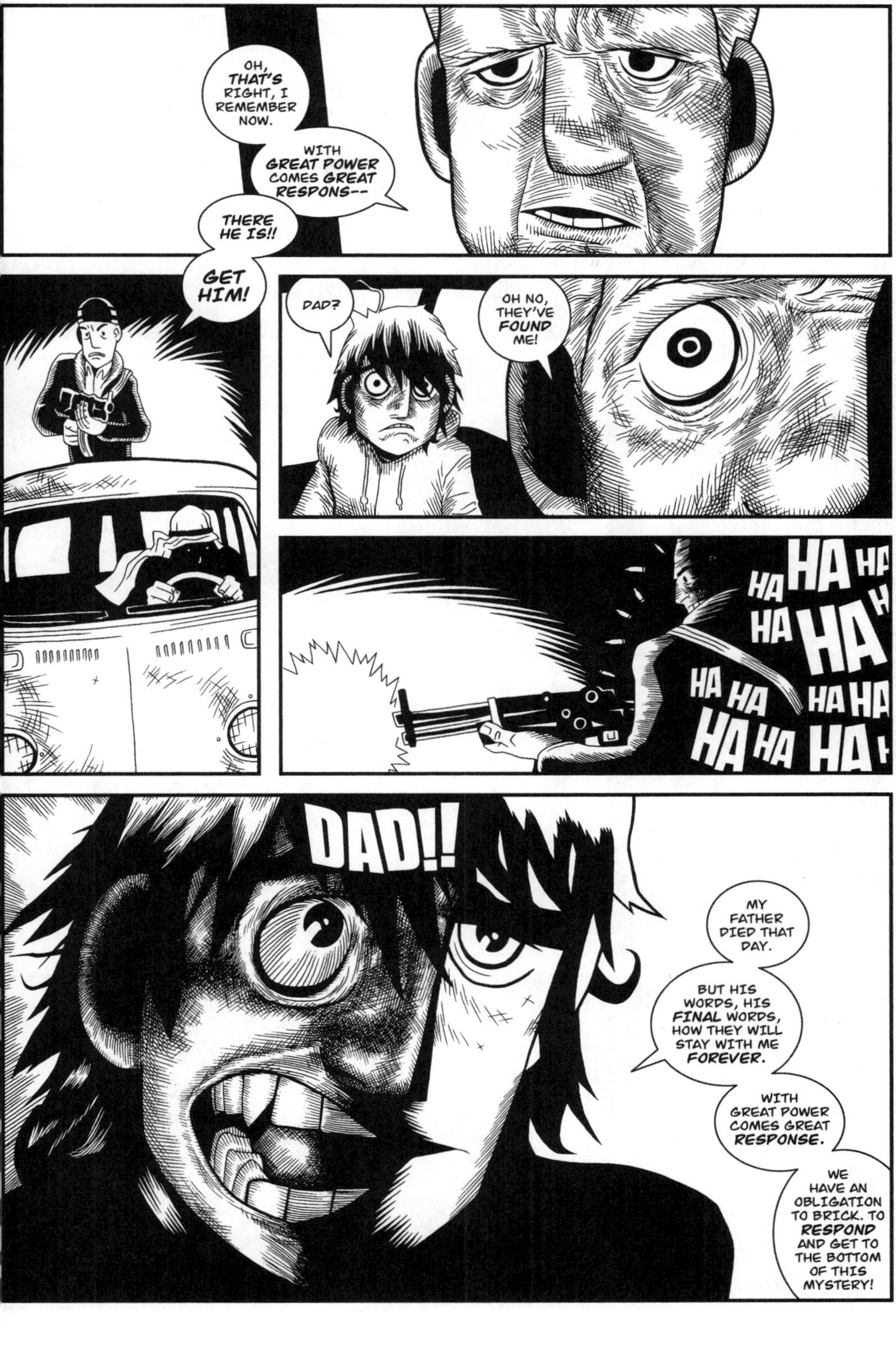
OH, THAT'S RIGHT, I REMEMBER NOW.
WITH GREAT POWER COMES GREAT RESPONS--
THERE HE IS!!
GET HIM!
DAD?
OH NO, THEY'VE FOUND ME!
HA HA HA HA HA HA HA HA HA HA HA HA HA HA
DAD!!
MY FATHER DIED THAT DAY.
BUT HIS WORDS, HIS FINAL WORDS, HOW THEY WILL STAY WITH ME FOREVER.
WITH GREAT POWER COMES GREAT RESPONSE.
WE HAVE AN OBLIGATION TO BRICK. TO RESPOND AND GET TO THE BOTTOM OF THIS MYSTERY!

I JUST GOT AN IDEA, BUT *FIRST* WE NEED MORGENSTEIN TO GET EVERYONE ON THE LOT IN THE SAME PLACE.

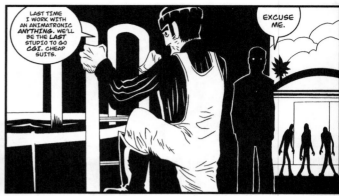

LAST TIME I WORK WITH AN ANIMATRONIC *ANYTHING*, WE'LL BE THE *LAST* STUDIO TO GO *CGI*. CHEAP SUITS.

EXCUSE ME.

EH? WHAT IS IT, PAL?

COULD YOU DO ME A *FAVOR*, PLEASE?

I WANT YOU TO DO *EXACTLY* WHAT I SAY, PLEASE.

NO. I...

JOIN ME.

NUH... YES.

JOIN ME NOW!

YES, HYPNO. TO HEAR IS TO OBEY.

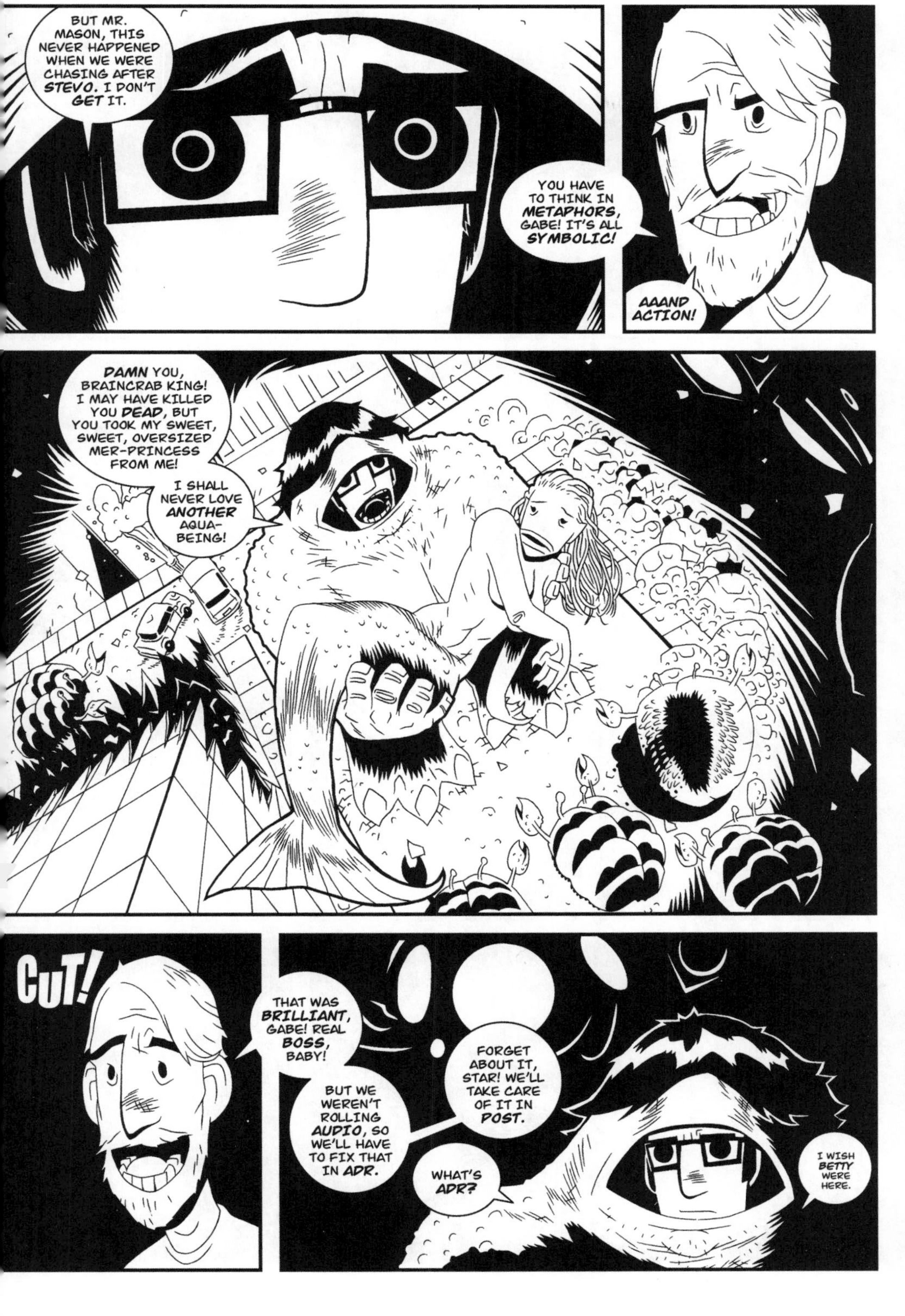
BUT MR. MASON, THIS NEVER HAPPENED WHEN WE WERE CHASING AFTER STEVO. I DON'T GET IT.
YOU HAVE TO THINK IN METAPHORS, GABE! IT'S ALL SYMBOLIC!
AAAND ACTION!
DAMN YOU, BRAINCRAB KING! I MAY HAVE KILLED YOU DEAD, BUT YOU TOOK MY SWEET, SWEET, OVERSIZED MER-PRINCESS FROM ME!
I SHALL NEVER LOVE ANOTHER AQUA-BEING!
CUT!
THAT WAS BRILLIANT, GABE! REAL BOSS, BABY!
BUT WE WEREN'T ROLLING AUDIO, SO WE'LL HAVE TO FIX THAT IN ADR.
WHAT'S ADR?
FORGET ABOUT IT, STAR! WE'LL TAKE CARE OF IT IN POST.
I WISH BETTY WERE HERE.

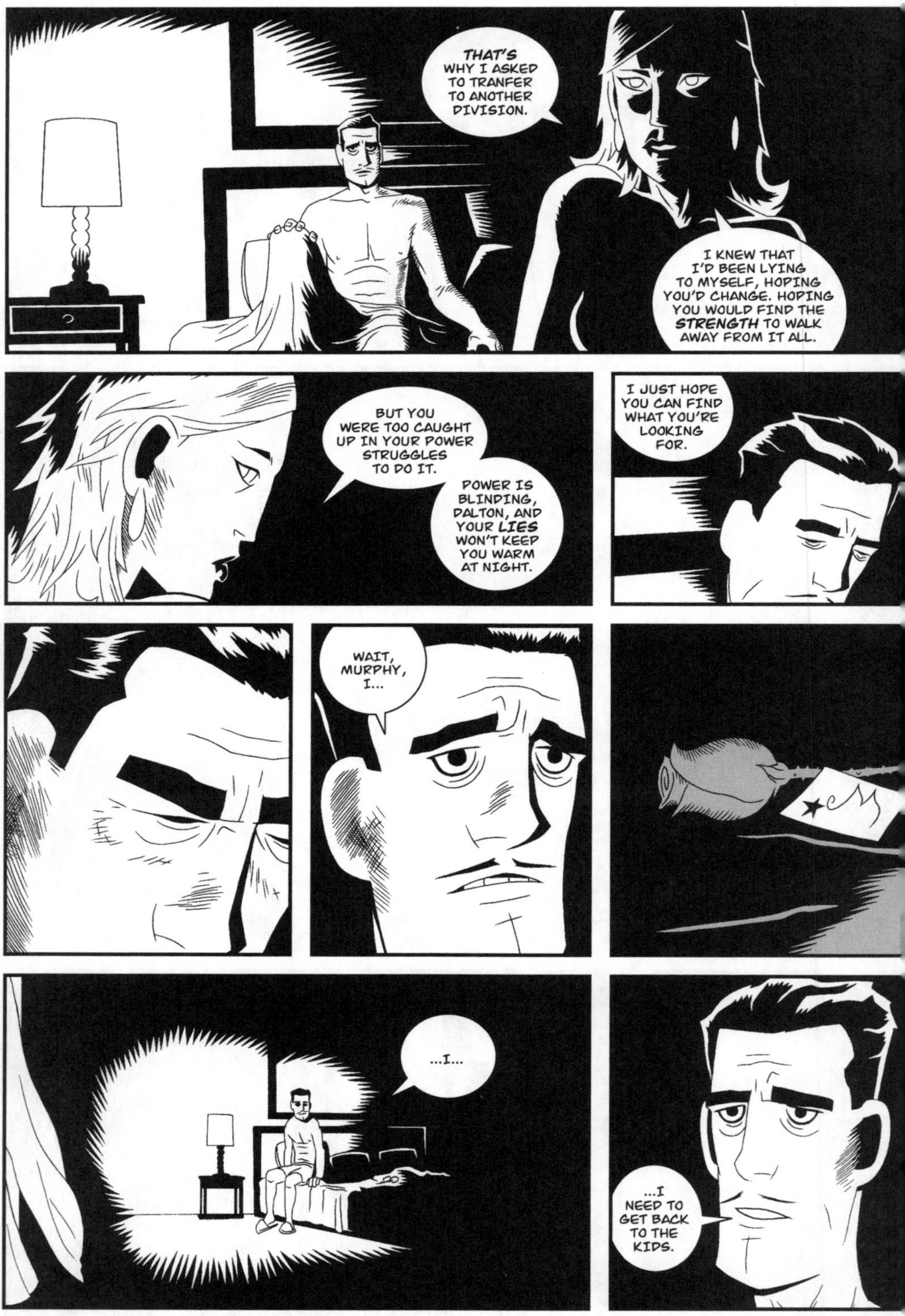

THAT'S WHY I ASKED TO TRANFER TO ANOTHER DIVISION.
I KNEW THAT I'D BEEN LYING TO MYSELF, HOPING YOU'D CHANGE. HOPING YOU WOULD FIND THE STRENGTH TO WALK AWAY FROM IT ALL.
BUT YOU WERE TOO CAUGHT UP IN YOUR POWER STRUGGLES TO DO IT.
POWER IS BLINDING, DALTON, AND YOUR LIES WON'T KEEP YOU WARM AT NIGHT.
I JUST HOPE YOU CAN FIND WHAT YOU'RE LOOKING FOR.
WAIT, MURPHY, I...
...I...
...I NEED TO GET BACK TO THE KIDS.

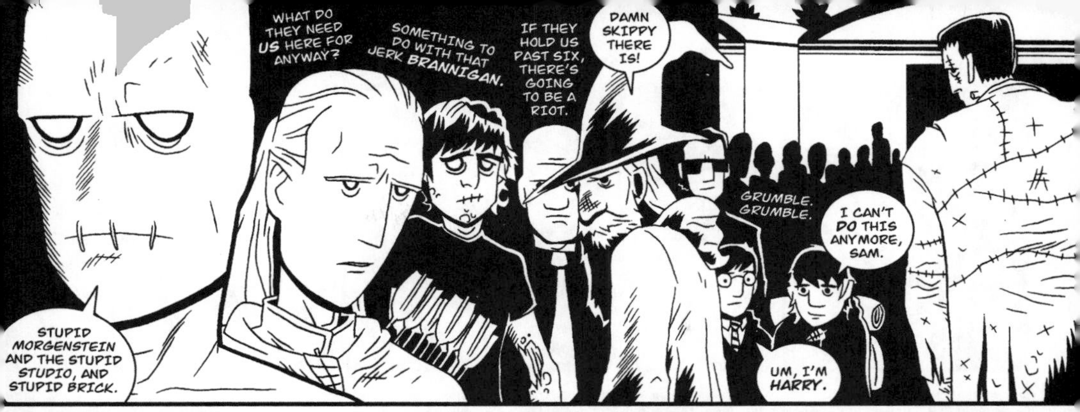
STUPID MORGENSTEIN AND THE STUPID STUDIO, AND STUPID BRICK.
WHAT DO THEY NEED US HERE FOR ANYWAY?
SOMETHING TO DO WITH THAT JERK BRANNIGAN.
IF THEY HOLD US PAST SIX, THERE'S GOING TO BE A RIOT.
DAMN SKIPPY THERE IS!
GRUMBLE. GRUMBLE.
I CAN'T DO THIS ANYMORE, SAM.
UM, I'M HARRY.

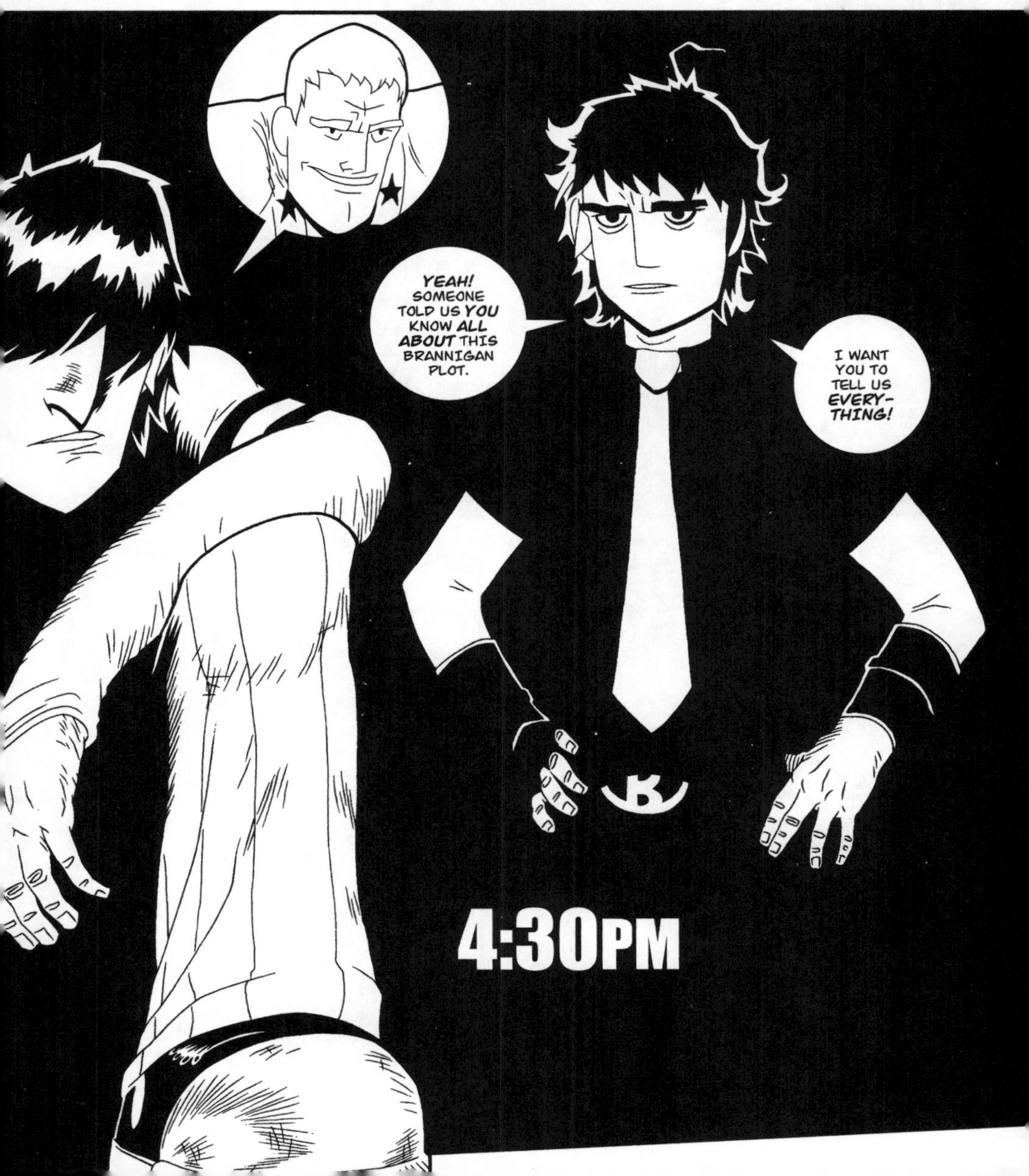
YEAH! SOMEONE TOLD US YOU KNOW ALL ABOUT THIS BRANNIGAN PLOT.
I WANT YOU TO TELL US EVERYTHING!
4:30PM

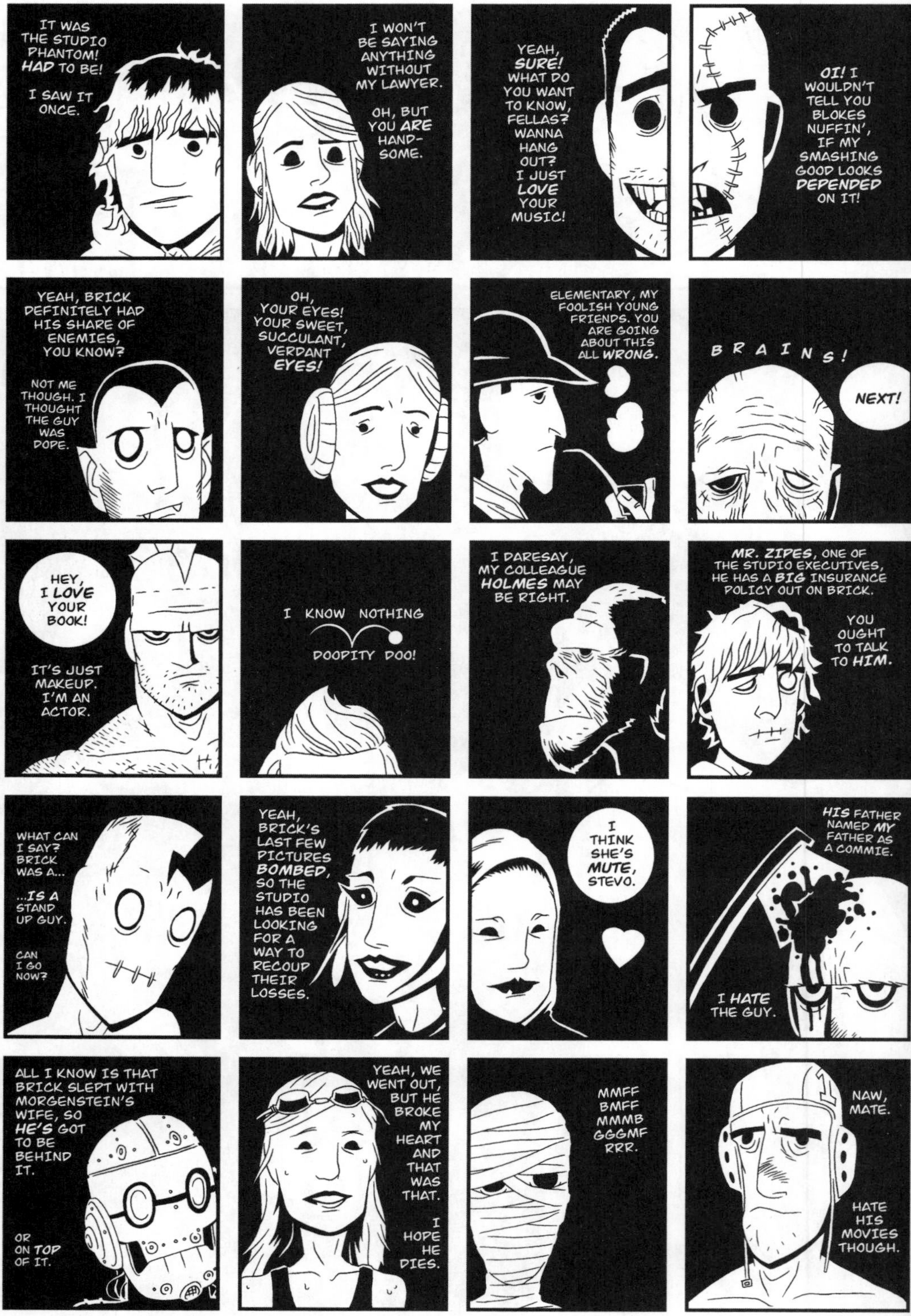
IT WAS THE STUDIO PHANTOM! HAD TO BE!
I SAW IT ONCE.
I WON'T BE SAYING ANYTHING WITHOUT MY LAWYER.
OH, BUT YOU ARE HAND-SOME.
YEAH, SURE! WHAT DO YOU WANT TO KNOW, FELLAS? WANNA HANG OUT? I JUST LOVE YOUR MUSIC!
OI! I WOULDN'T TELL YOU BLOKES NUFFIN', IF MY SMASHING GOOD LOOKS DEPENDED ON IT!
YEAH, BRICK DEFINITELY HAD HIS SHARE OF ENEMIES, YOU KNOW?
NOT ME THOUGH. I THOUGHT THE GUY WAS DOPE.
OH, YOUR EYES! YOUR SWEET, SUCCULANT, VERDANT EYES!
ELEMENTARY, MY FOOLISH YOUNG FRIENDS. YOU ARE GOING ABOUT THIS ALL WRONG.
B R A I N S!
NEXT!
HEY, I LOVE YOUR BOOK!
IT'S JUST MAKEUP. I'M AN ACTOR.
I KNOW NOTHING
DOOPITY DOO!
I DARESAY, MY COLLEAGUE HOLMES MAY BE RIGHT.
MR. ZIPES, ONE OF THE STUDIO EXECUTIVES, HE HAS A BIG INSURANCE POLICY OUT ON BRICK.
YOU OUGHT TO TALK TO HIM.
WHAT CAN I SAY? BRICK WAS A...
...IS A STAND UP GUY.
CAN I GO NOW?
YEAH, BRICK'S LAST FEW PICTURES BOMBED, SO THE STUDIO HAS BEEN LOOKING FOR A WAY TO RECOUP THEIR LOSSES.
I THINK SHE'S MUTE, STEVO.
HIS FATHER NAMED MY FATHER AS A COMMIE.
I HATE THE GUY.
ALL I KNOW IS THAT BRICK SLEPT WITH MORGENSTEIN'S WIFE, SO HE'S GOT TO BE BEHIND IT.
OR ON TOP OF IT.
YEAH, WE WENT OUT, BUT HE BROKE MY HEART AND THAT WAS THAT.
I HOPE HE DIES.
MMFF BMFF MMMB GGGMF RRR.
NAW, MATE.
HATE HIS MOVIES THOUGH.

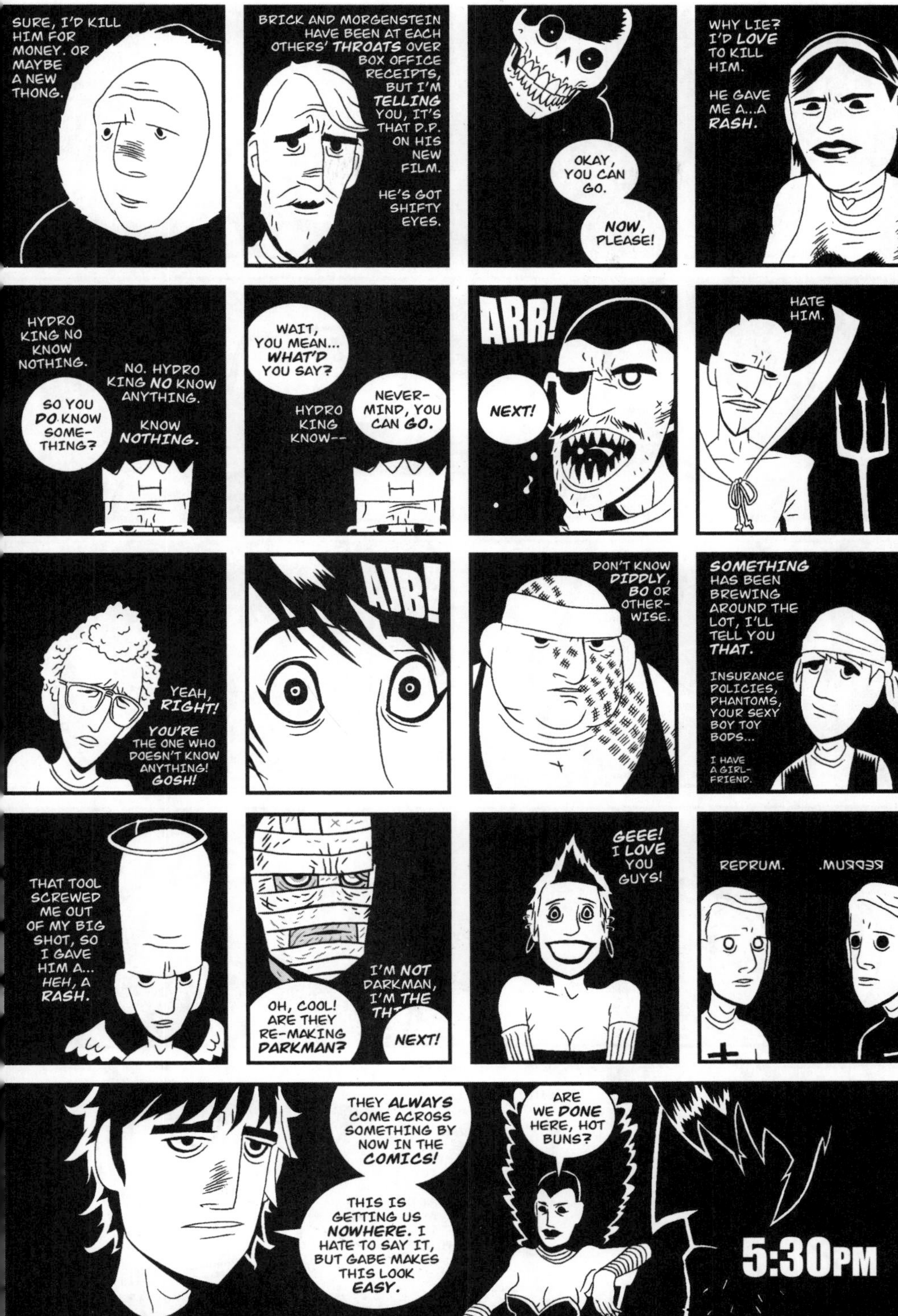
SURE, I'D KILL HIM FOR MONEY. OR MAYBE A NEW THONG.
BRICK AND MORGENSTEIN HAVE BEEN AT EACH OTHERS' THROATS OVER BOX OFFICE RECEIPTS, BUT I'M TELLING YOU, IT'S THAT D.P. ON HIS NEW FILM.
HE'S GOT SHIFTY EYES.
OKAY, YOU CAN GO.
NOW, PLEASE!
WHY LIE? I'D LOVE TO KILL HIM.
HE GAVE ME A...A RASH.
HYDRO KING NO KNOW NOTHING.
SO YOU DO KNOW SOME-THING?
NO. HYDRO KING NO KNOW ANYTHING.
KNOW NOTHING.
WAIT, YOU MEAN... WHAT'D YOU SAY?
HYDRO KING KNOW--
NEVER-MIND, YOU CAN GO.
ARR!
NEXT!
HATE HIM.
YEAH, RIGHT!
YOU'RE THE ONE WHO DOESN'T KNOW ANYTHING! GOSH!
AJB!
DON'T KNOW DIDDLY, BO OR OTHER-WISE.
SOMETHING HAS BEEN BREWING AROUND THE LOT, I'LL TELL YOU THAT.
INSURANCE POLICIES, PHANTOMS, YOUR SEXY BOY TOY BODS...
I HAVE A GIRL-FRIEND.
THAT TOOL SCREWED ME OUT OF MY BIG SHOT, SO I GAVE HIM A... HEH, A RASH.
OH, COOL! ARE THEY RE-MAKING DARKMAN?
I'M NOT DARKMAN, I'M THE TH
NEXT!
GEEE! I LOVE YOU GUYS!
REDRUM.
REDRUM.
THEY ALWAYS COME ACROSS SOMETHING BY NOW IN THE COMICS!
THIS IS GETTING US NOWHERE. I HATE TO SAY IT, BUT GABE MAKES THIS LOOK EASY.
ARE WE DONE HERE, HOT BUNS?
5:30PM

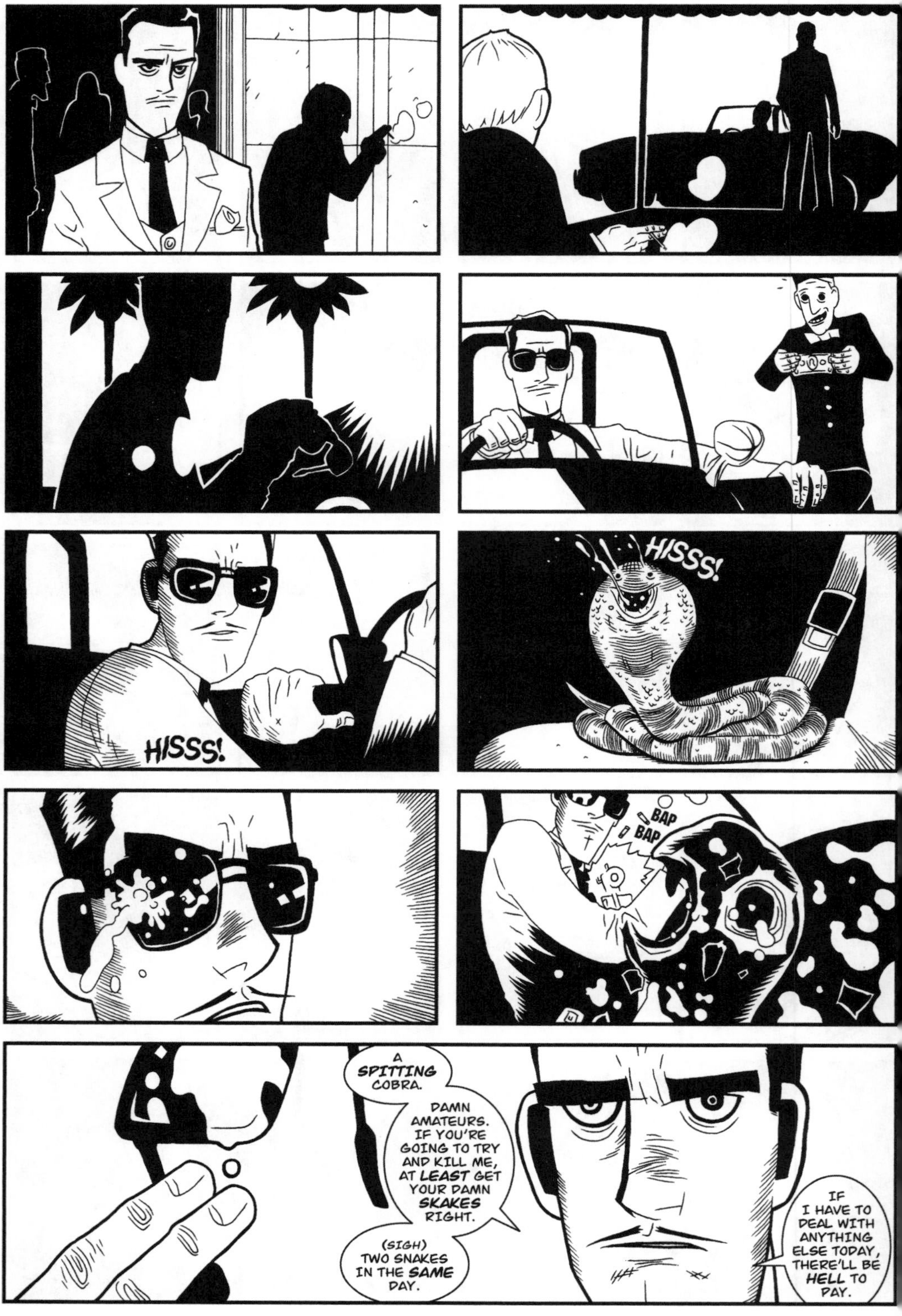
HISSS!
HISSS!
BAP
BAP
A SPITTING COBRA.
DAMN AMATEURS. IF YOU'RE GOING TO TRY AND KILL ME, AT LEAST GET YOUR DAMN SKAKES RIGHT.
(SIGH) TWO SNAKES IN THE SAME DAY.
IF I HAVE TO DEAL WITH ANYTHING ELSE TODAY, THERE'LL BE HELL TO PAY.

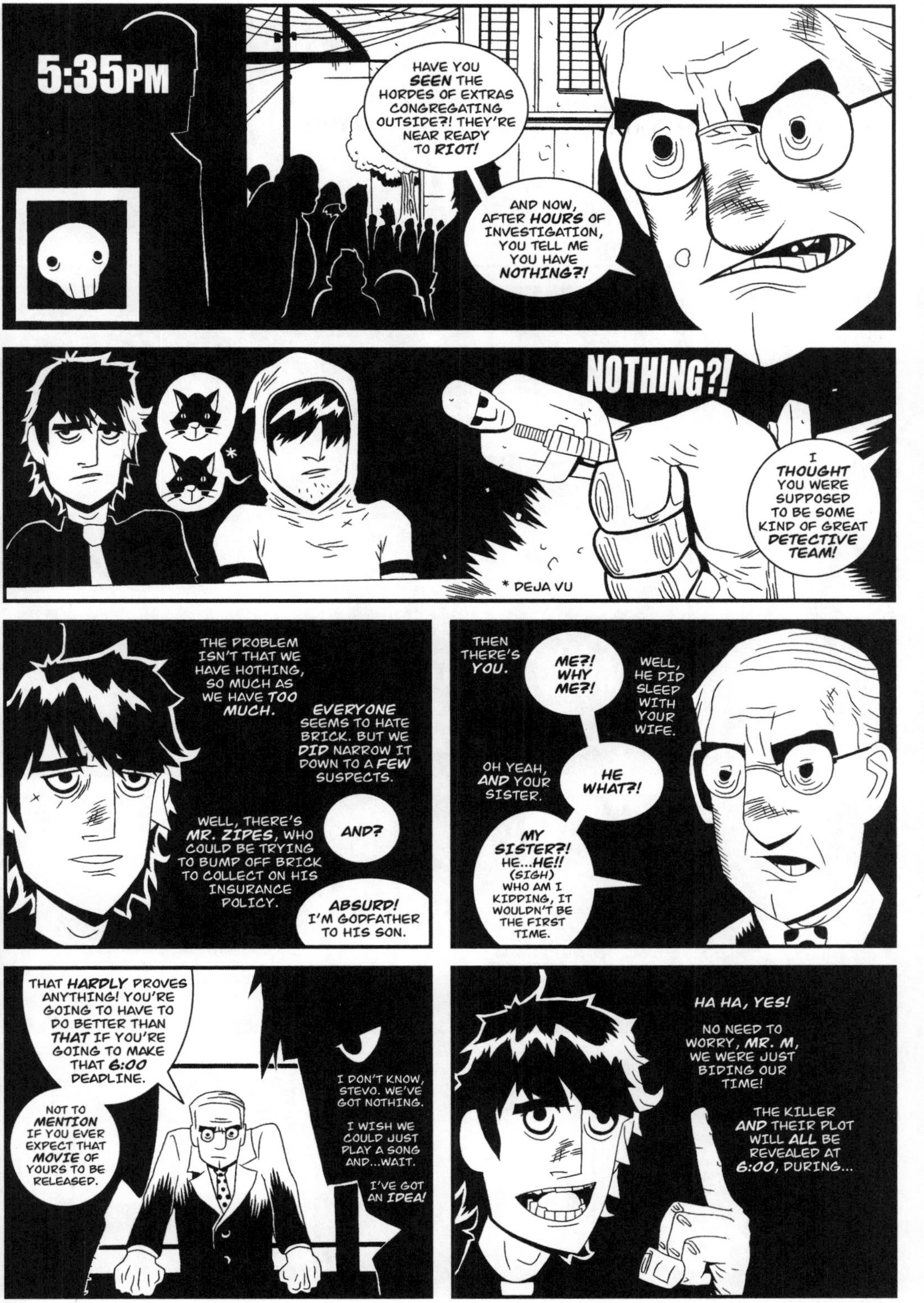
5:35PM
HAVE YOU SEEN THE HORDES OF EXTRAS CONGREGATING OUTSIDE?! THEY'RE NEAR READY TO RIOT!
AND NOW, AFTER HOURS OF INVESTIGATION, YOU TELL ME YOU HAVE NOTHING?!
NOTHING?!
I THOUGHT YOU WERE SUPPOSED TO BE SOME KIND OF GREAT DETECTIVE TEAM!
* DEJA VU
THE PROBLEM ISN'T THAT WE HAVE HOTHING, SO MUCH AS WE HAVE TOO MUCH.
EVERYONE SEEMS TO HATE BRICK. BUT WE DID NARROW IT DOWN TO A FEW SUSPECTS.
AND?
WELL, THERE'S MR. ZIPES, WHO COULD BE TRYING TO BUMP OFF BRICK TO COLLECT ON HIS INSURANCE POLICY.
ABSURD! I'M GODFATHER TO HIS SON.
THEN THERE'S YOU.
ME?! WHY ME?!
WELL, HE DID SLEEP WITH YOUR WIFE.
HE WHAT?!
OH YEAH, AND YOUR SISTER.
MY SISTER?! HE...HE!! (SIGH) WHO AM I KIDDING, IT WOULDN'T BE THE FIRST TIME.
THAT HARDLY PROVES ANYTHING! YOU'RE GOING TO HAVE TO DO BETTER THAN THAT IF YOU'RE GOING TO MAKE THAT 6:00 DEADLINE.
NOT TO MENTION IF YOU EVER EXPECT THAT MOVIE OF YOURS TO BE RELEASED.
I DON'T KNOW, STEVO. WE'VE GOT NOTHING.
I WISH WE COULD JUST PLAY A SONG AND...WAIT.
I'VE GOT AN IDEA!
HA HA, YES!
NO NEED TO WORRY, MR. M, WE WERE JUST BIDING OUR TIME!
THE KILLER AND THEIR PLOT WILL ALL BE REVEALED AT 6:00, DURING...

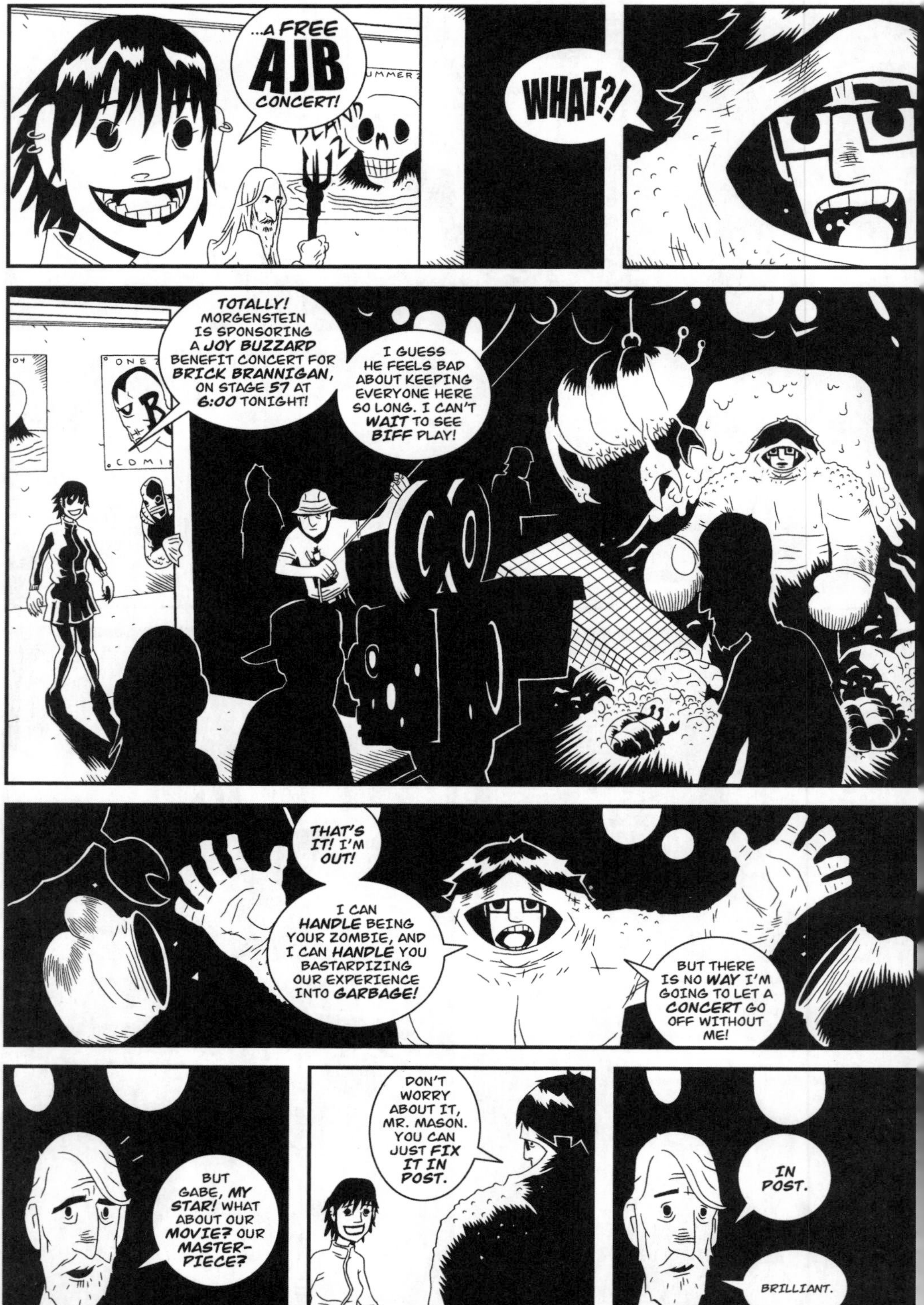
...A FREE AJB CONCERT!
WHAT?!
TOTALLY! MORGENSTEIN IS SPONSORING A JOY BUZZARD BENEFIT CONCERT FOR BRICK BRANNIGAN, ON STAGE 57 AT 6:00 TONIGHT!
I GUESS HE FEELS BAD ABOUT KEEPING EVERYONE HERE SO LONG. I CAN'T WAIT TO SEE BIFF PLAY!
THAT'S IT! I'M OUT!
I CAN HANDLE BEING YOUR ZOMBIE, AND I CAN HANDLE YOU BASTARDIZING OUR EXPERIENCE INTO GARBAGE!
BUT THERE IS NO WAY I'M GOING TO LET A CONCERT GO OFF WITHOUT ME!
BUT GABE, MY STAR! WHAT ABOUT OUR MOVIE? OUR MASTER-PIECE?
DON'T WORRY ABOUT IT, MR. MASON. YOU CAN JUST FIX IT IN POST.
IN POST.
BRILLIANT.

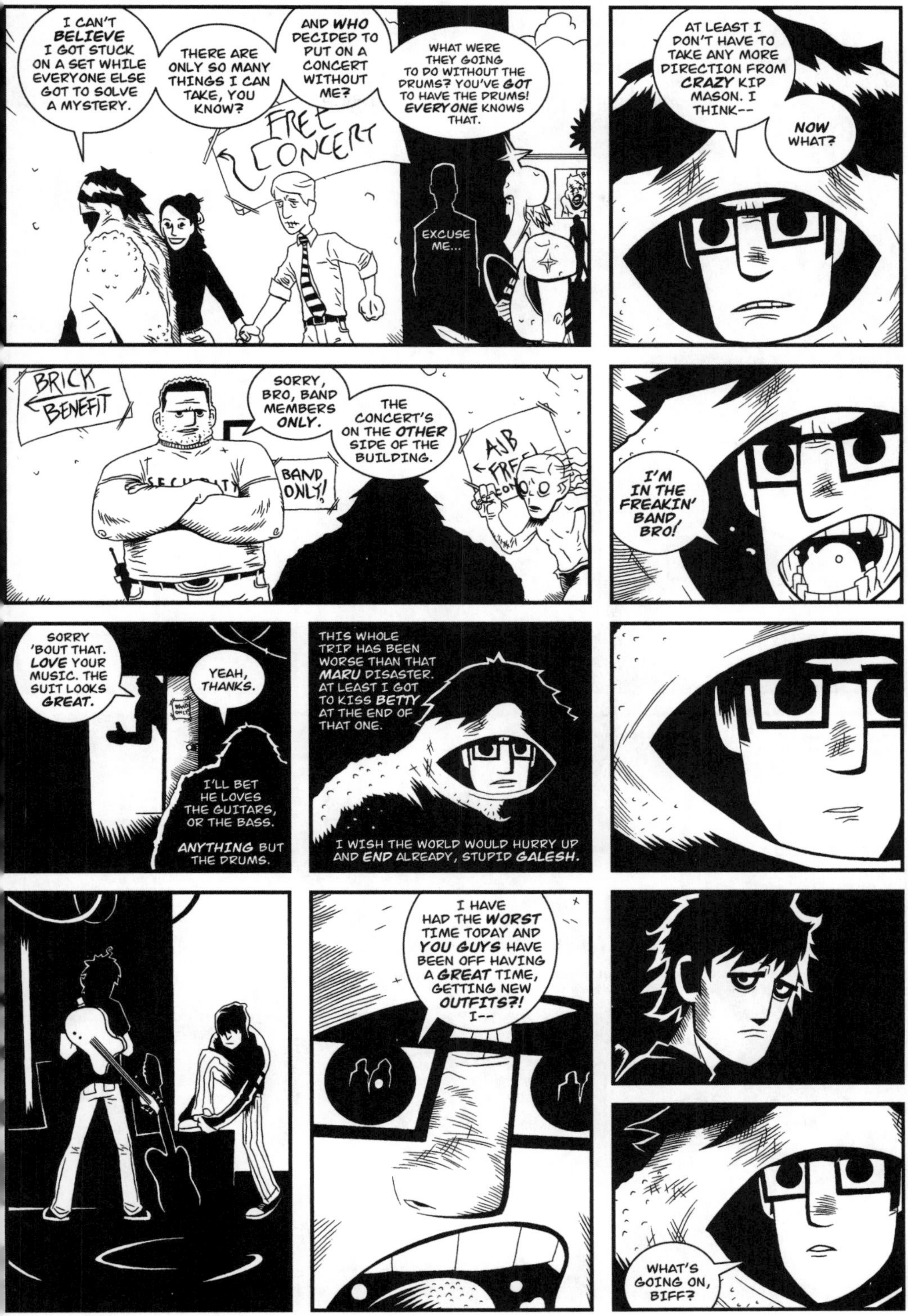

I CAN'T BELIEVE I GOT STUCK ON A SET WHILE EVERYONE ELSE GOT TO SOLVE A MYSTERY.
THERE ARE ONLY SO MANY THINGS I CAN TAKE, YOU KNOW?
AND WHO DECIDED TO PUT ON A CONCERT WITHOUT ME?
FREE CONCERT
WHAT WERE THEY GOING TO DO WITHOUT THE DRUMS? YOU'VE GOT TO HAVE THE DRUMS! EVERYONE KNOWS THAT.
EXCUSE ME...
AT LEAST I DON'T HAVE TO TAKE ANY MORE DIRECTION FROM CRAZY KIP MASON. I THINK--
NOW WHAT?
BRICK BENEFIT
SORRY, BRO, BAND MEMBERS ONLY.
THE CONCERT'S ON THE OTHER SIDE OF THE BUILDING.
BAND ONLY!
I'M IN THE FREAKIN' BAND, BRO!
SORRY 'BOUT THAT. LOVE YOUR MUSIC. THE SUIT LOOKS GREAT.
YEAH, THANKS.
I'LL BET HE LOVES THE GUITARS, OR THE BASS.
ANYTHING BUT THE DRUMS.
THIS WHOLE TRIP HAS BEEN WORSE THAN THAT MARU DISASTER. AT LEAST I GOT TO KISS BETTY AT THE END OF THAT ONE.
I WISH THE WORLD WOULD HURRY UP AND END ALREADY, STUPID GALESH.
I HAVE HAD THE WORST TIME TODAY AND YOU GUYS HAVE BEEN OFF HAVING A GREAT TIME, GETTING NEW OUTFITS?! I--
WHAT'S GOING ON, BIFF?

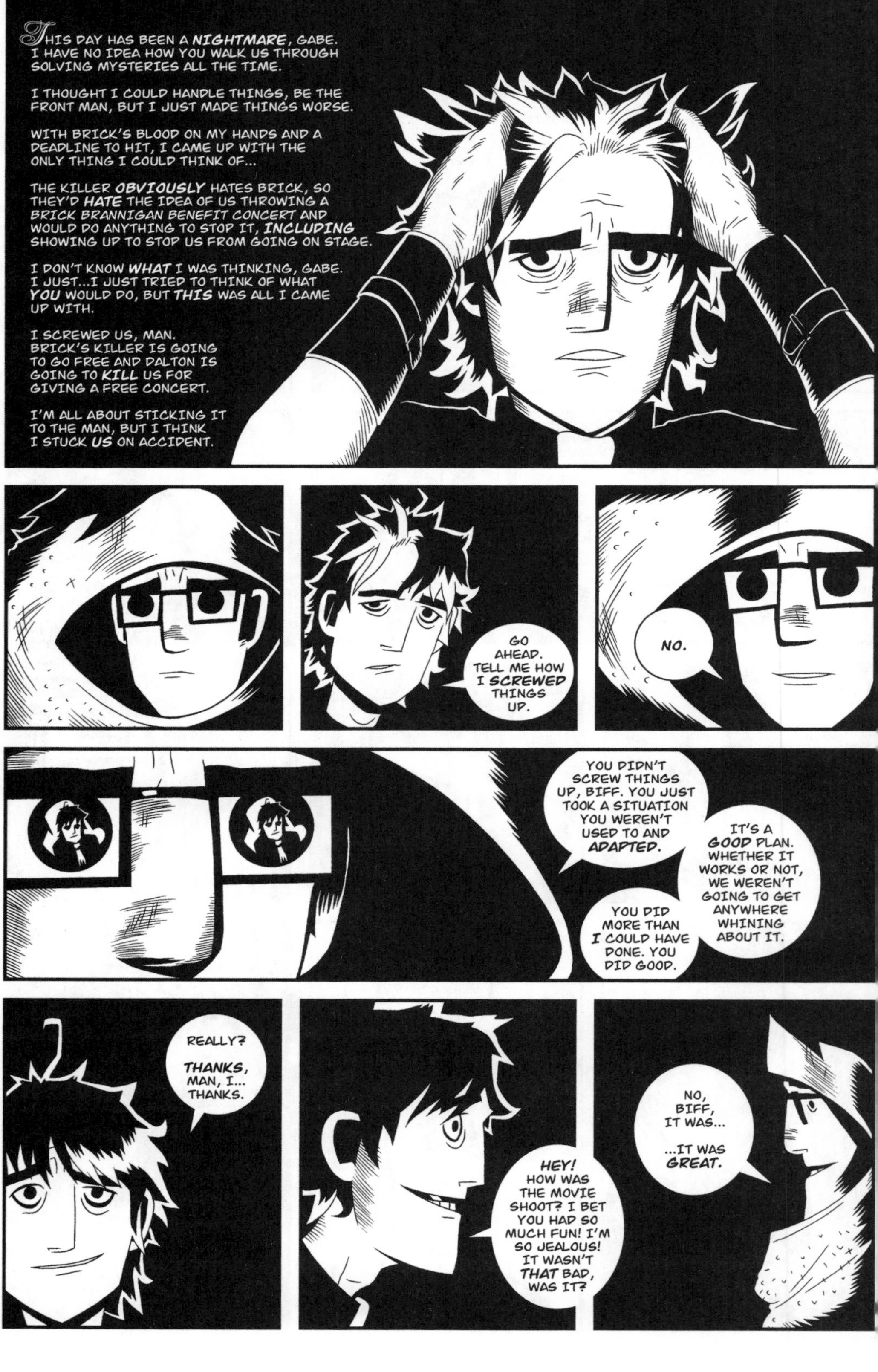
THIS DAY HAS BEEN A NIGHTMARE, GABE. I HAVE NO IDEA HOW YOU WALK US THROUGH SOLVING MYSTERIES ALL THE TIME.
I THOUGHT I COULD HANDLE THINGS, BE THE FRONT MAN, BUT I JUST MADE THINGS WORSE.
WITH BRICK'S BLOOD ON MY HANDS AND A DEADLINE TO HIT, I CAME UP WITH THE ONLY THING I COULD THINK OF...
THE KILLER OBVIOUSLY HATES BRICK, SO THEY'D HATE THE IDEA OF US THROWING A BRICK BRANNIGAN BENEFIT CONCERT AND WOULD DO ANYTHING TO STOP IT, INCLUDING SHOWING UP TO STOP US FROM GOING ON STAGE.
I DON'T KNOW WHAT I WAS THINKING, GABE. I JUST...I JUST TRIED TO THINK OF WHAT YOU WOULD DO, BUT THIS WAS ALL I CAME UP WITH.
I SCREWED US, MAN. BRICK'S KILLER IS GOING TO GO FREE AND DALTON IS GOING TO KILL US FOR GIVING A FREE CONCERT.
I'M ALL ABOUT STICKING IT TO THE MAN, BUT I THINK I STUCK US ON ACCIDENT.
GO AHEAD. TELL ME HOW I SCREWED THINGS UP.
NO.
YOU DIDN'T SCREW THINGS UP, BIFF. YOU JUST TOOK A SITUATION YOU WEREN'T USED TO AND ADAPTED.
IT'S A GOOD PLAN. WHETHER IT WORKS OR NOT, WE WEREN'T GOING TO GET ANYWHERE WHINING ABOUT IT.
YOU DID MORE THAN I COULD HAVE DONE. YOU DID GOOD.
REALLY?
THANKS, MAN, I... THANKS.
HEY! HOW WAS THE MOVIE SHOOT? I BET YOU HAD SO MUCH FUN! I'M SO JEALOUS! IT WASN'T THAT BAD, WAS IT?
NO, BIFF, IT WAS...
...IT WAS GREAT.

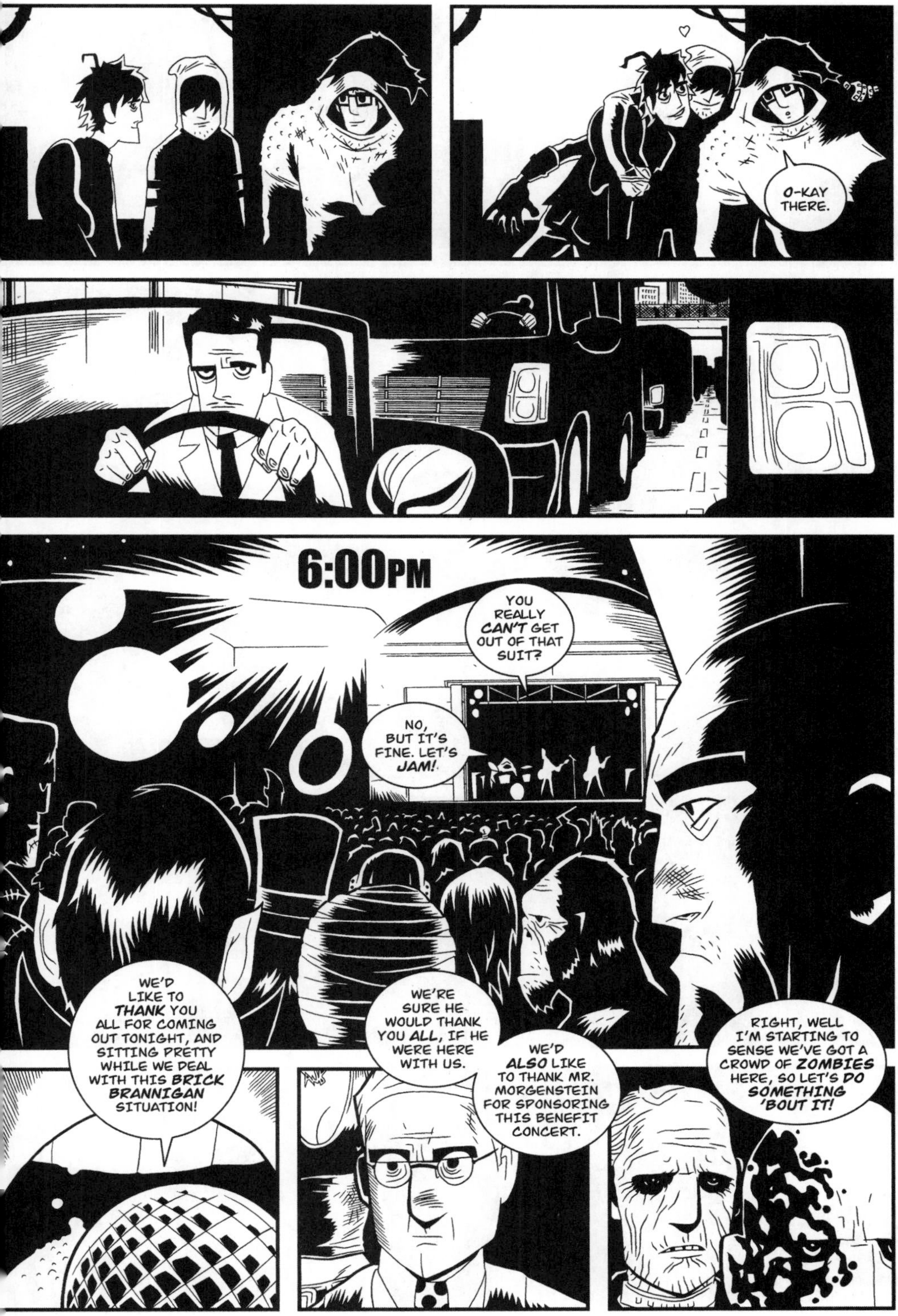
O-KAY THERE.
6:00PM
YOU REALLY CAN'T GET OUT OF THAT SUIT?
NO, BUT IT'S FINE. LET'S JAM!
WE'D LIKE TO THANK YOU ALL FOR COMING OUT TONIGHT, AND SITTING PRETTY WHILE WE DEAL WITH THIS BRICK BRANNIGAN SITUATION!
WE'RE SURE HE WOULD THANK YOU ALL, IF HE WERE HERE WITH US.
WE'D ALSO LIKE TO THANK MR. MORGENSTEIN FOR SPONSORING THIS BENEFIT CONCERT.
RIGHT, WELL I'M STARTING TO SENSE WE'VE GOT A CROWD OF ZOMBIES HERE, SO LET'S DO SOMETHING 'BOUT IT!

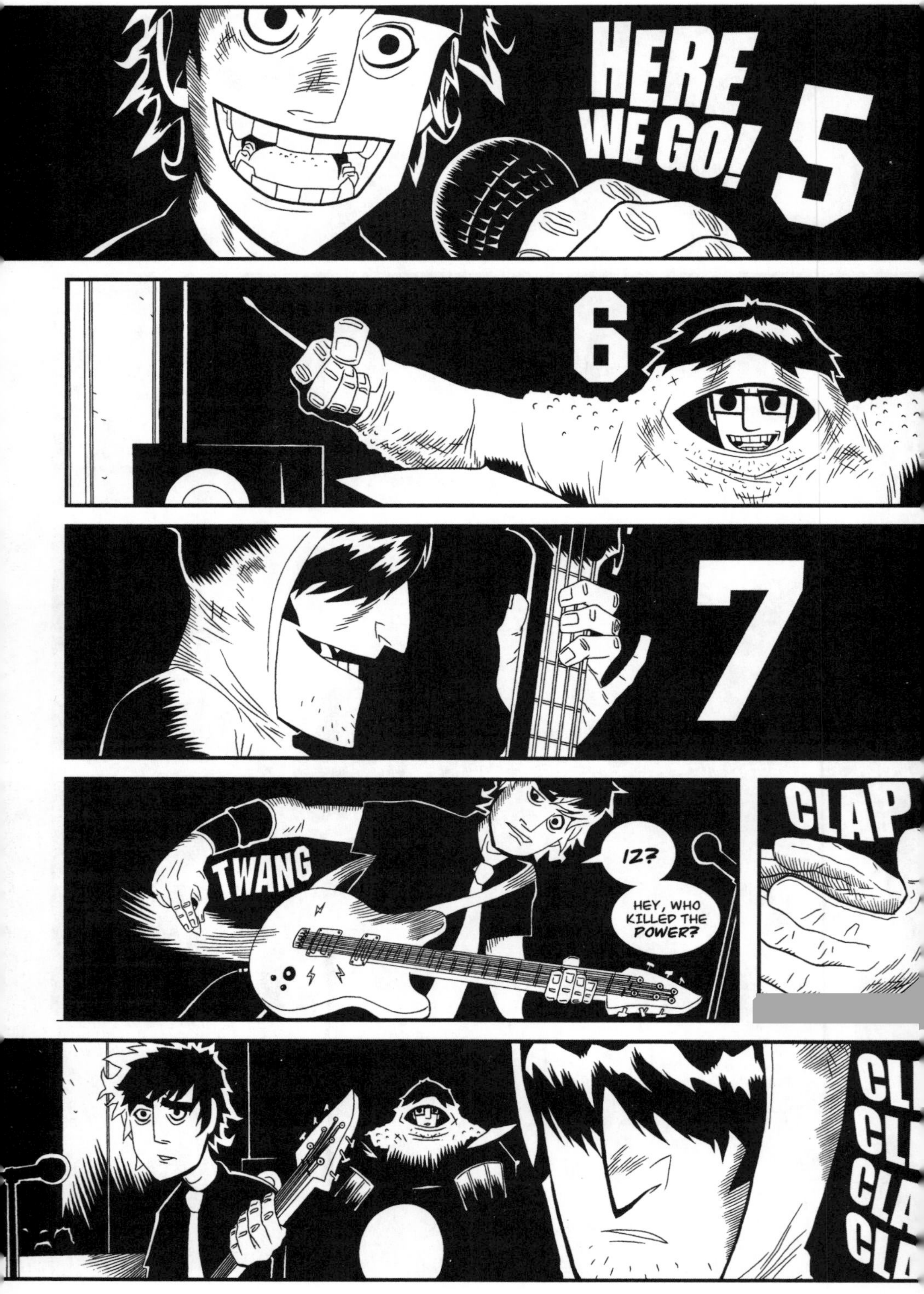
HERE WE GO!
5
6
7
TWANG
12?
HEY, WHO KILLED THE POWER?
CLAP
CL
CL
CLA
CLA

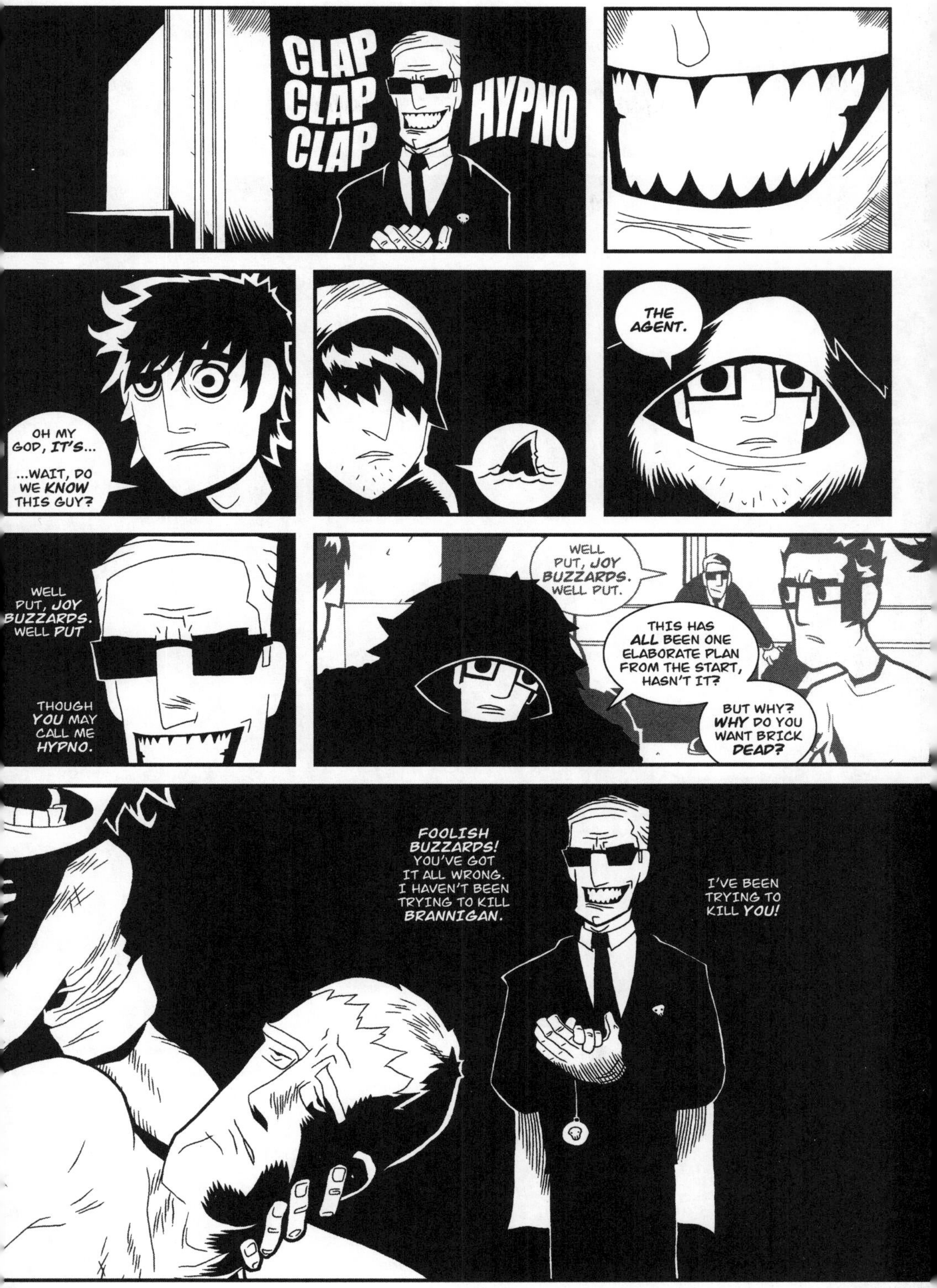
CLAP
CLAP
CLAP
HYPNO
OH MY GOD, IT'S...
...WAIT, DO WE KNOW THIS GUY?
THE AGENT.
WELL PUT, JOY BUZZARDS. WELL PUT
THOUGH YOU MAY CALL ME HYPNO.
WELL PUT, JOY BUZZARDS. WELL PUT.
THIS HAS ALL BEEN ONE ELABORATE PLAN FROM THE START, HASN'T IT?
BUT WHY? WHY DO YOU WANT BRICK DEAD?
FOOLISH BUZZARDS! YOU'VE GOT IT ALL WRONG. I HAVEN'T BEEN TRYING TO KILL BRANNIGAN.
I'VE BEEN TRYING TO KILL YOU!

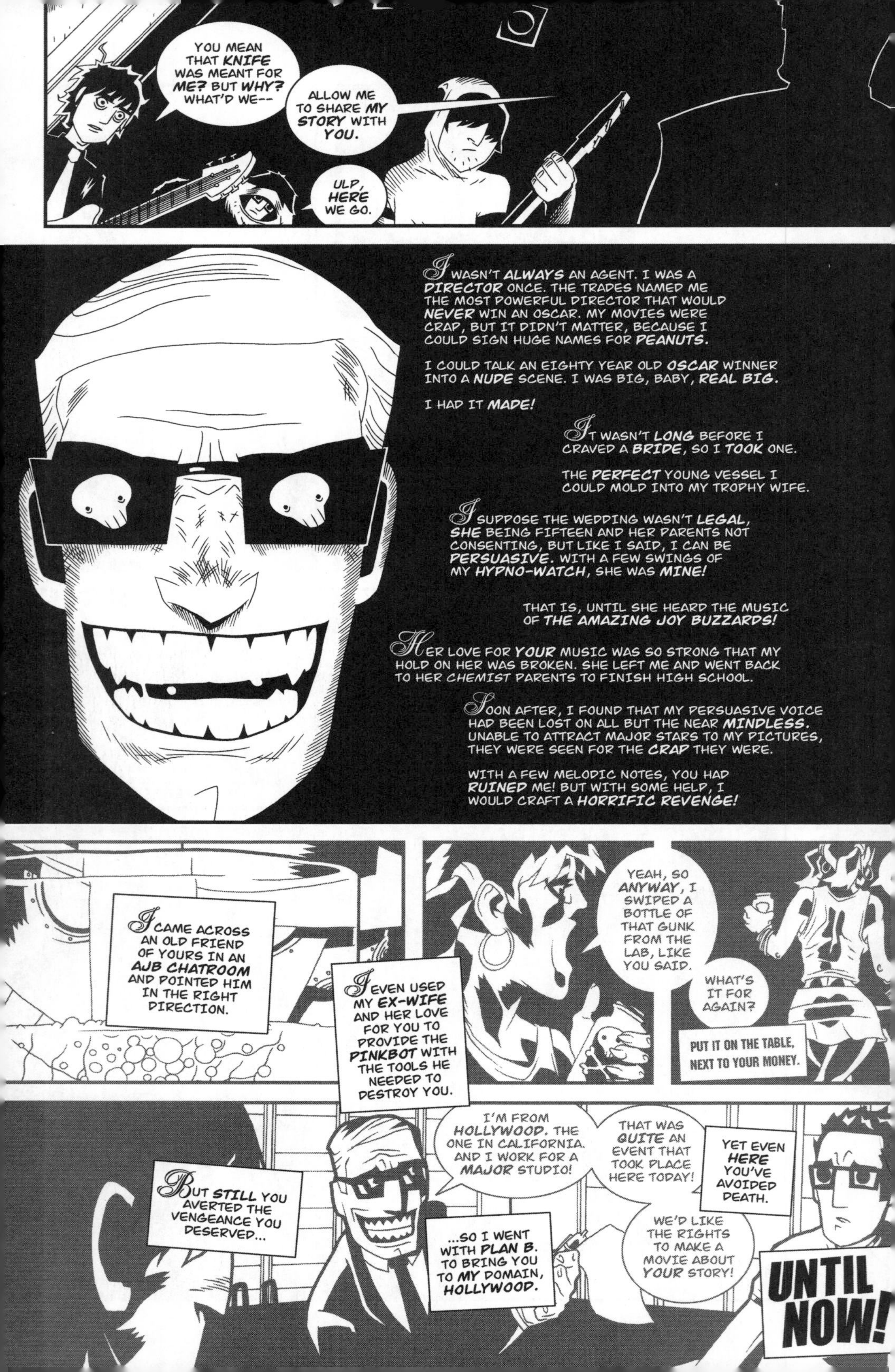

YOU MEAN THAT KNIFE WAS MEANT FOR ME? BUT WHY? WHAT'D WE--
ALLOW ME TO SHARE MY STORY WITH YOU.
ULP, HERE WE GO.
I WASN'T ALWAYS AN AGENT. I WAS A DIRECTOR ONCE. THE TRADES NAMED ME THE MOST POWERFUL DIRECTOR THAT WOULD NEVER WIN AN OSCAR. MY MOVIES WERE CRAP, BUT IT DIDN'T MATTER, BECAUSE I COULD SIGN HUGE NAMES FOR PEANUTS.
I COULD TALK AN EIGHTY YEAR OLD OSCAR WINNER INTO A NUDE SCENE. I WAS BIG, BABY, REAL BIG.
I HAD IT MADE!
IT WASN'T LONG BEFORE I CRAVED A BRIDE, SO I TOOK ONE.
THE PERFECT YOUNG VESSEL I COULD MOLD INTO MY TROPHY WIFE.
I SUPPOSE THE WEDDING WASN'T LEGAL, SHE BEING FIFTEEN AND HER PARENTS NOT CONSENTING, BUT LIKE I SAID, I CAN BE PERSUASIVE. WITH A FEW SWINGS OF MY HYPNO-WATCH, SHE WAS MINE!
THAT IS, UNTIL SHE HEARD THE MUSIC OF THE AMAZING JOY BUZZARDS!
HER LOVE FOR YOUR MUSIC WAS SO STRONG THAT MY HOLD ON HER WAS BROKEN. SHE LEFT ME AND WENT BACK TO HER CHEMIST PARENTS TO FINISH HIGH SCHOOL.
SOON AFTER, I FOUND THAT MY PERSUASIVE VOICE HAD BEEN LOST ON ALL BUT THE NEAR MINDLESS. UNABLE TO ATTRACT MAJOR STARS TO MY PICTURES, THEY WERE SEEN FOR THE CRAP THEY WERE.
WITH A FEW MELODIC NOTES, YOU HAD RUINED ME! BUT WITH SOME HELP, I WOULD CRAFT A HORRIFIC REVENGE!
I CAME ACROSS AN OLD FRIEND OF YOURS IN AN AJB CHATROOM AND POINTED HIM IN THE RIGHT DIRECTION.
I EVEN USED MY EX-WIFE AND HER LOVE FOR YOU TO PROVIDE THE PINKBOT WITH THE TOOLS HE NEEDED TO DESTROY YOU.
YEAH, SO ANYWAY, I SWIPED A BOTTLE OF THAT GUNK FROM THE LAB, LIKE YOU SAID.
WHAT'S IT FOR AGAIN?
PUT IT ON THE TABLE, NEXT TO YOUR MONEY.
BUT STILL YOU AVERTED THE VENGEANCE YOU DESERVED...
...SO I WENT WITH PLAN B. TO BRING YOU TO MY DOMAIN, HOLLYWOOD.
I'M FROM HOLLYWOOD. THE ONE IN CALIFORNIA. AND I WORK FOR A MAJOR STUDIO!
THAT WAS QUITE AN EVENT THAT TOOK PLACE HERE TODAY!
WE'D LIKE THE RIGHTS TO MAKE A MOVIE ABOUT YOUR STORY!
YET EVEN HERE YOU'VE AVOIDED DEATH.
UNTIL NOW!

POOR. BRICK.

(POOR PINKBOT)

POOR YOU, PAL!

DO YOU HAVE **ANY** IDEA WHAT YOU'VE DONE TO **BRICK**, OR **PINKBOT**, OR **THAT GIRL**, FOR CRYING OUT LOUD?!

I MEAN, **FIFTEEN** YEARS OLD?! **SICK!**

YOU SAY PO-TAY-TO, **I** SAY PO-TA-TO.

I'VE HAD JUST ABOUT ALL I CAN TAKE FROM YOU, **HYPNO-CRAZY-GUY!**

DID YOU THINK YOU'D JUST **STROLL** ON STAGE AT A **PACKED** CONCERT, ANNOUNCE YOUR PLANS TO **KILL** US AND EXPECT US **OR OUR FANS** TO STAND BY WHILE YOU DID YOUR BUSINESS?!

I DON'T THINK SO, BUDDY!

I'VE ALREADY WADED THROUGH **ENOUGH** CRAP TODAY, MISTER, AND I'M **NOT** ABOUT TO TAKE A STEP INTO **YOURS!**

UH, BIFF.

BIFF.

IT'S TIME FOR A--

BIFF!

WHAT, GABE?! WHAT?!

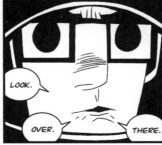

LOOK.

OVER.

THERE.

OH.

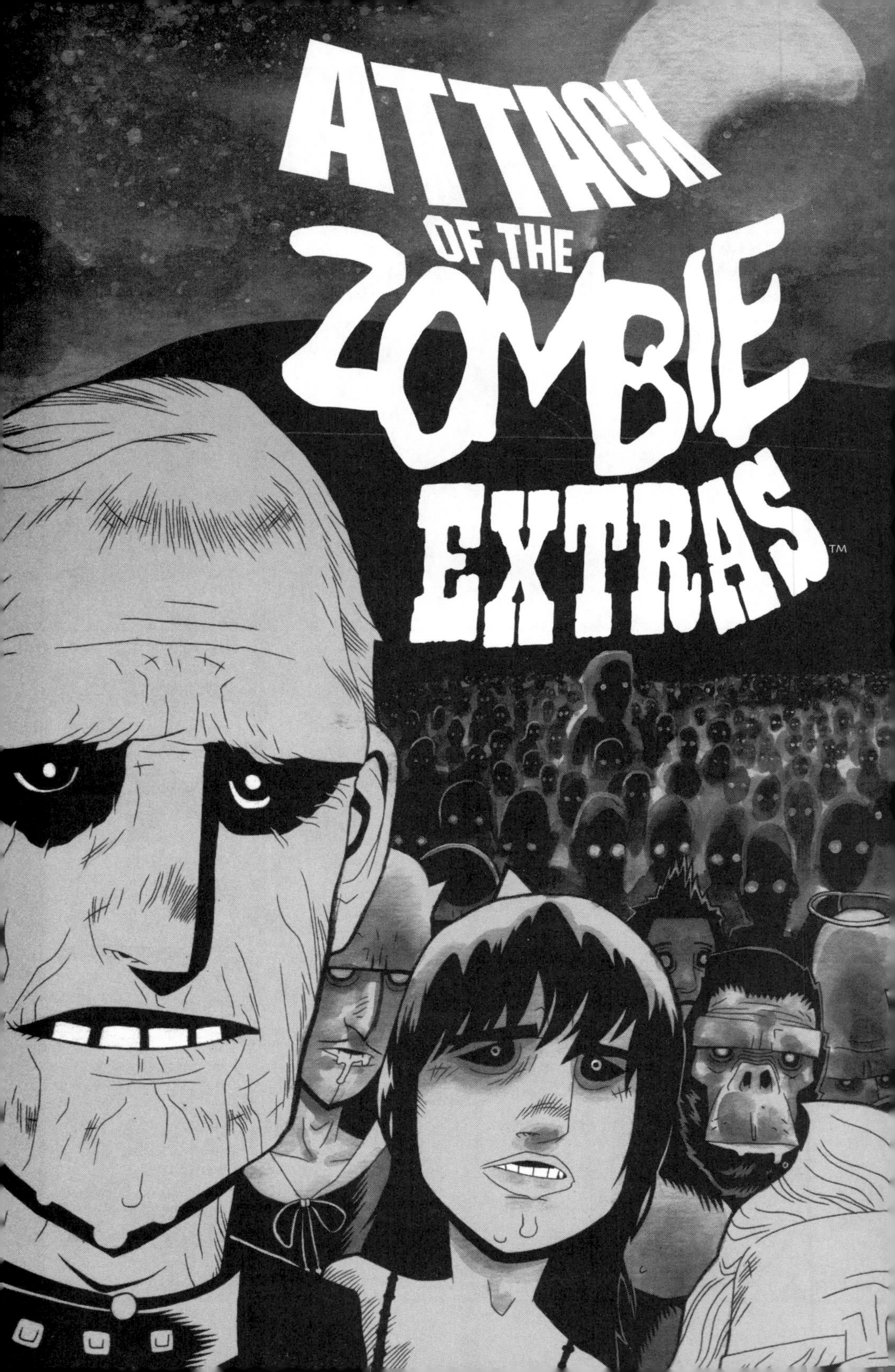
ATTACK
OF THE
ZOMBIE
EXTRAS™

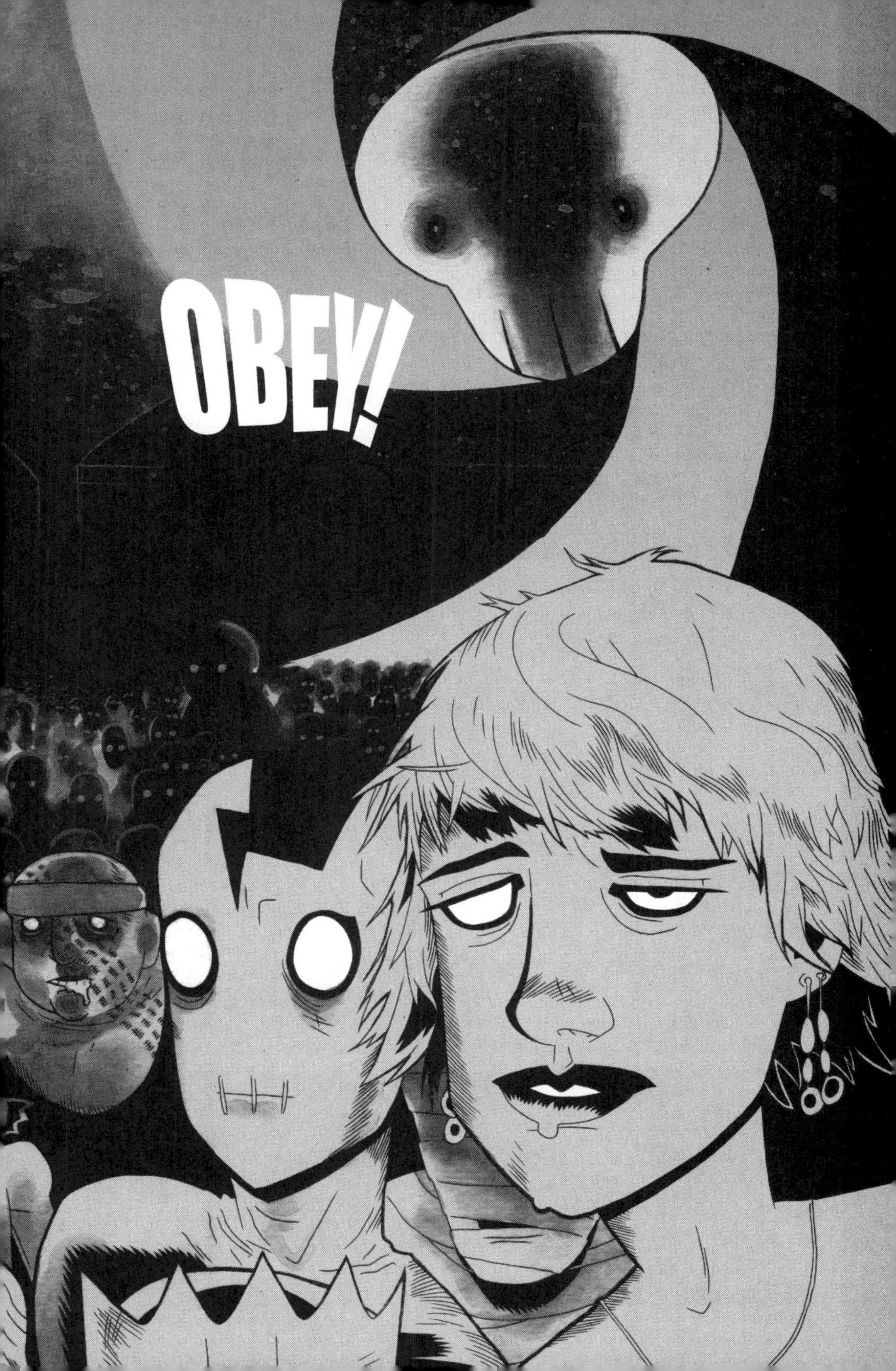
OBEY!

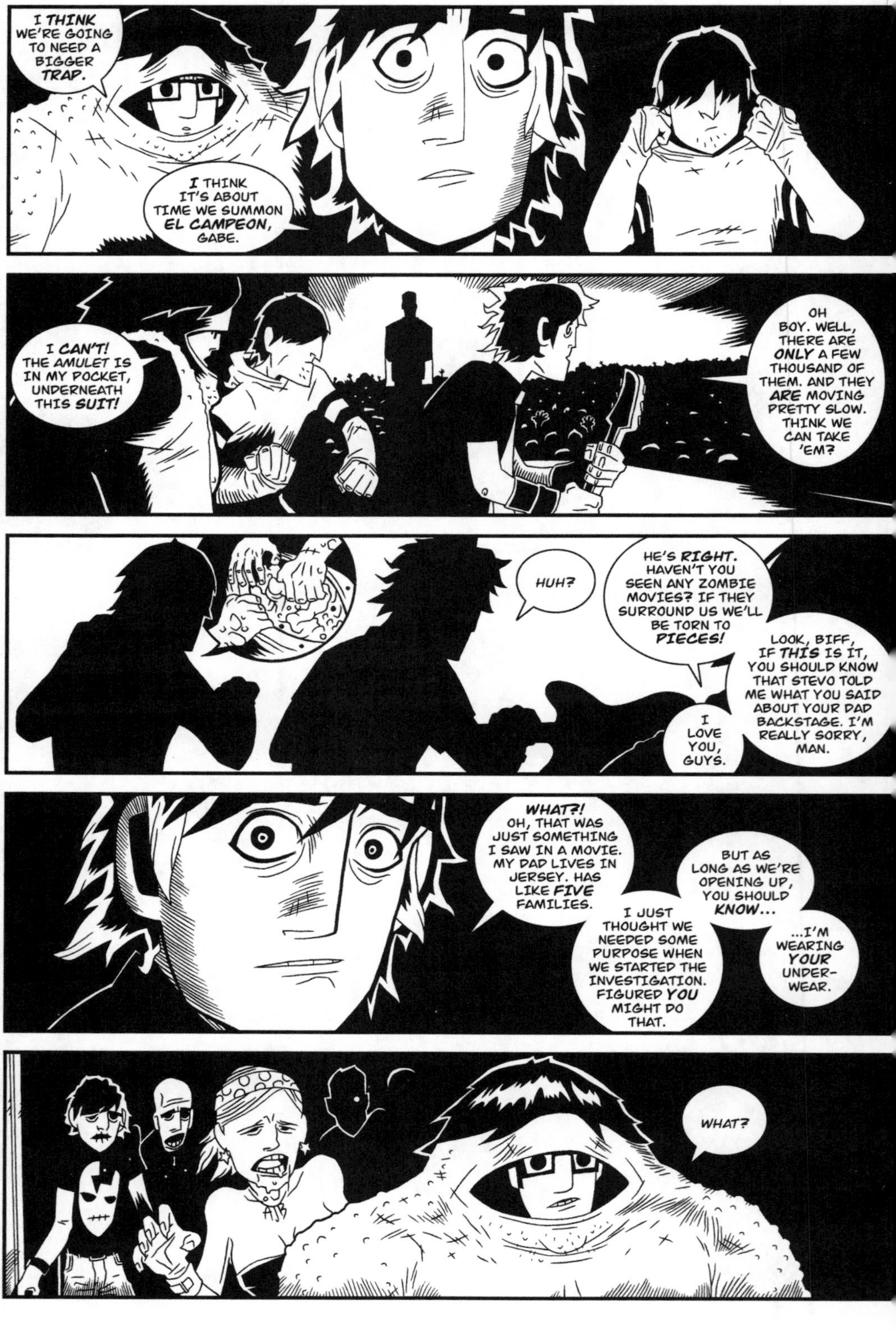
I THINK WE'RE GOING TO NEED A BIGGER TRAP.
I THINK IT'S ABOUT TIME WE SUMMON EL CAMPEON, GABE.
I CAN'T! THE AMULET IS IN MY POCKET, UNDERNEATH THIS SUIT!
OH BOY. WELL, THERE ARE ONLY A FEW THOUSAND OF THEM. AND THEY ARE MOVING PRETTY SLOW. THINK WE CAN TAKE 'EM?
HUH?
HE'S RIGHT. HAVEN'T YOU SEEN ANY ZOMBIE MOVIES? IF THEY SURROUND US WE'LL BE TORN TO PIECES!
I LOVE YOU, GUYS.
LOOK, BIFF, IF THIS IS IT, YOU SHOULD KNOW THAT STEVO TOLD ME WHAT YOU SAID ABOUT YOUR DAD BACKSTAGE. I'M REALLY SORRY, MAN.
WHAT?! OH, THAT WAS JUST SOMETHING I SAW IN A MOVIE. MY DAD LIVES IN JERSEY. HAS LIKE FIVE FAMILIES.
I JUST THOUGHT WE NEEDED SOME PURPOSE WHEN WE STARTED THE INVESTIGATION. FIGURED YOU MIGHT DO THAT.
BUT AS LONG AS WE'RE OPENING UP, YOU SHOULD KNOW...
...I'M WEARING YOUR UNDER-WEAR.
WHAT?

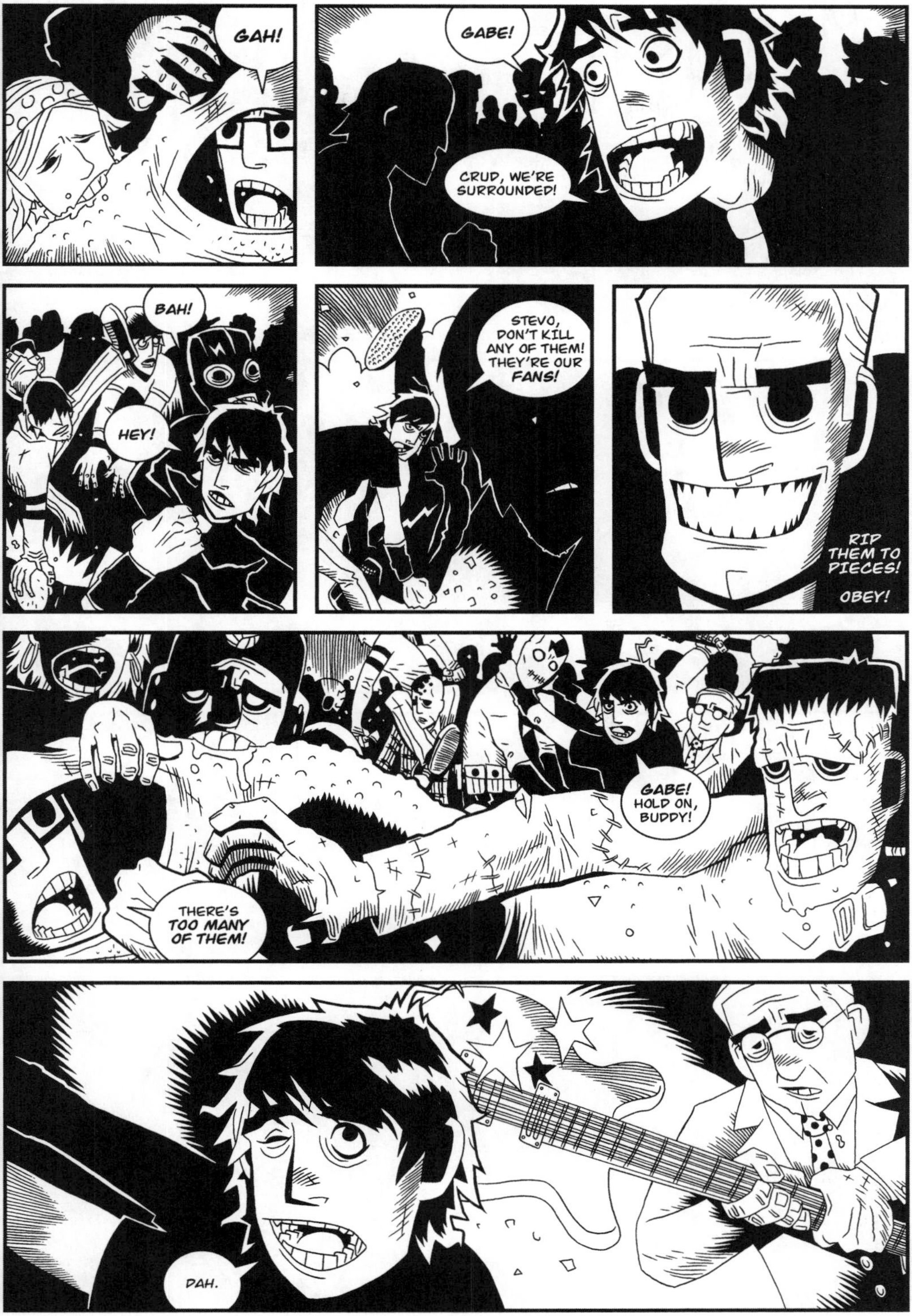
GAH!
GABE!
CRUD, WE'RE SURROUNDED!
BAH!
HEY!
STEVO, DON'T KILL ANY OF THEM! THEY'RE OUR FANS!
RIP THEM TO PIECES!
OBEY!
GABE! HOLD ON, BUDDY!
THERE'S TOO MANY OF THEM!
DAH.

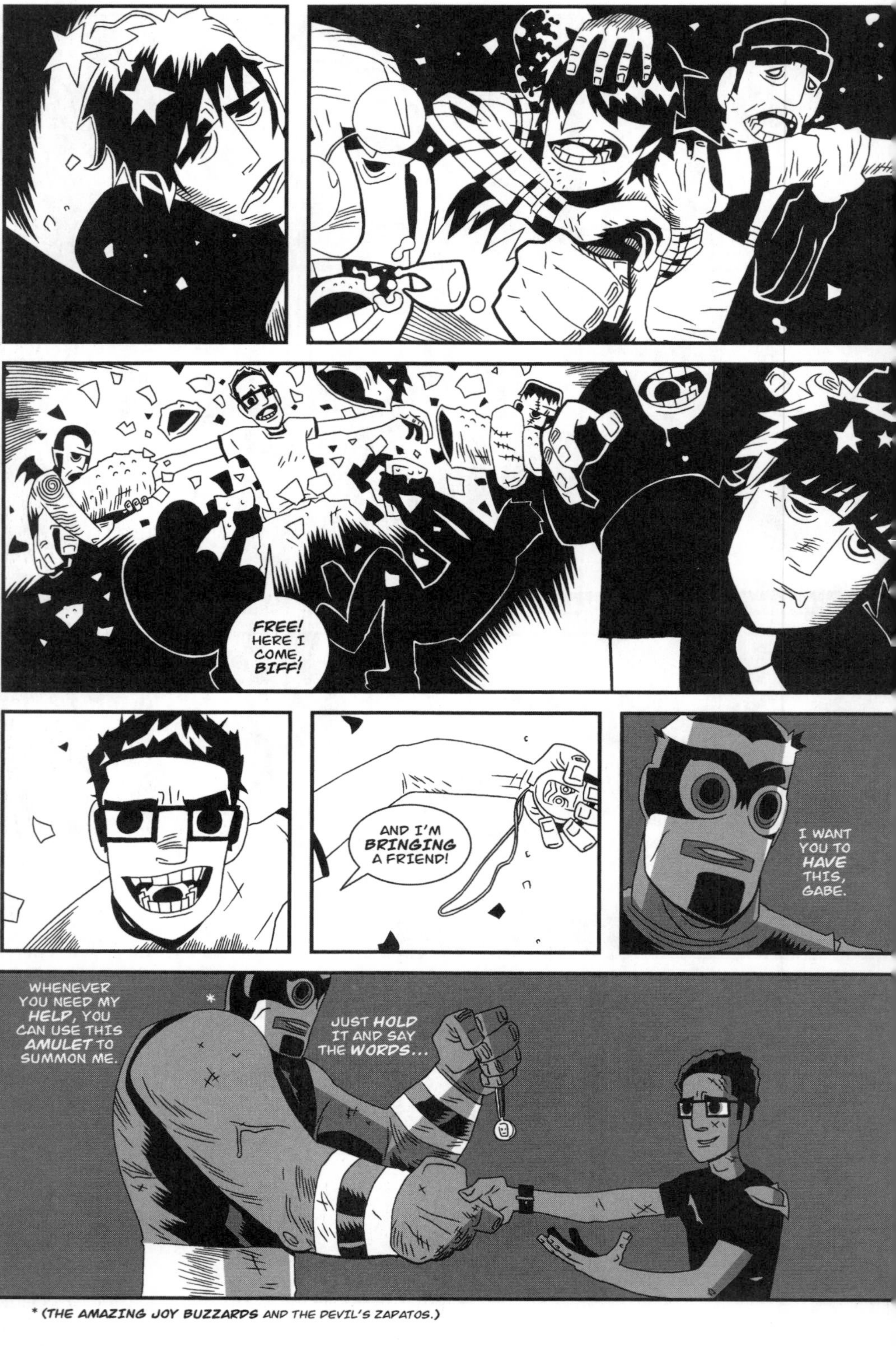
FREE! HERE I COME, BIFF!
AND I'M BRINGING A FRIEND!
I WANT YOU TO HAVE THIS, GABE.
WHENEVER YOU NEED MY HELP, YOU CAN USE THIS AMULET TO SUMMON ME.
*
JUST HOLD IT AND SAY THE WORDS...

* (THE AMAZING JOY BUZZARDS AND THE DEVIL'S ZAPATOS.)

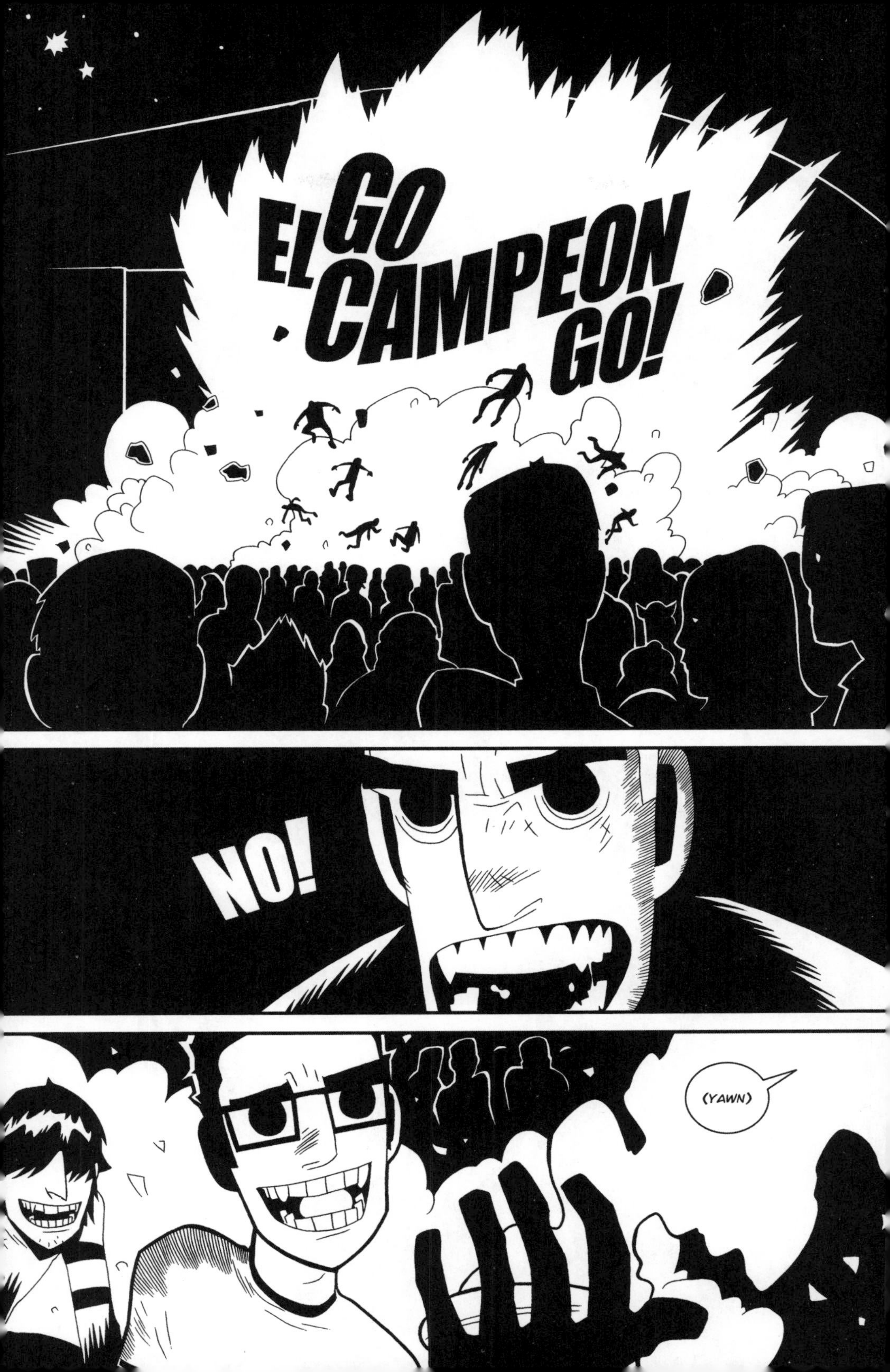
GO EL CAMPEON GO!
NO!
(YAWN)

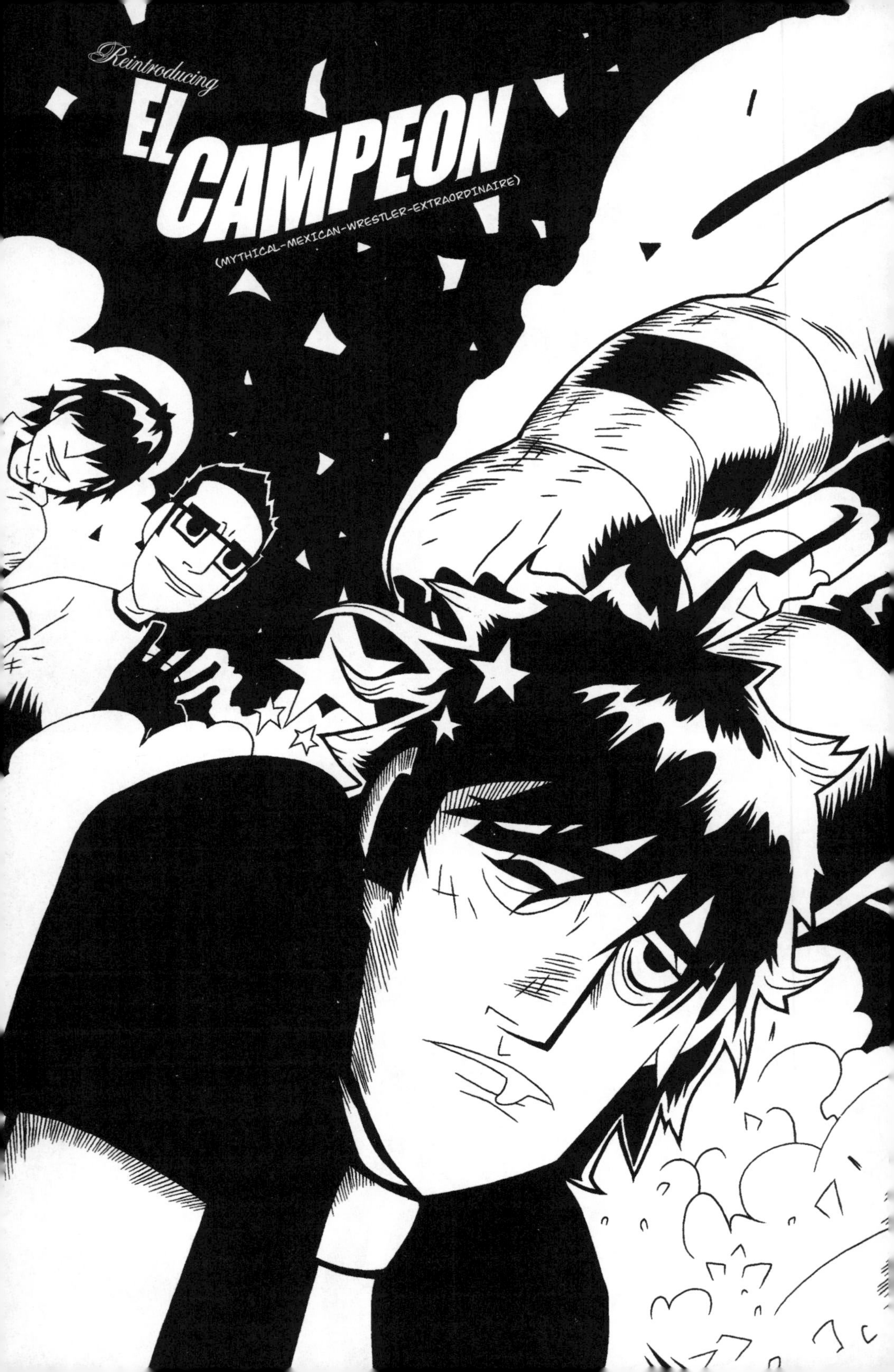
Reintroducing
EL CAMPEON
(MYTHICAL-MEXICAN-WRESTLER-EXTRAORDINAIRE)

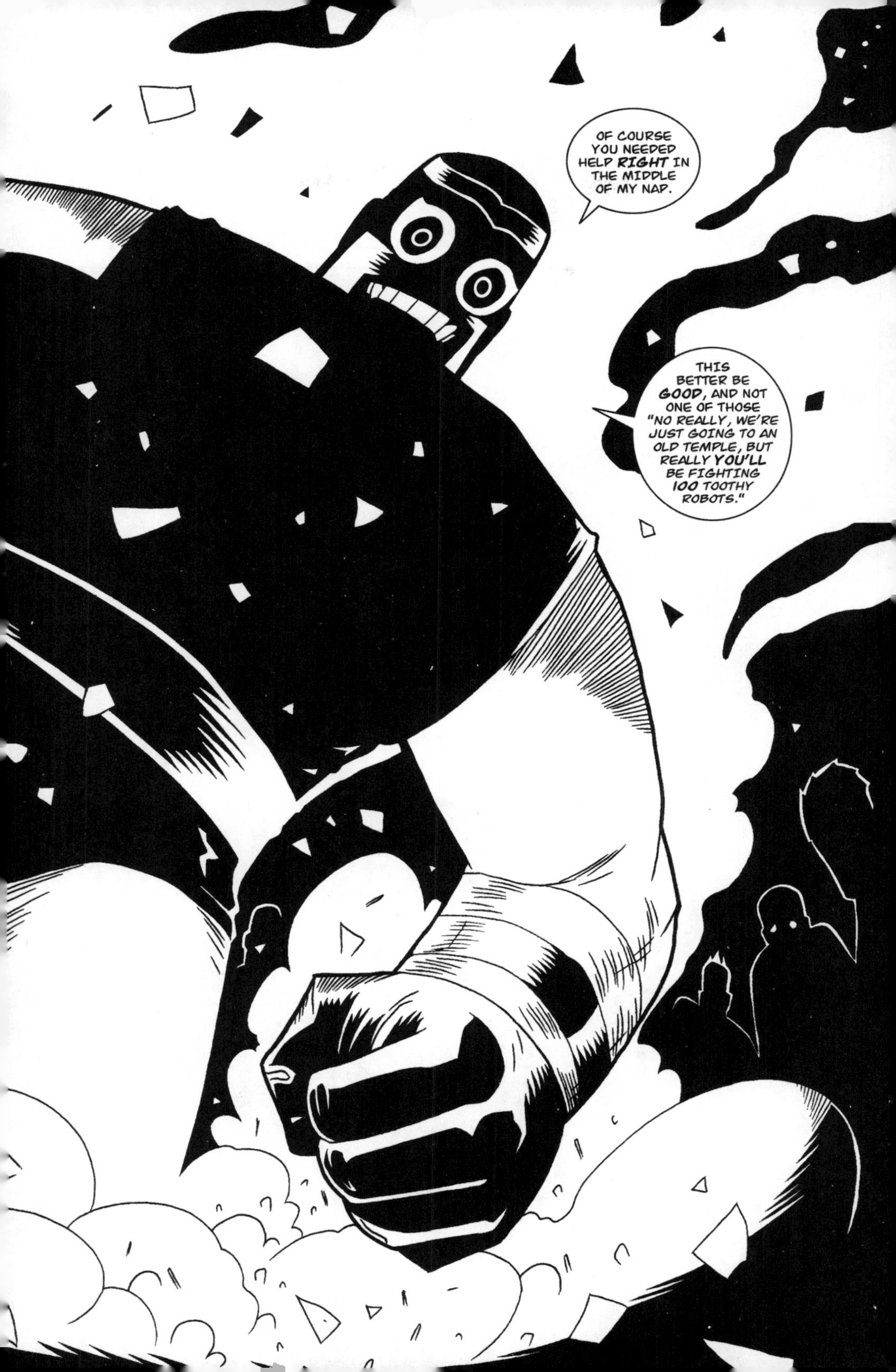
OF COURSE YOU NEEDED HELP RIGHT IN THE MIDDLE OF MY NAP.
THIS BETTER BE GOOD, AND NOT ONE OF THOSE "NO REALLY, WE'RE JUST GOING TO AN OLD TEMPLE, BUT REALLY YOU'LL BE FIGHTING 100 TOOTHY ROBOTS."

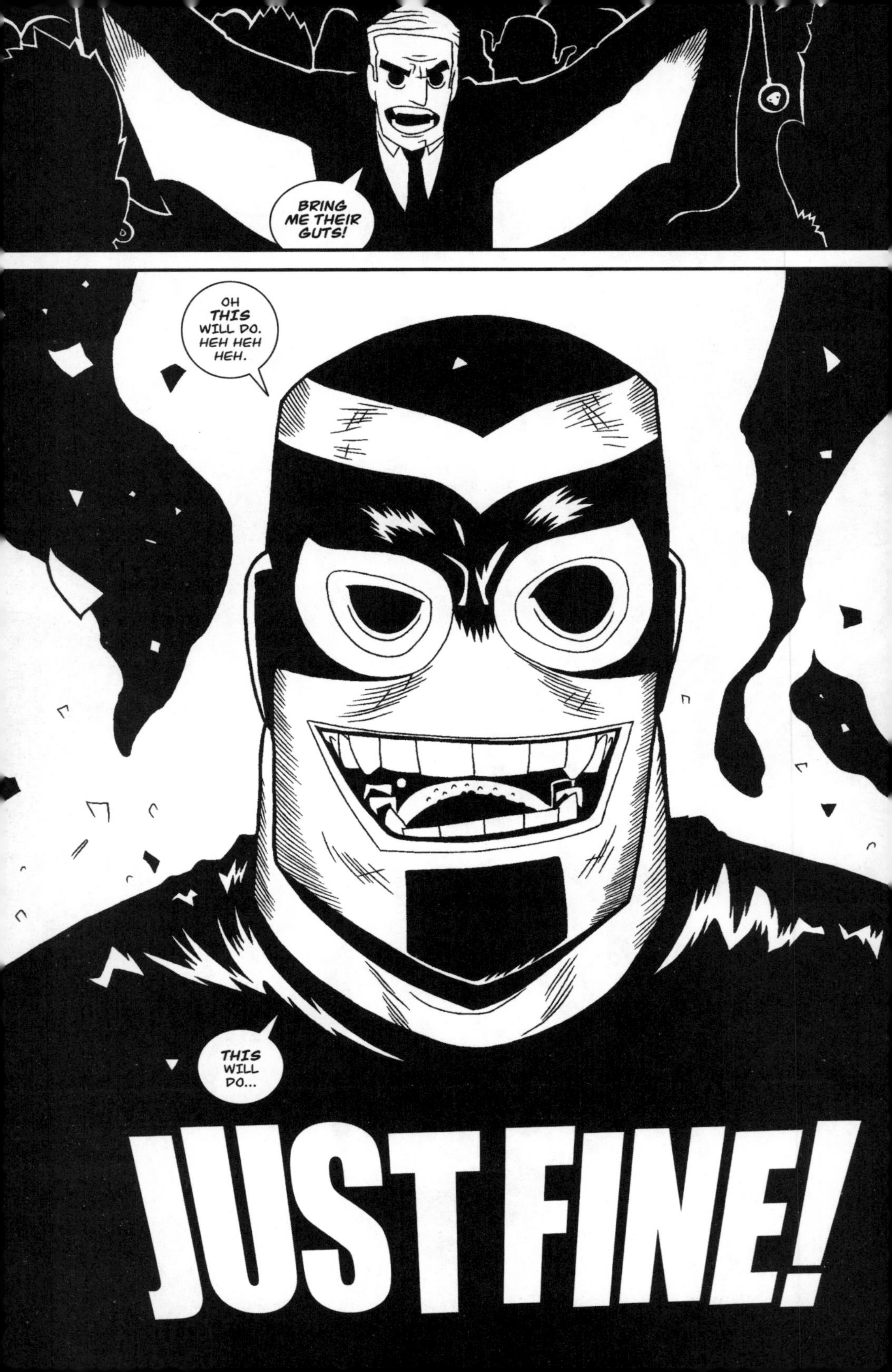
BRING ME THEIR GUTS!
OH THIS WILL DO. HEH HEH HEH.
THIS WILL DO...
JUST FINE!

Pull the car over and take a potty break...

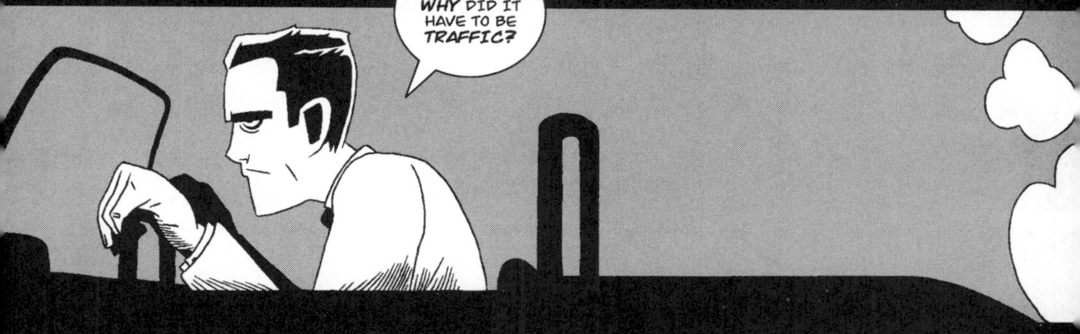
TRAFFIC. WHY DID IT HAVE TO BE TRAFFIC?

...or don't. The part 4 finale begins now.

(DIM THE LIGHTS...)

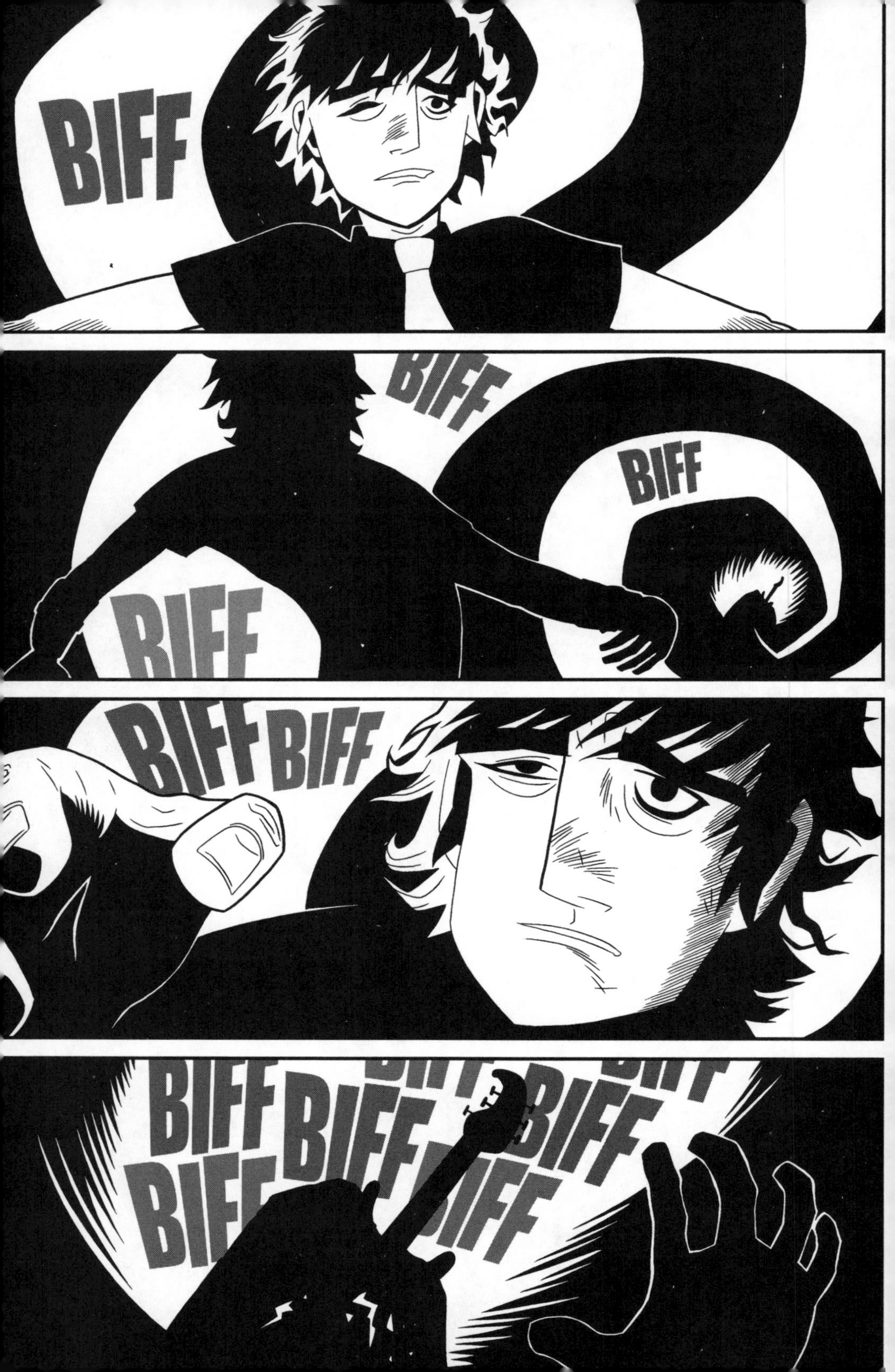
BIFF
BIFF
BIFF
BIFF
BIFF
BIFF
BIFF
BIFF
BIFF
BIFF
BIFF

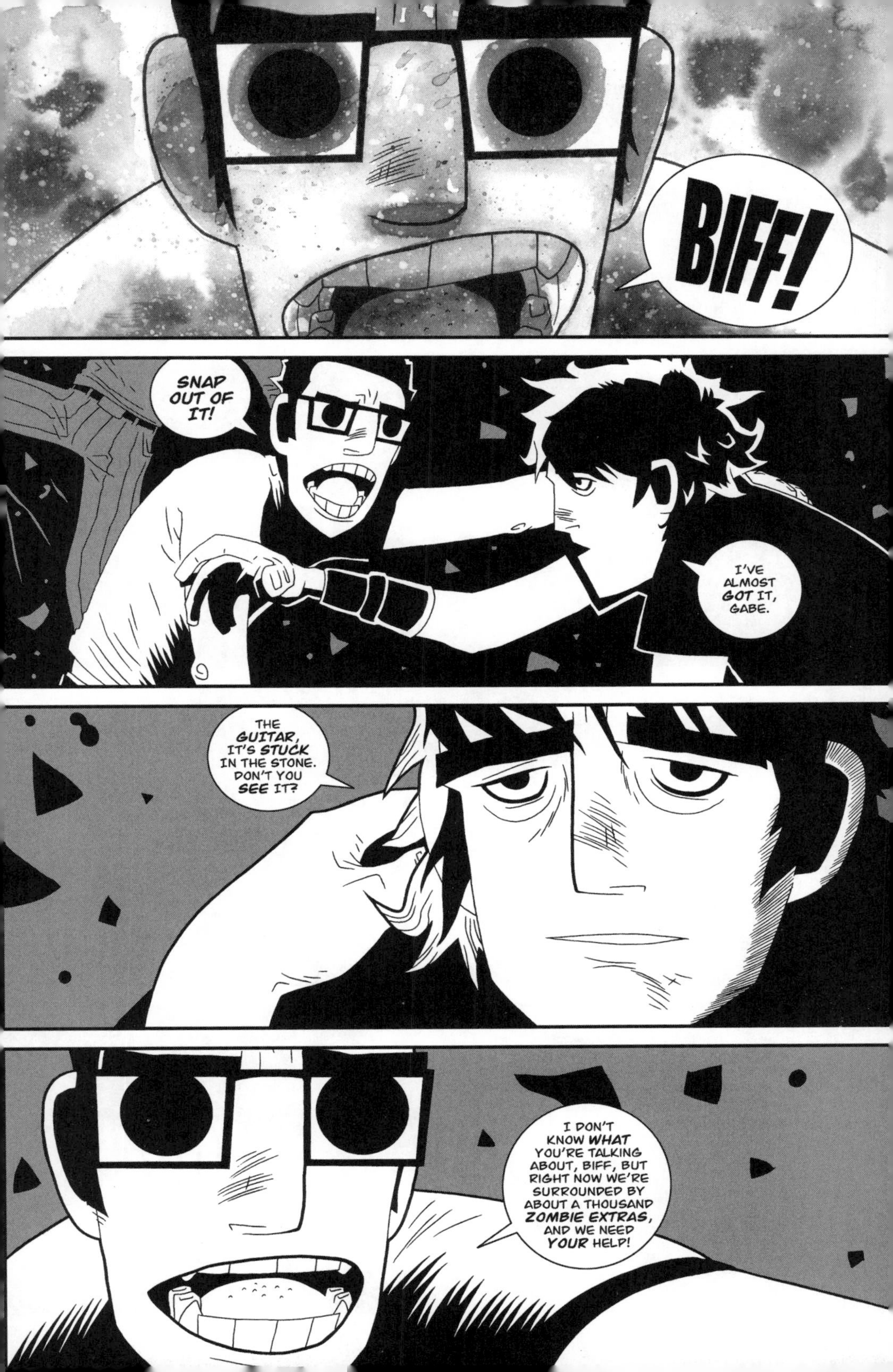
BIFF!
SNAP OUT OF IT!
I'VE ALMOST GOT IT, GABE.
THE GUITAR, IT'S STUCK IN THE STONE. DON'T YOU SEE IT?
I DON'T KNOW WHAT YOU'RE TALKING ABOUT, BIFF, BUT RIGHT NOW WE'RE SURROUNDED BY ABOUT A THOUSAND ZOMBIE EXTRAS, AND WE NEED YOUR HELP!

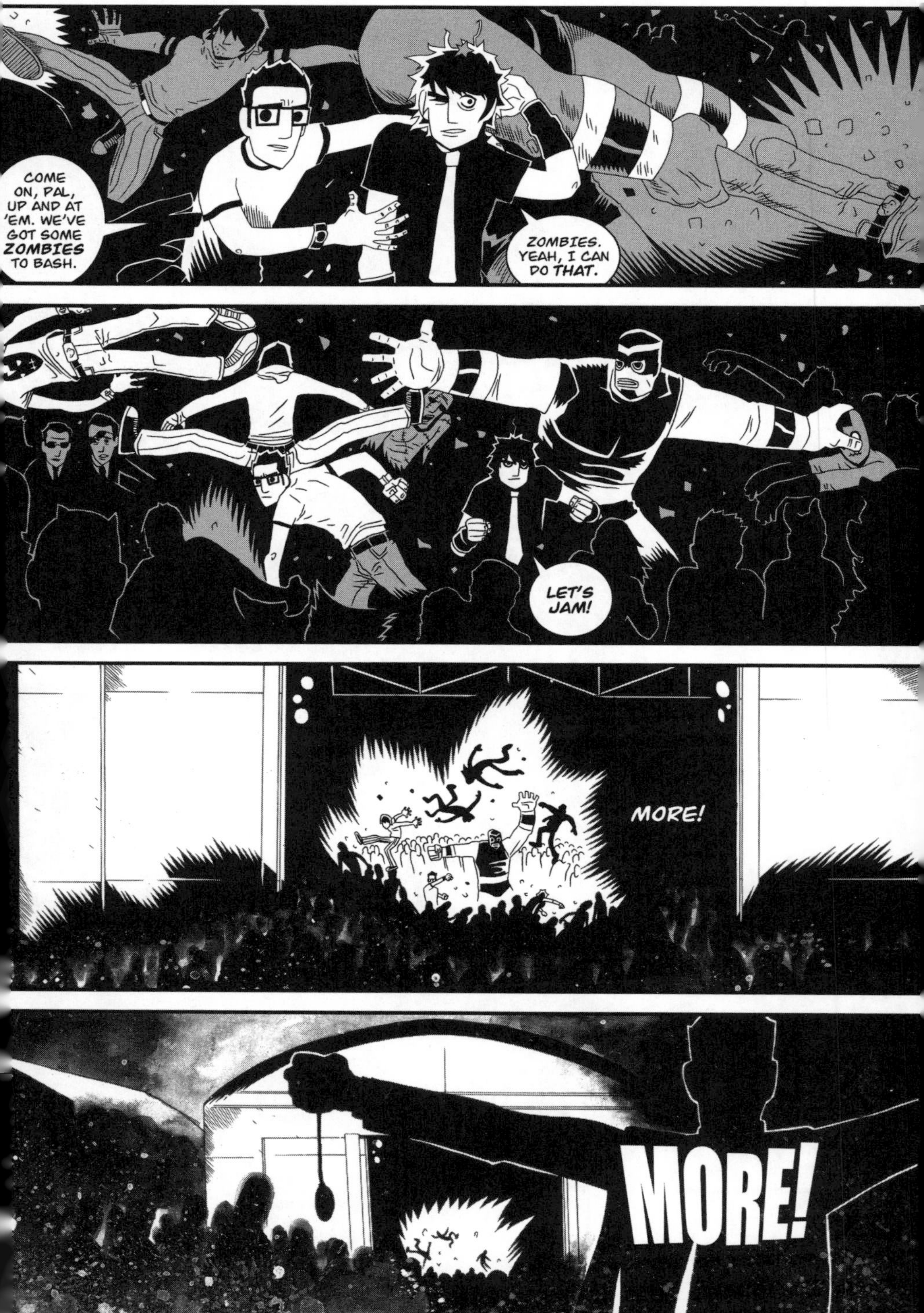

COME ON, PAL, UP AND AT 'EM. WE'VE GOT SOME ZOMBIES TO BASH.
ZOMBIES. YEAH, I CAN DO THAT.
LET'S JAM!
MORE!
MORE!

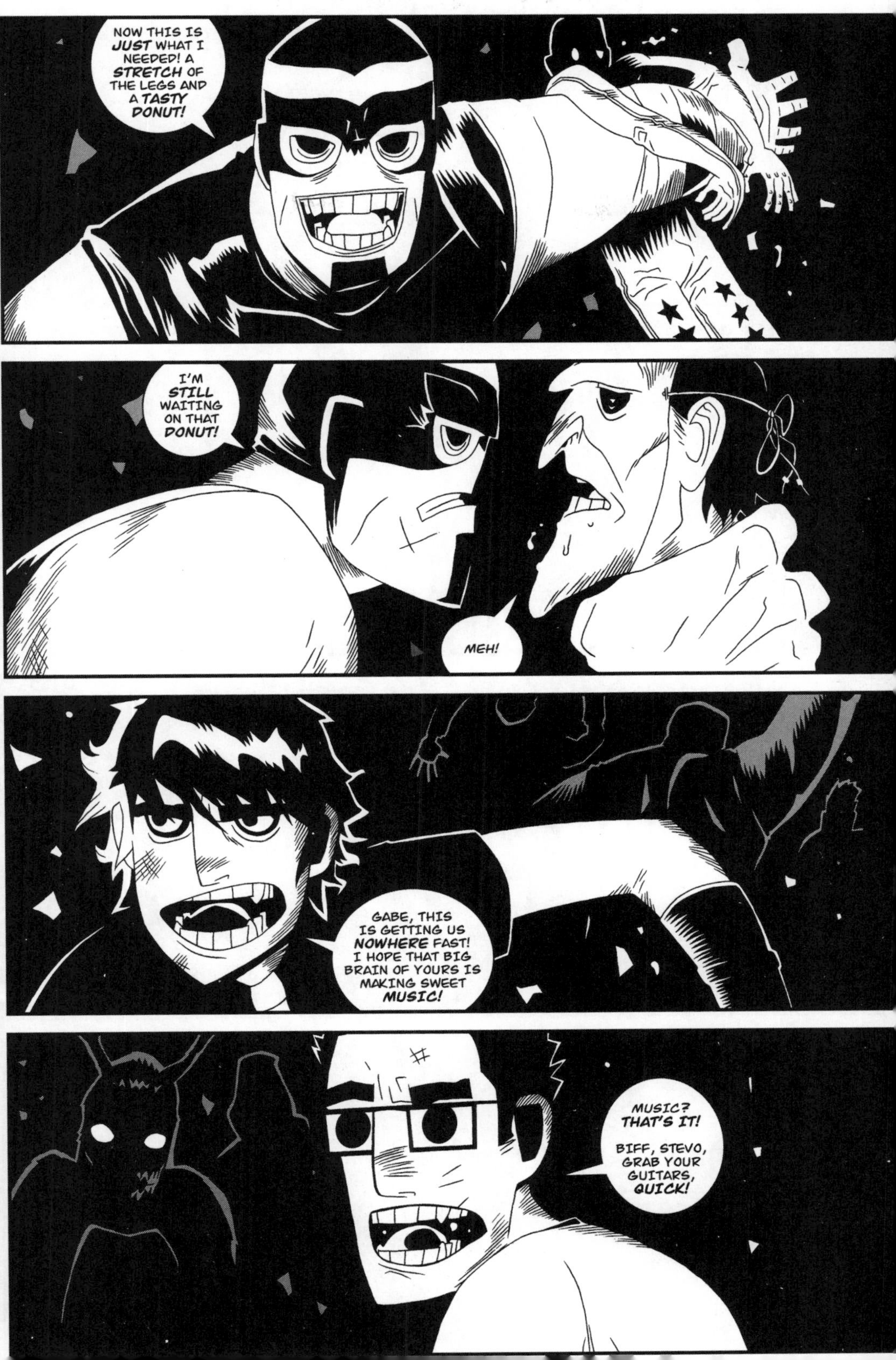
NOW THIS IS JUST WHAT I NEEDED! A STRETCH OF THE LEGS AND A TASTY DONUT!
I'M STILL WAITING ON THAT DONUT!
MEH!
GABE, THIS IS GETTING US NOWHERE FAST! I HOPE THAT BIG BRAIN OF YOURS IS MAKING SWEET MUSIC!
MUSIC? THAT'S IT!
BIFF, STEVO, GRAB YOUR GUITARS, QUICK!

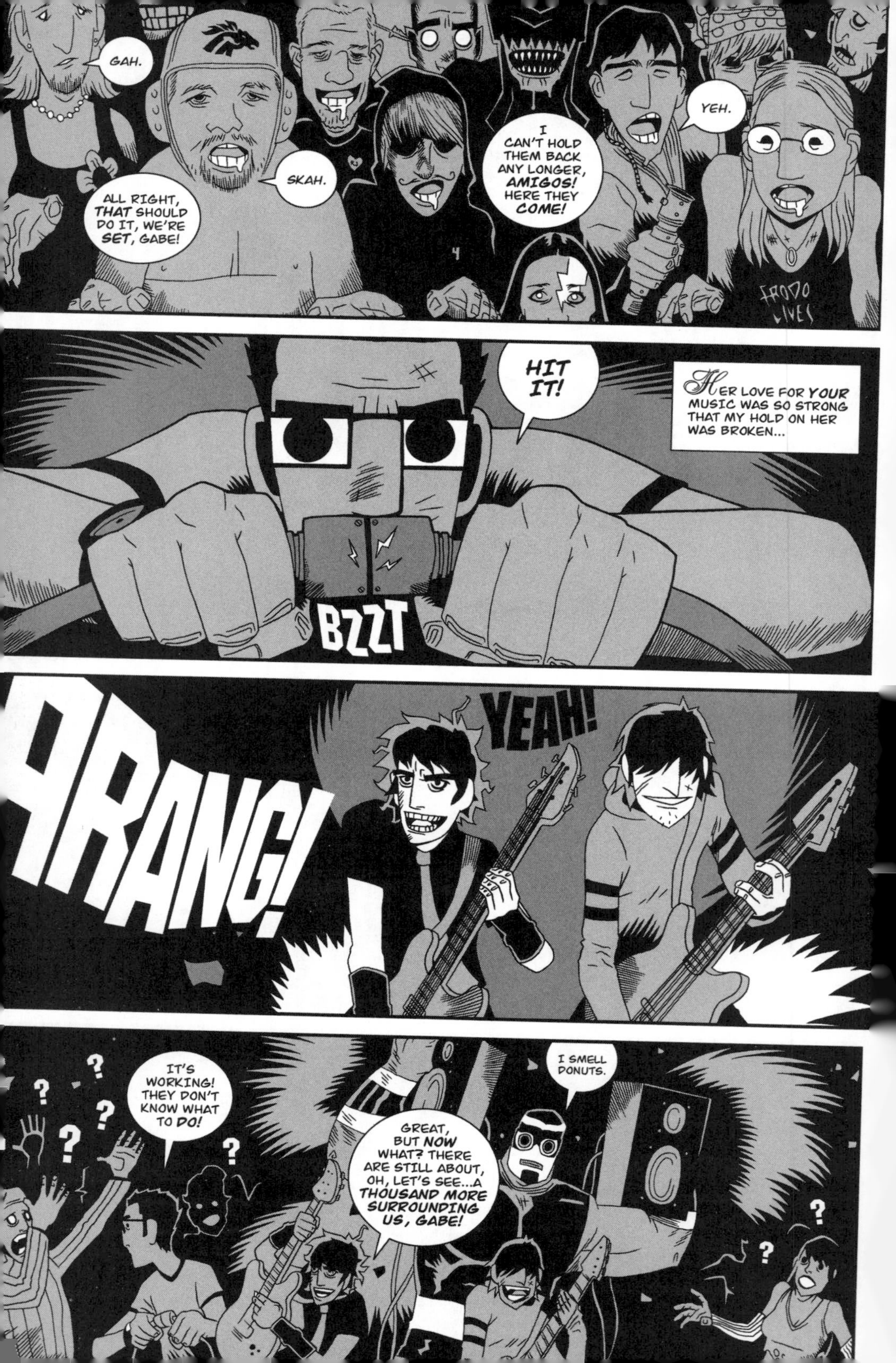
GAH.
SKAH.
ALL RIGHT, THAT SHOULD DO IT, WE'RE SET, GABE!
I CAN'T HOLD THEM BACK ANY LONGER, AMIGOS! HERE THEY COME!
YEH.
FRODO LIVES
HIT IT!
HER LOVE FOR YOUR MUSIC WAS SO STRONG THAT MY HOLD ON HER WAS BROKEN...
BZZT
BRANG!
YEAH!
IT'S WORKING! THEY DON'T KNOW WHAT TO DO!
GREAT, BUT NOW WHAT? THERE ARE STILL ABOUT, OH, LET'S SEE...A THOUSAND MORE SURROUNDING US, GABE!
I SMELL DONUTS.

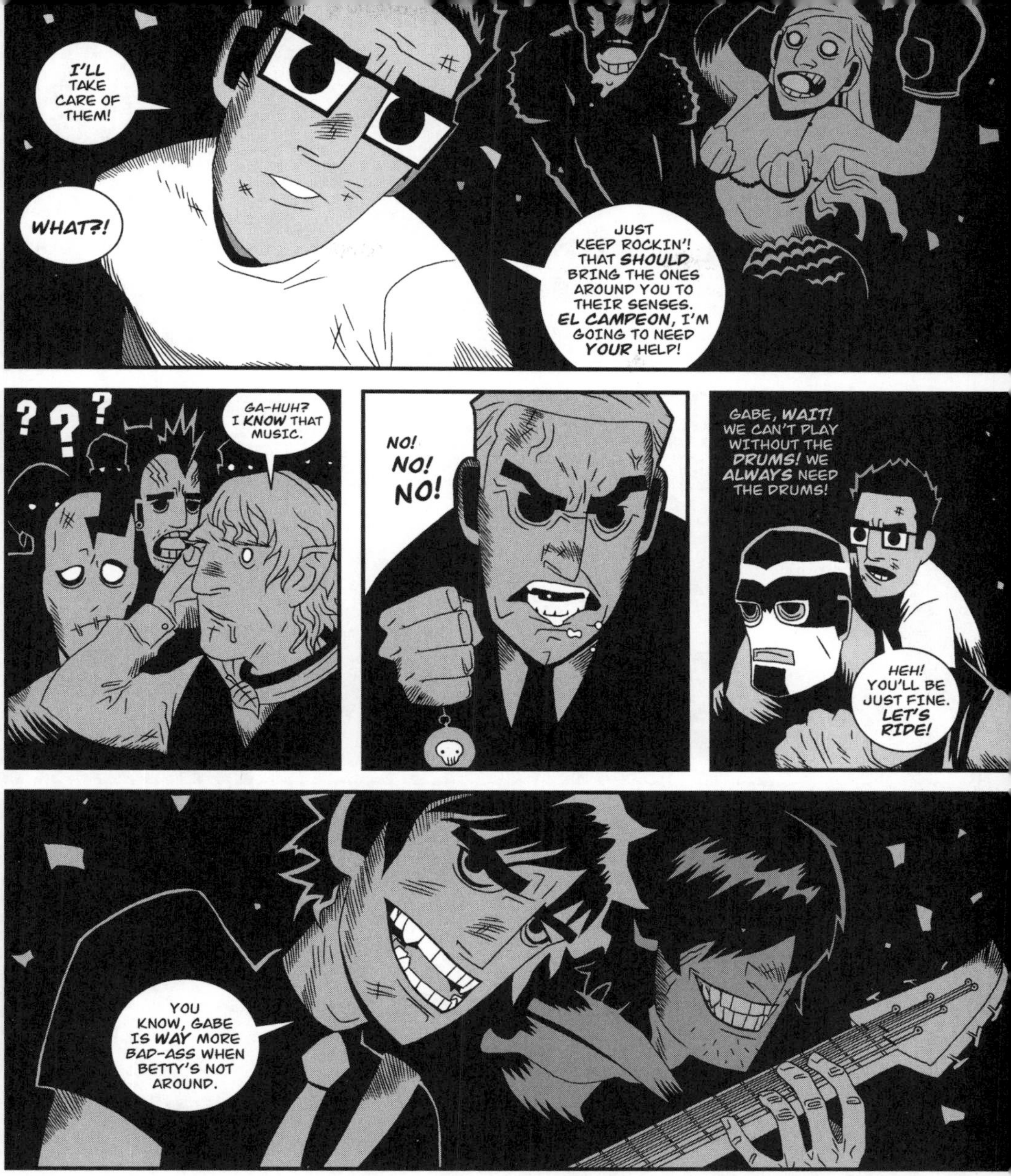
I'LL TAKE CARE OF THEM!
WHAT?!
JUST KEEP ROCKIN'! THAT SHOULD BRING THE ONES AROUND YOU TO THEIR SENSES. EL CAMPEON, I'M GOING TO NEED YOUR HELP!
???
GA-HUH? I KNOW THAT MUSIC.
NO! NO! NO!
GABE, WAIT! WE CAN'T PLAY WITHOUT THE DRUMS! WE ALWAYS NEED THE DRUMS!
HEH! YOU'LL BE JUST FINE. LET'S RIDE!
YOU KNOW, GABE IS WAY MORE BAD-ASS WHEN BETTY'S NOT AROUND.

Dear Betty,
You were right, Hollywood isn't the slice of paradise I'd hoped it might be. Tabloids have us wishing we were part of this world, but it seems at the cost of your soul.

Being a part of this band has been an incredible experience. I won't squander it by becoming a zombie drone of any industry.

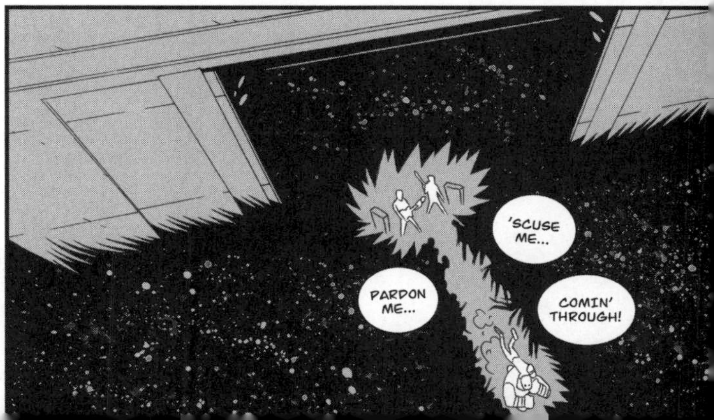
'SCUSE ME...
PARDON ME...
COMIN' THROUGH!

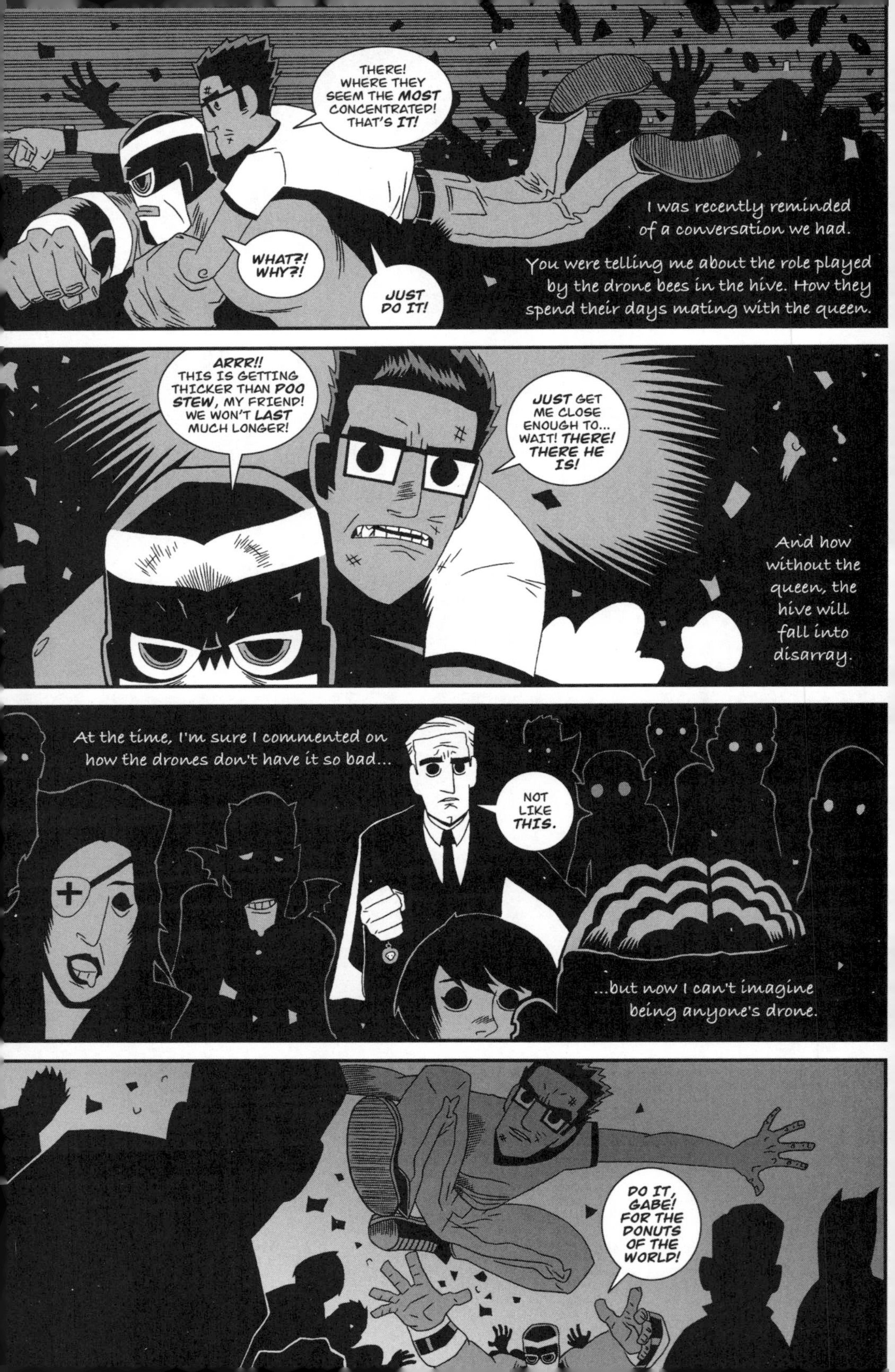
THERE! WHERE THEY SEEM THE MOST CONCENTRATED! THAT'S IT!
WHAT?! WHY?!
JUST DO IT!
I was recently reminded of a conversation we had.
You were telling me about the role played by the drone bees in the hive. How they spend their days mating with the queen.
ARRR!! THIS IS GETTING THICKER THAN POO STEW, MY FRIEND! WE WON'T LAST MUCH LONGER!
JUST GET ME CLOSE ENOUGH TO... WAIT! THERE! THERE HE IS!
And how without the queen, the hive will fall into disarray.
At the time, I'm sure I commented on how the drones don't have it so bad...
NOT LIKE THIS.
...but now I can't imagine being anyone's drone.
DO IT, GABE! FOR THE DONUTS OF THE WORLD!

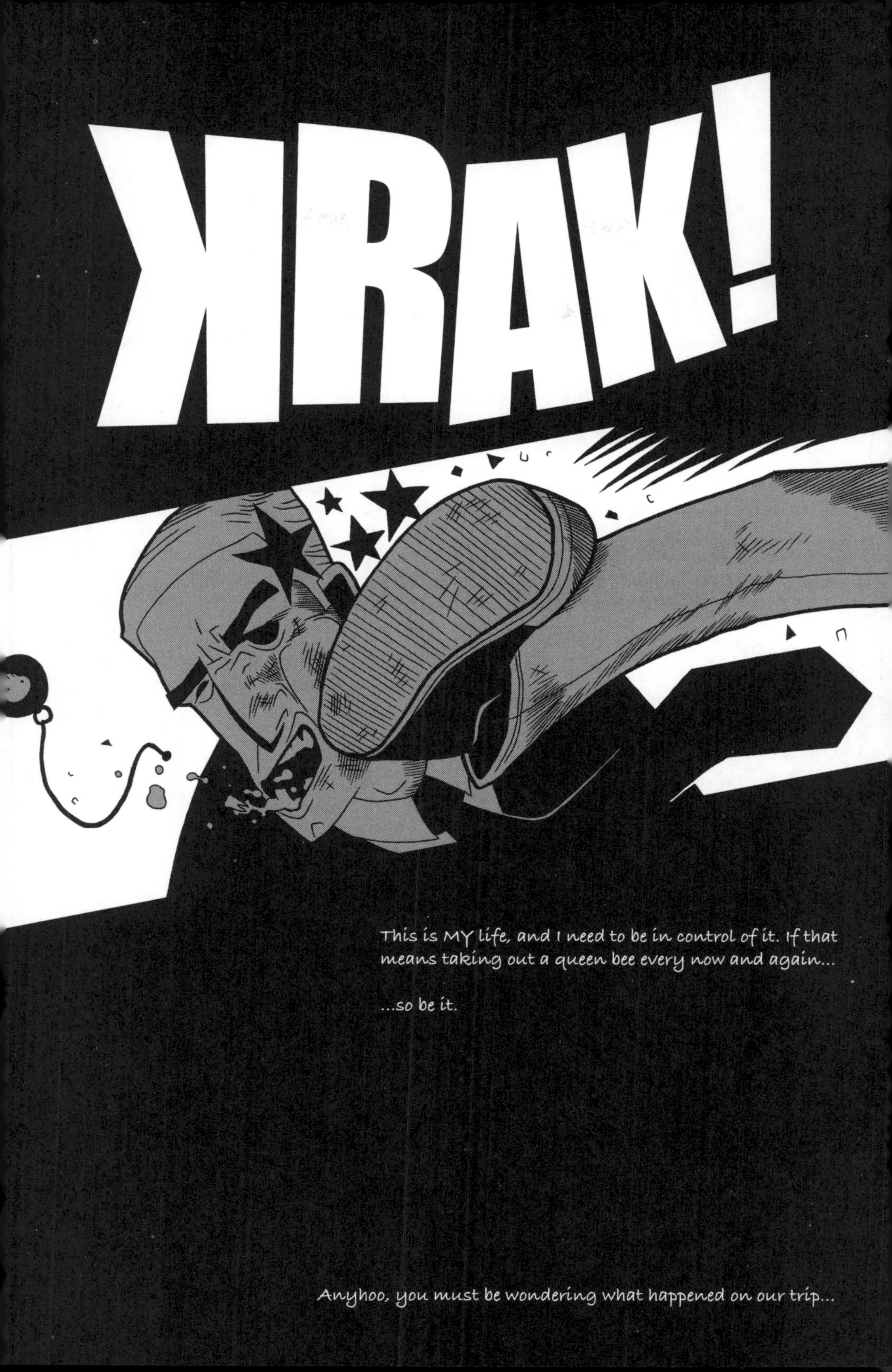
KRAK!
This is MY life, and I need to be in control of it. If that means taking out a queen bee every now and again...
...so be it.
Anyhoo, you must be wondering what happened on our trip...

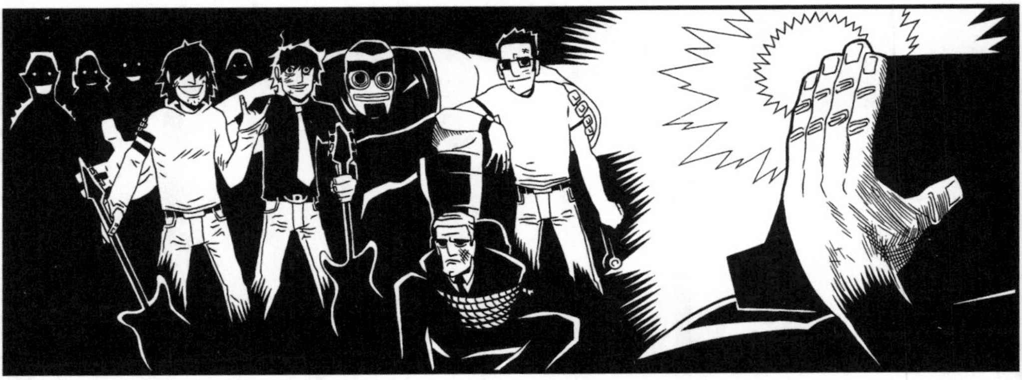

Aside from making a crap movie, we managed to take out some jerk bad guy that was after us. We had El Campeon's help, but he expected a free meal out of it, so he didn't stay long.

After beating on a couple thousand of our fans to keep from being ripped apart, we threw a free concert to show our gratitude for the lumps they took. By the end of the first song they didn't seem to mind the breaks and bruises.

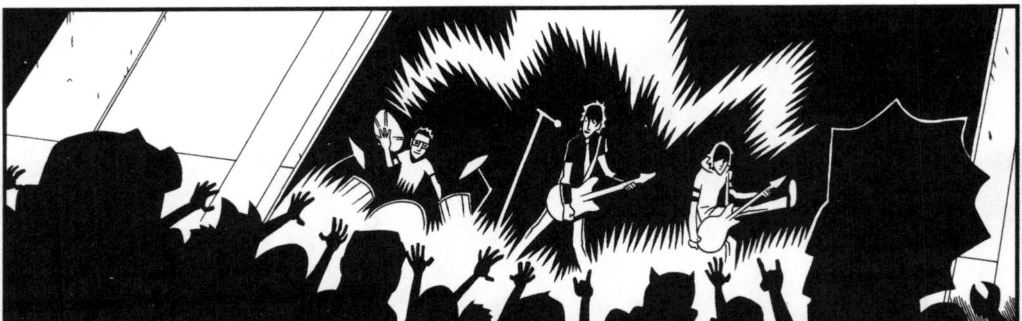

Dalton left us to fend for ourselves all day long, so when he finally showed up we had a few words with the man before he could explode over the free concert we gave.

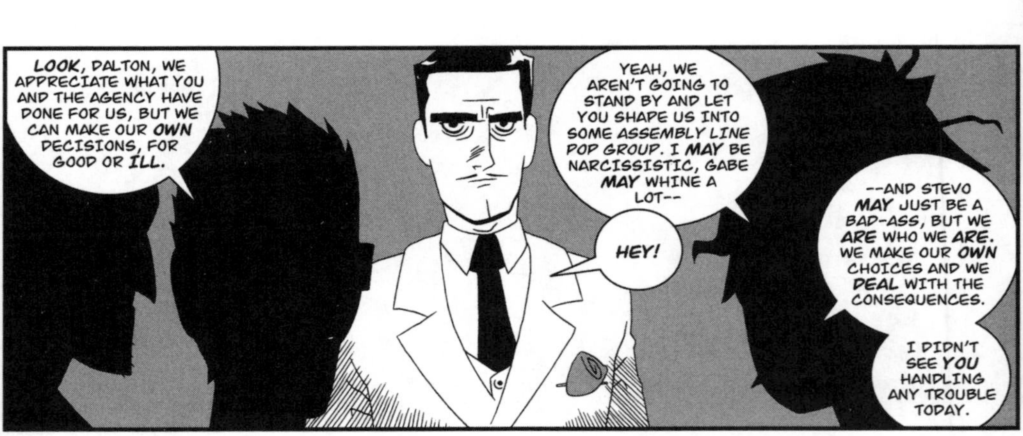
LOOK, DALTON, WE APPRECIATE WHAT YOU AND THE AGENCY HAVE DONE FOR US, BUT WE CAN MAKE OUR OWN DECISIONS, FOR GOOD OR ILL.
YEAH, WE AREN'T GOING TO STAND BY AND LET YOU SHAPE US INTO SOME ASSEMBLY LINE POP GROUP. I MAY BE NARCISSISTIC, GABE MAY WHINE A LOT--
HEY!
--AND STEVO MAY JUST BE A BAD-ASS, BUT WE ARE WHO WE ARE. WE MAKE OUR OWN CHOICES AND WE DEAL WITH THE CONSEQUENCES.
I DIDN'T SEE YOU HANDLING ANY TROUBLE TODAY.

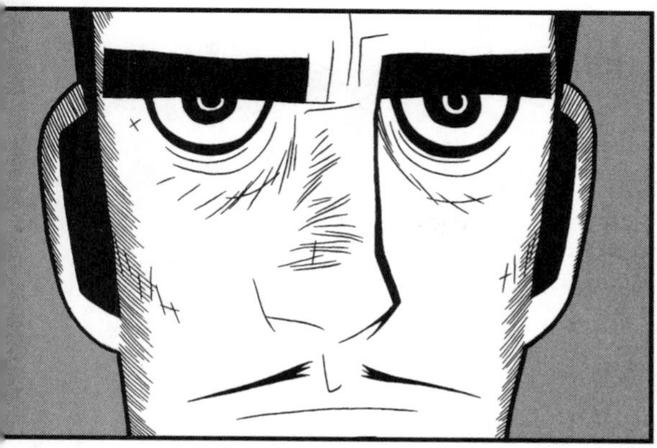

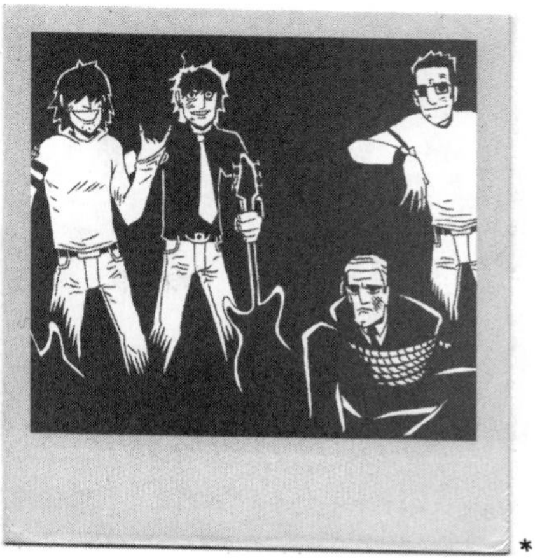

*

I don't think he took it well. You could see it in his eyes. They were like gelatinous volcanoes.

We did our best to explain that El Campeon saved the day, but we didn't have any evidence of that actually happening*, and the big guy refused to come out of the amulet again.

Did I tell you about the amulet? Anyway, I guess Dalton's never actually seen El Campeon, so he agreed to disagree before storming off. Oh (and this is bizarro), before he left, he had a few words with Mr. Morgenstein (studio villian) before hauling Hypno (villian villian) off in his Cobra.

We didn't see Dalton again until we were at the airport.

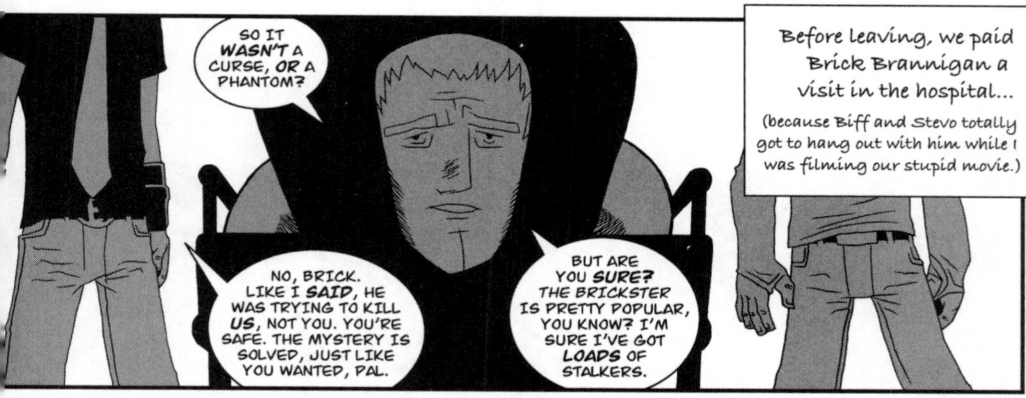
Before leaving, we paid Brick Brannigan a visit in the hospital...
(because Biff and Stevo totally got to hang out with him while I was filming our stupid movie.)
SO IT WASN'T A CURSE, OR A PHANTOM?
NO, BRICK. LIKE I SAID, HE WAS TRYING TO KILL US, NOT YOU. YOU'RE SAFE. THE MYSTERY IS SOLVED, JUST LIKE YOU WANTED, PAL.
BUT ARE YOU SURE? THE BRICKSTER IS PRETTY POPULAR, YOU KNOW? I'M SURE I'VE GOT LOADS OF STALKERS.

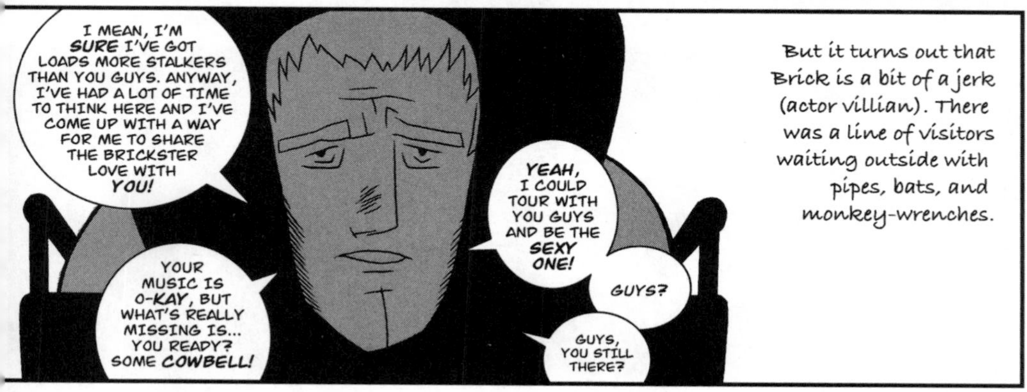
I MEAN, I'M SURE I'VE GOT LOADS MORE STALKERS THAN YOU GUYS. ANYWAY, I'VE HAD A LOT OF TIME TO THINK HERE AND I'VE COME UP WITH A WAY FOR ME TO SHARE THE BRICKSTER LOVE WITH YOU!
YOUR MUSIC IS O-KAY, BUT WHAT'S REALLY MISSING IS... YOU READY? SOME COWBELL!
YEAH, I COULD TOUR WITH YOU GUYS AND BE THE SEXY ONE!
GUYS?
GUYS, YOU STILL THERE?
But it turns out that Brick is a bit of a jerk (actor villian). There was a line of visitors waiting outside with pipes, bats, and monkey-wrenches.

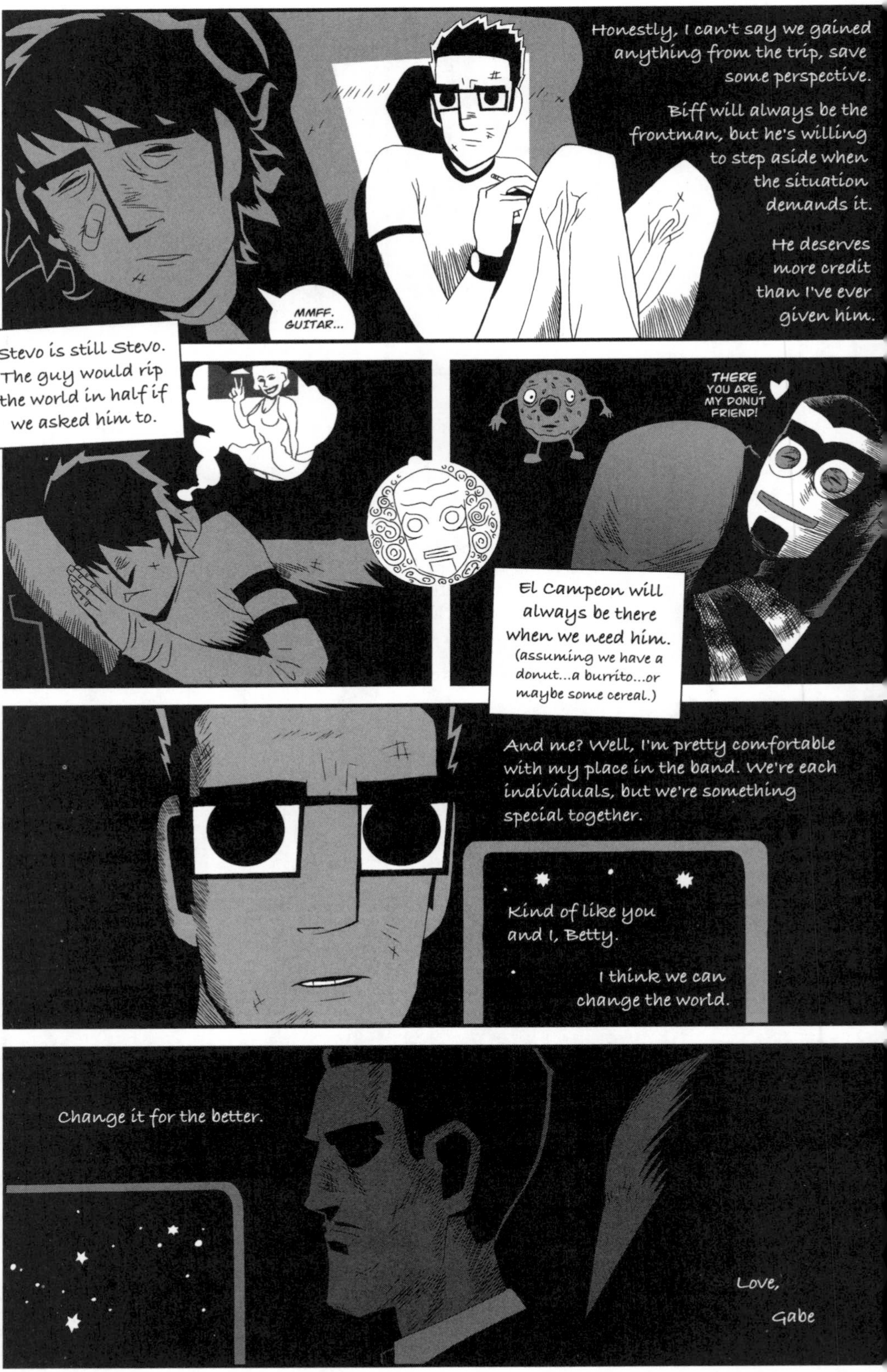
Honestly, I can't say we gained anything from the trip, save some perspective.
Biff will always be the frontman, but he's willing to step aside when the situation demands it.
He deserves more credit than I've ever given him.
MMFF. GUITAR...
Stevo is still Stevo. The guy would rip the world in half if we asked him to.
THERE YOU ARE, MY DONUT FRIEND!
El Campeon will always be there when we need him. (assuming we have a donut...a burrito...or maybe some cereal.)
And me? Well, I'm pretty comfortable with my place in the band. We're each individuals, but we're something special together.
Kind of like you and I, Betty.
I think we can change the world.
Change it for the better.
Love,
Gabe

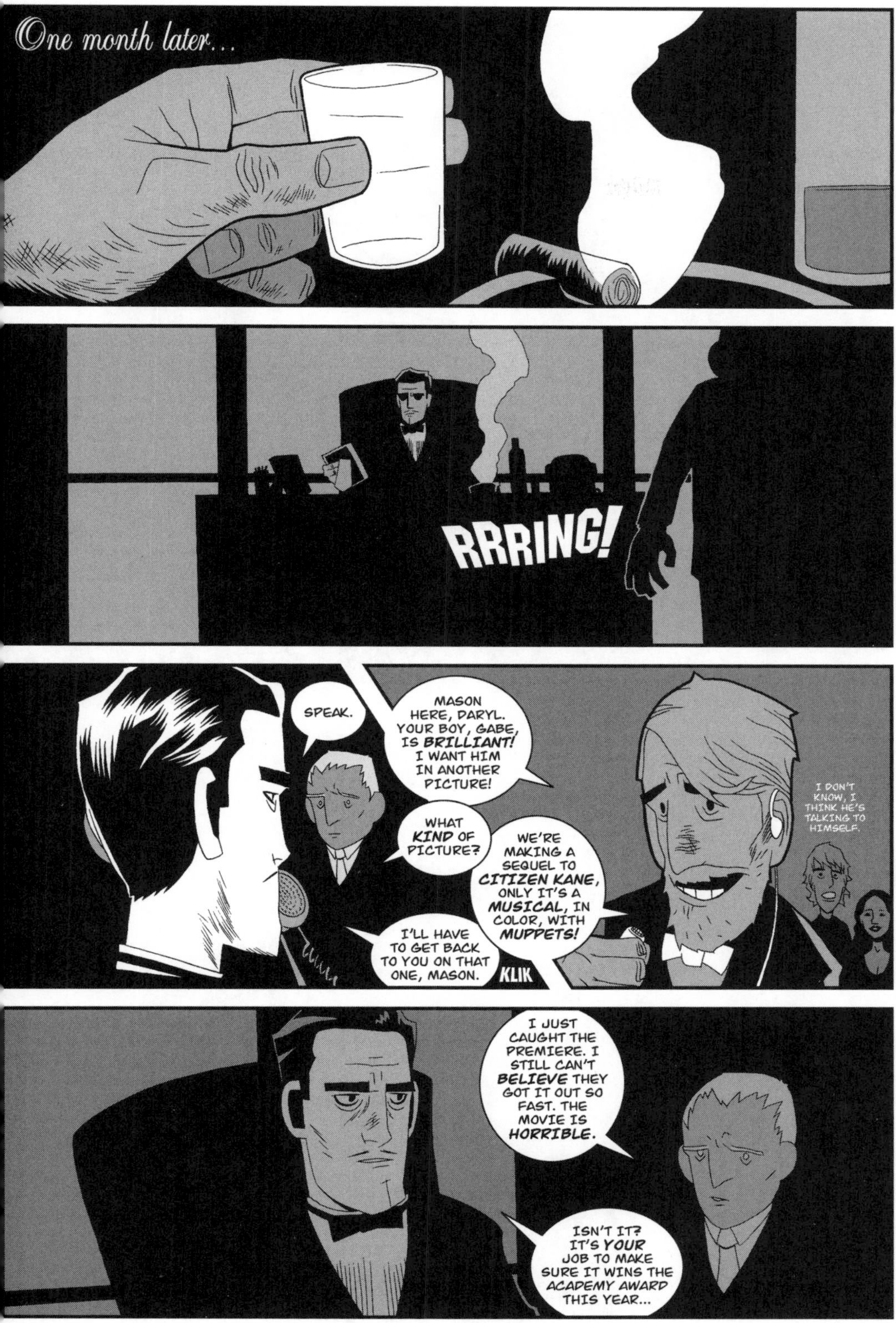
One month later...
RRRING!
SPEAK.
MASON HERE, DARYL. YOUR BOY, GABE, IS BRILLIANT! I WANT HIM IN ANOTHER PICTURE!
WHAT KIND OF PICTURE?
WE'RE MAKING A SEQUEL TO CITIZEN KANE, ONLY IT'S A MUSICAL, IN COLOR, WITH MUPPETS!
I DON'T KNOW, I THINK HE'S TALKING TO HIMSELF.
I'LL HAVE TO GET BACK TO YOU ON THAT ONE, MASON.
KLIK
I JUST CAUGHT THE PREMIERE. I STILL CAN'T BELIEVE THEY GOT IT OUT SO FAST. THE MOVIE IS HORRIBLE.
ISN'T IT? IT'S YOUR JOB TO MAKE SURE IT WINS THE ACADEMY AWARD THIS YEAR...

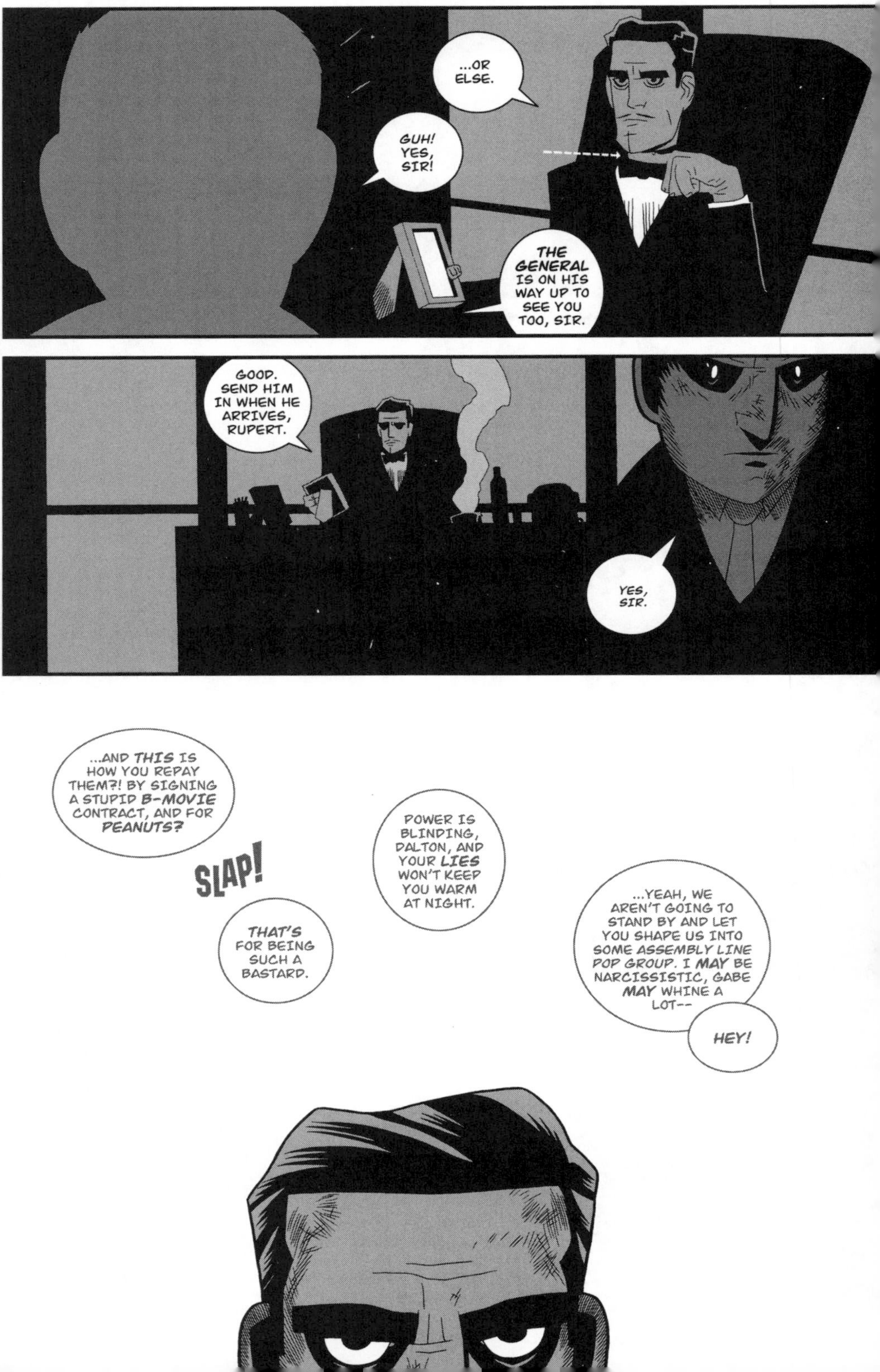
...OR ELSE.
GUH! YES, SIR!
THE GENERAL IS ON HIS WAY UP TO SEE YOU TOO, SIR.
GOOD. SEND HIM IN WHEN HE ARRIVES, RUPERT.
YES, SIR.
...AND THIS IS HOW YOU REPAY THEM?! BY SIGNING A STUPID B-MOVIE CONTRACT, AND FOR PEANUTS?
SLAP!
THAT'S FOR BEING SUCH A BASTARD.
POWER IS BLINDING, DALTON, AND YOUR LIES WON'T KEEP YOU WARM AT NIGHT.
...YEAH, WE AREN'T GOING TO STAND BY AND LET YOU SHAPE US INTO SOME ASSEMBLY LINE POP GROUP. I MAY BE NARCISSISTIC, GABE MAY WHINE A LOT--
HEY!

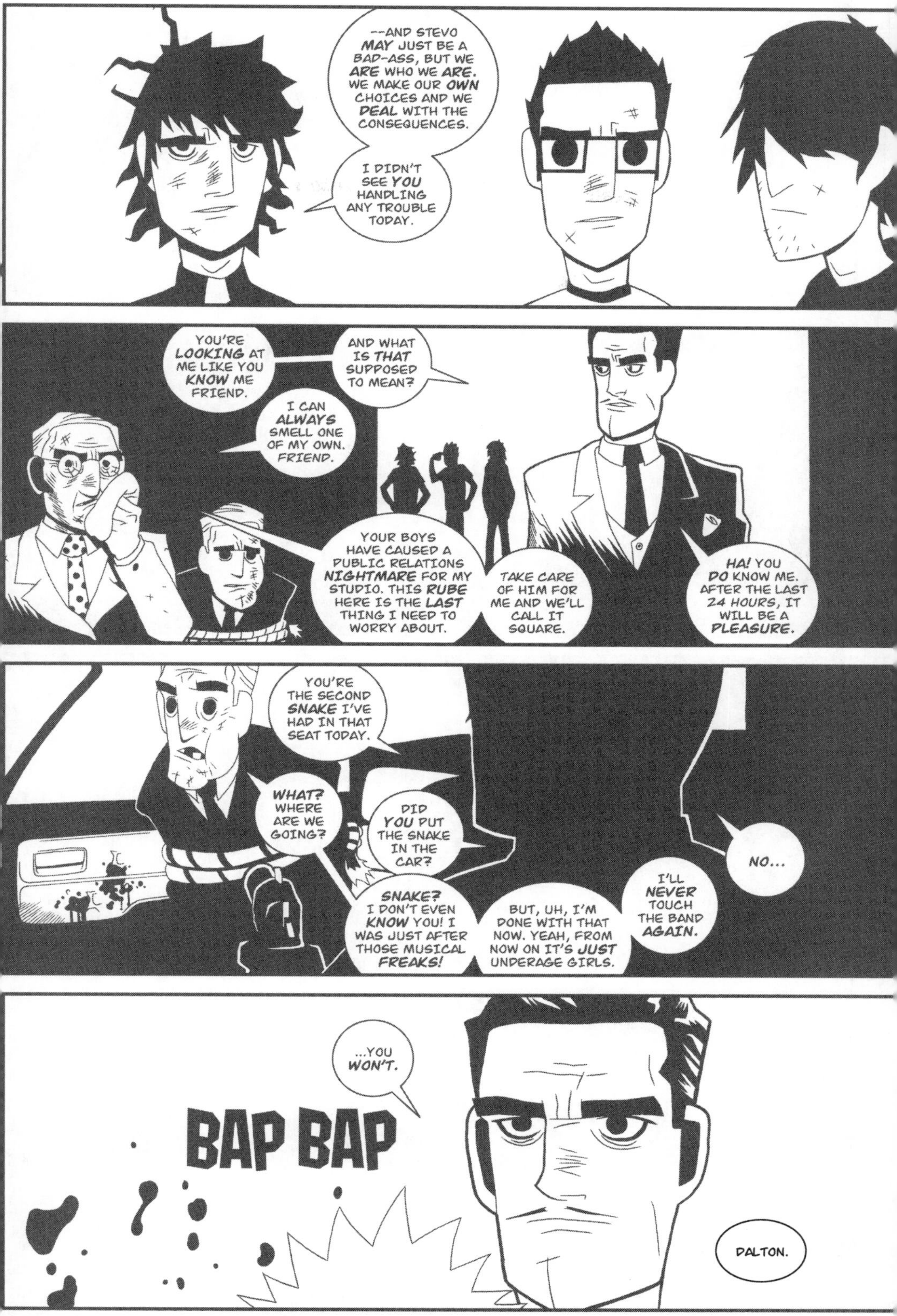
--AND STEVO MAY JUST BE A BAD-ASS, BUT WE ARE WHO WE ARE. WE MAKE OUR OWN CHOICES AND WE DEAL WITH THE CONSEQUENCES.
I DIDN'T SEE YOU HANDLING ANY TROUBLE TODAY.
YOU'RE LOOKING AT ME LIKE YOU KNOW ME FRIEND.
AND WHAT IS THAT SUPPOSED TO MEAN?
I CAN ALWAYS SMELL ONE OF MY OWN. FRIEND.
YOUR BOYS HAVE CAUSED A PUBLIC RELATIONS NIGHTMARE FOR MY STUDIO. THIS RUBE HERE IS THE LAST THING I NEED TO WORRY ABOUT.
TAKE CARE OF HIM FOR ME AND WE'LL CALL IT SQUARE.
HA! YOU DO KNOW ME. AFTER THE LAST 24 HOURS, IT WILL BE A PLEASURE.
YOU'RE THE SECOND SNAKE I'VE HAD IN THAT SEAT TODAY.
WHAT? WHERE ARE WE GOING?
DID YOU PUT THE SNAKE IN THE CAR?
SNAKE? I DON'T EVEN KNOW YOU! I WAS JUST AFTER THOSE MUSICAL FREAKS!
BUT, UH, I'M DONE WITH THAT NOW. YEAH, FROM NOW ON IT'S JUST UNDERAGE GIRLS.
I'LL NEVER TOUCH THE BAND AGAIN.
NO...
...YOU WON'T.
BAP BAP
DALTON.

THE GENERAL

DALTON.

SIR?

I WANTED TO COMMEND YOU *AGAIN* ON THE WAY YOU HANDLED THAT *HOLLYWOOD NONSENSE*, DALTON.

THANK YOU, SIR.

THOSE BOYS OF YOURS MAY GET INTO A LOT OF TROUBLE, BUT THEY SURE DO COME IN HANDY, DON'T THEY?

YES, SIR.

HA HA! IT'S NEVER *BEEN* SO EASY TO GET IN AND OUT OF THIRD WORLD COUNTRIES.

NOT TO *MENTION* THE NUMBER OF THREATS TO NATIONAL SECURITY THEY MANAGE TO TAKE OUT ON THEIR OWN.

ARE YOU *SURE* THEY STILL HAVE NO IDEA *WHO* THEY ARE WORKING FOR, DALTON?

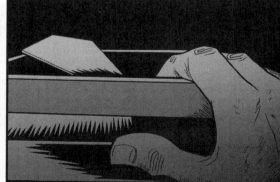

NO, SIR. THEY'RE YOUNG AND CLUELESS.

GOOD. YOUNG AND DUMB.

JUST THE WAY WE LIKE 'EM.

END SCENE.

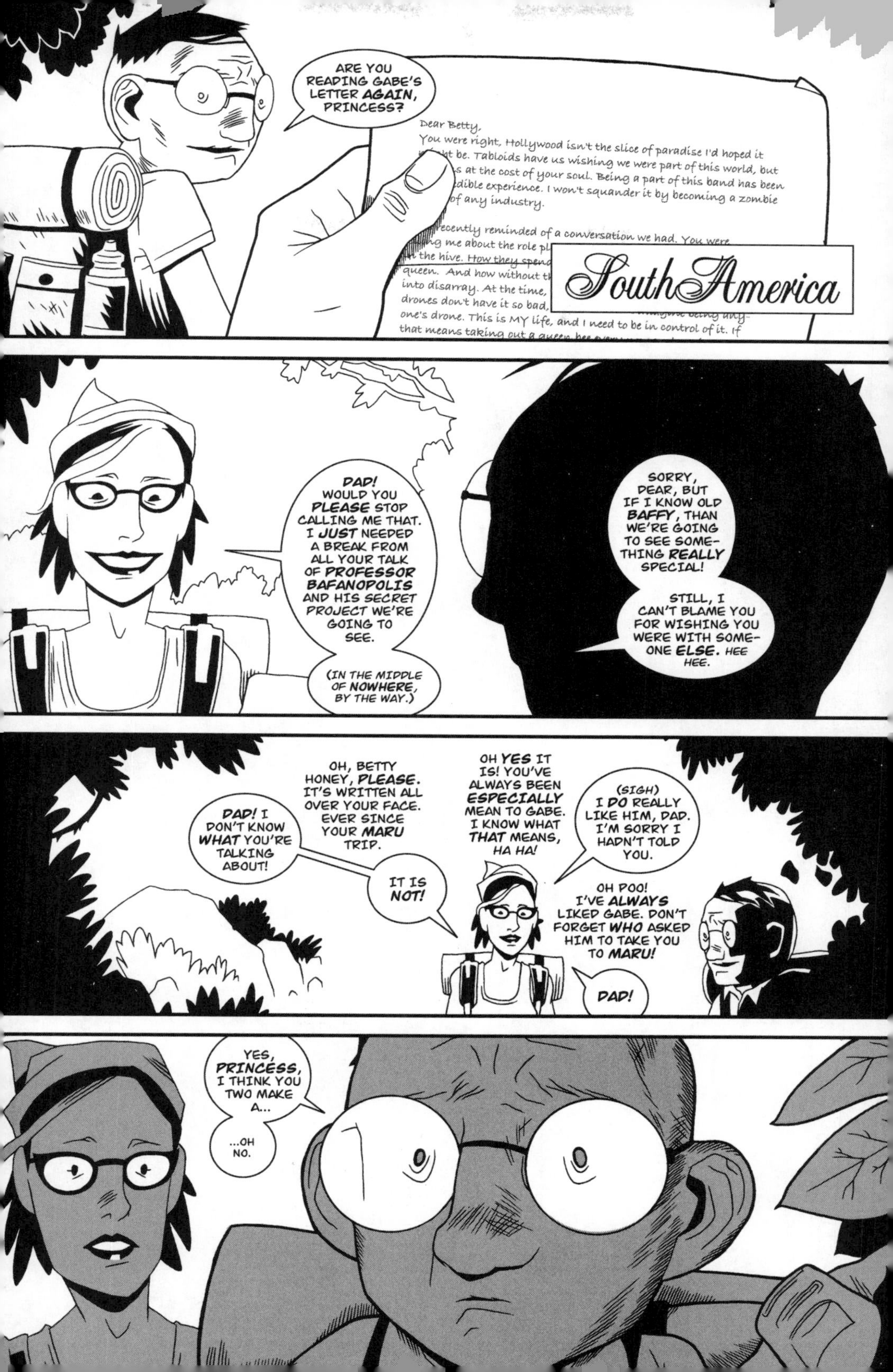
ARE YOU READING GABE'S LETTER AGAIN, PRINCESS?
Dear Betty,
You were right, Hollywood isn't the slice of paradise I'd hoped it
t be. Tabloids have us wishing we were part of this world, but
s at the cost of your soul. Being a part of this band has been
dible experience. I won't squander it by becoming a zombie
of any industry.
ecently reminded of a conversation we had. You were
g me about the role pl
the hive. How they spend
queen. And how without t
into disarray. At the time,
drones don't have it so bad,
one's drone. This is MY life, and I need to be in control of it. If
South America
DAD! WOULD YOU PLEASE STOP CALLING ME THAT. I JUST NEEDED A BREAK FROM ALL YOUR TALK OF PROFESSOR BAFANOPOLIS AND HIS SECRET PROJECT WE'RE GOING TO SEE.
(IN THE MIDDLE OF NOWHERE, BY THE WAY.)
SORRY, DEAR, BUT IF I KNOW OLD BAFFY, THAN WE'RE GOING TO SEE SOMETHING REALLY SPECIAL!
STILL, I CAN'T BLAME YOU FOR WISHING YOU WERE WITH SOMEONE ELSE. HEE HEE.
DAD! I DON'T KNOW WHAT YOU'RE TALKING ABOUT!
OH, BETTY HONEY, PLEASE. IT'S WRITTEN ALL OVER YOUR FACE. EVER SINCE YOUR MARU TRIP.
IT IS NOT!
OH YES IT IS! YOU'VE ALWAYS BEEN ESPECIALLY MEAN TO GABE. I KNOW WHAT THAT MEANS, HA HA!
(SIGH) I DO REALLY LIKE HIM, DAD. I'M SORRY I HADN'T TOLD YOU.
OH POO! I'VE ALWAYS LIKED GABE. DON'T FORGET WHO ASKED HIM TO TAKE YOU TO MARU!
DAD!
YES, PRINCESS, I THINK YOU TWO MAKE A...
...OH NO.

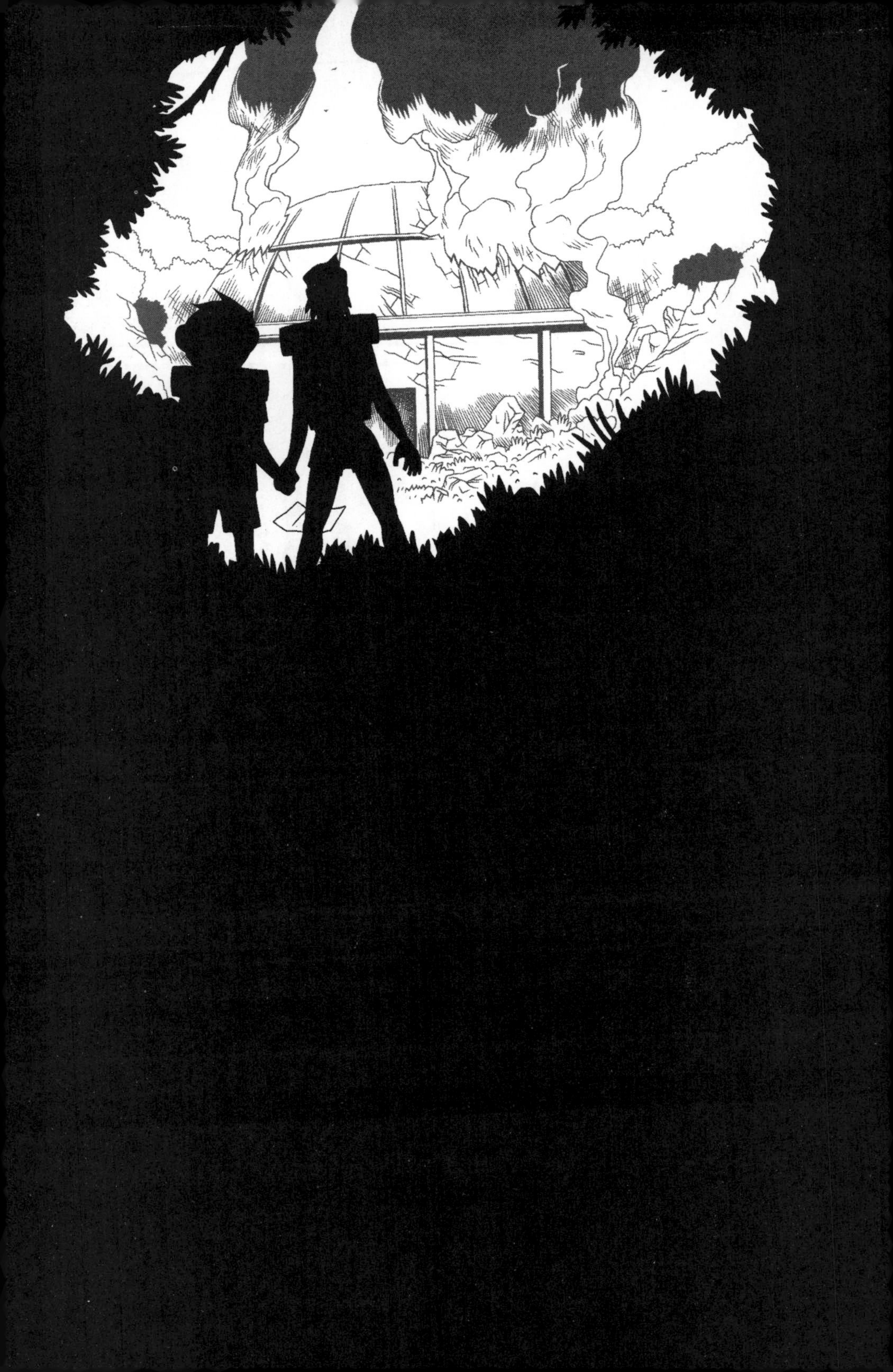

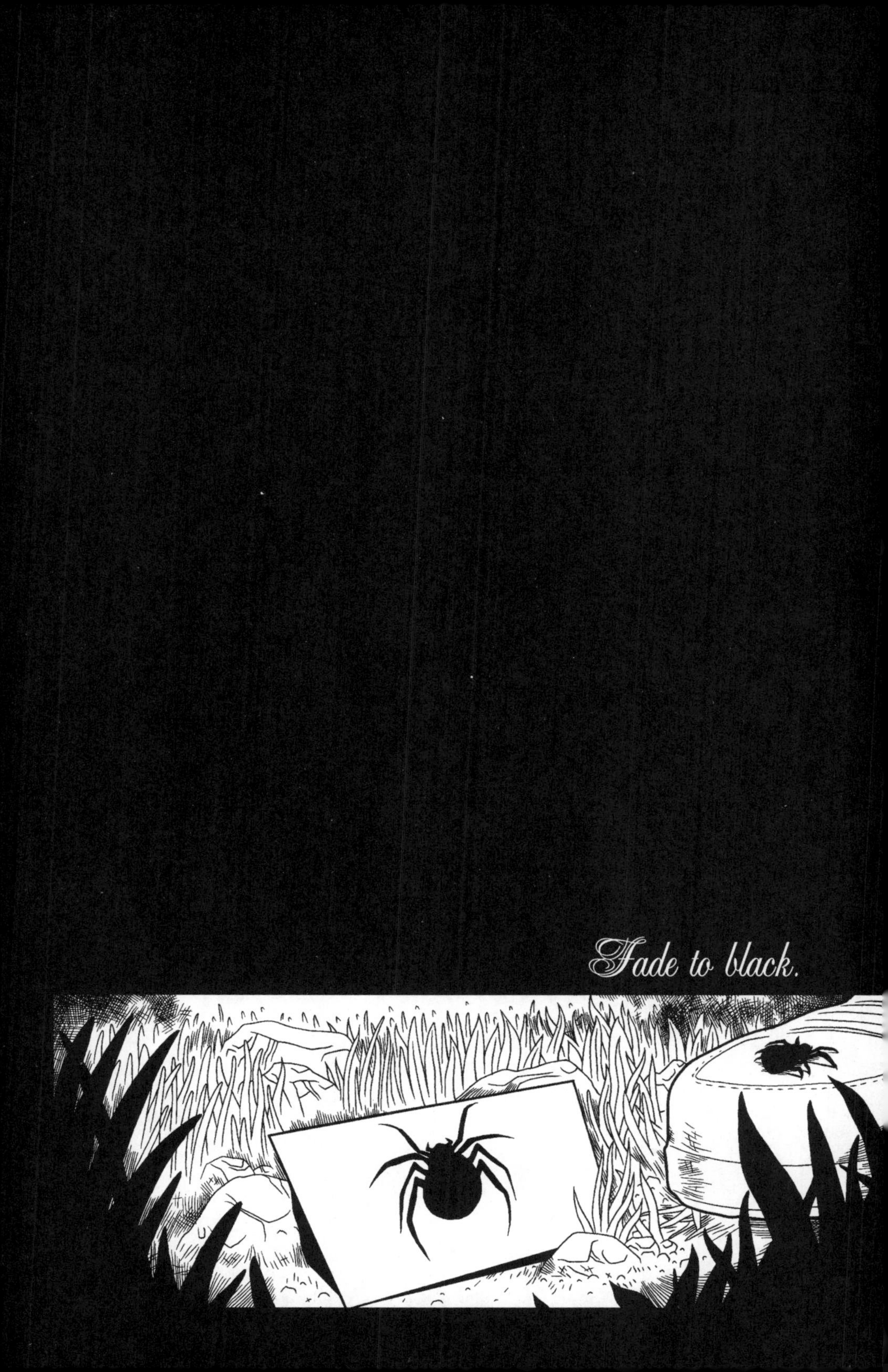
Fade to black.

PART FIVE

HERE COME THE SPIDERS

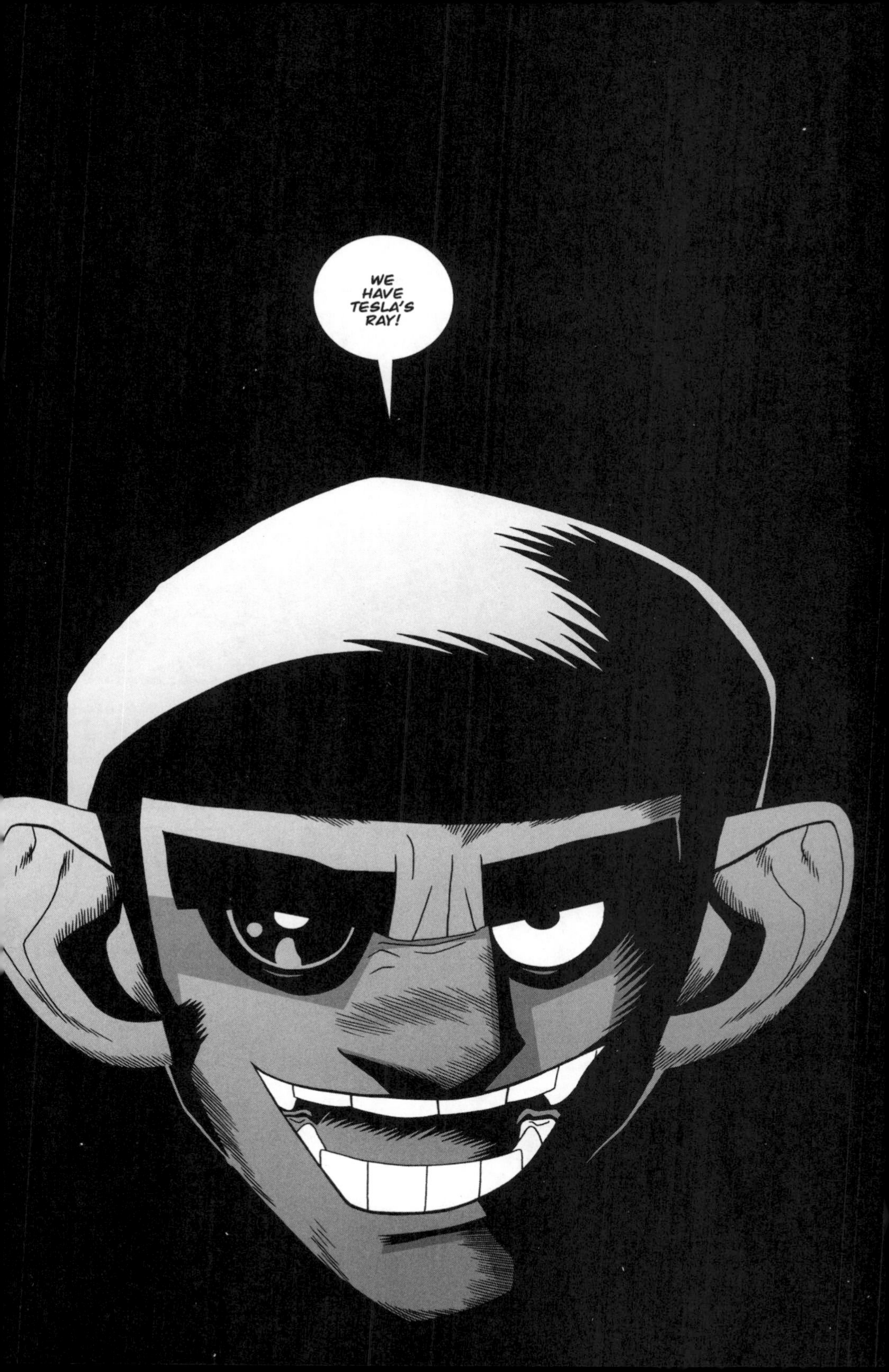
WE HAVE TESLA'S RAY!

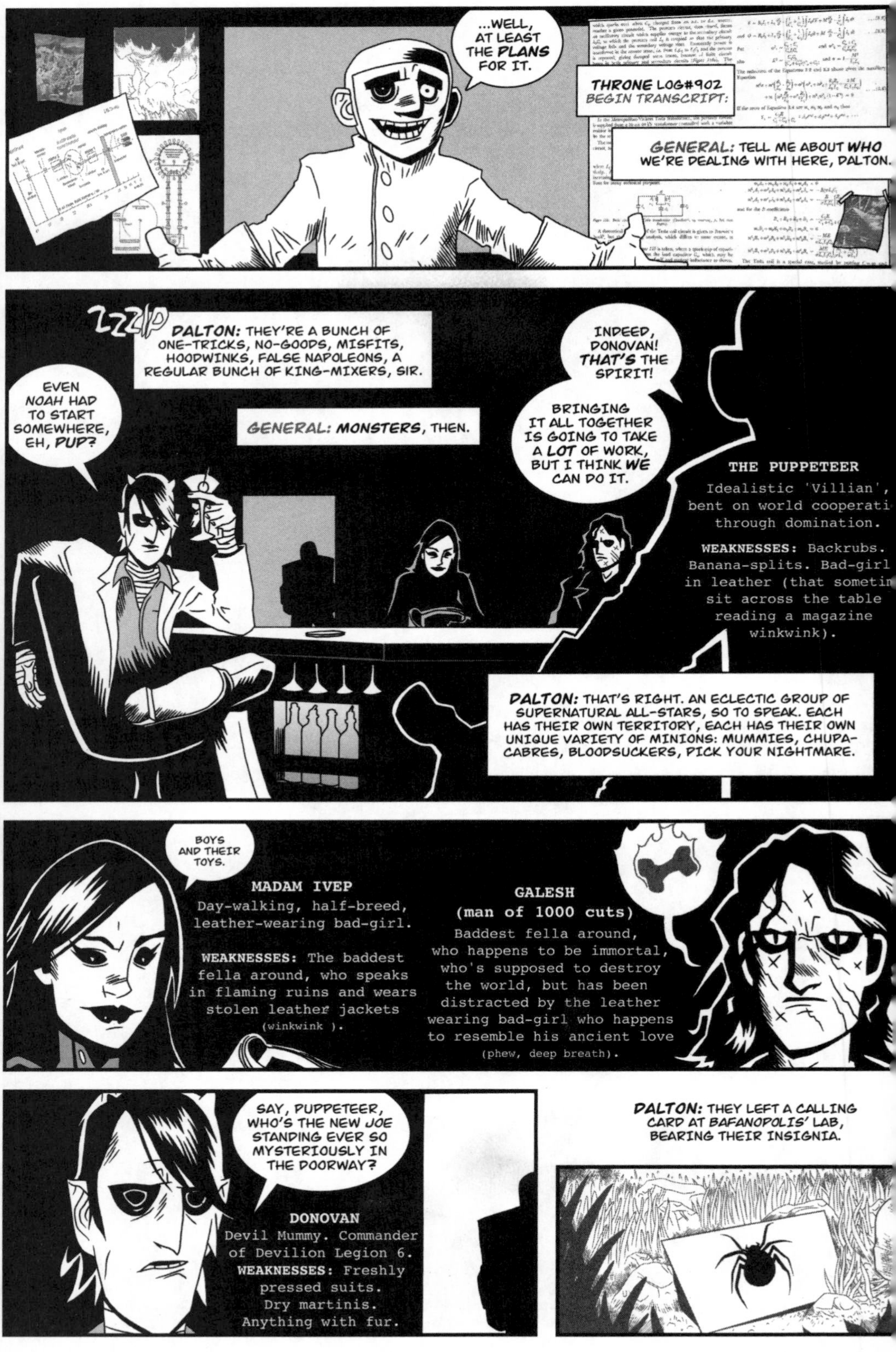
...WELL, AT LEAST THE PLANS FOR IT.
THRONE LOG#902 BEGIN TRANSCRIPT:
GENERAL: TELL ME ABOUT WHO WE'RE DEALING WITH HERE, DALTON.
ZZZIP
DALTON: THEY'RE A BUNCH OF ONE-TRICKS, NO-GOODS, MISFITS, HOODWINKS, FALSE NAPOLEONS, A REGULAR BUNCH OF KING-MIXERS, SIR.
EVEN NOAH HAD TO START SOMEWHERE, EH, PUP?
GENERAL: MONSTERS, THEN.
INDEED, DONOVAN! THAT'S THE SPIRIT!
BRINGING IT ALL TOGETHER IS GOING TO TAKE A LOT OF WORK, BUT I THINK WE CAN DO IT.
THE PUPPETEER
Idealistic 'Villian', bent on world cooperati through domination.
WEAKNESSES: Backrubs. Banana-splits. Bad-girl in leather (that someti sit across the table reading a magazine winkwink).
DALTON: THAT'S RIGHT. AN ECLECTIC GROUP OF SUPERNATURAL ALL-STARS, SO TO SPEAK. EACH HAS THEIR OWN TERRITORY, EACH HAS THEIR OWN UNIQUE VARIETY OF MINIONS: MUMMIES, CHUPA-CABRES, BLOODSUCKERS, PICK YOUR NIGHTMARE.
BOYS AND THEIR TOYS.
MADAM IVEP
Day-walking, half-breed, leather-wearing bad-girl.
WEAKNESSES: The baddest fella around, who speaks in flaming ruins and wears stolen leather jackets (winkwink).
GALESH
(man of 1000 cuts)
Baddest fella around, who happens to be immortal, who's supposed to destroy the world, but has been distracted by the leather wearing bad-girl who happens to resemble his ancient love (phew, deep breath).
SAY, PUPPETEER, WHO'S THE NEW JOE STANDING EVER SO MYSTERIOUSLY IN THE DOORWAY?
DONOVAN
Devil Mummy. Commander of Devilion Legion 6.
WEAKNESSES: Freshly pressed suits. Dry martinis. Anything with fur.
DALTON: THEY LEFT A CALLING CARD AT BAFANOPOLIS' LAB, BEARING THEIR INSIGNIA.

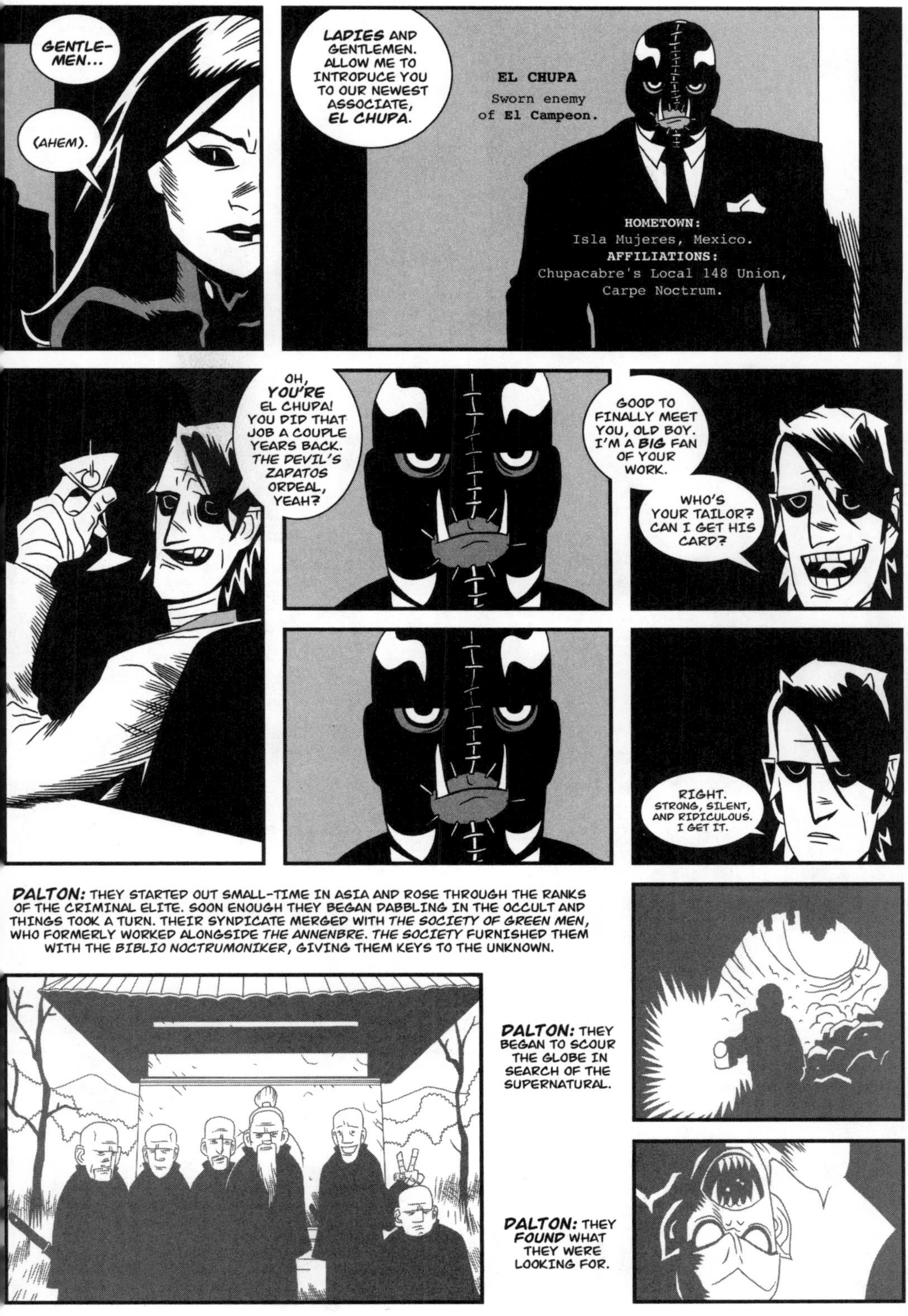

GENTLE-MEN...
(AHEM).
LADIES AND GENTLEMEN. ALLOW ME TO INTRODUCE YOU TO OUR NEWEST ASSOCIATE, EL CHUPA.
EL CHUPA
Sworn enemy of El Campeon.
HOMETOWN:
Isla Mujeres, Mexico.
AFFILIATIONS:
Chupacabre's Local 148 Union, Carpe Noctrum.
OH, YOU'RE EL CHUPA! YOU DID THAT JOB A COUPLE YEARS BACK. THE DEVIL'S ZAPATOS ORDEAL, YEAH?
GOOD TO FINALLY MEET YOU, OLD BOY. I'M A BIG FAN OF YOUR WORK.
WHO'S YOUR TAILOR? CAN I GET HIS CARD?
RIGHT. STRONG, SILENT, AND RIDICULOUS. I GET IT.
DALTON: THEY STARTED OUT SMALL-TIME IN ASIA AND ROSE THROUGH THE RANKS OF THE CRIMINAL ELITE. SOON ENOUGH THEY BEGAN DABBLING IN THE OCCULT AND THINGS TOOK A TURN. THEIR SYNDICATE MERGED WITH THE SOCIETY OF GREEN MEN, WHO FORMERLY WORKED ALONGSIDE THE ANNENBRE. THE SOCIETY FURNISHED THEM WITH THE BIBLIO NOCTRUMONIKER, GIVING THEM KEYS TO THE UNKNOWN.
DALTON: THEY BEGAN TO SCOUR THE GLOBE IN SEARCH OF THE SUPERNATURAL.
DALTON: THEY FOUND WHAT THEY WERE LOOKING FOR.

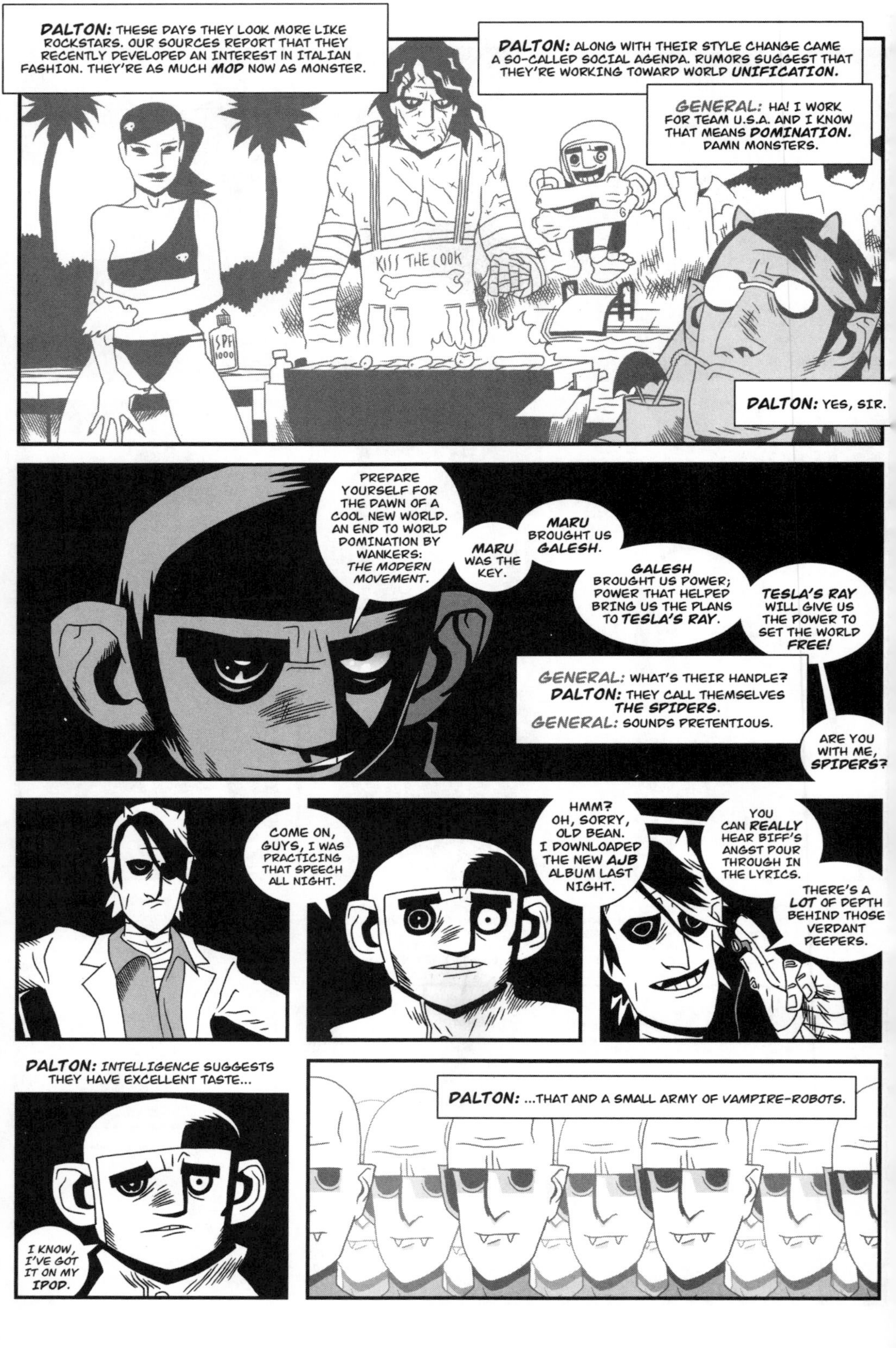
DALTON: THESE DAYS THEY LOOK MORE LIKE ROCKSTARS. OUR SOURCES REPORT THAT THEY RECENTLY DEVELOPED AN INTEREST IN ITALIAN FASHION. THEY'RE AS MUCH MOD NOW AS MONSTER.
DALTON: ALONG WITH THEIR STYLE CHANGE CAME A SO-CALLED SOCIAL AGENDA. RUMORS SUGGEST THAT THEY'RE WORKING TOWARD WORLD UNIFICATION.
GENERAL: HA! I WORK FOR TEAM U.S.A. AND I KNOW THAT MEANS DOMINATION. DAMN MONSTERS.
KISS THE COOK
SPF 1000
DALTON: YES, SIR.
PREPARE YOURSELF FOR THE DAWN OF A COOL NEW WORLD. AN END TO WORLD DOMINATION BY WANKERS: THE MODERN MOVEMENT.
MARU WAS THE KEY.
MARU BROUGHT US GALESH.
GALESH BROUGHT US POWER; POWER THAT HELPED BRING US THE PLANS TO TESLA'S RAY.
TESLA'S RAY WILL GIVE US THE POWER TO SET THE WORLD FREE!
GENERAL: WHAT'S THEIR HANDLE?
DALTON: THEY CALL THEMSELVES THE SPIDERS.
GENERAL: SOUNDS PRETENTIOUS.
ARE YOU WITH ME, SPIDERS?
COME ON, GUYS, I WAS PRACTICING THAT SPEECH ALL NIGHT.
HMM? OH, SORRY, OLD BEAN. I DOWNLOADED THE NEW AJB ALBUM LAST NIGHT.
YOU CAN REALLY HEAR BIFF'S ANGST POUR THROUGH IN THE LYRICS.
THERE'S A LOT OF DEPTH BEHIND THOSE VERDANT PEEPERS.
DALTON: INTELLIGENCE SUGGESTS THEY HAVE EXCELLENT TASTE...
I KNOW, I'VE GOT IT ON MY IPOD.
DALTON: ...THAT AND A SMALL ARMY OF VAMPIRE-ROBOTS.

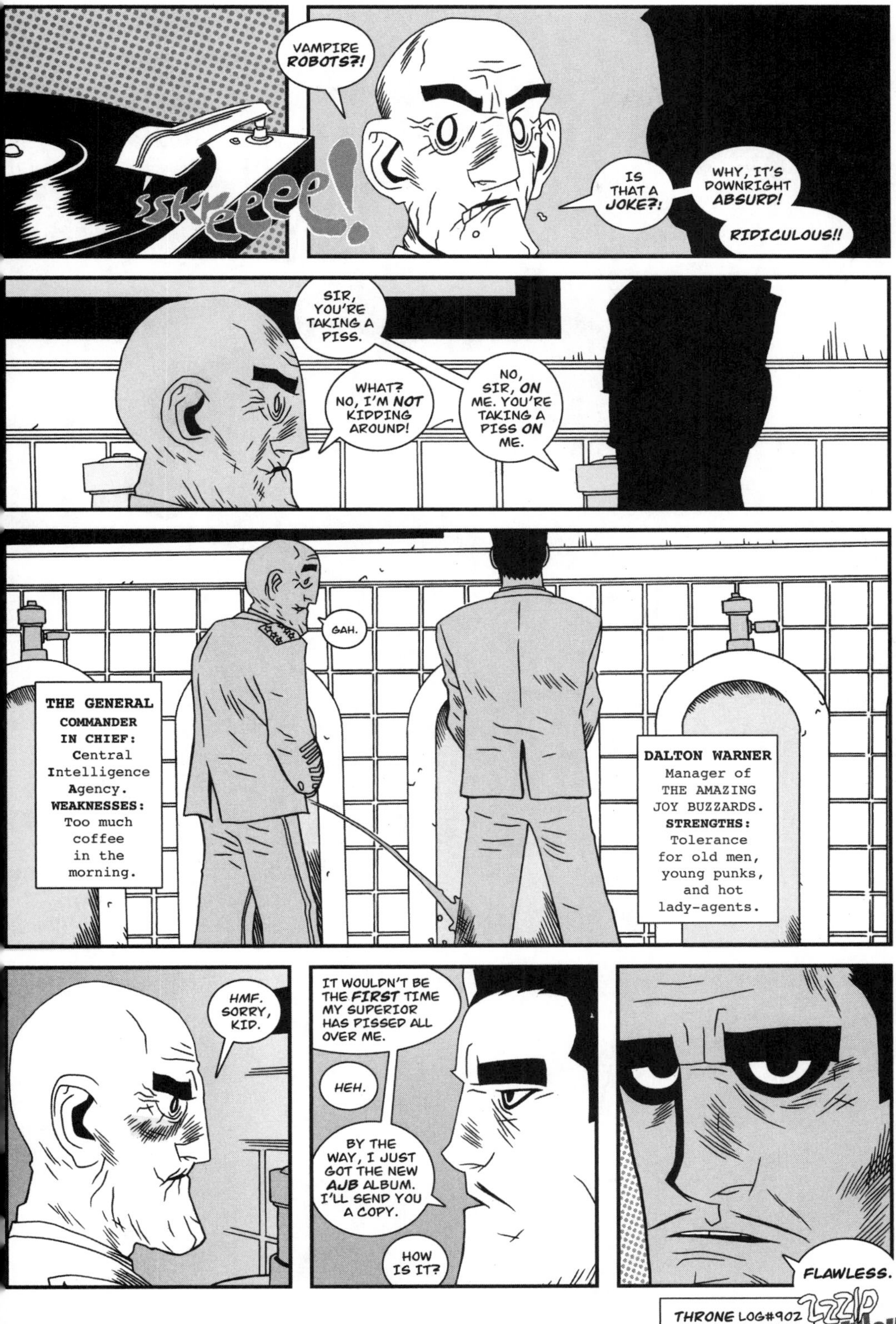

VAMPIRE ROBOTS?!
SSKREEEE!
IS THAT A JOKE?!
WHY, IT'S DOWNRIGHT ABSURD!
RIDICULOUS!!
SIR, YOU'RE TAKING A PISS.
WHAT? NO, I'M NOT KIDDING AROUND!
NO, SIR, ON ME. YOU'RE TAKING A PISS ON ME.
GAH.
THE GENERAL
COMMANDER IN CHIEF: Central Intelligence Agency.
WEAKNESSES: Too much coffee in the morning.
DALTON WARNER
Manager of THE AMAZING JOY BUZZARDS.
STRENGTHS: Tolerance for old men, young punks, and hot lady-agents.
HMF. SORRY, KID.
IT WOULDN'T BE THE FIRST TIME MY SUPERIOR HAS PISSED ALL OVER ME.
HEH.
BY THE WAY, I JUST GOT THE NEW AJB ALBUM. I'LL SEND YOU A COPY.
HOW IS IT?
FLAWLESS.
THRONE LOG#902
END TRANSCRIPT
ZZZIP
FLUSH

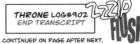

CONTINUED ON PAGE AFTER NEXT.

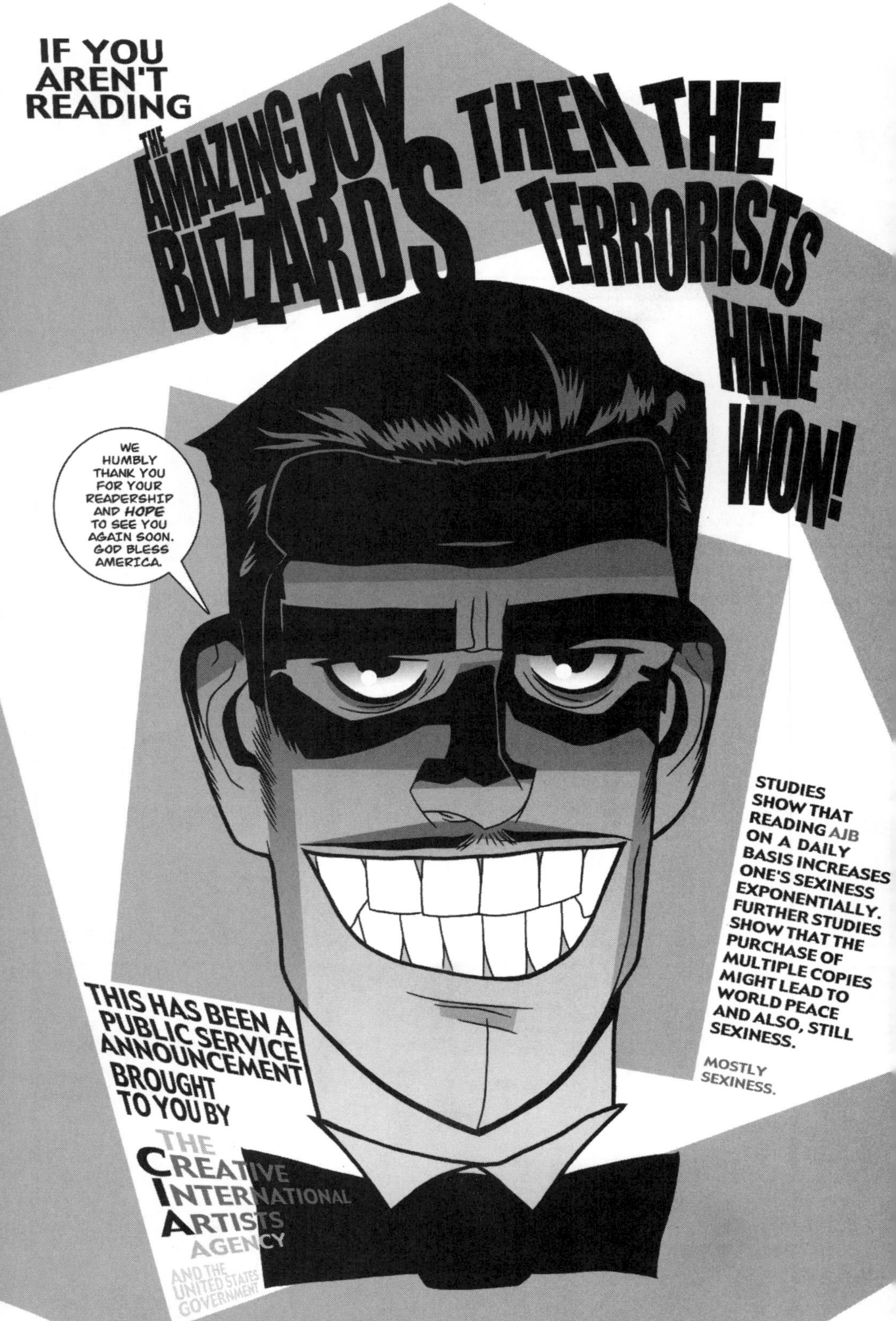
IF YOU AREN'T READING
THE AMAZING JOY BUZZARDS THEN THE TERRORISTS HAVE WON!
WE HUMBLY THANK YOU FOR YOUR READERSHIP AND HOPE TO SEE YOU AGAIN SOON. GOD BLESS AMERICA.
STUDIES SHOW THAT READING AJB ON A DAILY BASIS INCREASES ONE'S SEXINESS EXPONENTIALLY. FURTHER STUDIES SHOW THAT THE PURCHASE OF MULTIPLE COPIES MIGHT LEAD TO WORLD PEACE AND ALSO, STILL SEXINESS.
MOSTLY SEXINESS.
THIS HAS BEEN A PUBLIC SERVICE ANNOUNCEMENT BROUGHT TO YOU BY
THE CREATIVE INTERNATIONAL ARTISTS AGENCY
AND THE UNITED STATES GOVERNMENT

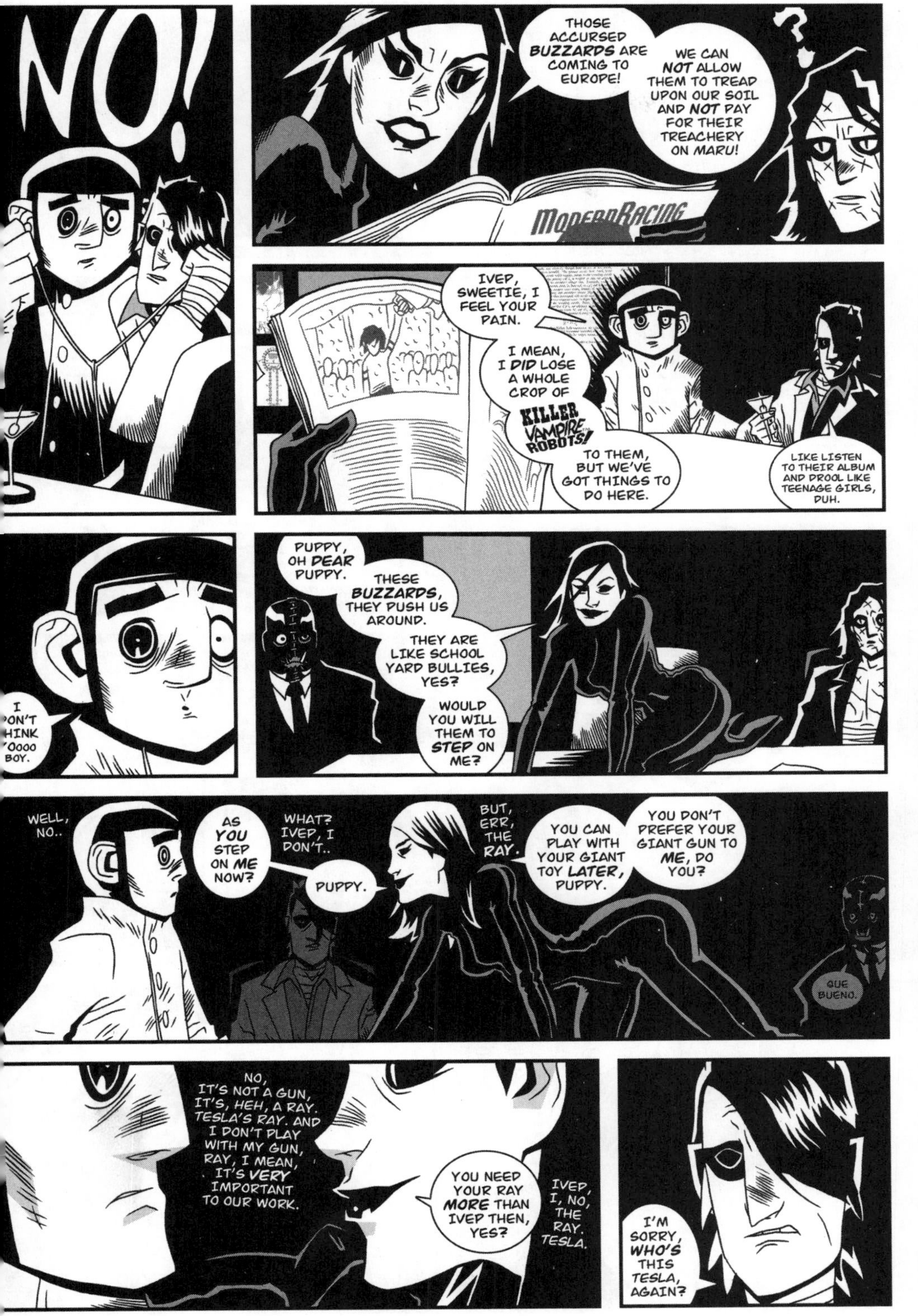
NO!
THOSE ACCURSED BUZZARDS ARE COMING TO EUROPE!
WE CAN NOT ALLOW THEM TO TREAD UPON OUR SOIL AND NOT PAY FOR THEIR TREACHERY ON MARU!
?
MODERN RACING
IVEP, SWEETIE, I FEEL YOUR PAIN.
I MEAN, I DID LOSE A WHOLE CROP OF
KILLER VAMPIRE ROBOTS!
TO THEM, BUT WE'VE GOT THINGS TO DO HERE.
LIKE LISTEN TO THEIR ALBUM AND DROOL LIKE TEENAGE GIRLS, DUH.
I DON'T THINK YOOOO BOY.
PUPPY, OH DEAR PUPPY.
THESE BUZZARDS, THEY PUSH US AROUND.
THEY ARE LIKE SCHOOL YARD BULLIES, YES?
WOULD YOU WILL THEM TO STEP ON ME?
WELL, NO..
AS YOU STEP ON ME NOW?
WHAT? IVEP, I DON'T..
PUPPY.
BUT, ERR, THE RAY.
YOU CAN PLAY WITH YOUR GIANT TOY LATER, PUPPY.
YOU DON'T PREFER YOUR GIANT GUN TO ME, DO YOU?
QUE BUENO.
NO, IT'S NOT A GUN, IT'S, HEH, A RAY. TESLA'S RAY. AND I DON'T PLAY WITH MY GUN, RAY, I MEAN, IT'S VERY IMPORTANT TO OUR WORK.
YOU NEED YOUR RAY MORE THAN IVEP THEN, YES?
IVEP, I, NO, THE RAY. TESLA.
I'M SORRY, WHO'S THIS TESLA, AGAIN?

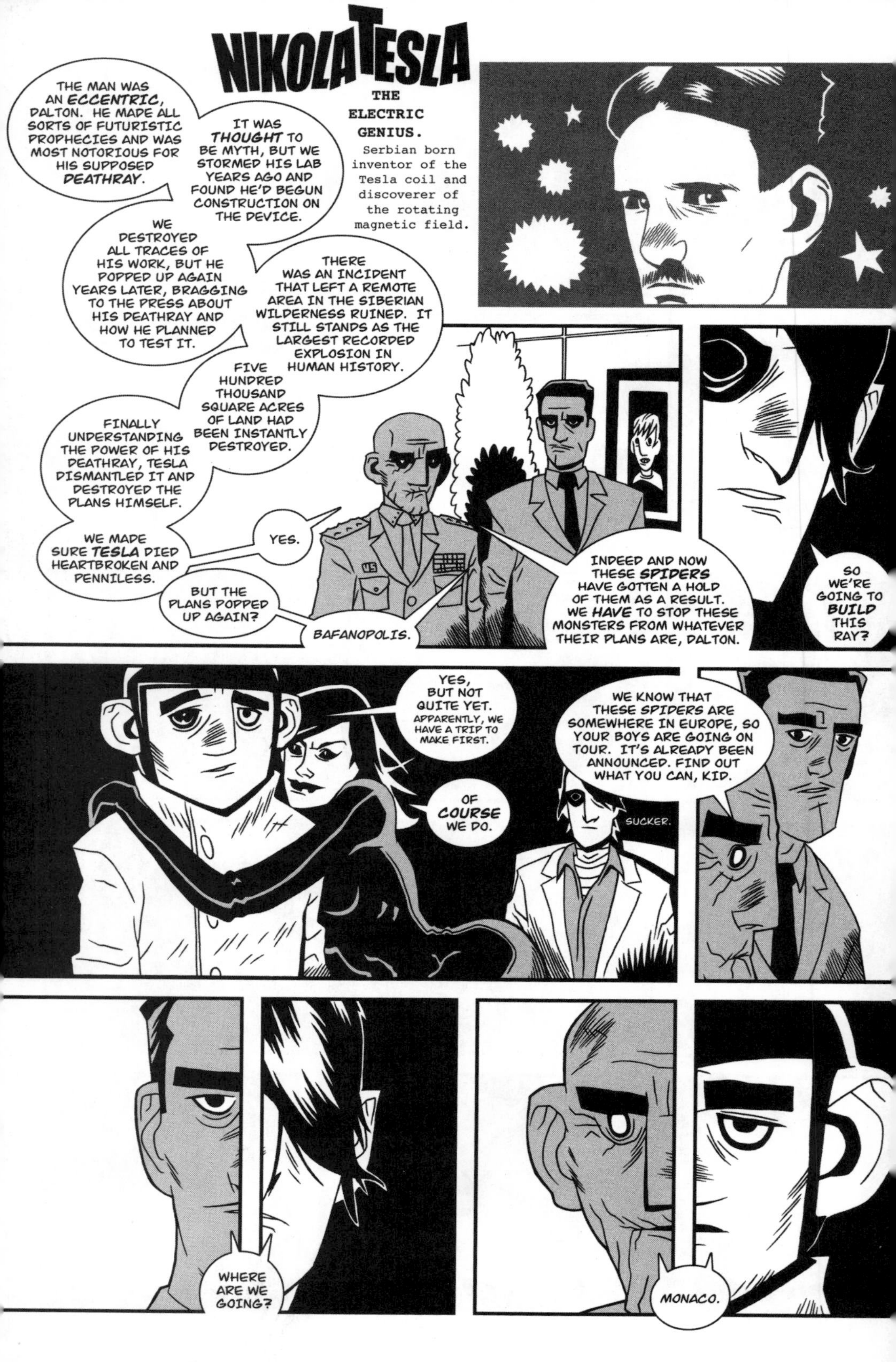
NIKOLA TESLA
THE ELECTRIC GENIUS.
Serbian born inventor of the Tesla coil and discoverer of the rotating magnetic field.
THE MAN WAS AN ECCENTRIC, DALTON. HE MADE ALL SORTS OF FUTURISTIC PROPHECIES AND WAS MOST NOTORIOUS FOR HIS SUPPOSED DEATHRAY.
IT WAS THOUGHT TO BE MYTH, BUT WE STORMED HIS LAB YEARS AGO AND FOUND HE'D BEGUN CONSTRUCTION ON THE DEVICE.
WE DESTROYED ALL TRACES OF HIS WORK, BUT HE POPPED UP AGAIN YEARS LATER, BRAGGING TO THE PRESS ABOUT HIS DEATHRAY AND HOW HE PLANNED TO TEST IT.
THERE WAS AN INCIDENT THAT LEFT A REMOTE AREA IN THE SIBERIAN WILDERNESS RUINED. IT STILL STANDS AS THE LARGEST RECORDED EXPLOSION IN HUMAN HISTORY.
FIVE HUNDRED THOUSAND SQUARE ACRES OF LAND HAD BEEN INSTANTLY DESTROYED.
FINALLY UNDERSTANDING THE POWER OF HIS DEATHRAY, TESLA DISMANTLED IT AND DESTROYED THE PLANS HIMSELF.
WE MADE SURE TESLA DIED HEARTBROKEN AND PENNILESS.
YES.
BUT THE PLANS POPPED UP AGAIN?
BAFANOPOLIS.
INDEED AND NOW THESE SPIDERS HAVE GOTTEN A HOLD OF THEM AS A RESULT. WE HAVE TO STOP THESE MONSTERS FROM WHATEVER THEIR PLANS ARE, DALTON.
SO WE'RE GOING TO BUILD THIS RAY?
YES, BUT NOT QUITE YET. APPARENTLY, WE HAVE A TRIP TO MAKE FIRST.
OF COURSE WE DO.
WE KNOW THAT THESE SPIDERS ARE SOMEWHERE IN EUROPE, SO YOUR BOYS ARE GOING ON TOUR. IT'S ALREADY BEEN ANNOUNCED. FIND OUT WHAT YOU CAN, KID.
SUCKER.
WHERE ARE WE GOING?
MONACO.

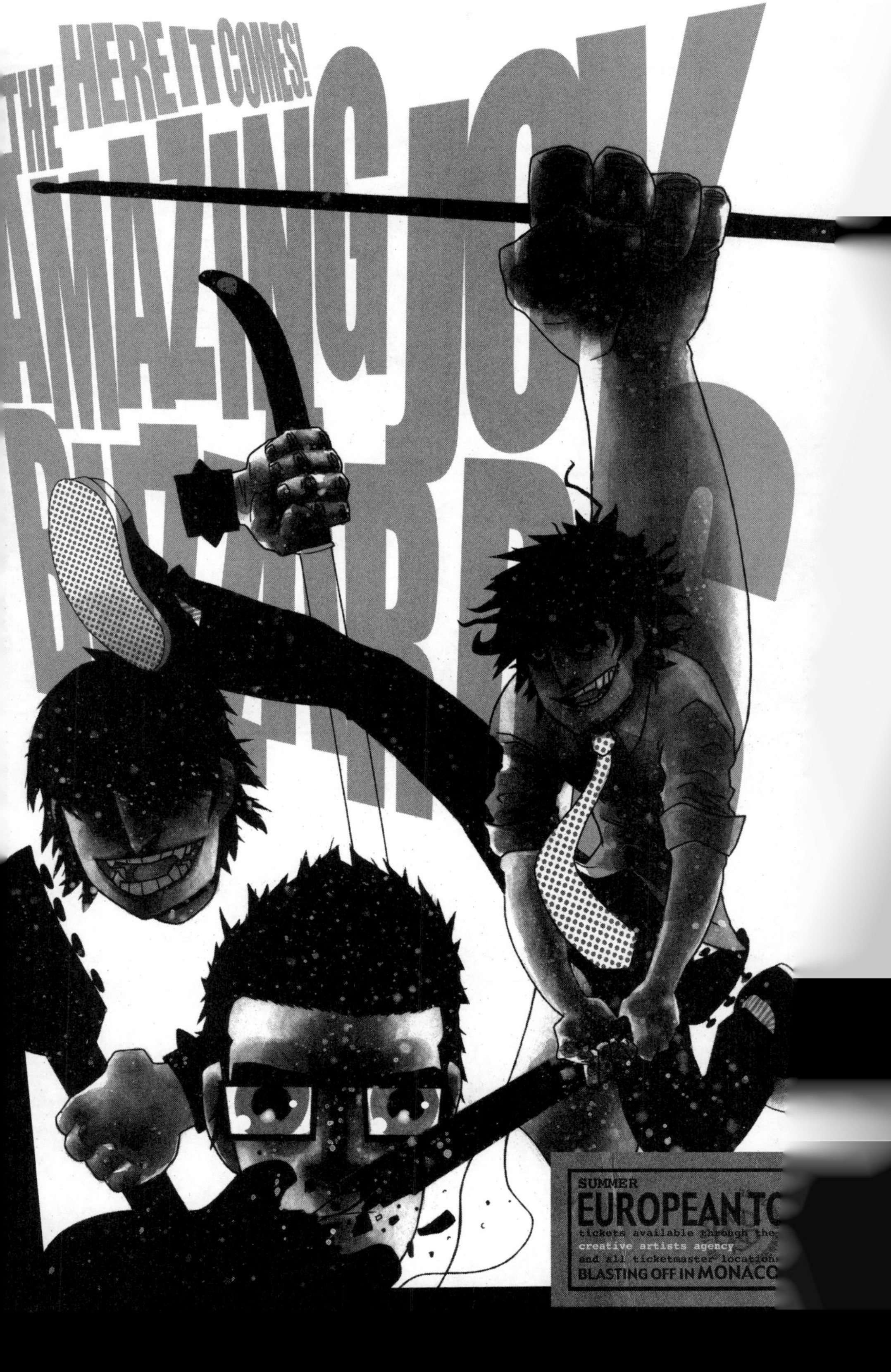
THE
HERE IT COMES!
AMAZING JOY
SUMMER
EUROPEAN
tickets available through the
creative artists agency
and all ticketmaster
BLASTING OFF IN MONACO

THE AMAZING JOY BUZZARDS

Rock-band of legendary proportion. Often involved in matters of supernatural interest. Unwitting pawn of the CIA

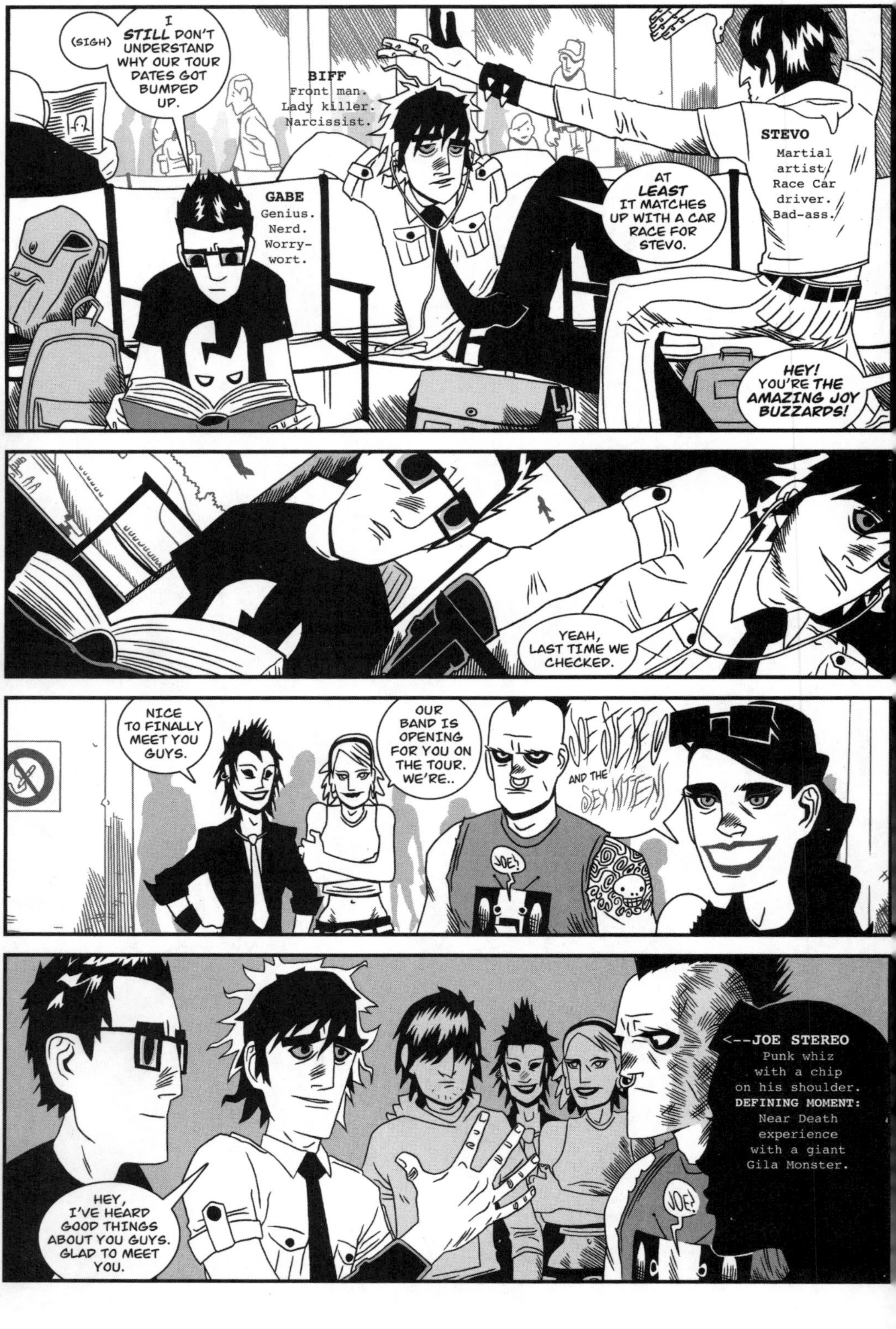
(SIGH)
I STILL DON'T UNDERSTAND WHY OUR TOUR DATES GOT BUMPED UP.
BIFF
Front man. Lady killer. Narcissist.
GABE
Genius. Nerd. Worry-wort.
AT LEAST IT MATCHES UP WITH A CAR RACE FOR STEVO.
STEVO
Martial artist. Race Car driver. Bad-ass.
HEY! YOU'RE THE AMAZING JOY BUZZARDS!
YEAH, LAST TIME WE CHECKED.
NICE TO FINALLY MEET YOU GUYS.
OUR BAND IS OPENING FOR YOU ON THE TOUR. WE'RE..
JOE STEREO AND THE SEX KITTENS
JOE!
<--JOE STEREO
Punk whiz with a chip on his shoulder.
DEFINING MOMENT:
Near Death experience with a giant Gila Monster.
HEY, I'VE HEARD GOOD THINGS ABOUT YOU GUYS. GLAD TO MEET YOU.
JOE!

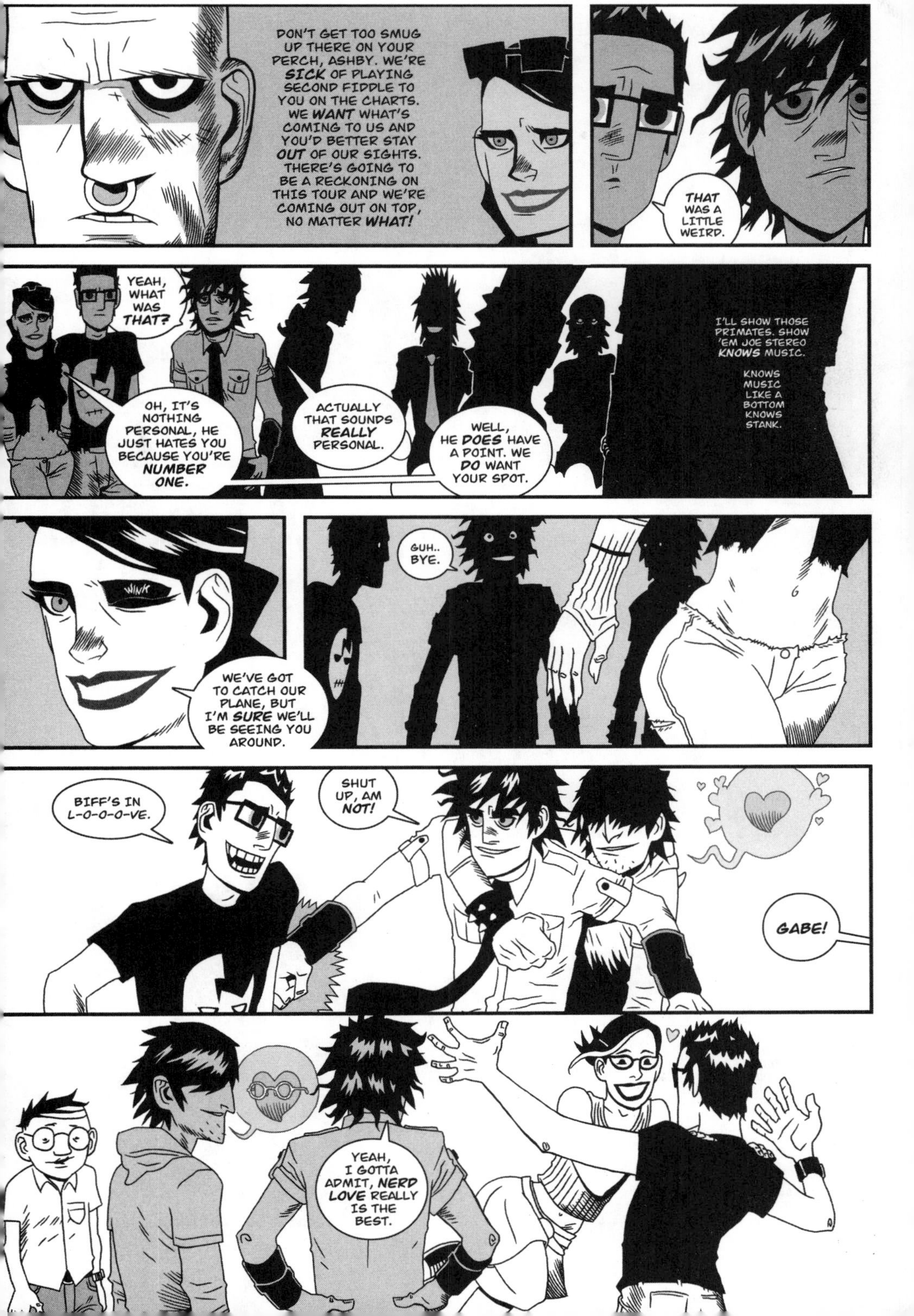
DON'T GET TOO SMUG UP THERE ON YOUR PERCH, ASHBY. WE'RE SICK OF PLAYING SECOND FIDDLE TO YOU ON THE CHARTS. WE WANT WHAT'S COMING TO US AND YOU'D BETTER STAY OUT OF OUR SIGHTS. THERE'S GOING TO BE A RECKONING ON THIS TOUR AND WE'RE COMING OUT ON TOP, NO MATTER WHAT!
THAT WAS A LITTLE WEIRD.
YEAH, WHAT WAS THAT?
OH, IT'S NOTHING PERSONAL, HE JUST HATES YOU BECAUSE YOU'RE NUMBER ONE.
ACTUALLY THAT SOUNDS REALLY PERSONAL.
WELL, HE DOES HAVE A POINT. WE DO WANT YOUR SPOT.
I'LL SHOW THOSE PRIMATES. SHOW 'EM JOE STEREO KNOWS MUSIC.
KNOWS MUSIC LIKE A BOTTOM KNOWS STANK.
WINK
WE'VE GOT TO CATCH OUR PLANE, BUT I'M SURE WE'LL BE SEEING YOU AROUND.
GUH.. BYE.
BIFF'S IN L-O-O-O-VE.
SHUT UP, AM NOT!
GABE!
YEAH, I GOTTA ADMIT, NERD LOVE REALLY IS THE BEST.

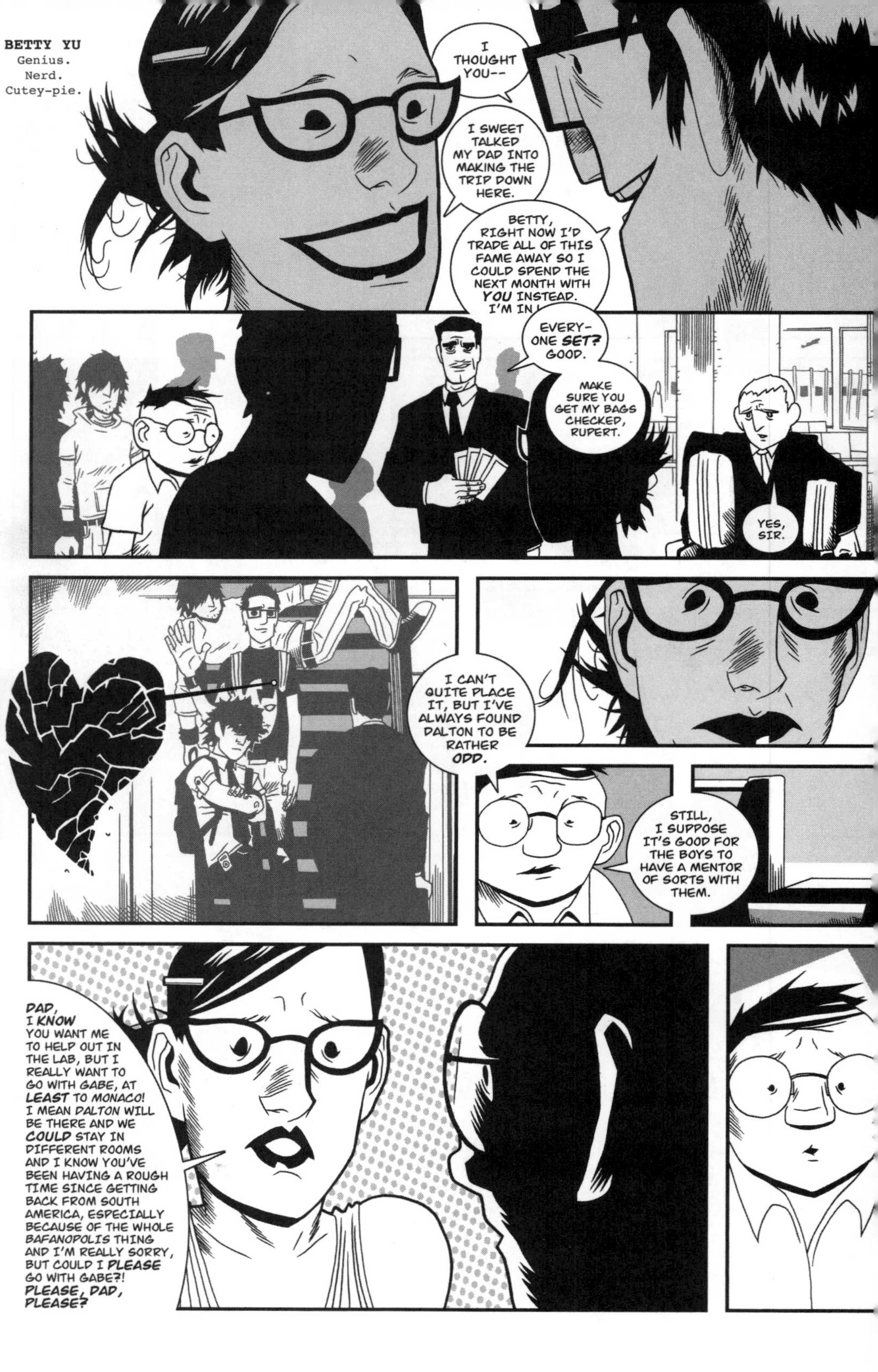
BETTY YU
Genius.
Nerd.
Cutey-pie.
I THOUGHT YOU--
I SWEET TALKED MY DAD INTO MAKING THE TRIP DOWN HERE.
BETTY, RIGHT NOW I'D TRADE ALL OF THIS FAME AWAY SO I COULD SPEND THE NEXT MONTH WITH YOU INSTEAD.
EVERY-ONE SET? GOOD.
MAKE SURE YOU GET MY BAGS CHECKED, RUPERT.
YES, SIR.
I CAN'T QUITE PLACE IT, BUT I'VE ALWAYS FOUND DALTON TO BE RATHER ODD.
STILL, I SUPPOSE IT'S GOOD FOR THE BOYS TO HAVE A MENTOR OF SORTS WITH THEM.
DAD, I KNOW YOU WANT ME TO HELP OUT IN THE LAB, BUT I REALLY WANT TO GO WITH GABE, AT LEAST TO MONACO! I MEAN DALTON WILL BE THERE AND WE COULD STAY IN DIFFERENT ROOMS AND I KNOW YOU'VE BEEN HAVING A ROUGH TIME SINCE GETTING BACK FROM SOUTH AMERICA, ESPECIALLY BECAUSE OF THE WHOLE BAFANOPOLIS THING AND I'M REALLY SORRY, BUT COULD I PLEASE GO WITH GABE?! PLEASE, DAD, PLEASE?

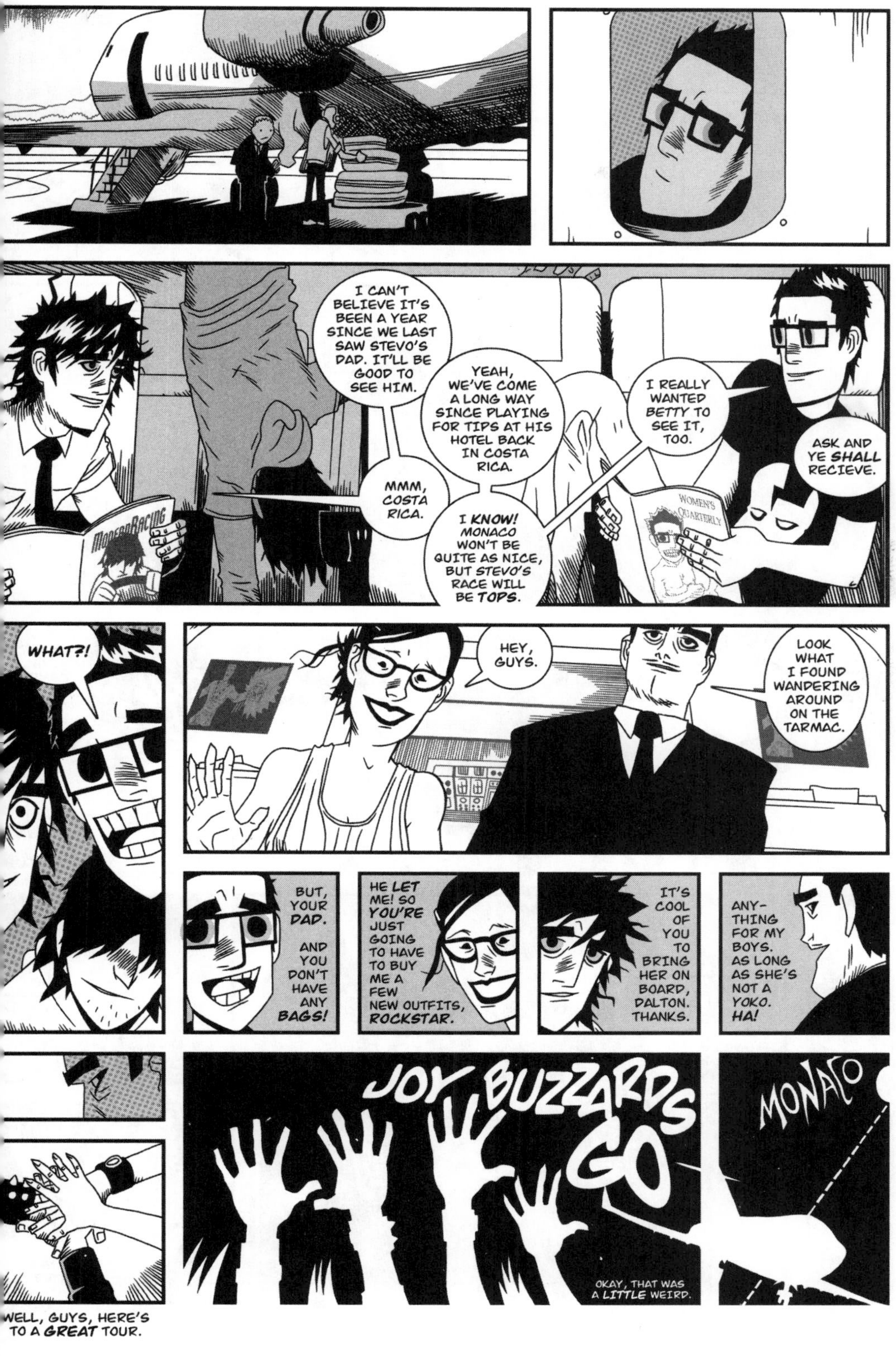
I CAN'T BELIEVE IT'S BEEN A YEAR SINCE WE LAST SAW STEVO'S DAD. IT'LL BE GOOD TO SEE HIM.
YEAH, WE'VE COME A LONG WAY SINCE PLAYING FOR TIPS AT HIS HOTEL BACK IN COSTA RICA.
MMM, COSTA RICA.
I KNOW! MONACO WON'T BE QUITE AS NICE, BUT STEVO'S RACE WILL BE TOPS.
I REALLY WANTED BETTY TO SEE IT, TOO.
ASK AND YE SHALL RECIEVE.
WOMEN'S QUARTERLY
MODERN RACING
WHAT?!
HEY, GUYS.
LOOK WHAT I FOUND WANDERING AROUND ON THE TARMAC.
BUT, YOUR DAD.
AND YOU DON'T HAVE ANY BAGS!
HE LET ME! SO YOU'RE JUST GOING TO HAVE TO BUY ME A FEW NEW OUTFITS, ROCKSTAR.
IT'S COOL OF YOU TO BRING HER ON BOARD, DALTON. THANKS.
ANY-THING FOR MY BOYS. AS LONG AS SHE'S NOT A YOKO. HA!
WELL, GUYS, HERE'S TO A GREAT TOUR.
JOY BUZZARDS GO
OKAY, THAT WAS A LITTLE WEIRD.
MONACO

ABRAHAM VARGAS

Rich, lazy man of leisure. Father to a bad-ass bass player.

EXCUSE OF CHOICE: "But I'm delicate, baby."

BOYS!

HEY, POPPA VARGAS.

STEVO, MY BOY! I'M SO PROUD OF YOU! COME HERE!

GOOD TO SEE YOU, VARGAS.

I'VE TOLD YOU, DALTON, CALL ME ABE.

BOYS, LOOK AT YOU!

ONE YEAR AND YOU ARE NEARLY MEN.

AND YOU'VE BROUGHT A PRINCESS!

HA! HELLO, SIR.

NOW, BOYS, LISTEN TO ME. WE'VE GOT TO GET YOU **OUT** OF HERE. IT'S A **MAD** HOUSE OUT THERE!

OH, COME ON. IT **CAN'T** B ANY WORS THAN OUR ARRIVAL I HOLLYWOO

ACTUALLY, THAT WAS **LOS** ANGELES, BIFF.

WHATEVER

YOU SEE? MONACO **LOVES** YOU BOYS! THE SURROUNDING TOWNS HAVE ALL SHUT DOWN.

I...IT.. THERE.. UH..PAGO BAH..

YOU BOYS MAY AS WELL GIVE THEM WHAT THEY WANT.

THE PLANE CREW IS UNLOADING YOUR GEAR. I'LL HAVE THEM SET IT UP.

SOMEON BETTER CAL AIR TRAFFI CONTRO

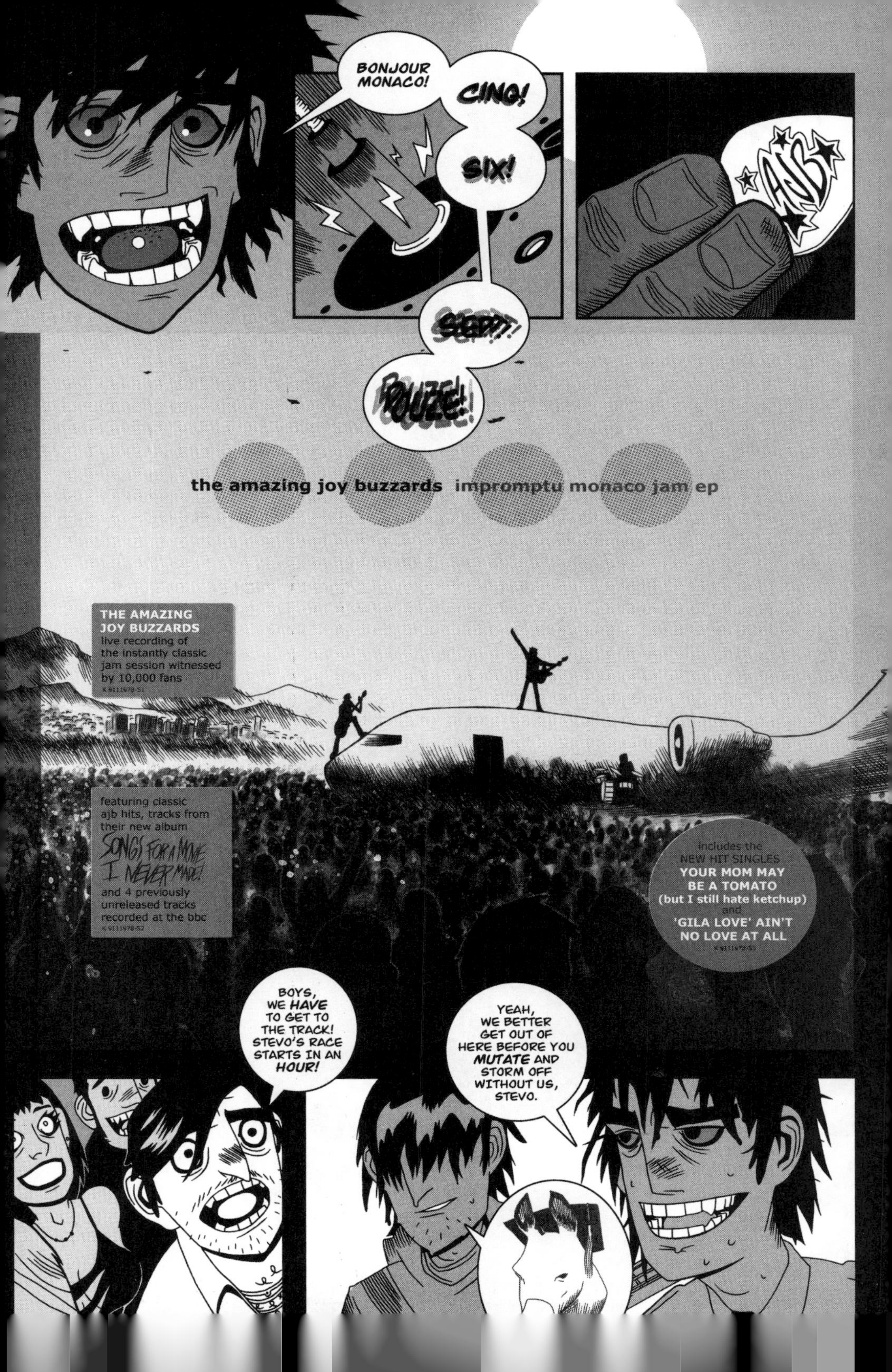
BONJOUR MONACO!
CINQ!
SIX!
the amazing joy buzzards impromptu monaco jam ep
THE AMAZING JOY BUZZARDS live recording of the instantly classic jam session witnessed by 10,000 fans
featuring classic ajb hits, tracks from their new album SONGS FOR A MOVIE I NEVER MADE! and 4 previously unreleased tracks recorded at the bbc
includes the NEW HIT SINGLES YOUR MOM MAY BE A TOMATO (but I still hate ketchup) and 'GILA LOVE' AIN'T NO LOVE AT ALL
BOYS, WE HAVE TO GET TO THE TRACK! STEVO'S RACE STARTS IN AN HOUR!
YEAH, WE BETTER GET OUT OF HERE BEFORE YOU MUTATE AND STORM OFF WITHOUT US, STEVO.

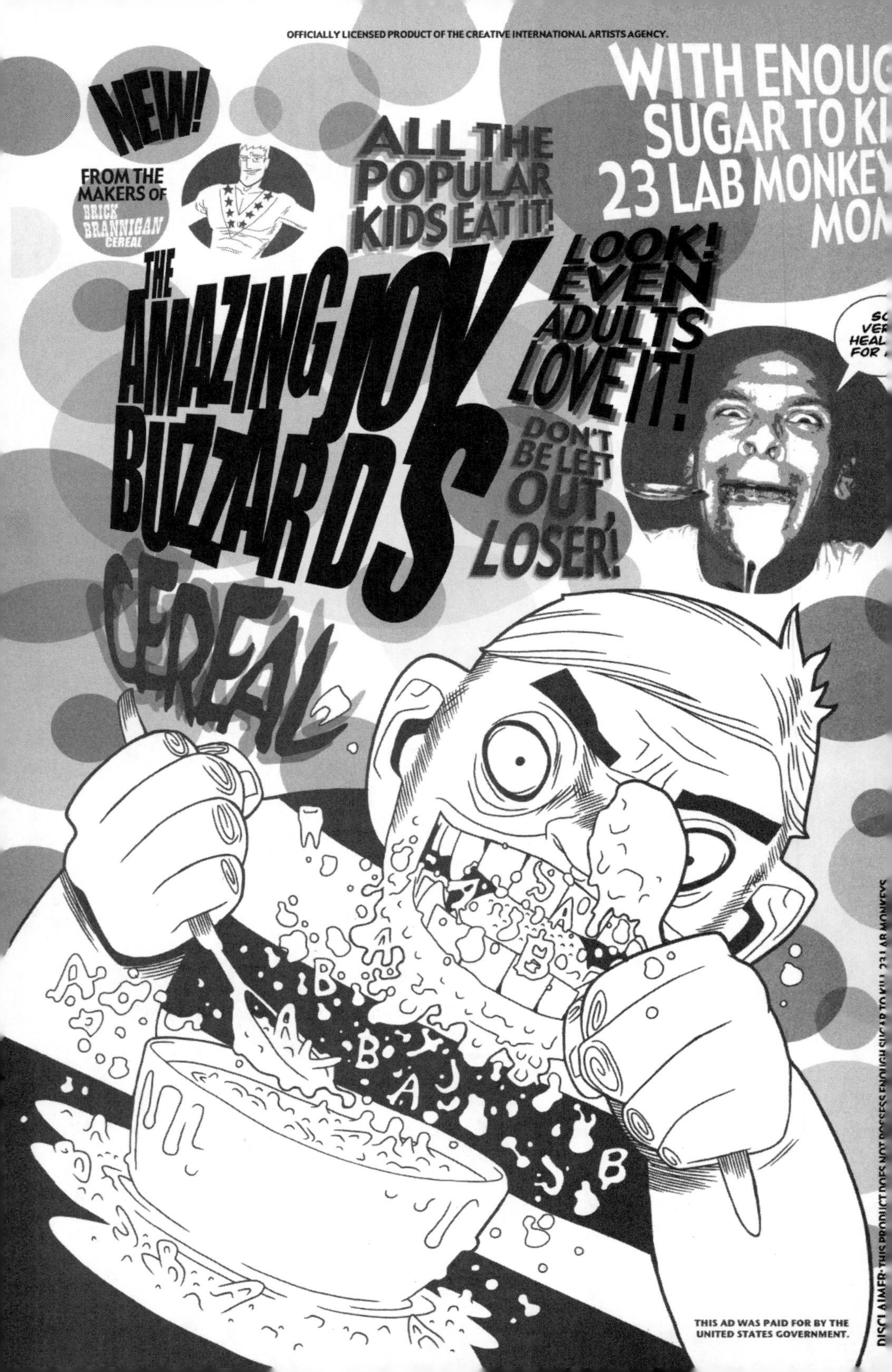

OFFICIALLY LICENSED PRODUCT OF THE CREATIVE INTERNATIONAL ARTISTS AGENCY.
NEW!
FROM THE MAKERS OF
BRICK BRANNIGAN CEREAL
ALL THE POPULAR KIDS EAT IT!
WITH ENOUG
SUGAR TO KI
23 LAB MONKEY
MON
THE AMAZING JOY BUZZARDS
CEREAL
LOOK! EVEN ADULTS LOVE IT!
DON'T BE LEFT OUT, LOSER!
DISCLAIMER: THIS PRODUCT DOES NOT POSSESS ENOUGH SUGAR TO KILL 23 LAB MONKEYS
THIS AD WAS PAID FOR BY THE UNITED STATES GOVERNMENT.

READY, SET, IGNITION!

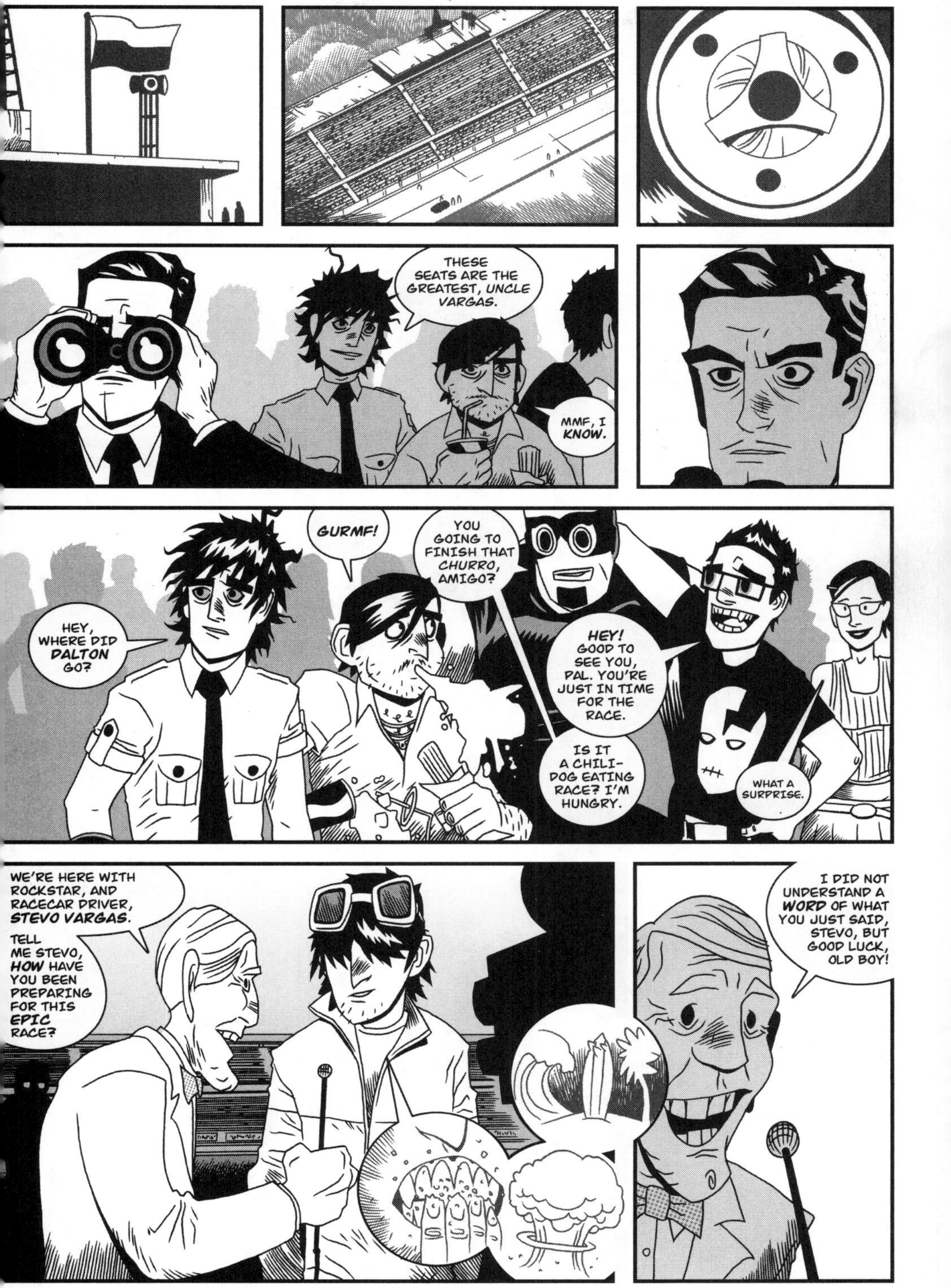
THESE SEATS ARE THE GREATEST, UNCLE VARGAS.
MMF, I KNOW.
GURMF!
YOU GOING TO FINISH THAT CHURRO, AMIGO?
HEY, WHERE DID DALTON GO?
HEY! GOOD TO SEE YOU, PAL. YOU'RE JUST IN TIME FOR THE RACE.
IS IT A CHILI-DOG EATING RACE? I'M HUNGRY.
WHAT A SURPRISE.
WE'RE HERE WITH ROCKSTAR, AND RACECAR DRIVER, STEVO VARGAS.
TELL ME STEVO, HOW HAVE YOU BEEN PREPARING FOR THIS EPIC RACE?
I DID NOT UNDERSTAND A WORD OF WHAT YOU JUST SAID, STEVO, BUT GOOD LUCK, OLD BOY!

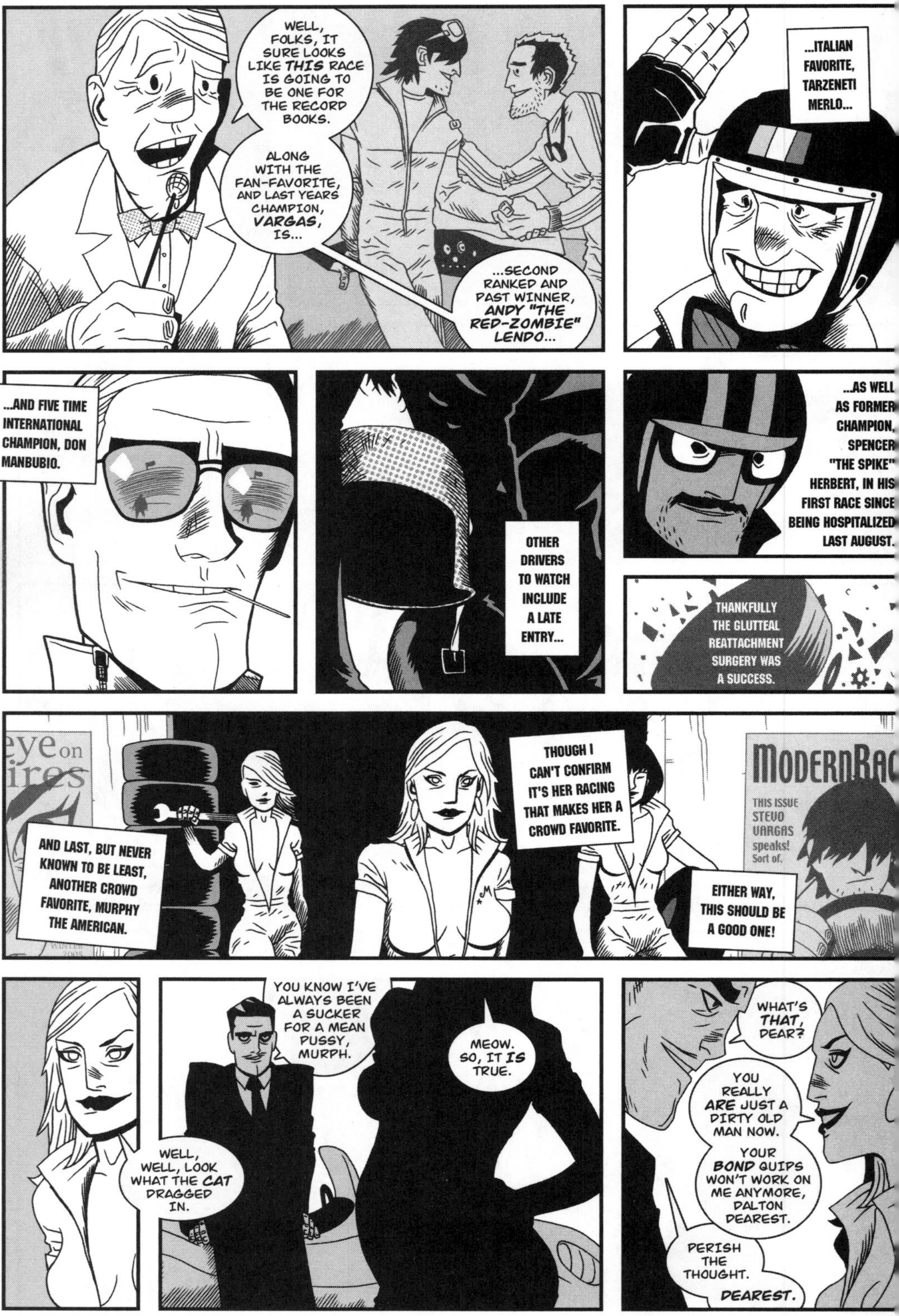
WELL, FOLKS, IT SURE LOOKS LIKE THIS RACE IS GOING TO BE ONE FOR THE RECORD BOOKS.
ALONG WITH THE FAN-FAVORITE, AND LAST YEARS CHAMPION, VARGAS, IS...
...SECOND RANKED AND PAST WINNER, ANDY "THE RED-ZOMBIE" LENDO...
...ITALIAN FAVORITE, TARZENETI MERLO...
...AND FIVE TIME INTERNATIONAL CHAMPION, DON MANBUBIO.
OTHER DRIVERS TO WATCH INCLUDE A LATE ENTRY...
...AS WELL AS FORMER CHAMPION, SPENCER "THE SPIKE" HERBERT, IN HIS FIRST RACE SINCE BEING HOSPITALIZED LAST AUGUST.
THANKFULLY THE GLUTTEAL REATTACHMENT SURGERY WAS A SUCCESS.
eye on tires
MODERNRAC
THIS ISSUE STEVO VARGAS speaks! Sort of.
AND LAST, BUT NEVER KNOWN TO BE LEAST, ANOTHER CROWD FAVORITE, MURPHY THE AMERICAN.
THOUGH I CAN'T CONFIRM IT'S HER RACING THAT MAKES HER A CROWD FAVORITE.
EITHER WAY, THIS SHOULD BE A GOOD ONE!
WELL, WELL, LOOK WHAT THE CAT DRAGGED IN.
YOU KNOW I'VE ALWAYS BEEN A SUCKER FOR A MEAN PUSSY, MURPH.
MEOW. SO, IT IS TRUE.
WHAT'S THAT, DEAR?
YOU REALLY ARE JUST A DIRTY OLD MAN NOW.
YOUR BOND QUIPS WON'T WORK ON ME ANYMORE, DALTON DEAREST.
PERISH THE THOUGHT.
DEAREST.

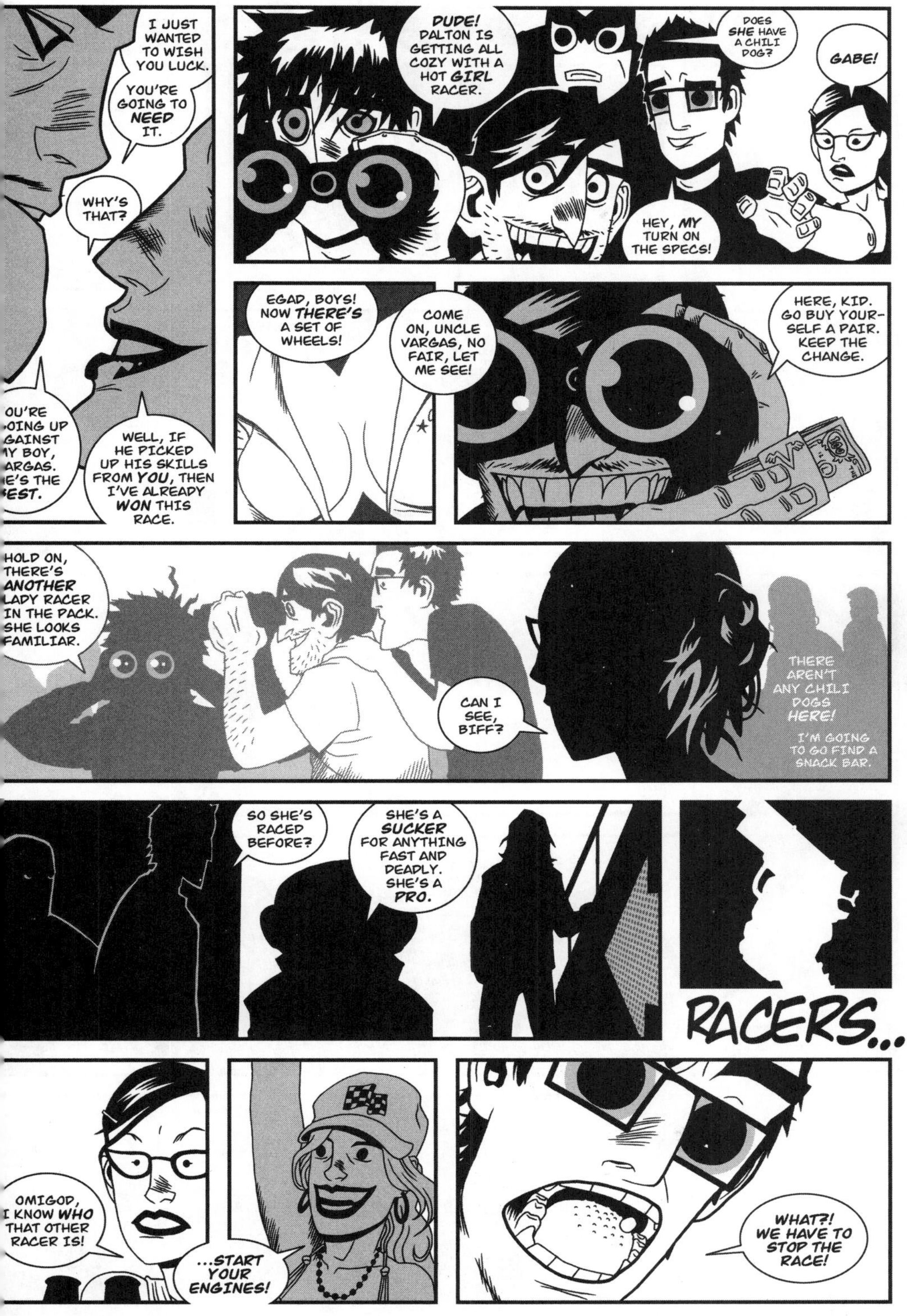
I JUST WANTED TO WISH YOU LUCK.
YOU'RE GOING TO NEED IT.
WHY'S THAT?
OU'RE OING UP GAINST MY BOY, VARGAS. E'S THE EST.
WELL, IF HE PICKED UP HIS SKILLS FROM YOU, THEN I'VE ALREADY WON THIS RACE.
DUDE! DALTON IS GETTING ALL COZY WITH A HOT GIRL RACER.
DOES SHE HAVE A CHILI DOG?
GABE!
HEY, MY TURN ON THE SPECS!
EGAD, BOYS! NOW THERE'S A SET OF WHEELS!
COME ON, UNCLE VARGAS, NO FAIR, LET ME SEE!
HERE, KID. GO BUY YOURSELF A PAIR. KEEP THE CHANGE.
HOLD ON, THERE'S ANOTHER LADY RACER IN THE PACK. SHE LOOKS FAMILIAR.
CAN I SEE, BIFF?
THERE AREN'T ANY CHILI DOGS HERE!
I'M GOING TO GO FIND A SNACK BAR.
SO SHE'S RACED BEFORE?
SHE'S A SUCKER FOR ANYTHING FAST AND DEADLY. SHE'S A PRO.
RACERS...
OMIGOD, I KNOW WHO THAT OTHER RACER IS!
...START YOUR ENGINES!
WHAT?! WE HAVE TO STOP THE RACE!

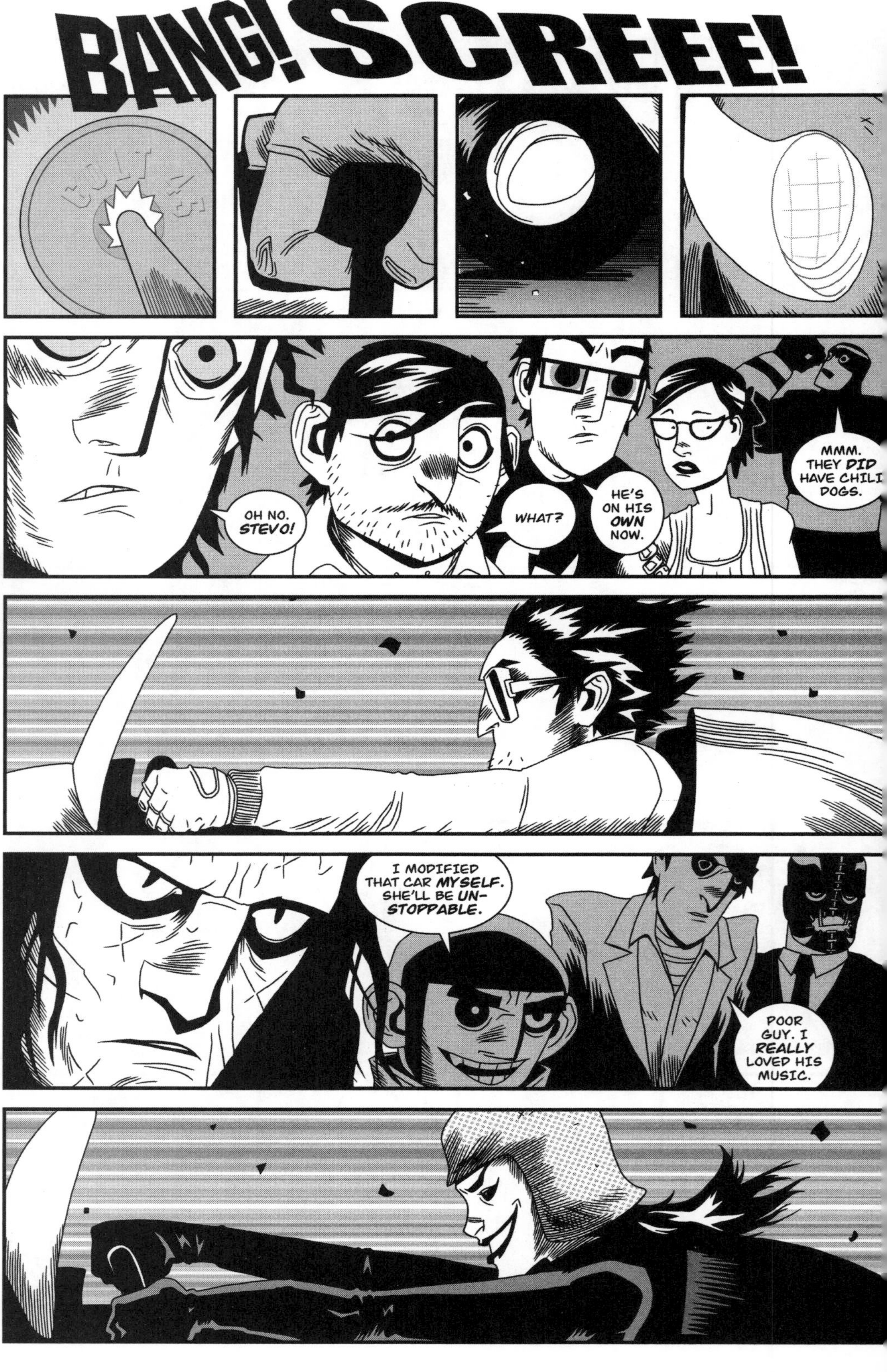
BANG!
SCREEE!
COLT 45
OH NO. STEVO!
WHAT?
HE'S ON HIS OWN NOW.
MMM. THEY DID HAVE CHILI DOGS.
I MODIFIED THAT CAR MYSELF. SHE'LL BE UN-STOPPABLE.
POOR GUY. I REALLY LOVED HIS MUSIC.

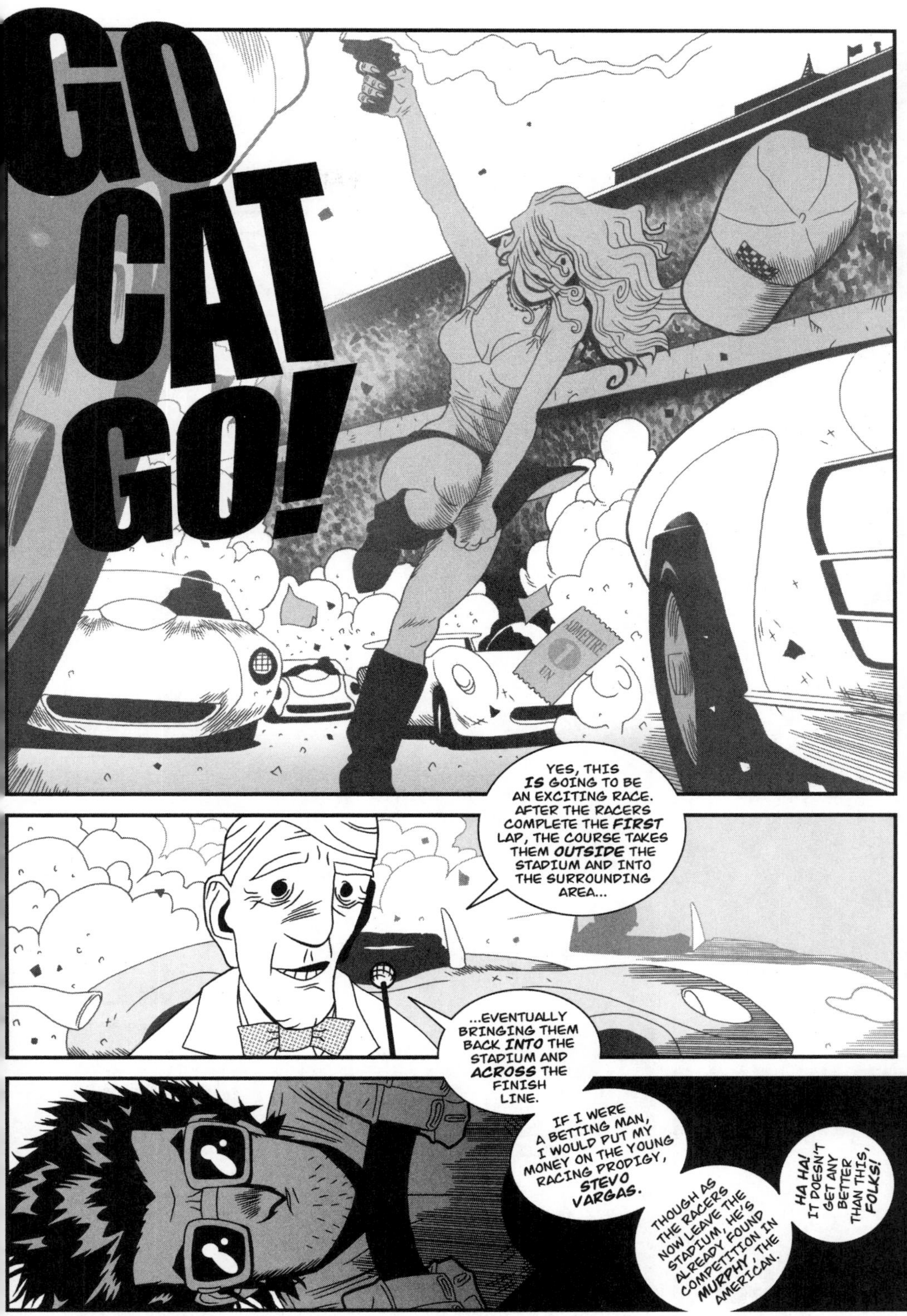
GO CAT GO!
YES, THIS IS GOING TO BE AN EXCITING RACE. AFTER THE RACERS COMPLETE THE FIRST LAP, THE COURSE TAKES THEM OUTSIDE THE STADIUM AND INTO THE SURROUNDING AREA...
...EVENTUALLY BRINGING THEM BACK INTO THE STADIUM AND ACROSS THE FINISH LINE.
IF I WERE A BETTING MAN, I WOULD PUT MY MONEY ON THE YOUNG RACING PRODIGY, STEVO VARGAS.
THOUGH AS THE RACERS NOW LEAVE THE STADIUM, HE'S ALREADY FOUND COMPETITION IN MURPHY, THE AMERICAN.
HA HA! IT DOESN'T GET ANY BETTER THAN THIS, FOLKS!

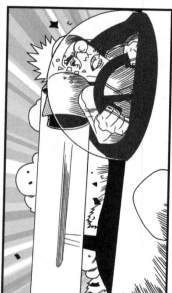

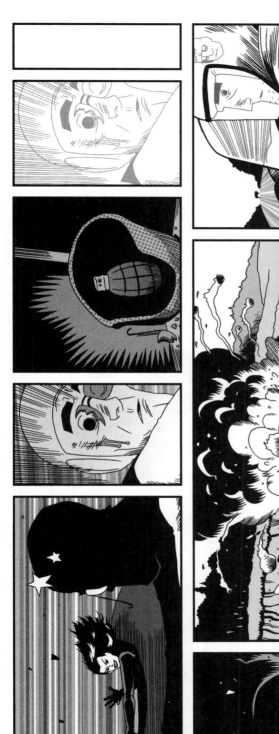

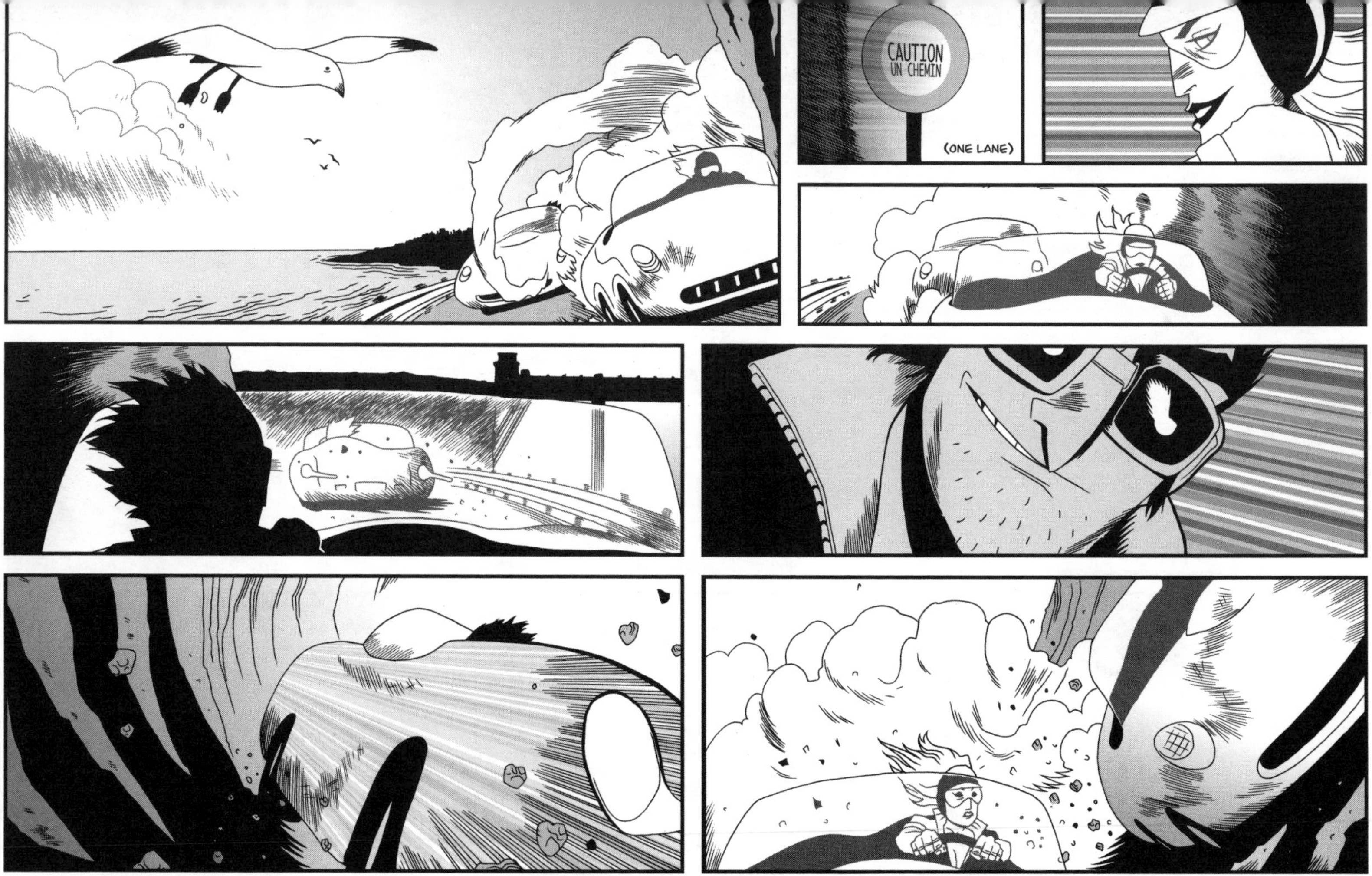
CAUTION
UN CHEMIN
(ONE LANE)

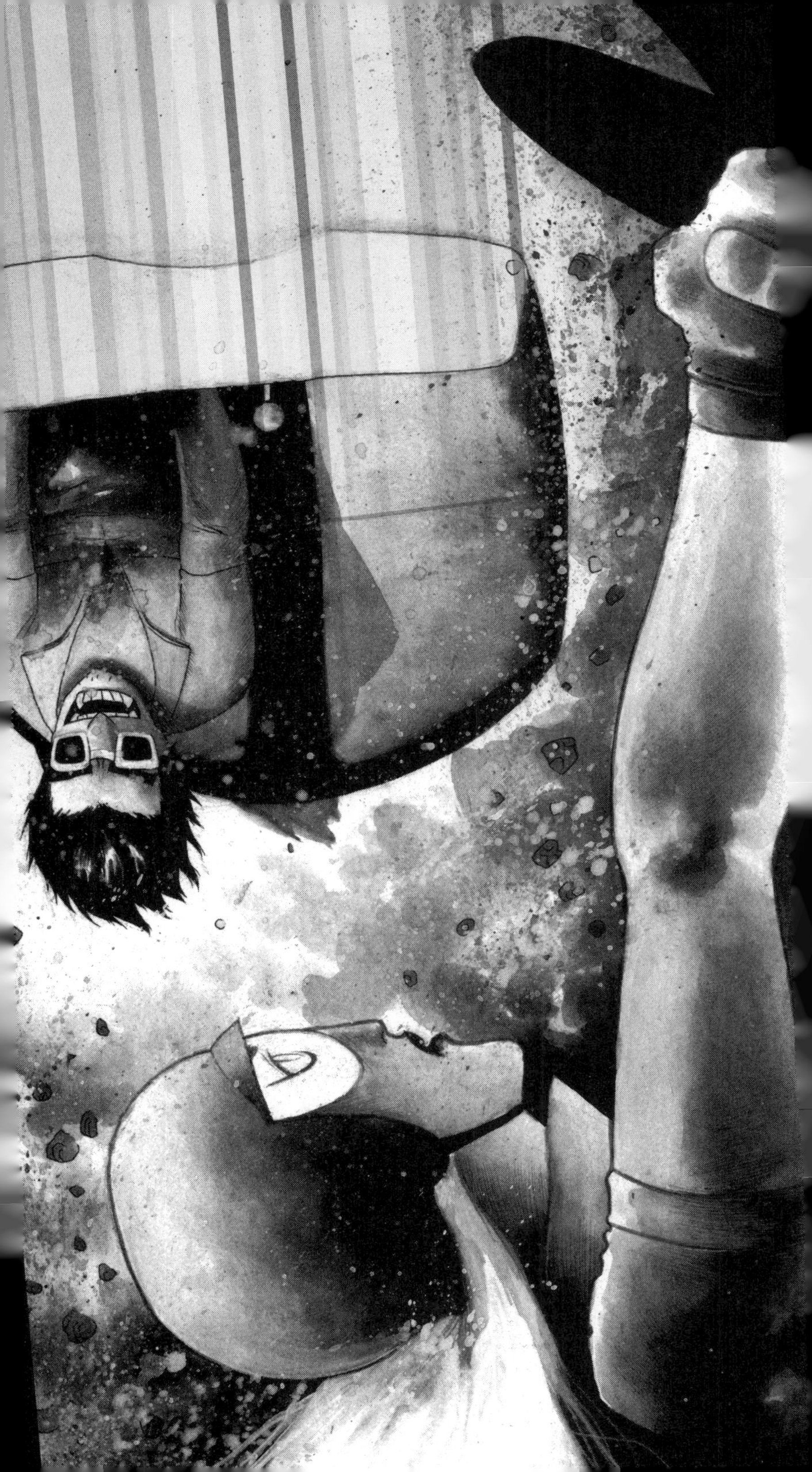

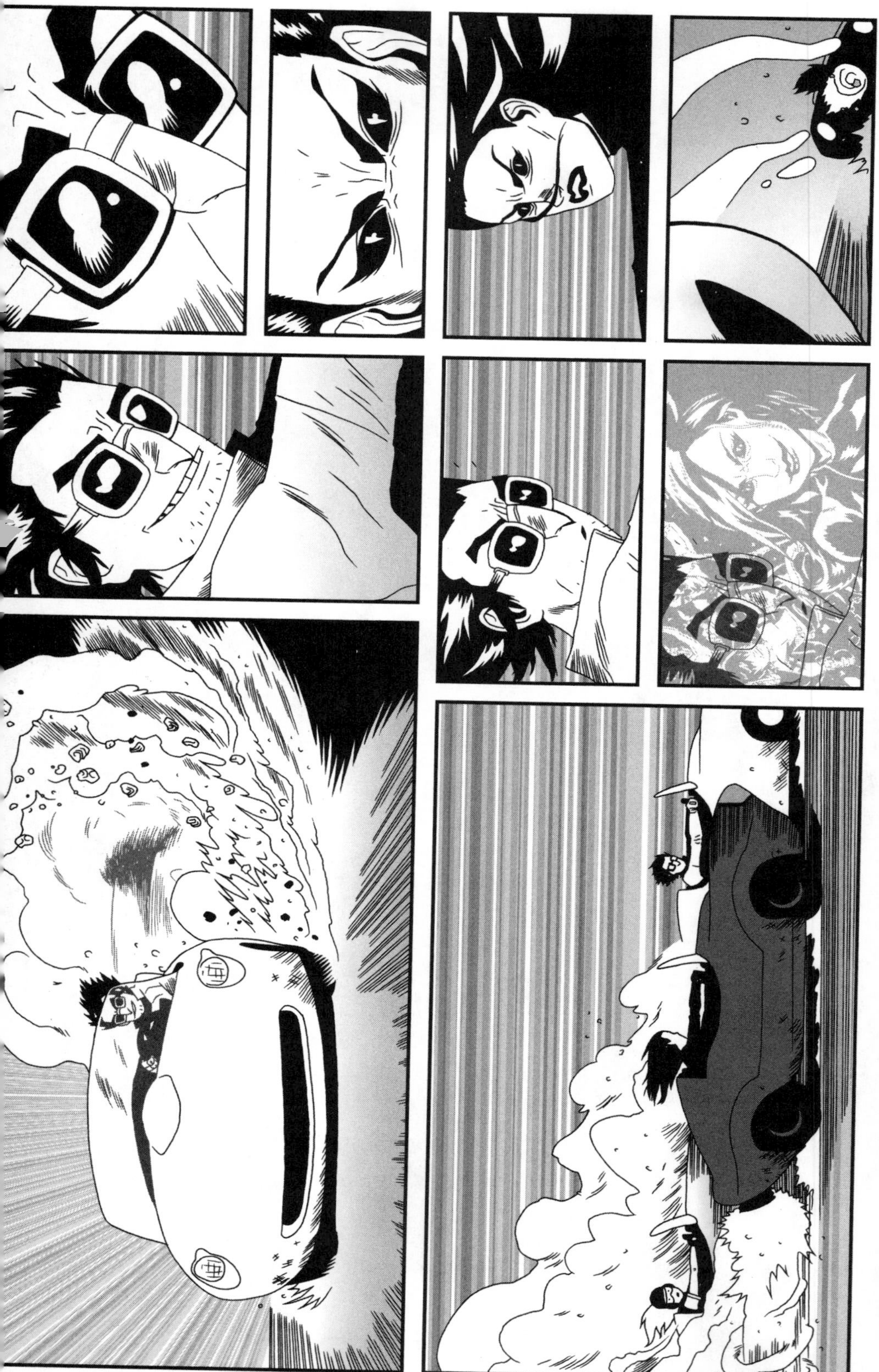

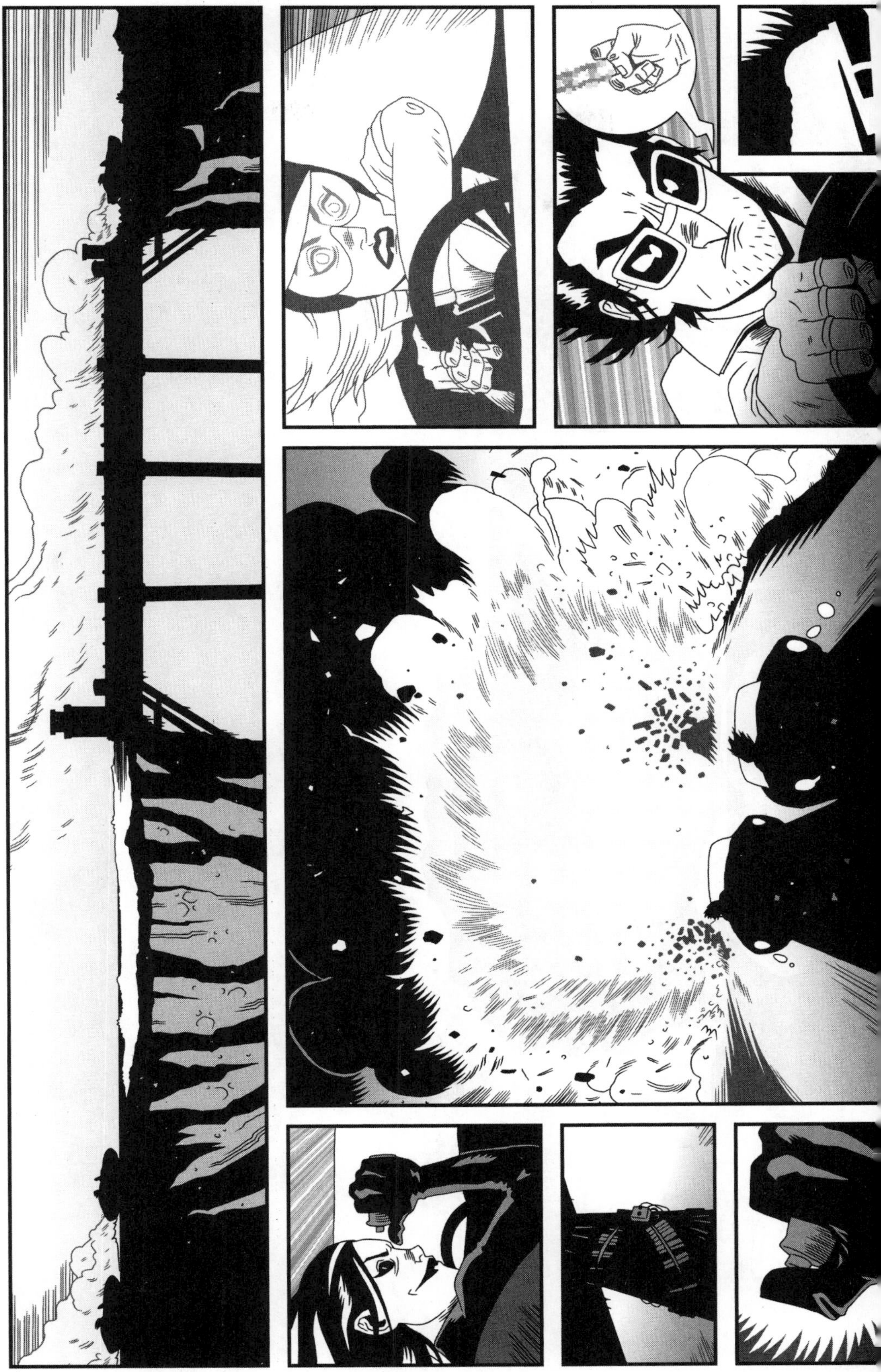

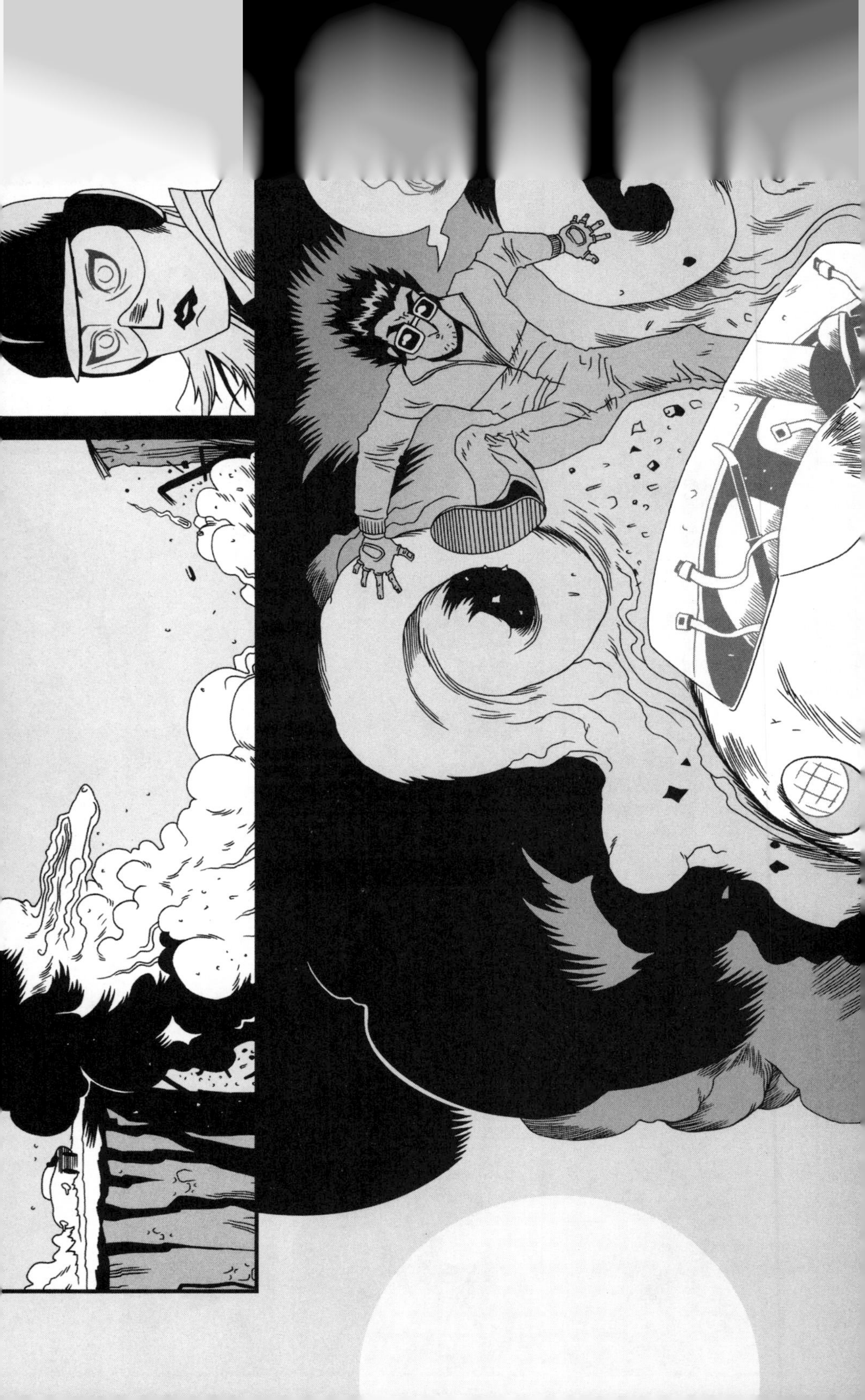

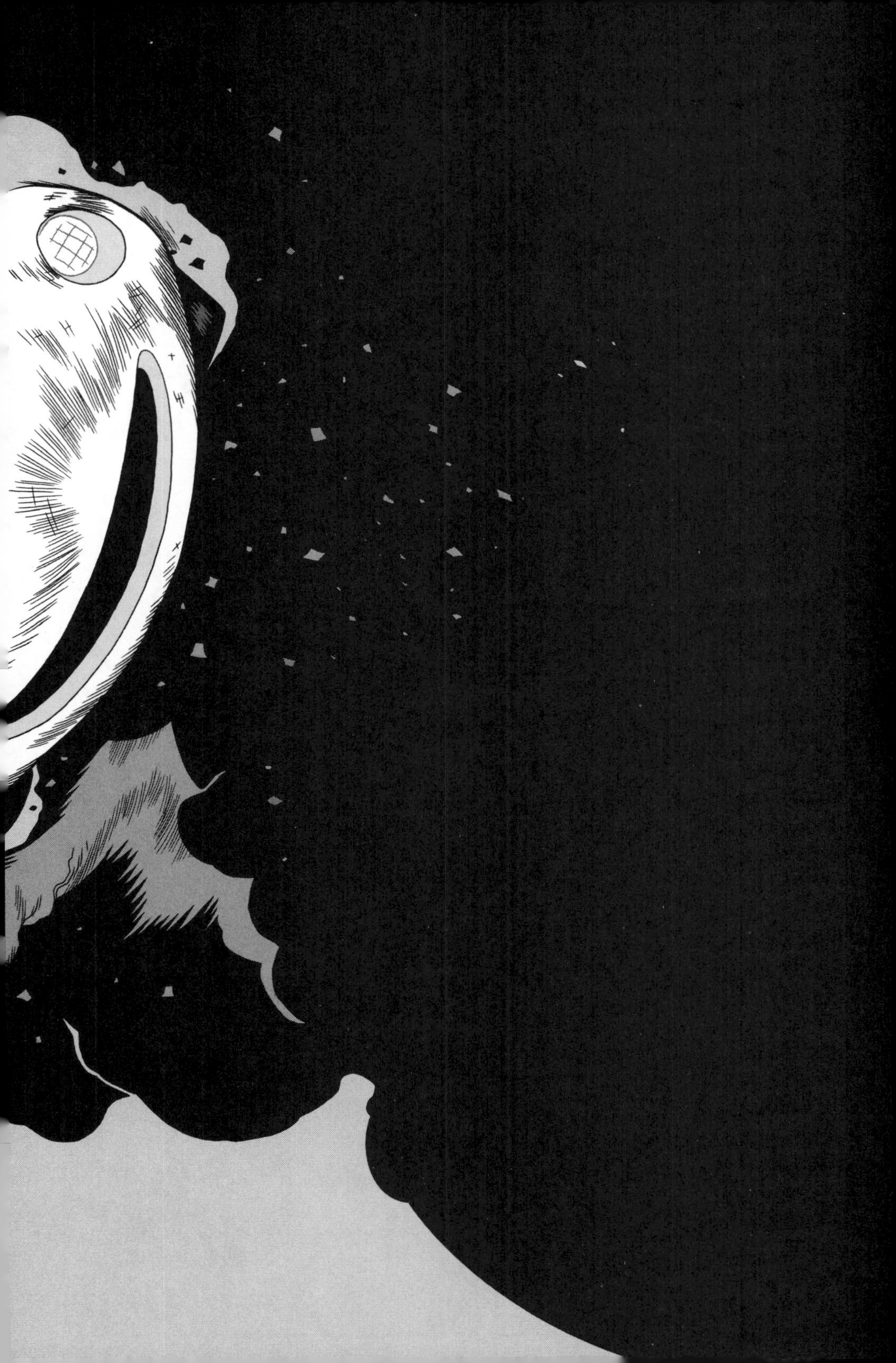

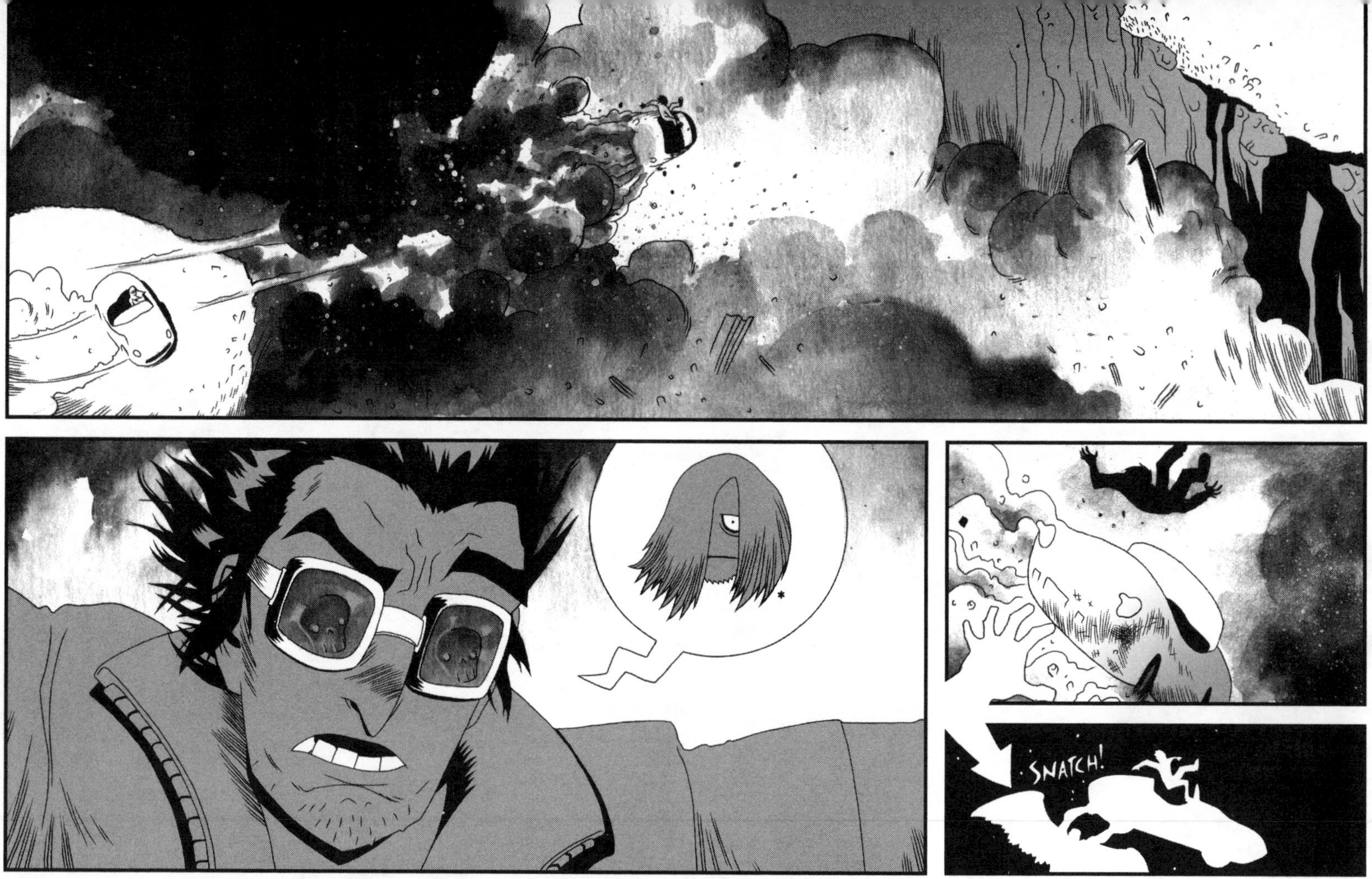
*
SNATCH!

* **EDITOR'S NOTE:** DON'T ASK ***US*** WHAT IT MEANS, WE JUST WORK HERE!

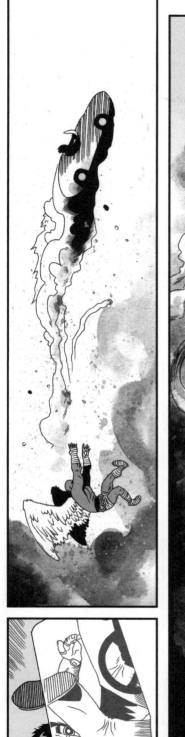

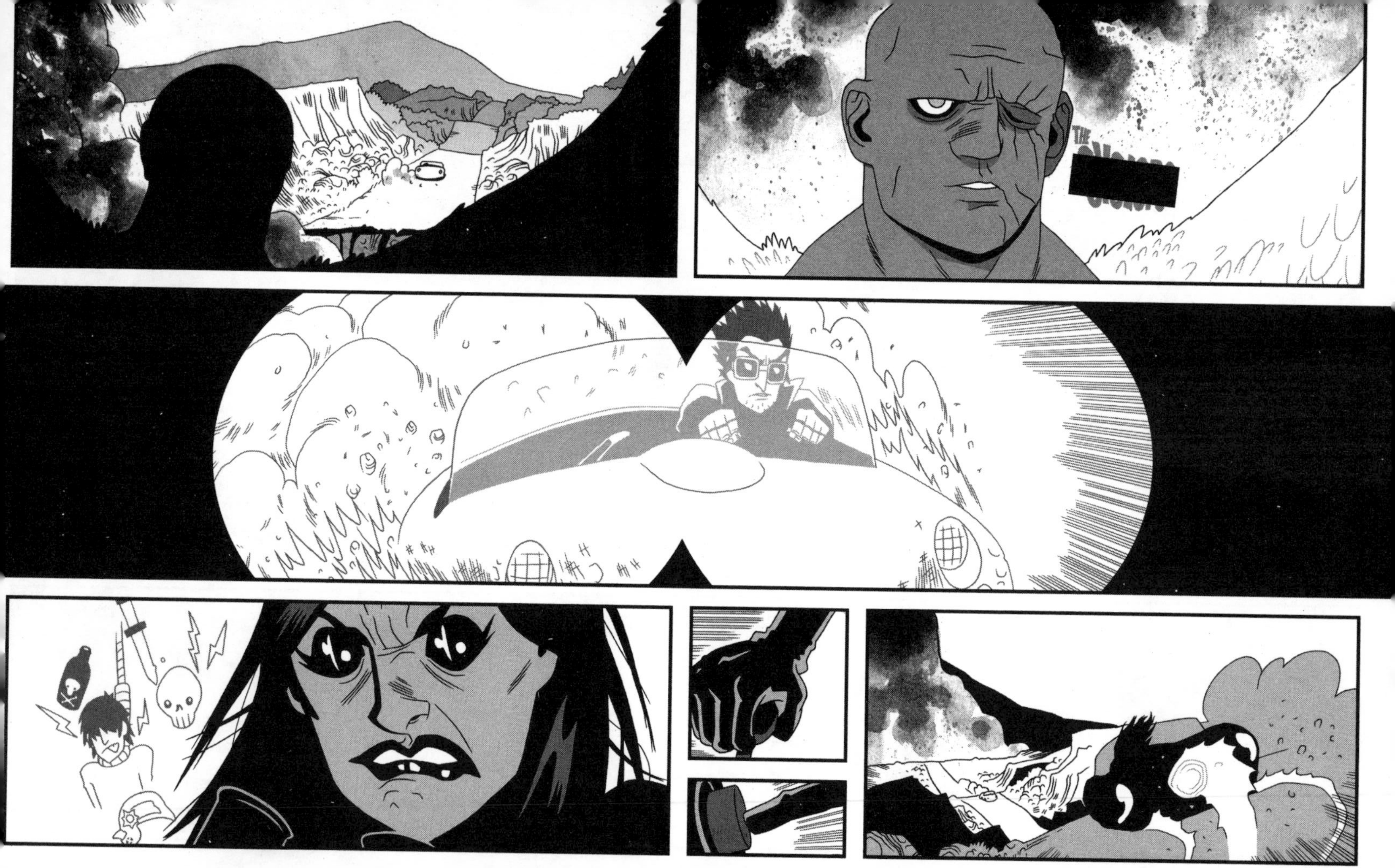
THE [redacted]

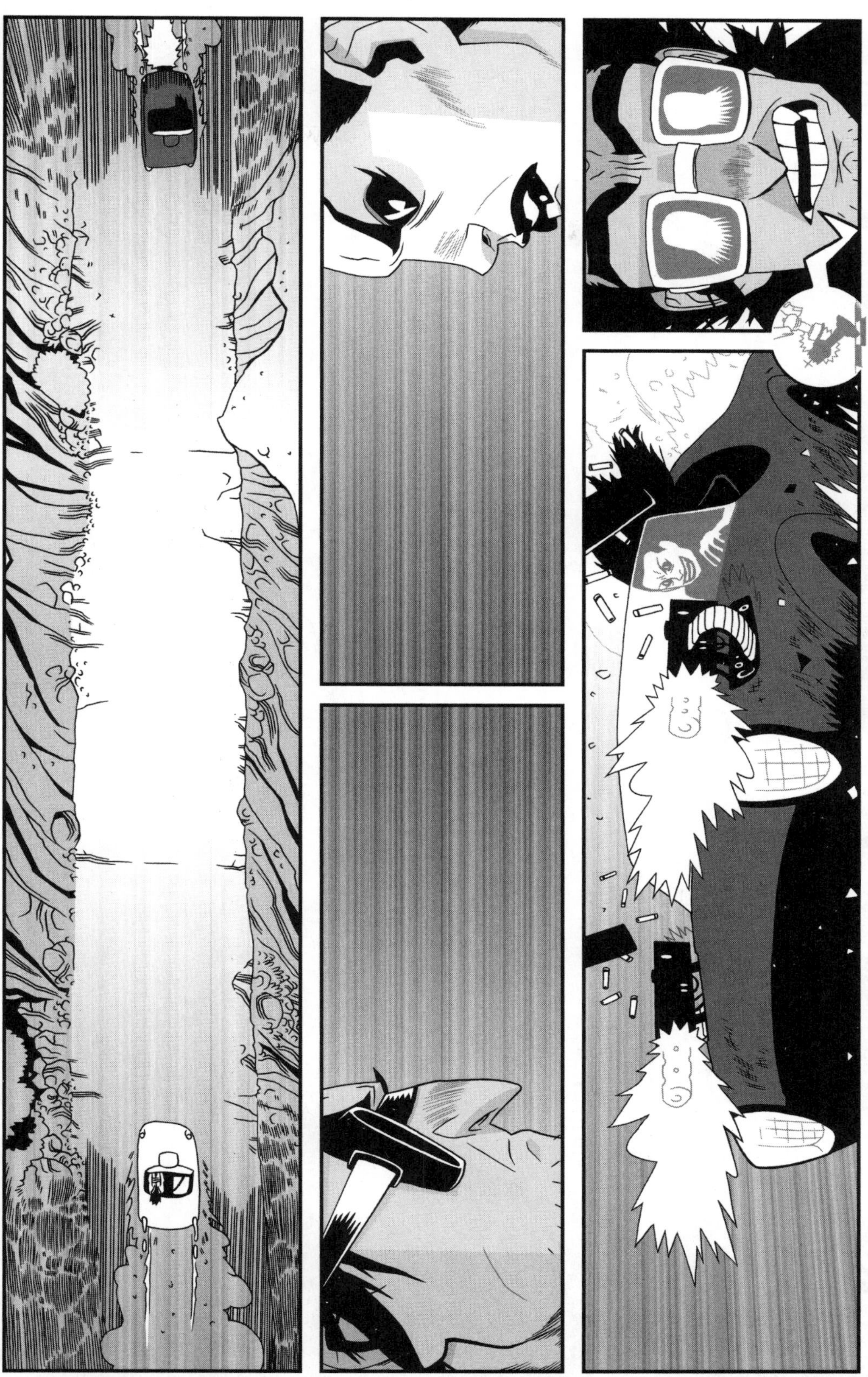

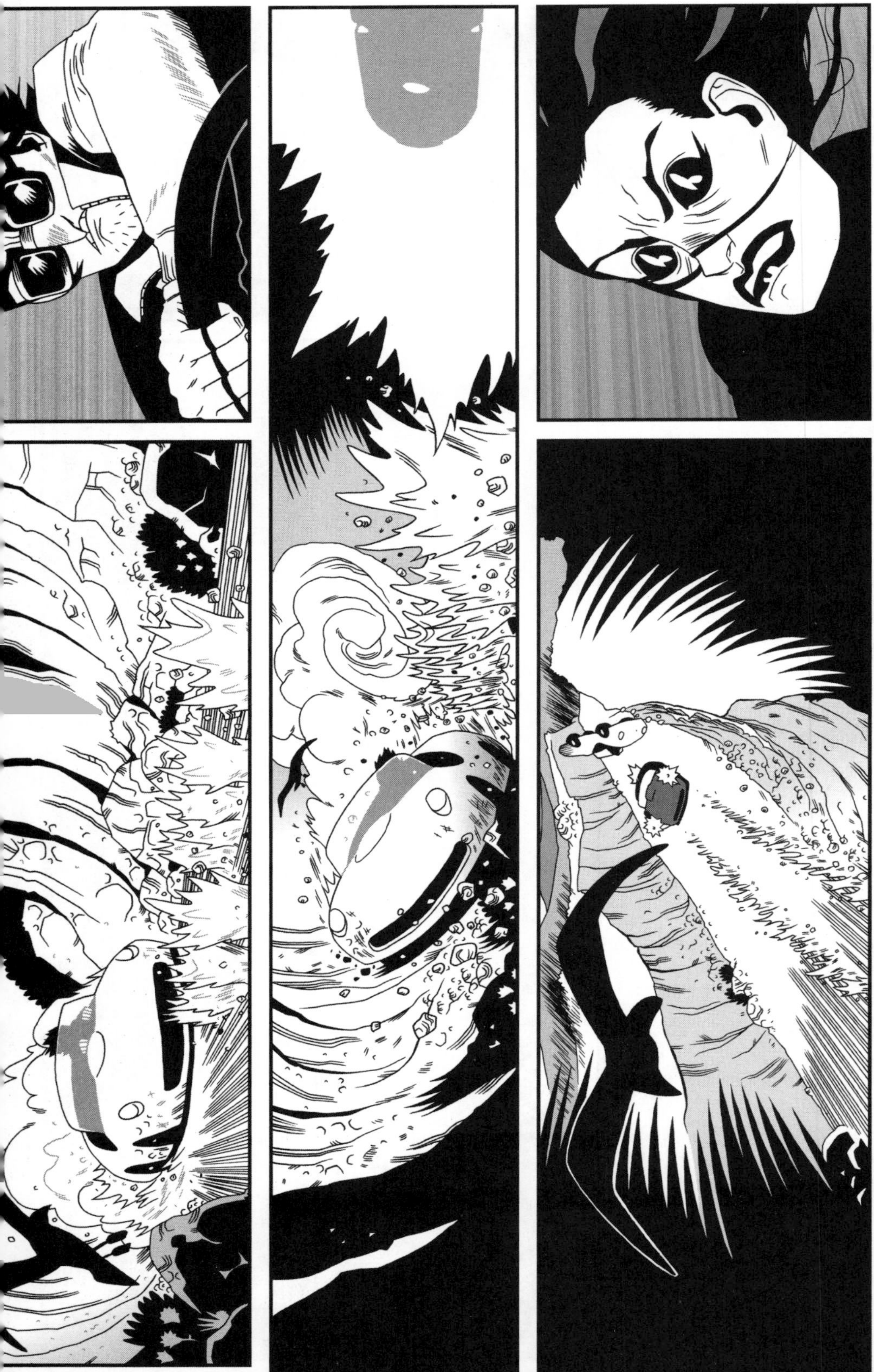

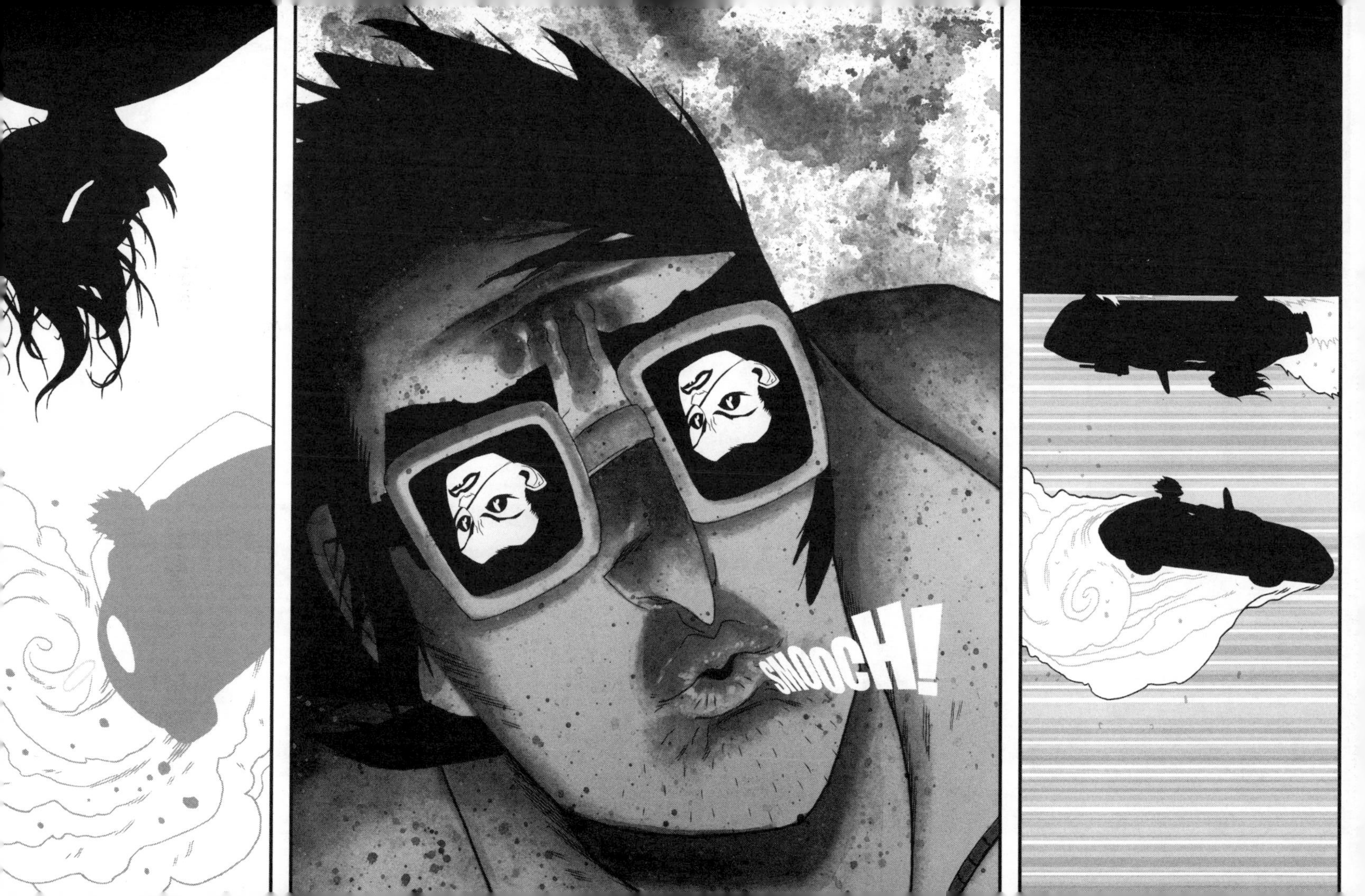
SMOOCH!

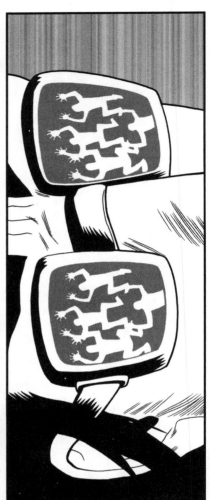

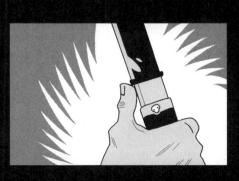

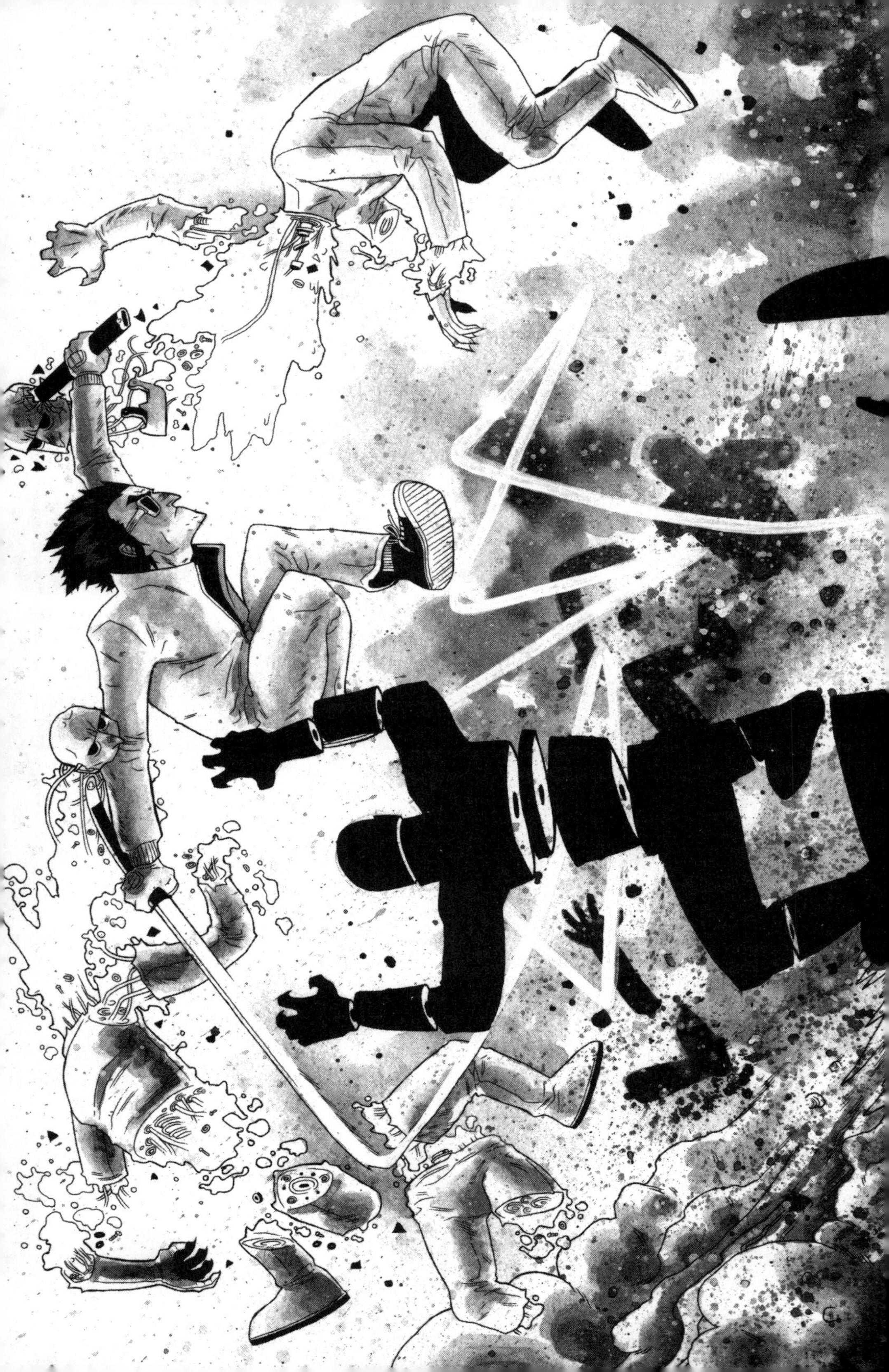

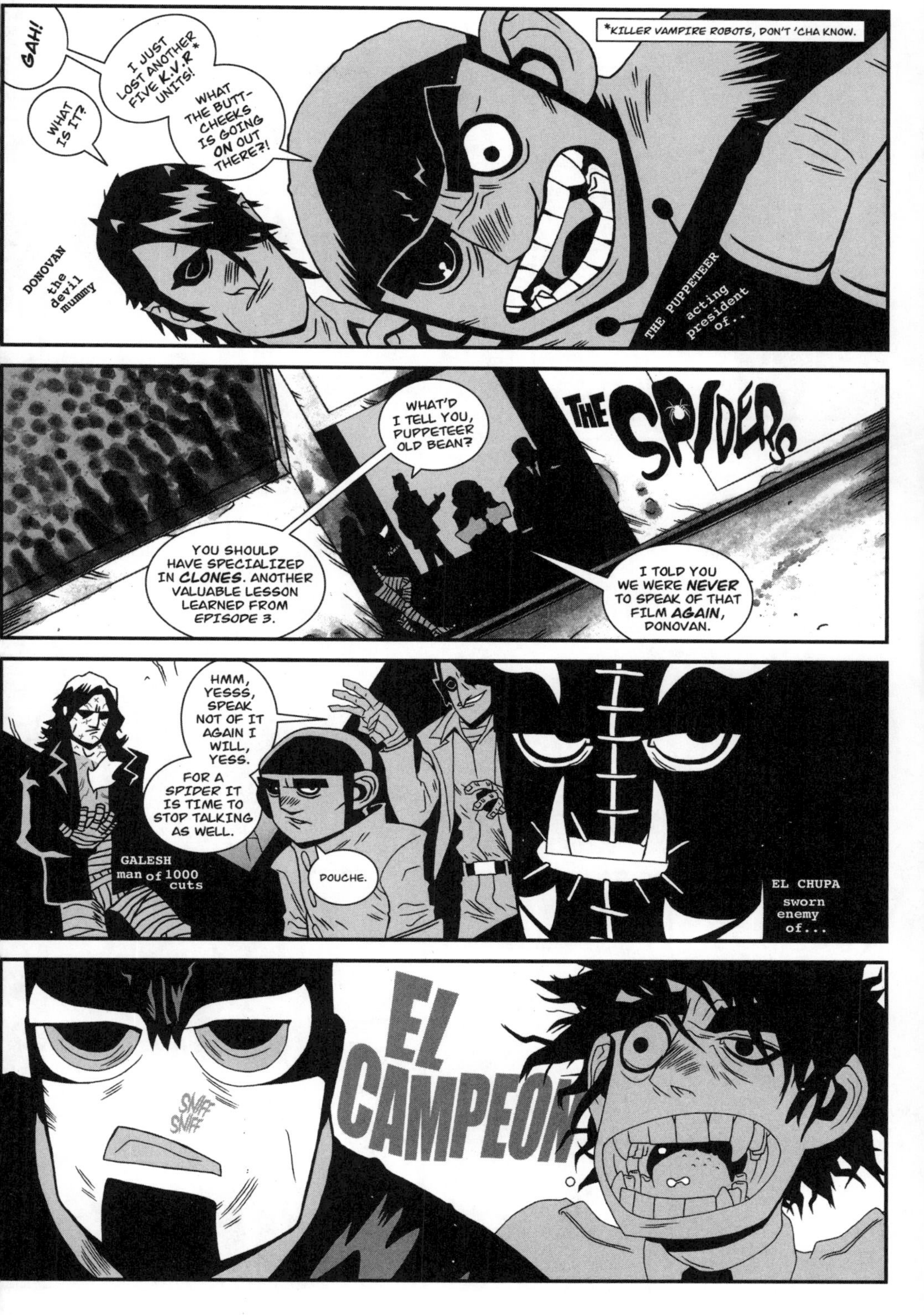
*KILLER VAMPIRE ROBOTS, DON'T 'CHA KNOW.
GAH!
WHAT IS IT?
I JUST LOST ANOTHER FIVE K.V.R* UNITS!
WHAT THE BUTT-CHEEKS IS GOING ON OUT THERE?!
DONOVAN the devil mummy
THE PUPPETEER acting president of..
THE SPIDERS
WHAT'D I TELL YOU, PUPPETEER OLD BEAN?
YOU SHOULD HAVE SPECIALIZED IN CLONES. ANOTHER VALUABLE LESSON LEARNED FROM EPISODE 3.
I TOLD YOU WE WERE NEVER TO SPEAK OF THAT FILM AGAIN, DONOVAN.
HMM, YESSS, SPEAK NOT OF IT AGAIN I WILL, YESS.
FOR A SPIDER IT IS TIME TO STOP TALKING AS WELL.
DOUCHE.
GALESH man of 1000 cuts
EL CHUPA sworn enemy of...
EL CAMPEON
SNIFF SNIFF

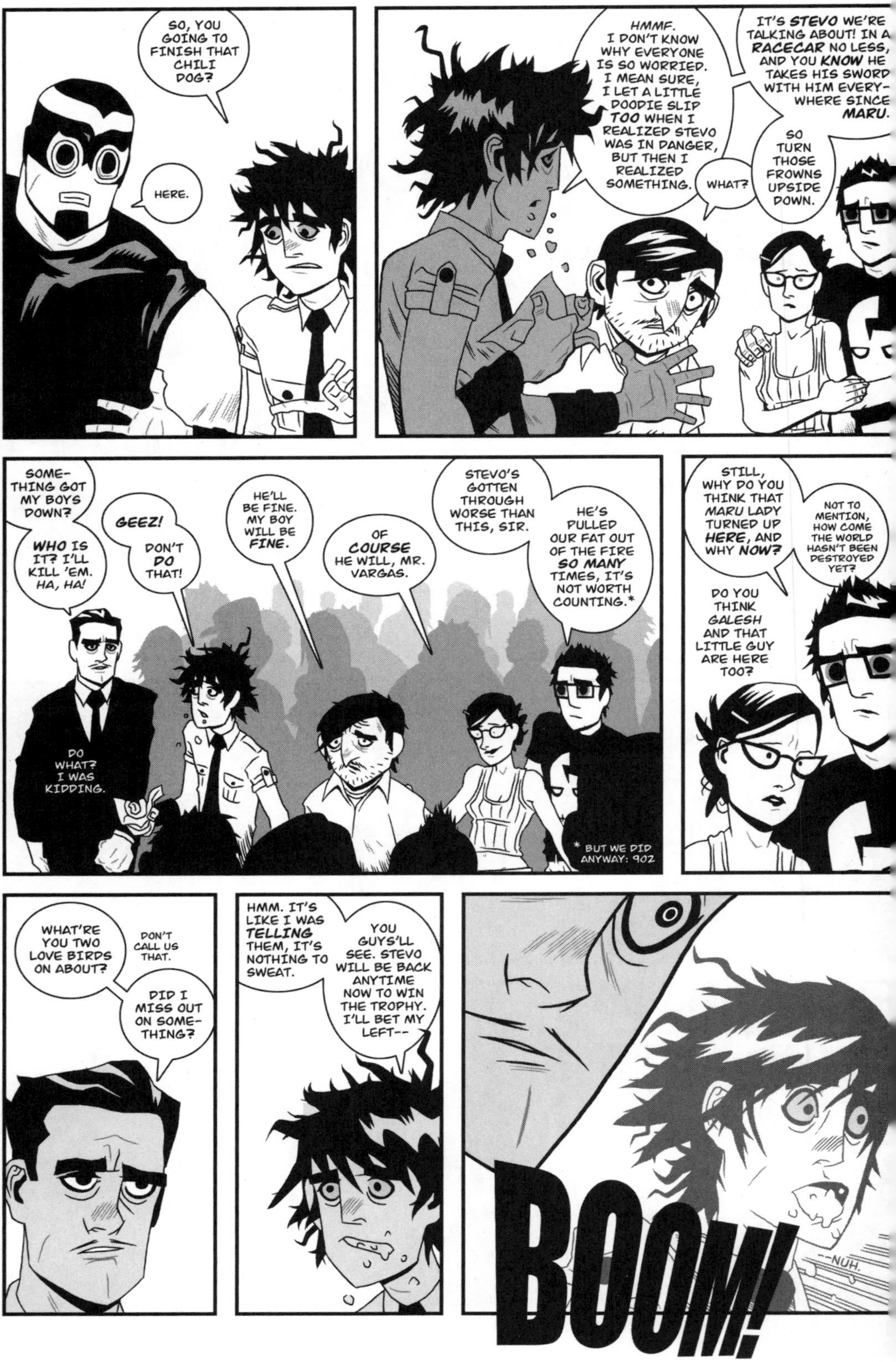

SO, YOU GOING TO FINISH THAT CHILI DOG?
HERE.
HMMF. I DON'T KNOW WHY EVERYONE IS SO WORRIED. I MEAN SURE, I LET A LITTLE DOODIE SLIP TOO WHEN I REALIZED STEVO WAS IN DANGER, BUT THEN I REALIZED SOMETHING.
WHAT?
IT'S STEVO WE'RE TALKING ABOUT! IN A RACECAR NO LESS, AND YOU KNOW HE TAKES HIS SWORD WITH HIM EVERY-WHERE SINCE MARU.
SO TURN THOSE FROWNS UPSIDE DOWN.
SOME-THING GOT MY BOYS DOWN?
WHO IS IT? I'LL KILL 'EM. HA, HA!
GEEZ!
DON'T DO THAT!
DO WHAT? I WAS KIDDING.
HE'LL BE FINE. MY BOY WILL BE FINE.
OF COURSE HE WILL, MR. VARGAS.
STEVO'S GOTTEN THROUGH WORSE THAN THIS, SIR.
HE'S PULLED OUR FAT OUT OF THE FIRE SO MANY TIMES, IT'S NOT WORTH COUNTING.*
* BUT WE DID ANYWAY: 902
STILL, WHY DO YOU THINK THAT MARU LADY TURNED UP HERE, AND WHY NOW?
NOT TO MENTION, HOW COME THE WORLD HASN'T BEEN DESTROYED YET?
DO YOU THINK GALESH AND THAT LITTLE GUY ARE HERE TOO?
WHAT'RE YOU TWO LOVE BIRDS ON ABOUT?
DON'T CALL US THAT.
DID I MISS OUT ON SOME-THING?
HMM. IT'S LIKE I WAS TELLING THEM, IT'S NOTHING TO SWEAT.
YOU GUYS'LL SEE. STEVO WILL BE BACK ANYTIME NOW TO WIN THE TROPHY. I'LL BET MY LEFT--
BOOM!
--NUH.

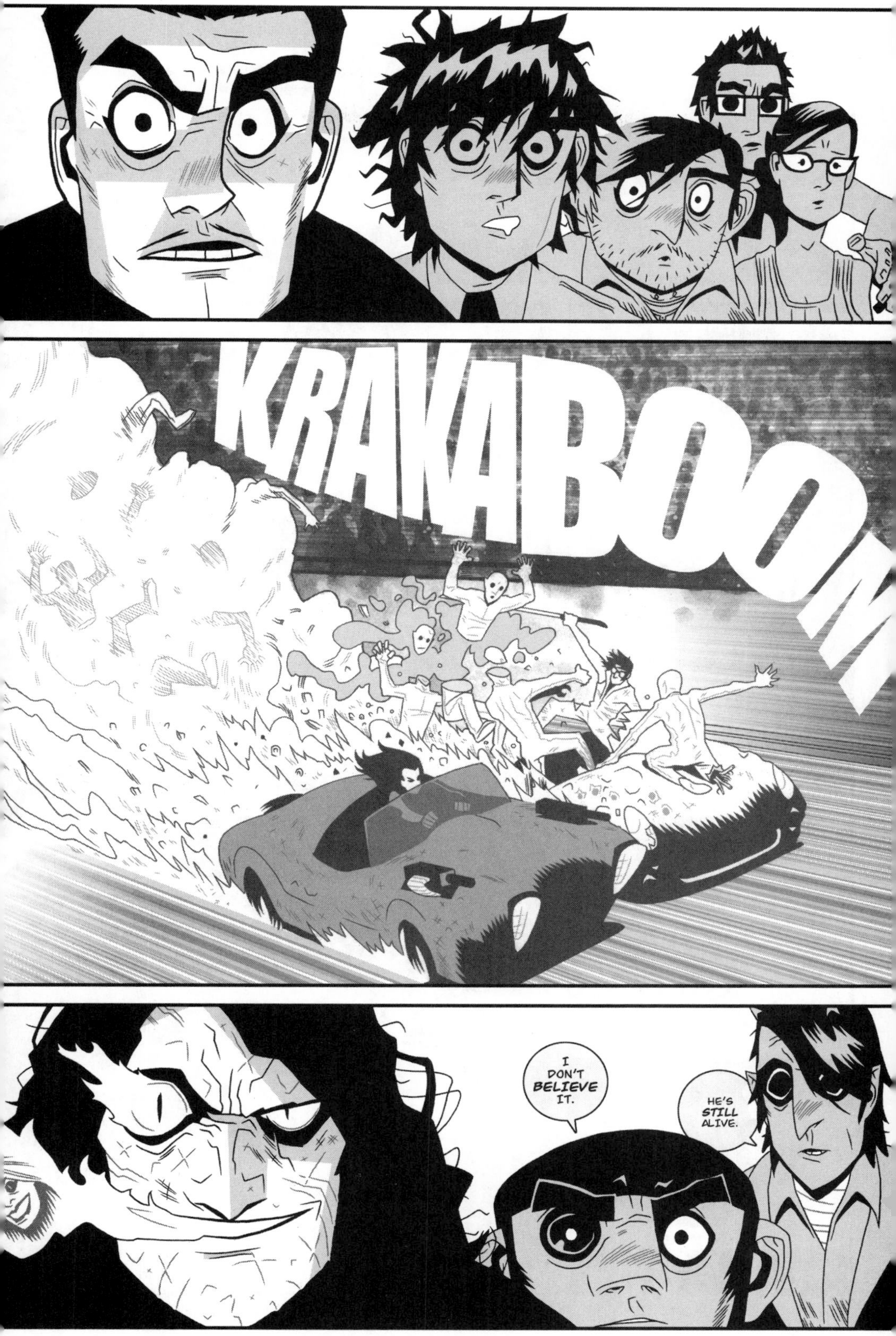
KRAKABOOOM
I DON'T BELIEVE IT.
HE'S STILL ALIVE.

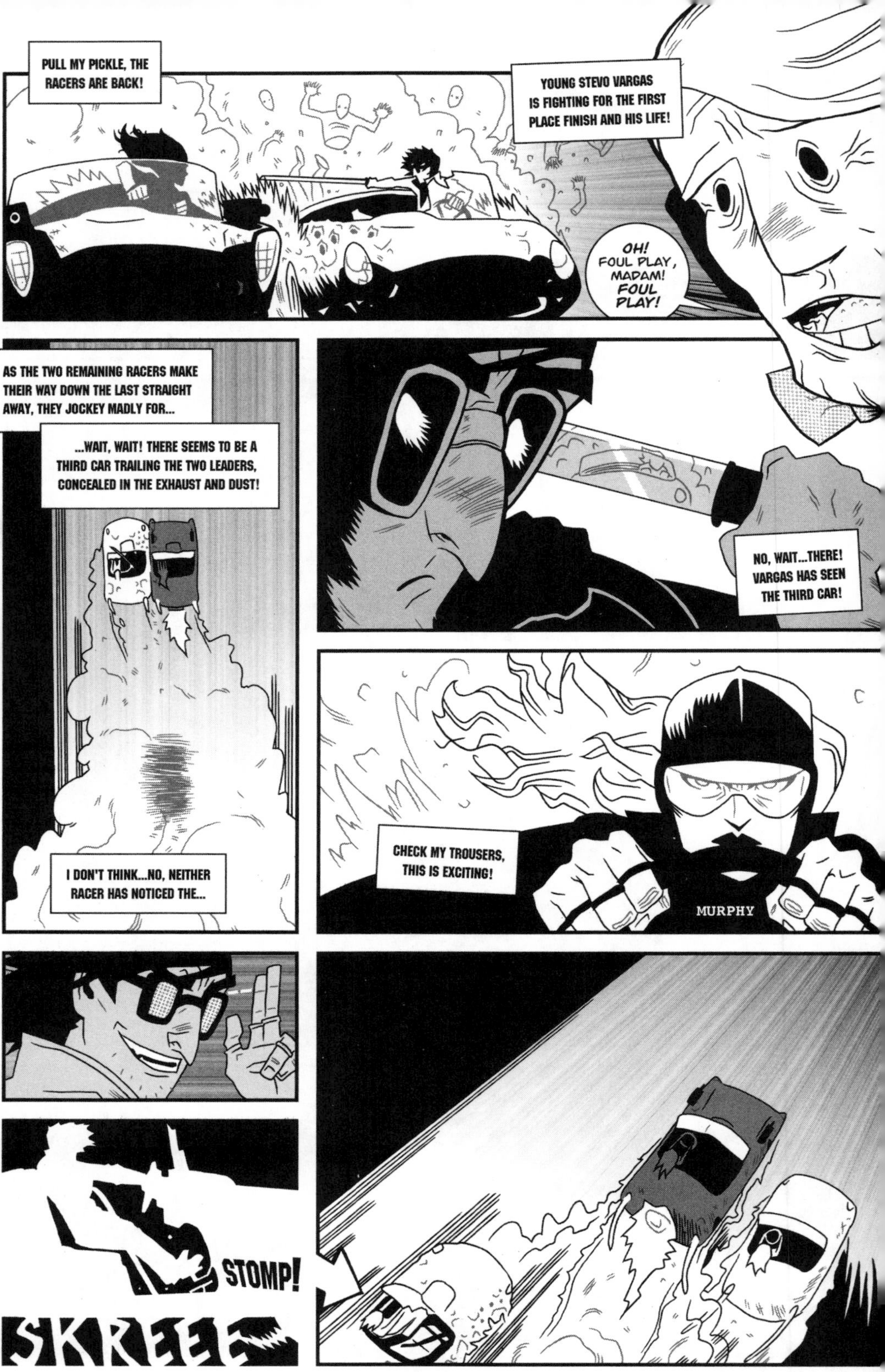

PULL MY PICKLE, THE RACERS ARE BACK!
YOUNG STEVO VARGAS IS FIGHTING FOR THE FIRST PLACE FINISH AND HIS LIFE!
OH! FOUL PLAY, MADAM! FOUL PLAY!
AS THE TWO REMAINING RACERS MAKE THEIR WAY DOWN THE LAST STRAIGHT AWAY, THEY JOCKEY MADLY FOR...
...WAIT, WAIT! THERE SEEMS TO BE A THIRD CAR TRAILING THE TWO LEADERS, CONCEALED IN THE EXHAUST AND DUST!
I DON'T THINK...NO, NEITHER RACER HAS NOTICED THE...
NO, WAIT...THERE! VARGAS HAS SEEN THE THIRD CAR!
CHECK MY TROUSERS, THIS IS EXCITING!
MURPHY
STOMP!
SKREEE

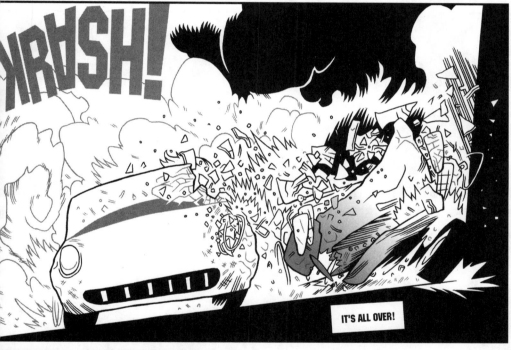

IT'S ALL OVER!

MURPHY THE AMERICAN HAS WON THE RACE, FOLLOWED CLOSELY BY STEVO VARGAS!

THE CROWD IS GOING WILD, AND WHY NOT? A GOOD SHOW INDEED!

A FINE BIT OF TEAM-WORK!

BRINGS TEARS TO MY EYES. WHO SAYS THE GOOD GUYS NEVER WIN?

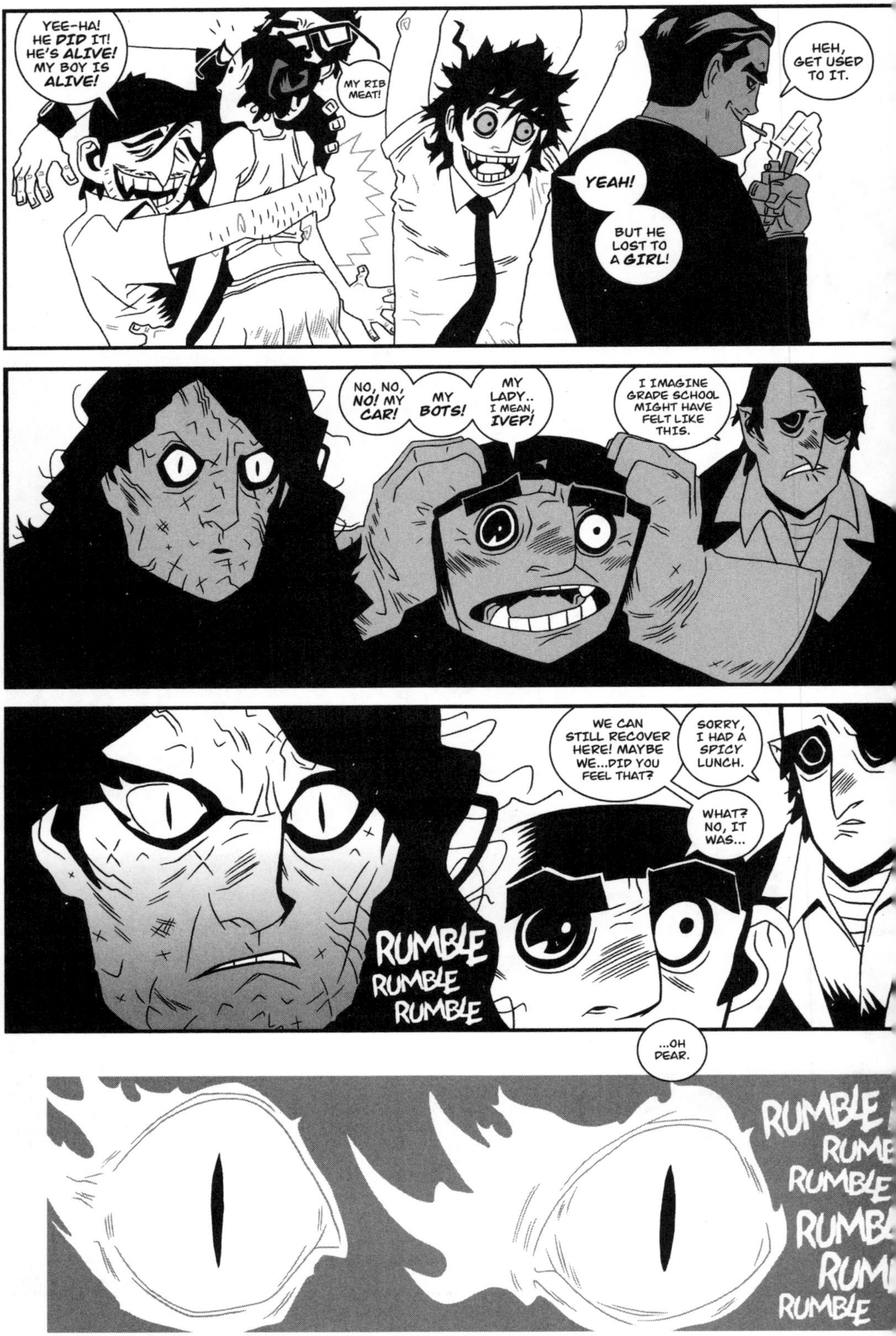
YEE-HA! HE DID IT! HE'S ALIVE! MY BOY IS ALIVE!
MY RIB MEAT!
YEAH!
BUT HE LOST TO A GIRL!
HEH, GET USED TO IT.
NO, NO, NO! MY CAR!
MY BOTS!
MY LADY.. I MEAN, IVEP!
I IMAGINE GRADE SCHOOL MIGHT HAVE FELT LIKE THIS.
WE CAN STILL RECOVER HERE! MAYBE WE...DID YOU FEEL THAT?
SORRY, I HAD A SPICY LUNCH.
WHAT? NO, IT WAS...
RUMBLE
RUMBLE
RUMBLE
...OH DEAR.
RUMBLE
RUMBLE
RUMBLE

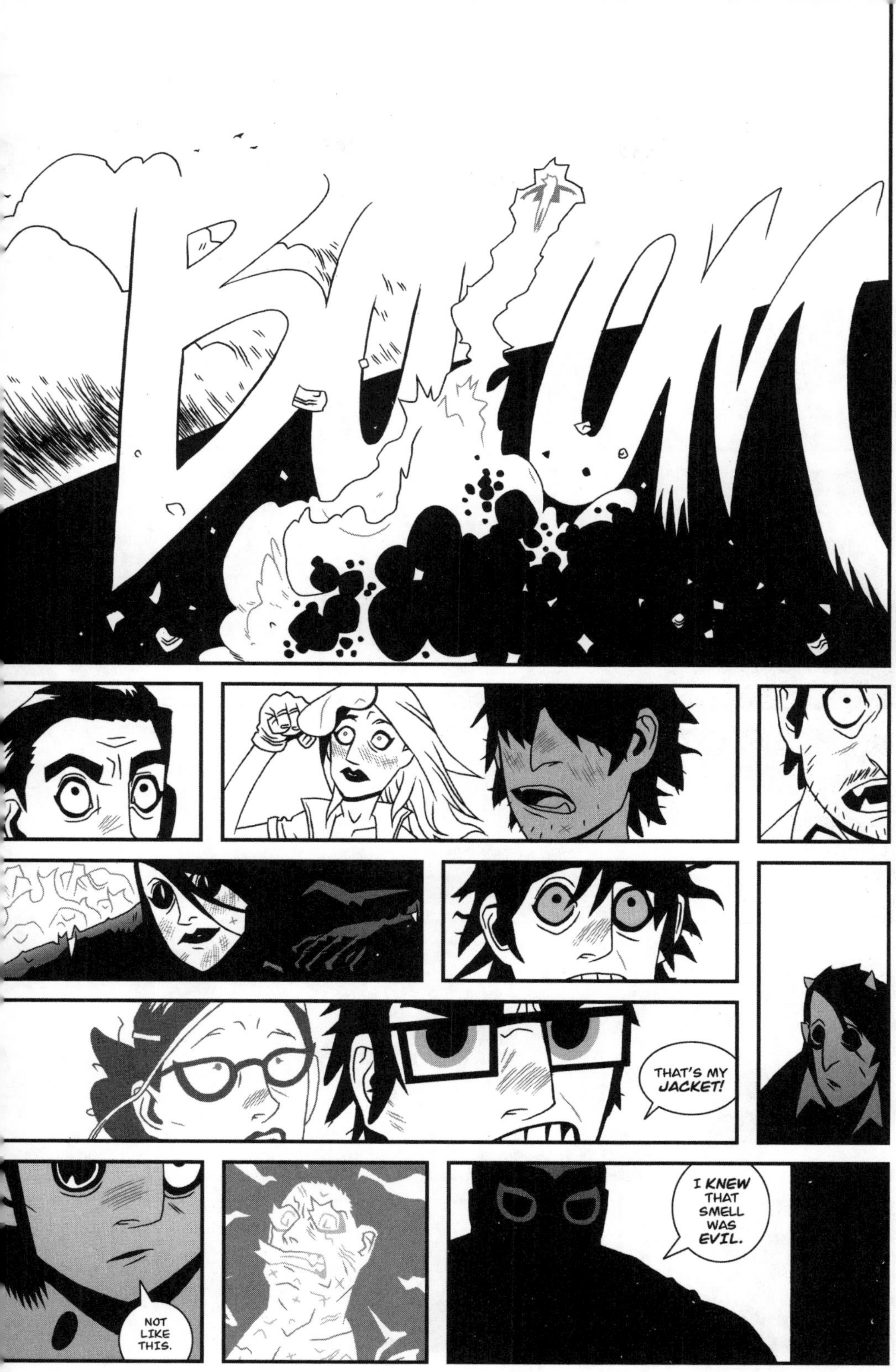

THAT'S MY JACKET!
NOT LIKE THIS.
I KNEW THAT SMELL WAS EVIL.

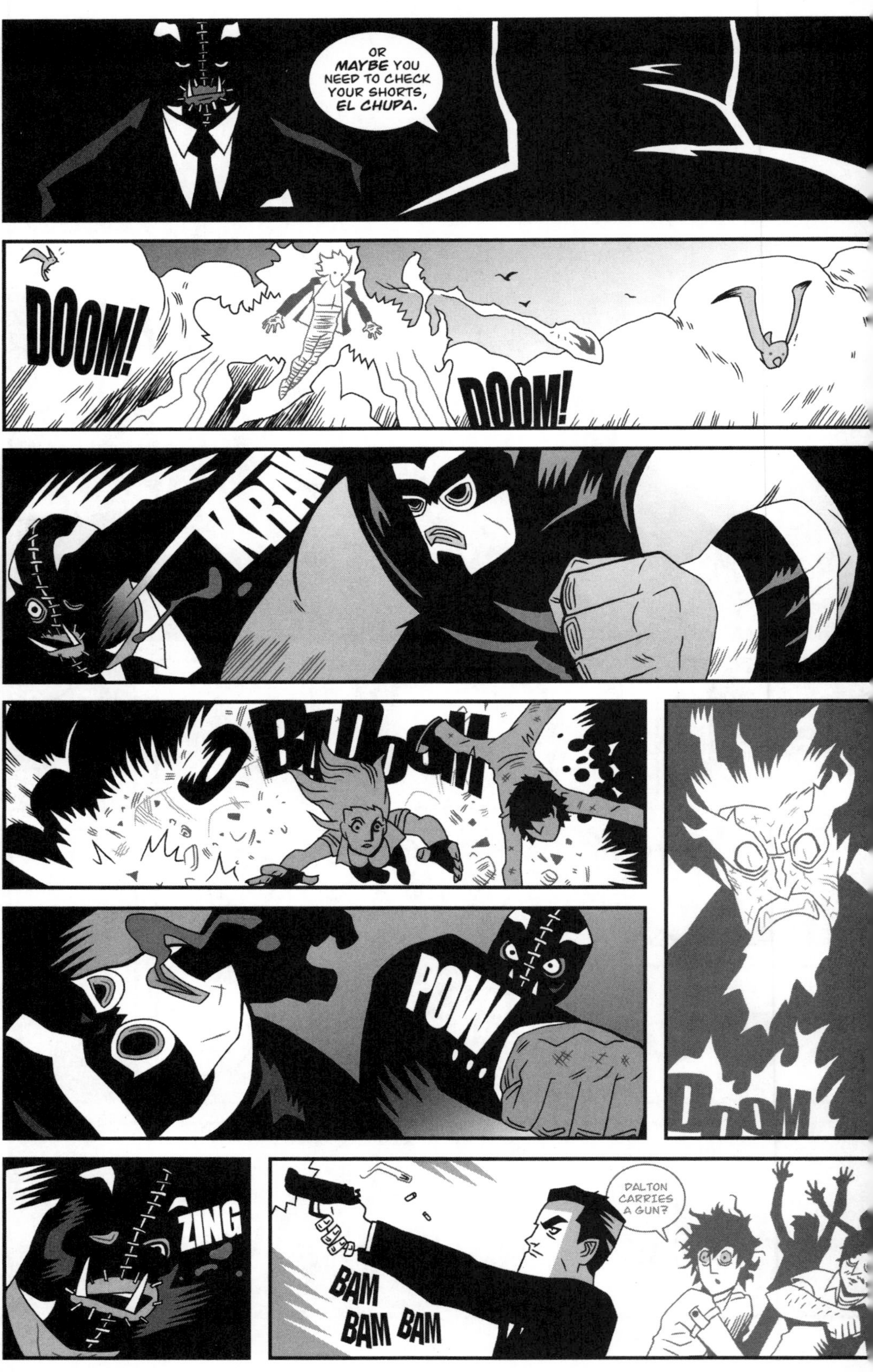
OR MAYBE YOU NEED TO CHECK YOUR SHORTS, EL CHUPA.
DOOM!
DOOM!
KRAK
BADOOM
POW
DOOM
ZING
BAM
BAM BAM
DALTON CARRIES A GUN?

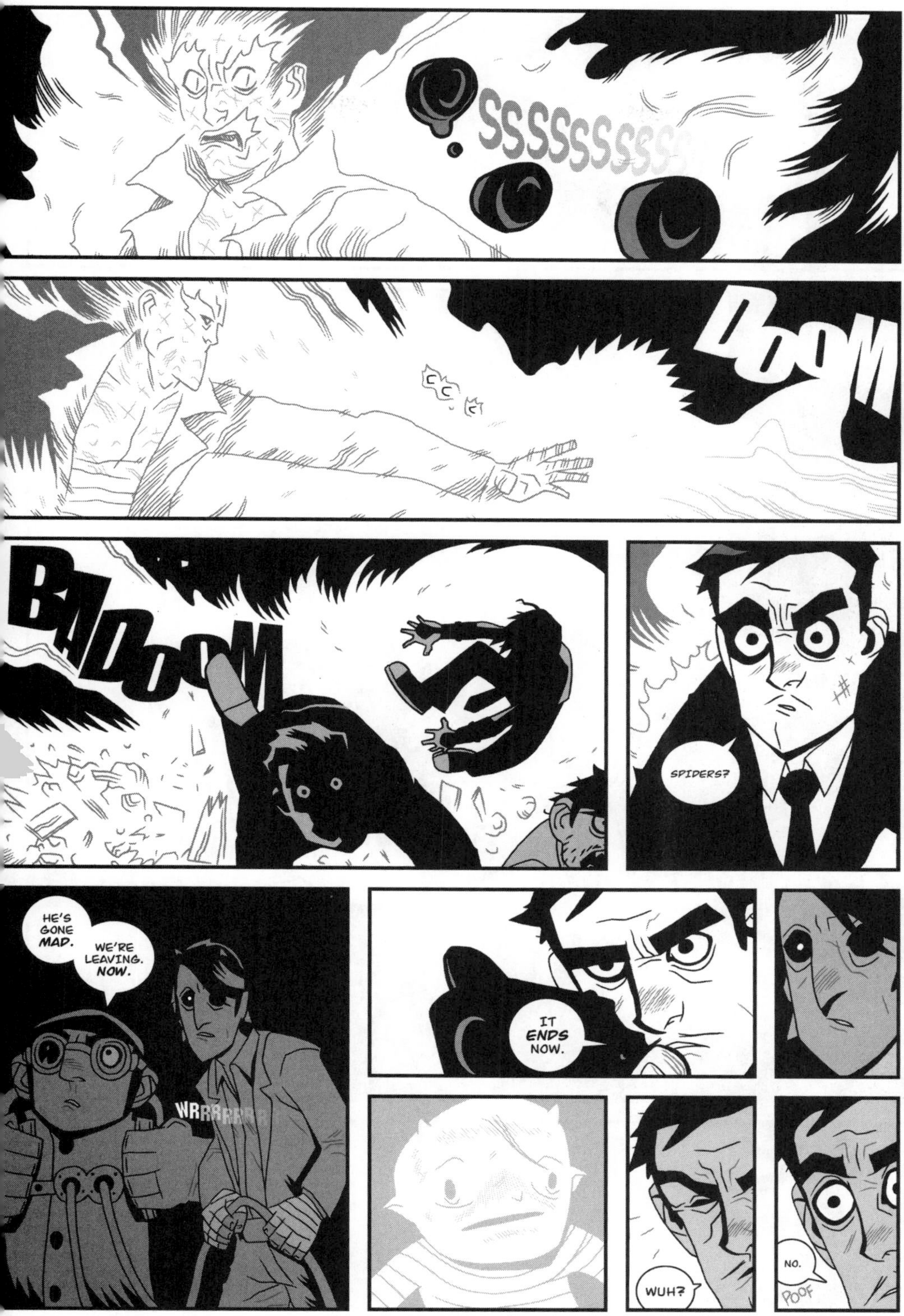
SSSSSSSSSS
DOOM
BADOOM
SPIDERS?
HE'S GONE MAD.
WE'RE LEAVING. NOW.
WRRRRRRR
IT ENDS NOW.
WUH?
NO.
POOF

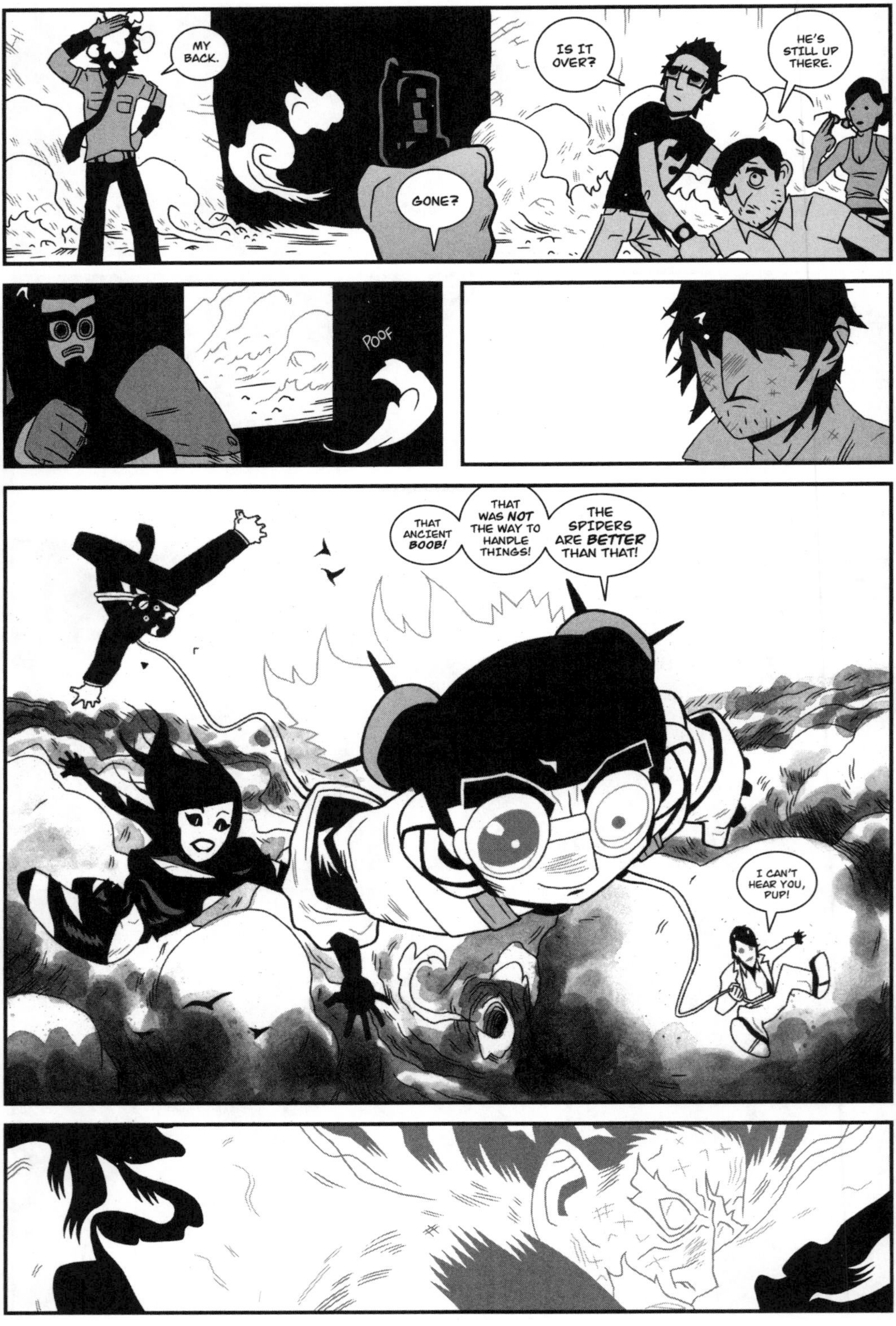
MY BACK.
GONE?
IS IT OVER?
HE'S STILL UP THERE.
POOF
THAT ANCIENT BOOB!
THAT WAS NOT THE WAY TO HANDLE THINGS!
THE SPIDERS ARE BETTER THAN THAT!
I CAN'T HEAR YOU, PUP!

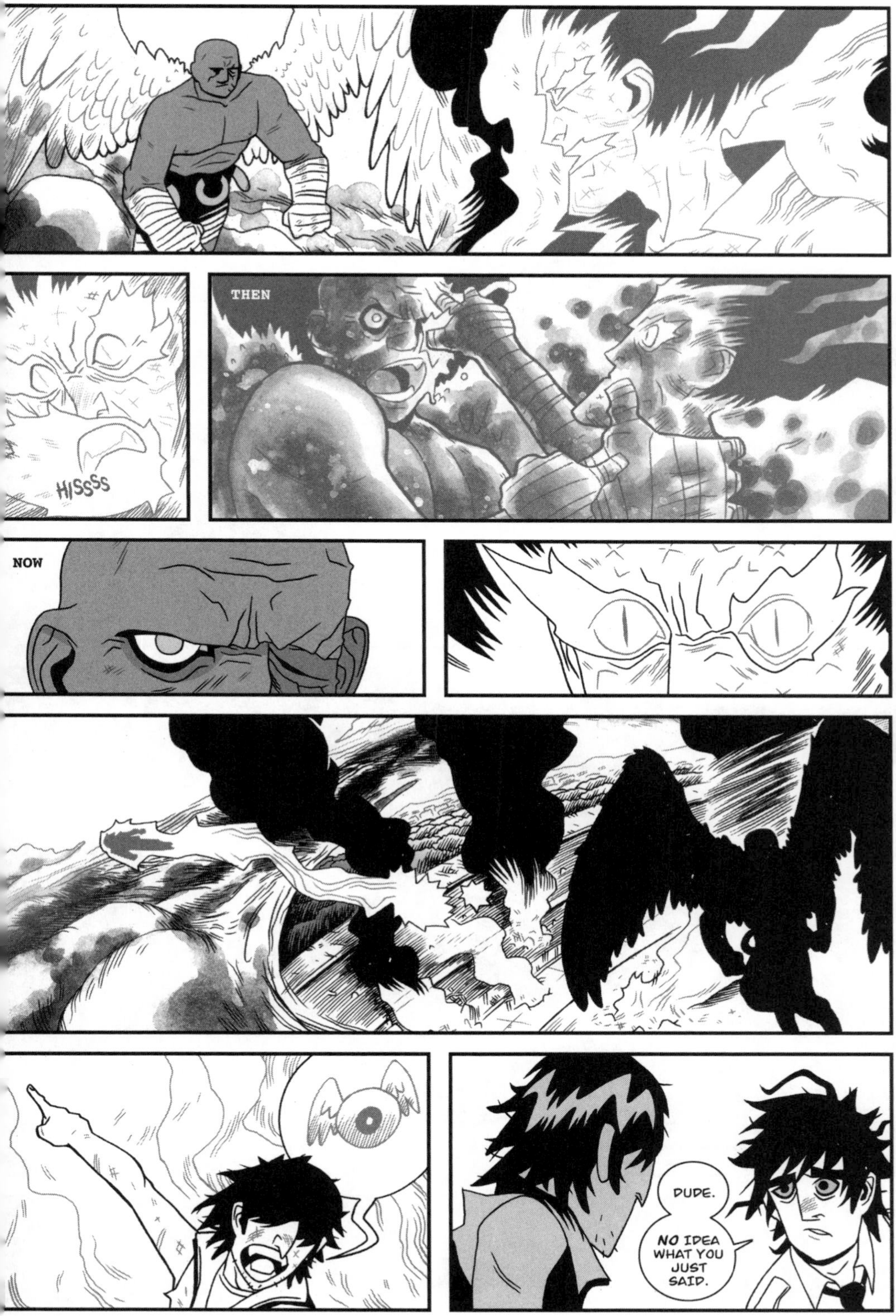
HISSSS
THEN
NOW
DUDE.
NO IDEA WHAT YOU JUST SAID.

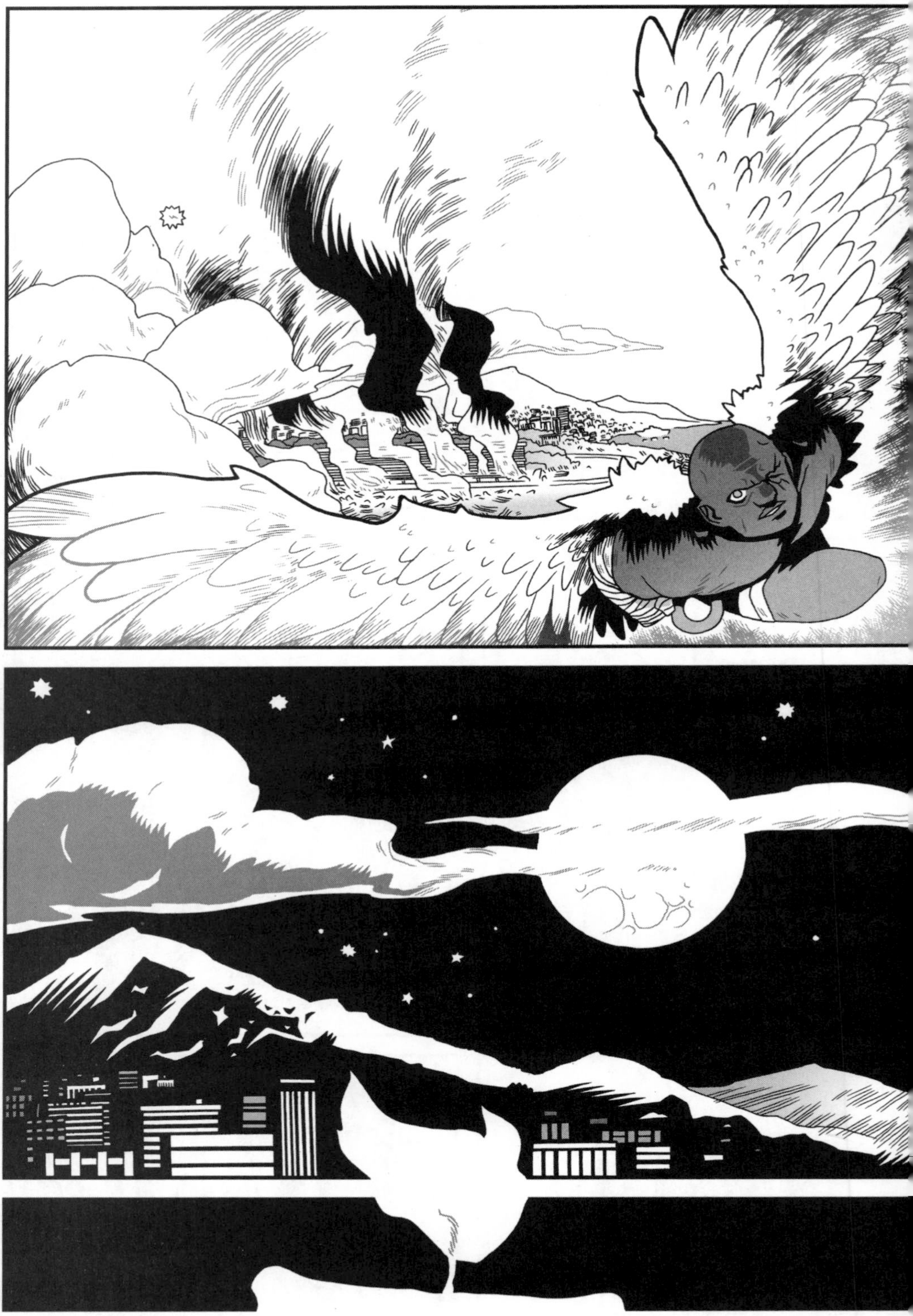

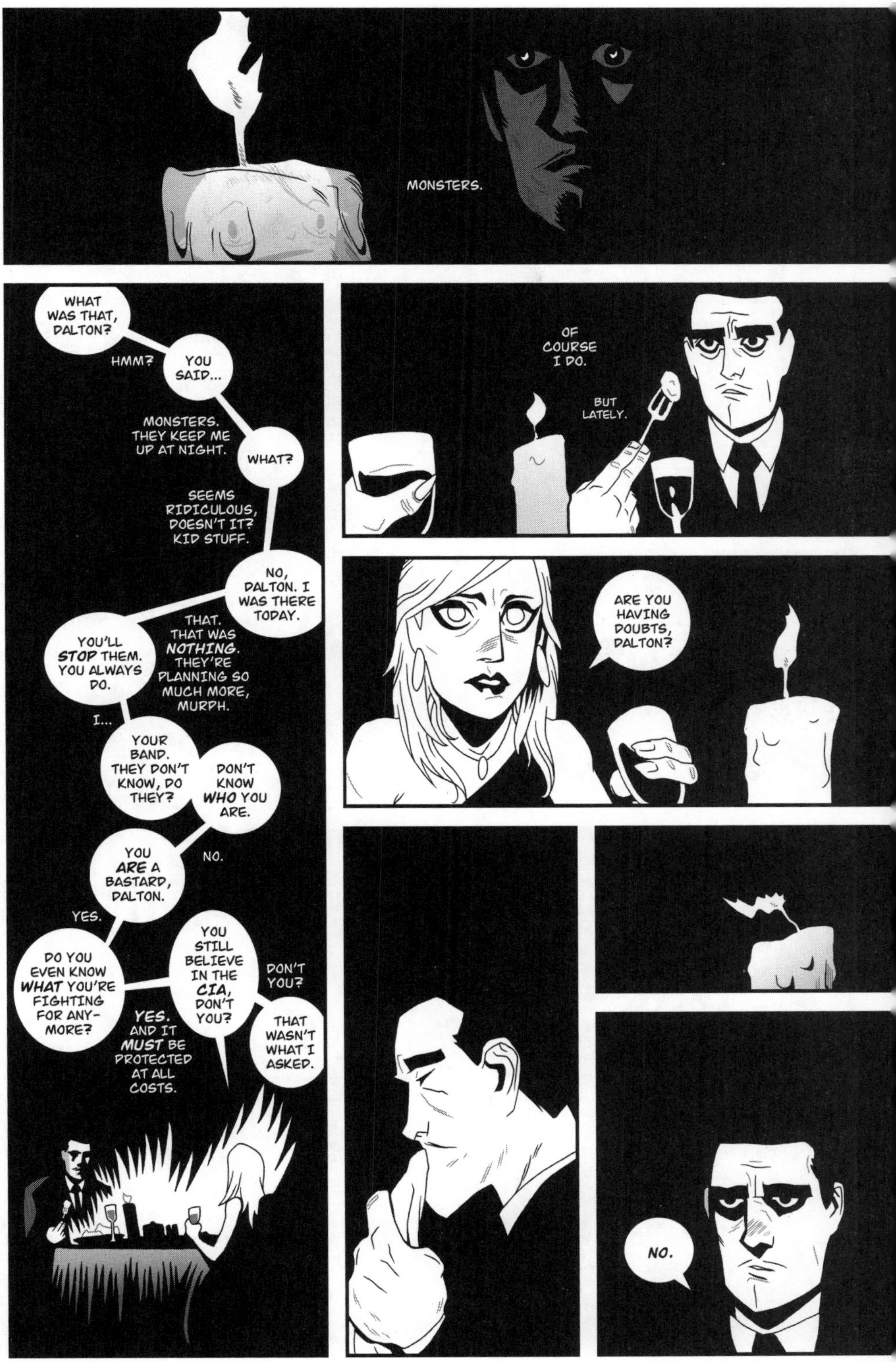
MONSTERS.
WHAT WAS THAT, DALTON?
HMM?
YOU SAID...
MONSTERS. THEY KEEP ME UP AT NIGHT.
WHAT?
SEEMS RIDICULOUS, DOESN'T IT? KID STUFF.
NO, DALTON. I WAS THERE TODAY.
THAT. THAT WAS NOTHING. THEY'RE PLANNING SO MUCH MORE, MURPH.
YOU'LL STOP THEM. YOU ALWAYS DO.
I...
YOUR BAND. THEY DON'T KNOW, DO THEY?
DON'T KNOW WHO YOU ARE.
NO.
YOU ARE A BASTARD, DALTON.
YES.
DO YOU EVEN KNOW WHAT YOU'RE FIGHTING FOR ANYMORE?
YES. AND IT MUST BE PROTECTED AT ALL COSTS.
YOU STILL BELIEVE IN THE CIA, DON'T YOU?
DON'T YOU?
THAT WASN'T WHAT I ASKED.
OF COURSE I DO.
BUT LATELY.
ARE YOU HAVING DOUBTS, DALTON?
NO.

BACK AT THE SPIDER'S LAIR...

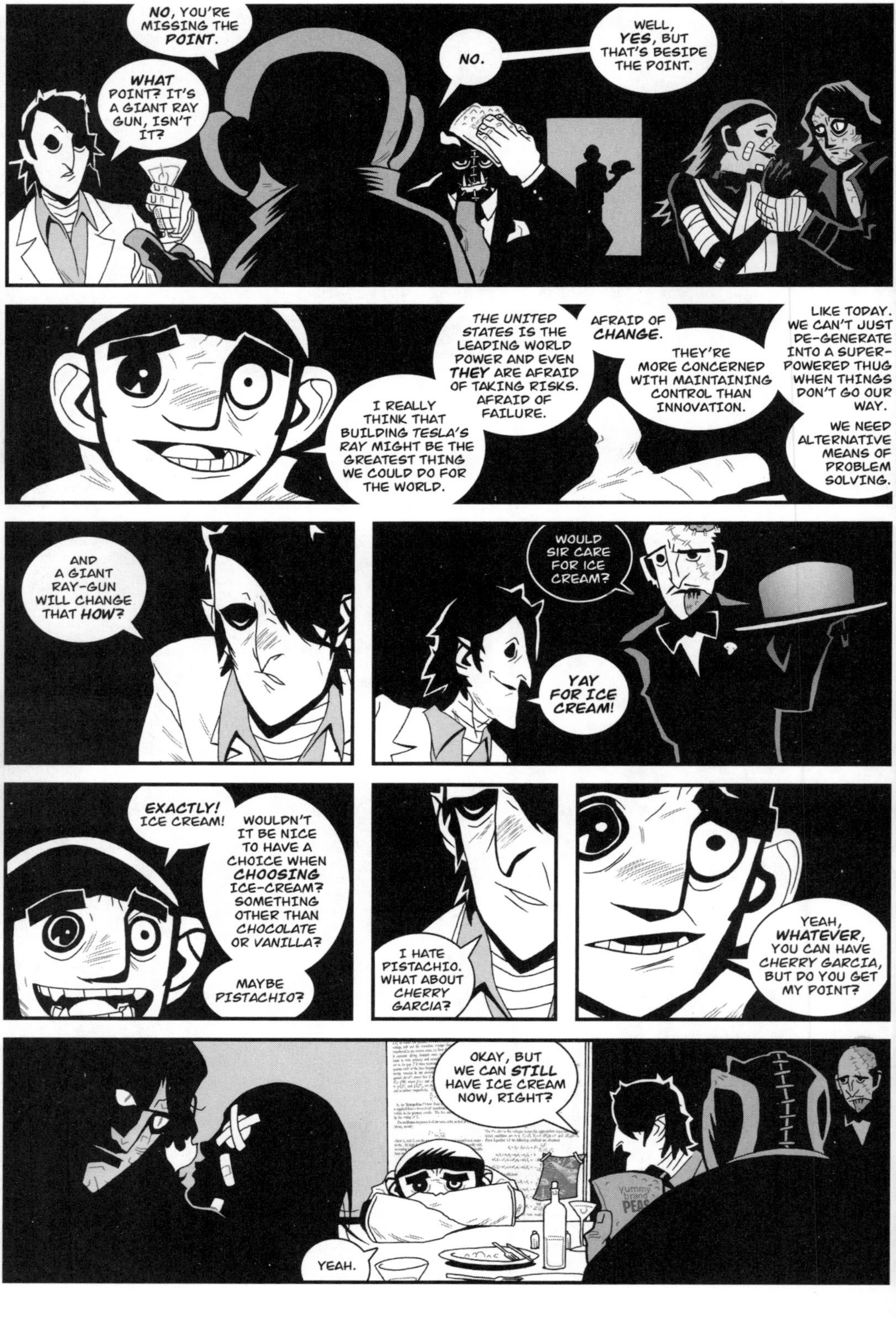
NO, YOU'RE MISSING THE POINT.
WHAT POINT? IT'S A GIANT RAY GUN, ISN'T IT?
NO.
WELL, YES, BUT THAT'S BESIDE THE POINT.
I REALLY THINK THAT BUILDING TESLA'S RAY MIGHT BE THE GREATEST THING WE COULD DO FOR THE WORLD.
THE UNITED STATES IS THE LEADING WORLD POWER AND EVEN THEY ARE AFRAID OF TAKING RISKS. AFRAID OF FAILURE.
AFRAID OF CHANGE.
THEY'RE MORE CONCERNED WITH MAINTAINING CONTROL THAN INNOVATION.
LIKE TODAY. WE CAN'T JUST DE-GENERATE INTO A SUPER-POWERED THUG WHEN THINGS DON'T GO OUR WAY.
WE NEED ALTERNATIVE MEANS OF PROBLEM SOLVING.
AND A GIANT RAY-GUN WILL CHANGE THAT HOW?
WOULD SIR CARE FOR ICE CREAM?
YAY FOR ICE CREAM!
EXACTLY! ICE CREAM!
WOULDN'T IT BE NICE TO HAVE A CHOICE WHEN CHOOSING ICE-CREAM? SOMETHING OTHER THAN CHOCOLATE OR VANILLA?
MAYBE PISTACHIO?
I HATE PISTACHIO. WHAT ABOUT CHERRY GARCIA?
YEAH, WHATEVER, YOU CAN HAVE CHERRY GARCIA, BUT DO YOU GET MY POINT?
OKAY, BUT WE CAN STILL HAVE ICE CREAM NOW, RIGHT?
yummy brand PEAS
YEAH.

THE VARGAS PENTHOUSE, MONACO

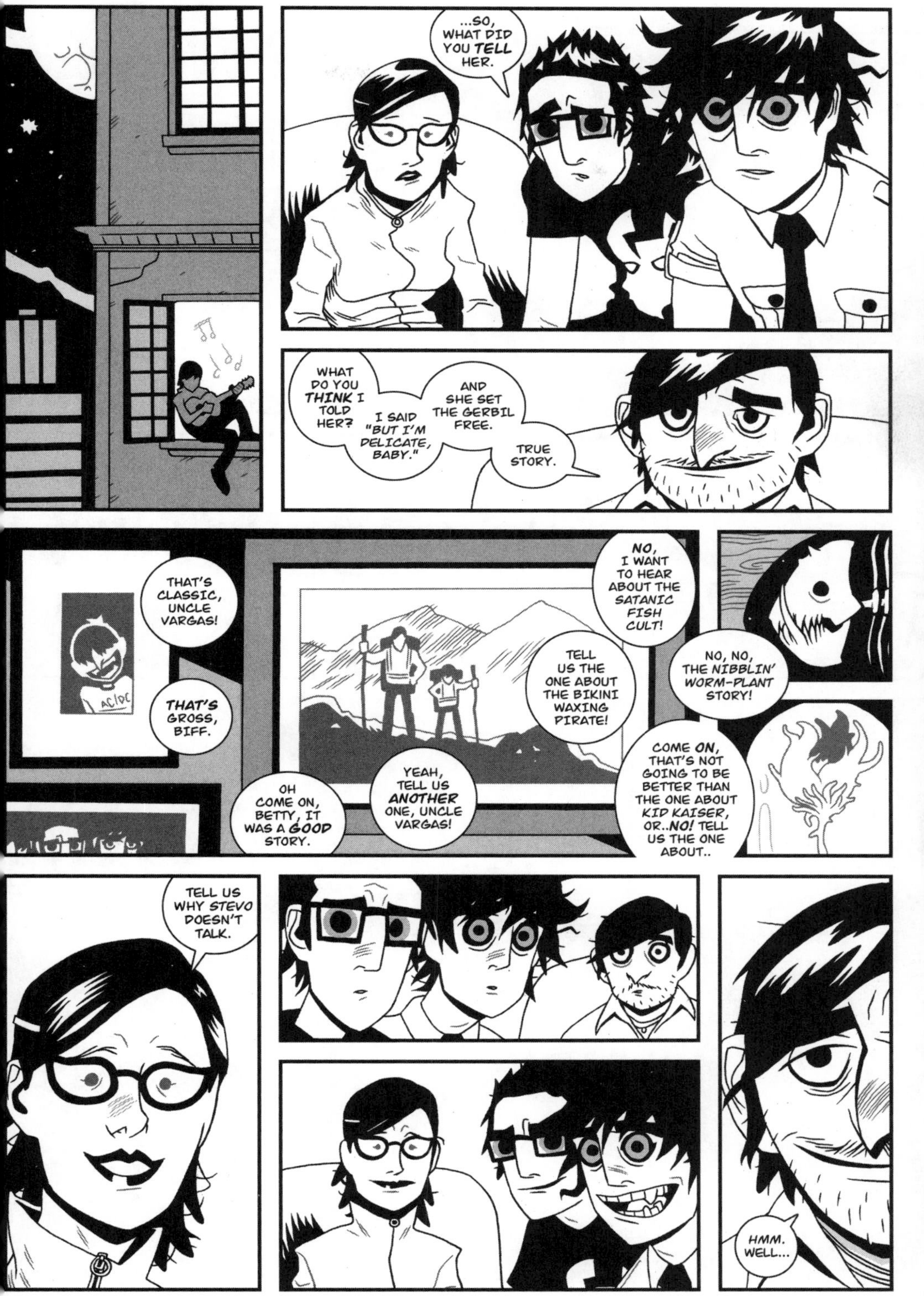
...SO, WHAT DID YOU TELL HER.
WHAT DO YOU THINK I TOLD HER?
I SAID "BUT I'M DELICATE, BABY."
AND SHE SET THE GERBIL FREE.
TRUE STORY.
THAT'S CLASSIC, UNCLE VARGAS!
THAT'S GROSS, BIFF.
OH COME ON, BETTY, IT WAS A GOOD STORY.
YEAH, TELL US ANOTHER ONE, UNCLE VARGAS!
AC/DC
NO, I WANT TO HEAR ABOUT THE SATANIC FISH CULT!
TELL US THE ONE ABOUT THE BIKINI WAXING PIRATE!
NO, NO, THE NIBBLIN' WORM-PLANT STORY!
COME ON, THAT'S NOT GOING TO BE BETTER THAN THE ONE ABOUT KID KAISER, OR..NO! TELL US THE ONE ABOUT..
TELL US WHY STEVO DOESN'T TALK.
HMM. WELL...

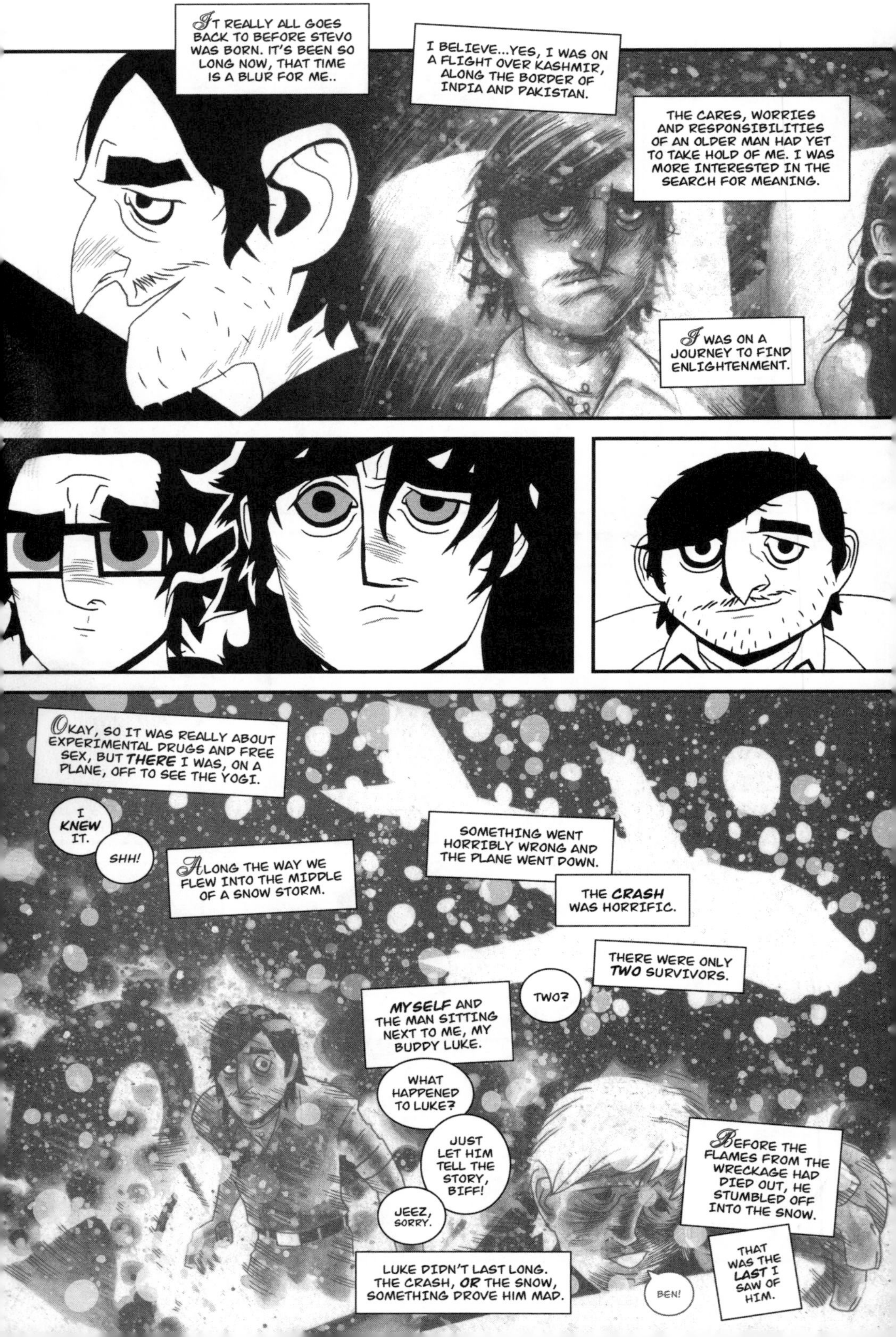
IT REALLY ALL GOES BACK TO BEFORE STEVO WAS BORN. IT'S BEEN SO LONG NOW, THAT TIME IS A BLUR FOR ME..
I BELIEVE...YES, I WAS ON A FLIGHT OVER KASHMIR, ALONG THE BORDER OF INDIA AND PAKISTAN.
THE CARES, WORRIES AND RESPONSIBILITIES OF AN OLDER MAN HAD YET TO TAKE HOLD OF ME. I WAS MORE INTERESTED IN THE SEARCH FOR MEANING.
I WAS ON A JOURNEY TO FIND ENLIGHTENMENT.
OKAY, SO IT WAS REALLY ABOUT EXPERIMENTAL DRUGS AND FREE SEX, BUT THERE I WAS, ON A PLANE, OFF TO SEE THE YOGI.
I KNEW IT.
SHH!
ALONG THE WAY WE FLEW INTO THE MIDDLE OF A SNOW STORM.
SOMETHING WENT HORRIBLY WRONG AND THE PLANE WENT DOWN.
THE CRASH WAS HORRIFIC.
THERE WERE ONLY TWO SURVIVORS.
TWO?
MYSELF AND THE MAN SITTING NEXT TO ME, MY BUDDY LUKE.
WHAT HAPPENED TO LUKE?
JUST LET HIM TELL THE STORY, BIFF!
JEEZ, SORRY.
BEFORE THE FLAMES FROM THE WRECKAGE HAD DIED OUT, HE STUMBLED OFF INTO THE SNOW.
LUKE DIDN'T LAST LONG. THE CRASH, OR THE SNOW, SOMETHING DROVE HIM MAD.
BEN!
THAT WAS THE LAST I SAW OF HIM.

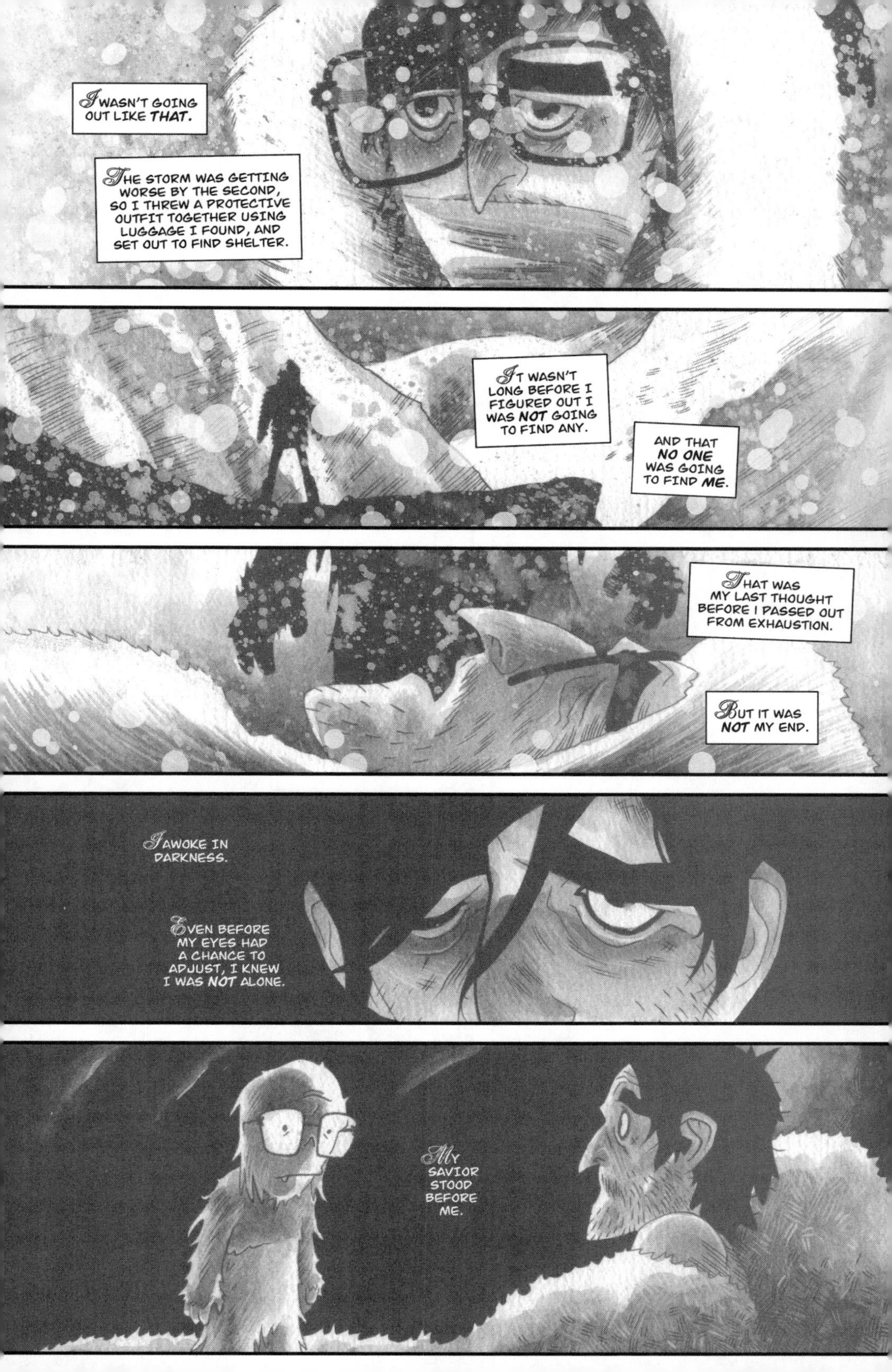
I WASN'T GOING OUT LIKE THAT.
THE STORM WAS GETTING WORSE BY THE SECOND, SO I THREW A PROTECTIVE OUTFIT TOGETHER USING LUGGAGE I FOUND, AND SET OUT TO FIND SHELTER.
IT WASN'T LONG BEFORE I FIGURED OUT I WAS NOT GOING TO FIND ANY.
AND THAT NO ONE WAS GOING TO FIND ME.
THAT WAS MY LAST THOUGHT BEFORE I PASSED OUT FROM EXHAUSTION.
BUT IT WAS NOT MY END.
I AWOKE IN DARKNESS.
EVEN BEFORE MY EYES HAD A CHANCE TO ADJUST, I KNEW I WAS NOT ALONE.
MY SAVIOR STOOD BEFORE ME.

BUT THERE WAS SOMETHING *ELSE* I HAD YET TO ANSWER TO.

IT'S *MOTHER.*

A YETI BEAST. SAVAGE, ALONE, YEARNING THE HARD TOUCH OF A MALE, LONG LOST TO THE BITTER COLD.

I COULD SEE THE FORBIDDEN WANT IN HER EYES AND FOR THE FIRST TIME I FELT A LONGING THAT WAS NOT DICTATED BY POSITION OR AESTHETIC.

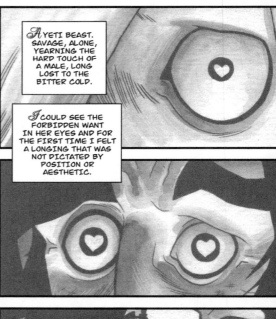

IN A SINGLE MOMENT, I UNDERSTOOD LOVE IN IT'S MOST RAW FORM.

AND IT WAS GOOD.

TIME PASSED AND THE WINTER RAGED ON.

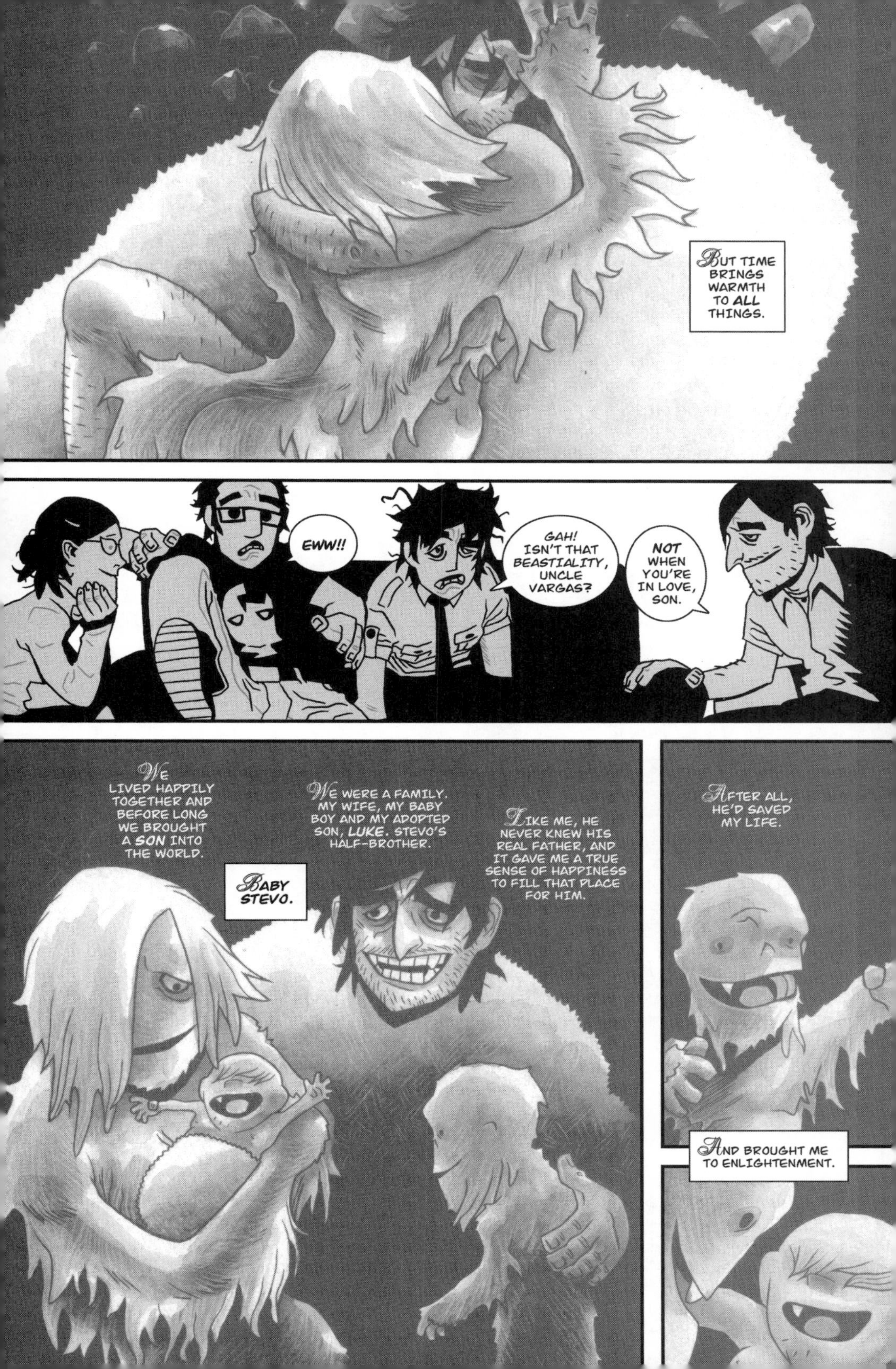
But time brings warmth to ALL things.
EWW!!
GAH! ISN'T THAT BEASTIALITY, UNCLE VARGAS?
NOT WHEN YOU'RE IN LOVE, SON.
We lived happily together and before long we brought a SON into the world.
Baby Stevo.
We were a family. My wife, my baby boy and my adopted son, LUKE. Stevo's half-brother.
Like me, he never knew his real father, and it gave me a true sense of happiness to fill that place for him.
After all, he'd saved my life.
And brought me to enlightenment.

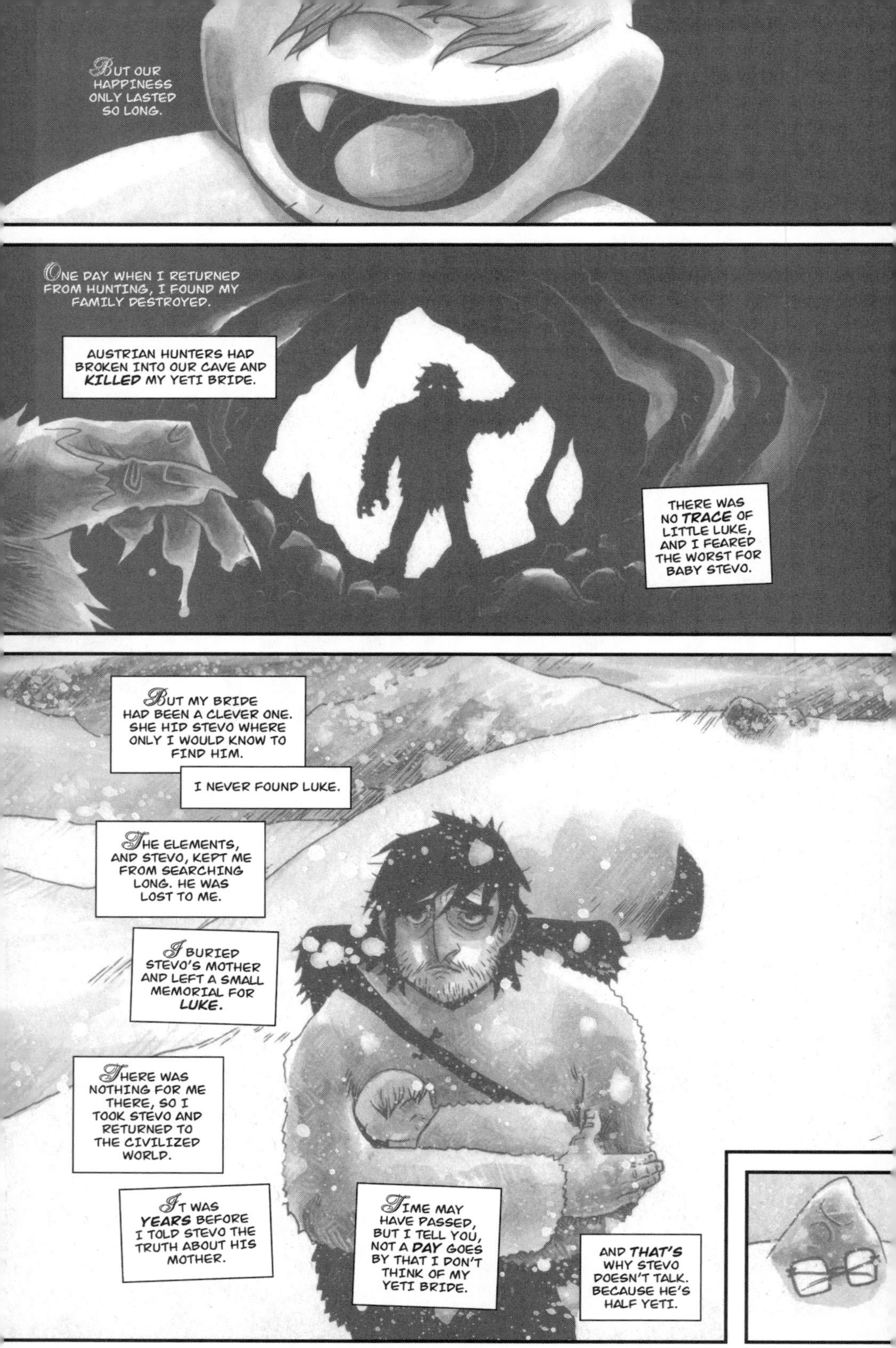

BUT OUR HAPPINESS ONLY LASTED SO LONG.
ONE DAY WHEN I RETURNED FROM HUNTING, I FOUND MY FAMILY DESTROYED.
AUSTRIAN HUNTERS HAD BROKEN INTO OUR CAVE AND KILLED MY YETI BRIDE.
THERE WAS NO TRACE OF LITTLE LUKE, AND I FEARED THE WORST FOR BABY STEVO.
BUT MY BRIDE HAD BEEN A CLEVER ONE. SHE HID STEVO WHERE ONLY I WOULD KNOW TO FIND HIM.
I NEVER FOUND LUKE.
THE ELEMENTS, AND STEVO, KEPT ME FROM SEARCHING LONG. HE WAS LOST TO ME.
I BURIED STEVO'S MOTHER AND LEFT A SMALL MEMORIAL FOR LUKE.
THERE WAS NOTHING FOR ME THERE, SO I TOOK STEVO AND RETURNED TO THE CIVILIZED WORLD.
IT WAS YEARS BEFORE I TOLD STEVO THE TRUTH ABOUT HIS MOTHER.
TIME MAY HAVE PASSED, BUT I TELL YOU, NOT A DAY GOES BY THAT I DON'T THINK OF MY YETI BRIDE.
AND THAT'S WHY STEVO DOESN'T TALK. BECAUSE HE'S HALF YETI.

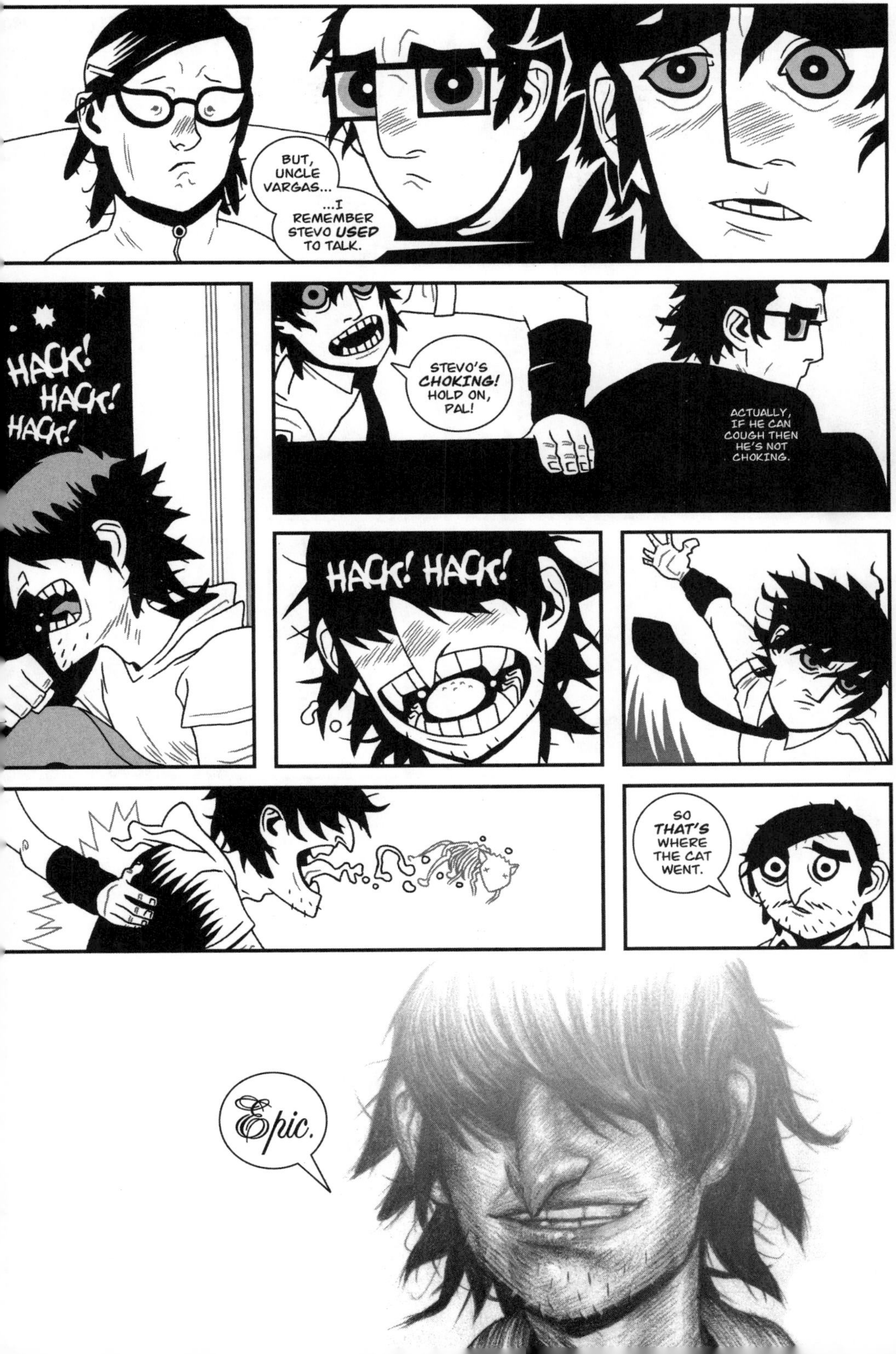

BUT, UNCLE VARGAS...
...I REMEMBER STEVO USED TO TALK.
HACK! HACK! HACK!
STEVO'S CHOKING! HOLD ON, PAL!
ACTUALLY, IF HE CAN COUGH THEN HE'S NOT CHOKING.
HACK! HACK!
SO THAT'S WHERE THE CAT WENT.
Epic.

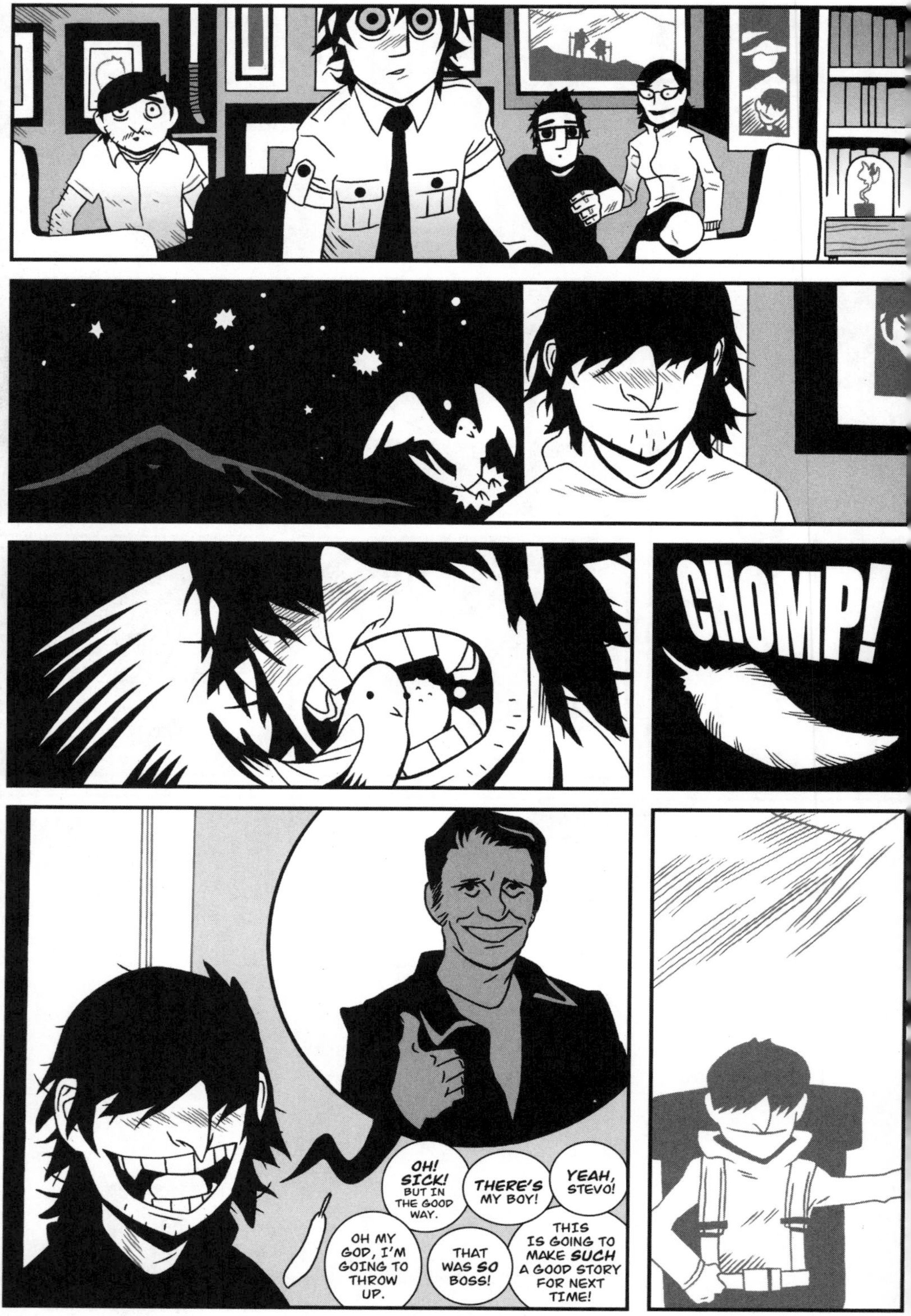
CHOMP!
OH! SICK! BUT IN THE GOOD WAY.
THERE'S MY BOY!
YEAH, STEVO!
OH MY GOD, I'M GOING TO THROW UP.
THAT WAS SO BOSS!
THIS IS GOING TO MAKE SUCH A GOOD STORY FOR NEXT TIME!

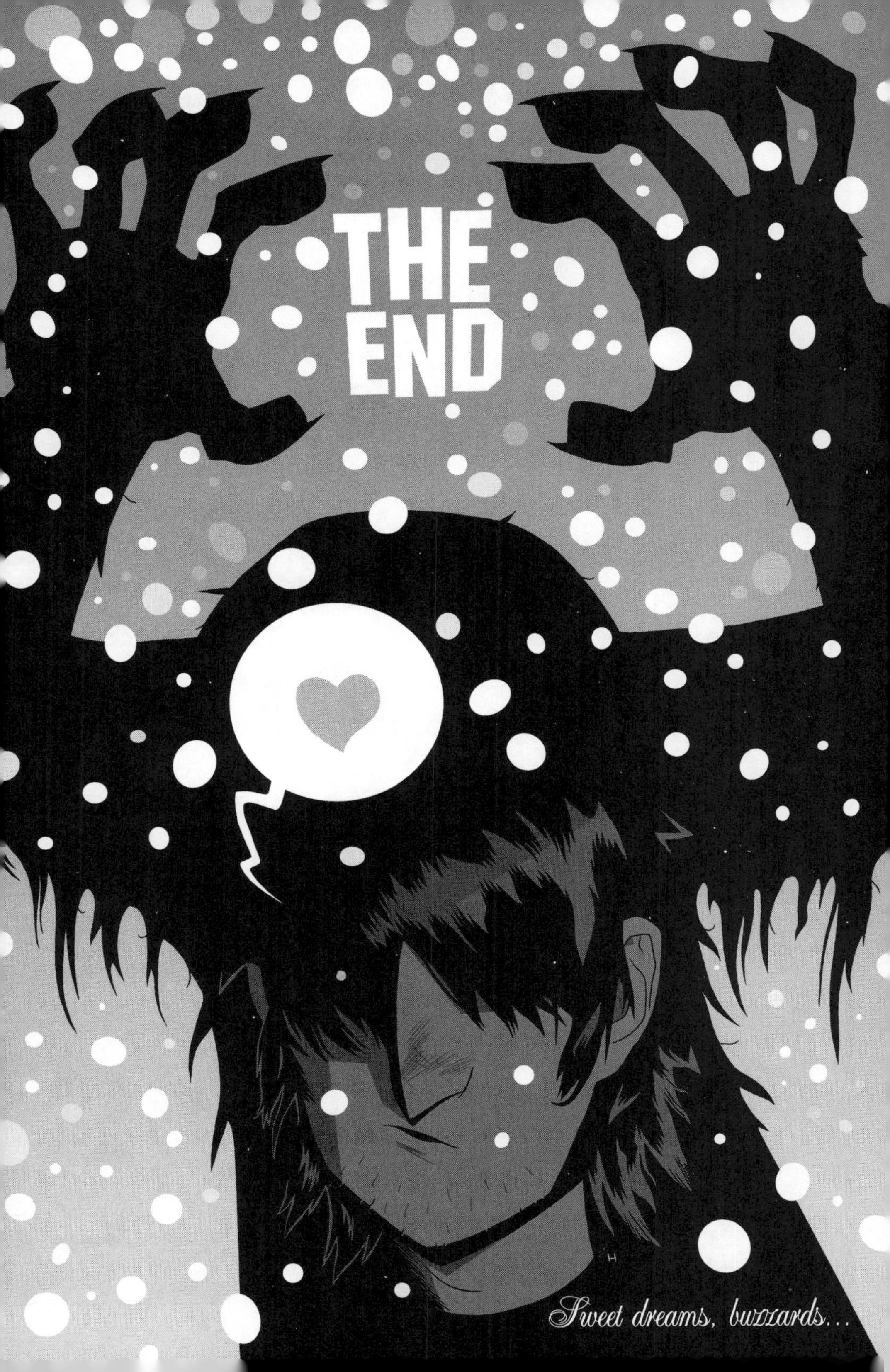
THE END
Sweet dreams, buzzards...

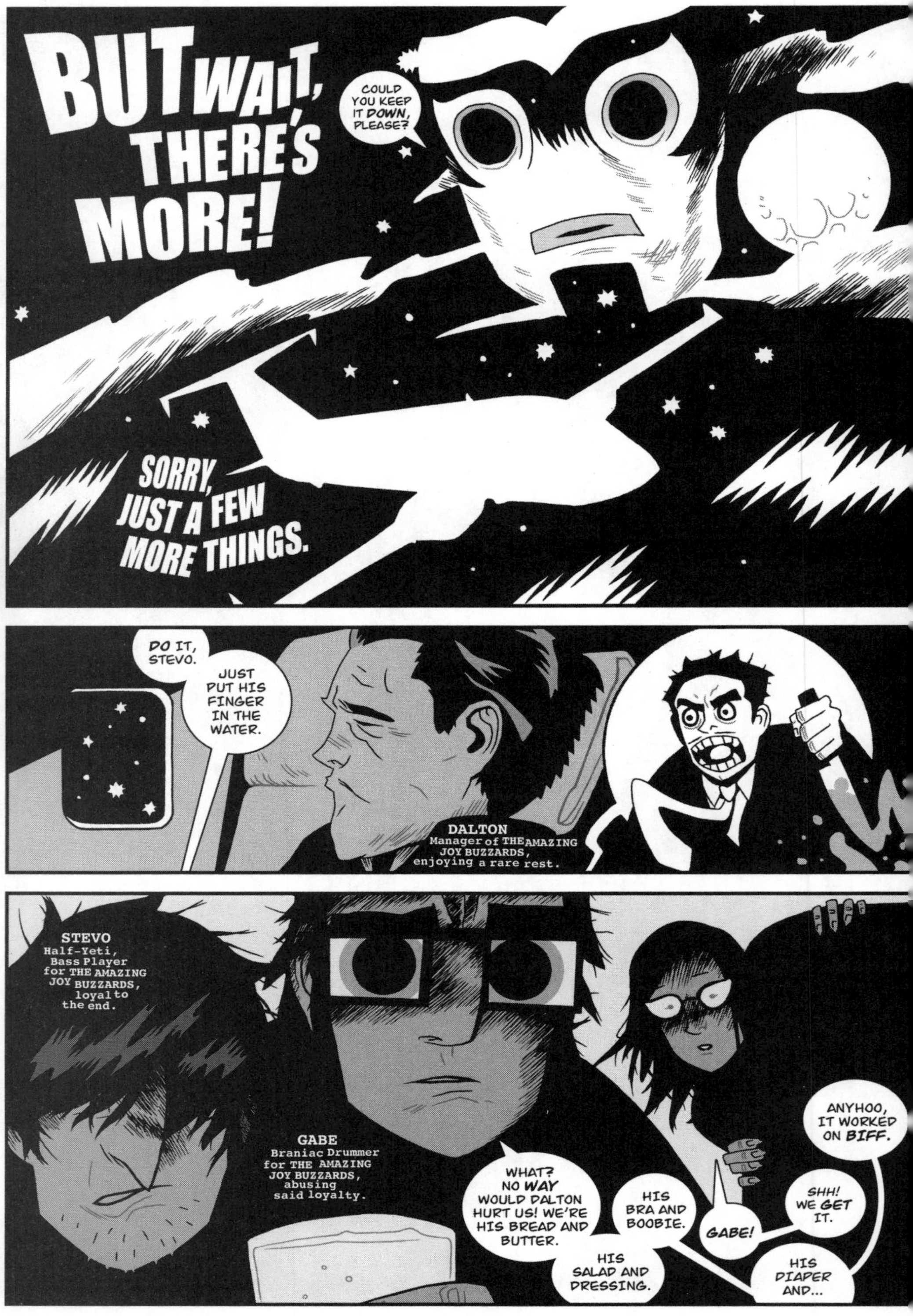

BUT WAIT, THERE'S MORE!
COULD YOU KEEP IT DOWN, PLEASE?
SORRY, JUST A FEW MORE THINGS.
DO IT, STEVO.
JUST PUT HIS FINGER IN THE WATER.
DALTON
Manager of THE AMAZING JOY BUZZARDS, enjoying a rare rest.
STEVO
Half-Yeti, Bass Player for THE AMAZING JOY BUZZARDS, loyal to the end.
GABE
Braniac Drummer for THE AMAZING JOY BUZZARDS, abusing said loyalty.
WHAT? NO WAY WOULD DALTON HURT US! WE'RE HIS BREAD AND BUTTER.
HIS SALAD AND DRESSING.
HIS BRA AND BOOBIE.
GABE!
HIS DIAPER AND...
SHH! WE GET IT.
ANYHOO, IT WORKED ON BIFF.

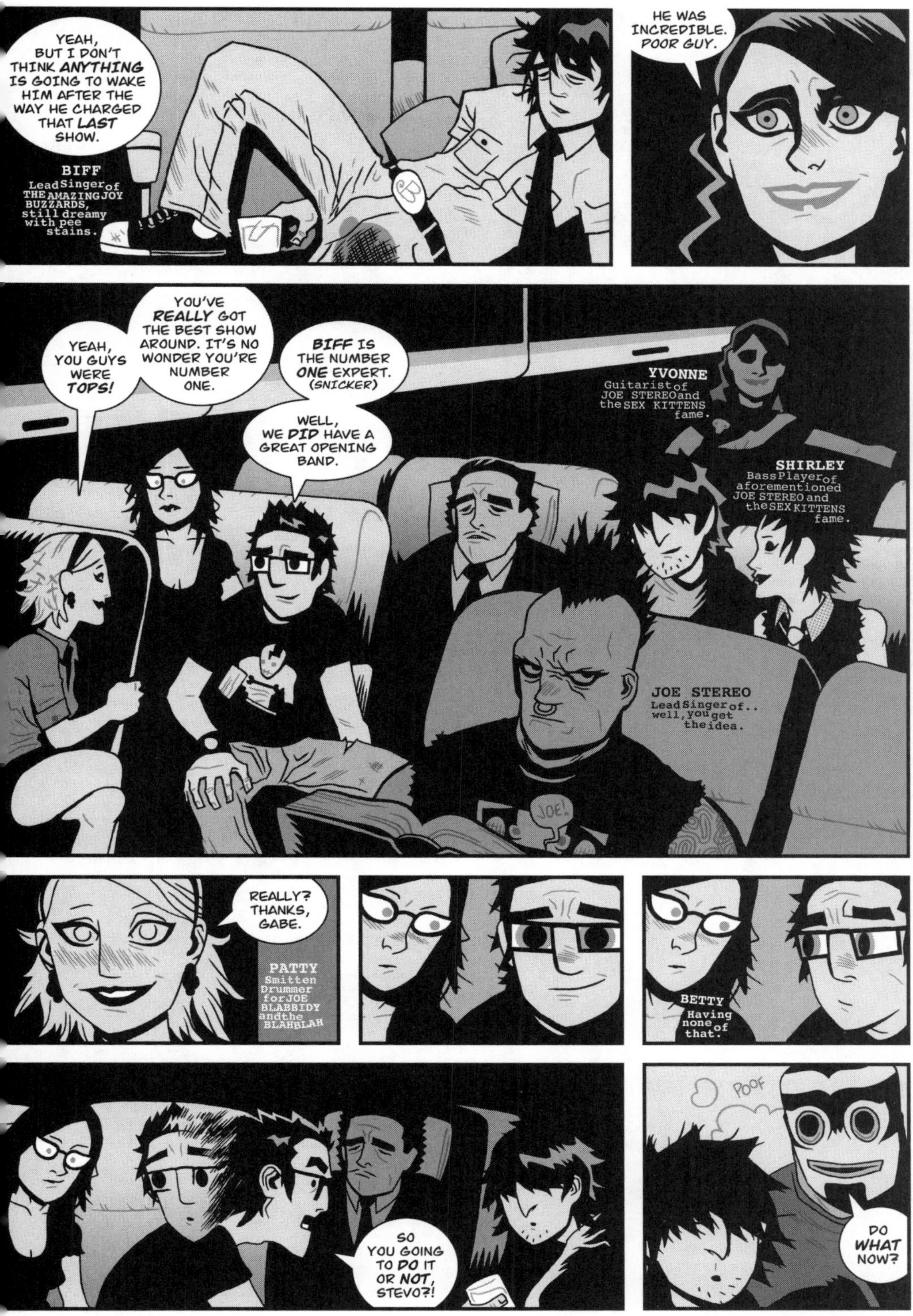
YEAH, BUT I DON'T THINK ANYTHING IS GOING TO WAKE HIM AFTER THE WAY HE CHARGED THAT LAST SHOW.
BIFF
Lead Singer of THE AMAZING JOY BUZZARDS, still dreamy with pee stains.
HE WAS INCREDIBLE. POOR GUY.
YEAH, YOU GUYS WERE TOPS!
YOU'VE REALLY GOT THE BEST SHOW AROUND. IT'S NO WONDER YOU'RE NUMBER ONE.
BIFF IS THE NUMBER ONE EXPERT. (SNICKER)
WELL, WE DID HAVE A GREAT OPENING BAND.
YVONNE
Guitarist of JOE STEREO and the SEX KITTENS fame.
SHIRLEY
Bass Player of aforementioned JOE STEREO and the SEX KITTENS fame.
JOE STEREO
Lead Singer of.. well, you get the idea.
JOE!
REALLY? THANKS, GABE.
PATTY
Smitten Drummer for JOE BLABBIDY and the BLAHBLAH
BETTY
Having none of that.
SO YOU GOING TO DO IT OR NOT, STEVO?!
POOF
DO WHAT NOW?

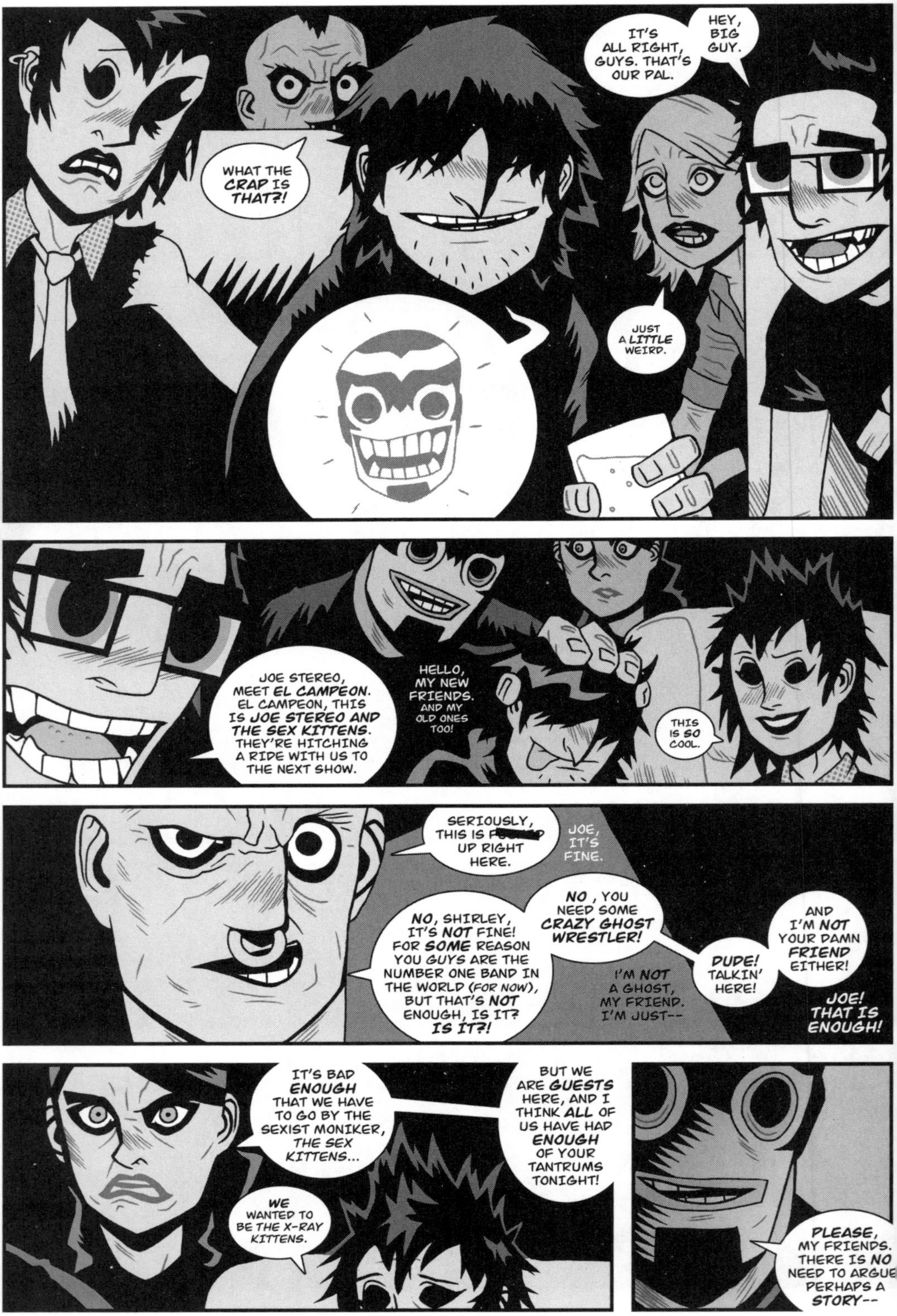

WHAT THE CRAP IS THAT?!
IT'S ALL RIGHT, GUYS. THAT'S OUR PAL.
HEY, BIG GUY.
JUST A LITTLE WEIRD.
JOE STEREO, MEET EL CAMPEON. EL CAMPEON, THIS IS JOE STEREO AND THE SEX KITTENS. THEY'RE HITCHING A RIDE WITH US TO THE NEXT SHOW.
HELLO, MY NEW FRIENDS. AND MY OLD ONES TOO!
THIS IS SO COOL.
SERIOUSLY, THIS IS F[redacted] UP RIGHT HERE.
JOE, IT'S FINE.
NO, SHIRLEY, IT'S NOT FINE! FOR SOME REASON YOU GUYS ARE THE NUMBER ONE BAND IN THE WORLD (FOR NOW), BUT THAT'S NOT ENOUGH, IS IT? IS IT?!
NO , YOU NEED SOME CRAZY GHOST WRESTLER!
I'M NOT A GHOST, MY FRIEND. I'M JUST--
DUDE! TALKIN' HERE!
AND I'M NOT YOUR DAMN FRIEND EITHER!
JOE! THAT IS ENOUGH!
IT'S BAD ENOUGH THAT WE HAVE TO GO BY THE SEXIST MONIKER, THE SEX KITTENS...
BUT WE ARE GUESTS HERE, AND I THINK ALL OF US HAVE HAD ENOUGH OF YOUR TANTRUMS TONIGHT!
WE WANTED TO BE THE X-RAY KITTENS.
PLEASE, MY FRIENDS. THERE IS NO NEED TO ARGUE PERHAPS A STORY--

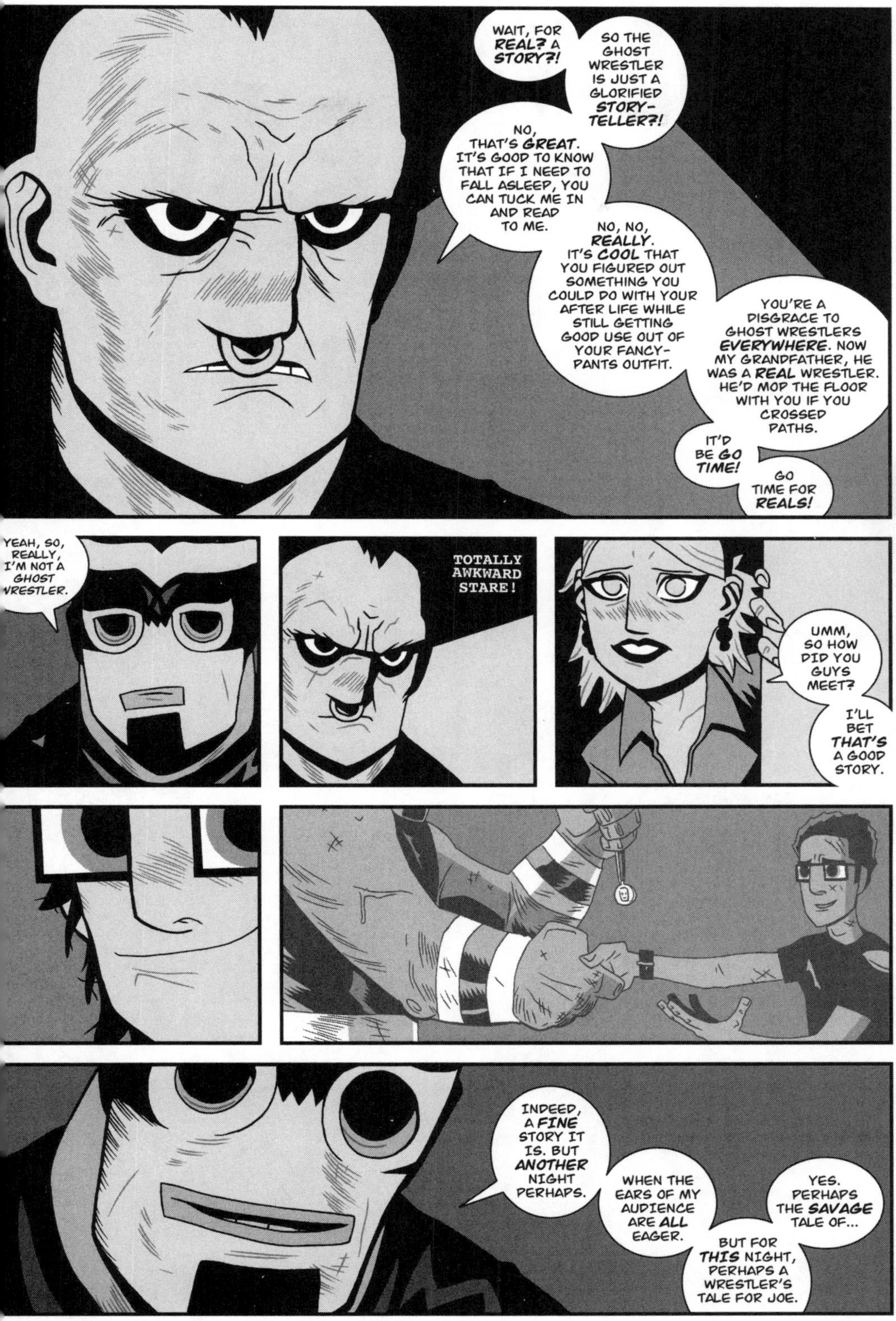
WAIT, FOR REAL? A STORY?!
SO THE GHOST WRESTLER IS JUST A GLORIFIED STORY-TELLER?!
NO, THAT'S GREAT. IT'S GOOD TO KNOW THAT IF I NEED TO FALL ASLEEP, YOU CAN TUCK ME IN AND READ TO ME.
NO, NO, REALLY. IT'S COOL THAT YOU FIGURED OUT SOMETHING YOU COULD DO WITH YOUR AFTER LIFE WHILE STILL GETTING GOOD USE OUT OF YOUR FANCY-PANTS OUTFIT.
YOU'RE A DISGRACE TO GHOST WRESTLERS EVERYWHERE. NOW MY GRANDFATHER, HE WAS A REAL WRESTLER. HE'D MOP THE FLOOR WITH YOU IF YOU CROSSED PATHS.
IT'D BE GO TIME!
GO TIME FOR REALS!
YEAH, SO, REALLY, I'M NOT A GHOST WRESTLER.
TOTALLY AWKWARD STARE!
UMM, SO HOW DID YOU GUYS MEET?
I'LL BET THAT'S A GOOD STORY.
INDEED, A FINE STORY IT IS. BUT ANOTHER NIGHT PERHAPS.
WHEN THE EARS OF MY AUDIENCE ARE ALL EAGER.
YES. PERHAPS THE SAVAGE TALE OF...
BUT FOR THIS NIGHT, PERHAPS A WRESTLER'S TALE FOR JOE.

"WHEN THE DIAPER BANDIT CAME A KNOCKIN'!"

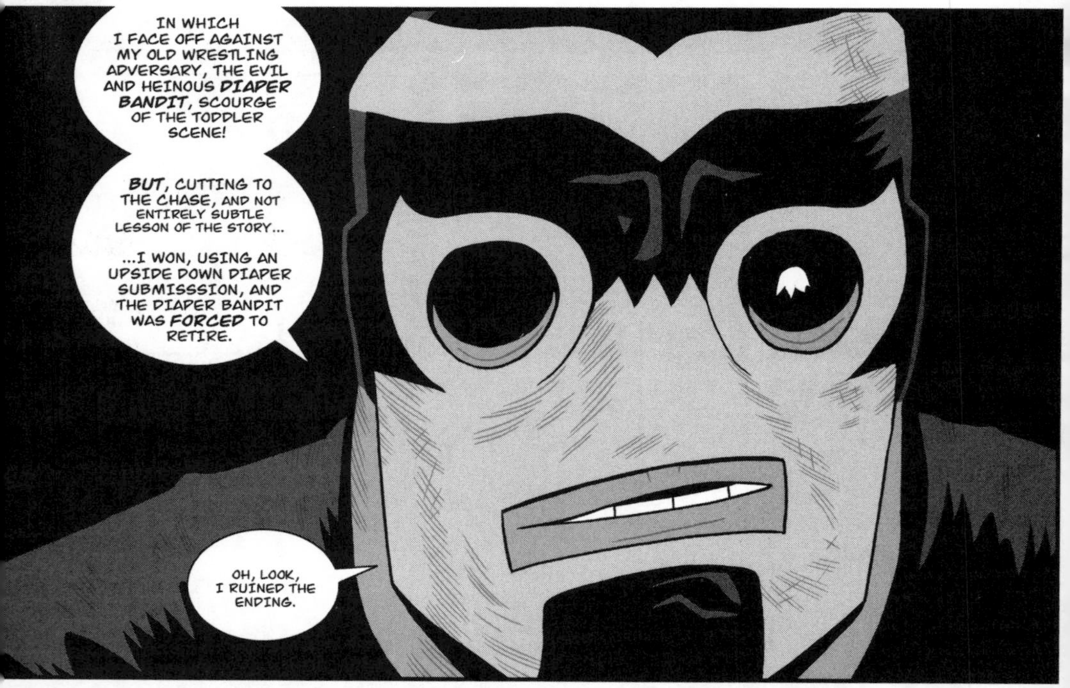
IN WHICH I FACE OFF AGAINST MY OLD WRESTLING ADVERSARY, THE EVIL AND HEINOUS DIAPER BANDIT, SCOURGE OF THE TODDLER SCENE!
BUT, CUTTING TO THE CHASE, AND NOT ENTIRELY SUBTLE LESSON OF THE STORY...
...I WON, USING AN UPSIDE DOWN DIAPER SUBMISSSION, AND THE DIAPER BANDIT WAS FORCED TO RETIRE.
OH, LOOK, I RUINED THE ENDING.

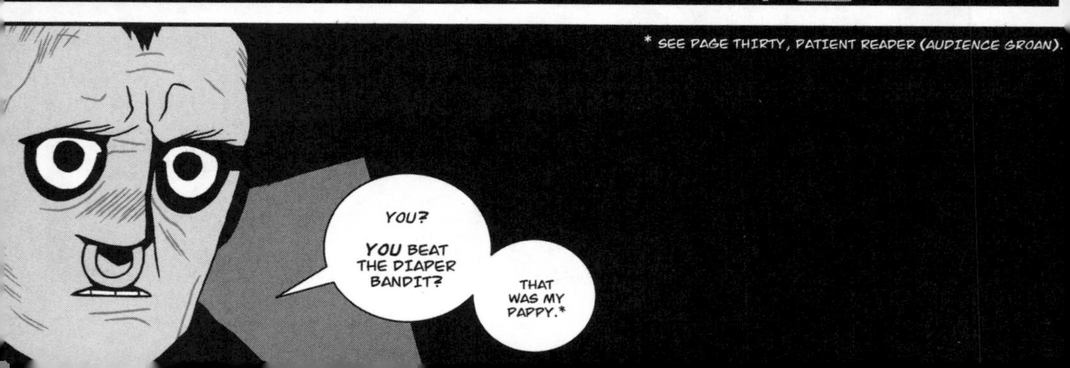
* SEE PAGE THIRTY, PATIENT READER (AUDIENCE GROAN).
YOU?
YOU BEAT THE DIAPER BANDIT?
THAT WAS MY PAPPY.*

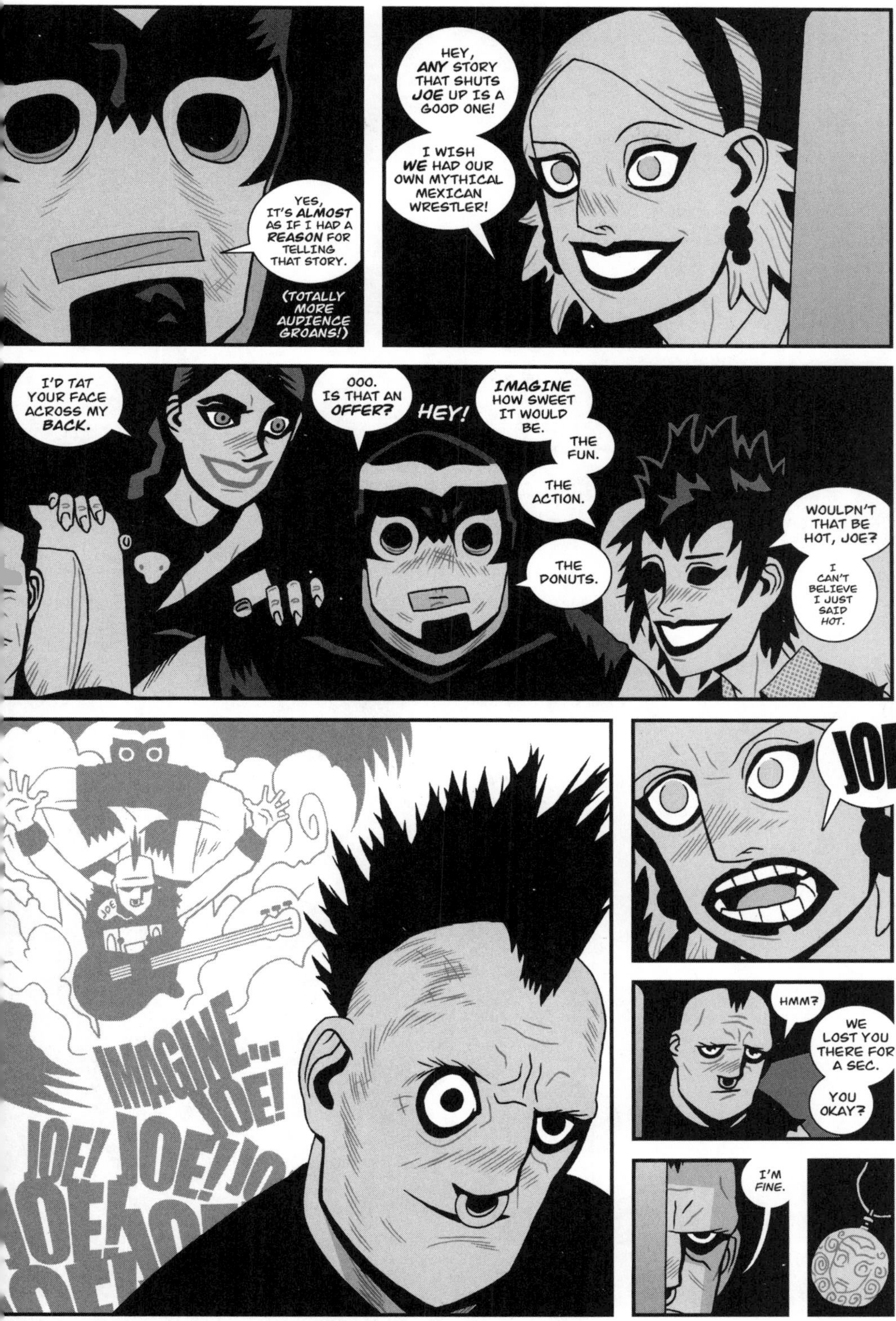
YES, IT'S ALMOST AS IF I HAD A REASON FOR TELLING THAT STORY.
(TOTALLY MORE AUDIENCE GROANS!)
HEY, ANY STORY THAT SHUTS JOE UP IS A GOOD ONE!
I WISH WE HAD OUR OWN MYTHICAL MEXICAN WRESTLER!
I'D TAT YOUR FACE ACROSS MY BACK.
OOO. IS THAT AN OFFER?
HEY!
IMAGINE HOW SWEET IT WOULD BE.
THE FUN.
THE ACTION.
THE DONUTS.
WOULDN'T THAT BE HOT, JOE?
I CAN'T BELIEVE I JUST SAID HOT.
IMAGINE...
JOE!
JOE! JOE! JO
JOE!
HMM?
WE LOST YOU THERE FOR A SEC.
YOU OKAY?
I'M FINE.

IMAGINE...

WHAT WOULD YOU DO IF YOU FOUND A GENIE IN A BOTTLE?

WOULD YOU DEMAND *Glory?*
Fame?
Love?

WOULD YOU FIND *Adventure?*
OR WOULD ADVENTURE FIND ***YOU?***

IMAGINE, IF YOU WILL...

BUT PERHAPS THAT IS ***NOT*** THE WAY SUCH THINGS WORK.

PERHAPS IT IS NOT UP TO ***YOU*** TO FIND THE ***GENIE***.

PERHAPS IT IS UP TO THE ***GENIE*** TO FIND ***YOU***...

AND WHEN HE DOES, WHAT ***THEN?***

WOULD YOU TAKE IT AS AN ***ACCIDENT?***

OR IS ***FATE*** SHOWING YOU THE PATH TO YOUR DESTINY?

Imagine...

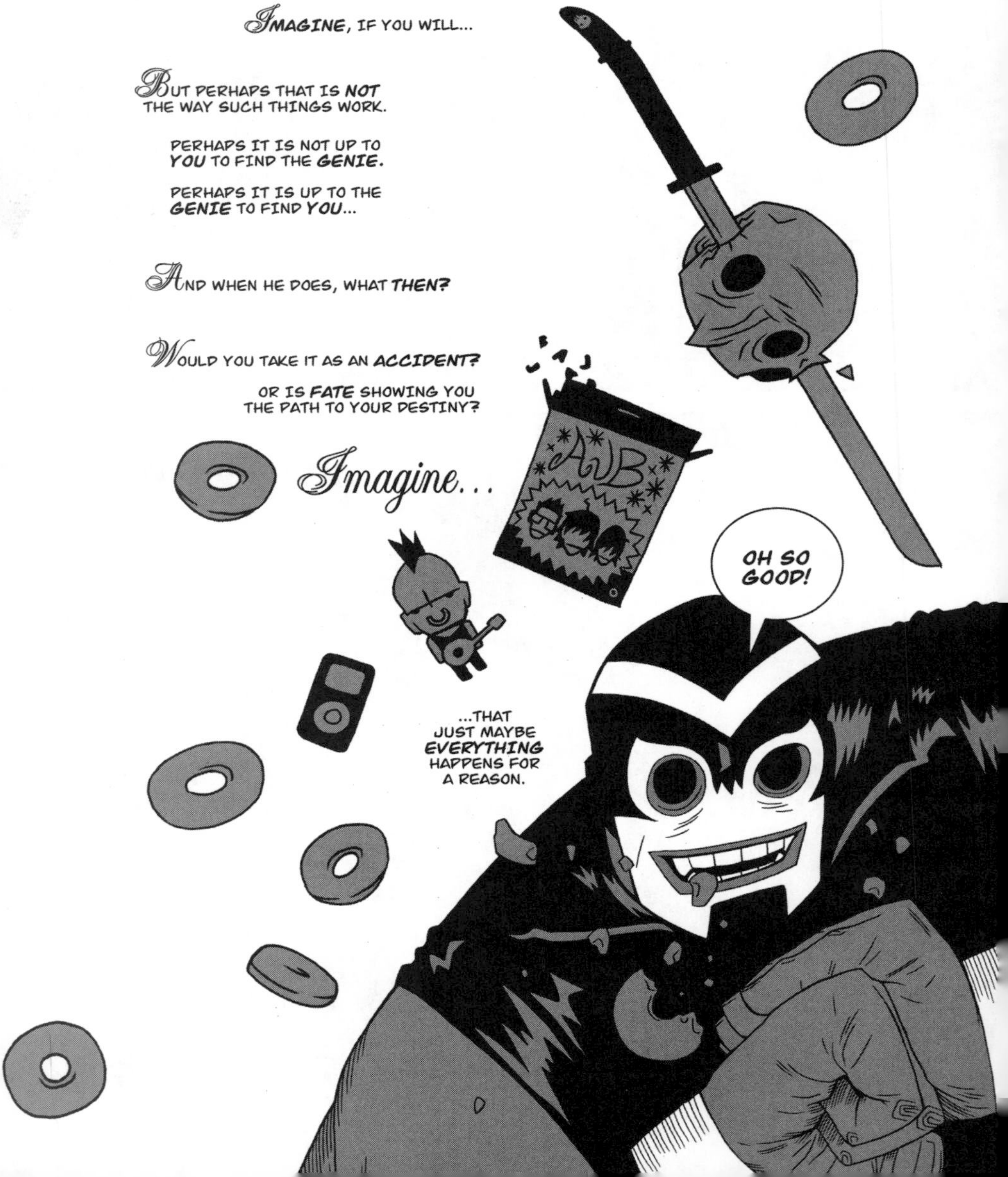

...THAT JUST MAYBE ***EVERYTHING*** HAPPENS FOR A REASON.

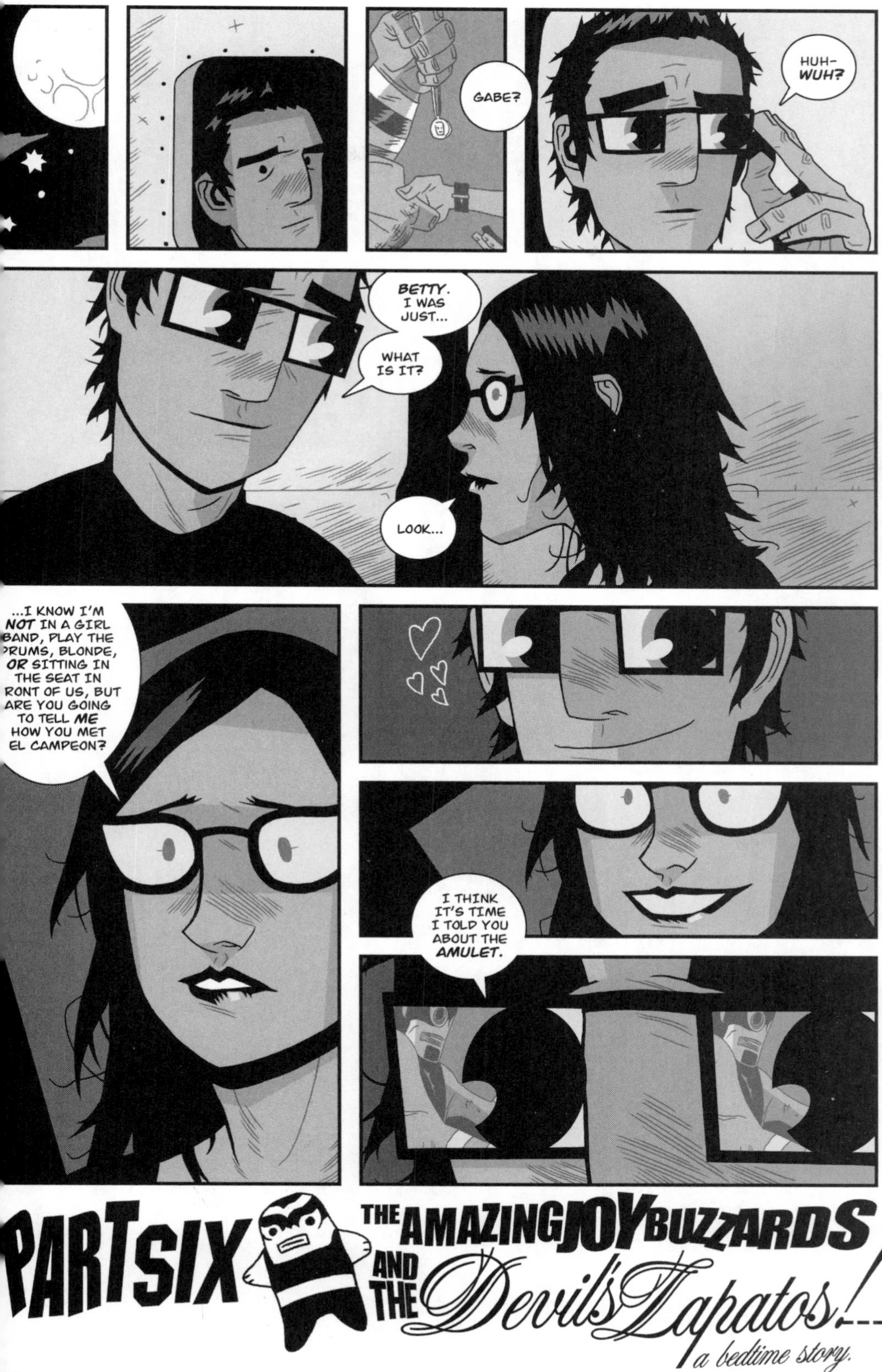
GABE?
HUH-WUH?
BETTY. I WAS JUST...
WHAT IS IT?
LOOK...
...I KNOW I'M NOT IN A GIRL BAND, PLAY THE RUMS, BLONDE, OR SITTING IN THE SEAT IN RONT OF US, BUT ARE YOU GOING TO TELL ME HOW YOU MET EL CAMPEON?
I THINK IT'S TIME I TOLD YOU ABOUT THE AMULET.

PART SIX THE AMAZING JOY BUZZARDS AND THE Devil's Zapatos!

a bedtime story.

FEDERAL ALERT #SD902
CHAPTER

MISSING

FOR YOUR SAFETY AND PROTECTION, AND IN ACCORDANCE WITH THE MAGICAL IMMIGRATIONS AND SECRECIES ACT, THIS CHAPTER HAS BEEN REMOVED.

POSSESSION OF SAID MISSING CHAPTER IN THIS, OR ANY OTHER, EDITION WILL LEAD TO DETAINMENT, PROSECUTION AND ANY ASSOCIATED PENALTIES.

END FEDERAL ALERT #SD902

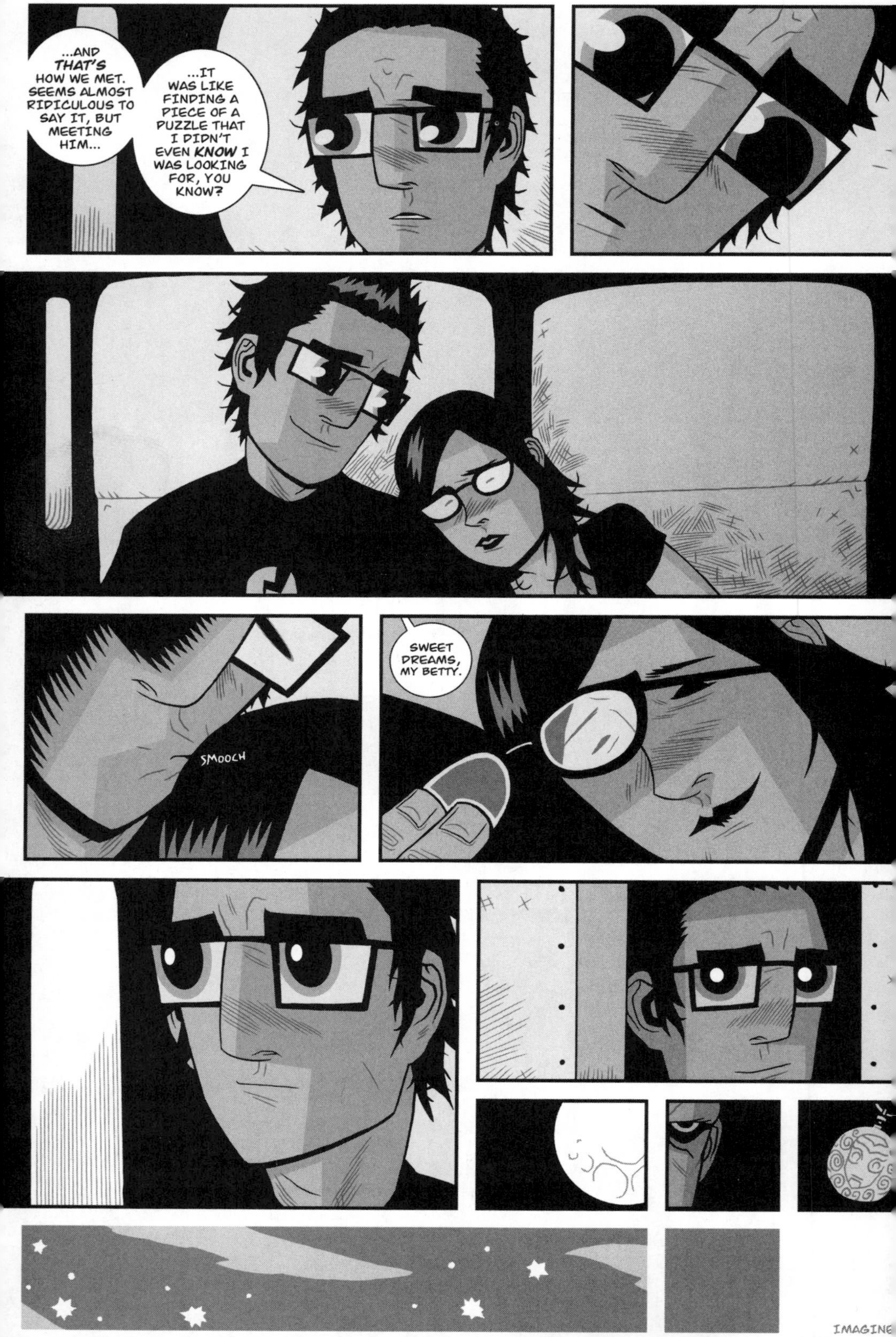
...AND THAT'S HOW WE MET. SEEMS ALMOST RIDICULOUS TO SAY IT, BUT MEETING HIM...
...IT WAS LIKE FINDING A PIECE OF A PUZZLE THAT I DIDN'T EVEN KNOW I WAS LOOKING FOR, YOU KNOW?
SMOOCH
SWEET DREAMS, MY BETTY.

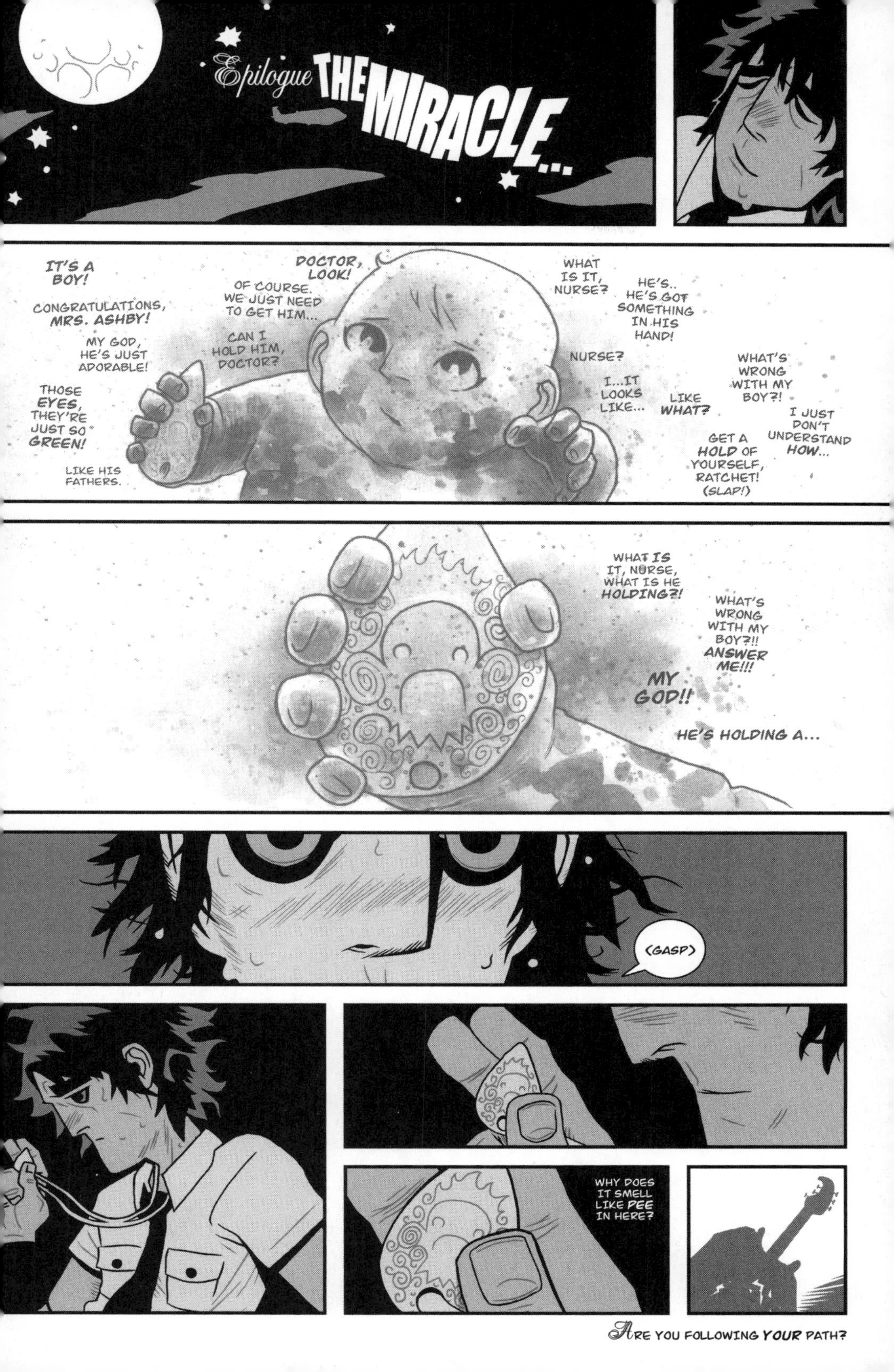
Epilogue THE MIRACLE...
IT'S A BOY!
CONGRATULATIONS, MRS. ASHBY!
MY GOD, HE'S JUST ADORABLE!
THOSE EYES, THEY'RE JUST SO GREEN!
LIKE HIS FATHERS.
OF COURSE. WE JUST NEED TO GET HIM...
CAN I HOLD HIM, DOCTOR?
DOCTOR, LOOK!
WHAT IS IT, NURSE?
HE'S.. HE'S GOT SOMETHING IN HIS HAND!
NURSE?
I...IT LOOKS LIKE...
LIKE WHAT?
WHAT'S WRONG WITH MY BOY?!
I JUST DON'T UNDERSTAND HOW...
GET A HOLD OF YOURSELF, RATCHET! (SLAP!)
WHAT IS IT, NURSE, WHAT IS HE HOLDING?!
WHAT'S WRONG WITH MY BOY?!! ANSWER ME!!!
MY GOD!!
HE'S HOLDING A...
(GASP)
WHY DOES IT SMELL LIKE PEE IN HERE?
ARE YOU FOLLOWING YOUR PATH?

THE
END
again.

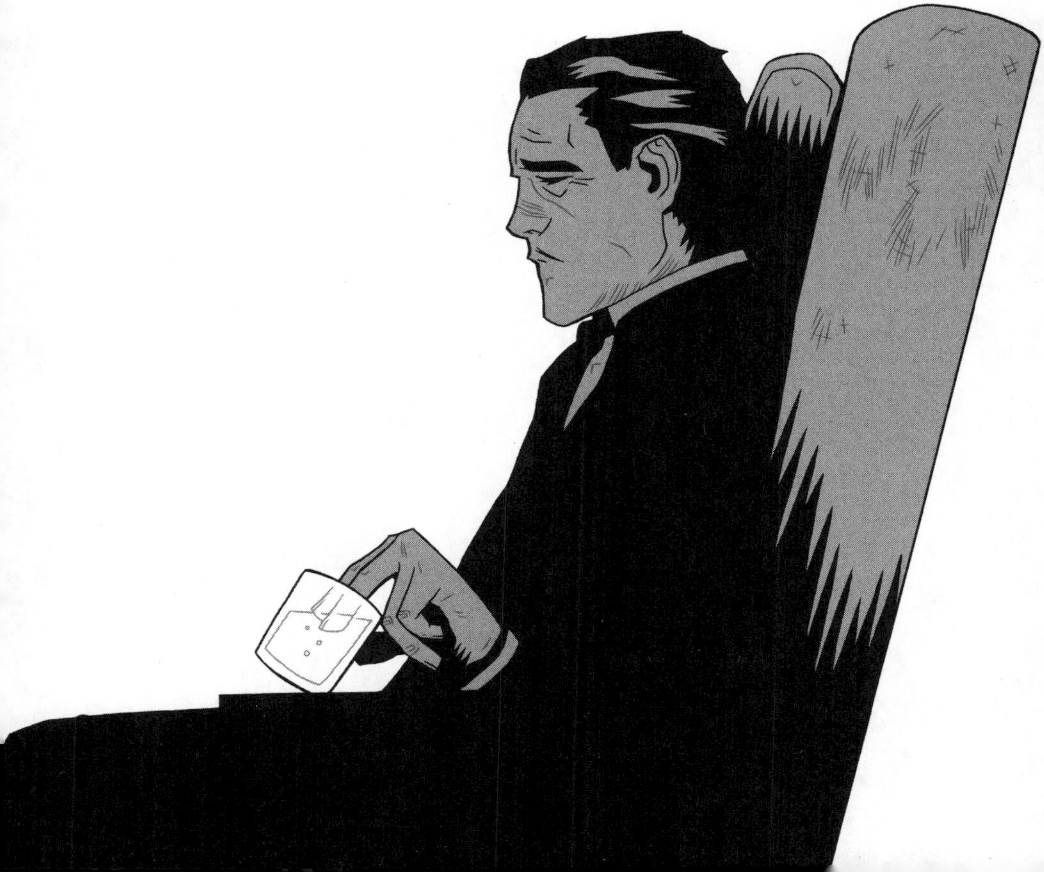

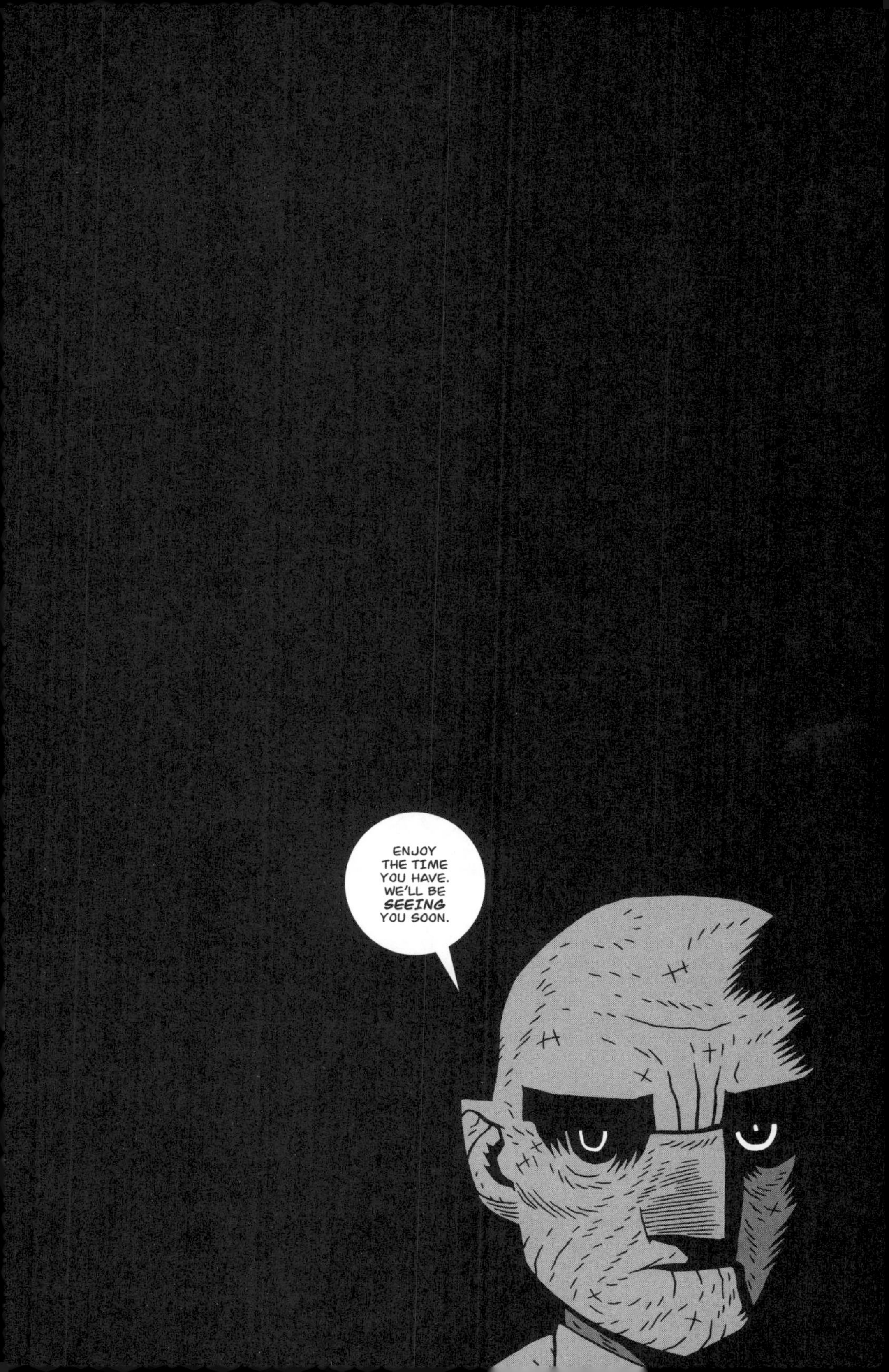
ENJOY THE TIME YOU HAVE. WE'LL BE **SEEING** YOU SOON.

THE FOLLOWING PAGES CONTAIN

EVIDENCE

AGAINST WANTED AUTHORS

MARK ANDREW SMITH AND DANIEL SPENCER HIPP

TO BE USED IN THE SECRET TRIBUNAL TRIAL OF THE UNITED STATES GOVERNMENT VS. SMITH AND HIPP.

ALL EXHIBITS ARE TO REMAIN IN THIS EDITION AND ARE NOT TO BE REMOVED, OR COPIED IN ANY WAY, UNDER PENALTY OF DEATH AND/OR DISEMBOWLMENT.

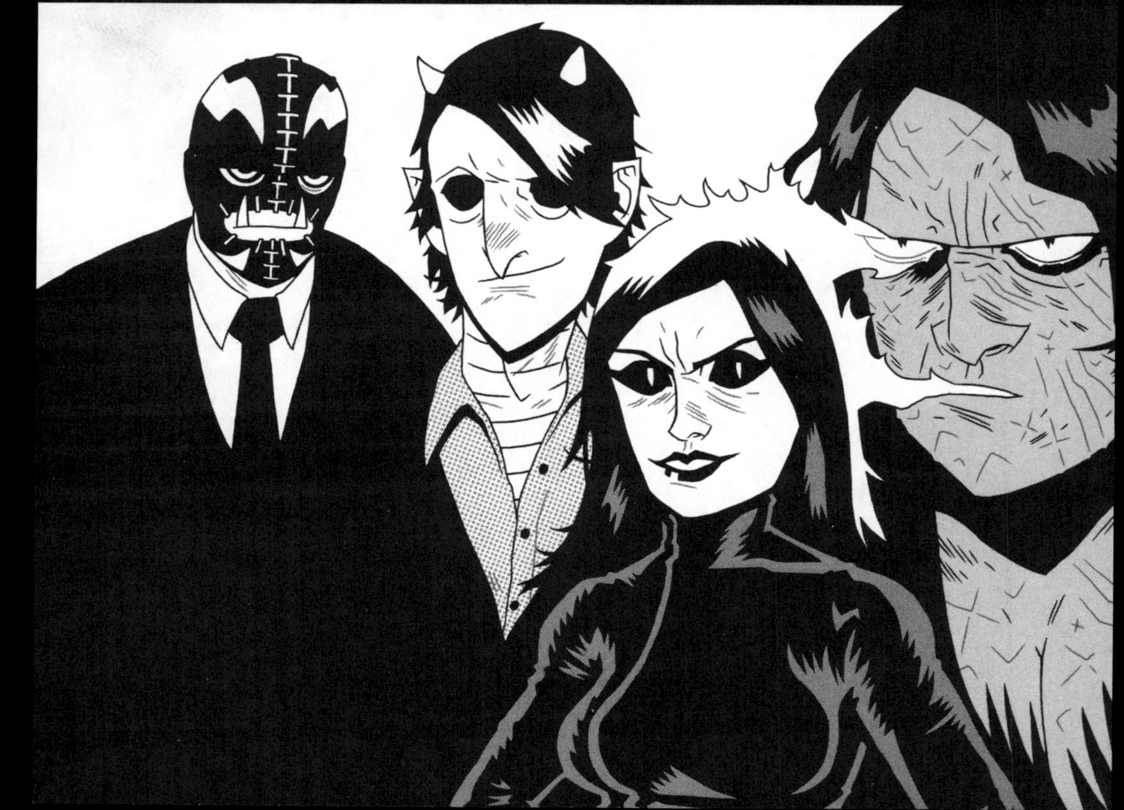

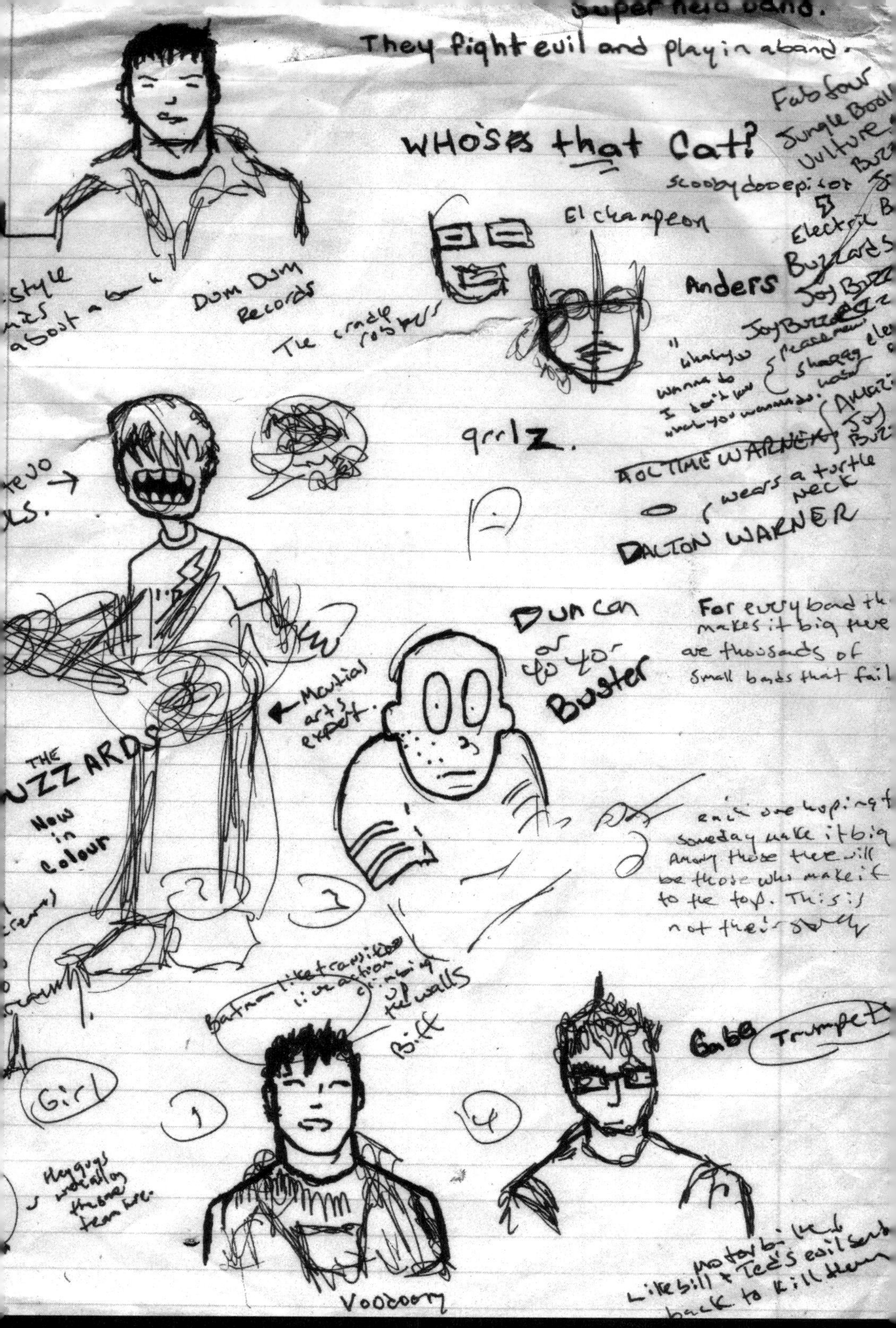
They fight evil and play in a band.
WHO'S that Cat?
Fab four
El champeon
Anders Buzzards
grrlz.
wears a turtle neck
DALTON WARNER
Duncan
Buster
For every band that makes it big there are thousands of small bands that fail
Martial arts expert.
THE BUZZARDS
Now in colour
each one hoping to someday make it big. Among those there will be those who make it to the top. This is not their story
Dum Dum Records
Girl
Gabe
Trumpet
Biff
Vooroom
Like Bill & Ted's evil sent back to kill them

EXHIBIT A1: A SMITH NOTEBOOK PAGE, PRE-DATING THE FIRST PUBLISHED APPEARANCE OF THE AMAZING JOY BUZZARDS.

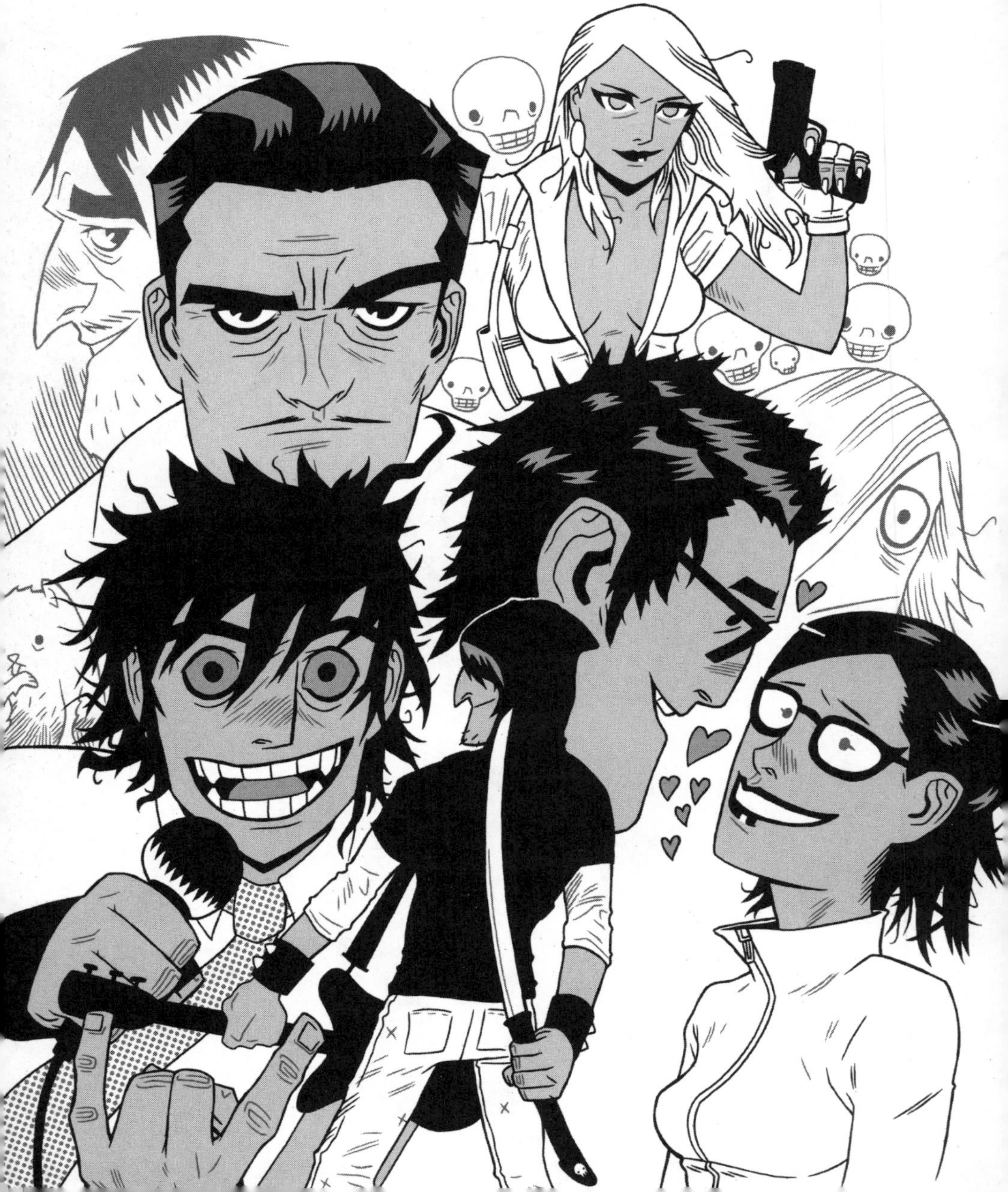

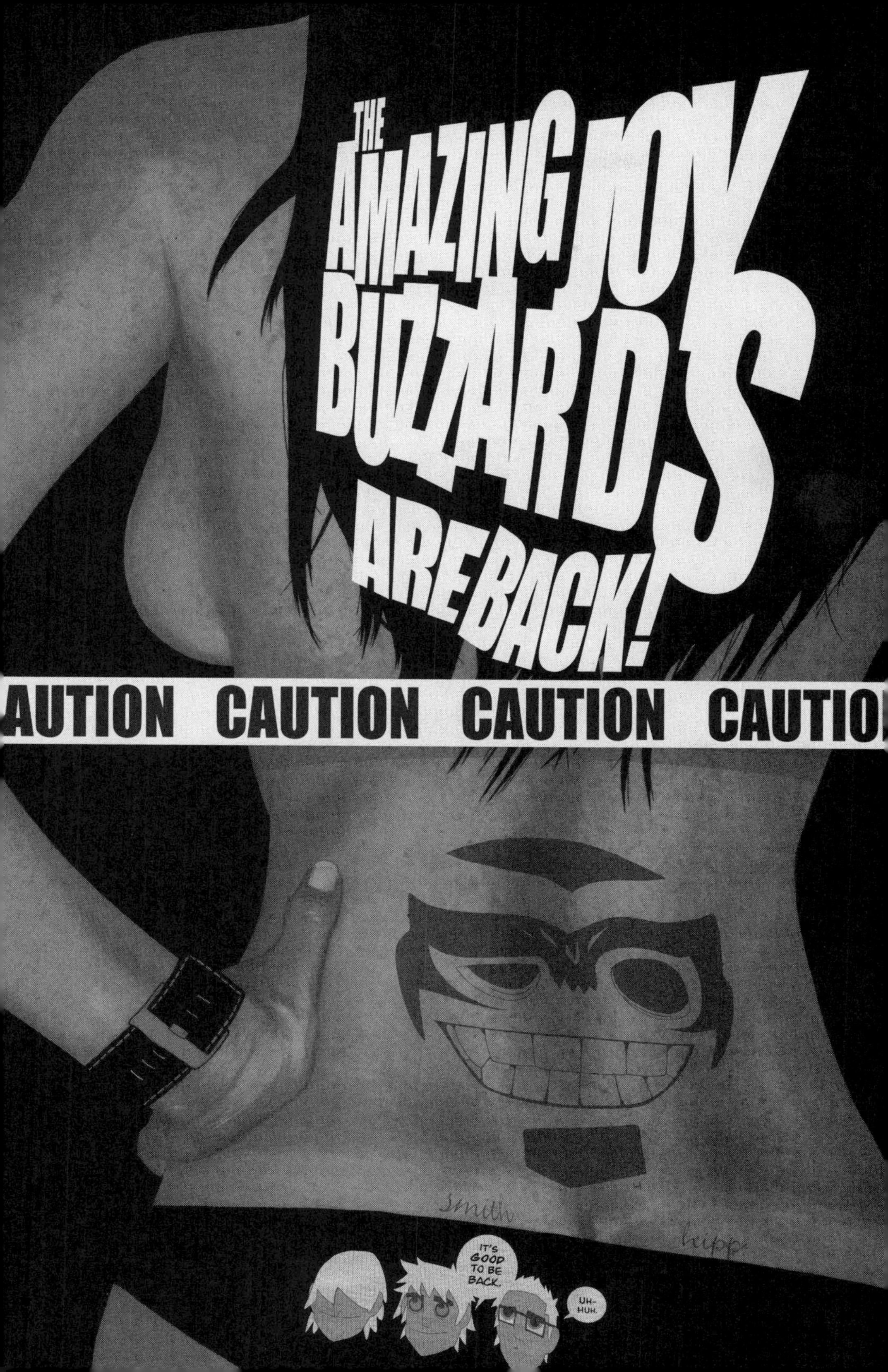
THE AMAZING JOY BUZZARDS ARE BACK!
CAUTION CAUTION CAUTION CAUTIO
smith
hipp
IT'S GOOD TO BE BACK.
UH-HUH.

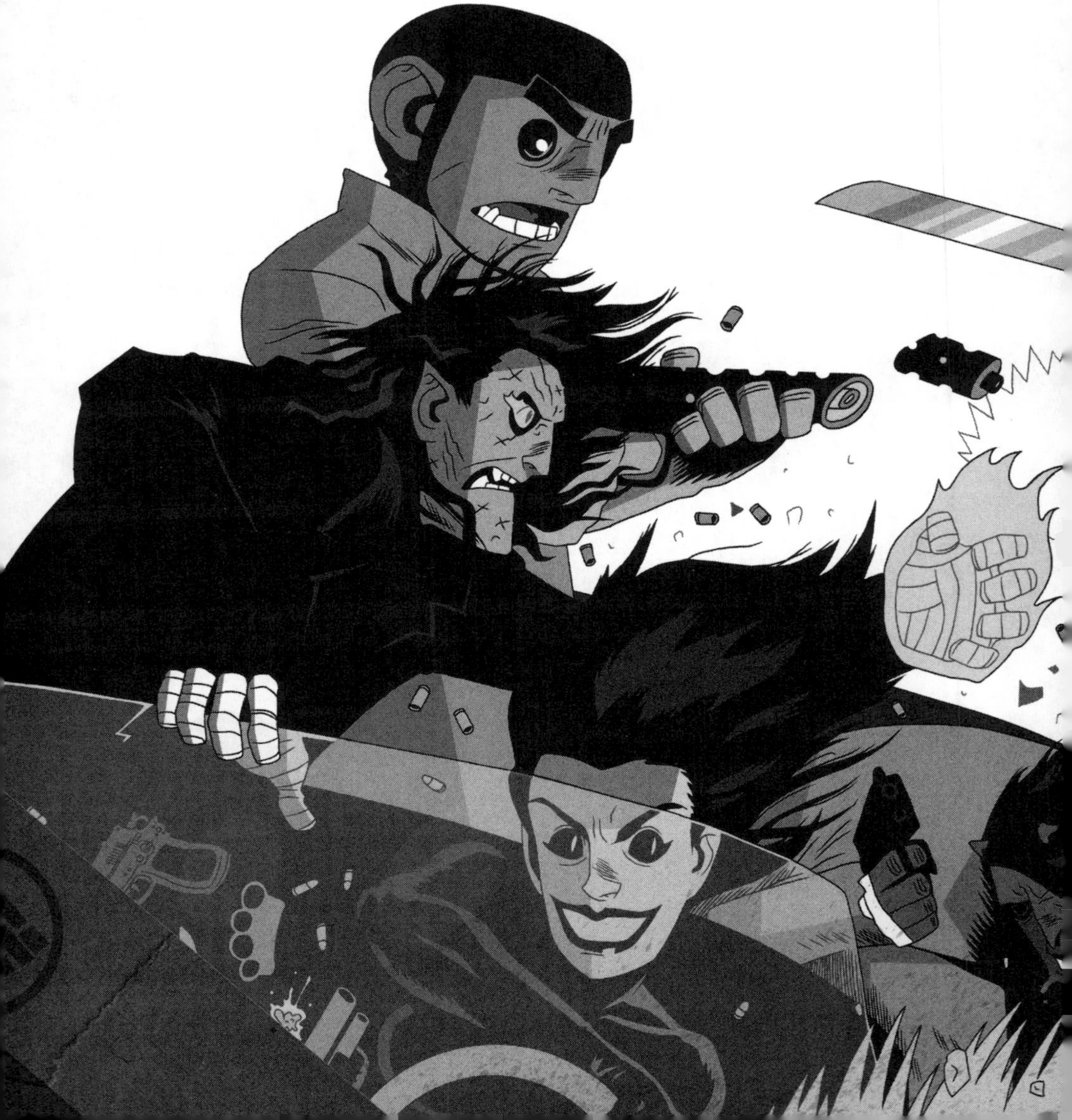

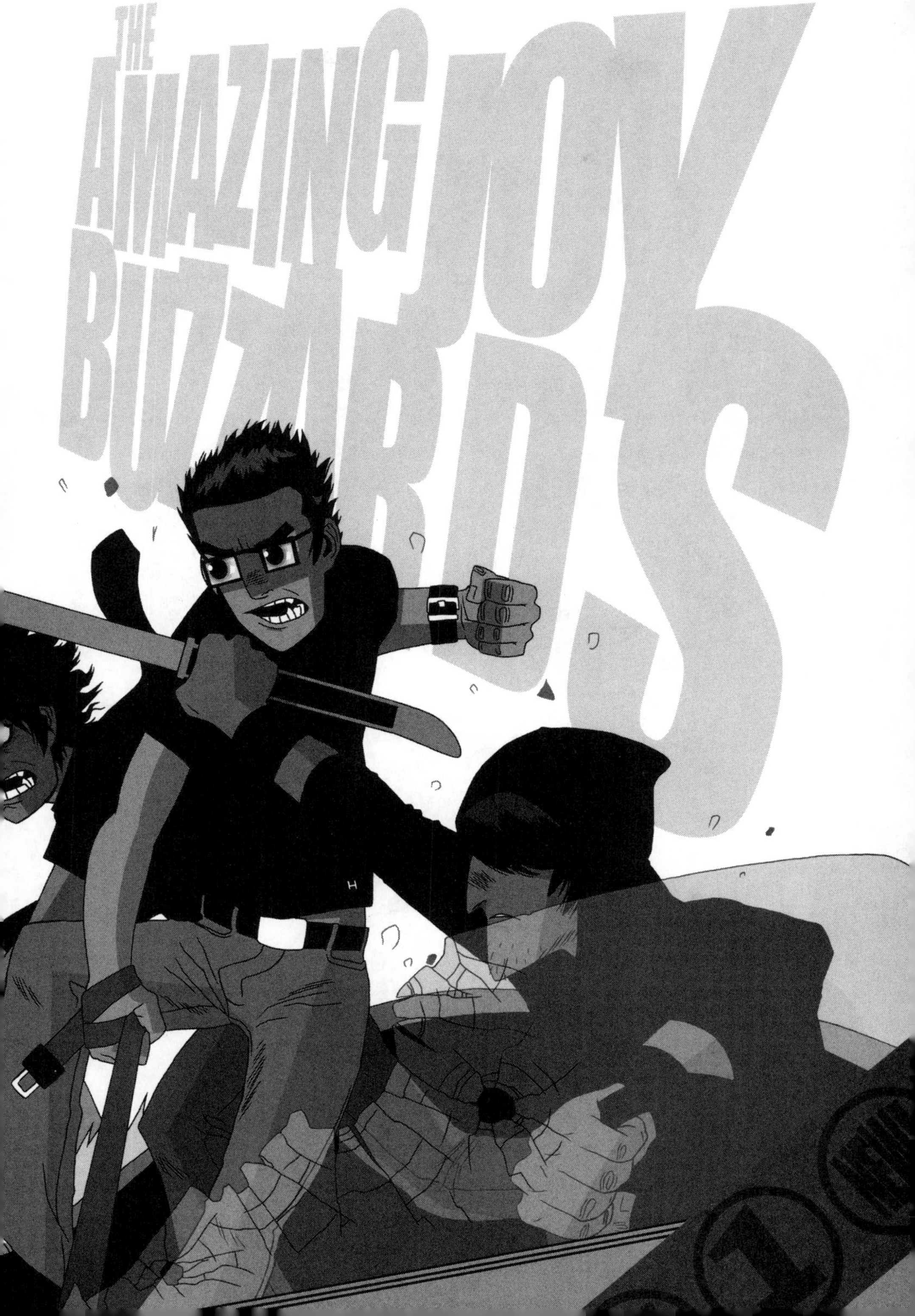
THE AMAZING JOY BUZZARDS

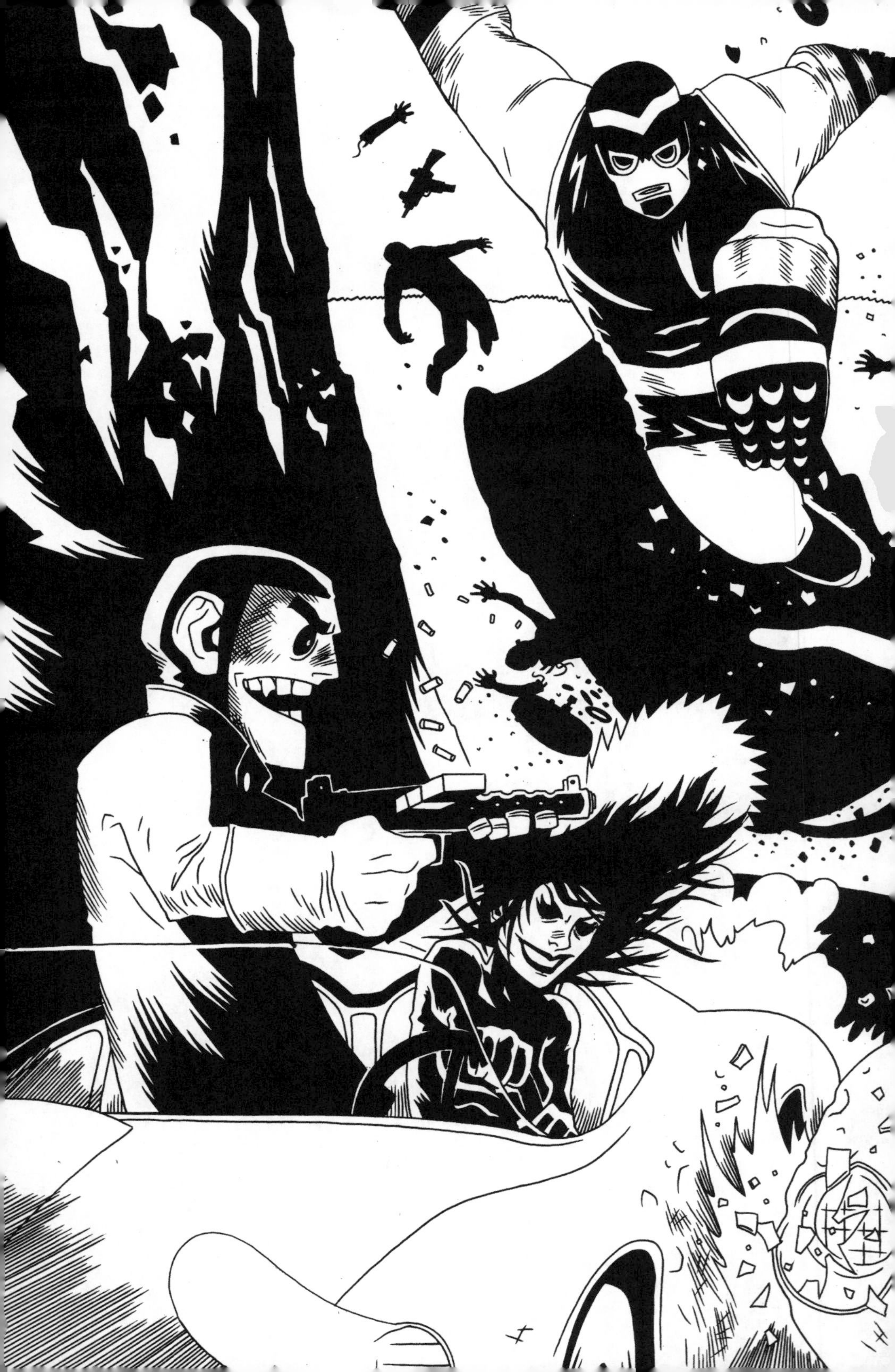

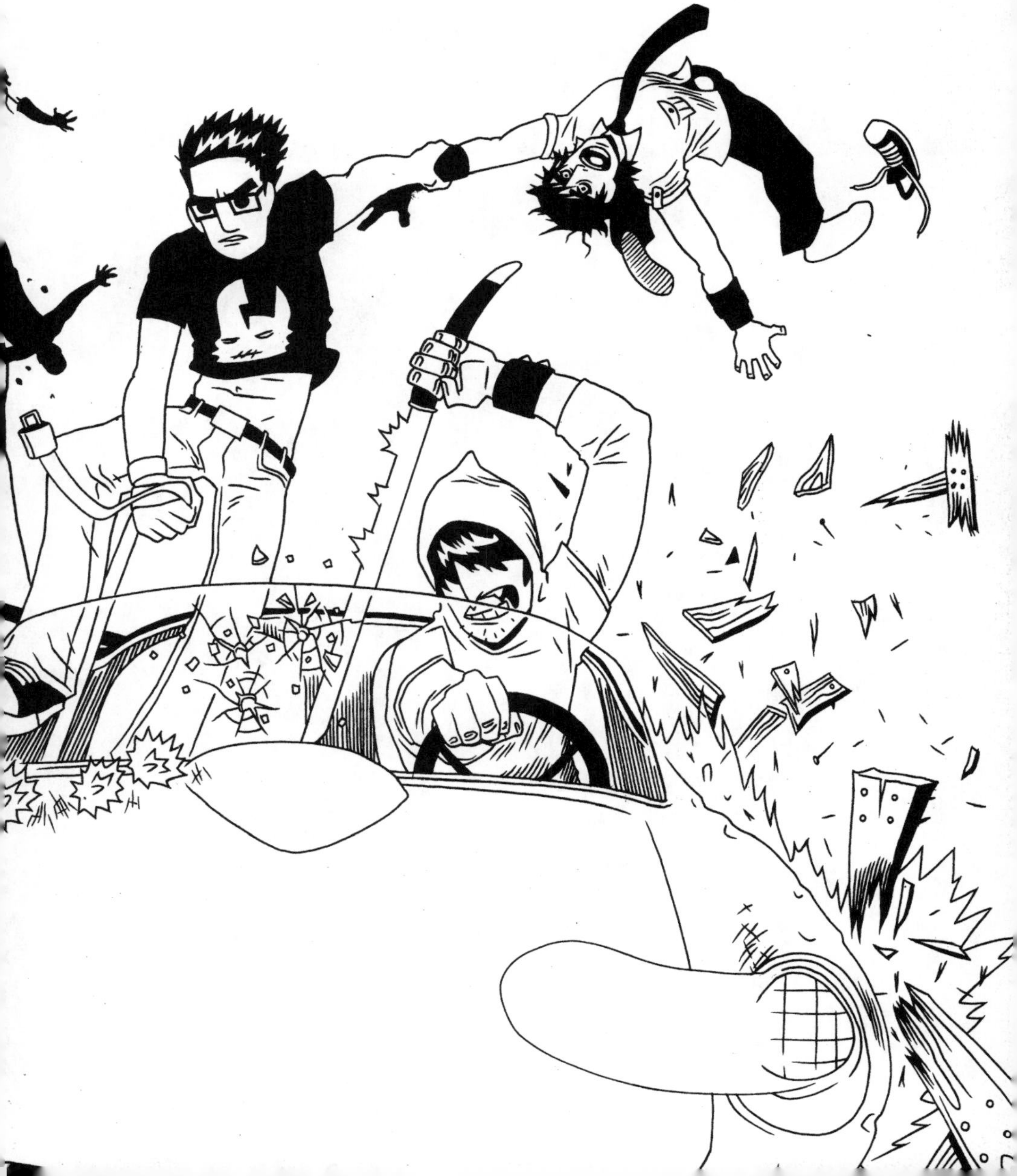

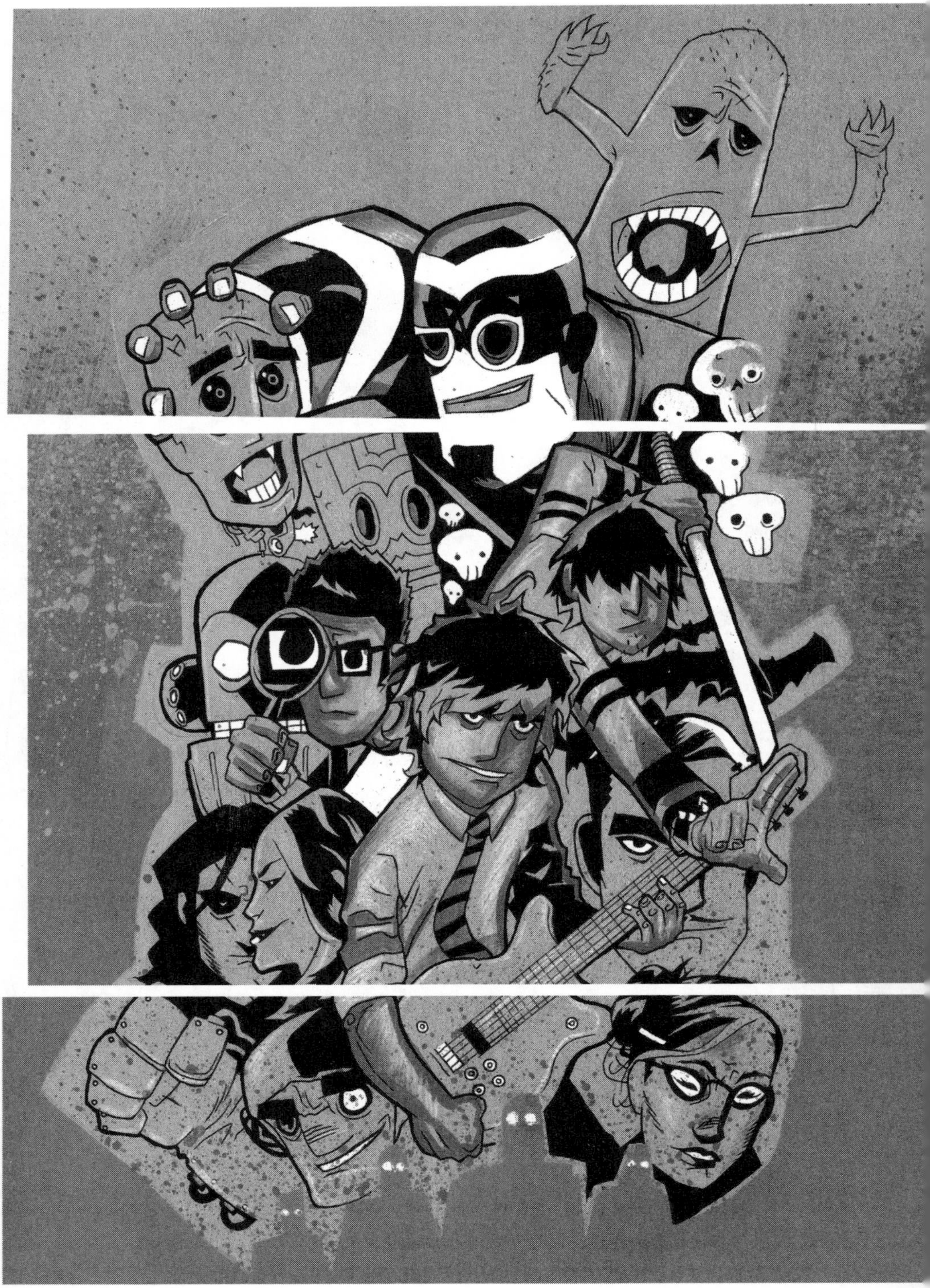

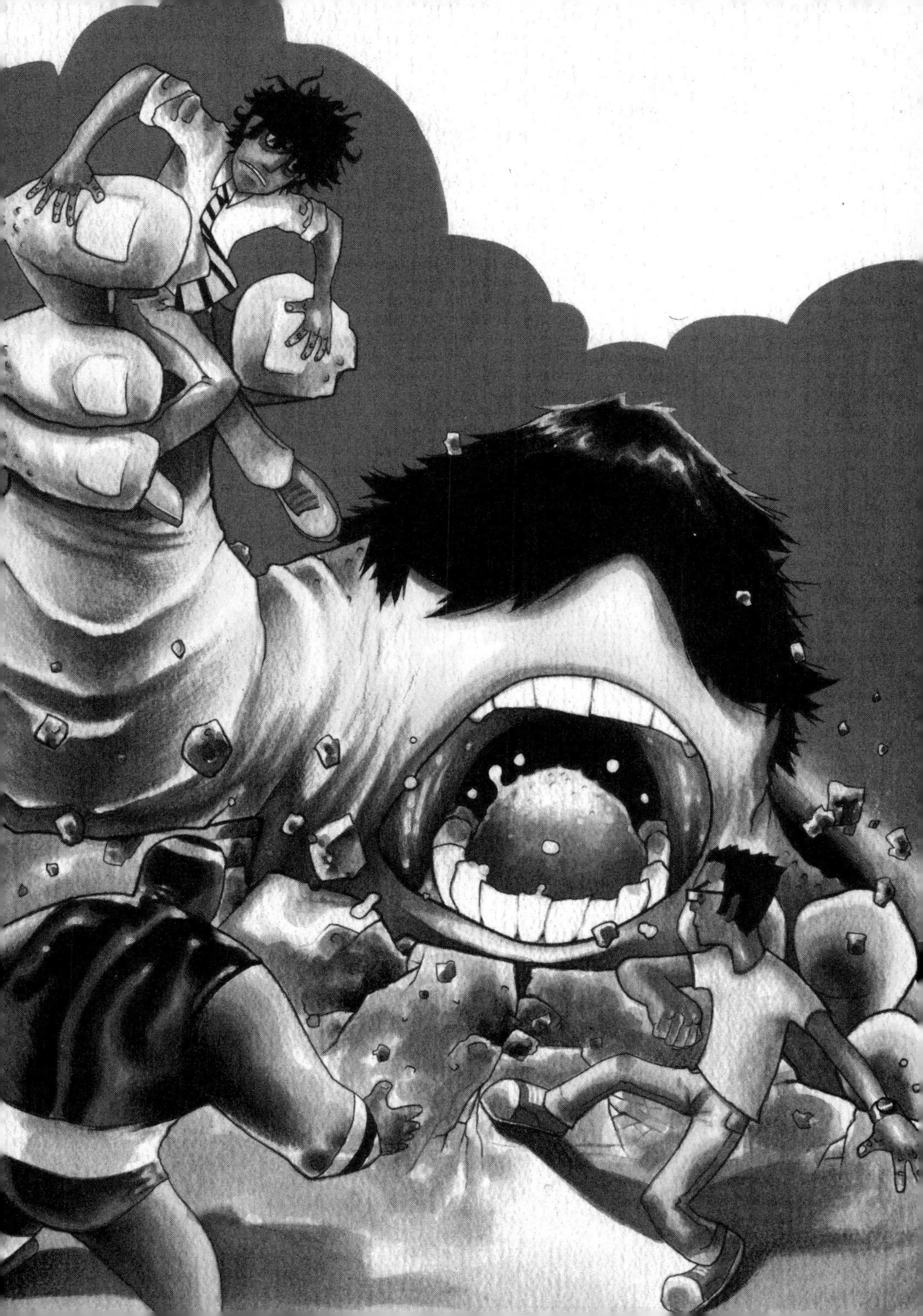

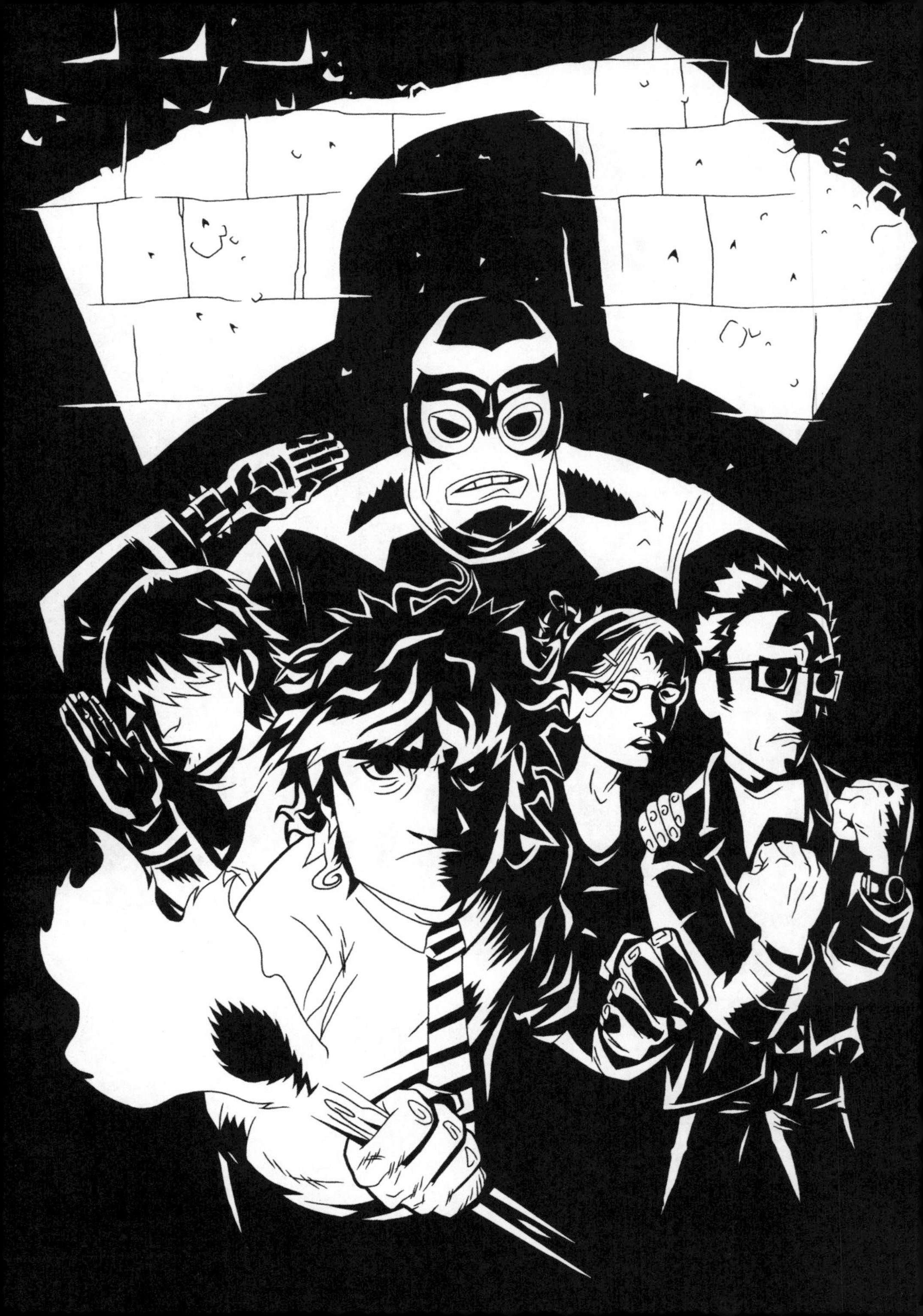

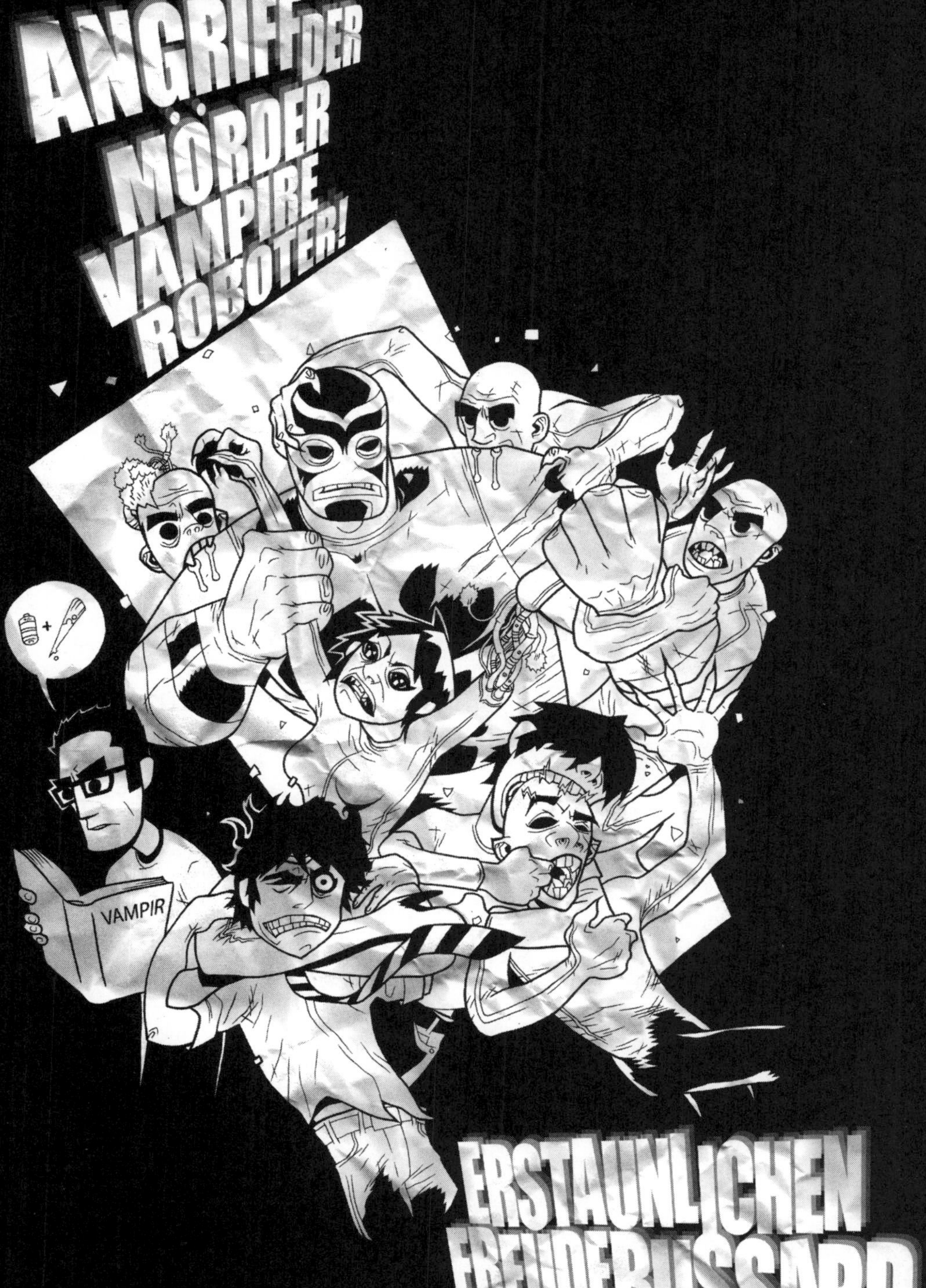

ANGRIFF DER
MÖRDER
VAMPIRE
ROBOTER!
VAMPIR
ERSTAUNLICHEN
FREUDEBUSSARD

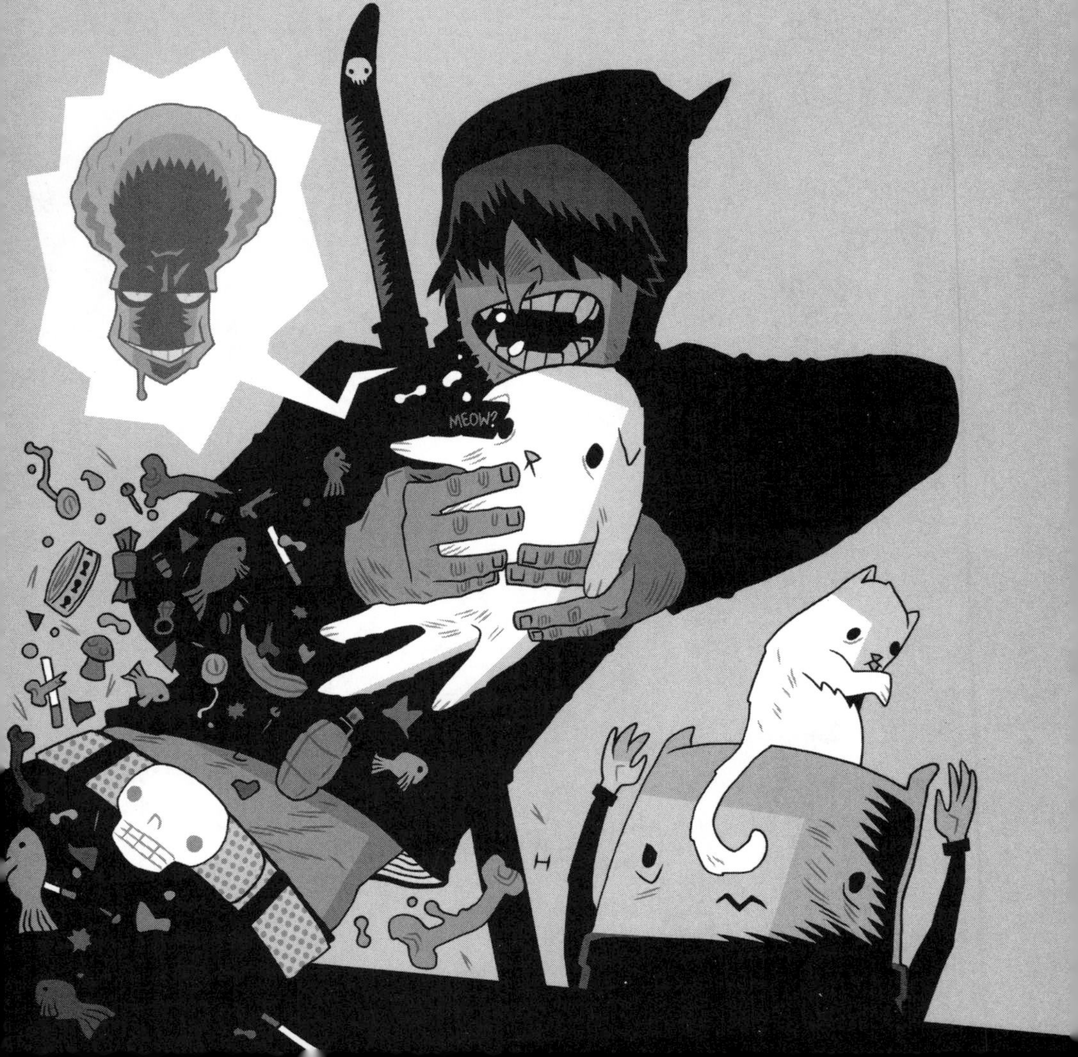
MEOW?

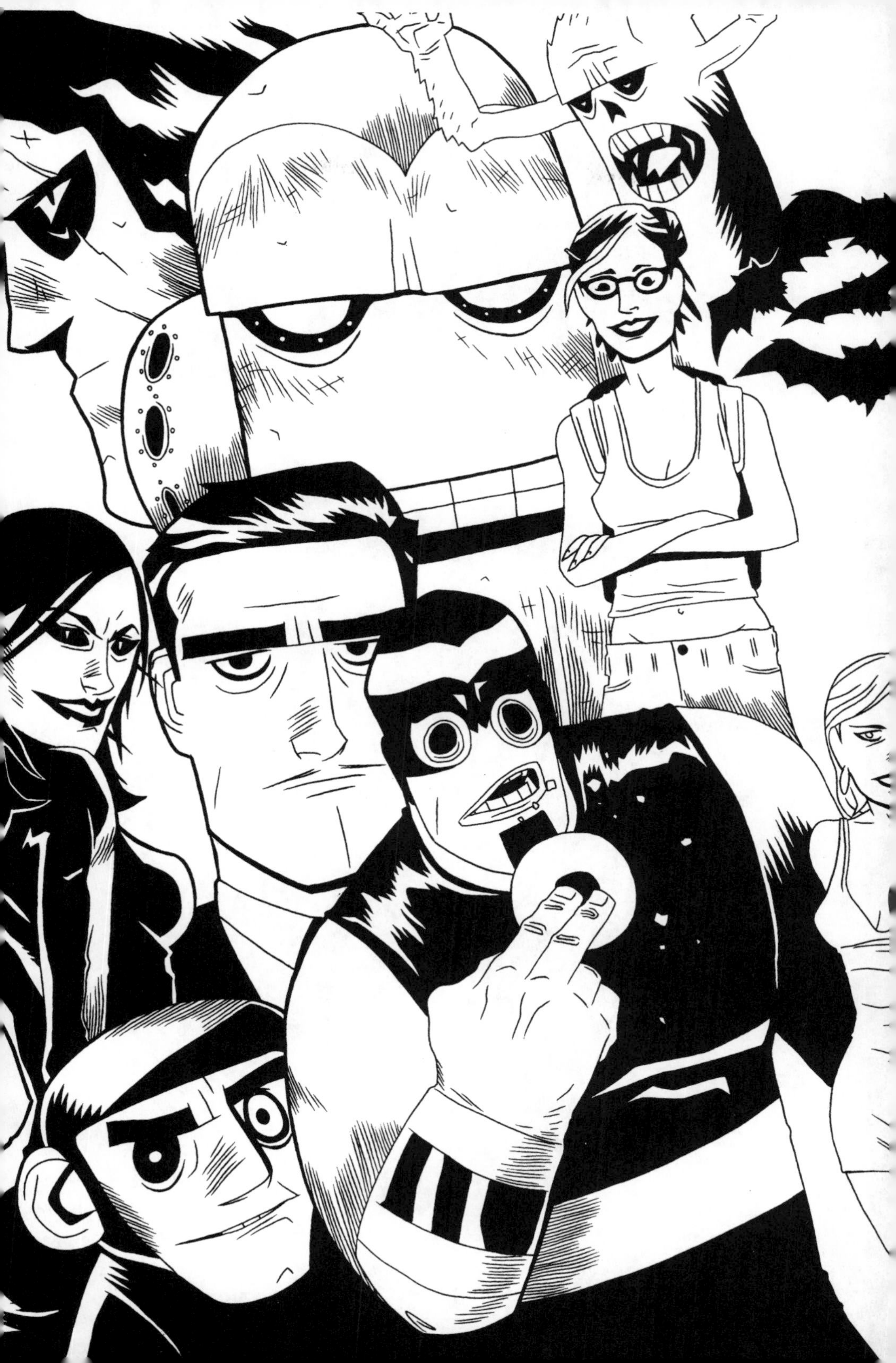

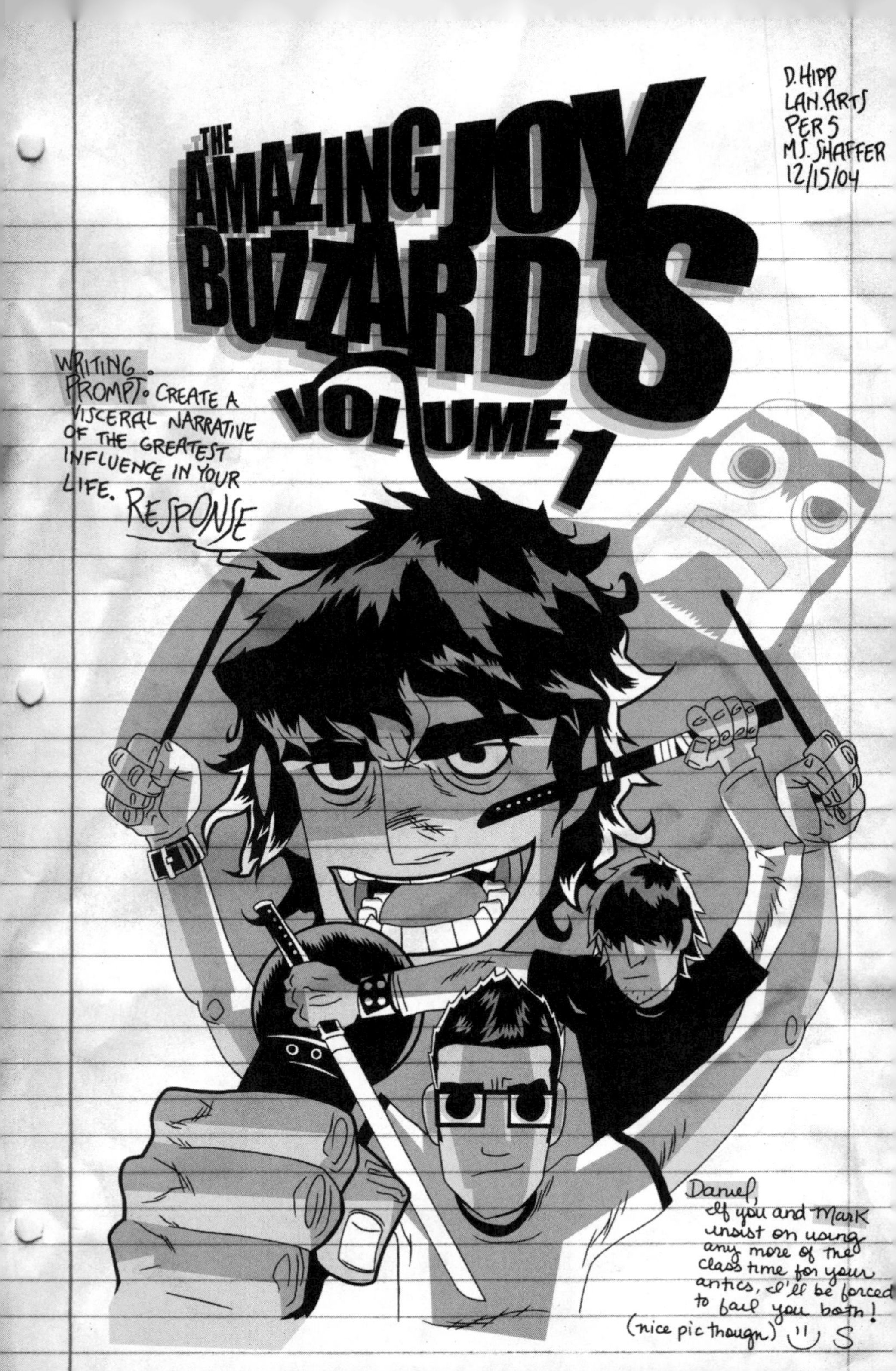

D. HIPP
LAN. ARTS
PER 5
MS. SHAFFER
12/15/04
THE AMAZING JOY BUZZARDS
VOLUME 1
WRITING PROMPT: CREATE A VISCERAL NARRATIVE OF THE GREATEST INFLUENCE IN YOUR LIFE. RESPONSE
Daniel,
If you and Mark insist on using any more of the class time for your antics, I'll be forced to fail you both!
(nice pic though) :) S

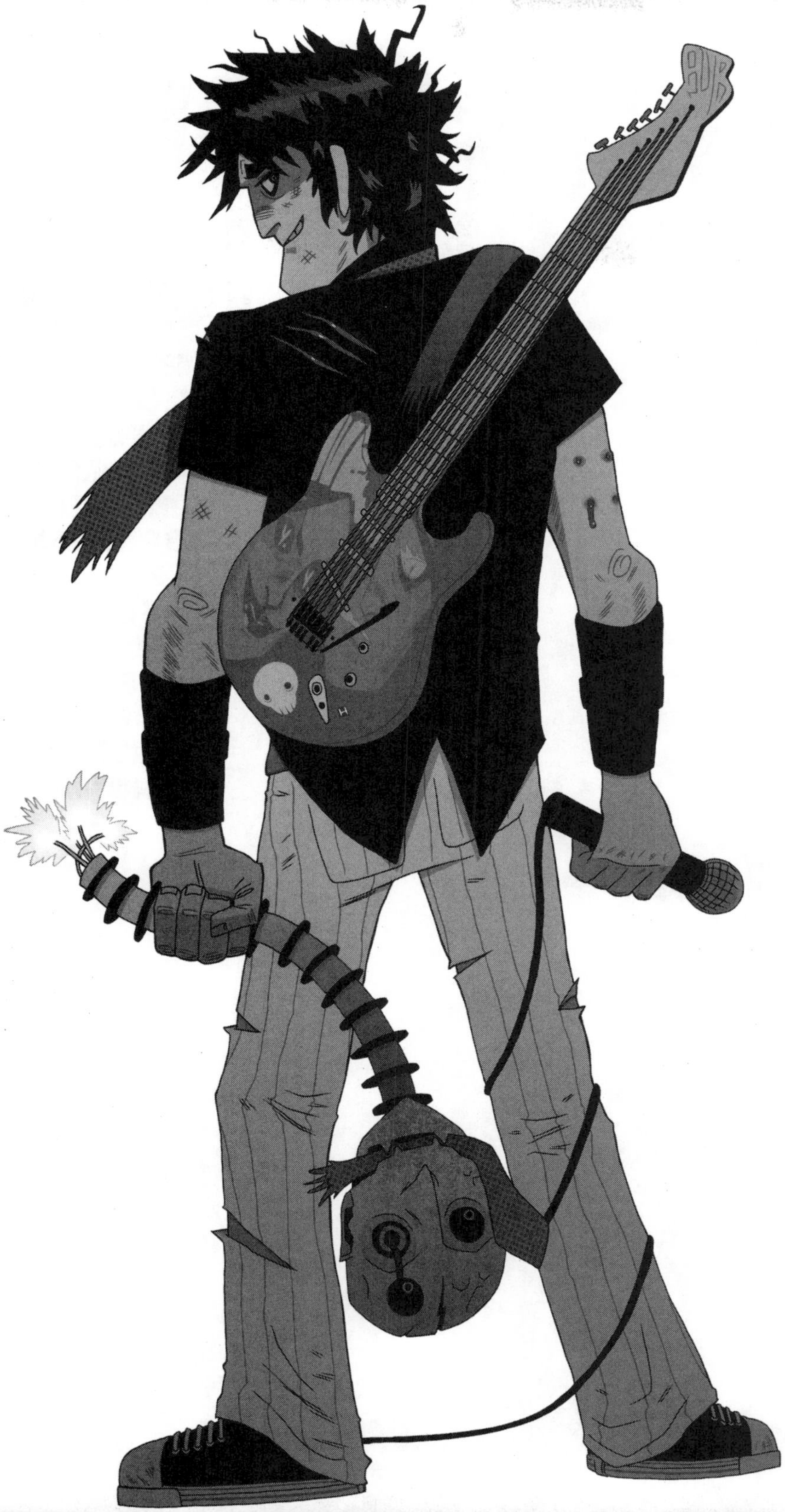

LIST OF KNOWN ACCOMPLICES:

ISRAEL SANCHEZ   JIM MAHFOOD
BRIAN CHURILLA   JOSE GARIBALDI
MIKE HUDDLESTON   RICK CORTES
DOUG HOLGATE   JOEY MASON
DAVE COLLINSON   JIM PEZZETTI
SAM MCKENZIE   ENRICO CASAROSA
JIM RUGG   SCOTT MORSE
CHUCK BB   OVI NEDELCU
JAMES STOKOE   GREG KIRKPATRICK
NATE BELLEGARDE   JAY STEVENS
DAVE CROSLAND   RAGNAR
KHARY RANDOLPH   CHRIS FASON
SEAN GALLOWAY   JASON HOWARD

IF YOU HAVE ANY INFORMATION REGARDING THE WHEREABOUTS OF ANY OF THE
ABOVE MENTIONED INDIVIDUALS, PLEASE CONTACT YOUR LOCAL AUTHORITIES.

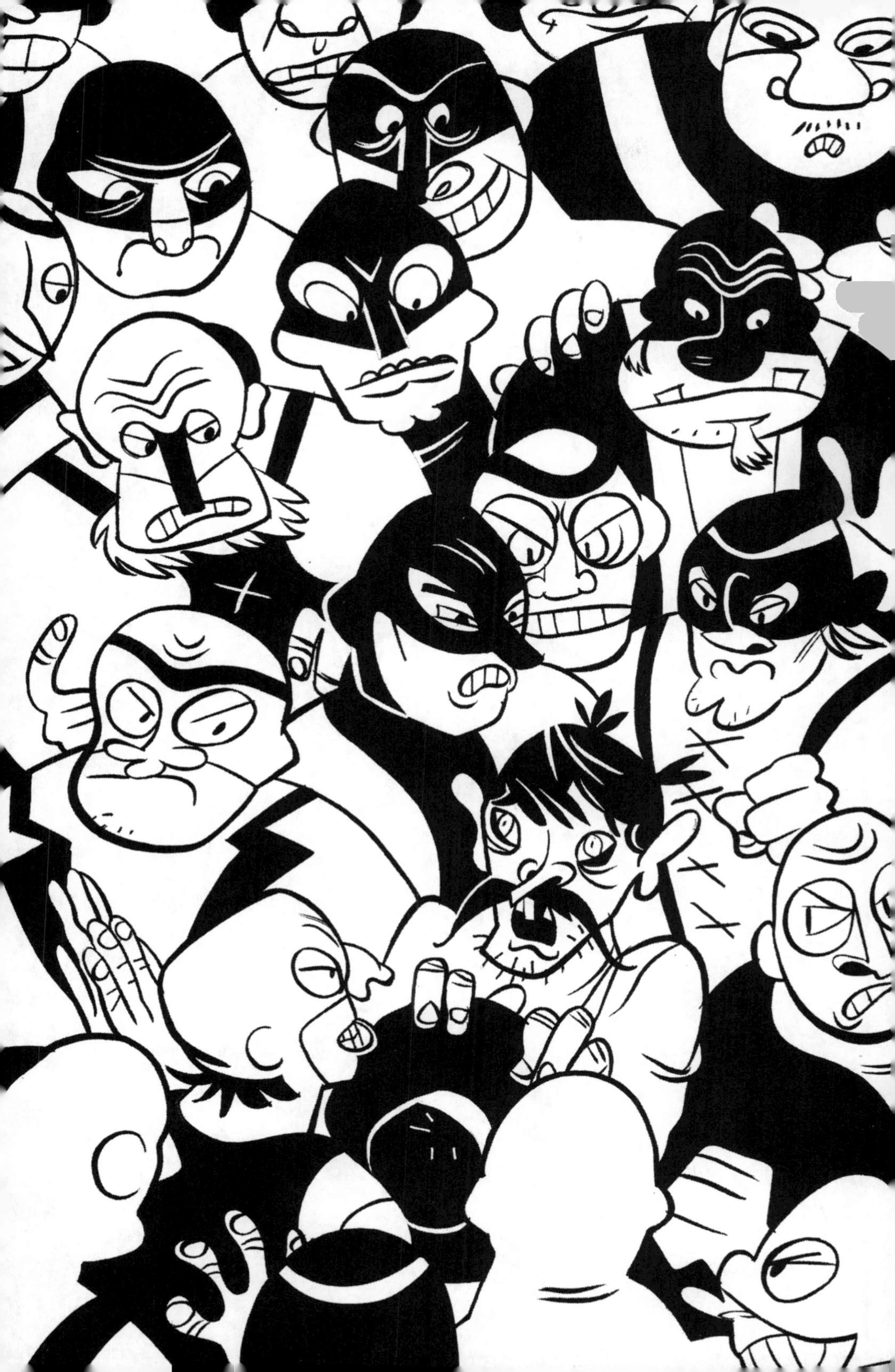

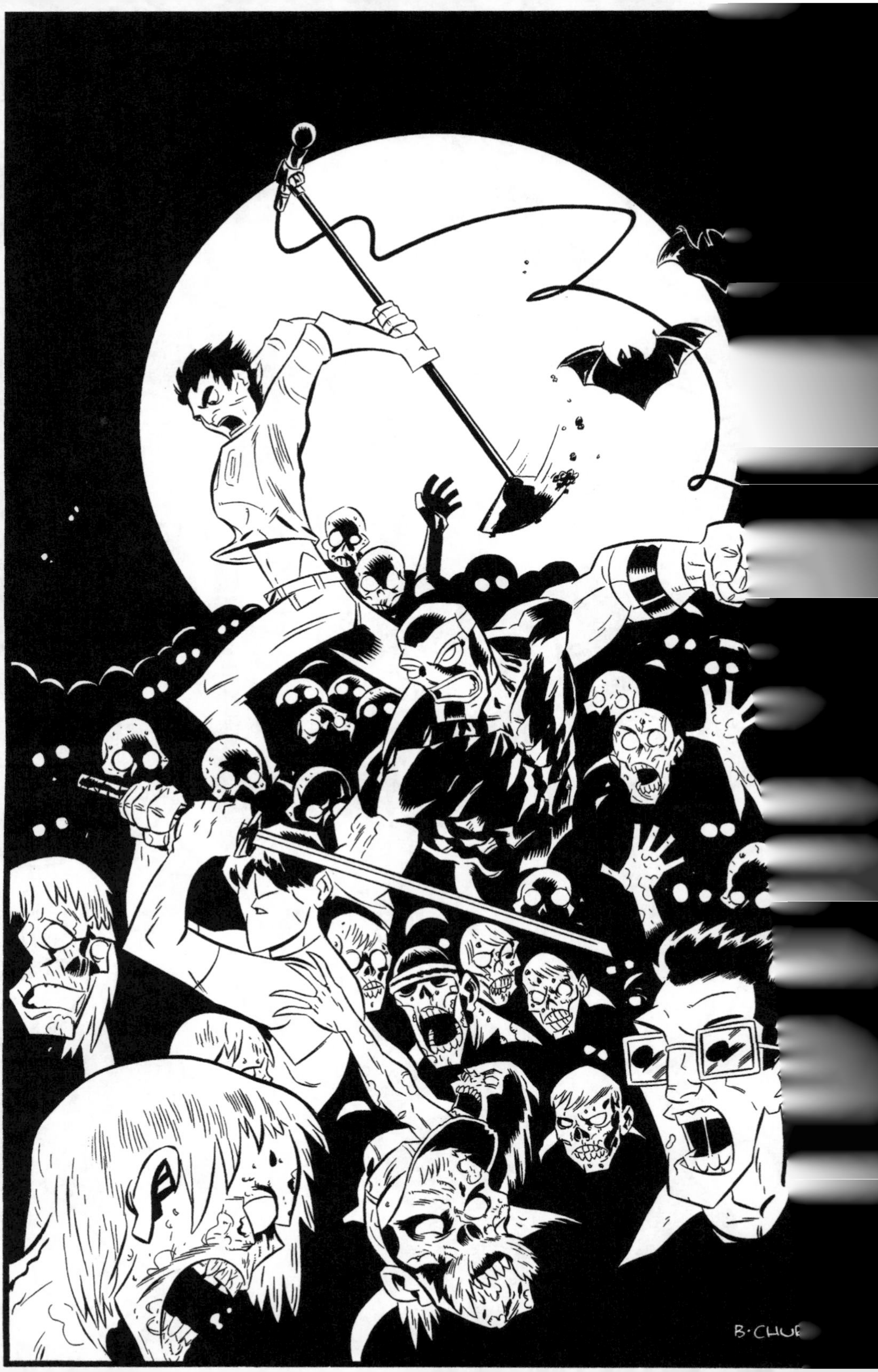

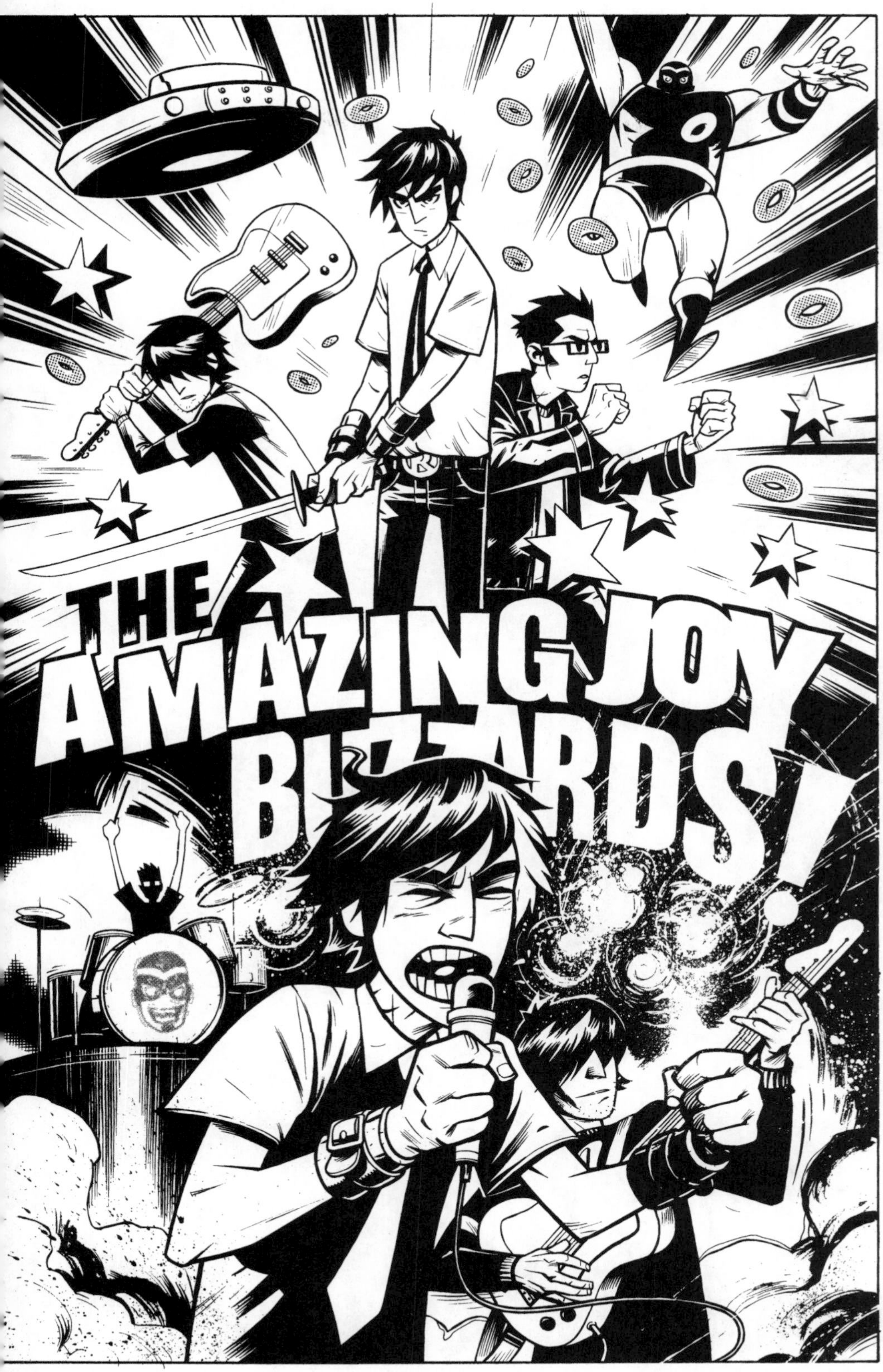
THE AMAZING JOY BUZZARDS!

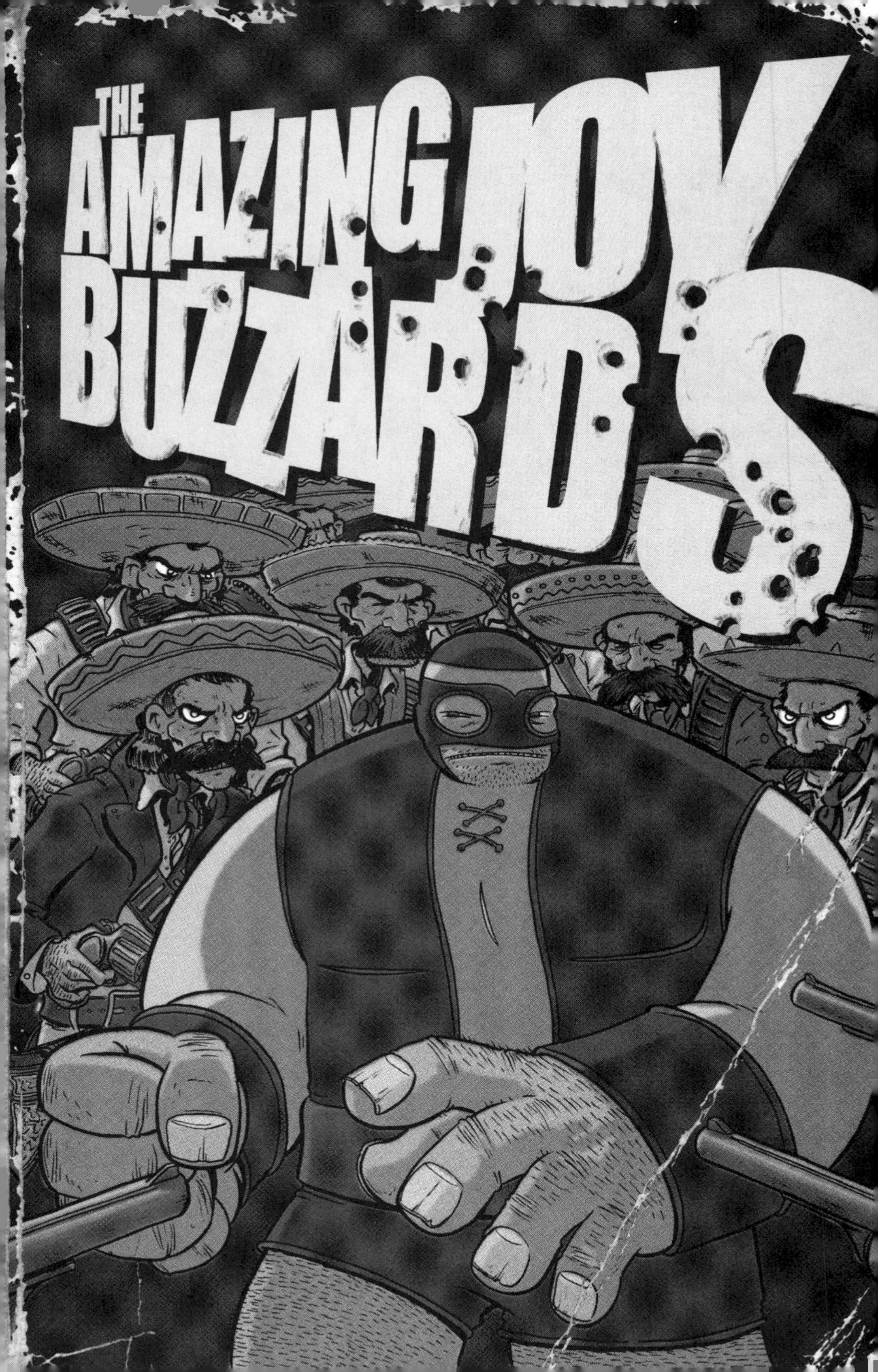
THE AMAZING JOY BUZZARDS

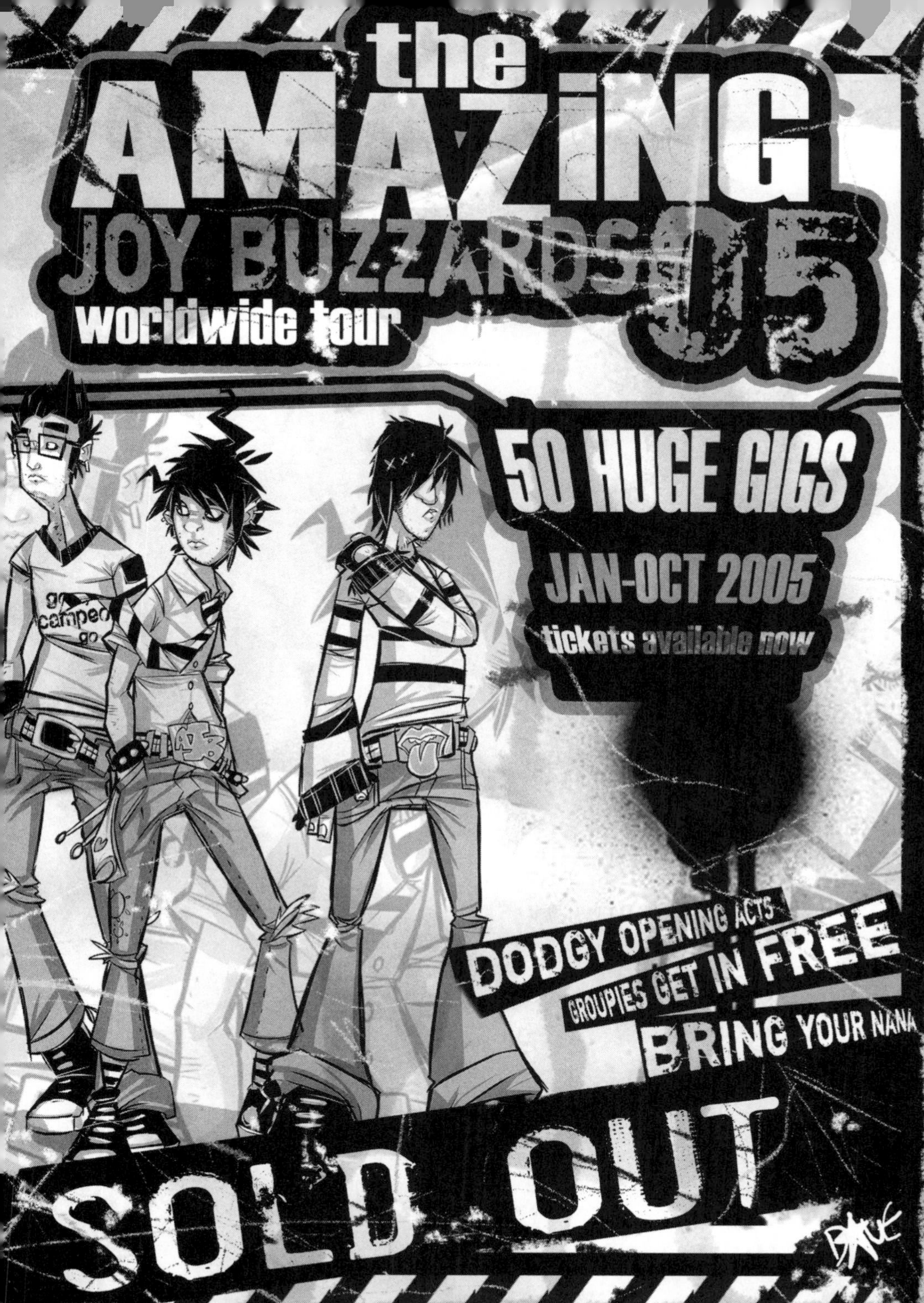
the AMAZING JOY BUZZARDS
worldwide tour
05
50 HUGE GIGS
JAN-OCT 2005
tickets available now
go campeon go
DODGY OPENING ACTS
GROUPIES GET IN FREE
BRING YOUR NANA
SOLD OUT

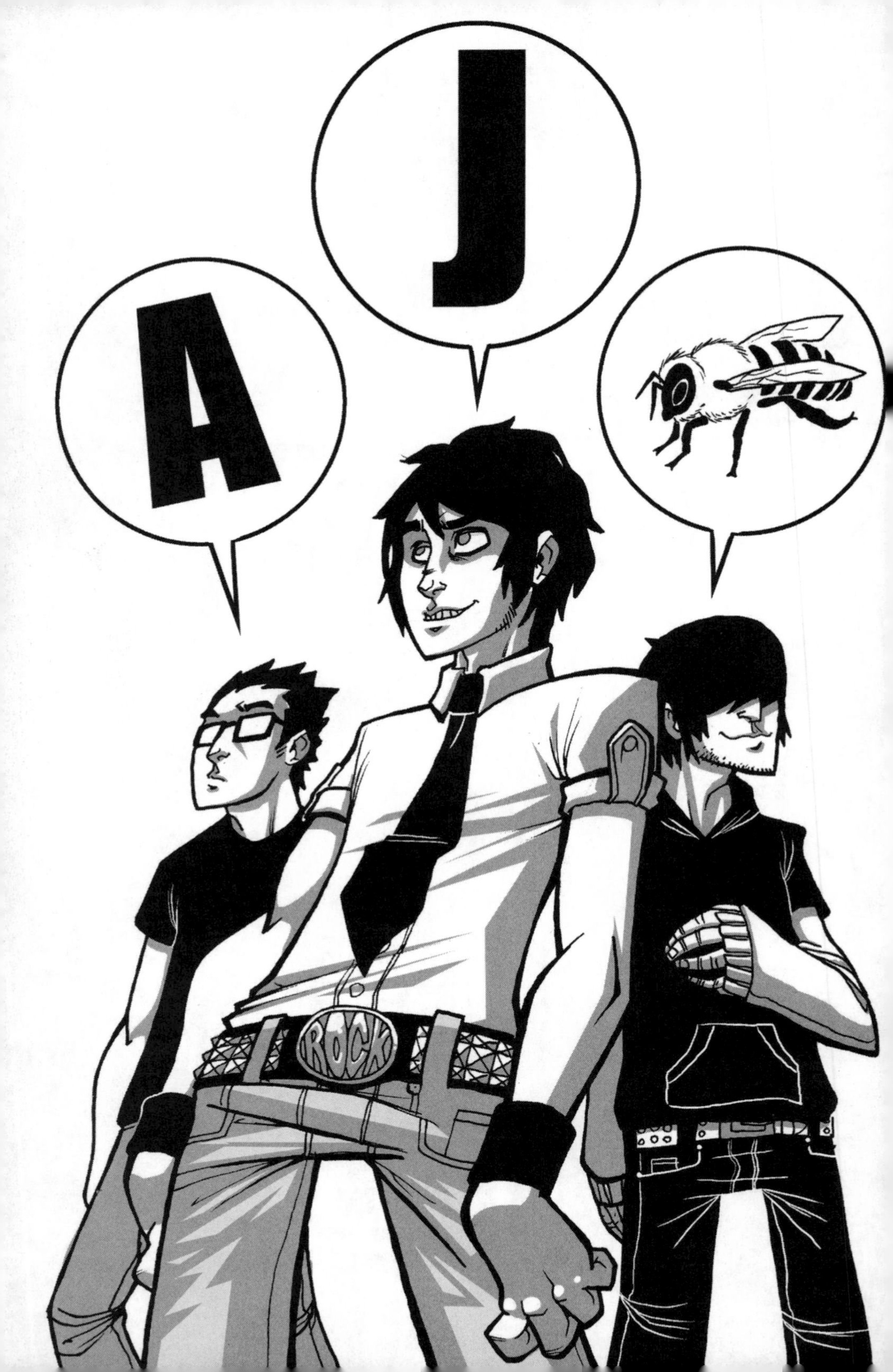
A
J
ROCK

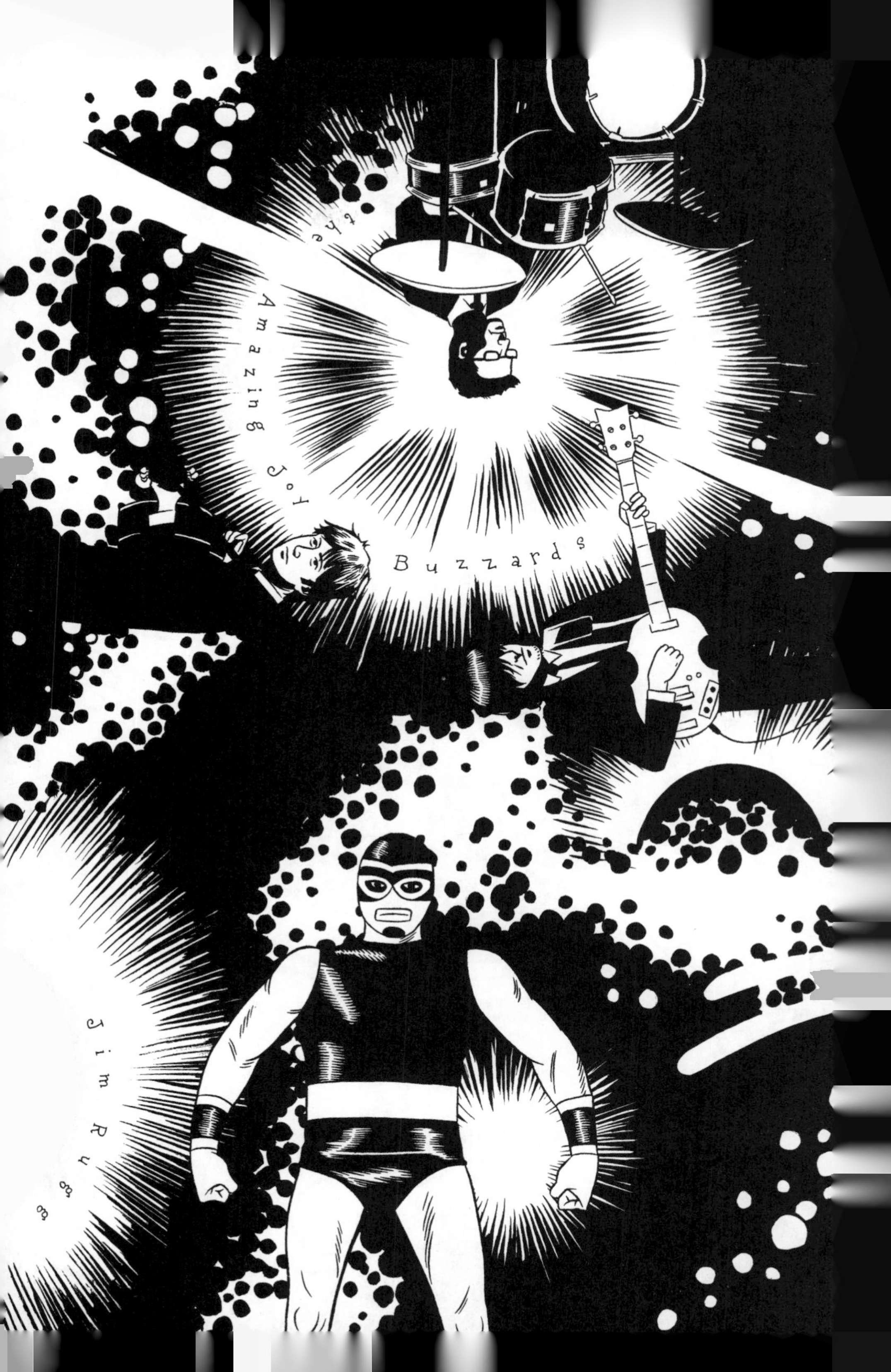
the Amazing Joy Buzzards
Jim Rugg

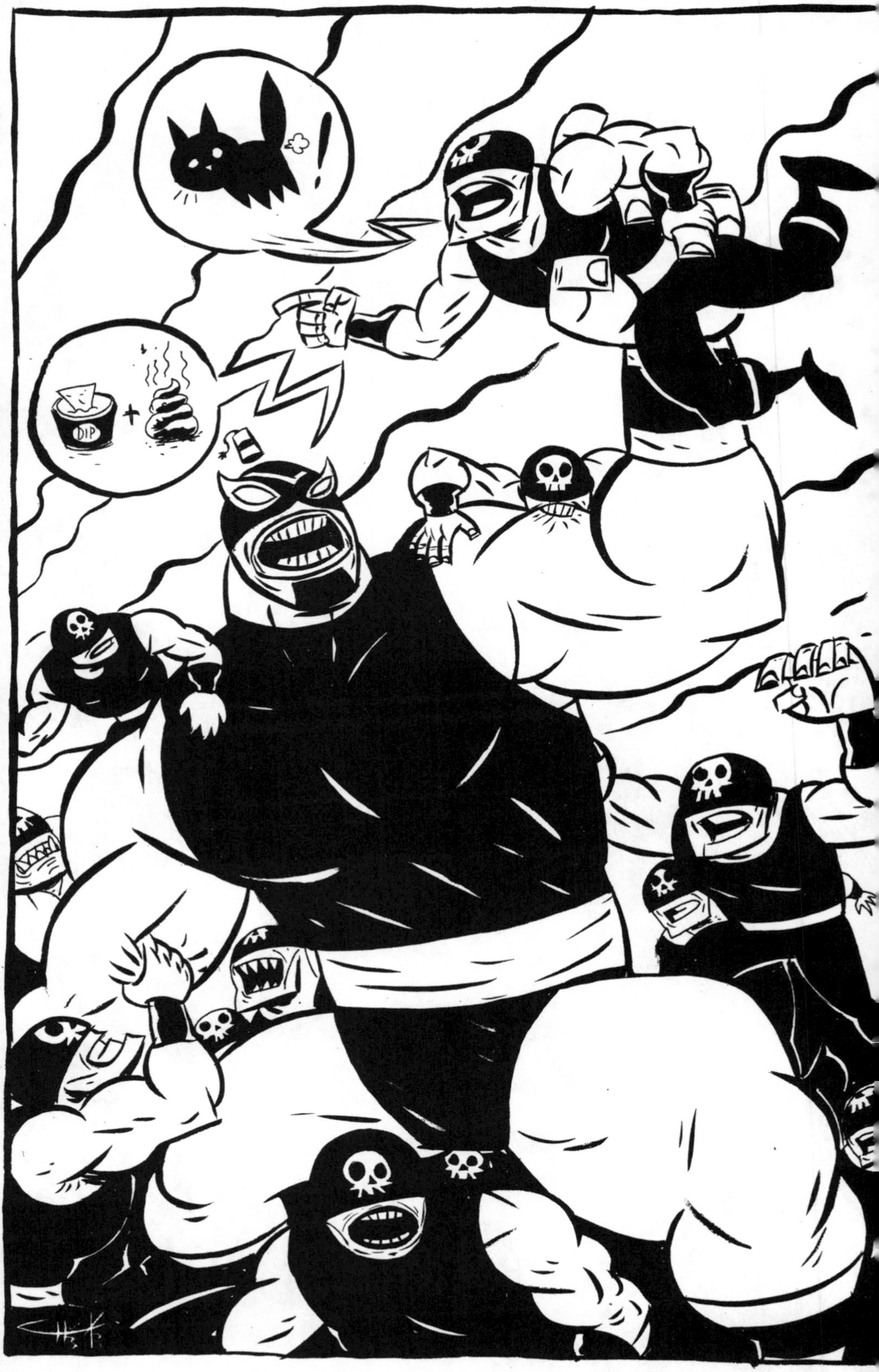
!
DIP

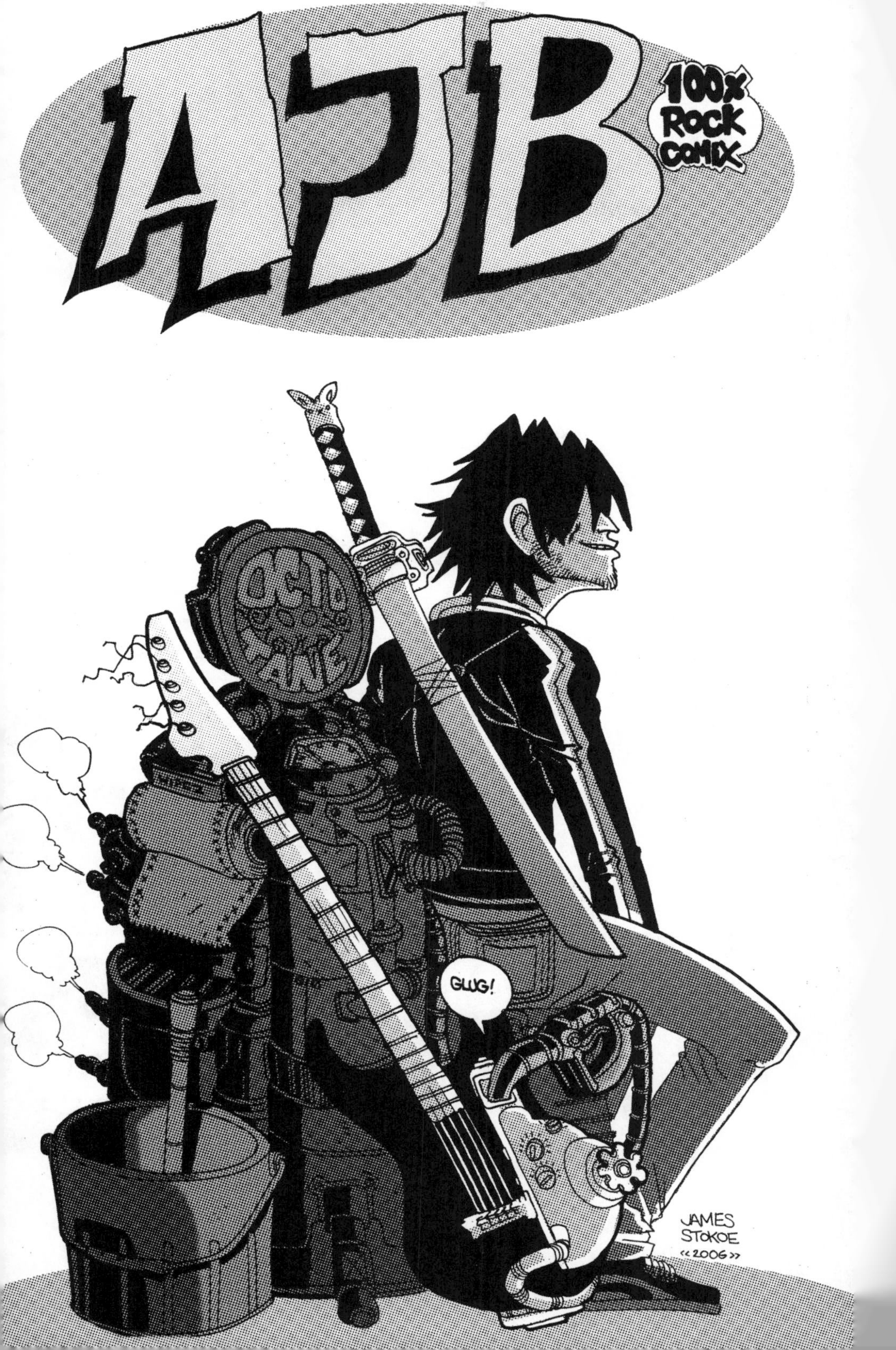
AJB
100% ROCK COMIX
GLUG!
JAMES STOKOE
<<2006>>

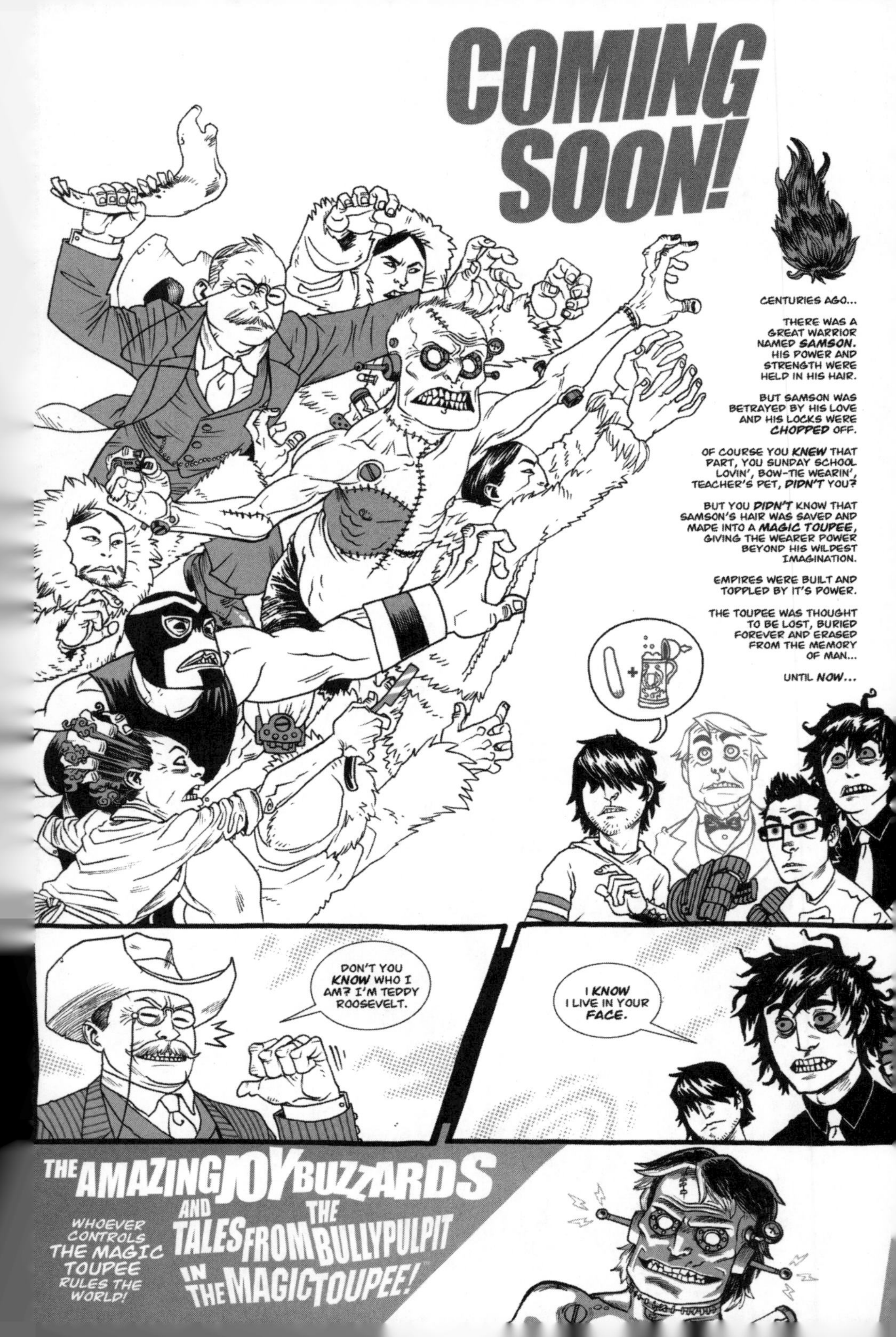

COMING SOON!
CENTURIES AGO...
THERE WAS A GREAT WARRIOR NAMED SAMSON. HIS POWER AND STRENGTH WERE HELD IN HIS HAIR.
BUT SAMSON WAS BETRAYED BY HIS LOVE AND HIS LOCKS WERE CHOPPED OFF.
OF COURSE YOU KNEW THAT PART, YOU SUNDAY SCHOOL LOVIN', BOW-TIE WEARIN', TEACHER'S PET, DIDN'T YOU?
BUT YOU DIDN'T KNOW THAT SAMSON'S HAIR WAS SAVED AND MADE INTO A MAGIC TOUPEE, GIVING THE WEARER POWER BEYOND HIS WILDEST IMAGINATION.
EMPIRES WERE BUILT AND TOPPLED BY IT'S POWER.
THE TOUPEE WAS THOUGHT TO BE LOST, BURIED FOREVER AND ERASED FROM THE MEMORY OF MAN...
UNTIL NOW...
DON'T YOU KNOW WHO I AM? I'M TEDDY ROOSEVELT.
I KNOW I LIVE IN YOUR FACE.
THE AMAZING JOY BUZZARDS AND THE TALES FROM THE BULLYPULPIT IN THE MAGIC TOUPEE!™
WHOEVER CONTROLS THE MAGIC TOUPEE RULES THE WORLD!

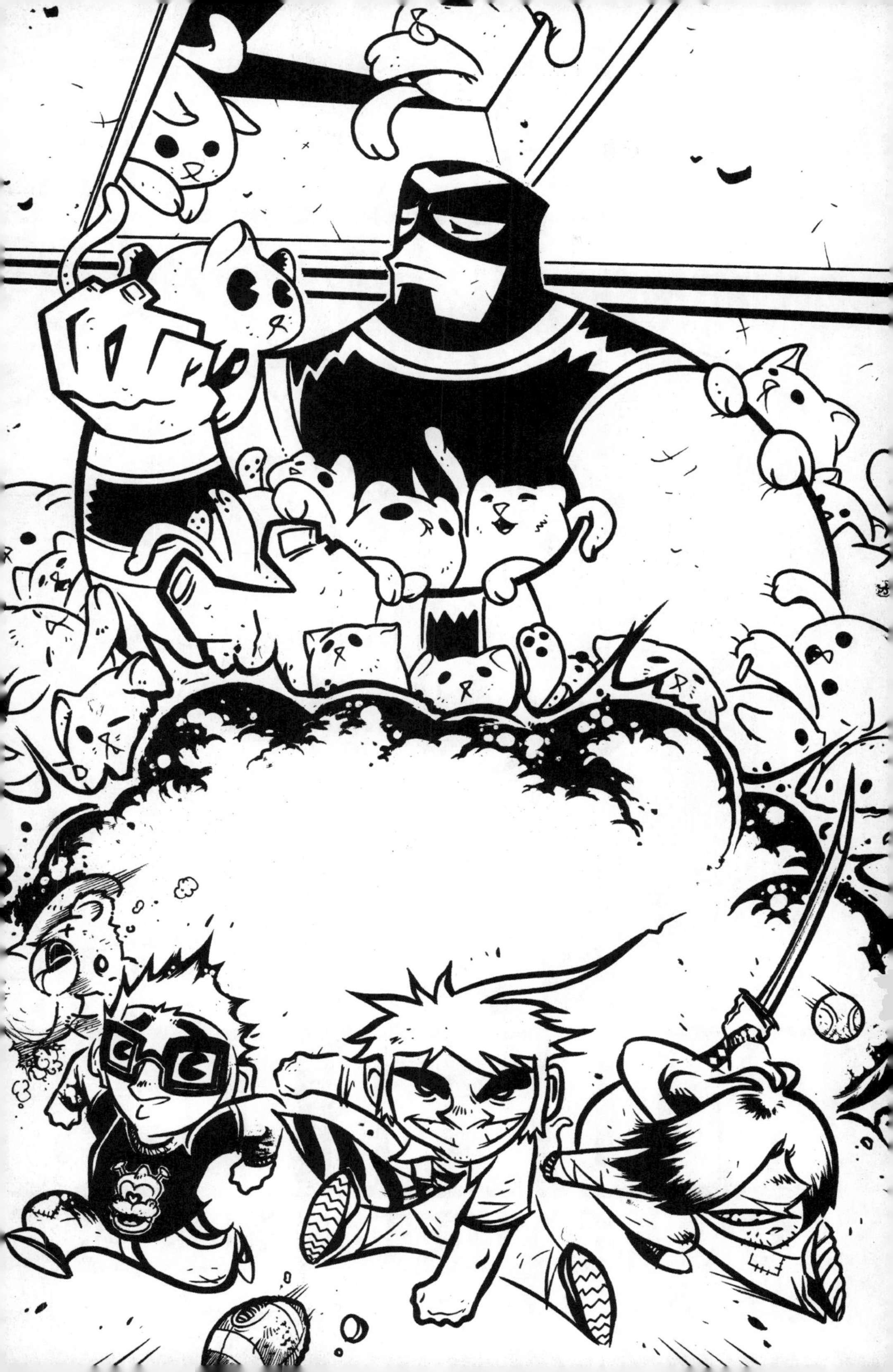

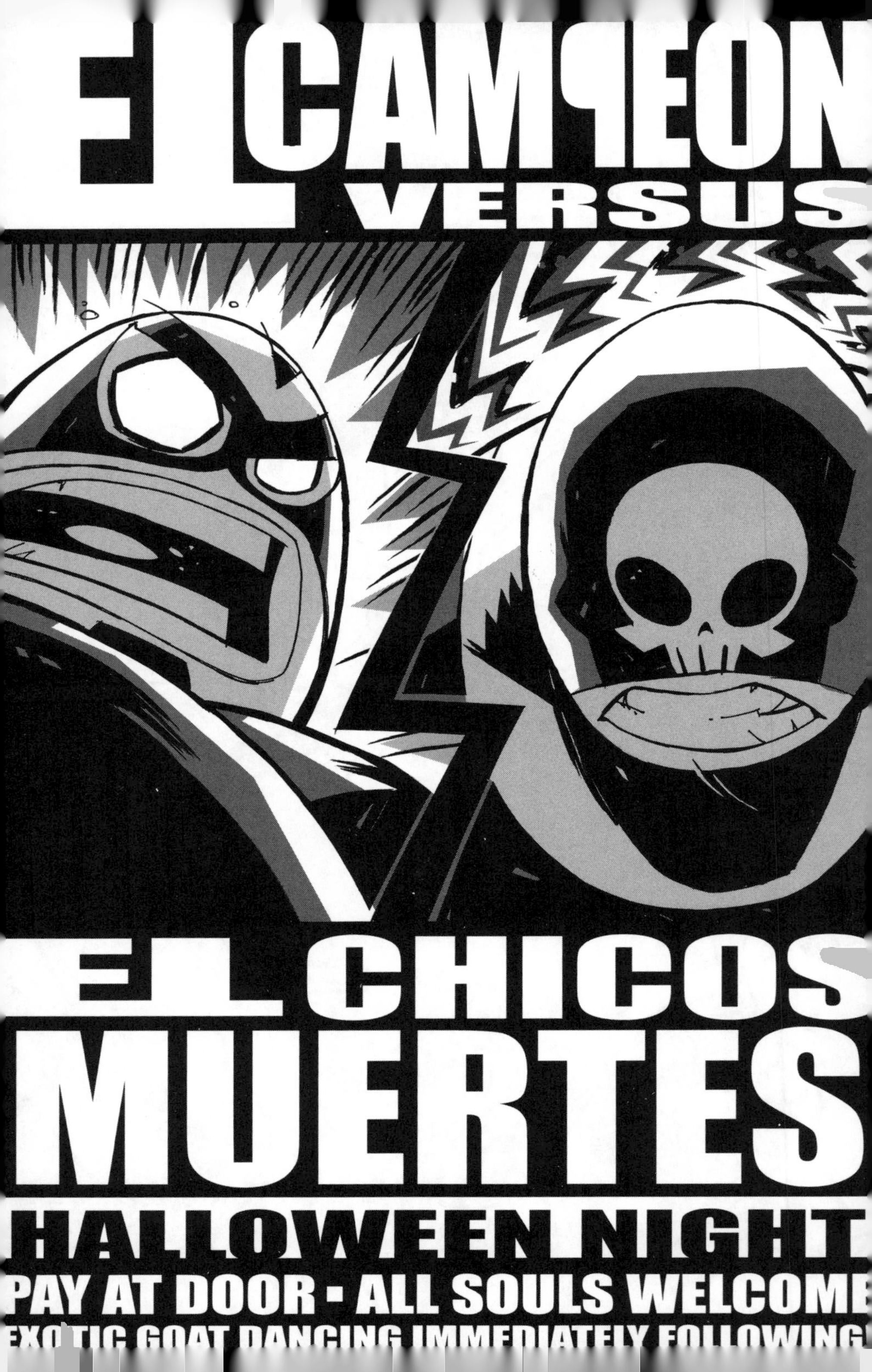
EL CAMPEON
VERSUS
EL CHICOS
MUERTES
HALLOWEEN NIGHT
PAY AT DOOR - ALL SOULS WELCOME
EXOTIC GOAT DANCING IMMEDIATELY FOLLOWING!

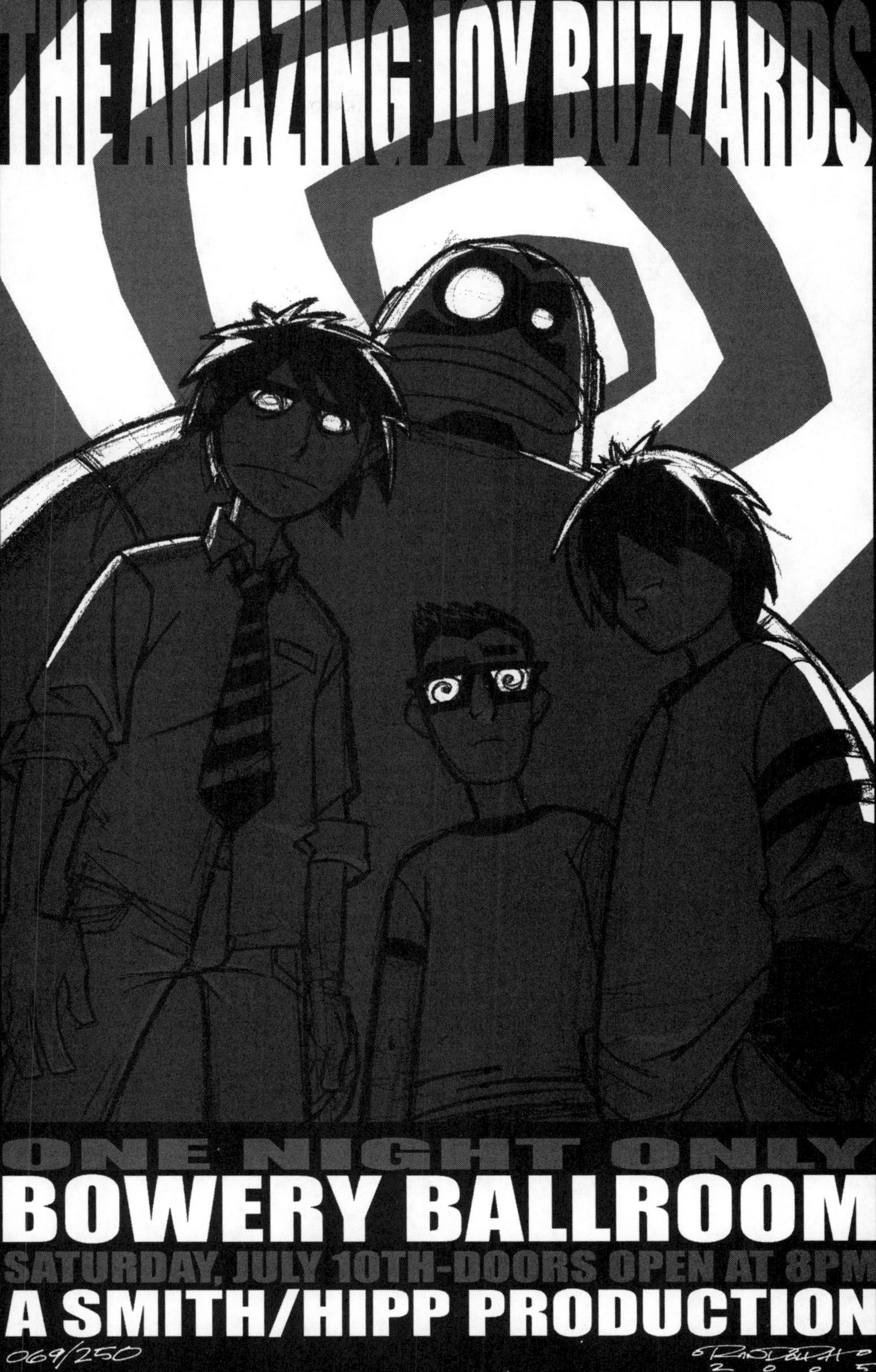
THE AMAZING JOY BUZZARDS
ONE NIGHT ONLY
BOWERY BALLROOM
SATURDAY, JULY 10TH-DOORS OPEN AT 8PM
A SMITH/HIPP PRODUCTION
069/250

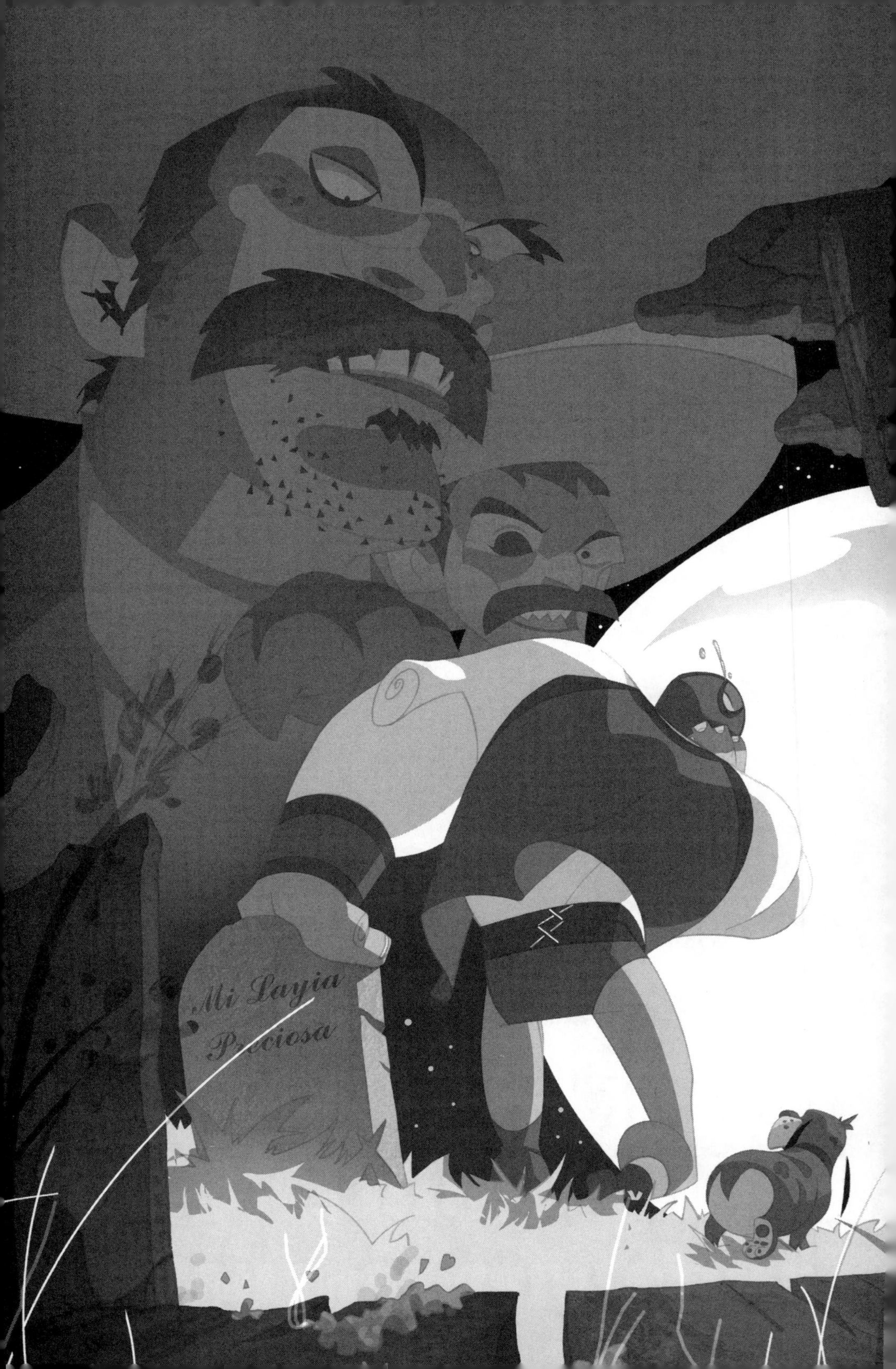
Mi Layia
Preciosa

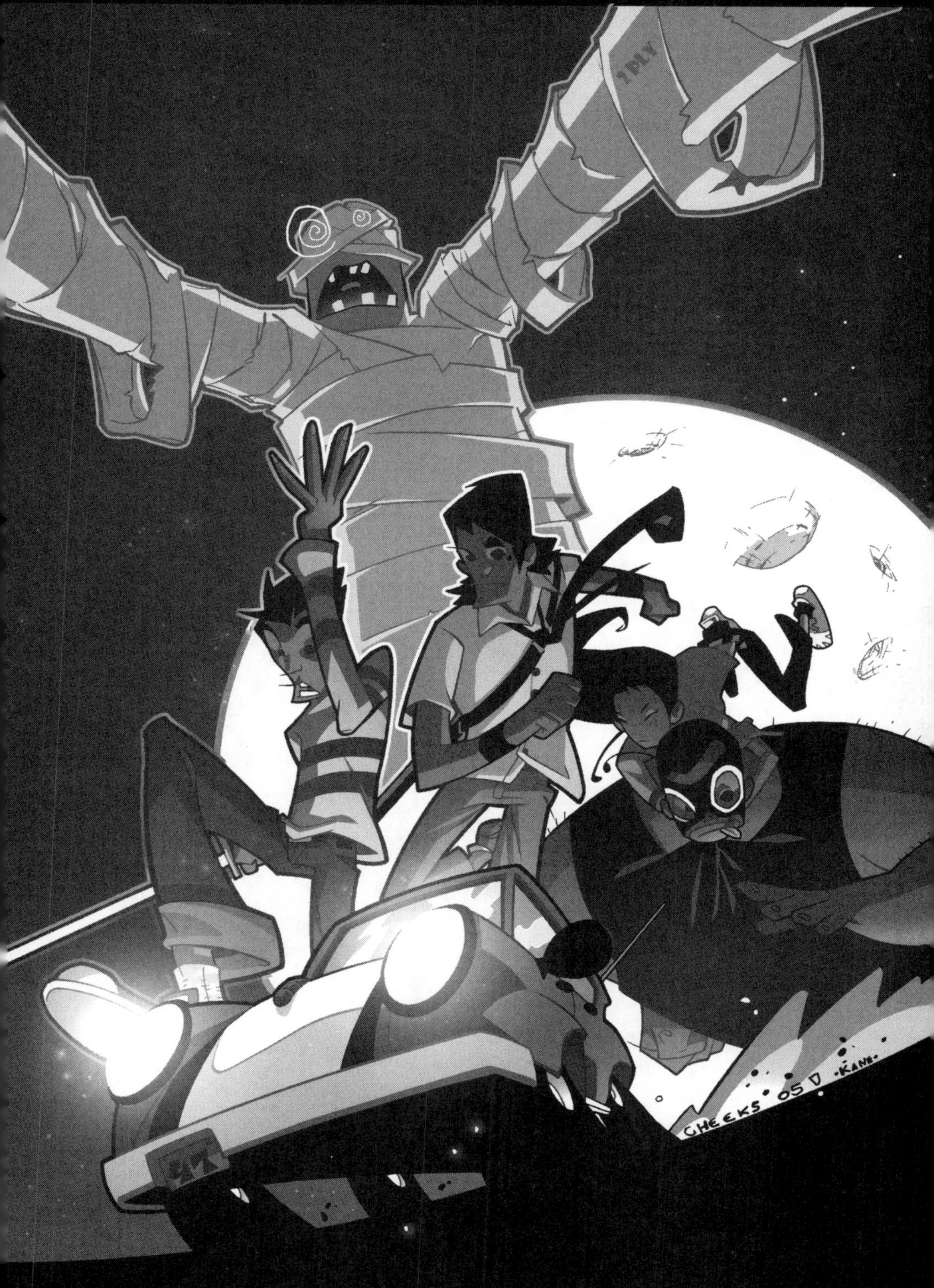
CHEEKS 05
KANE

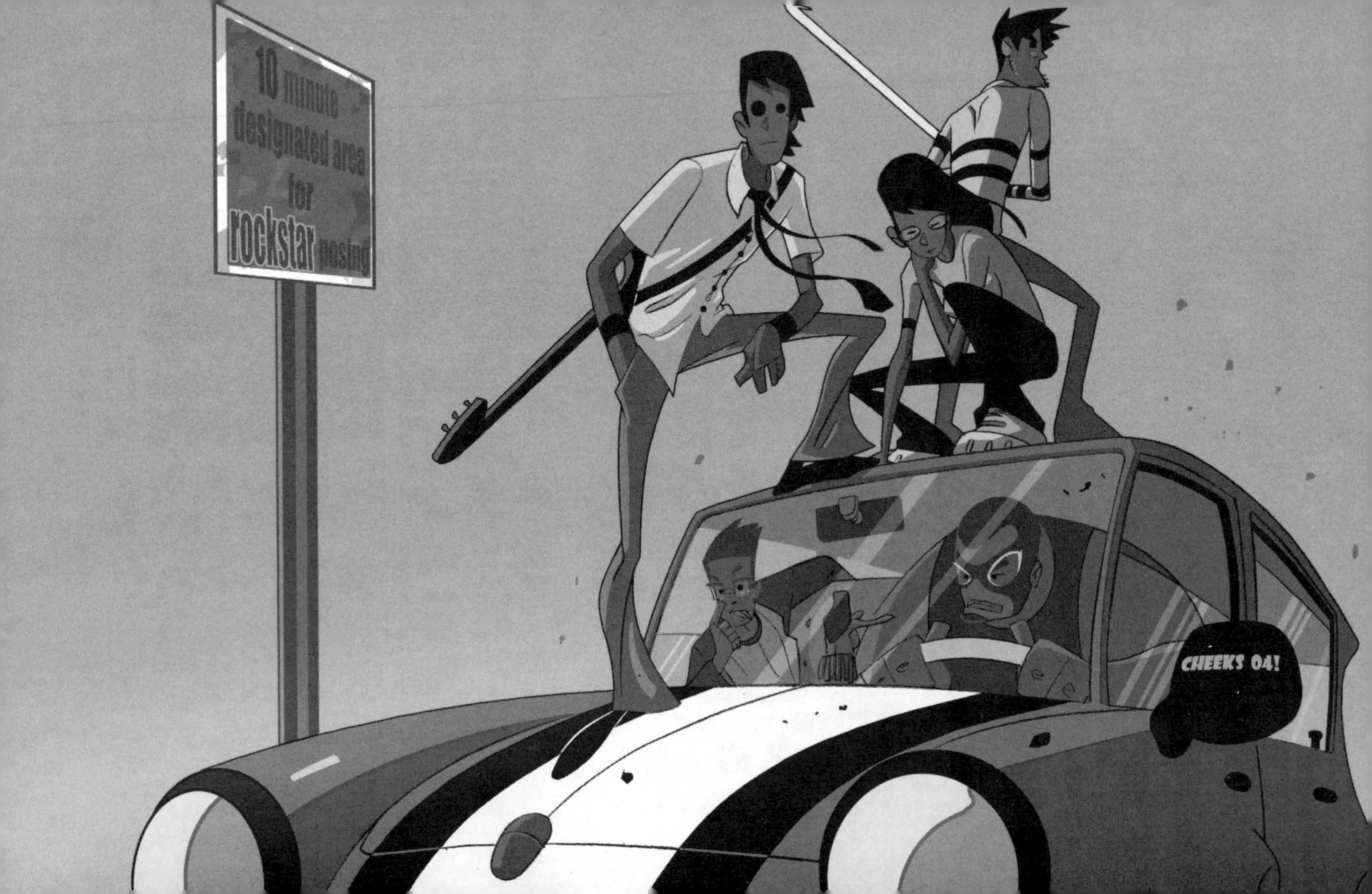
10 minute designated area for rockstar posing
CHEEKS 04!

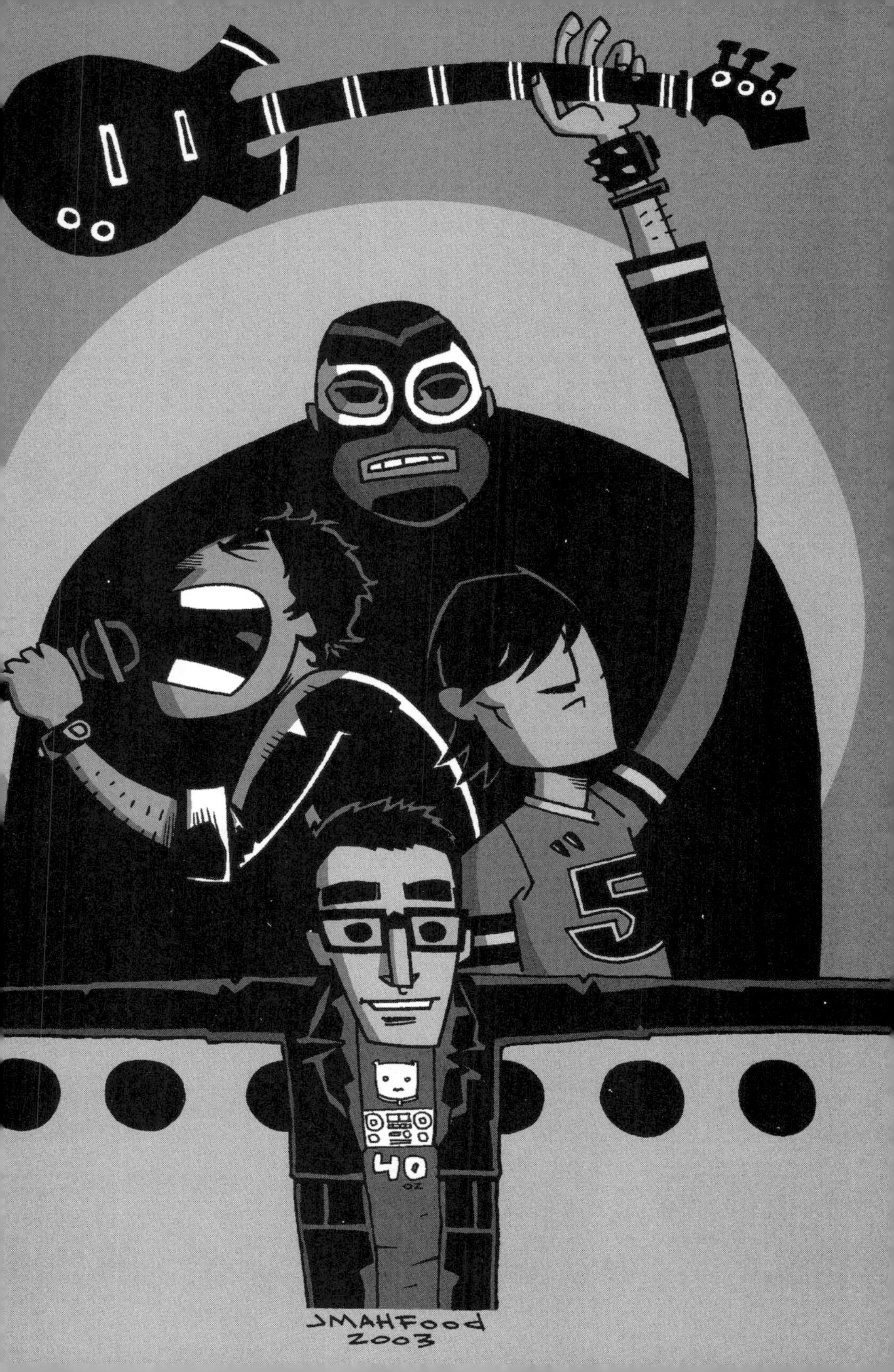
5
40
JMAHFood
2003

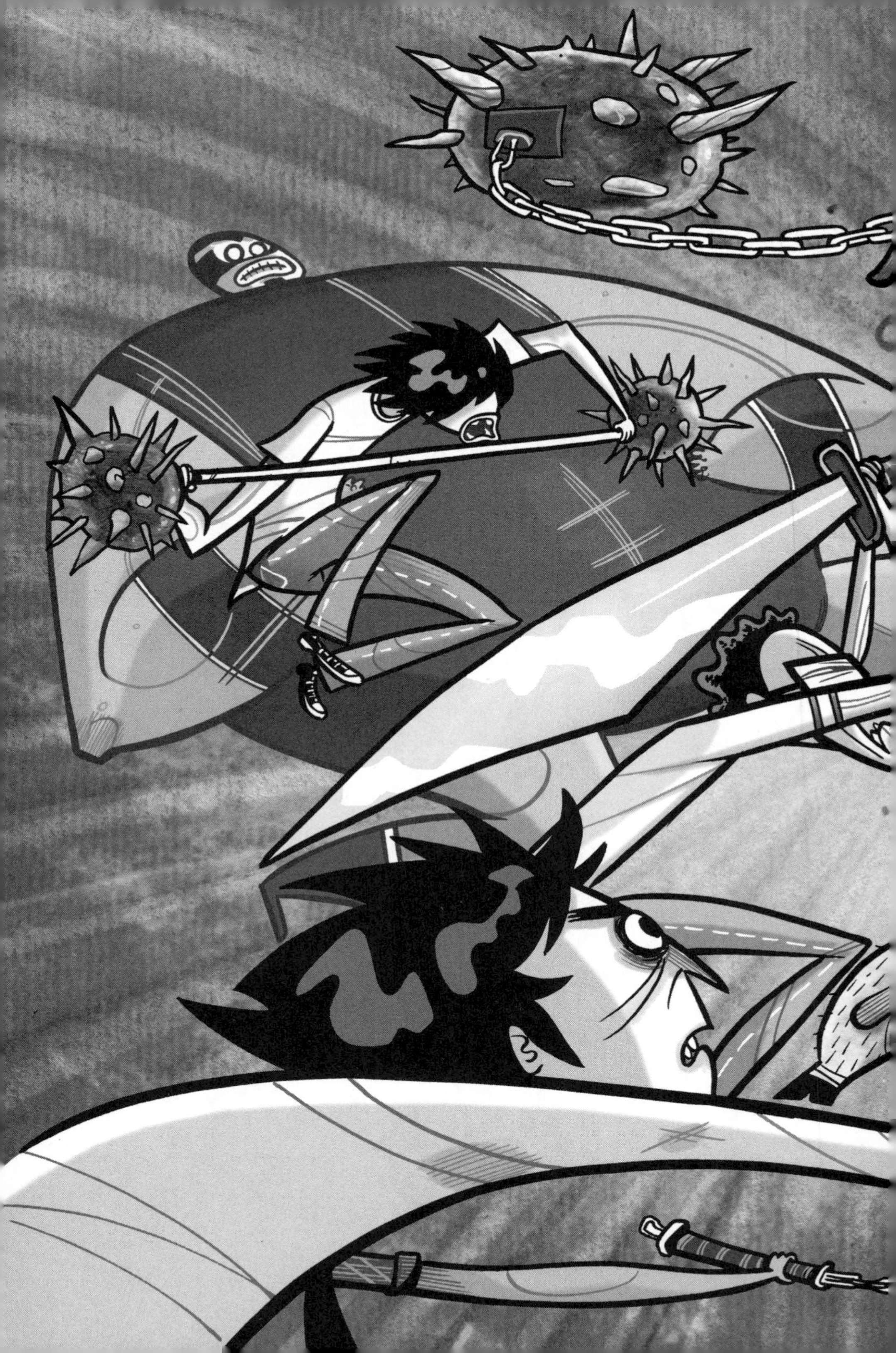

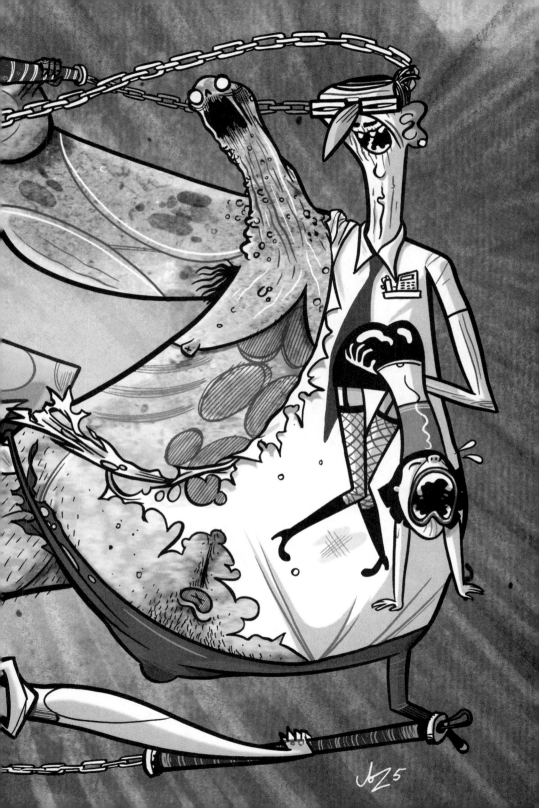

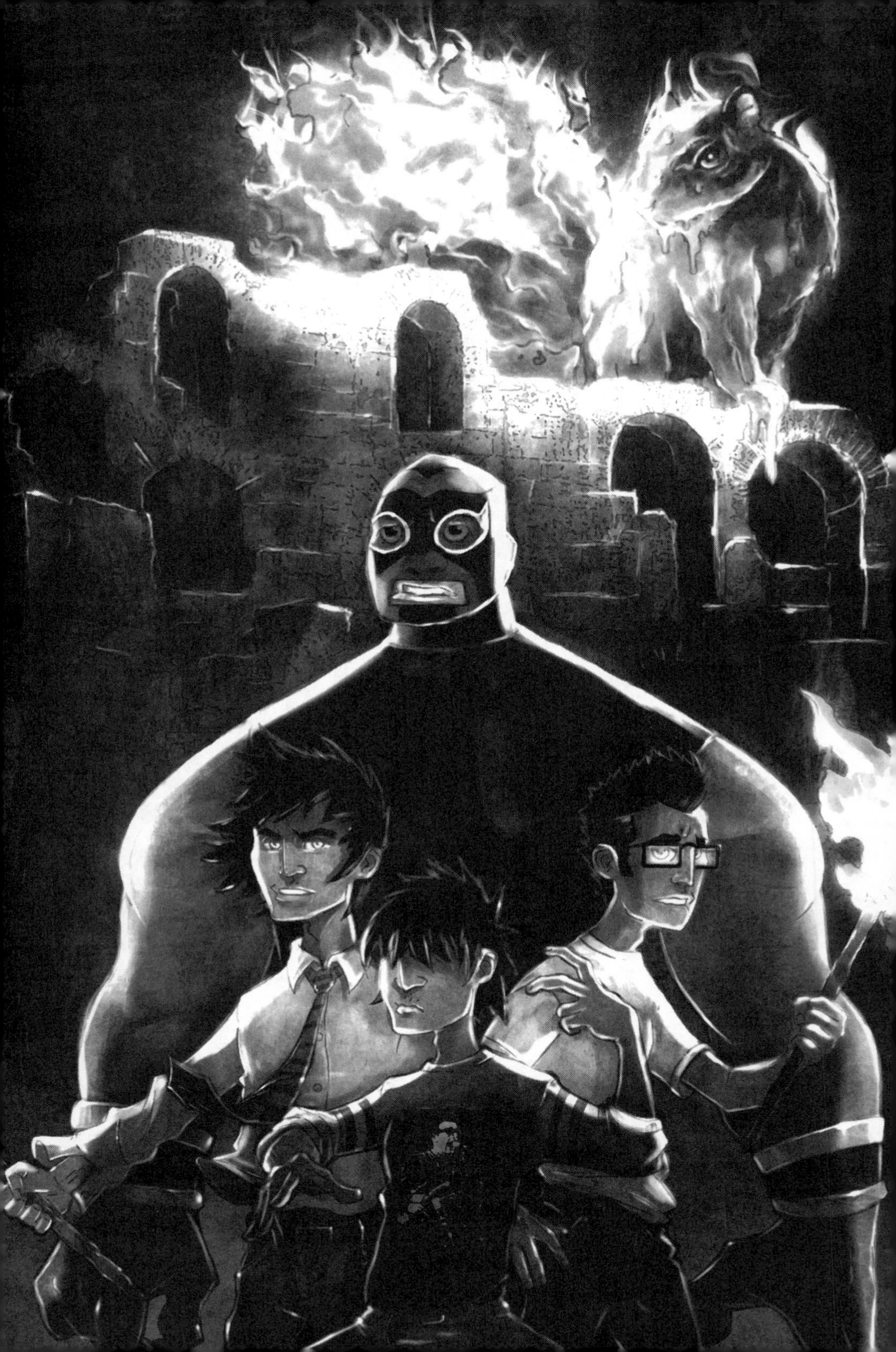

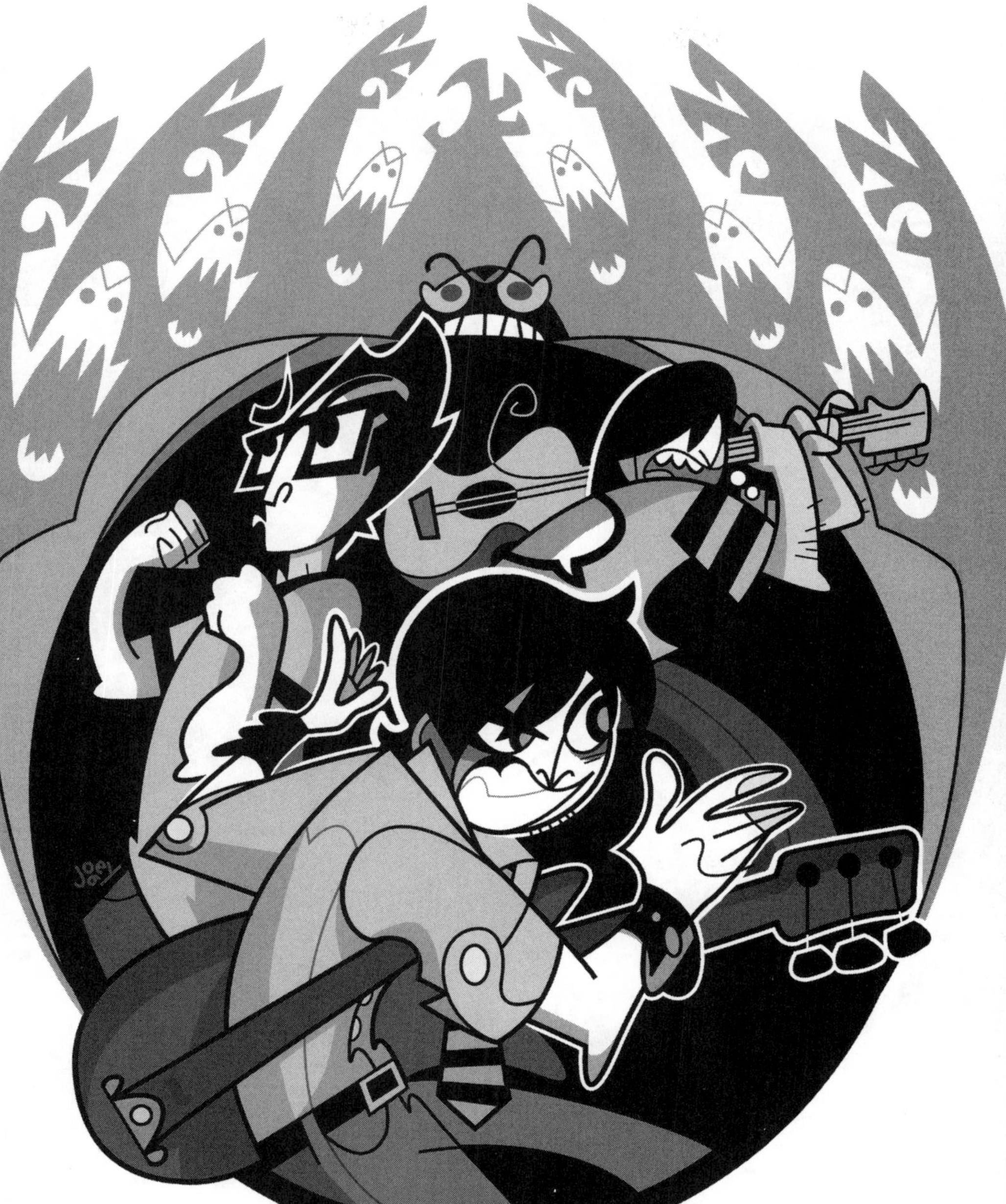

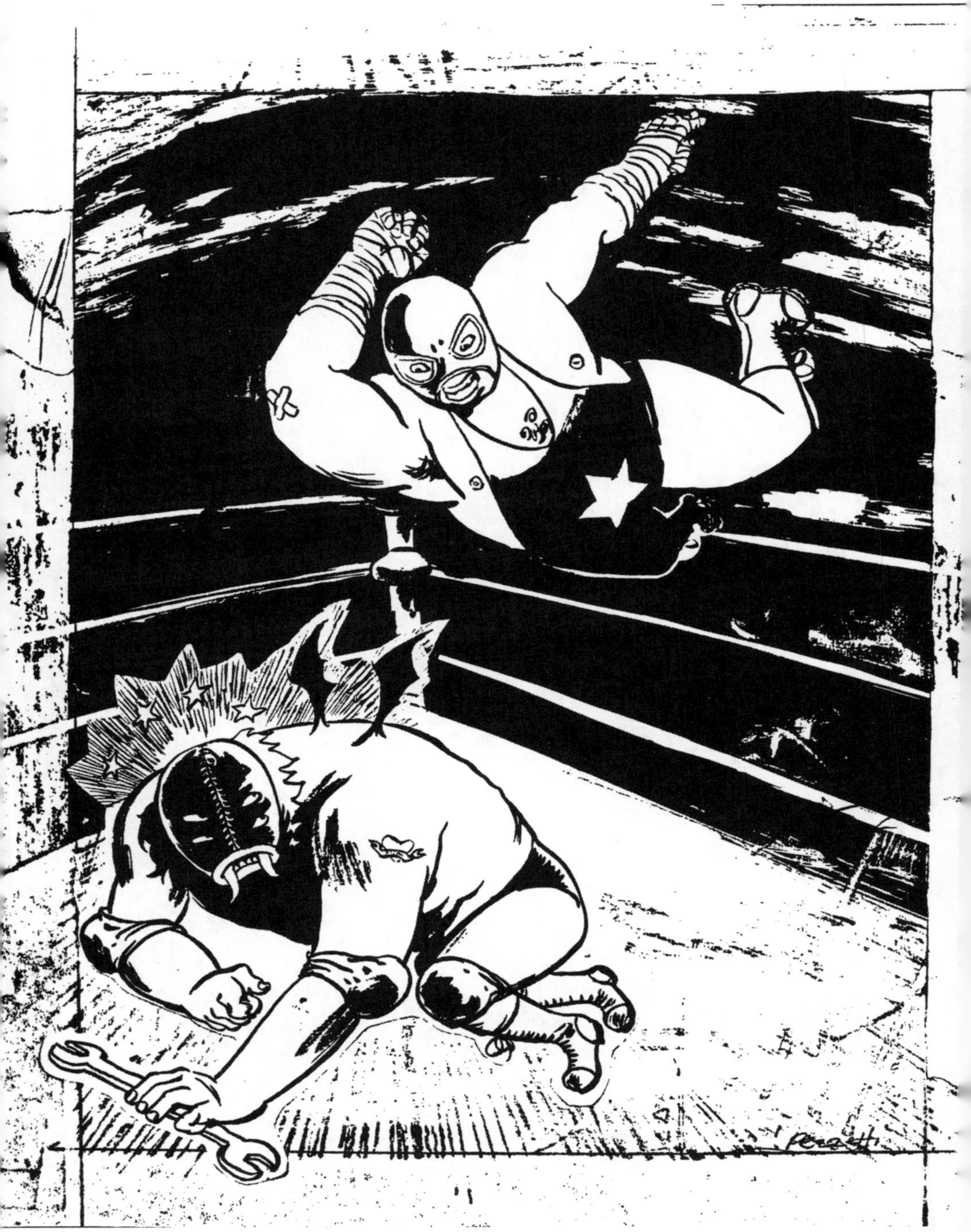

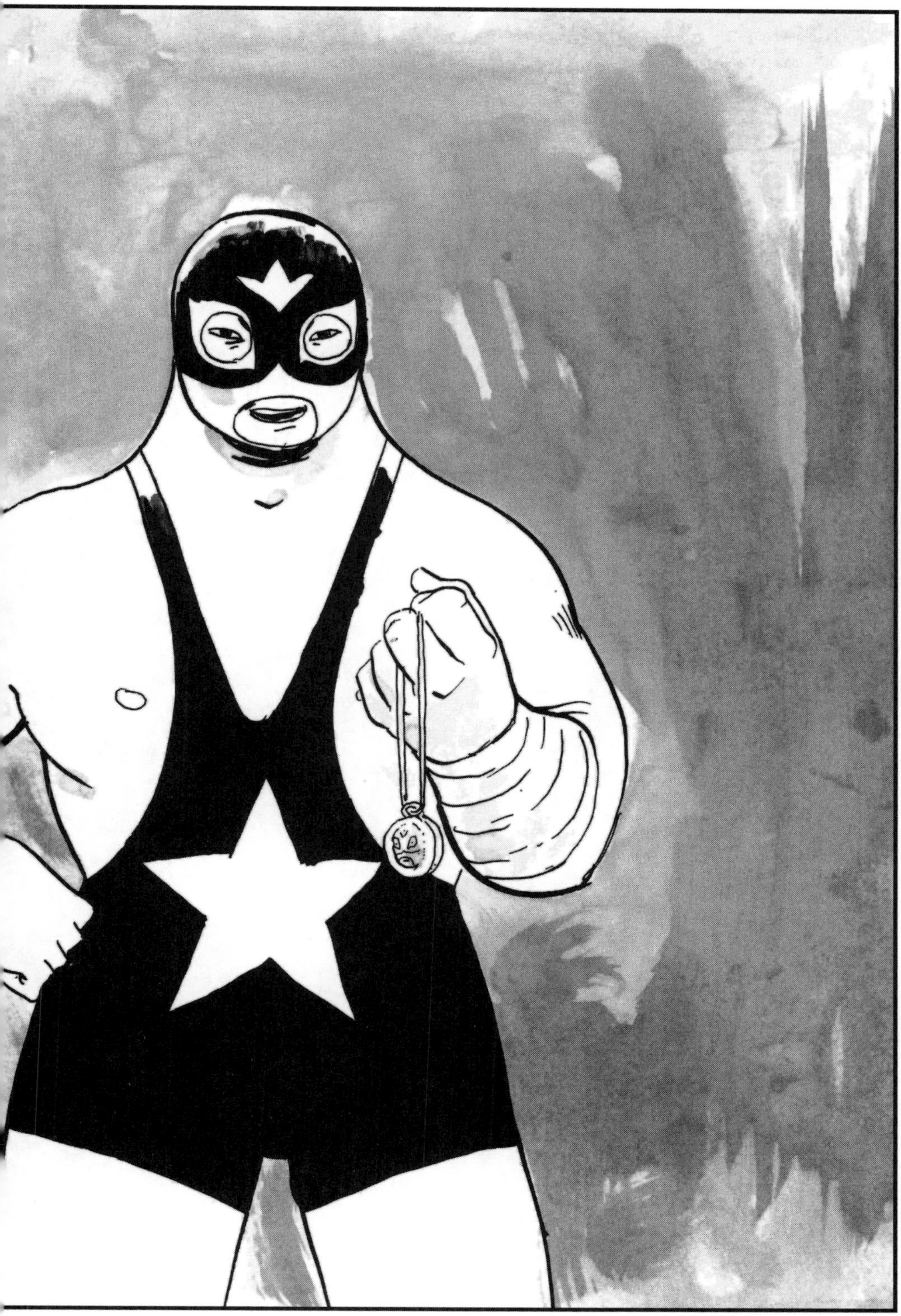

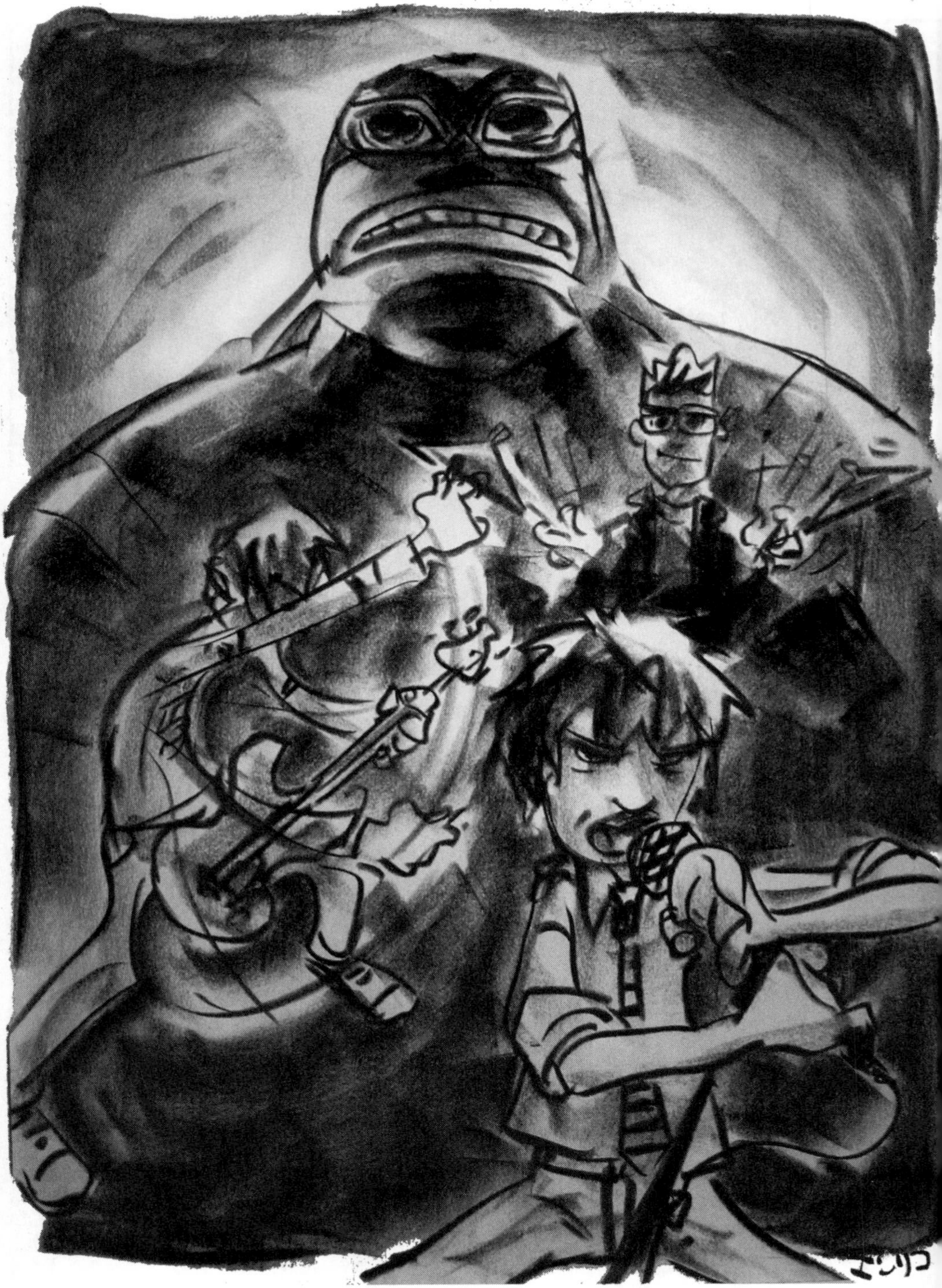

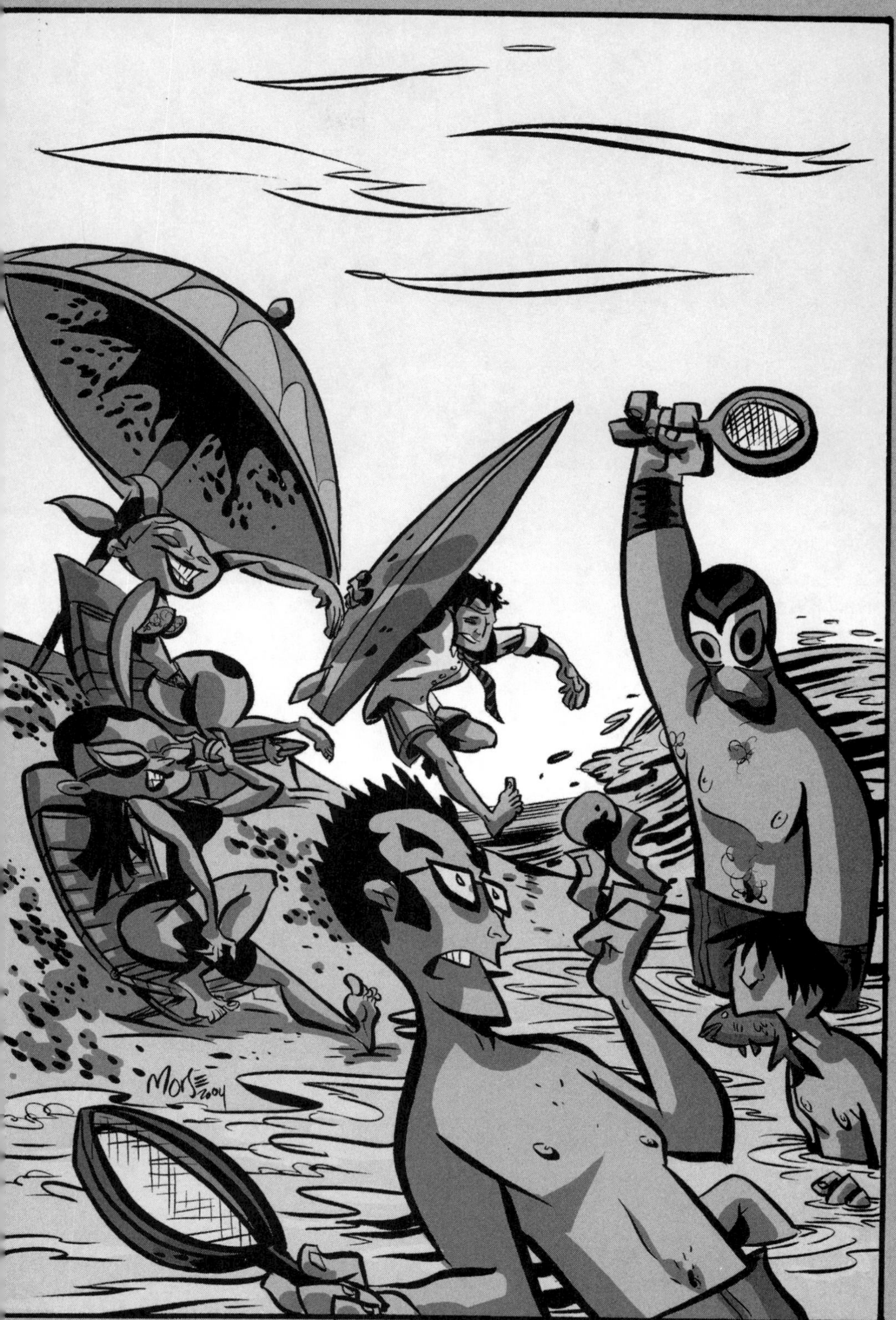
Morse 2004

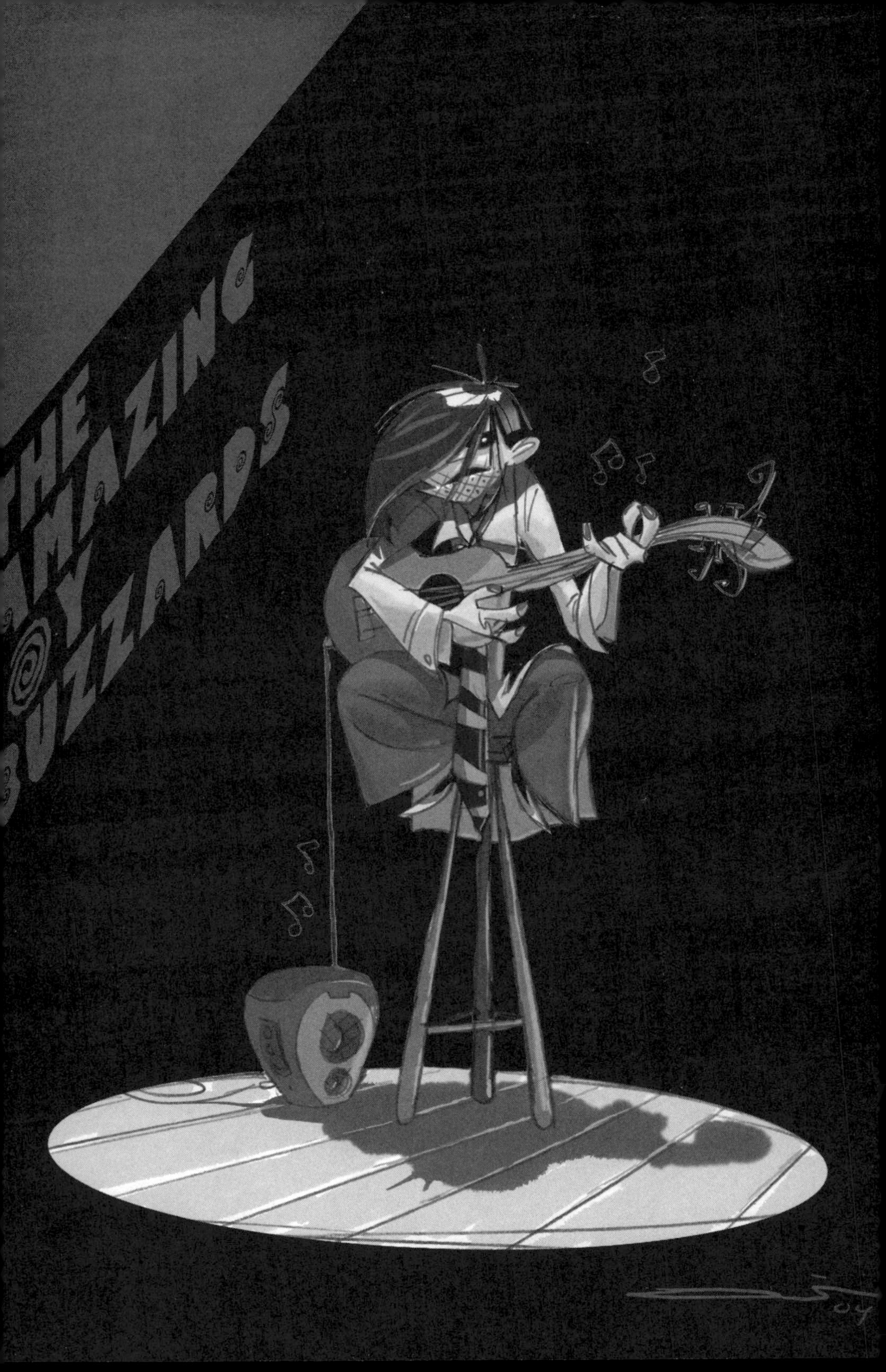

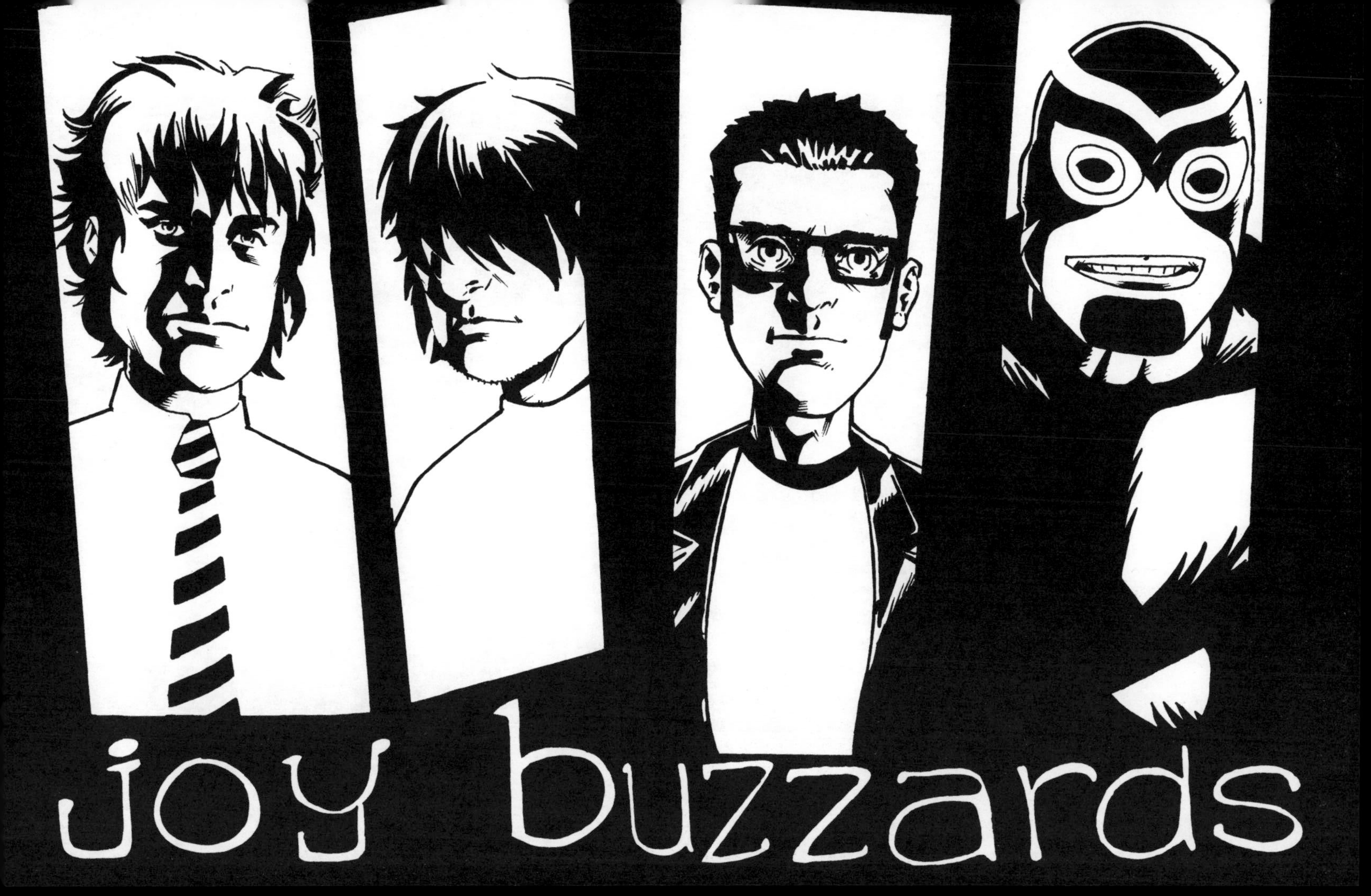
joy buzzards

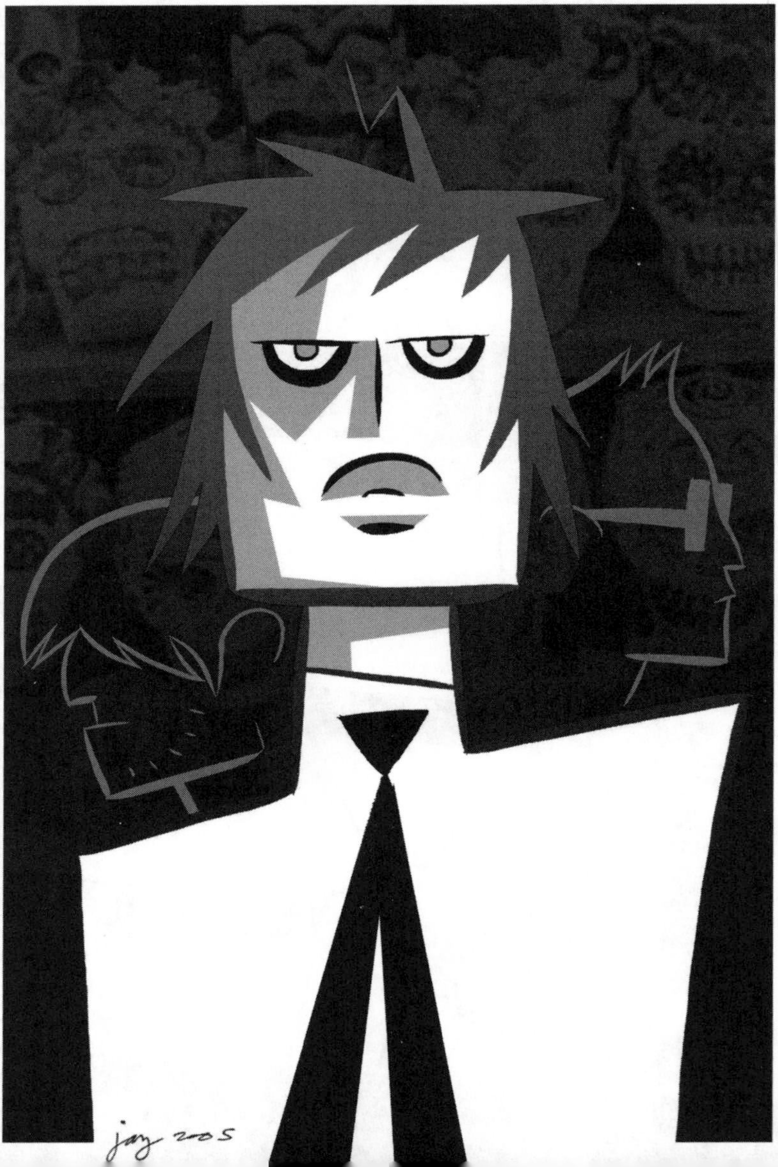
jay 2005

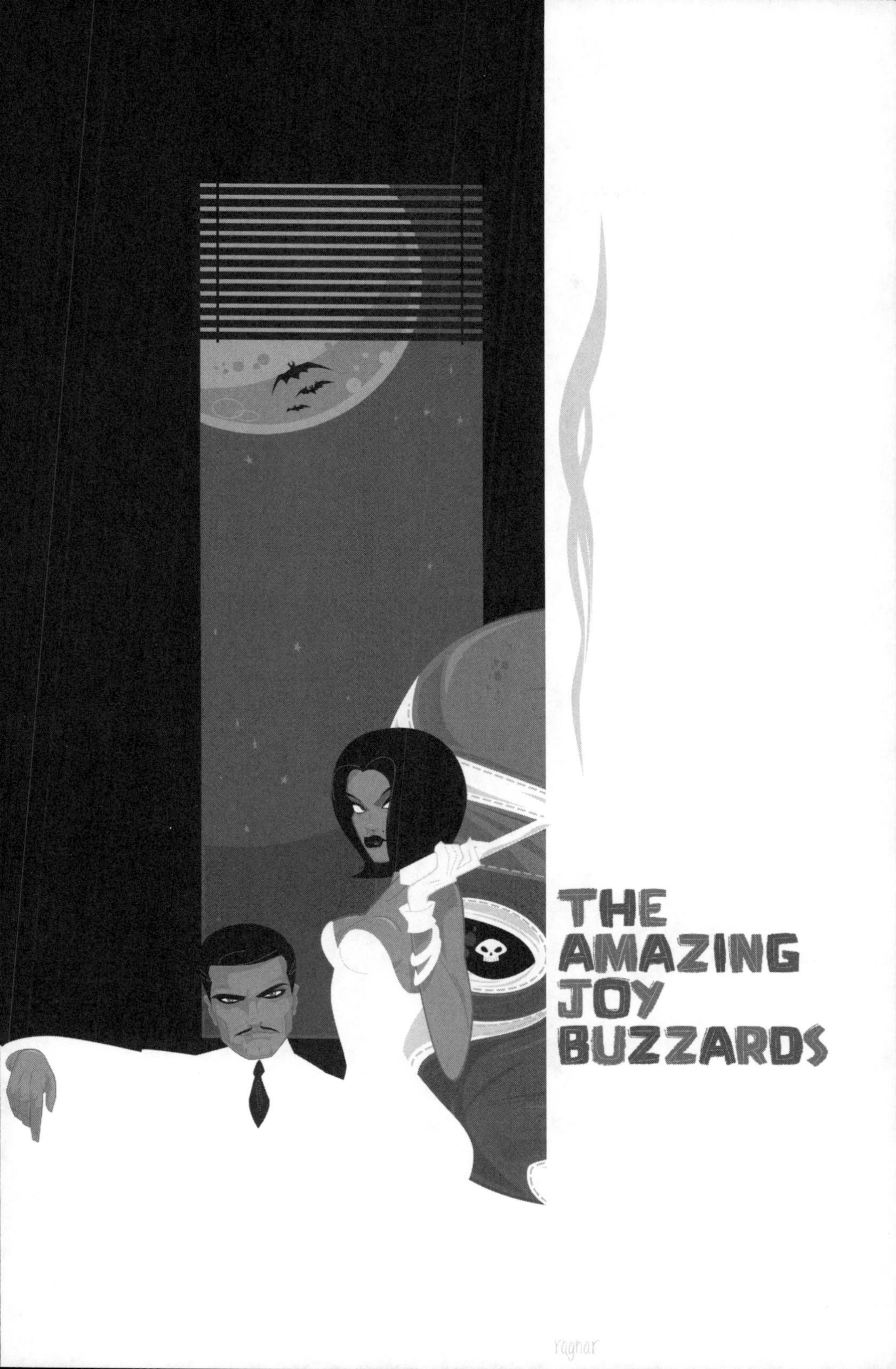
THE
AMAZING
JOY
BUZZARDS
Yaghar

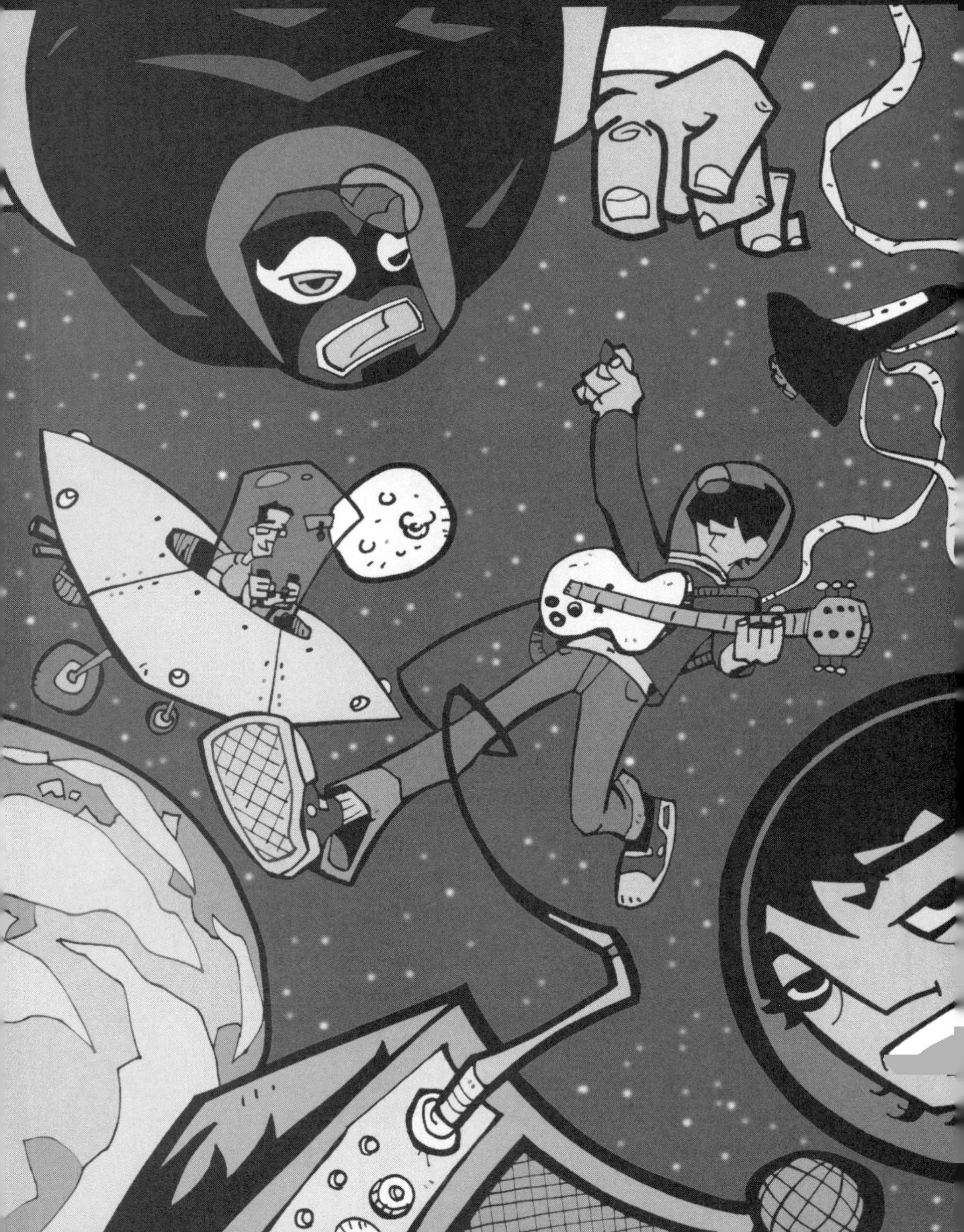

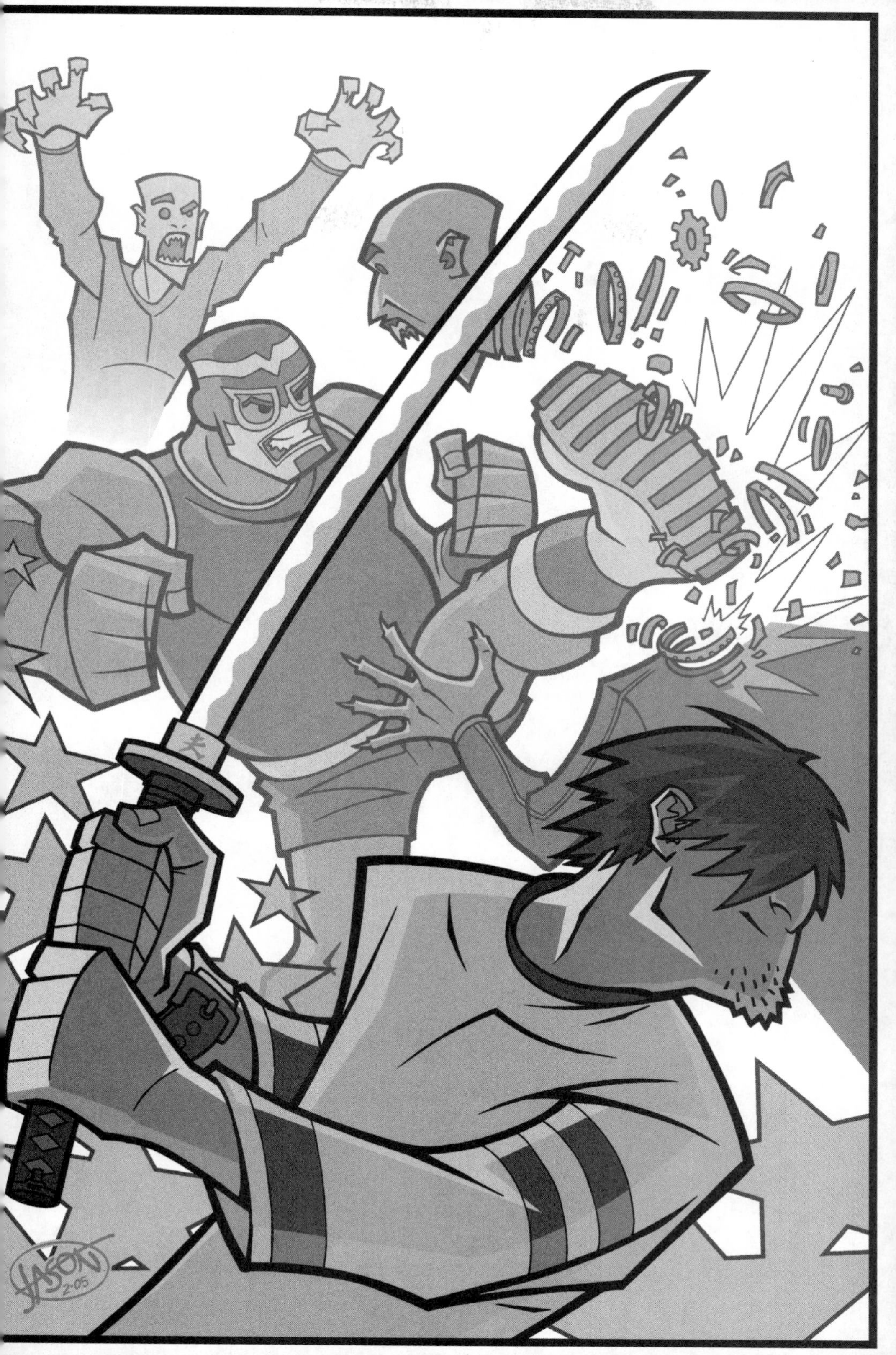
JASON
2-05

NOW FOR AN AMAZING JOY BUZZARDS *Masterpiece Moment...*

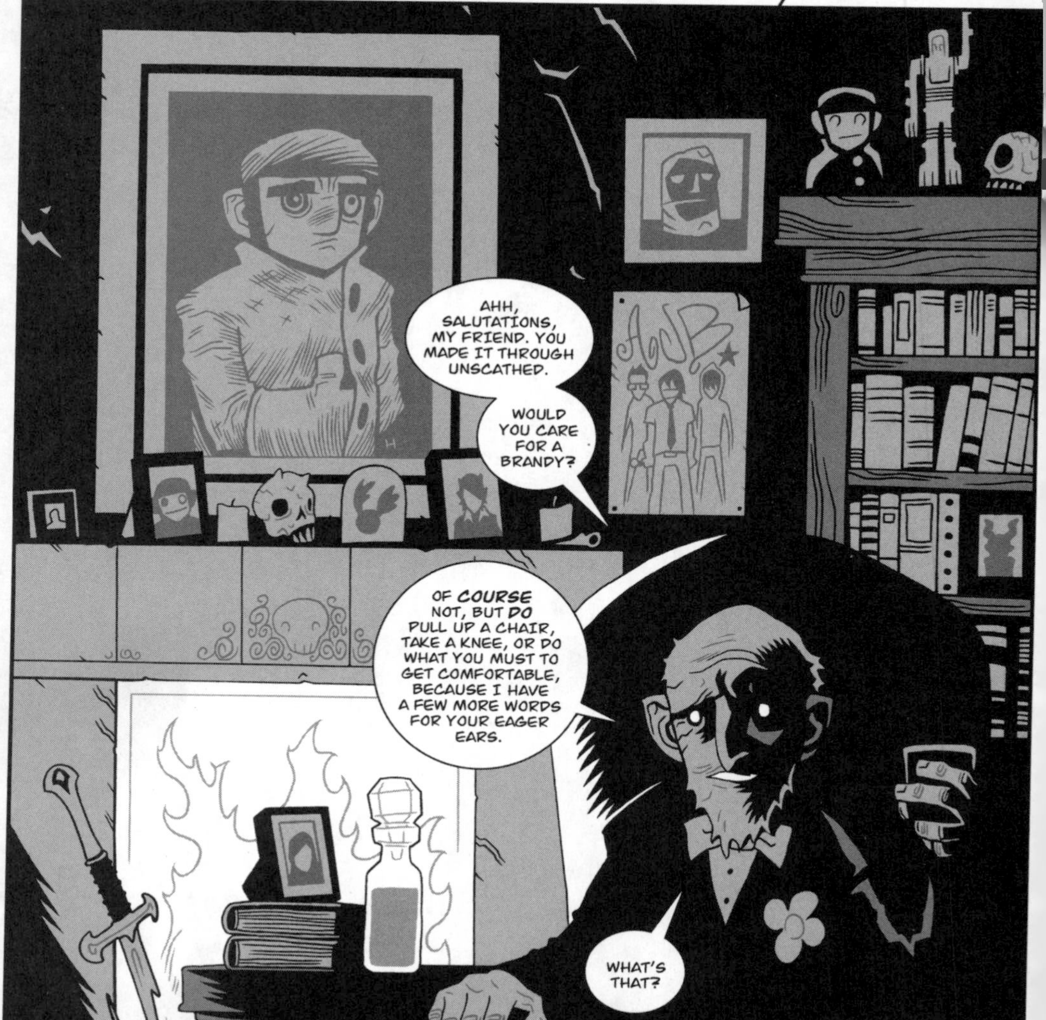
AHH, SALUTATIONS, MY FRIEND. YOU MADE IT THROUGH UNSCATHED.
WOULD YOU CARE FOR A BRANDY?
OF COURSE NOT, BUT DO PULL UP A CHAIR, TAKE A KNEE, OR DO WHAT YOU MUST TO GET COMFORTABLE, BECAUSE I HAVE A FEW MORE WORDS FOR YOUR EAGER EARS.
WHAT'S THAT?

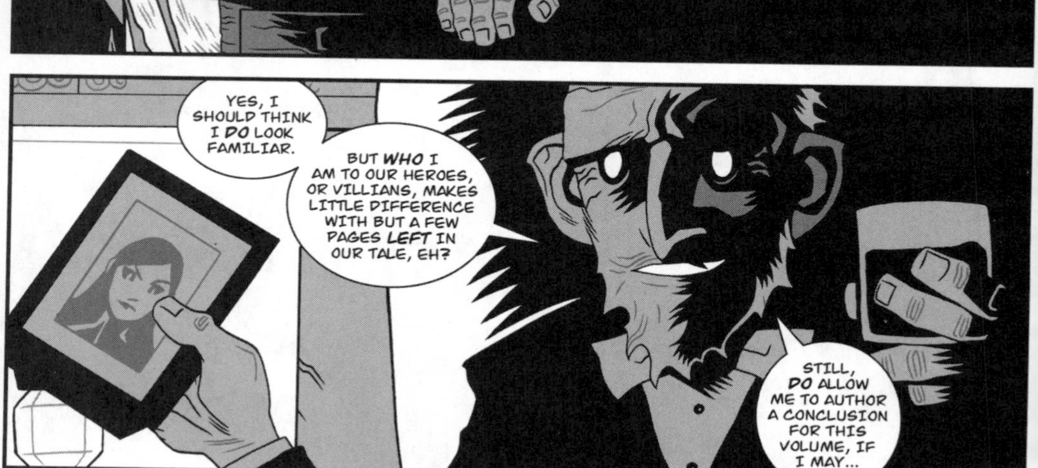
YES, I SHOULD THINK I DO LOOK FAMILIAR.
BUT WHO I AM TO OUR HEROES, OR VILLIANS, MAKES LITTLE DIFFERENCE WITH BUT A FEW PAGES LEFT IN OUR TALE, EH?
STILL, DO ALLOW ME TO AUTHOR A CONCLUSION FOR THIS VOLUME, IF I MAY...

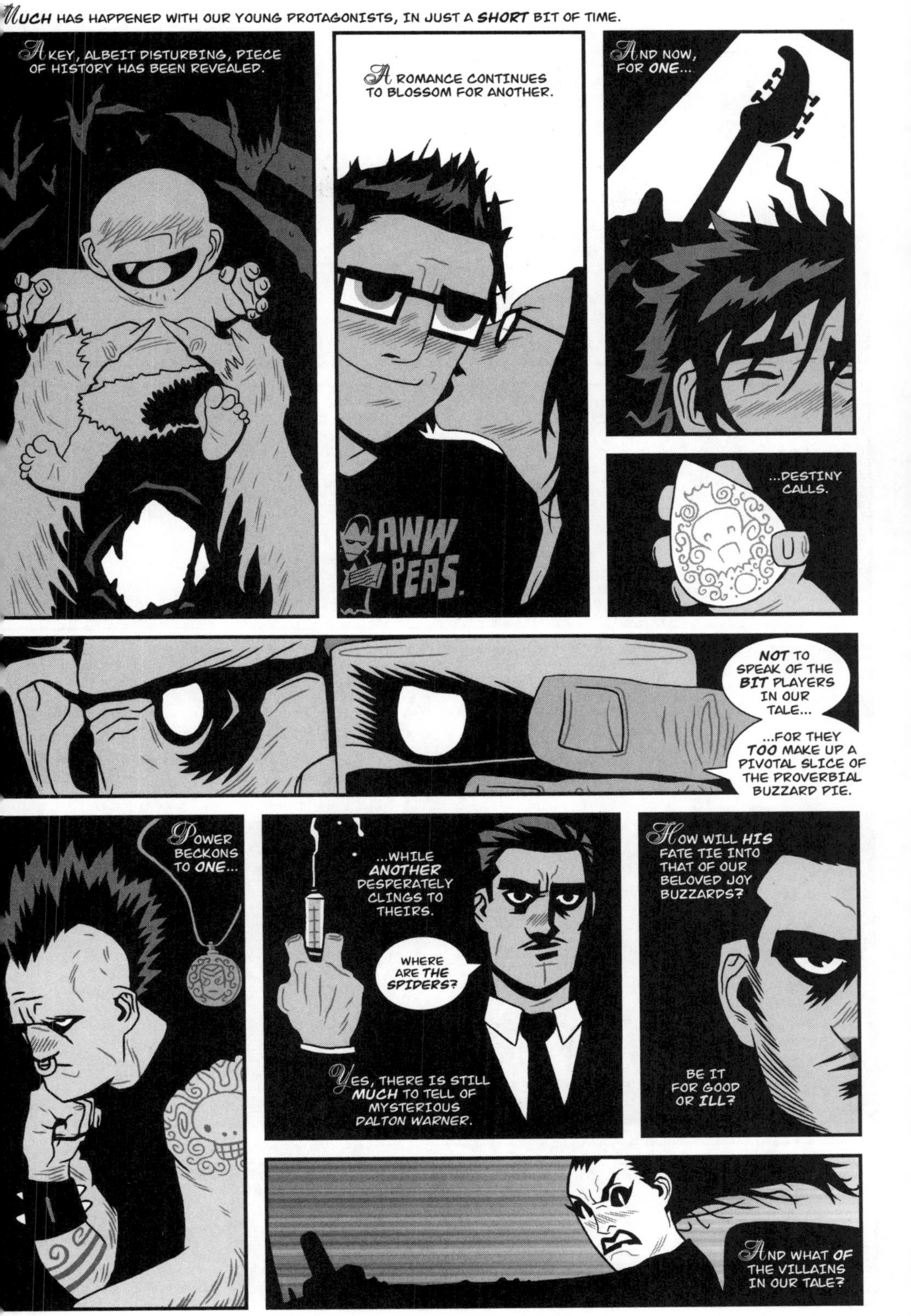
MUCH HAS HAPPENED WITH OUR YOUNG PROTAGONISTS, IN JUST A SHORT BIT OF TIME.
A KEY, ALBEIT DISTURBING, PIECE OF HISTORY HAS BEEN REVEALED.
A ROMANCE CONTINUES TO BLOSSOM FOR ANOTHER.
AWW PEAS.
AND NOW, FOR ONE...
...DESTINY CALLS.
NOT TO SPEAK OF THE BIT PLAYERS IN OUR TALE...
...FOR THEY TOO MAKE UP A PIVOTAL SLICE OF THE PROVERBIAL BUZZARD PIE.
POWER BECKONS TO ONE...
...WHILE ANOTHER DESPERATELY CLINGS TO THEIRS.
WHERE ARE THE SPIDERS?
YES, THERE IS STILL MUCH TO TELL OF MYSTERIOUS DALTON WARNER.
HOW WILL HIS FATE TIE INTO THAT OF OUR BELOVED JOY BUZZARDS?
BE IT FOR GOOD OR ILL?
AND WHAT OF THE VILLAINS IN OUR TALE?

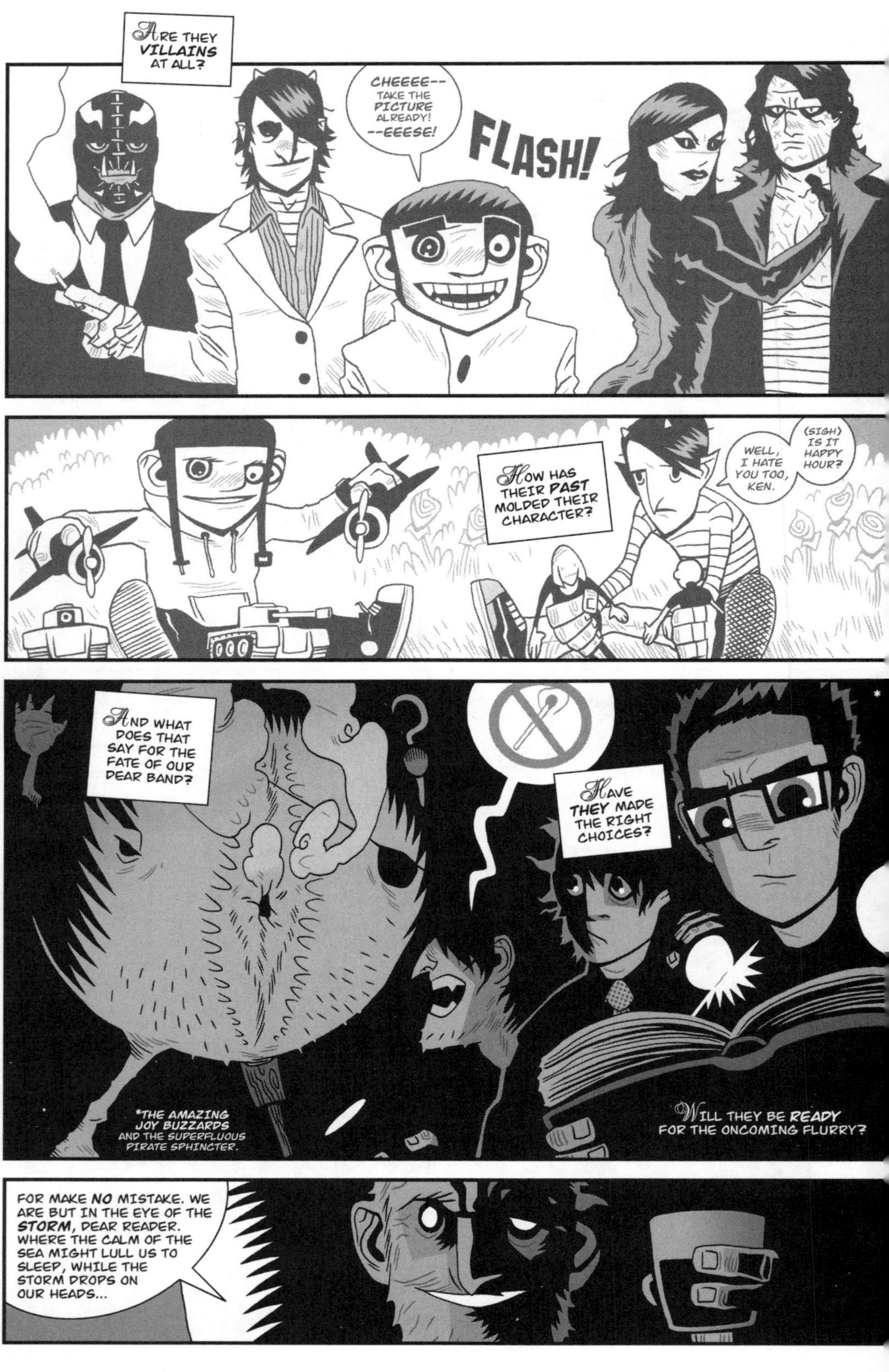

ARE THEY VILLAINS AT ALL?
CHEEEE-- TAKE THE PICTURE ALREADY! --EEESE!
FLASH!
HOW HAS THEIR PAST MOLDED THEIR CHARACTER?
WELL, I HATE YOU TOO, KEN.
(SIGH) IS IT HAPPY HOUR?
AND WHAT DOES THAT SAY FOR THE FATE OF OUR DEAR BAND?
HAVE THEY MADE THE RIGHT CHOICES?
*THE AMAZING JOY BUZZARDS AND THE SUPERFLUOUS PIRATE SPHINCTER.
WILL THEY BE READY FOR THE ONCOMING FLURRY?
FOR MAKE NO MISTAKE. WE ARE BUT IN THE EYE OF THE STORM, DEAR READER. WHERE THE CALM OF THE SEA MIGHT LULL US TO SLEEP, WHILE THE STORM DROPS ON OUR HEADS...

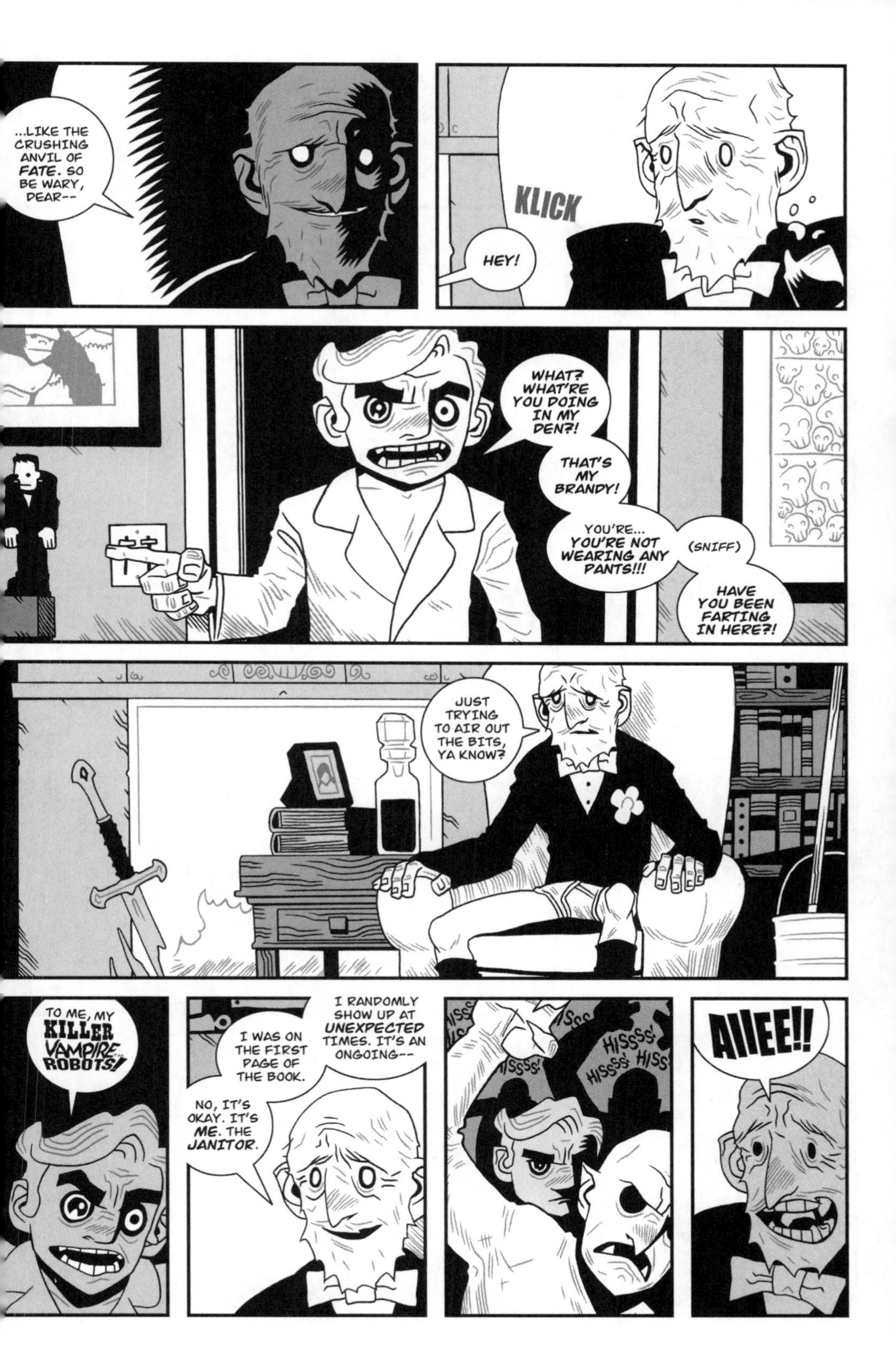
...LIKE THE CRUSHING ANVIL OF FATE. SO BE WARY, DEAR--
KLICK
HEY!
WHAT? WHAT'RE YOU DOING IN MY DEN?!
THAT'S MY BRANDY!
YOU'RE... YOU'RE NOT WEARING ANY PANTS!!!
(SNIFF)
HAVE YOU BEEN FARTING IN HERE?!
JUST TRYING TO AIR OUT THE BITS, YA KNOW?
TO ME, MY KILLER VAMPIRE ROBOTS!
I WAS ON THE FIRST PAGE OF THE BOOK.
I RANDOMLY SHOW UP AT UNEXPECTED TIMES. IT'S AN ONGOING--
NO, IT'S OKAY. IT'S ME. THE JANITOR.
HISSSS! HISSSS! HISSSS! HISSSS! HISS!
AIIEE!!

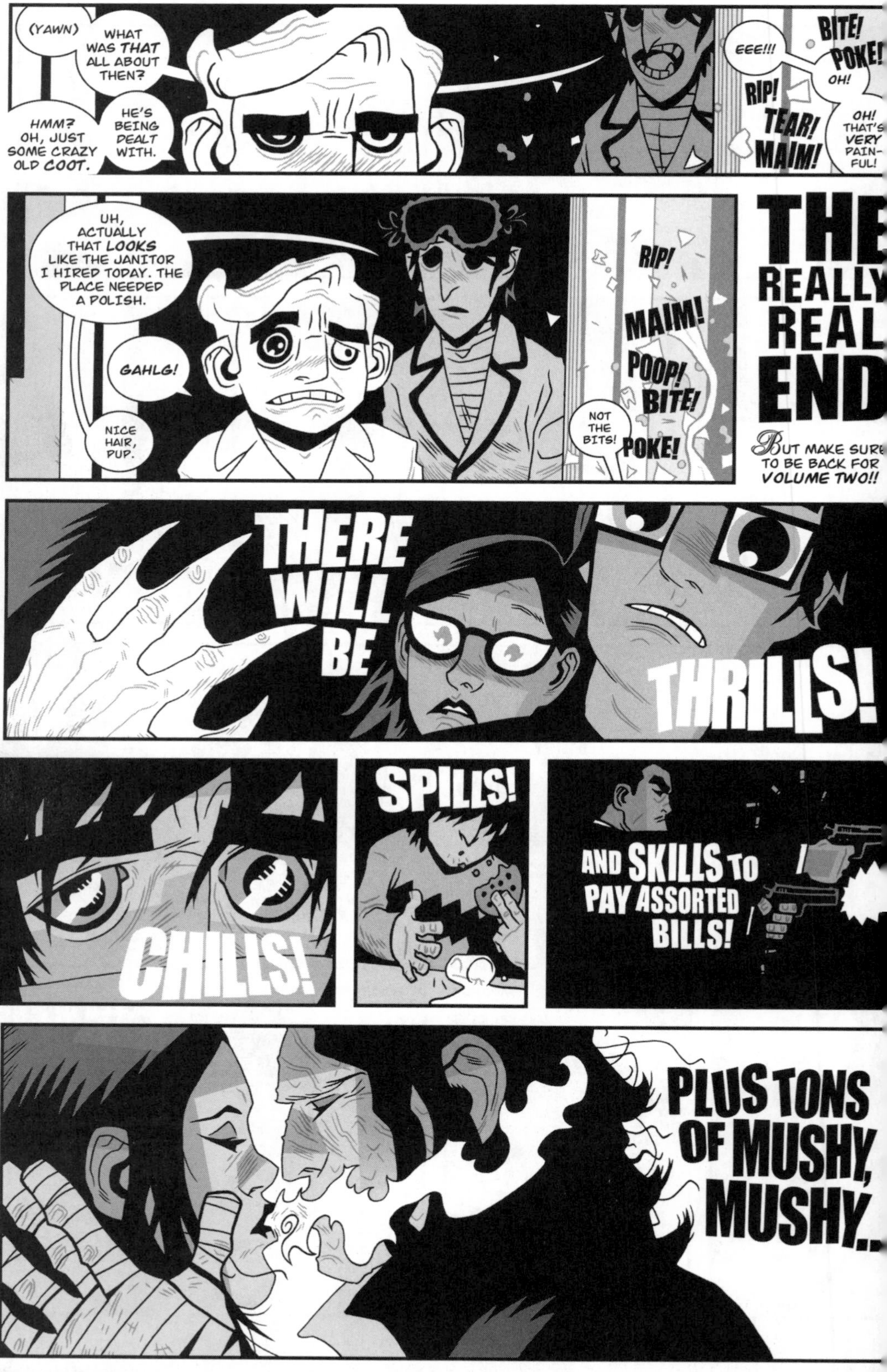

(YAWN)
WHAT WAS THAT ALL ABOUT THEN?
HMM? OH, JUST SOME CRAZY OLD COOT.
HE'S BEING DEALT WITH.
EEE!!!
BITE!
POKE!
OH!
RIP!
TEAR!
MAIM!
OH! THAT'S VERY PAIN-FUL!
UH, ACTUALLY THAT LOOKS LIKE THE JANITOR I HIRED TODAY. THE PLACE NEEDED A POLISH.
GAHLG!
NICE HAIR, PUP.
RIP!
MAIM!
POOP!
BITE!
NOT THE BITS!
POKE!
THE REALLY REAL END
BUT MAKE SURE TO BE BACK FOR VOLUME TWO!!
THERE WILL BE
THRILLS!
CHILLS!
SPILLS!
AND SKILLS TO PAY ASSORTED BILLS!
PLUS TONS OF MUSHY, MUSHY...

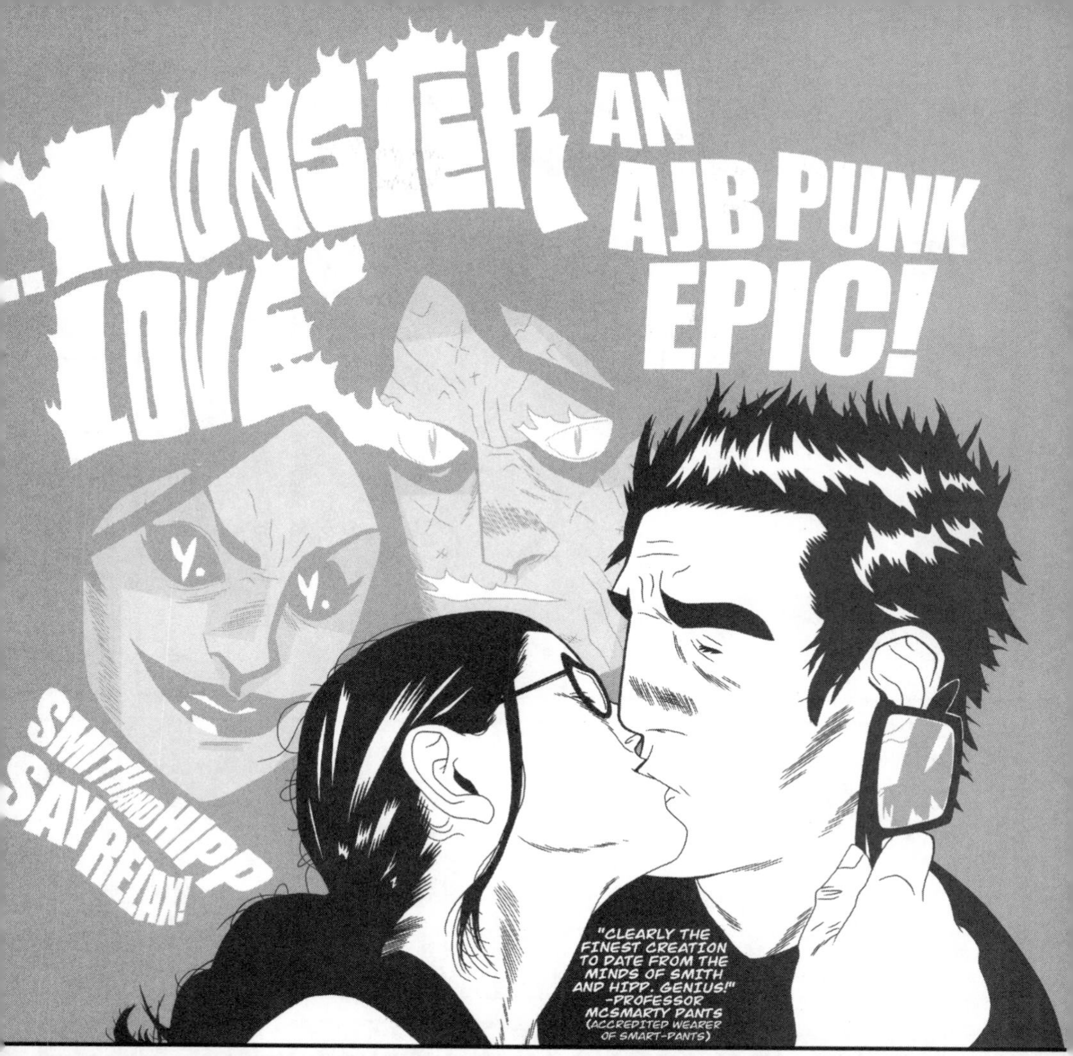
"MONSTER LOVE"
AN AJB PUNK EPIC!
SMITH AND HIPP SAY RELAX!
"CLEARLY THE FINEST CREATION TO DATE FROM THE MINDS OF SMITH AND HIPP. GENIUS!" -PROFESSOR MCSMARTY PANTS (ACCREDITED WEARER OF SMART-PANTS)

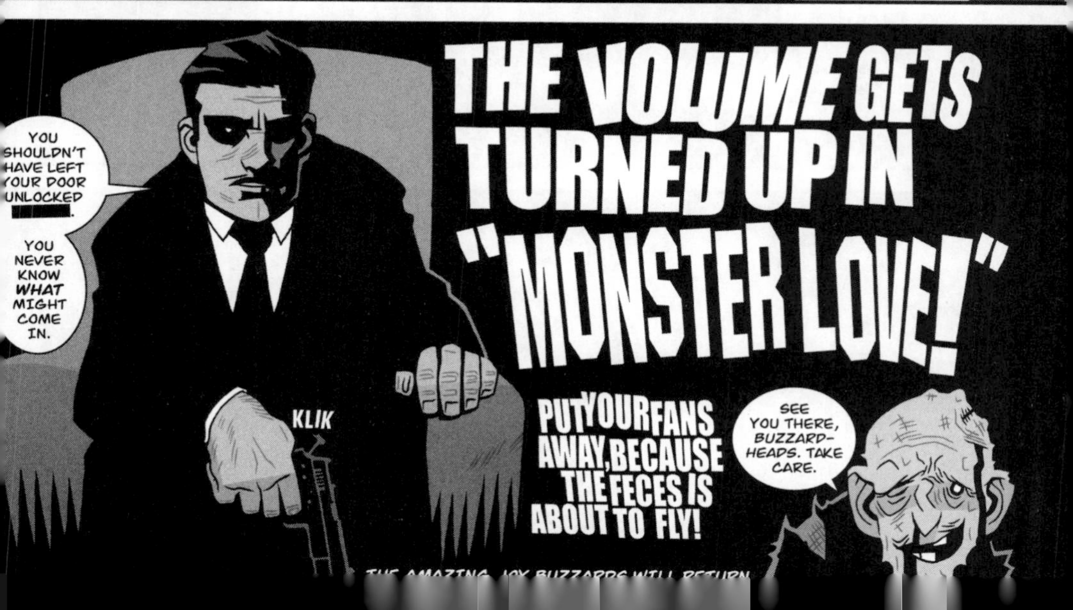
YOU SHOULDN'T HAVE LEFT YOUR DOOR UNLOCKED [redacted].
YOU NEVER KNOW WHAT MIGHT COME IN.
KLIK
THE VOLUME GETS TURNED UP IN "MONSTER LOVE!"
PUT YOUR FANS AWAY, BECAUSE THE FECES IS ABOUT TO FLY!
SEE YOU THERE, BUZZARD-HEADS. TAKE CARE.
THE AMAZING JOY BUZZARDS WILL RETURN

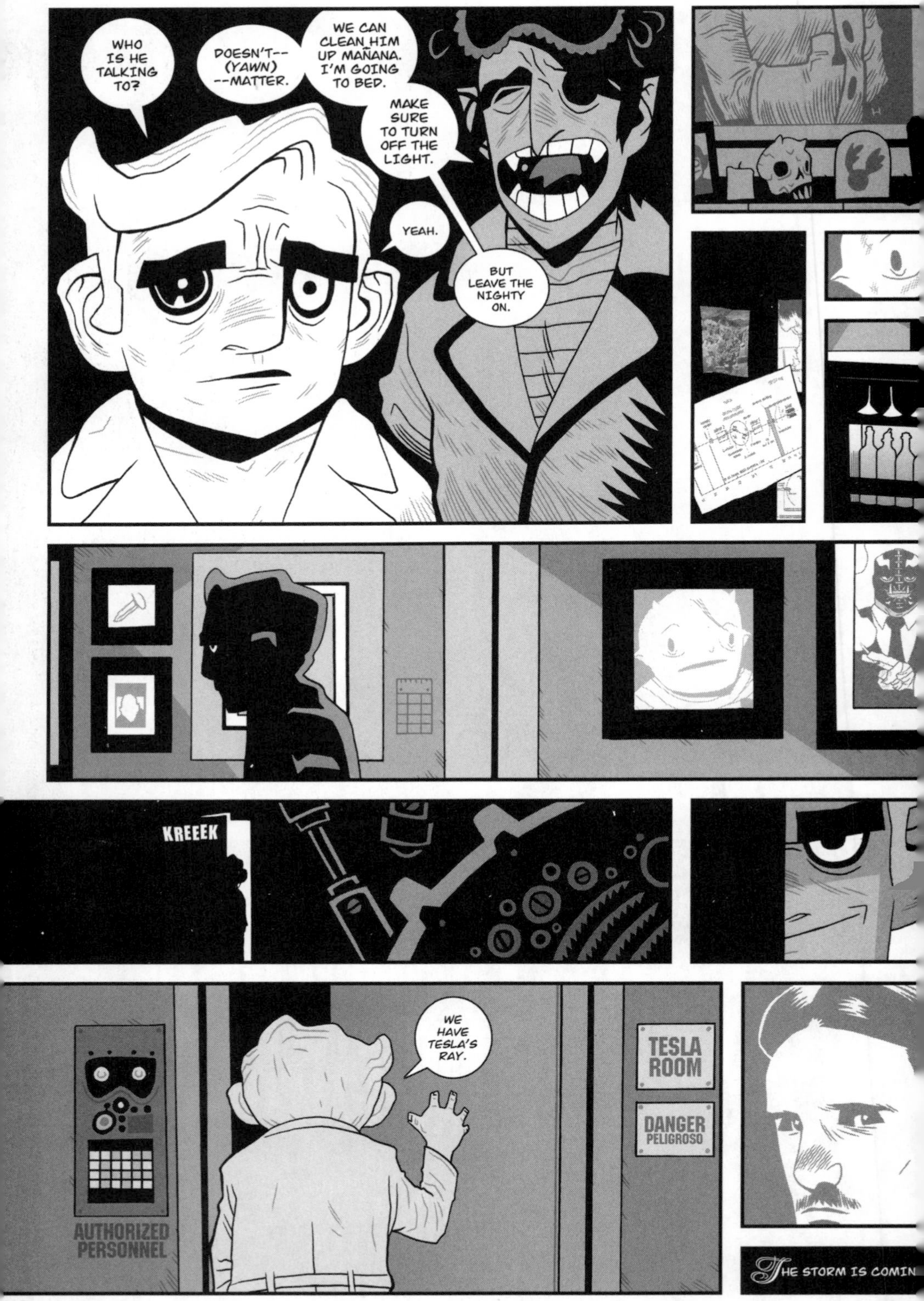
WHO IS HE TALKING TO?
DOESN'T-- (YAWN) --MATTER.
WE CAN CLEAN HIM UP MAÑANA. I'M GOING TO BED.
MAKE SURE TO TURN OFF THE LIGHT.
YEAH.
BUT LEAVE THE NIGHTY ON.
KREEEK
WE HAVE TESLA'S RAY.
TESLA ROOM
DANGER
PELIGROSO
AUTHORIZED PERSONNEL
THE STORM IS COMIN